WAR MAID'S CHOICE

BAEN BOOKS by DAVID WEBER

HONORVERSE NOVELS

On Basilisk Station
The Honor of the Queen
The Short Victorious War
Field of Dishonor
Flag in Exile
Honor Among Enemies
In Enemy Hands
Echoes of Honor
Ashes of Victory
War of Honor
At All Costs
Mission of Honor
Crown of Slaves (with Eric Flint)
Torch of Freedom (with Eric Flint)
The Shadow of Saganami
Storm from the Shadows
A Rising Thunder

HONORVERSE ANTHOLOGIES

More than Honor
Worlds of Honor
Changer of Worlds
The Service of the Sword
In Fire Forged

HONORVERSE YOUNG ADULT NOVEL

A Beautiful Friendship
Fire Season (with Jane Lindskold)*

EMPIRE FROM THE ASHES

Mutineers' Moon
The Armageddon Inheritance
Heirs of Empire
Empire from the Ashes (omnibus)

WAR GOD SERIES

Oath of Swords
The War God's Own
Wind Rider's Oath
War Maid's Choice

Path of the Fury
In Fury Born

The Apocalypse Troll

The Excalibur Alternative

WITH STEVE WHITE

Insurrection
Crusade
In Death Ground
The Shiva Option
The Stars at War I
The Stars at War II

WITH JOHN RINGO

March Upcountry
March to the Sea
March to the Stars
We Few

WITH ERIC FLINT

1633
1634: The Baltic War

WITH LINDA EVANS

Hell's Gate
Hell Hath No Fury

*forthcoming

WAR MAID'S CHOICE

DAVID WEBER

War Maid's Choice

This is a work of fiction. All the characters and events portrayed in this book are fictional, and any resemblance to real people or incidents is purely coincidental.

A Baen Books Original

Baen Publishing Enterprises
P.O. Box 1403
Riverdale, NY 10471
www.baen.com

ISBN: 978-1-4516-3835-6

Cover art by Dominic Harman
Map by Eleanor Kostyk

First printing, July 2012

Distributed by Simon & Schuster
1230 Avenue of the Americas
New York, NY 10020

Library of Congress Cataloging-in-Publication Data

Weber, David, 1952–
War maid's choice / David Weber.
p. cm.
ISBN 978-1-4516-3835-6 (hc)
I. Title.
PS3573.E217W374 2012
813'.54—dc23

2012009326

10 9 8 7 6 5 4 3 2 1

Pages by Joy Freeman (www.pagesbyjoy.com)
Printed in the United States of America

For Indiana Graham

September 20, 1990 – March 23, 2012

Son of Bruce and Treysa

Brother of Rebecca, Dakota, and Mackenzie

A fighter who never surrendered and who, by the life he lived,
showed all of us the promise we've lost...
and left us a legacy of love and inspiration we can never lose.

God Bless, Indy.

Fly high.

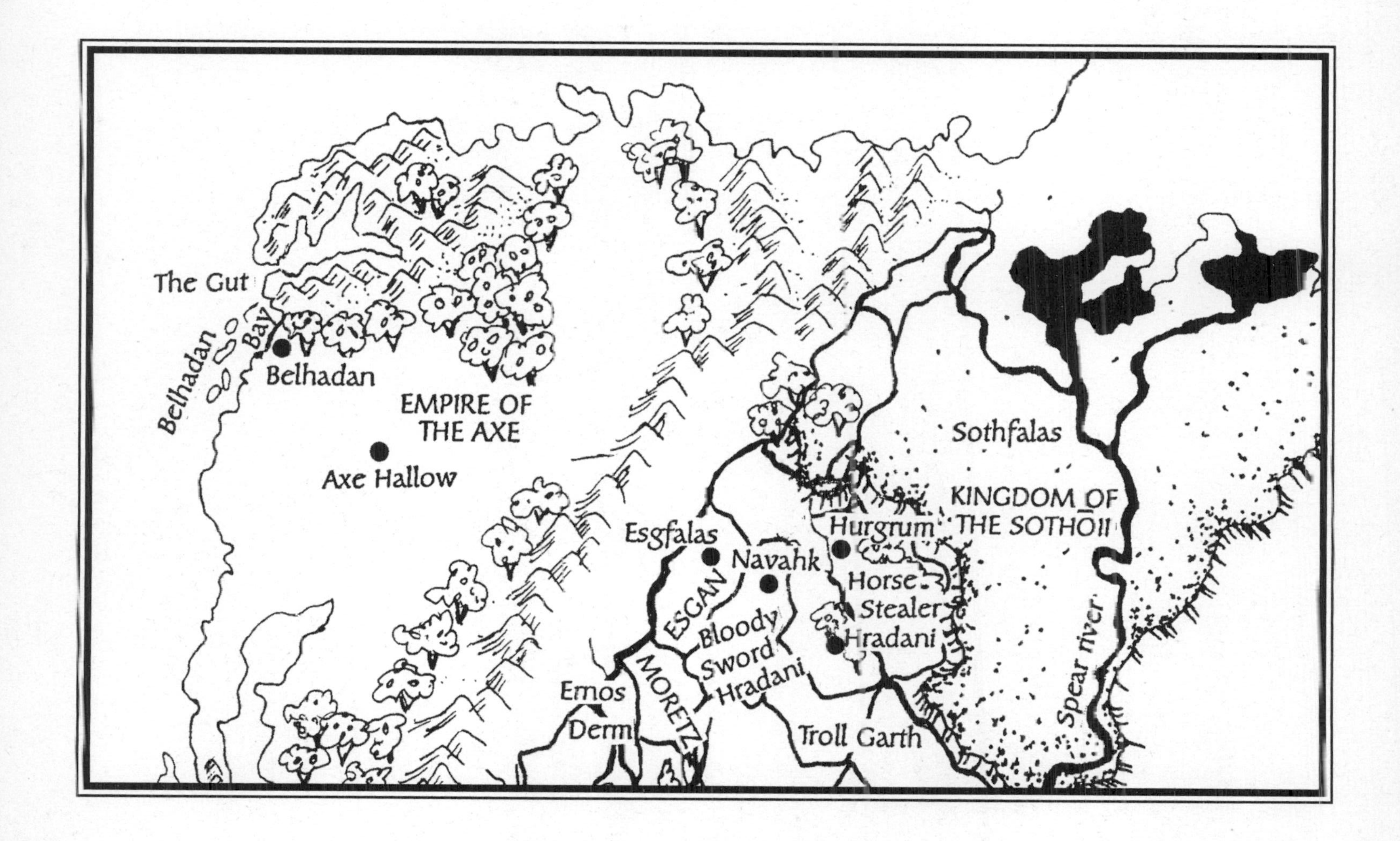
The Gut
Belhadan Bay
Belhadan
EMPIRE OF THE AXE
Axe Hallow
Sothfalas
KINGDOM OF THE SOTHŌII
Hurgrum
Horse Stealer Hradani
Esgfalas
Navahk
ESGAN
Bloody Sword Hradani
MORETZ
Emos
Derm
Troll Garth
Spear river

Prologue

Cables of blue-white lightning, tangled with knots of livid green, streaked down the ebon heavens, crashing to earth in a coruscating circle around the stupendous, many-turreted structure. The shortest of those turrets towered hundreds of feet above the endless, smooth pavement stretching away in every direction as far as any mortal eye might have seen, and the glare of lightning danced and glittered from the mirror-smooth obsidian of which the enormous palace had been built. Or *formed*, perhaps. There were no tool marks, no lines between blocks of masonry, on that titanic façade, and the light—such as it was—that glowed from its narrow window slits was a pestilential green, less brilliant than the corruption of that lightning yet more sullen, more . . . poisonous.

Fresh lightning hammered down, replenishing the glaring circle, feeding it, keeping it alive while thunder echoed and rolled and bellowed. Each braided strand lit the purple-bellied clouds from within, momentarily etching their swirling depths upon the eye, and strange, unclean shapes flew in those briefly illuminated deeps. One of those shapes plummeted from the clouds, sweeping lower, riding through the chinks of darkness between the lightning's pickets. Larger it grew, and larger, insectlike head armed with brutal pincers, enormous bat wings and mighty talons throwing back the glare of lightning until it seemed gilded in the eye-tearing fury of the seething heavens.

At the very last moment it flared its wings and settled upon the balcony of the very highest turret, a thousand feet and more above the lightning-crowned pavement. The size of that obsidian palace dwarfed even its stature, and a rider stepped from its back to the balcony and disappeared within.

More lightning sizzled and howled out of the darkness, smashing into the earth with redoubled ferocity, bolt following bolt, driving that circle of fury higher and brighter as if that flying shape's arrival had been a signal, and perhaps it had.

✧ ✧ ✧

The throne room was impossibly vast.

It couldn't possibly have been as large as it seemed, and yet it was. In some way no mortal could have described, it was vaster than whole worlds and yet small enough that the purple-cloaked figure which swept into it could cross it in no more than a dozen strides, and a strange perfume—sweet and seductive, yet undergirt by the scent of something long dead—drifted on its air. The newcomer ignored the six others who had been gathered there, awaiting his arrival. He stalked past them, ascending the high throne against the huge chamber's rear wall, and seated himself, and the wan, green radiance which had filled the room flared abruptly higher and brighter as he sat. A nimbus of deadly green fire hissed above his hooded head, and balls of the same lurid radiance crackled into existence high overhead, dancing and swirling beneath the soaring, vaulted ceiling like lost galaxies trapped in the throne room's miasma of incense.

Like the palace itself, the throne was a single, seamlessly extruded outcropping of obsidian, but this obsidian was veined with gold, and its surface glittered with diamonds, emeralds, and precious gems. The arms ended in carven demon's faces, each encrusted with more gold, more gems, and each held a mangled, dismembered body in its fangs. Rubies dripped from their jaws in glittering, lovingly detailed streams of blood, and a huge, haughty face looked down from the wall above the throne, etched across the stone in bas-relief and glittering with still more gold. As the figure seated upon the throne threw back the hood of his cloak, the face which was revealed matched that upon the wall.

Phrobus Orfro, once the seventh son of Orr All-Father and Kontifrio, gazed down upon his chosen mate and their children, and his expression was not a happy one.

"I wonder, sometimes, which of you is the least competent," he said abruptly. "The competition is so fierce I can't make up my mind between you."

His voice was deep, beautifully modulated, yet something seemed to scream somewhere inside those resonant, perfectly articulated tones, and only one of the six beings gathered before him returned his glare levelly. Krashnark Phrofro stood with square shoulders, arms crossed, refusing to cringe, and Phrobus' eyes glittered. Yet he let the defiance—if such it was—pass. Krashnark was the strongest of his children, the only one who might have openly challenged his own position, but there was scant fear of that. Not from Krashnark. There was no lack of ambition or surfeit of mercy in his second son, and he was the most powerful of all of Phrobus' children. Yet that strength was hobbled by his perverse, inner code of honor. He neither gave nor asked quarter, but his oath was unbreakable, which was why Phrobus felt no fear of Krashnark's rebellion, for he had sworn fealty to his father. It was unthinkable that he might raise his hand against Phrobus after swearing that oath . . . and none of the others, not even—or perhaps especially—Shīgū would ever have dared.

"All of you know the stakes for which we play," he continued, "yet none of you seems capable of accomplishing even the simplest task."

"In fairness, Father," one of his other children said, raising her head and using one hand to draw glorious red hair back from her face to reveal pupil-less eyes as black as his throne's obsidian, "that isn't precisely correct. Things have gone . . . poorly in several universes. That's unfortunately true, but we've succeeded in others."

Her voice was calm, respectful, yet pointed, and Phrobus gritted his teeth. Carnadosa was his youngest child, and although she'd been careful not to say it, many of those other successes had been her doing—a point she obviously wasn't above making by *not* making it. Yet not even a god or a goddess could deal with all the possible alternative realities of every potential universe. There had to be some division of labor, and in all too many of those realities which Carnadosa—and Krashnark—had not overseen, Phrobus' plans had failed catastrophically. He could feel his other children's, and his wife's, hatred seething like the lightning outside his palace as they glared at Carnadosa for underlining their failures, yet they dared not speak.

"Yes," he said after a moment. "We *have* succeeded in some, but we've failed in far too many others. We can afford no more losses, especially in those where victory had seemed within our grasp. Too much hangs on what happens there, which is the reason your accursed uncle is striving so hard to snatch them back from us, yet none of you seem capable of stopping him. I've looked into the future, Carnadosa. If we fail to stop this slide of events in the Light's favor, if Tomanāk's successes continue, our power—the power of *all* of us—may suffer catastrophic damage."

He paused, letting the implications sink into all of his listeners. It wasn't as if they shouldn't have been able to figure out for themselves just how dire their situation might become, but sometimes they needed to be shaken by the scruff of their collective necks before they could step back from their plotting and mutual betrayals long enough to really think about the nature of their struggle with the Gods of Light.

He leaned back in his throne, glaring down at them, his own thoughts running back over the ages since his failed rebellion against his own father. It was his brother's fault, he told himself once more, thunder rolling outside the palace in echo of his inner rage. It had been Tomanāk who'd rallied the others after the devastating surprise of Phrobus' initial attack. Tomanāk who'd personally struck Phrobus down, taken his original name from him and given him the one he bore now. "Truth Bender," that was what his name meant, and in the depth of his defeat, he'd been unable to reject it when his brother fastened it upon him forever. Not even he now remembered what his name had once been, and he thought perhaps he hated Tomanāk most of all for that.

Yet much as he hated—and feared—Tomanāk, he hated the myriad worlds of mortals even more.

His attempt to seize Orr's power as his own had very nearly succeeded, but in the moment in which Tomanāk ripped it back out of his grasp, that power had fractured, broken into more pieces than even a god could count. Worse, each of those pieces had taken on its own life, its own existence, and when that happened, the fates of all the gods had become captive to those insignificant, puny mites crawling about all of the worlds upon worlds which had spilled from the riven, shattered power he'd hungered to make his own. A new concept had come into existence in that moment—the concept of *time*. The concept of a future . . . and an end. And not even the gods themselves were immune to it, able to ignore the endless, steady trickle of years sliding one after another into the maw of eternity. Yet worse still, far worse, was the intolerable discovery that those ephemeral mortals held *his* fate in their hands.

In many ways, only the fragmenting of Orr's power had preserved Phrobus' own life, for there was no doubt what Tomanāk would have done with him if only he could. But all of them were entrapped in the uncertain fate Phrobus had unwittingly, unintentionally created. Orr himself had been diminished, weakened, stripped of his ability to command the tides of fate and left as captive to those capricious mortals as Phrobus himself. The restoration of his power was beyond his own reach, and neither the remaining Gods of Light nor Phrobus could repair it for him. It must heal itself in the fullness of that mortal creation—time.

But *how* would it heal itself? It had taken Phrobus centuries to realize the question could even be asked, for no one had ever considered the possibility that Orr's power *could* be shattered, and so no one had ever considered what might happen if it was. He knew how frustrated Tomanāk was that the cataclysmic collision of so many potential alternate futures had prevented him from slaying him for his treachery, yet Tomanāk had no choice. The death of a god, *any* god, would have released far too much additional power, poured far too much additional uncertainty into the shattered present and chaotic future of Orr's realm. And so Tomanāk had been forced to let him live, let him leave the home from which he'd been cast for his crimes, let him carve out his own realm in the broken confusion of too many realities.

And as he'd paced the confines of that lesser realm, contemplating the far vaster one he'd held so tantalizingly within his fingers, it had come to him.

The entire universe—the original, un-shattered universe, his father's great creation—had broken with Orr's power. It was as if a glass had been dropped upon a stone floor, and the shattered bits and pieces had flown in every direction. It had been impossible for anyone, even a god, to predict where any of them might land, far less where *all* of them might end their bouncing journeys across the stone. Now they lay scattered, tumbled into confused windrows without rhyme or reason, separated from one another and yet longing on some deep, fundamental level to become whole once more. To become *one* once again. And as they lay, they could be gathered back up by the proper set of hands. They could be . . . reassembled, put back together, and the hands which put them back together would control what they became on the day that they *were* one once more.

If he could reclaim them, gather enough of them together in the pattern of his choosing, he could remake them not as a reflection and restoration of *Orr's* power, but of his own.

Of course, that infernal busybody Semkirk had reasoned it out before him, and his accursed brothers and sisters—even that flighty fool Hirahim and that pathetic simpleton Sorbus—had set themselves to restoring the broken bits and pieces themselves. But there was a catch. Those bits and pieces had minds of their own. They were . . . malleable. They could be shaped, convinced, seduced, even *taken*, but only from within. In the end, they would choose their own fates on the basis of their own decisions, and those choices—and *only* those choices—would decide whose hands they came into in the fullness of time.

It was a race between him and his brothers and sisters, and so he'd taken to himself a wife and begotten children of his own to aid him in the struggle. Even with them, he was badly outnumbered, but not all of the Gods of Light were equally suited to the nature of the struggle between them. And the most ironic thing of all was that individual strength was of secondary importance, at best. They were forced to contend for each reality separately, individually, and the nature of the contest leveled the difference between their abilities. *Any* god could have destroyed any single fragment of that broken power, yet none of them knew how *many* fragments could be destroyed before the whole failed, and so none of them dared to destroy any of them. They must confront one another within the limits and constraints each individual mortal reality could endure, until that reality reached its tipping point and fell as the possession of the Light . . . or of the Dark.

And in the fullness of time, enough of those individual realities would fall to one side to give that side possession of them all. Which meant, that despite his failure all those ages ago, Phrobus might yet win all he'd sought.

But that could happen only if those mortals he loathed with all his being—loathed because they ultimately held his fate in their hands—*gave* him that victory. Fortunately, only a tiny fraction of them realized the prize for which the gods truly contended, and their puny lifespans made most of them shortsighted and easily duped. Many of them could scarcely *wait* to give themselves to him and to his children, and his hatred for them only made the taste of their souls still sweeter.

Yet not all of them were blind, not all were easily seduced. Their resistance to the Dark ran through their realities like ribs of steel, and some of them . . . oh, yes, *some* of them were far more dangerous than others.

"All of you know how much Tomanāk has poured into Orfressa," he said now. "All of you know how many possible outcomes run through that single cable of universes."

His eyes burned even hotter as he glared at them, his anger smoking in the air as he contemplated how close they'd come to victory, to seeing that reality—*all* the facets of that reality—safely locked into their possession twelve hundred of the mortals' years ago, only to have it slip through their fingers at the last moment. It lay now like a strand of fire wrapped in shadow, its central core surrounded by the penumbra of all its potentialities, not quite within his grasp, not quite beyond it, and the long wait to determine the side to which it must ultimately fall burned in his bones like slow poison. To be sure, centuries were but the blinks of an eye to one such as himself. Or they should have been, at least . . . had he been one bit less aware of the galling chains the mortal concept of "time" had set upon him.

"Father, the advantage is still ours," another voice said. "No one in all of Norfressa—except, perhaps, Wencit—even imagines what's preparing in Kontovar. Surely—"

"Don't speak to me of '*surely*,' Fiendark!" Phrobus snapped, turning the full power of his glare upon his eldest son. "There was a time when Orr's power was 'surely' mine! And I tell you that I've looked long and hard into the future of this reality and all those spinning from it, and I see confusion. I see uncertainty. And I see threads of Tomanāk's weaving that lead to places I *cannot* see. Places where this reality—*all* of these realities, and all the myriad others which might spring from them yet—fall from our hands into his unless we cut those threads of his, and do it quickly."

"But how, Father?" Carnadosa asked. "As Fiendark says, the advantage is still clearly ours, and Tomanāk can no more act openly in Orfressa than we can. So how can those threads of his snatch it away from us now?"

"The answer to that lies in those places beyond my vision."

Phrobus growled his reply, and Carnadosa frowned as the thunder outside the palace rolled darker and louder. Her father was stronger than any of them, and his ability to see the strands of future and past was greater. Yet there were limits even for him, for no one could predict what future any given reality would experience. There were too many variables, too many uncertainties, and until an event actually occurred, all possible outcomes of that event were equally valid, equally possible. Some were more *likely* than others, and outcomes became increasingly more likely—or unlikely—as a reality approached that particular event. Yet that uncertainty meant no one could predict precisely what would happen, or exactly *how* it would come about, and that, too, was the fault of those maddening, unpredictable mortals.

Still . . .

"But it continues to depend upon Bahzell, doesn't it?" she asked. Her father glared at her, and she bent her head slightly. "I ask because that's my own reading of this reality, Father. If yours is different . . . ?"

She let her voice trail off on a questioning note, fading into the rolling peals of distant thunder, and her father glared at her. Yet the question lingered, requiring an answer.

"Yes," Phrobus replied after a fulminating moment. "Bahzell is the key, but perhaps not precisely as you think. It revolves *about* Bahzell; yet there are so many elements in play, and Tomanāk has worked so skillfully to confuse the possibilities, that I truly can't say it depends *upon* him. Still, certain aspects are clear enough, aren't they? The hradani are supposed to be *our* tools, not Tomanāk's. They and the Sothōii are supposed to be at one another's throats, not *allies*, and these accursed 'war maids' are an entirely new ingredient. Whatever else may be happening, Tomanāk and his meddling 'champions' are in the process of creating a fundamental realignment which threatens all our future plans for that reality, and Bahzell is the catalyst that brought all of them together."

"I would never question your analysis, Father," Fiendark said, his voice an alloy of obsequiousness and arrogance, "yet it seems unlikely to me that anything Tomanāk might accomplish where the hradani and Sothōii are concerned could truly threaten our ultimate plans."

"You think not?" Phrobus returned his attention to Fiendark.

For better or worse, Fiendark was his senior deputy, yet there were times when his son's delight in destruction for destruction's sake got in the way of more . . . constructive approaches to a problem. He was too likely sometimes to think in terms of simply destroying an opponent to look for more subtle opportunities... or threats.

"I admit what I *have* seen shows it could be highly inconvenient," Fiendark replied now. "Their efforts might make our task more difficult, yet what if it does? In the end, the destruction will only grow greater and even more complete as their resistance delays their final defeat, and that can only serve our own ends."

"That might seem reasonable enough," Phrobus conceded after a moment. "But Tomanāk's invested too much in the effort for me to simply assume it to be true, and I don't like those threads I can't see. No. We will assume *nothing*, and we will bring this Bahzell Bahnakson and all those other threads which revolve about him *to* nothing. Am I understood?"

Heads nodded around the throne as fresh thunder exploded outside the palace to underscore his question.

"Good," he said with a thin smile. But his smile was only fleeting, and a frown replaced it as he gazed at Carnadosa thoughtfully.

Of all his children, she was the most subtle. Indeed, there were times when even he sometimes wondered exactly what game she might be playing. And, whether he chose to admit it or not, she was the one who most worried him. Not because he thought she was actively plotting to supplant him, but because if she ever did decide to overthrow him as he'd attempted to overthrow his own father, she was the one most likely to succeed. She was unimpressed with the taste for cruelty which infused Sharnā, just as she disdained Krahana's hunger and Fiendark's lust for destruction. But neither did she have any use for Krashnark's perverse sense of honor. Pragmatism was all that mattered to her, and she was a past mistress of the indirect approach. Very few of her victims ever even suspected her presence until she pounced from the shadows.

Yet she was also capable of direct—*very* direct—action when it seemed called for, and her status as the patron of dark wizardry and knowledge made her followers a force to be reckoned with in any mortal reality. It was possible—indeed, probable, given the outcome—he should have given her primary responsibility for the last attempt to disrupt Tomanāk's plans for this Bahzell Bahnakson, whatever those plans might be. He'd chosen not to because it had seemed a case in which wizardry couldn't be openly utilized—not yet, at least. And, he admitted, because Shīgū had been so insistent on doing it *her* way.

But now his options were limited. Sharnā and Shīgū had both been badly damaged in their recent confrontations with Tomanāk and his accursed champions, and it would be mortal decades yet before even Krahana fully recovered.

There were times Phrobus was forced to admit there were at least some advantages to the fashion in which Tomanāk and the other Gods of Light interacted with mortals. Their insistence that their "champions" had to give their allegiance knowingly, aware of the implications of their choices, made it far more difficult for them to enlist followers, and their refusal to simply enter into those champions and turn them into avatars limited their freedom of action. Seduction and corruption made recruitment far simpler for the Dark Gods, especially for mortals too foolish to suspect what their ultimate fate would be, and far more could be accomplished by turning those strong enough to bear the touch of godhood without being instantly destroyed into mere appendages. Not every mortal *was* strong enough, by any means, to be turned into an avatar, but those who were became conduits and anchors—doorways (so long as they lasted), through which their masters and mistresses could reach into the reality of mortals at will.

But Tomanāk and his fellows' refusal to suborn the wills of mortals meant they could act in the mortal world only when they were allowed to—when they were *invited* to—by those who'd chosen to serve them. And their refusal to burn out their servants limited the total amount of their own power and presence with which they could invest them. No mortal could long survive the direct embrace of godhood, even when the god in question sought to protect him, and so the Gods of Light treated their champions with silk gloves. They gave only so much of their power as their servants could channel, and in the process they surrendered control of what their champions *did* with that power.

No Dark God would give up that control, nor would one of them worry himself unduly over the fate of one of his servants. Avatars existed to be used, after all, even if they tended to be... consumed quickly. Replacing them could be inconvenient, yet that was acceptable, because while they lasted, they gave their masters direct access to their own reality, and there were always others who could be recruited to replace them afterward.

Yet there was a disadvantage to that, as well, as Sharnā and Shīgū had both discovered. It was one thing for a god to decide to withdraw his power from an avatar in an orderly fashion; it was quite another when that avatar was destroyed *before* he could withdraw. When that happened, the power, the fragment of his own essence, which had been poured into his mortal tool was lost with the avatar. Worse, it left him temporarily maimed, unable to reach back into that particular reality until the strength he'd lost regenerated itself once more, and that was precisely what had happened to Sharnā and Shīgū.

Sharnā had largely recovered from the damage he'd taken when Bahzell slew Harnak Churnazhson, but he'd been foolish enough to invest even more of his essence in the sword with which he'd armed Harnak. He'd seen that as a way to ensure Harnak's victory and *avoid* his avatar's destruction, but it hadn't worked out that way, and the sword touched by his essence now lay at the bottom of the sea. It would be centuries before he recovered from *that*, and until he did—or until the sword could be recovered from Korthrala's keeping and returned to him—he had no personal access to that reality.

Phrobus knew his son well enough to feel confident Sharnā was far from brokenhearted by the knowledge that he couldn't have faced Bahzell and Tomanāk in personal combat once more even if he'd *wanted* to . . . which he most definitely did not.

Shīgū had managed not to leave any of her being lying around in cursed weapons, but she'd never been noted for her rationality, and she'd poured herself wildly and recklessly into her avatar when she confronted Dame Kaeritha Seldansdaughter. Indeed, she would have emptied even more of herself into her tool, even at the risk of completely destroying that reality, had Tomanāk not blocked her. Given the possible consequences of any universe's destruction, it was as well Tomanāk had, but that same block had prevented her from withdrawing any of the power she'd invested, and her avatar's destruction had cost her even more dearly than Prince Harnak's death had cost Sharnā.

Krahana—wiser than her brother and saner than her mother—had committed her most powerful servants to the attack on Bahzell Bahnakson, but she'd declined to face him directly through an avatar of her own. As a result, she continued to have access to Bahzell's reality, but her resources there had been seriously curtailed. Until she could recruit or breed new servants powerful enough to replace those she'd lost, her capabilities would be only a shadow of what they had been.

And Fiendark had too many other responsibilities elsewhere (and was too fond of sheer destruction to be trusted with this task, anyway), which left only Carnadosa . . . and perhaps Krashnark.

"I think this has become a task for you, Carnadosa," he said finally.

Her expression never changed, but her obsidian eyes glittered as she contemplated the possibilities. She'd been involved only peripherally in the last attempt, as the coordinator and link between Shīgū and Krahana, and her mortal servants had been wise enough to remain safely in the shadows rather than confront Tomanāk's champions directly. More than that, she was unique among the Dark Gods in that she practically never used avatars of her own. Her wizard followers were usually quite powerful enough for her ends, and she had no desire at all to see *her* power diminished if a confrontation with one of the Light's champions went poorly. Giving her primary responsibility in this instance would increase the odds that she would be forced to confront Tomanāk or one of the others openly, whether she wished to or not, and it would definitely raise the probability that sorcery would be used openly sooner than Phrobus could have wished. She was too canny and too well informed not to recognize at least some of the potential consequences of reintroducing the arcane into the long, simmering conflict between Norfressa and Kontovar too soon, yet if she succeeded where Sharnā, Shīgū, and Krahana had all failed, that entire reality would become her personal possession, and all the power generated by every mortal living in it would be added to her own.

"Obviously, our original strategy failed miserably," he continued. "You have a free hand to formulate your own approach to the problem, although I want nothing done without my approval. We've failed twice already; I refuse to fail a *third* time. And because I refuse to fail yet again, Krashnark will assist you."

A flicker of disappointment showed in her eyes as she contemplated being forced to share the spoils of victory with her brother, but she was too wise to protest. And too wise not to recognize what a powerful ally Krashnark could be, as well.

"I understand, Father," she said, bending her head.

"I'm sure you do."

Phrobus sat back in his throne once more, listening to the crash and bellow of the thunder, and his eyes were hard.

"I'm sure you do," he repeated.

Chapter One

"I always love watching this part," Brandark Brandarkson, of the Bloody Sword hradani, murmured from behind his hand.

He and Bahzell Bahnakson stood in an enormous lantern-lit tunnel, surrounded by what anyone would have had to call "an unlikely crowd." He and Bahzell were its only hradani members, and Bahzell was a Horse Stealer of Clan Iron Axe, which had been the Bloody Swords' fiercest rival for generations. In fact, he wasn't just "a" Horse Stealer; he was the youngest son of Prince Bahnak Karathson, ruler of the Northern Confederation of Hradani... who'd *conquered* the Bloody Sword little more than six years ago. As if that pairing weren't bad enough, there were the dozen or so dwarves, a matching number of humans, and the huge roan stallion behind Bahzell. Up until a very few years ago, the possibility of that eclectic blend being gathered in one place without swordplay, bloodshed and mayhem would have been ridiculous. And the fact that all of the humans in question were Sothōii, the bitter traditional enemies of *all* hradani, Horse Stealers and Bloody Swords alike, would only have made it even more unlikely.

Of course, Brandark was a pretty unlikely sight all by himself. Very few Norfressans would have been prepared to behold a six-foot, two-inch hradani dressed in the very height of foppish fashion, from his embroidered silken doublet to his brilliantly shined riding boots—black, with tasteful silver tassels—and the long feather adorning the soft cloth cap adjusted to the perfect rakish angle on his head. The balalaika slung across his back would only have completed their stupefaction.

His towering companion, who was well over a foot and a half taller than he, was an almost equally unlikely sight, although in a very different way. Bahzell wore finely wrought chain mail and a polished steel breastplate, and instead of a balalaika, he carried a two-handed sword with a five-foot blade across *his* back. Aside from his size (which was enormous, even for a Horse Stealer) and the high quality of his gear, his martial appearance would have suited the stereotype of a hradani far better than Brandark's sartorial splendor... if not for his green surcoat, badged with the crossed mace and sword of Tomanāk Orfressa. The notion of a hradani champion of Tomanāk wasn't something the average Norfressan could be expected to wrap his mind around easily, and the roan courser watching alertly over his shoulder made it even worse. After all, if there was one being in all of Norfressa who could be counted upon to hate hradani even more than two-legged Sothōii did, it had to be a Sothōii *courser.*

"*Shhhhh!*" one of the dwarves scolded, turning to glare at Brandark. "If you distract her now, I'm going to have Walsharno step on you!"

"You don't scare me," Brandark retorted (albeit in an even softer tone), grinning down at him. Sermandahknarthas zoi'Harkanath was three times Brandark's age and the senior engineer on what had been dubbed the Gullet Tunnel, but he was also barely two-thirds as tall as the Bloody Sword, and his head barely topped Bahzell's belt buckle. "Walsharno *likes* me. He won't step on me without a lot better reason than your petty irritation!"

The colossal stallion—he stood over eight feet tall at the shoulder—tilted his head, ears cocked thoughtfully. Then he reached out and shoved Brandark between the shoulder blades with his nose. Despite his dandified appearance, the hradani was a solid, thick-boned plug of muscle and gristle, with shoulders so broad he looked almost squat, in spite of his height. He easily weighed two hundred and fifty pounds, none of it fat, and no one would have called him an easily-brushed-aside lightweight. But the stallion weighed over two tons, and Brandark staggered forward under the "gentle" push. He turned to look over his shoulder, his expression betrayed, and Bahzell laughed.

"Walsharno says as how he'll *always* have a 'better reason' when it comes to stepping on such as you, little man," he rumbled in an earthquake bass. "Mind, I think he's after exaggerating a *wee* bit . . . but not so much as all that."

"Will the both of you *please* be quiet?" Serman demanded. "This is a very ticklish moment and—"

"Yes, it is," a female voice agreed tartly. "And I would be grateful if all *three* of you could manage to keep your mouths shut for fifteen seconds at a time! Unless you'd like the next section of this tunnel to go straight down . . . and begin directly underneath you!"

Serman closed his mouth with an almost audible click, and Bahzell chuckled softly. It was a *very* soft chuckle, however. He didn't really think Chanharsadahknarthi zoihan'Harkanath would suddenly open a yawning pit under his feet, but he was in no tearing hurry to test the theory. Besides, she had a point.

Brandark contented himself with one last glower at Walsharno—who only curled his lips to show his teeth and shook his head in very horselike, mane-flipping amusement—then crossed his arms and concentrated on looking martyred. It wasn't a very convincing performance, especially given his obvious interest in what was about to happen, and Bahzell smiled and patted Walsharno's shoulder as he watched his friend's long nose almost quiver in fascination.

Quiet fell. It wasn't really a silence, for the shouts and sounds of construction gangs came up the steadily climbing tunnel from behind them, but those noises were distant. In a way, they only made the quiet even more profound, and Chanharsa closed her eyes once more. Her hands were outstretched, palms pressed flat against the smooth, vertical wall at the end of the tunnel, and she leaned forward, resting her forehead between them. She stood that way for several minutes, her posture relaxed, yet the others could literally feel the concentration pouring off of her.

It wasn't the first time Bahzell had watched this same scene, but the dwarvish art of sarthnaiskarmanthar was seldom seen outside the dwarves' subterranean cities, and like Brandark, he found it endlessly fascinating. Sarthnaiskarmanthar was the talent which truly set dwarves off from the other Races of Man and allowed them to undertake their monumental engineering projects, and they guarded their sarthnaisks (the word translated roughly as "stone herds" or "stone shepherds") like the priceless treasures they were.

There'd been occasions, especially during the dark and dreadful days of the Fall of Kontovar, when enslaved sarthnaisks had been valued by their captors above almost all other prisoners . . . and all too often driven until their talent consumed them. The dwarves had sworn that would never happen again, and any sarthnaisk was always accompanied by his personal armsman on any trip beyond the safe caverns of his—or, in this case, *her*—home city. Chanharsa, on the other hand, was accompanied by *eight* armsmen, and another sixteen waited at the tunnel's entrance for her return. It was an impressive display of security, but Chanharsadahknarthi zoihan'Harkanath wasn't just "any" sarthnaisk. According to Serman, the tunnel's chief engineer, she was the strongest sarthnaisk Dwarvenhame had seen in at least two generations (which Bahzell, having seen her work, readily believed), not to mention a blood kinswoman of Kilthandahknarthas dihna'Harkanath, the head of Clan Harkanath. It would be . . . unfortunate if anything were to happen to Lady Chanharsa.

At the moment, the diminutive sarthnaisk (she was well under four feet in height) didn't really look all that impressive. In fact, she didn't *look* as if she was doing anything more than simply leaning against the rock, but Bahzell knew how hard she was actually concentrating as she extended her senses, using her talent to run immaterial fingers through the solid stone in front of her. She was feeling fault lines, sampling quartz and rock, tasting the elusive flavor of minerals, metal ores and water. He also understood exactly why sarthnaiskarmanthar fascinated the keenly inquiring scholar who lived inside Brandark, but unlike his Bloody Sword friend, Bahzell *understood* what Chanharsa was doing, just as he understood why she could never truly explain it to Brandark or anyone who didn't possess the same talent. Or one very like it, at any rate.

As it happened, Bahzell did possess a similar talent. He had no ability to taste or shape stone, but he was a champion of Tomanāk, and the war god gifted his champions with the ability to heal. Yet not all of them were equally skilled as healers, for it was an ability which depended on the clarity with which the individual champion could open his mind to an injury or illness and truly believe he could do anything about it. It depended upon his ability to *understand* that damage, to accept it in all its often ghastly reality, and then to not only overlay his mental "map" of that damage with a vision of health but actually impose that vision upon the injury. To open himself as a channel or conduit between his deity and the mortal world and use that conduit—or allow *it* to use *him*, perhaps—to make that internal, personal image of restored well-being and vitality the reality. It all sounded simple enough, yet words could describe only the what, not the how of accomplishing it, and it was extraordinarily difficult to actually do.

Sarthnaiskarmanthar functioned in a similar fashion, although according to Wencit of Rūm (who certainly ought to know) a sarthnaisk's work was at least a little simpler because living creatures were in a constant state of change as blood pumped through their veins and oxygen flowed in and out of their lungs. Stone was in a constant state of change, as well, but it was a far slower and more gradual change, a process of ages and eons, not minute-to-minute or even second-to-second transformations. It didn't clamor and try to distract the way living bone and tissue did as the sarthnaisk formed the detailed mental image of what he intended to impose upon the stone's reality. Of course, stone was also more resistant *to* change, but that was where his training came in. Like a skilled mishuk martial artist, the sarthnaisk used balance and precision and focus against the monolithic resistance of stone and earth. He found the points within the existing matrix where a tiny push, a slight shift, began the process of change and put all the weight of the stone itself behind it, like deep mountain snow sliding down to drive boulders and shattered trees before it.

The trick was to stay in control, to *shape* the avalanche, to fit that instant of total plasticity to the sarthnaisk's vision, and steering an avalanche was always a . . . challenging proposition.

He smiled at the thought, and then his eyes narrowed and his foxlike ears folded back slightly as Chanharsa drew a deep, deep breath. Her shoulders rose as she filled her lungs, and then the stone *changed*.

Bahzell had seen her do this over a dozen times now, yet he still couldn't quite force what he saw to make sense. It wasn't that it happened too quickly for the eye to see, although that was what he'd thought the first time he'd watched it. No, the problem was that the eye wasn't *intended* to see it. Or perhaps that the mind hadn't been designed to understand it . . . or accept it. The smooth, flat wall of stone flowed like smoke under Chanharsa's palms, yet it was a *solid* smoke, a surface which continued to support her weight as she leaned even harder against it. A glow streamed out from her hands, spreading across the entire face of stone in a bright web of light, pulsing in time with her heartbeat, and that glow—that web—flowed away from her, sinking deeper and deeper into the smoky rock. In some way Bahzell would never be able to explain, he could *see* the glow stretching away from them, probing out through hundreds of cubic yards of stone and earth. He couldn't estimate how far into the rock he could "see," but the glow grew dimmer as it moved farther and farther away from him.

A minute slipped past. Then another. Three of them. And then—

Chanharsadahknarthi zoihan'Harkanath staggered ever so slightly as the stone under her hands vanished, and an abrupt, cool fist of breeze flowed over them from behind as air rushed up the tunnel to fill the suddenly created cavity before her. Her shoulders sagged, and one of her armsmen stepped forward quickly, taking her elbow and supporting her until she could regain her balance. She leaned against him for a moment, then inhaled again and shook her head, pushing herself back upright, and Bahzell heard a mutter of awe from the spectators... most of whom had seen her do exactly the same thing at least as often as he had.

On the other hand, it wasn't something a man got used to seeing.

The tunnel had suddenly grown at least sixty yards longer. The tunnel roof was thirty feet above its floor, and the tunnel walls were sixty-five feet apart, wide enough for three heavy freight wagons to pass abreast. Its sloped floor was ballroom-smooth yet textured to give feet or hooves solid traction, and two square-cut channels—six feet deep and two feet wide—ran the tunnel's full length, fifteen feet out from each wall. Every angle and surface was perfectly, precisely cut and shaped... and glossy smooth, gleaming as if they'd been hand polished, without a single tool mark anywhere. The new tunnel section had freed a sizable spring on its southern wall and water foamed and rushed from it like a fountain, but Chanharsa had allowed for that. Another, shorter channel had been cut across the tunnel floor, crossing the first two at right angles, this one deep enough that none of the newborn stream's water escaped into the first two as it flooded into its new bed and sent a wave front flowing across the tunnel to plunge gurgling and rushing into an opening in the northern wall. Two broad, gently arched bridges crossed the sudden musical chuckle of water—not built, but simply *formed*, as strong and immovably solid as the rock around them—and sunlight probed down from above through the air shaft piercing the tunnel roof. That shaft was two feet in diameter and over eighty feet deep, and patterns of reflected sunlight from the stream danced across the smooth stone walls.

"Well, I see I managed to get it mostly right despite all that distracting chatter going on behind me," Chanharsa observed, turning to give the hradani her best glare.

It was, Bahzell admitted, quite a good glare, considering that it was coming from someone less than half his own height. It wasn't remotely as potent as the one Kilthan could have produced, but she was twenty-five years younger than Serman, which made her less than half Kilthan's age. In another fifty years or so, possibly even as little as thirty or forty, he was sure she'd be able to match the panache Kilthan could put into the same expression.

"And it's not surprised I am, at all," he assured her with a broad smile. "For such a wee, tiny thing you've quite a way with rock."

"Which means I ought to have 'quite a way' with hradani *brains*, doesn't it?" she observed affably, and his smile turned into a laugh.

"You've a way to go still before you match old Kilthan, but I see you've the talent for it," he said. "I'm thinking it needs a bit more curl to the upper lip and the eyes a mite narrower, though, wouldn't you say, Brandark?"

"No, I most definitely *wouldn't* say," the Bloody Sword told him promptly. "I'm in enough trouble with her already."

Several people laughed, although at least one of Chanharsa's armsmen looked less than amused by the hradani's levity. Chanharsa only grinned. Despite the many differences between them, hradani and dwarves were very much alike in at least one respect. Their womenfolk enjoyed a far higher degree of freedom and equality—license, some might have called it—than those of the other Races of Man. Besides, Bahzell and Brandark were friends of the family.

"Uncle Kilthan always said you were smarter than you looked, Brandark," she said now. "Of course, being smarter than *you* look isn't that much of an accomplishment, is it?" She smiled sweetly.

"Why is it that *he's* the one who insulted your ability to glare properly and *I'm* the one who's getting whacked?" The Bloody Sword's tone was aggrieved, and he did his level best to look hurt.

"Because the world is full of injustice," she told him.

The sarthnaisk gave her armsman's shoulder a pat, then walked to the edge of the bridged channel and gazed down into the rushing water. Despite the tartness of her exchange with the two hradani, a curiously serene sense of joy seemed to fill the air about her, and Bahzell stepped up beside her. He understood that serenity; he felt something very like it every time he was privileged to heal, and he let one enormous hand rest very gently on her shoulder as he inhaled the damp, fresh breath of moisture rising from the boisterous stream.

"It's a fine piece of work you've done," he told her. "And it's grateful I am for your help. And for Kilthan's, of course."

"I suppose it's a bit undutiful of me to point out that Uncle Kilthan—and the rest of Silver Cavern—is going to be minting money when this little project is completed," she replied dryly, but her hand rose to touch his gently as she spoke.

"Aye," he acknowledged. "And so are my folk and Tellian's. Which isn't to say as how I'm any less grateful for it."

"Well, I imagine you've accomplished the odd little job or two to deserve it. That's what Uncle Kilthan said when he proposed this whole notion to the clan elders, anyway. Along with pointing out the fact that the clan was going to make fairly obscene amounts of profit, even by our standards, in the long haul, of course." She shook her head. "It's amazing how successful that second argument usually is with our folk."

She looked up at him, and the topaz eyes she shared with her uncle gleamed wickedly in the sunlight pouring through the air shaft. Of course, Kilthan wasn't *actually* her uncle, Bahzell reminded himself. Only a dwarf could possibly keep all of the intricacies of their family structures and clan relationships straight. Serman really was Kilthan's nephew, the son of his younger sister, but the exact nature of Chanharsa's relationship with Clan Harkanath's head was rather more complicated than that. In fact, Bahzell didn't have a clue what it truly was, although the fact that she was "*dah*knarthi" rather than "*al*knarthi" indicated that it was a blood relationship, rather than solely one by marriage, as did those eyes. And dwarves understood that *proper* explanations of consanguinity, collateral family lines, and connections by marriage quickly caused the eyes of the other Races of Man to glaze over, which made "uncle" or "aunt"—or the even more splendidly ambiguous "kinsman"—perfectly acceptable (if scandalously imprecise) substitutes.

"Aye, and money's not so bad an argument where my folk are concerned, come to that," he acknowledged. "Not that there's not those amongst us as would still prefer to be *plundering* those trade caravans like good, honest hradani! Still and all, I'm thinking my Da's in a fair way to convincing them to change their ways."

"True," Brandark said, stepping up on Chanharsa's other side. "I find it sad, somehow, to see so many good, unwashed barbarian Horse Stealers succumbing to the sweet sound of kormaks falling into their purses." He heaved a huge sigh. "Such decadence. Why, the next thing I know, they're all going to be taking *baths*!"

"Just you be keeping it up, little man," Bahzell rumbled. "I've no need to ask Walsharno to be stepping on you, and I'm thinking as how you'd be getting a bath of your own—aye, and making a fine dam—if I was after shoving your head into that drain hole yonder."

"Speaking of drains," the Bloody Sword said brightly, pointedly not glancing at Bahzell as he looked down at Chanharsa, "where does that one come out?"

"Into the Gullet, like the others." She shrugged. "By the time we're done, we'll probably have a river, or at least a fairly substantial stream, flowing back down it again. Year-round, I mean, not just whenever the snow melts up on the Wind Plain."

Brandark nodded, but his expression was thoughtful. They'd gotten farther and farther away from the narrow chasm, which twisted down the towering height of the Escarpment from Glanharrow to the hradani city-state of Hurgrum. The Balthar River had once flowed through that channel, before a massive earthquake had diverted it, long, long ago. That diversion had created The Bogs, as the vast, swampy area along the West Riding's border with the South Riding were called, when it pushed the diminished Balthar to the north and cut it off from the tributary which had drained them into the Hangnysti, below the Escarpment. The Gullet remained, however, still snaking its own broken-back way to the Hangnysti, which made it a natural place to dispose of any water that turned up in the course of boring the tunnel through the Escarpment. By now, though, the head of the tunnel was the better part of a mile from the Gullet, and he rubbed the tip of his truncated left ear as he cocked an eyebrow at her.

"I thought you could only do this sort of thing"—he waved at the newly created length of tunnel—"a few dozen yards at a time," he observed.

"*Most* sarthnaisks could only do 'this sort of thing' a few dozen *feet* at a time," she corrected him tartly. She gave him a sharp look for good measure, then shrugged. "Still, I take your point. But cutting a drainage channel is a lot simpler and more straightforward than cutting the tunnel itself. Each section of the tunnel is new and unique, and that requires a lot of concentration and focus, but I've made scores—probably even hundreds—of simple culverts and drainage systems. By now, it's almost more reflex than thought to throw one in whenever I need it, and it's even simpler than usual in this case. It's mostly just a matter of visualizing a straight line with the proper downslope, and I just . . . tell it which direction to go and what to do when it gets there." She shrugged again. "I'm sorry, Brandark. I know you're still trying to figure out how I do it, and I wish I could explain it better, but there it is."

"Unsatisfied curiosity is my lot in life," he told her with a smile. "Well, that and following Bahzell around from one scrape to another." He shook his head. "It's a dirty job, but someone has to do it. Hirahim only knows what would happen to him if I weren't there to pull him out again!"

"A *fine* dam, I'm thinking," Bahzell murmured, and Chanharsa laughed.

"You two deserve each other," she declared. "*I*, on the other hand, deserve a glass of good wine and a hot bath for my labors."

"And so you do," Bahzell agreed as Walsharno came over to join them.

Coursers, by and large, were only mildly curious about how the Races of Man, with the clever hands they themselves had been denied, accomplished all the things they seemed to find with which to occupy themselves. Those of them who bonded with human—or, in one highly unusual case, with hradani—riders tended to be more curious than others, but even Walsharno was more interested in results than processes. He looked down into the flowing water for a moment, then turned his head to Bahzell. The Horse Stealer looked back at him, listening to a voice only he could hear, then nodded.

"Walsharno's a suggestion," he told Chanharsa.

"He does?"

"Aye," Bahzell said simply, and then he picked her up like an infant and set her neatly on Walsharno's saddle.

The sarthnaisk gave a little squeak of astonishment and clutched at the saddle horn as she suddenly found herself perched more than twice her own height above the tunnel floor. A saddle sized for someone of Bahzell's dimensions was a very substantial seat for someone *her* size, however. In fact, it was almost large enough to serve her as a sofa as she sat sidesaddle on the courser's back.

The armsman who'd frowned at her exchange with the hradani took a quick step towards them, then stopped as Chanharsa relaxed and her face blossomed into a huge smile. However happy she might have been, *he* obviously wasn't at all pleased about having his charge on the back of such a monstrously tall mount. Even a small horse was huge for a dwarf, and a courser was anything but small. On the other hand, very few people were foolish enough to *argue* with a courser... and the coursers honored even fewer people by agreeing to bear them.

"I'd not be fretting about it too much," Bahzell told the armsman, with a sympathetic smile. "Walsharno's not one for letting folk fall off his back. Why, look at what he's put up with from me! And your lady's the right of it; she *is* after deserving that hot bath of hers, so what say we be getting her to it?"

Chapter Two

“Nobody better get between me and the hot tub tonight. That’s all *I’ve* got to say.” Garlahna Lorhanalfressa wiped sweat from her forehead with one muddy hand and glowered up at the sun. “Or the *cold* tub, either.”

“Oh?” Erlis Rahnafressa glanced across at her. “And just what makes you think you get priority over *me?* I believe the phrase is ‘Rank hath its privileges.’”

The commander of three hundred was a tough, sturdy looking woman, almost twice Garlahna’s age. Her fair hair was lightly streaked with gray, and she possessed an interesting collection of scars and only one arm. She was also the second in command of the Kalatha City Guard, and her brown eyes missed very little, even when they gleamed with amusement.

“Besides,” she continued, “my bones, not to mention other portions of my anatomy, are older than yours. They’re going to need longer to soak, and you uppity youngsters have to learn to respect your elders.”

“Goddess!” Garlahna shook her head. “I can’t believe you’re actually going to stand there—well, *sit* there, I suppose—and pile two platitudes on me at a time!”

“That’s ‘two platitudes at a time, *Ma’am,*’” Erlis said. Military duty was the only place war maids used that particular form of address with one another, and the three hundred’s smile grew broader as Garlahna rolled her eyes. “And we only get to argue about it if we win. Not that there’s going to *be* any argument, of course.”

"Tyrant," Garlahna muttered. "War maids are supposed to be free of this sort of petty oppression. It says so right in our charter."

"That's free of petty *male* oppression," Erlis pointed out. "Now watch your flank. I don't think Leeana's going to give up just because she missed us back at Thalar, do you?"

Garlahna stuck out her tongue, but she also turned her attention obediently back to the left flank of the small column making its way across the rolling grasslands of the Wardenship of Lorham towards the free town of Kalatha.

It didn't occur to her to think about the fact that that sort of exchange between a lowly commander of twenty and a commander of three hundred—the equivalent of a very junior lieutenant or a very *senior* noncom and a major in the Empire of the Axe—would never have been tolerated in most military organizations. She was aware that other armies put far more emphasis on things like saluting and standing at attention and titles of rank, but the awareness was purely intellectual and such antics left her with a sense of bemused semi-tolerance rather than any desire to emulate them, for war maids had little use for the sort of formality which infused those other armies. Most of them regarded the aristocratic, birth-based power structure of their own kingdom with outright contempt, and the spit and polish of standing armies like those of the Empire of the Axe and the Empire of the Spear filled them with amusement. Their own warriors were trained to operate as light infantry—scouts, skirmishers, and guerillas—and they valued initiative and ingenuity far more than unthinking obedience to orders. War maid officers came in all flavors and varieties, of course, but martinets were few and far between. Discipline was always maintained, yet that discipline rested upon an *esprit de corps* which didn't *require* formality, which had led more than one of their adversaries into underestimating them . . . with fatal consequences.

Unfortunately, there'd been quite a few of those adversaries over the years, given the disapproval with which Sothōii society regarded them, and there were those who wouldn't have hesitated for a moment to rob them. Some of those people would actually have felt a sense of virtuous justification at punishing such an uppity and unnatural bunch of women, if they could only figure out how to get away with it, which was the main reason Garlahna and her six woman detachment were out here sweltering in the heat. Erlis, on the other hand, was just a *bit* senior for this sort of nonsense. The three hundred would normally have let Garlahna get on with her routine task without looking over her shoulder this way, but she'd had business of her own in Thalar, so she'd decided to come along and turn the trip into a training exercise.

Not that anyone was taking the trip lightly. "Routine" was quite a different thing from "unimportant," and the two large wagons at the heart of the formation were piled high with supplies and raw materials for Kalatha's craftswomen, especially for Theretha, the town glassblower. Garlahna didn't know exactly how much their contents were worth, but the weight of the purse Erlis had turned over to their agent in Thalar had been impressive, and the wagons were heavily laden enough to be an unmitigated pain in the arse. That would probably have been true under any circumstances, but the condition of the road didn't help a bit.

The muddy track (even Sothōii notions of a "highway" would have made an Axeman engineer cringe, and *this* ribbon of muck was little better than a country lane) ran between tall walls of prairie grass. The good news was that it was still early enough in the summer that the grass hadn't had time to turn into the sort of sun-dried tinder which all too often flared into rolling walls of flame later in the year. The bad news was that there was absolutely no wind today, and the rains of spring, while nourishing the grass quite nicely, had not only turned the road into a quagmire which seemed bottomless in spots but also stoked a humidity that turned the grass-hemmed roadbed into a steam bath.

The entire escort, including Erlis, had just finished helping the drivers and their assistants wrestle both wagons out of yet another knee-deep pothole full of soupy mud, and Garlahna had *not* been amused. Nor had her horse, when he'd found himself hitched to the lead wagon to add his own weight to the effort. The gelding was no prize example of the Sothōii warhorses which were the pride of the Kingdom, but he'd obviously found the role of dray horse *far* beneath his dignity... as he'd demonstrated with an indignant crow hop or two when she'd climbed back into the saddle.

Garlahna wasn't the horsewoman her friend Leeana was. Most war maids were infantry, more comfortable on their feet than in a saddle under the best of conditions, and she'd been born to a family of yeomen, not in the house of a great noble. For her, horses were simply a means of transportation—a way to get from one place to another without using her own feet—and while Leeana would undoubtedly have taken the gelding's misbehavior in stride and actually enjoyed it, Garlahna was just relieved she hadn't parted company with her saddle. Well, by that and the fact that her spine seemed not to have collapsed after all.

She chuckled at the thought and wiped another stripe of mud across her forehead as she blotted fresh sweat and thought longingly of her chari and yathu. The short, kiltlike chari was definitely not the most comfortable garment for a lengthy horseback ride, however. Trousers were a far better idea for that (*another* reason to prefer feet to saddles, she thought darkly). They were also at least a *little* less offensive to traditional Sothōii patriarchs than the short, revealing, *comfortable* chari (and even more scandalous yathu!), and unlike some of her sister war maids, Garlahna didn't have a problem being unconfrontational for trips to non-war maid towns, at least when it could be done without appearing weak. Outside such towns, the traditionalists could like it or lump it as far as she was concerned, and if she'd been traveling on foot, she'd have worn chari and yathu this time, as well, and let the townsfolk think whatever they liked. The war maids weren't about to kowtow to anyone's prejudices after their long, bitter fight for equality. Yet she had to admit that, as towns went, Thalar was more accustomed to and comfortable with war maids than most. Now, at least. Garlahna wasn't going to object if the trousers she'd donned for utilitarian reasons soothed any potential ruffled feathers someplace like Thalar—she wasn't *that* enamored of making a statement everywhere she went—but that didn't mean she liked the wet, sticky misery her present attire helped create in this kind of humid heat.

At least her horseback perch put her high enough to see across the green sea of grass baking under the windless sun. That was fortunate, given what she was pretty sure was out there somewhere doing its best to sneak up on them, and she shaded her eyes with one hand, making a slow, conscientious sweep of her own area of responsibility. So far, so good, with no sign of trouble, and she nodded in satisfaction, then glanced back at those muddy, creaking wagons with mixed feelings. She would far rather have spent the last couple of days in one of the Kalatha Guard's nice, shady barracks, but she did have a proprietary interest in the larger of the two vehicles, since it carried (among a host of other things) a dozen bolts of fabric in rich colors and textures destined for Tomarah Felisfressa. Tomarah and her freemate Selistra were the best seamstresses and dressmakers in Kalatha, and Garlahna had paid the better part of two months of income for the length of amber-colored silk that was going to turn into her new gathering gown. At, she reflected, the expense of another week or so of her income for Tomarah . . . whose skilled fingers and flair for design would be worth every copper kormak.

Of course, my income would be a little better if it wasn't my year for Guard service, Garlahna reflected wryly. *Still, even with little jaunts like today's, serving in the Guard isn't* that *bad. Aside from Erlis' and Ravlahn's idea of "restful" morning calisthenics, that is!*

Unlike certain others of Kalatha's younger citizens, she didn't really object to serving her stint in the City Guard. It was inconvenient, and it interfered with her thriving business as a tinker, yet she'd never even considered hiring a substitute, as quite a few Kalathans did. Partly because it would have cost at least half of her earnings, but also because she was young enough it was no physical hardship . . . and because it was important for the town to maintain a reserve of trained and experienced war maids to back up the standing Guard just in case. It wasn't all that many years since Kalatha had come entirely too close to finding itself under attack, after all, even if the town hadn't known anything about it until it was all over.

Garlahna's good humor dimmed at the memory, and she grimaced and reached down to adjust the short sword at her hip. No one in Kalatha liked to think about how close the Dark Gods had come to setting the town and Trisu of Lorham at one another's throats. And Garlahna suspected very few in Kalatha liked to think about the fact that Trisu had been in the right during their bitter dispute over land and water rights, either. There was no love lost between Kalatha and Trisu even now, but any fair-minded war maid would have been forced to acknowledge that he'd actually shown remarkable restraint under the circumstances. Not that all war maids were precisely fair-minded, of course. In fact, *some* of them seemed to prefer to go on blaming Trisu rather than accept that Shīgū had perverted the Kingdom of the Sothōii's most sacred temple of Lillinara and affected the minds of quite a few Kalathans along the way. If it hadn't been for Dame Kaeritha Seldansdaughter . . .

Garlahna decided—again—not to think about where it all could have ended. War maids were accustomed to being less than popular, especially with hard-core traditionalists like Trisu Pickaxe, but it was frightening to think how close Shīgū had come to provoking an open, violent confrontation between them and the rest of the Kingdom. If the Twisted One had succeeded, the consequences would have been catastrophic. Indeed, she might have achieved her goal of destroying the war maids once and for all.

That hadn't happened, and it wasn't going to, either, but it had come frighteningly close to reality, and relations with Thalar had become strained and overtly hostile as a result. They'd recovered their normal, even tenor once the townsfolk realized what had happened, though . . . which was actually quite generous of them, given the way Jolhanna Evahlafressa, Kalatha's previous agent in Thalar, had acted. Jolhanna was one of the war maids who'd gone completely over to the Dark, and she'd done her very best to utterly destroy Kalatha's relations with the largest town in the Wardenship of Lorham. Thalar's willingness to accept Dame Kaeritha's explanation of what had led to Jolhanna's actions—and that they'd been *her* actions, not Kalatha's—was one reason Garlahna didn't mind making at least a few concessions to the town's sensibilities where things like attire were concerned.

The war maids had taken the lesson to heart, however, and no one was ready to assume Shīgū and the other Dark Gods had simply given up on the project, either. That was the reason the Kalatha City Guard was half again the size it had been and why the tradition of requiring war maids between the ages of eighteen and thirty-eight to contribute one year in four to militia service had been revived. There'd been a few changes to the militia requirements, too. One new profession—that of glassblower—had been added to the exempted trades list, and the town charter had been amended to allow people to discharge their entire Guard obligation in a single five-year stint, if that was their preference, rather than breaking it up into five separate terms of service. Garlahna was seriously considering combining at least two years of her own service into a single term, but she hadn't made up her mind yet. There were arguments in favor of either decision, but the biggest one against it was Barlahn.

He didn't have any objection to her discharging her militia responsibility; it only made the logistics complicated because she had to be on-post every night, except when she could get leave. It wasn't too bad during the winter months, when he was able to share her assigned quarters in town at least three or four nights a week, but that wasn't very practical once he could get his crops into the ground again. She'd grown up around farmers, and she knew all about the hours they worked. It would have been silly for him to be hiking the six miles in and out of town every morning and every evening, especially when he was already worn out from his labors, and she knew it. None of which made her any happier about the currently empty state of her bed. It would be nice to get her present year of service out of the way and get settled back in with him, but then again if she discharged two of her remaining three years of obligation back to back, she'd have six years, not just three, in which to do that settling. That would be nice. Time enough for a couple of children, perhaps, and to help get them past the toddler stage before Mommy had to report for duty again....

One of the wagon drivers swore wearily, and Garlahna turned in the saddle to look back over her shoulder as the front wheels of the woman's wagon splashed down into a puddle which was obviously even deeper and muckier than usual. Garlahna's gelding had automatically made his way around the pothole's lip on one side while Erlis circled it on the other, but the wagons didn't have that option, and the hole was the next best thing to wheel hub-deep. The lead wagon came to an abrupt halt, the mules whuffing against their collars in surprise, and Erlis shook her head as she drew rein.

"Mother, this one's deeper than the *last* one!" the three hundred said sourly.

"Looks like it," Garlahna agreed even more sourly. "I *hate* paying Trisu the road toll, but I have to admit he keeps the main roads in a lot better shape than this! Maybe *we* should start charging tolls?"

"Who'd pay them?" Erlis snorted. "We're the only ones who use this miserable excuse for a road. And in case you've forgotten, *we* only use it because the shortcut lets us stay *off* his stupid toll road. Not that our 'shortcut' seems to be saving us all that much time today, does it?"

"Not so you'd notice. But it's the principle that counts, isn't it? Well, that and the kormaks, I suppose. And at least this damned swamp isn't as *wide* as the last one. It's only big enough to eat one wagon at a time."

"And this is supposed to make me feel better because—?" Erlis inquired, turning her mount and trotting back towards the mired wagon.

"Give me a few minutes and I'll think of a reason," Garlahna promised from behind her, and Erlis chuckled. But then she shook her head and swung down from the saddle in a creak of stirrup leather.

"Best be getting on with it, I guess," she sighed.

Garlahna nodded and touched the gelding's sides with her heels, heading back towards the wagons in Erlis' wake as the three hundred looped her reins around the stump of her left arm, pressing them in against her side, and walked up to the edge of the pothole to survey the problem. The rest of the escort had already dismounted as well, and the six of them were uncoiling their saddle ropes as they prepared to add their own horses' efforts to disinterring the wagon. Garlahna knew all about leading by example, but she'd already done that three times today, and her boots and trousers were caked with dried mud to the knee to prove it. "Follow me!" was all very well when it came time to lead her people into actual combat, but *this* time, she decided, she was perfectly prepared to let the members of her detachment wade out into the mud while she confined herself to a proper supervisory role. She knew she was going to have to climb down from the saddle and help out eventually—the hole was so deep it was undoubtedly going to take all of them to wrestle the wagons across it—but there was no point doing it until somebody *else* had gotten thoroughly muddy this time around, and she drew up beside Erlis on the lip of the swamp.

"That really *is* a deep hole," she commented, swatting irritably at a horsefly as two of the other war maids kicked off their boots and started wading towards the wagon. Erlis looked up at her, smiling faintly as she found Garlahna still in the saddle, and the younger woman shook her head. "The wagons were even more heavily loaded on the way *to* Thalar. Thank Lillinara we didn't put one of them into this mess then!"

"Absolutely," Erlis agreed fervently. She looked back at the mud-hole stretching almost all the way across the road. "That *would* have been the perfect way to start this little expedition, wouldn't it?"

Garlahna nodded, but then she frowned as another thought struck her. Why *hadn't* they encountered the pothole on the way out? As wide as it was, it should have been impossible to avoid. It was possible one of the spring thunderstorms could have dumped enough rain on this stretch of the road to make the hole worse without having rained on them in Thalar, but it wasn't all that likely. Besides, enough fresh rain to have created this morass should have generated even more mud along the road's shoulders, shouldn't it? But that meant—

"I think—" she began sharply, but it was already too late.

A chalk-covered beanbag came flying out of the grass on the south side of the lane and smacked Erlis right between the shoulder blades in a puff of colored dust. The three hundred jerked, then whirled around with an oath born of twenty-plus years' service as a professional soldier . . . just as three more beanbags thudded into the trio of war maids standing in the mud on the north side of the road. An instant later, more of them smacked into two of the three on the *south* side of the road, as well, and the single dismounted war maid who hadn't already been hit ducked under the wagon in a geyser of muddy water, snatching out her short sword with one hand and reaching for her bandolier of throwing stars with the other. Despite her own surprise, Garlahna knew better than to try to stand and fight. Instead, she reined her gelding's head around and slapped her heels in—hard—trying to break free of the ambush before one of those infernal beanbags found *her*. If she could circle back around to counterattack—

It was a good idea, but before the horse had even moved, a very tall, red-haired young woman bounded out of a stretch of grass Garlahna would have sworn couldn't have hidden a rabbit. The newcomer took three strides, tucked a bare foot into the front of Garlahna's offside stirrup, pinning her own foot in place, grabbed the saddle horn with her right hand, and pivoted on the stirrup, swinging her left leg over the horse's croup and dropping to sit neatly behind the saddle. It happened too quickly for Garlahna to react, and the newcomer's hands settled on her shoulders and gripped tightly.

"You're turning blue, Garlahna!" the red-haired war maid announced cheerfully. "Too bad, I really *liked* you."

"Very funny, Leeana," Garlahna growled, looking over her shoulder with a disgusted expression as the last war maid of the escort, despite the protection of the wagon, was hit by three different beanbags flying in from three different directions.

"You're dead, too, Saltha!" another voice crowed from the grass.

"Oh, yeah?" Saltha Mahrlafressa, the war maid under the wagon, sounded as disgusted as Garlahna felt. "Well, I'm mucky enough already, Raythas," she retorted, raking a glob of mud out of her graying hair and looking at it distastefully. "If you think I'm going to die dramatically and bellyflop into this mudhole, you've got another think coming!"

"Spoilsport."

Raythas Talafressa emerged from the grass with a grin, followed by two more, equally delighted young women in traditional war-maid garb. They'd added leather leg guards to protect their otherwise bare legs from the prairie grass, but aside from that, they looked revoltingly cool and comfortable, Garlahna thought from inside her sweaty trousers and shirt. They also looked revoltingly *pleased* with themselves.

"Nicely done," Erlis acknowledged, shaking her head as she looked at their attackers. "Not that we didn't help you by acting like drooling idiots who shouldn't be let out without a keeper." She grimaced. "What a *convenient* mudhole you just happened to find to stop us for you."

"Yes, it was, wasn't it?" Leeana agreed. She slid down from the back of Garlahna's horse and grinned impudently up at her friend as her left hand twirled the garrotte she hadn't wrapped around Garlahna's neck. "It only took us four or five hours to get it dug. The biggest problem was hauling in the water to fill it after we got it properly excavated." She looked back at Erlis. "We were only an hour or two behind you on the way out, so the mud had plenty of time to cure."

"So I see."

Erlis stretched out her hand to help Saltha out of the mudhole while she considered the victors. The three hundred didn't like losing, but she had to admire Leeana's tactics. The manufactured pothole had been a masterstroke, an obstacle which was certain to stop the wagons but which hadn't set off any mental alarms because they'd already had to deal with so many mudholes. And as she looked further into the grass on either side of the road, she saw the blinds Leeana and her three companions had painstakingly constructed to conceal them until they struck.

It's a good thing they weren't really trying to kill us, she reflected with more than a little chagrin. All eight members of the escort—except Garlahna—bore large, bright splotches of chalk dust from the beanbags which had been substituted for the far more lethal throwing stars (or knives) which would have come their way if Leeana had been serious. *I must be getting old to let the young hellion get away with it this way!*

Yet even as she thought that, she knew that wasn't the true reason. Yes, she really should have been more suspicious—or alert, at least—but that wouldn't have mattered in the end, given how carefully Leeana had organized things. The girl had come a long way in the six and a half years since she'd fled to the war maids. She was still not quite twenty-two years old, yet she was already a commander of seventy-five, and whether she realized it or not, Erlis and Balcartha Evahnalfressa, the commander of five hundred who commanded the City Guard, were quietly grooming her for far higher rank. Indeed, Erlis was beginning to wonder if Kalatha would be allowed to keep her. The war maids were legally obligated to provide troops in the Crown's service in return for the royal charter which had created them in the first place, and any field commander in his (or her) right mind was going to want an officer of Leanna Hanathafressa's caliber. No matter what challenge Erlis and Balcartha threw at her, she took it in stride, and she was so cheerful even old sweats like Saltha couldn't seem to take offense when she effortlessly ran rings around them.

Or got promoted *past* them, for that matter.

"All right," she said finally. "You won; we lost. So you get the bathhouse first tonight and you get the three-day passes."

Leeana and the other members of her team looked at one another with broad grins, and Erlis let them have their moment before she gave them a rather nasty smile of her own.

"And now that you've won, why don't the four of you just wade out into that marvelous mudhole of yours and help us get this wagon out of it?"

Chapter Three

The small, carefully nondescript man sat back in his chair and rubbed his eyes as the flickering glow died in the heart of the water-clear gramerhain crystal on the desk before him. His name was Varnaythus, or that was the one he most commonly went by among those who knew who (and what) he truly was, at any rate. He looked to be no more than in his mid-forties, yet he was actually well past eighty—there were some advantages to being a wand wizard willing to manipulate blood magic—and no one had learned his true name in at least the last sixty years. It was safer that way.

Of course, "safe" was a relative term.

He climbed out of his chair and began pacing back and forth across the small, luxurious (and carefully hidden) room. There were no windows, and the light from the oil lamps was dim, despite the highly polished reflectors, to eyes which had become accustomed to the grammerhain's brilliance. He could have flooded the room with clear, sourceless light, but black wizards who wanted to stay alive in Norfressa avoided that sort of self-indulgence. Wizardry was outlawed upon pain of death in virtually all Norfressan realms, and however much Varnaythus might resent that, he couldn't pretend he didn't *understand* it. That reaction had been inevitable after the Wizard Wars destroyed the Empire of Ottovar and turned the entire continent of Kontovar into a blasted wasteland which had needed a thousand years to recover. It was actually quite useful to Vanaythus' Lady and her fellows, in many ways. It certainly reduced the opposition's strength and ability to respond to arcane attacks, at any rate.

There *were* wizards here, but most of them tended to be at best a dingy shade of gray. The fact that they were already outlawed and condemned made it far easier for the Carnadosans to recruit them, as well, and not even the ones unwilling to actively serve the Dark themselves would be interested in calling attention to himself if he happened to notice that another wizard was practicing the art in his vicinity. Unfortunately, if Varnaythus didn't have to worry about being turned in by another *wizard*, he did have to worry about magi.

He puffed his lips in familiar frustration as he paced. The wizard lords of Kontovar still didn't understand how the mage talents worked. Varnaythus himself had picked up far more about the effects and consequences of their various abilities, including some interesting . . . intersections with the art, but he'd gathered that information very cautiously indeed. Much of it had been gleaned by picking the brains (in some cases literally) of other nonmagi, while the rest had come from wary, circumspect observation with the stealthiest scrying spells he could command. And all of it, unfortunately, remained largely theoretical, since he had absolutely no desire to risk his own personal hide in order to test his conjectures. Quite a few wizards who'd done that sort of thing had never found the opportunity to report back on their success, for some reason.

Still, they did know at least a *little* about them. For instance, it was obvious the talents themselves were products of the Wizard Wars, the result of some deep change in the very being of the current magi's ancestors, although it had never manifested in Kontovar even after the Fall. He suspected there'd been very, very few of them in the beginning, when refugees from all of Kontovar first flooded into Norfressa. There couldn't have been many, since no one had really recognized their existence at all for over seven hundred years, and they'd only become sufficiently numerous to begin organizing their mage academies in the last three or four centuries.

The Carnadosan lords of Kontovar hadn't even noticed them at first, and by the time they'd begun to realize just how . . . inconvenient they might prove to their own ultimate plans, the magi had been too firmly entrenched to eliminate. Efforts to acquire live magi for study hadn't worked out well, either. The bastards were slippery as fish and even more elusive, and *trained* magi had a nasty tendency to die, often taking any wizard unfortunate enough to have been interrogating them at the moment with them, if they were captured. Not to mention the fact that many of them could call for help telepathically over even lengthy distances. Varnaythus knew of at least three expeditions to capture magi which had come to unfortunate ends when the magi in question managed to guide cruisers of the Royal and Imperial Navy to intercept the ships carrying them to Kontovar. The effort hadn't been abandoned, but it was one of those tasks to be approached very, very cautiously, and he was more than happy to leave it to someone else, like Tremala. Or even better, now that he thought about it—however serious a rival Tremala might be, he actually *liked* her, after all—someone like that insufferable, egotistical, *irritating* pain Rethak.

More to the point, however, the accursed magi could sense the use of the art. Some were more sensitive than others—in fact, some of them were damned bloodhounds where sorcery was concerned!—but *all* of them had at least some sensitivity to it. And unlike Norfressan wizards, they had no reason not to report any sorcery they detected. In fact, the mage academies' Oath of Semkirk *required* magi to fight dark wizardry and blood magic, and the bastards had been growing steadily into ever more of a pain in the arse for the last two hundred years.

Nor was their ability to sense wizardry the only threat they posed to Kontovaran ambitions. They had other talents as well—from the ability to speak mind-to-mind across vast distances, to healing, to distance-viewing, to the ability to unerringly detect lies, plus Phrobus only knew what else. Thankfully, none of them had more than three or four such talents each, but groups of them could combine their abilities into the sort of threat which had to make any wizard wary, and they were oathbound to use their abilities to serve others, which made them disgustingly popular with the very people who most hated and feared wizardry. Many rulers welcomed them into their realms, often relying upon them as agents, investigators, and representatives, and King Markhos of the Sothōii had opened his arms even more broadly to them than most. There was no mage academy in his kingdom—Sothōii magi were trained in one of their Axeman allies' academies, usually at either Axe Hallow or Belhadan—but there were *dozens* of them wandering around Markhos' capital of Sothōfalas, and all it would take was for one of them to stroll past when Varnaythus was using the art, at which point all manner of unpleasant things would happen.

A soft, musical tone sounded out of the empty air, and Varnaythus turned towards one of the office's featureless walls. Nothing happened for a moment; then the outline of a doorframe appeared in the middle of the wall. It glowed dimly, seeming to quiver a little around the edges, then solidified.

"Enter," he said, and the glowing door swung open to admit two other men.

One of them looked to be about the same age as Varnaythus, and he was even more nondescript and bland looking. The other was younger, with red-blond hair and gray eyes. At just over six feet, he was also considerably taller than the other two, and his clothing was much richer, that of a mid-level functionary at court, perhaps. Looking through the door by which they'd entered the office, it was as if that single door had opened into two totally separate locations... which was fair enough, since that was exactly what it had done.

"You're late," Varnaythus observed brusquely, waving the newcomers to chairs in front of his desk. He waited until they'd seated themselves, then sank back into his own chair, leaned his elbows on the blotter on either side of his gramerhain with his fingers interlaced above it, and leaned forward to rest his chin on the backs of his raised hands. "I don't want to belabor the point," he said then, "but using the art is risky enough without having our timetable screwed up."

"I couldn't get to the portal," the older of his two guests said. He shrugged. "Someone decided to choose today to drop off two dray loads of tea. Somehow I didn't think you'd want me activating it from my end with half a dozen warehousemen carrying crates of tea in and out."

"No, I don't suppose that would have been a very good idea," Varnaythus acknowledged. He straightened, then leaned back in his chair and folded his hands across his stomach. "I never was very happy about that location. Unfortunately, moving it at this point would be too risky. As a matter of fact, it would be safer to build an entirely new portal somewhere else." He raised one eyebrow. "Would you happen to have a more convenient—and safer—spot in mind, Salgahn?"

"Not right this minute, no," Salgahn replied. "I'll think about it. There aren't really all that many options, though. Not unless I want to risk letting some of the other dog brothers find out about it."

His final sentence ended on the rising note of a question and he raised one eyebrow.

"Not yet." Varnaythus shook his head quickly.

"With all due respect, Varnaythus," the younger of the two newcomers said, "we've been saying 'not yet' for over six years now. Are we ever really going to move at all?"

Varnaythus regarded him thoughtfully. Unlike himself, Magister Malahk Sahrdohr truly was as young as he looked, but he'd proven himself to be smart, ambitious, and capable. As his title indicated, he ranked well below a master wizard like Varnaythus in both training and raw strength, but he'd risen high and quickly in the service of the Church of Carnadosa through a combination of the intelligent use of the skills he did possess and a degree of absolute ruthlessness Varnaythus had seldom seen equaled.

"You do remember what happened the last time we 'moved' here in the Kingdom, don't you?" he inquired mildly.

"Of course I do." Sahrdohr shrugged. "I read all the reports before I even left Trōfrōlantha. And I understand why we had to let things settle back down. But it's been six *years*. Forgive me for pointing this out, but the original plan indicated we were rapidly approaching one of the critical cusp points, and it's only gotten closer since. If we don't do something soon, it's going to be right on top of us!"

Varnaythus nodded. Sahrdohr had a valid point, although Varnaythus suspected his impatience had more to do with his current role here in Sothōfalas than with approaching "cusp points." In his alter ego as Mahrahk Firearrow, Sahrdohr was a mid-level bureaucrat in the Exchequer. His position gave him access to all sorts of sensitive information, but it was junior enough to keep him from attracting unwanted attention, and he did his job well. Unfortunately, it restricted him to a much less luxurious lifestyle than the one to which he had been accustomed in Kontovar and required him to be civil to and even take orders from men without so much as a trace of the magical ability which would have given them authority there. That had to be irksome enough by itself, yet his very position inside the Palace meant he dared not employ the art at all. The King kept at least two or three magi at court permanently, and the magister would have been promptly detected if he'd done anything of the sort.

Varnaythus felt an unwilling ripple of sympathy for the younger man. Being forced to restrict his use of the art was hard for any wizard; renouncing it entirely, even if only temporarily, as Sahrdohr's role had required him to do, was the next best thing to intolerable. All questions of power and ambition aside, there was a splendor to the art, a glory no wizard could truly resist. He *had* to reach out to it, for better or for worse, and Sahrdohr had been denied the chance to do that for over four years, ever since his own arrival here in Sothōfalas. No wonder he was feeling impatient.

"If you've read the reports, Malahk," the older wizard said after a moment, "then you know I'm the only one of the senior agents originally assigned to this operation who's still alive. Salgahn here and I did our jobs just about perfectly, and I still barely got away with my skin. Jerghar and Paratha were less fortunate, and Farrier is . . . still laboring under the Spider's disapproval, shall we say?"

He grimaced at the thought of how the Twisted One had chosen to express Her unhappiness with Dahlaha Farrier. He'd never liked the woman, but seeing what had happened to *her* made him uncomfortably aware of what could happen to *him*. And that was with Shīgū's decision to be "lenient" with the servant who'd failed Her.

"Worse," he continued, "our last little escapade almost certainly warned the other side—Wencit, at the very least—that we've become far more interested in the Sothōii than we ever were before. Don't you think it makes sense to proceed with a modicum of caution when all of that is true?"

"Caution, yes," Sahrdohr agreed. "But we can't afford to allow ourselves to be paralyzed, either. Especially not if we really are coming up on one of the cusp points."

"And would you happen to know *why* it's a cusp point?" Varnaythus asked mildly, extending his thumbs and tapping them together. He raised both eyebrows and cocked his head, and Sahrdohr looked back with a stubborn expression for several seconds. Then the younger man shrugged irritably.

"No," he said shortly.

"Neither do I," Varnaythus told him. It was Sahrdohr's eyebrows' turn to shoot upward, and his eyes widened with surprise. Surprise that turned into skepticism almost instantly, Varnaythus noticed.

"I'm telling you the truth," he said. "I realize that's a novel approach, but we're in rather an unusual situation here. They haven't told me why They want us to do what They want us to do. All They've told me is *what* They want us to do. Now, to me that suggests this may be even more important than They're prepared to admit even to us. Either that or *They* don't know everything that's involved here. Either way, there's no way I'm going to rush in and blow this operation a second time. Is that understood?"

Sahrdohr gazed at him for at least a minute. Then he nodded slowly, and Varnaythus nodded back just a bit more emphatically. Both of them understood the subtext of what Varnaythus had just said. He'd avoided the Dark Gods' displeasure because, unlike his deceased associates, he'd carried out his own portion of the operation almost flawlessly. Perhaps even more importantly, he'd covered his backside by carefully sending very complete reports—including reports of the several times he'd warned those associates that things were slipping—back to Kontovar. Coupled with the years of successful service he'd given to Carnadosa, that had sufficed to protect him from divine wrath. It was unusual for one of the Dark Gods' minions to survive the failure of a single mission remotely this important, however; it was unheard of for one of them to survive a *second* failure.

Varnaythus understood that, and he had no intention of failing, yet he wished passionately that his mistress had explained more about the reasons for this operation. What he'd said to Sahrdohr was nothing but the truth, and he *hated* operating blindly. It wouldn't be the first time he'd had to do it, but he'd never liked it. It was difficult—and risky—to improvise or modify strategies when he didn't even know what the ultimate motives of and reasons for his orders were.

The orders themselves were remarkably clear and unambiguous, however. That was something.

"All right," he said after a moment, allowing his chair to come back upright. "Having just told you we're not going to move until we're ready, now I'm going to tell you that we *are* ready... almost."

"We are?" Sahrdohr straightened with a jerk, and even Salgahn's eyes narrowed speculatively.

"'Almost,' I said," Varnaythus cautioned, raising one index finger. "There's been a certain degree of... discussion back and forth, and I've convinced Them we need a narrower focus this time. One of the reasons we failed last time was that each of Them had His or Her own objectives and strategies. This time *our* Lady is in charge, Sahrdohr, and we're going to avoid the kinds of distractions that got in the way last time."

Both Sahrdohr and Salgahn nodded in understanding. The Dark Gods' greatest weakness was their unwillingness to truly cooperate with one another. The same weakness afflicted their servants, but it was even worse among the gods themselves.

"That's good to hear," Sahrdohr said after a moment, and to his credit, he sounded as if he actually meant it. Which he might, Varnaythus reflected. The mortality rate among the Dark Gods' servants who had actually faced Bahzell Bahnakson or Tomanāk's other champions here on the Wind Plain had been effectively total. Sahrdohr could well be analyzing how his own position might be improved if something unfortunate happened to Varnaythus.

Of course, if whatever happens to me is truly *unfortunate, it'll probably happen to* him, *too. I wonder if he's factoring* that *into his analysis?*

"I think it's good news, too," he replied aloud. "But let's not any of us start thinking this is going to be simple, because it's not."

"If it were going to be simple, they wouldn't need *us*," Sahrdohr said with a grin which made him look even younger.

"A reassuring thought, I'm sure," Varnaythus said dryly, and Salgahn surprised him with a chuckle.

"All right," the elder wizard continued. "We've been 'authorized' to assassinate Bahzell and Tellian ourselves if we can find a way to do it." He rolled his eyes, and both of his companions grimaced. The Dark Gods had tried that approach more than once now... with uniformly disastrous results for their mortal instruments. None of the present trio were in favor of encountering those same results in person.

"Obviously," he continued, "there are limits to how directly we can approach that sort of thing. I'm, ah... doing my best to encourage our good frind Arthnar to organize an attempt, and he's certainly got more than enough motivation, given what their canal projects are going to do to his own arrangements. Unfortunately, he's not an idiot, either, so I don't know how successful

I'll be in getting him to move." He shrugged. "I think we can probably get him to at least see what a few anonymously hired mercenaries can accomplish, but it would be foolish to expect a high chance of success out of that sort of attempt."

"I can understand his reluctance," Sahrdohr said drily. "On the other hand, what about an attempt on Bahnak or Kilthandahknarthas? Killing either of them would probably derail their damned project, as well, wouldn't it? I'll admit they could probably survive better without the dwarf than without Bahnak, even if Kilthan was the one who got Silver Cavern and Dwarvenhame to put their weight behind Bahnak in the first place. But losing him would still have to be a major blow. And Bahnak, now . . . he's the glue holding this entire hradani 'Confederation' together, and there have to be enough Bloody Swords who'd love to see him dead."

Varnaythus regarded him thoughtfully for a moment, then glanced at Salgahn.

"Would *you* care to undertake either of those assignments?" he asked the assassin, and Salgahn snorted harshly.

"Get an assassin close enough to Kilthan of Silver Cavern? Not bloody likely! We don't have that many dwarven dog brothers to begin with, and the security around any clan head—and especially *that* clan head—is far too tight for any stranger to get to him. We *might* be able to manage it the next time he heads out with the trade caravans, but do we have the time to wait that long?"

He looked the question at Varnaythus, who shook his head.

"Almost certainly not. And, frankly, it sounds like investing the effort it would take to get to him would be a waste of our resources. Not to mention coming entirely too close to spreading ourselves too thin with the same kind of 'let's kill everyone in sight' stupidity that screwed up Their plans *last* time."

"That's about what I thought." Salgahn shrugged. "And as far as Bahnak is concerned, his security's almost as good as Kilthan's. I'm pretty sure we could get to him, but there's no way we could make it look like anything except a very obvious assassination . . . and not by hradani."

"We couldn't simply . . . assist one of the Bloody Swords who hate him?" Sahrdohr asked.

"There aren't as many of them as you might think," Varnaythus said grimly. "He's actually making this Confederation of his work, and the Bloody Swords who still have enough of a power base to risk going after him and infuriating every single Horse Stealer in Norfressa are smart enough to recognize that they've never been as well off as they are now. For that matter, they remember how Harnak's and Chalgaz's association with us turned even some of their fellow Bloody Swords against Navahk before the war. They're not going to be in any hurry to do anything that could make people think *they're* signing up with Sharnā and the dog brothers. Besides, Bahnak's done too damned good a job of training up those children of his. *All* of them, not just Bahzell. He may be the glue that put the hradani together in the first place, but I think Barondir and the rest would almost certainly manage to hold them together if he were to die suddenly."

"You're probably right about that," Salgahn agreed after considering it for a moment or two. "And, to be honest, hradani are hard to kill under the best of circumstances. You may remember how much trouble we had trying to take Bahzell and Brandark even before Bahzell became a champion! Of course, they're both special cases, even for hradani, but trying to get through Bahnak's bodyguard with anything except a full frontal assault would be . . . unlikely. And hradani are damned near impossible to poison with anything except an instantly fatal dose. Considering all the difficulties, taking Bahnak with any normal tactics would probably be at least as hard as taking Bahzell. Our best odds would be with Tellian, frankly, and even that would be a challenge. Not impossible, by any stretch, mind you, but definitely a challenge. Which is the reason Arthnar's not going to be all that keen on trying it, I suspect."

"Oh, I agree," Varnyathus said. "Which doesn't mean I won't be trying as hard as I can to talk him into it. In fact, I think we're going to have to get you involved in that as well, Salgahn."

"Oh?" The assassin raised an eyebrow at him, his expression wary. "And just how did you have it in mind for *that* to work?"

"I need someone to help do that convincing . . . and to make sure things are properly organized if we can talk him into it. He's cleverer than Cassan thinks he is, but he *does* have a certain tendency towards brute force solutions. We need something a bit more subtle than that. Or, at least, we need it to be something that steers any suspicion towards Tellian's purely local adversaries, since *we*"—he met his fellows' gazes levelly—"are specifically forbidden to make any attempt which could be traced back to us."

"We are?" If Sahrdohr was dismayed by the restriction, he hid it remarkably well, Varnaythus thought dryly.

"The overall operation is too important, and the odds against a successful assassination are too high, to justify risking it," he said calmly, not mentioning that *he* was the one who'd made that argument—successfully, thank Carnadosa!—when he first received his instructions. "If we launch a direct attack that's powerful enough to have a decent chance of success, the Order of Tomanāk is entirely too likely to be able to prove we were behind it . . . and that would prove *They* were behind it." Varnaythus shook his head. "We absolutely can't risk providing any evidence of that until all the other pieces are in place—not if we hope to succeed in our other plans, that is."

His fellows nodded gravely, and although it was obvious their approval had more to do with their own odds of personal survival than any tactical constraints, that didn't make anything he'd just said untrue. If—*if*—they succeeded in killing both Bahzell and Tellian, they would probably succeed in their overall mission. If they tried and failed, however, and if the effort proved the Dark Gods were trying to eliminate the two of them, it would strengthen Tellian's position in the Kingdom immeasurably. Sothōii were often impulsive and always prickly where things like honor and family feuds were concerned, but despite the stereotype certain of their enemies nourished, they weren't stupid. Certainly they weren't too slow to figure out that if the Dark Gods wanted someone dead it was because whoever they were trying to kill stood in their way, at any rate. That might not bother some of their . . . more self-serving nobles, perhaps, but whatever their internal political squabbles might be, the vast majority of the Sothōii could be expected to close ranks instantly against any recognized intrusion by Phrobus and his offspring.

And if that let Varnaythus stay far, far away from any direct attack on Bahzell Bloody Hand, that was a wonderful thing as far as he was concerned.

"That doesn't mean we won't be invloved, of course," he continued out loud, "but we *are* going to have to be as certain as we can that our cutouts will work. I think we're going to have to send you down to talk to Arthnar, Salgahn—I can arrange an introduction that will get you in to see him to help move him gently in the proper direction. We *don't* want the Guild openly involved. The last thing we need is any suggestion of dog brothers stirring up trouble, so we'll have to cover you as a mercenary with the right connections. I haven't decided yet whether or not we want you involved in the actual attempt or only in setting things in motion, and I don't see any way we *can* decide until we have a better idea of what he's willing to do, but I want to keep our options open in that respect."

Salgahn nodded, and if he looked less than delighted by the prospect, Varnaythus found that understandable enough.

"In the meantime," the wizard went on, "I've maintained my contacts with Cassan, and he's been kind enough to provide me with an introduction to Yeraghor, as well. Needless to say, neither of them is the least bit happy over what Tellian's up to, although I'm not positive Yeraghor truly realizes how close to finished that damned tunnel is. Or how profoundly the entire project—assuming it succeeds, of course—is going to change this part of Norfressa, for that matter."

"How close *are* they?" Sahrdohr asked, and Varnaythus shrugged irritably.

"I was just watching that unmitigated little pain Chanharsa." He gestured at the gramerhain. "She's putting in a forty- or fifty-yard section every day or so now, and she's only got about another three-quarters of a mile to go. That's only another two months. And the locks in the Balthar are already finished—they've had barges hauling construction materials all the way from from Hurgrum to The Gullet for two months now. The Derm Canal's taking longer, but I expect *it* to be finished by next spring, even allowing for construction shutting down over the winter months. In fact, they might even get it done before first snowfall, if the weather favors them over the summer."

Sahrdohr pursed his lips in a silent whistle, but Salgahn shook his head.

"That's all well and good," he pointed out, "but they've still got the River Brigands and the Ghoul Moor to worry about. As you just pointed out, Arthnar isn't going to take Bahnak's and Tellian's plans very cheerfully."

"Neither are the Purple Lords," Varnaythus agreed. "But exactly how do you think they're going to discourage a trio like Tellian, Kilthan, and Bahnak? Unless we—by which I'm afraid I really mean *you*, this time around—can convince Arthnar to try to kill them . . . and he succeeds, of course."

Salghan snorted in acknowledgment, but he also shook his head again.

"I'm just saying it's going to be a little more complicated than simply building a couple of canals and digging a tunnel," he said.

"And that's exactly what Yeraghor's been counting on—and Cassan, too, I suspect." Varnaythus shrugged. "Which, frankly, is . . . shortsighted of them, to say the least. Given the success rate Tellian and Bahnak—and Kilthan; let's not forget him—have demonstrated to date, how likely do *you* think it is that they won't succeed this time, as well?"

It was Salgahn's turn to shrug, conceding the point.

"As it happens, the Ghoul Moor is going to figure rather more prominently in our plans than I'd thought it was," Varnaythus continued. "I don't know that it's going to give us everything we want, although the chance that it might is actually better than I expected before She told me what resources we'll have there. Even if it doesn't work as well as expected"—he grimaced, and the others joined him as they recalled *other* plans which had failed to work exactly as the people who'd made them had expected—"it's still going to hurt them badly. It may actually stop the canal project completely, although I expect it's more likely just to slow them up for a year or two. More to the point, it ought to draw attention to the foot of the Escarpment and away from what we're really after on top of it. It may well fan the fire under Cassan and Yeraghor, as well, and whether it does or not, nothing that goes wrong for them on the Ghoul Moor is going to suggest any special interference on our part."

"Ah?" Sahrdohr cocked an eyebrow, and Varnaythus smiled unpleasantly.

"I don't have all the details yet, myself, but apparently the Ghouls are going to be receiving just a bit of a reinforcement. Quite a *sizeable* one, actually—possibly even enough of one to give one of those damned champions of Tomanāk pause. And since the Ghoul Moor's *always* been a . . . chancy proposition for the other side, let's say, no one's likely to be very surprised if this year's expedition suffers an accident or two, even if the accident is rather more spectacular than most."

The younger wizard nodded, and Varnaythus nodded back, then leaned back in his chair.

"The only downside in helping the ghouls slow them up is that if it *does* slow them up, it's likely to undercut the sense of urgency we've been trying to encourage among Tellian's opponents. One of my jobs is going to be keeping that urgency alive, and that means convincing Yeraghor and Cassan of just how close to success they are at court. Cassan's had too much personal experience with the ghouls to expect them to stop Tellian's and Bahzell's plans unless they succeed a lot more spectacularly than I expect, but Yeraghor will probably tend to overestimate their chances, and even Cassan's likely to see it as a reprieve. He'll expect it to give him more time to build opposition in Sothōfalas and on the Great Council, and he may figure the losses Tellian's about to take will help his own arguments that the entire idea is going to cost more than it's likely to be worth to the Kingdom in the long run. I need to knock both of those notions on the head, and for that I'm going to want access to Tellian's correspondence with Macebearer and Shaftmaster. Can you get it for me, Malahk?"

"I don't know." Sahrdohr frowned thoughtfully. "Shaftmaster's, yes. I'll have to be careful, but I can get to it without too much difficulty. If it will be all right to use a capture spell on it, that is?"

It was Varnaythus' turn to frown. A capture spell was a very minor working, one that even one of those accursed magi *probably* wouldn't notice unless he was right on top of it at the moment it was triggered. It required the use of a very small gramerhain, however, and if *that* was found on Sahrdohr's person...

"You're not concerned about carrying the stone with you?"

"I didn't say I wasn't concerned, but I think the risk would be manageable." The younger wizard smiled crookedly and held out his left hand, then tapped the ring on his second finger with his right index finger. It was an obviously old piece, set with a rather cheap looking opal. "I've been wearing this ever since I got here just for a moment like this one," Sahrdohr continued. "Everyone knows it has great sentimental value to me, despite the poor quality of the stone—it was a gift from my grandmother to my grandfather—so nobody thinks anything more about it. But—"

He touched the opal itself and it flashed into sudden clarity, like water-clear quartz. It stayed that way until he took his finger away again, when it turned just as quickly back into the milky stone it had been to begin with.

"Very nice," Varnaythus said sincerely.

The fact that Sahrdohr had put the ring into place so long

ago was yet another demonstration of his basic intelligence and foresight. And even at this short range, even after having had the glamour concealing the gramerhain demonstrated to him, Varnaythus could detect barely a whisper of the spell. If that was a sample of Sahrdohr's craftsmanship, he was further along towards the rank of master than Varnaythus had thought.

"All right, if you're comfortable using a capture spell, I'll leave that in your hands. But what about Macebearer?"

"That's going to be a lot harder," Sahrdohr replied. "I've at least got an excuse to be in Shaftmaster's office. I work for the man, after all. But I'm not high enough in the Exchequer to be wandering into the Prime Councilor's office and examining his personal correspondence with Baron Tellian."

"I really want to get our hands on those letters," Varnaythus said. "Shaftmaster's estimates will help—probably a lot—but Cassan's still keeping his head down, even without our gingering up the ghouls. I need proof of how much ground Tellian is gaining with Macebearer and Markhos to get him stirred back up again."

"Why don't we just forge it?" Sahrdohr asked. "It wouldn't be difficult—I can at least get samples of Macebearer's signature and his personal secretary's handwriting, and we already have samples of Tellian's. We could create correspondence that said whatever we needed it to say, then mix it in with genuine correspondence between Tellian and Shaftmaster."

"Tempting," Varnaythus conceded. "Unfortunately, Cassan's almost as good at this game as he thinks he is. I wouldn't be surprised to find out he's managed to get someone of his own inside Macebearer's staff. Probably not someone with the kind of access he'd *like* to have, but he might well have enough access to realize we're feeding him doctored documents."

"I might have a solution," Salgahn offered, and shrugged when both wizards looked at him. "I have a couple of men of my own inside the Palace. One of them's covered as a stable hand, but the other's on the housekeeping staff. He happens to be quite a good burglar, as a matter of fact."

"Does he, now?" Varnaythus considered the other man thoughtfully.

Like most dog brothers, Salgahn was officially a follower of Sharnā, although he was scarcely very devout. In fact, Varnaythus doubted Salgahn had ever seen one of Sharnā's actual rituals. It wasn't the sort of thing which would have appealed to him any more than it would have appealed to Varnaythus himself. But every profession required at least some support structure, and the Assassins' Guild had found *its* support in the church of Sharnā. Which meant that from time to time, whether they liked it or not, the dog brothers found themselves "urgently requested" to assist the church. Of course, the fact that Salgahn hadn't bothered to mention his men's presence in King Markho's palace until this very moment made Varnaythus wonder just how completely Salgahn had thrown himself into this operation.

And I don't blame him a bit if he's been thinking from the very beginning in terms of ratholes to dash down the instant this ship hits a reef, the wizard reflected, then chuckled mentally as he realized how liberally he'd just mixed metaphors.

"Just how obviously could your burglar burglarize the Prime Councilor's files?" he asked out loud.

"Obviously?" Salgahn raised an eyebrow.

"If everyone knows Macebearer's office was successfully broken into, then Cassan's a lot less likely to worry about whether or not we're trying to feed him forged documents. If we're going to physically steal them anyway, I'd like to leave enough evidence behind—evidence that Macebearer and the Crown would be able to keep from becoming *general* knowledge—to prime the pump with Cassan. His need to show how smart he is is his biggest weakness, when you come down to it. So if he knows about the 'secret burglary' when I show him copies—or even originals—from Macebearer's files, he'll be so smug about knowing how I got them that he won't even consider whether or not any alterations were made before he saw them. Letting someone convince himself always works better than trying to sell it to him from the outside."

"It'll make it a little riskier for my man," Salgahn pointed out.

"I'll triple the Guild's usual fee."

"Then I'm sure something can be worked out." Salgahn smiled, and Varnaythus chuckled.

"What about Borandas?" Sahrdohr asked, and Varnaythus frowned thoughtfully.

Borandas Daggeraxe was the Baron of Halthan and Lord Warden of the North Riding. The oldest of the four great barons of the Kingdom, he was also of no more than average intelligence, and he knew it. He was aware of the political power games swirling around at Court, but he was wise enough not to fish in such troubled waters and let himself be drawn into the toils of smarter but less scrupulous players. His son, Thorandas, was sharper than Borandas, and he'd been his father's primary political advisor for years. He understood the value of maintaining the North Riding's neutrality in the bitter power struggle between Cassan and Tellian. With Yeraghor of the East Riding supporting Cassan and the wind rider's representative supporting Tellian, that neutrality allowed the North Riding to effectively hold the balance of power on the Great Council, and Thorandas was unlikely to favor any course which would endanger that situation. On the other hand, he was also one of the hard-line anti-hradani bigots....

"I'm not sure about Borandas," Varnaythus admitted. "But if Tellian's correspondence with Macebearer says what I think it says, then showing certain select passages to *Thorandas* might pay a very nice dividend in the fullness of time. I'll have to think about that once we see what it actually does say."

Sahrdohr nodded, and Varnaythus drew a deep breath.

"Now," he said, "the reason I want to get my hands on all that documentation is that the time has come—or is coming very soon—for us to... restructure the Kingdom of the Sothōii. And this is how we're going to do it.

"First—"

Chapter Four

“*Careful*, lummox! That’s my head you’re dumping crap all over!”

The hradani stopped, parked the wheelbarrow carefully, and then leaned sideways, looking over the edge of the excavation.

“And would you be telling me what in Fiendark’s name you’re doing down there right this very minute?” he inquired testily.

“My *job*,” the dwarf standing in the bottom of the steep-walled cut replied in an even testier voice.

He took off his battered, well-used safety helmet to examine its top carefully, then rubbed a finger across the fresh patch of dust (and dent) the falling piece of rock had left in the steel and looked up accusingly. The hradani hadn’t actually “dumped” it on him—his wheelbarrow had simply dislodged a small stone in passing and knocked it over the edge—but the result had been the same.

“If I hadn’t been wearing this, you’d have splattered my brains all over the cut!” he said.

“Now that I wouldn’t have,” the hradani replied virtuously. “They’d not have covered more than a handspan of dirt at most, and likely less, come to think on it. And you’ve still not told me what it was you thought you were after doing down there when it was yourself told us to start pouring in the ballast.”

“Checking the form, if you must know,” the dwarf growled. “No one signed the check sheet.” He waved a clipboard irritably. “*Somebody* has to do a walkthrough before the voids get filled in!”

“Well, you’ll not be doing any ‘walkthroughs’ so very much longer if you don’t get your sawed-off arse out of the way.”

"'Sawed-off arse,' is it?" the dwarf demanded. He stumped over to the ladder fixed to the face of the massive, freestanding wooden form and started swarming up it. "For about one copper kormak I'll use *you* for ballast!"

"Ah? And how would you be doing that?" The hradani propped his hands on his hips and looked down at the dwarf from his towering inches. "I'm thinking a wee little fellow like you's likely to strain himself moving someone who's properly grown!"

The dwarf made it to the top of the ladder and across the wooden plank between the form and the solid ground beyond the cut, and stalked towards the enormous hradani. He was barely four feet tall, which made him less than two-thirds the hradani's height, and he looked even smaller beside a massive, hradani-scaled "wheelbarrow" larger than most pony carts. But his beard seemed to bristle and he jabbed an index finger like a sword as he halted in the wheelbarrow's shadow and glared up at the hradani.

"It's a pity all a hradani's growth goes into his height instead of his *brain*," he observed acidly. "Not that I should be *too* surprised, I suppose. After all, when a skull's that thick, there can't be all that much room for brains inside it!"

"Sure and I'm thinking such envy must be a hard thing to bear," the hradani replied. "Still and all," he gripped the wheelbarrow's handles again, "such as me, being full grown and all, would look right strange creeping about in those squinchy little tunnels your folk favor."

He lifted, straightening his spine with a slight grunt of effort, and the heavy wooden handles—well over six inches in diameter—flexed visibly as the wheelbarrow's massive load of gravel went thundering down into the excavation. A plume of dust rose, blowing on the hot afternoon breeze, and he glanced down with satisfaction.

"Which isn't to say such as *you* wouldn't be looking right strange pushing around wheelbarrows as are all grown up, either, now I think on it, now is it?"

The dwarf shook his head with a disgusted expression, but his lips twitched slightly, and the hradani smiled benignly down upon him.

"You're like to do yourself a mischief venting all that spleen, Gorsan, and a sad thing that would be," he said. "Well, sadder for some than for others, now I think on it."

"*Somebody's* going to suffer a mischief, at any rate," Gorsandahknarthas zoi'Felahkandarnas growled back.

"And so I have already, I'm thinking," the hradani sighed. "Why, I might be off lounging around on guard duty somewhere—or at least mucking out a stable—and instead, here I am, wheeling around loads of gravel to fill a hole I had the digging of my own self in the first place, and all of it with a wee little runt no higher than my knee yammering and whining the time." He shook his head dolefully. "It's enough to make a man tear up like a babe in arms, it is, and I'm after wondering just what it was I had the doing of that got me on Prince Bahnak's bad side and landed me here."

"You *really* don't want me to answer that one," the dwarf told him with a chuckle. "Or maybe you do. Listing all the reasons he doesn't want to trust you doing something *hard* would take long enough to keep both of us standing here till the end of the shift *after* yours, wouldn't it?"

The hradani grinned, conceding Gorsan the last word, and trundled back off for another load of fill. Gorsan watched him go, then stepped back out of the way as another hradani wheeled another massive wheelbarrow down the pathway of wooden planks which had been laid across the muddy ground. The newcomer had clearly heard most of the exchange, and he shook his head, foxlike ears cocked in amusement, as he dumped his own load of gravel into the gap between the form and the side of the excavation.

Gorsan shot him the expected grumpy look, but the dwarf's brown eyes twinkled when he did. The truth was that he got along extraordinarily well—indeed, far better than he'd expected—with the hradani laboring on the Derm Canal. The canal was the longest and (in most ways) most vital portion of the massive construction project conceived by Kilthandahknarthas of Silver Cavern, Bahnak of Hurgrum, and Tellian of Balthar six years earlier, and it had been an enormous professional compliment when Gorsan was named its chief engineer. It had been inevitable that it would go to *someone* from Clan Felahkandarnas, given that Felahkandarnas stood second to Clan Harkanath in Silver Cavern by only the slimmest of margins and that not even Harkanath had been in a position to finance something like this solely out of its own resources. All of Silver Cavern was deeply invested in it, and the other clans had a right to nominate their own fair share of its supervisors. There'd still been at least a dozen possible candidates for the assignment, however, and Kilthandahknarthas and Thersahkdahknarthas dinha'Felahkandarnas had made the choice based on proven ability. On the other hand, that ability had been demonstrated working with other *dwarves*, and although Gorsan would never have admitted it to a soul, he'd approached the notion of supervising a mixed crew of hradani, dwarves, and humans with pronounced trepidation.

Actually, he conceded, watching another outsized wheelbarrow approach, it hadn't been the *humans* who'd concerned him. The hradani's reputation as the most dangerous of the Races of Man had been well earned over the twelve hundred years since the fall of Kontovar. Their tendency to erupt in berserk, homicidal fury when struck by the Rage—the inherited madness of their race—was enough to make anyone nervous, especially people who'd lived in the same vicinity as them for the past several centuries, and the old adage about burned hands teaching best had come forcibly to mind when he first contemplated his assignment.

In theory that had all changed now, and Gorsan admitted that he'd seen no episodes of the Rage during the five and a half years he'd supervised the canal's construction. Despite that, he still wasn't certain he believed all the stories he'd heard about how the Rage had changed, even if they *were* vouched for by Wencit of Rūm and a champion of Tomanāk. For that matter, he still had a few problems wrapping his mind around the concept of a hradani champion at all!

But whatever might be true about the Rage, he'd discovered there were definite advantages to a work force whose laborers had the size, strength, and sheer stamina of hradani. They took workloads in stride which would have made even a dwarf blanch, and for the first time in Gorsan's experience, a job actually looked like it was going to come in *ahead* of schedule, even with the miserable weather of northern Norfressa to slow things up!

And there was no question that Prince Bahnak of Hurgrum was a far cry from the stereotypical barbarian brigand most people thought of when anyone said the word "hradani" to them, either. Gorsan had met the prince and most of his almost equally formidable offspring, and he suspected the rumor that Bahnak had suggested the project to Kilthan rather than the other way around might well be true. The dwarves of Dwarvenhame were far more accustomed to interacting with the other Races of Man than any of the ancestral clans had been back in Kontovar, and Kilthandahknarthas was even more accustomed to it than most, but the sheer boldness and scale of the Derm Canal—and its implications for all of Norfressa—were staggering.

We should *have thought of it years ago,* he reflected now, clasping his hands behind him as he strolled down the brink of the canal cut. *Except for the minor matter of its being impossible until Bahnak came along!*

He snorted at the thought, but it was undeniably true. Even for dwarven engineers, the thought of building a canal almost four hundred leagues long between the human city of Derm and the hradani city of Hurgrum could never have been anything but a fantasy as long as the hradani city-states had been at one another's throats. But Bahnak of Hurgrum's Clan Iron Axe had finally brought hundreds of years of ongoing conflict to an end.

For now, at least.

Gorsan grimaced as his mind insisted on adding the qualifier, yet it was hard to believe anyone or anything could truly turn the northern hradani into a single realm and keep it that way. But Bahnak and his Horse Stealers hadn't hammered the Bloody Swords into surrender by simple force of arms. Oh, he *had* hammered them—that was the only way anyone ever convinced a hradani to do *anything* he didn't want to, after all; that much hadn't changed, whatever might have happened to the Rage—yet it had been Bahnak's shrewd diplomacy which had made his victory possible . . . and which looked like making his conquest stand up. Even the name he'd chosen—the Northern Confederation—only underscored his shrewd understanding of his own people. No one doubted for a moment that the "Northern Confederation" was actually a kingdom and that Bahnak was its king, yet he'd been careful to avoid rubbing the other clans' stubborn, hardheaded, not to say intransigent noses in that reality. Instead, it remained a simple confederation, no more (officially) than an upgrade and an enlargement of the old Northern Alliance he'd forged amongst the Horse Stealers, and he remained a simple prince, no more (officially) than first among equals. It was true, perhaps, that he stood "first among equals" by a very considerable margin, yet he was careful to show what Gorsan believed was a genuine concern and respect for the opinions of the members of his newly created Council of Princes. No one was going to be so foolish as to cross him or mistake him for anyone but the Confederation's undisputed ruler, but that was due in no small part to his demonstration that he understood the *responsibilities* of a ruler.

The fact that he was already proving one of the canniest rulers in Norfressan history didn't hurt, either, Gorsan reflected. He wasn't afraid to *think*, as his ability to conceive of something like the Derm Canal and drive it through to success amply demonstrated. No doubt it had been difficult to convince the newly conquered Bloody Swords to take the proposal seriously, at least at first. Getting them to realize there could be more profit in supporting commerce than in plundering it couldn't have been *easy*, at any rate! It had probably helped that the canal would stretch right across the traditional Bloody Sword holdings, giving them ample opportunity to make plenty of money off of the freight it would soon be carrying. And, after the initial labor of building the thing, for far less effort than more traditional wealth-gathering hradani practices, like looting and pillaging.

And once shippers get accustomed to the notion of actually sending their cargoes through hradani lands, they'll probably take a certain comfort in the fact that the hradani will be providing security *rather than raiding their goods. It would take a lunatic to cross hradani guards on their own ground!*

He stopped and gazed out across the sprawling construction site. Close at hand, crews used rollers and muscle-powered, footed pile drivers to tamp down the gravel ballast filling the gap between the wall of the excavation and the finished wooden forms which awaited the concrete. Gorsan would have preferred to use even more gravel and have a sarthnaisk like Chanharsa fuse it, but other portions of the project were already eating up the efforts of at least two-thirds of Silver Cavern's available sarthnaisks, and concrete worked just fine for something as routine as a canal. Further west, the next lock in line was nearing completion, and more crews were tearing down the heavy forms now that the concrete had set. And, further west still, barges loaded with construction material moved steadily up and down the portion of the canal which was already operable.

The Derm Canal had been the most exhausting and exhilarating project of Gorsan's career, and his heart swelled with pride as he watched those barges moving across the gently rolling grasslands of Navahk. Another six months, he thought hopefully. Assuming they could finish before winter set in, that was. He shuddered as he remembered other winters, but he was determined they were going to beat this one. And with the Balthar locks already open and the Gullet Tunnel almost completed, the entire route could be ready and open as early as sometime next spring. He could hardly believe it even now, but those construction barges were the clearest possible proof that it really was going to work.

And those Purple Lord bastards down in Bortalik are going to be dropping in droves out of sheer apoplexy when it does, he thought with grim satisfaction. *Which suits* me *just fine.*

✧ ✧ ✧

"Do you think Shaftmaster's estimates are accurate?" the man across the table asked, and Cassan Axehammer reminded himself not to roll his eyes.

Yeraghor Stonecastle, Baron Ersok and Lord Warden of the East Riding, was of little more than average height for a Sothōii—two inches shorter than Cassan himself—and as dark and swarthy as Cassan was blond. He had very long arms, and his powerful wrists accurately reflected the rigorous traditional training regimen he maintained, despite his high rank. He and Cassan were kinsmen and close political allies, but there were times Yeraghor's ability to belabor the obvious grated on Cassan's nerves. In fact, it bothered him more because he knew how intelligent Yeraghor actually was, which only made his tendency to ask obviously rhetorical questions even more irritating.

"I don't know whether they're accurate or not," Cassan said once he was sure his voice would come out the way he wanted it to.

He sipped expensive Dwarvenhame whiskey, then set the crystal glass down very precisely in front of him and leaned back. His comfortable rattan chair creaked under his weight, and he gazed out across the rolling green fields of the Barony of Frahmahn. He could see literally for miles from the roofed balcony set on the west side of his castle's central keep, and everything he saw was his. But somewhere out there, beyond what he could see, beyond the borders of his own South Riding, lay Tellian of Balthar's *West* Riding, and he felt his jaw muscles clench as he considered the reason—the real reason—for this meeting with Yeraghor.

"I don't know whether they're accurate, but I think it's obvious Shaftmaster *thinks* they are—or *will* be, when all's said and done. And given that he's the Chancellor of the Exchequer, I'm not prepared to say he's wrong."

"And you're sure they're genuine?" Yeraghor asked, his eyes narrowing shrewdly. "Master Talthar's a resourceful soul, but we both know he has irons of his own in this fire."

"I'm sure," Cassan replied grimly. "And I've spent some time looking at the reports his estimates are based on, too." His expression wasn't getting any happier. "I'm not sure I agree with all of his analyses, but he can't be too far off."

"Shit," Yeraghor said flatly. Unlike Cassan, Yeraghor preferred beer to whiskey, and he buried his nose briefly in his silver-chased tankard. Then he slapped it back on the table and glowered at Cassan.

"And this business about Macebearer signing on? It all *looks* genuine enough. I doubt he'd hesitate to offer us false information or even outright forgeries if it would serve his purposes. And, capable or not, actually getting his hands on Macebearer's records—or even just getting *access* to them—couldn't have been easy. I know." He smiled thinly. "I've tried myself on more than one occasion!"

"They're not forgeries," Cassan said with a grimace. "I haven't managed to get anyone inside Macebearer's staff yet, either—not high enough to get his hands on this sort of documentation, at least—but I do have my sources in the Palace. Which is how I know someone broke into his office a few weeks ago. They've all done their best to hush it up, of course, but the investigation was as thorough as it was quiet. Talthar hasn't mentioned it to me specifically, but I'm pretty sure the 'servant' who disappeared the same night Macebearer got himself burglarized was his man." He shrugged. "I recognized Macebearer's handwriting, too. I don't think there's any question the documents are exactly what Talthar told me they are, and that means those estimates are about as accurate—or official, at least—as they get."

"Wonderful," Yeraghor said bitterly. "Things are bad enough the way they are. The last thing we need is Tellian getting Crown *approval* for that kind of boost to his revenues!"

It was nice that Yeraghor agreed with him, Cassan thought acidly, but it would have been even nicer if he could have foregone—just this once—his compulsion to restate the obvious. But then Cassan made himself stop and draw a deep breath. His temper, he reminded himself, remained closer to the surface and faster to flare than he would have liked, and however irritating Yeraghor might be, Cassan had no business taking out his ire on his kinsman. Nor was it reasonable to expect any other initial response out of him, given the circumstances. Yes, Yeraghor's conclusion was blindingly obvious, but Cassan had had the advantage of two additional weeks to study the documents the other baron had seen only in the last hour or so.

And, obvious or not, he had a point, Cassan conceded sourly.

One of the unfortunate realities of life was that the water transport of trade goods was far and away safer, faster, and much, much cheaper than trying to ship the same goods overland. That was true even in the Empire of the Axe, with its superb highways; here on the Wind Plain, or in the Empire of the Spear—where even the best of roads were dirt and the worst were . . . well, pretty terrible—moving anything remotely bulky by land over any really extended distance was far too expensive for anyone to show a profit on it.

As a consequence, it had always been difficult for Axeman merchants to ship their goods into the Kingdom of the Sothōii. It was possible to move at least some of them (mostly low-bulk luxury goods) overland from Dwarvenhame through the West Riding, but the Ordan Mountains and their foothills were a formidable barrier even over dwarf-designed high roads, and roads in the Duchy of Ordanfalas and the Duchy of Barondir, between Dwarvenhame and the West Riding, were no better than those of the Kingdom itself. For that matter, Barondir had a perennial problem with brigands and raiders, and the duke himself had been known to charge unexpected and sometimes extortionate "tolls" with very little warning.

Most of the Axeman goods that did reach the Sothōii made their way up the long, majestic stretch of the mighty Spear River, and even that was barely a tithe of what it might have been. Bortalik Bay, at the mouth of the Spear, lay well over twenty-five hundred leagues south of the Wind Plain. That was an enormous voyage, and Axeman goods coming up the river first had to sail clear down around Norfressa's western coast just to reach Bortalik. Yet distance was only the first hurdle they faced, for the half-elven Purple Lords who ruled Bortalik were deeply resentful of the Empire of the Axe's economic dominance, and they regarded the entire basin of the Spear as their own private preserve. The tolls they charged to permit Axeman goods to pass through Bortalik and up the river were damned close to confiscatory, and they also used their strategic position to fasten a stranglehold on the foreign trade of the Empire of the Spear—one that frequently drifted over into outright control of Spearman politics. Any Spearman noble who angered the Purple Lords was apt to find all access to foreign goods embargoed by them, with consequences ranging from the merely painful to the ruinous.

Neither Cassan nor Yeraghor had any particular problem with that arrangement. What happened in the Empire of the Spear was no concern of theirs, and if Axeman goods found it difficult to make the voyage from Bortalik to Nachfalas, Cassan's clifftop port above the Escarpment, *Purple Lord* goods made the trip just fine. True, it made the Kingdom's economy almost as vulnerable to Purple Lord manipulation as the Empire of the Spear's in some ways, but that was actually advantageous in many respects, especially from Cassan's viewpoint. That "unavoidable Purple Lord pressure" gave the Kingdom another card to play when it came to managing its relationship with its Axeman allies, who could be counted upon to cough up occasional concessions to sweeten the alliance as a counterbalance. And, on a more personal level, Cassan showed a pretty profit on all of the trade, Purple Lord or not, that passed through his lands on its way to Sothōfalas and other points north. As for Yeraghor, the East Riding was the site of most of the Kingdom's iron mines and smithies, and Yeraghor's smiths and craftsmen had absolutely no desire to find themselves competing with the smithies and forges of Dwarvenhame.

But that, unfortunately, was exactly what was going to happen if Tellian succeeded in his latest intolerable scheme. The so-called Derm Canal was going to make it possible for Axeman merchant barges to sail up the Morvan River to Derm, the highest navigable point on that river, and then across to the Hangnysti River at Bahnak's capital of Hurgrum and up the Balthar River to the very foot of the Escarpment and their accursed "Gullet Tunnel." Once their goods reached the top of the Escarpment, the Balthar would be available again to ferry them all the way to Tellian's capital, or they could be delivered directly to Sothōfalas by way of Glanharrow in less than a third of the time it took for them to reach the capital from Nachfalas... all without paying a single kormak in tolls to the South Riding. And worst of all, it would break the Purple Lords' monopoly on the Spear River. Those same barges could sail down the Hangnysti to the Spear and as far south as they pleased with cargos of Axeman goods and return the same way with cargoes from *Spearman* merchants without ever going near Bortalik Bay. The Purple Lords were about to lose a disastrous portion of their wealth and power, and while Cassan would have lost no sleep over *that*, the thought that largish chunks of that same wealth and power would be pouring into Bahnak's accursed Northern Confederation and the West Riding, instead, was another matter entirely. While it was likely his own income would actually increase, given Nachfalas' location and the greater volume of trade which would be passing up and down the upper Spear, that increase would be only a shadow—and a very thin, *dim* shadow, at that—of the revenue increase *Tellian* was about to see.

Cassan's nostrils flared as he contemplated that grim future, and a dull tide of resentment burned through him yet again as he remembered how *close* he'd come to defeating Tellian for good.

The two of them had been locked in combat for dominance on the Great Council for over twenty years now, and their respective *houses* had fought that same battle still longer—all the way back to the Kingdom's very first Time of Troubles—with the struggle seesawing back and forth with the shifting of political tides. Under King Sandahl, the present King's father, the House of Axehammer had enjoyed a pronounced advantage, but Cassan's position had slipped under King Markhos . . . thanks, in no small part, to the advice the King had received from his younger brother, Yurokhas. Prince Yurokhas had been fostered at Balthar under Tellian's father at the insistence of the Great Council, which had feared the South Riding's influence with King Sandahl. He'd known the present baron since boyhood, and to make bad worse, he too was a wind rider, like Tellian. Besides, Cassan was forced to admit that he'd overplayed his own hand during Markhos' brief regency.

Markhos had been fostered at Toramos, the seat of the Barons of Frahmahn, under *Cassan's* father, and Cassan had expected to capitalize on that relationship. It had been a mistake. He admitted that freely, if not happily. He'd put the boy's hackles up, and he'd probably been just a bit too open—well, heavy-handed, if he was going to be honest—about using the advantages of his riding's position on the Spear. He'd been younger then, himself, barely a dozen years Markhos' senior, and he'd come to his own dignities only a few years before, but that was no excuse for his clumsiness, and he knew it.

Still, he'd been confident of regaining all the ground he'd lost, and then some, when Tellian "surrendered" over four thousand of his men to less than eighty *hradani*. The hatred between the Sothōii and their hradani "neighbors" was deep as the sea and bitter as brine, and Tellian had passed up the perfect opportunity to ride down into the Horse Stealers' lands and burn their cities behind them while their own warriors were off battling their Bloody Sword enemies. He'd been right there, poised to carry through the attack, with plenty of reinforcements available to follow his original spearhead down The Gullet. He could have destroyed "Prince" Bahnak's alliance and prevented the Phrobus-damned abortion of a unified hradani "Confederation" on the Wind Plain's very flank before it even began, but he'd let *eighty* of the barbarians stop him! And, even worse in some ways, he'd actually accepted the blasphemous claim that Tomanāk Orfro could conceivably have chosen a *hradani* as one of His champions! For that matter, he'd accepted Wencit of Rūm's preposterous lie that it was the *Sothōii* who'd begun the millennium and more of bitter, brutal warfare between themselves and the hradani.

The court faction which had been most concerned about the possibility of a unified hradani realm had been furious, nor had they been alone in that. Even some of those who'd been prepared to take a wait-and-see attitude had been shocked—and more than a little frightened, whether they'd wanted to admit it or not—by the idea that Tellian had actually connived to *create* the "Northern Confederation." And the notion that he should recognize the champion status of a Horse Stealer hradani, the most hated and reviled of all the hradani clans, had triggered an upsurge of bitter anger. Cassan would never be certain, but he strongly suspected that only Prince Yurokhas' support for Tellian—and his acceptance that Tomanāk might actually have been so insane as to take a hradani as His champion—had motivated Markhos to resist the furious demands that Tellian be stripped of his membership on the Great Council. Indeed, there'd been demands that he be stripped of his barony and lord wardenship, as well.

Yet even though Markhos had stopped short of accepting those demands, Cassan had known how thin the ice had become under Tellian's feet, and he'd been confident that *this* time he could finish off his rival's influence in Sothōfalas once and for all.

Unfortunately, it hadn't worked out that way. His strategy to undermine Tellian's rule with a series of safely deniable attacks on Festian of Glanharrow would have been bad enough, but then that bastard Bahzell had been given credit for saving the tattered remnants of the Warm Springs courser herd and actually going on to defeat a pack of demons set upon the coursers by none other than Krahana herself! Cassan still found that tale too ridiculous to accept. He was willing to admit Bahzell might have had something to do with rescuing the surviving coursers—certainly *something* had inspired them to accept him as a wind rider, which was almost as blasphemous as the idea that he might actually be a champion—but Cassan Axehammer would believe Tomanāk had accepted Bahzell Bahnakson as one of His champions when Tomanāk turned up in person in his own great hall to tell him so!

And then, as if that hadn't been enough, that meddlesome, common-born bitch Kaeritha Seldansdaughter had seen fit to interfere in the Kingdom's internal affairs, as well. Of course Cassan wouldn't have wanted someone like Shīgū to succeed in destroying an entire temple of *any* God of Light, but Lillinara was scarcely his favorite deity, either. If it had had to happen to someone's temple, he would have managed to bear up under the knowledge that it had been Hers. And as for the war maids—! Anything that got rid of those unnatural bitches once and for all couldn't be *all* bad.

King Markhos appeared to see things differently, however. Worse, he'd sent his accursed magi to investigate Tellian's and Kaeritha's claims.

Personally, Cassan had never trusted the magi, anyway. Oh, he knew all about their precious Oath of Semkirk and how it bound all of them to use their powers only within the law . . . and as far as he was concerned, that and a silver kormak would get him a cup of hot chocolate. No one with the unnatural powers the magi claimed could be trusted. If for no other reason, how could anyone but the magi themselves verify that they were telling the truth about what they did—or didn't—do with those powers of theirs? And the last thing he wanted was anyone peering around inside his head, which was why he *always* wore the amulet that blocked any mage from doing just that. Fortunately, at least some people had naturally strong blocks which made them all but impossible to read without a major—and obvious—effort (assuming the magi were telling the truth about their abilities, at least), and since his amulet simply duplicated that natural block, its protection hadn't triggered any alarms in and of itself.

That had prevented the magi from denouncing him as part of the "plot" against Tellian. But it *hadn't* prevented them from uncovering almost all of the minor lords warden who'd been involved, and one of them—Saratic Redhelm of Golden Vale—had been Cassan's own vassal and distant kinsman. *That* had almost proved disastrous, but Cassan had installed enough layers of insulation between him and Saratic to at least confuse the issue. The danger that Saratic might have chosen to trade his testimony against Cassan for some sort of clemency, or even outright immunity, from the Crown had presented itself . . . but only until Darnas Warshoe, that useful armsman, saw to it that Saratic suffered an accident.

And given what Saratic had been up to, at least a sizable minority of the Kingdom's nobles strongly suspected Tellian had been behind that "accident," not Cassan. It wasn't the sort of thing Tellian normally did, but mercenaries hired by another Sothōii noble didn't normally try to kill Tellian's nephew and heir-adoptive, either. There were some provocations no one could allow to pass unanswered.

Cassan doubted anyone in the entire Kingdom believed he hadn't been behind the raids, yet with Saratic's death, there'd been no proof, and not even an irate monarch proceeded against one of the four most powerful nobles of his realm without incontrovertible proof. Not openly, at any rate. Still, whatever anyone else might think, King Markhos obviously knew who'd instigated it all, and he'd made his displeasure clear by stripping Golden Vale from the South Riding and incorporating it into Tellian's *West* Riding . . . officially as a form of reparations for *Saratic's* actions, although everyone knew whose wrist he'd actually been smacking. Nor had he stopped there.

He'd summarily dismissed Garthmahn Ironhelm, Lord Warden of Chersa, who'd been his Prime Councilor—and Cassan's firm ally—for over ten years. And he'd also informed Cassan in a cold, painful personal interview that he himself would be unwelcome in Sothōfalas for the next year or two. The King had stopped short of expelling Cassan formally from the Great Council, yet Ironhelm's dismissal and his own banishment from Sothōfalas, however temporary it might be, had reduced his web of alliances and influence to tatters. He'd only recently begun putting those alliances back together, and they remained a ghost of what they had been.

Which was, after all, one of the reasons Yeraghor had become even more vital to all of his future plans.

"You're right, of course, Yeraghor," he said finally. "And it's not just the revenues Tellian's looking at, either. There's the correspondence from Macebearer, as well. This isn't just about money. Tellian's climbing deeper and deeper into bed with the Axemen and that bastard Bahnak. He's not only going to drag the entire Kingdom into actually *endorsing* Bahnak's rule, but he's going to get our foreign policy tied directly to Dwarvenhame! And when the dust settles, he's going to be the real power broker here on the Wind Plain. Don't think for a minute that that isn't exactly what he has in mind in the long run, and when he gets it, don't think he's going to forget anyone who's ever done him an injury, either."

He looked across the table into Yeraghor's eyes, and his own were grim.

"He can rhapsodize about how much good this is going to do our economy, but Shaftmaster and Macebearer are blind, drooling idiots if they can't see the downside! And even if they don't think it's a downside for the rest of the Kingdom, it's damned well going to be one for *us*. Assuming, of course"—he smiled thinly—"that we were so foolish as to let Tellian and Bahnak get away with it."

Chapter Five

The clouds looked less than promising, Lady Sharlassa Dragonclaw thought, gazing unhappily at the overcast settling lower about the shoulders of Hill Guard Castle.

Lady Sharlassa sat under the branches of the castle's apple orchard, but they were barely beginning to bud, and it was far too early in the year to expect them to offer her any protection if Chemalka decided to go ahead and release the rain hovering in those clouds. The breeze was strengthening, too, blowing through the apple branches and lifting stray locks of auburn hair on puffs of blossom-scented perfume, and her nostrils flared as she drew the green, living incense of the world deep into her lungs. She felt alive at moments like this in a way she'd never really been able to explain even to herself, far less to anyone else. It was as if her nerves were connected directly to the trunks of the apple trees, as if she could feel them yearning towards fruit, tossing their branches like widespread fingers to the caress of the wind.

Her mother had only smiled fondly and mentioned things like active imaginations when a much younger Sharlassa tried to describe moments like this, and Sharlassa knew she was right. Yet, imagination or not, she did feel the life moving with the breeze, tantalizing her with that damp kiss of rain to come. Personally, Sharlassa had no desire to find herself soaked to the skin, but that sense of oneness with the apple trees whispered to her that *they* were looking forward to it.

Well, it was nice that *someone* was looking forward to *something*, she thought, and heaved a deep, mournful sigh as the reflection returned her to the reason she was sitting here on a rather damp wall of rough, unmortared stone in an apple orchard almost two hundred leagues from her home. Or, rather, from her *new* home, since she'd been born and raised less than six miles from where she sat at that very moment. That was another reason she found this apple orchard so restful; she'd spent enough hours sitting here as a little girl for the trees to be old friends. Or gleaning windfallen fruit between meals. Or clambering around in their branches like a squirrel during harvest. In fact, one of those trees, not so very far from where she sat at this very moment, had her initials carved into its bark. She could still remember the thrashing she'd gotten from her mother for "defacing" one of the Baron's trees!

A smile flickered across her face at the memory, and she put her palms flat on the top of the wall, leaning back slightly to rest her weight on them while she arched her spine and looked up at those clouds. Life had been so much simpler then, without as many opportunities, perhaps, but without as many prices, either. And no one—except her parents, of course—had really been that concerned if a hoyden teenager wandered off to sit in an apple orchard somewhere once her chores were done. Now, of course, *everyone* cared, and the nature of her "chores" had changed rather drastically.

She looked back at the castle whose walls had loomed protectively over her parents' modest stone house when she was a girl. Somewhere inside those walls, at this very moment, Tahlmah Bronzebow, her harassed maid, was undoubtedly searching for her. On the basis of past Sharlassa hunts, she estimated that Tahlmah wouldn't quite be ready to call out Duke Tellian's armsmen yet. That would take, oh . . . another hour and a half. Possibly two. Unless, of course, it occurred to Tahlmah to come check the orchard again. Sharlassa was certain her maid had looked here first, but the initial phase of Sharlassa's current truancy had taken her to the stables, instead, to spend fifteen or twenty minutes communing with the one being in all the world who *always* commiserated with her. Muddy—known on official occasions as Summer Rain Falling—might not understand the reasons for his mistress' moodiness and occasional aspirations to rebellion, but he never stinted on his sympathy.

Which, she sometimes reflected, probably had something to do with the lumps of sugar that were customarily nestled in her pocket when she went to call upon him.

She smiled at the thought and took her right hand off the wall long enough to pull one of the dark green ribbons out of her hair. She held it up between thumb and forefinger, listening to it snap gently as the breeze played with it, then opened her hand and let it fly. It swooped up into the branches of one of the trees, wrapped itself around a limb, and flew bravely, like a banner against the steadily darkening charcoal of the sky.

You're being silly, she told herself... again. *Every single one of the girls you grew up with would give her eyeteeth for your life, and you know it! Well, all but* one *of them, maybe. Of course, her life went the opposite direction from yours, didn't it?*

She laughed at the thought, but that didn't make it untrue. Yet what all those other girls she'd grown up with probably wouldn't believe for a moment was that she'd never wanted to be a lord warden's daughter. She'd been perfectly happy—well, *almost* perfectly happy—as the daughter of a simple armsman. Oh, she'd been proud of her father and the officer's rank he'd gained. And being a wind rider's daughter had made her even prouder. She could still remember the first time Kengayr, her father's courser companion, had presented his huge, soft nose to a grubby five-year-old's hand, towering over her like a vast gray mountain. A single one of his forehooves had been as big as she was, and his head had been bigger—she could have used one of his horseshoes for the seat of a swing, and he could have squashed her with a thought—but all she'd felt was the wonder of him, and she'd known even then that Kengayr meant her father really was as wonderful as she'd always thought he was.

But Sir Jahsak Dragonclaw could have stopped at Major Dragonclaw in Baron Tellian's service, as far as Sharlassa was concerned. In fact, she wished he had!

If wishes were fishes, we'd never want food, she told herself tartly, quoting one of her mother's favorite maxims. Yet there were times she suspected Lady Sharmatha wasn't a lot happier about the "Lady" in front of her name than Sharlassa was about the one in front of hers. In fact, she was certain there were, although Lady Sharmatha would no more ever admit that than her father might admit that he, too, must cherish occasional second thoughts about the consequences of the honor Baron Tellian had bestowed upon him.

And it is *an honor, you twit,* Sharlassa told herself sternly. *From a common armsman to a knight and a wind rider and a major all the way to* lord warden?! *It's the kind of honor other people only* dream *of, and you should spend your time being happy for him—and proud of him—instead of worrying about all the problems it's made for* you!

Unfortunately, it was easier for Sir Jahsak—and for her brothers—than it was for Sharlassa . . . or her mother. The rules were so *hard* for a girl who'd been raised as a tomboy until she was thirteen years old. She was still trying to figure them out, six years later, and she dreaded the even greater number of rules—the *endless* number of rules—she'd have to worry about in years to come. She knew her mother found her new role as Lady Golden Vale an uncomfortable fit, and not just because so many of "their" retainers and tenants hated and resented them as interlopers and usurpers. It would take someone much braver than Sharlassa to show Lady Sharmatha disrespect to her face, yet Sharmatha had to be aware of the way all those hostile eyes scrutinized her, watching for any miscue or misstep they could pounce upon as fresh proof of how uncouth and unworthy of his lord wardenship Sir Jahsak was.

Sharlassa was only too well aware of it, at any rate.

Yet she could have handled that hostility if it had been the only problem. Or she thought she could have. She might have been wrong about that, the way she'd been wrong about so many other things in her life.

She sighed again and leaned forward, picking at a bit of moss on the stone wall, feeling the unseen, damp pressure of the rain growing slowly more omnipresent. A patch of the moss came loose and she held it up, studying it, feeling the velvety softness of it against the ball of her thumb. The back, where it had kissed against the stone, was rougher grained, papery, so *different* from its front, and she wondered if that was some sort of metaphor for her life . . . or if she was only being maudlin again.

She snorted softly, with bittersweet regret for what might have happened. It was strange, and it made her feel guilty sometimes, but she could hardly remember what Sathek had truly looked like. They'd been supposed to have his miniature painted for her before he'd ridden off with Sir Trianal to deal with the mystery attacks being launched on Lord Warden Glanharrow's herds and fields. She ought to remember anyway, painting or no painting—she'd been madly in love with him, hadn't she?—but she didn't. Not truly. She remembered how she'd *felt* about him, how she'd looked forward to the marriage as soon as she was old enough, sometimes she even remembered the feel of his arms around her, but his *face* was slipping away from her. In an odd way, and one which frequently made her feel almost unbearably guilty, she had a far clearer memory of Sir Trianal's face on the day he'd personally ridden up to her father's house to tell her that Sathek Smallsword had died in his baron's service and under Sir Trianal's command.

Well, of course you remember Sir Trianal's face better! Her inner voice was tart this time. *Sathek is gone, and you never got that miniature painted, and they say the mind forgets what the heart remembers. Besides, Sir Trianal* isn't *dead, now is he? It's been—what? All of three hours since you saw him at breakfast? That probably tends to keep him a little fresher in your memory, don't you think?*

True enough. That was true enough. And it still didn't keep her from feeling guilty when she couldn't remember. Just as the fact that life was what it was, and Lillinara knew Sharlassa couldn't change it just by wishing it was different, didn't make her any happier about it.

At least Mother knows you need all the help you can get, she reminded herself. *No matter* how *much you wish she'd stop beating herself up for "not having done right by you" when you were a girl! She didn't know where we were going to wind up any more than Father did. Or than* you *did, for that matter! And when it comes down to it, teaching you to think of yourself as a fine lady would have been the cruelest thing she could have done before Father became a lord warden.*

So, yes, she was deeply grateful to Lady Sharmatha for sending her where she could get the schooling she needed as a proper Sothôii noblewoman, even if it did seem like one of Hirahim's worse jokes to find herself in that position. And no one could possibly have been more understanding or kinder or a better teacher than Baroness Hanatha. Yet sending Sharlassa *here*—sending her to the place she still thought of deep in her bones as "home"—had its own sharp, jagged edges. She was no longer the person she'd been when she'd lived here in one of the neat little houses maintained for the garrison's officers. The girls she'd grown up with—those that weren't married, at any rate—had no better idea of how to act around her now than she had of how to act around them. Even her closest friends felt awkward and uncomfortable, divided by that invisible armor of rank which lay between them, afraid someone—possibly even Sharlassa herself—would think they were being overly familiar if they dared to treat their old friend *as* a friend.

She sighed yet again—she was getting a lot of practice at that this afternoon—and tossed the moss up into the air. Unlike the ribbon, it plummeted to the ground, disappearing into the orchard's grass, and she found herself wishing she could do the same.

It was a potentially dangerous thought, especially here in Balthar, and she knew her mother was concerned about that, however careful she'd been to never discuss it with her daughter in so many words. But there wasn't any point pretending the idea hadn't crossed Sharlassa's mind more than once.

Lady Leeana Bowmaster had been just as much a tomboy as ever Sharlassa Dragonclaw had been, and she'd gone through life with a fearlessness Sharlassa deeply envied. She'd wondered sometimes if that was because Leeana was not simply one of the most nobly born young women in the entire Kingdom but also an only child, treated more like a son than even she'd realized at the time. Now, with her own closer acquaintance with Baron Tellian and Baroness Hanatha, Sharlassa knew it wasn't that Leeana's parents had treated her like a son but that they'd treated her as a unique person in her own right. Baroness Hanatha treated Sharlassa the same way, and she'd seen the easy affection and love—the trust—in the way they treated Sir Trianal, as well.

Yet there was no denying that Sharlassa had deeply admired and respected Leeana. Of course, Leanna had been not simply the daughter of her liege lord but also over two years older than Sharlassa. They'd never been anything someone might have described as friends, for they'd lived in different worlds which simply happened to overlap from time to time. But those worlds *had* overlapped—sometimes in one of the paddocks or the stables, sometimes right here in this orchard when both of them had helped gather apples—and whenever they had, Leeana had been unfailingly friendly and kind. More than that, she'd . . . *radiated* something, something Sharlassa had seemed to sense the way she sensed the apple trees around her now. There'd been a sparkle, a strength, a sense of vibrant, flickering energy. No doubt that was as much her imagination as sometimes dreaming she was a tree, but that hadn't made the sensation *feel* any less real, and she couldn't quite convince herself that it had *all* been imagination.

She frowned moodily, with the expression her father had always called "scratching a mental itch" when she'd been younger, just before he chucked her under the chin or snatched her up onto his shoulder or tickled her unmercifully. She wished he was here to do that now and distract her from her brown, unreasonably moody mood, although it would, of course, be unspeakably improper for Lord Jahsak to do such a thing with Lady Sharlassa.

In a way, that feeling that she could almost reach out and touch the innermost being of the orchard's trees was to blame for much of her present mood, and she knew it. She treasured the feeling, took strength from it as if it helped to center her and remind her of who she was deep down inside, not simply who she had to learn to be as *Lady* Sharlassa. Yet she'd always secretly thought she would someday outgrow the absurd fancy that she could sense the trees at all, and she hadn't. In fact, it was actually growing stronger, and she sometimes thought she was reaching deeper and further.

Was the problem that she *wanted* to be able to do that? That she was so unhappy, so uncertain, about who she must learn to be that she longed for escape into some warm, comforting dream? Or into something which could distract her from learning the lessons her life had set her? Or was she simply losing her mind in a pleasantly harmless sort of way?

Her lips twitched at that last thought, remembering Granny Marlys. All Balthar's children had loved Granny growing up, although even the youngest of them had realized she was what some of the adults in their lives called "not quite right." As she'd grown older, Sharlassa had realized that people who *were* "quite right" didn't firmly believe they were the goddess Chemalka and could summon rain on a whim or make the sun shine whenever they wanted to. Yet aside from that minor foible, Granny Marlys had been the warmest, kindest person—and greatest storyteller—imaginable. Not a parent in Balthar would have hesitated for a moment to ask Granny to care for a child, and her kitchen had been a magic land where the scent of fresh cookies or gingerbread had a habit of ambushing a youthful visitor.

But, no, she wasn't another Granny. Granny had simply ignored the fact that she *couldn't* always make the sun shine whenever she wanted to . . . and that she frequently managed to get herself drenched working in her kitchen garden because that rain she'd forbidden to fall had fallen anyway. And she'd regarded all of the mortals around her with a benign sense that they were there to serve her whims but that she didn't really need them to do anything for her just at the moment, so they might as well go ahead and get along with their own lives until she *did* need them.

Sharlassa didn't live in that comfortable sort of imaginary world. That was the problem, after all! And that was why it . . . worried her, if that wasn't putting it too strongly, that she seemed to be becoming more sensitive, not less, to at least portions of the world around her.

And if you're going to become "more sensitive" to part of the world, why not all of it? she asked herself bitingly. *But, no, you can't do that, can you? It has to be just* some *of the world and just* some *of the people in it!*

To be fair, she'd always thought she could sense Kengayr whenever the courser was around. And there'd been that feeling that she could tell thirty seconds ahead of time when her father or her mother was about to walk through a door or someone like Leeana had been about to come around a corner. She'd mentioned that to her mother once, and Lady Sharmatha (only, of course, she hadn't been "Lady" Sharmatha at that point) had told her about something called "*syn shai'hain*." Sharlassa had never heard of it, but her mother had explained that it meant "something seen before" or "something already seen" in ancient Kontovaran. Sometimes, Sharmatha had told her eleven-year-old daughter seriously as they'd peeled apples—apples from this very orchard, in fact—for one of Sharmatha's peerless pies, someone had a flash, a feeling, that they'd already done or seen or experienced something. No one knew exactly why or exactly how it worked, but it happened to a lot of people, especially those—she looked up under her eyelashes with a smile—who had particularly *active* imaginations.

For a long time, Sharlassa had simply accepted that her awareness of the world about her was simply *syn shai'hain*, something she was imagining after the fact but so quickly it seemed to have come *before* the fact. Unfortunately, that had been easier when it happened less often. Because the truth was, whether she really wanted to admit it or not, that it was happening more and more often. Practically every time she saw Prince Bahzell, for example. Or Walsharno. Or, on a lesser scale, Dathgar or Gayrhalan. Or... one or two other people.

She grimaced and ran her hands over her wind-tousled hair, trying not to feel... trapped. That wasn't the word for it, but it came so close. She was being hammered and squeezed into a shape that wasn't hers, and the fact that the people who were doing the shaping had only her best interests at heart—that so many of them genuinely loved her—made it no more pleasant to be turned into someone she wasn't.

Which was why her mother was concerned about her youthful admiration for Lady Leeana, she knew. Lady Sharmatha would never say so, but she had to worry that Sharlassa might decide to follow Leeana's example and seek refuge among the war maids' free-towns. And, truth to tell, there were times when Sharlassa *had* been tempted, especially now that she'd had the opportunity to meet Leeana *Hanathafressa* on her occasional, brief visits to Balthar. That sense of energy and focused purpose and sheer passion for living which she'd sensed—or thought she'd sensed—in Leeana when they'd both been so much younger was brighter and stronger than ever. She never had the sense that there weren't things about Leeana's life and the decisions she'd made which she regretted, some of them bitterly, but regret was part of life, wasn't it? Sometimes there were no perfect solutions or choices, only better ones... or worse. And Sharlassa had never once sensed from Leeana any feeling that she'd made the *wrong* decisions, given the choices which had lain open to her.

Yet Sharlassa faced a life of very different choices, for much as she'd admired Leeana, Leeana Hanathafressa was larger-than-life. Like Prince Bahzell, she met the world head-on, unflinchingly, making the choice that seemed best to her and accepting the consequences, whatever they might be. And she was braver than Sharlassa. Or perhaps not so much *braver* as more fearless, for there was a difference between those two things. And when it came down to it, as unhappy as Sharlassa might feel about who she was being forced to become, she wasn't brave enough to give up the parents she loved so dearly. She'd seen Baron Tellian and Baroness Hanatha, and she knew they'd never stopped loving their daughter for a moment. She was confident Lord Jahsak and Lady Sharmatha would never have stopped loving her, even if she'd done something as outrageous as to run away to the war maids. But she also knew how deeply that separation would pain them—and her—and at least there was no prospect of her being forced into marriage with someone as disgusting as Rulth Blackhill! In fact—

She stopped that thought ruthlessly in its tracks. She wasn't going to think about that again, even though it did seem bitterly unfair that she should be forced out of the world in which she'd grown up and yet not allowed *into* the world in which—

Stop that! she scolded herself. *It's* not *going to happen. Or at least the moon will fall and the sun will freeze before it does! And how much of all this doom and gloom and worrying about being able to "sense" trees is all about that kind of foolishness? A lot, I'll bet.* She gave herself a shake. *Maybe it's a pity you're too old for Mother to put over her knee when you start being this foolish! Your brain always seemed to work better as a child when she stimulated your posterior, after all.*

She startled herself with a giggle at the image that thought evoked, given that she was two inches taller than her mother these days. Not that Lady Sharmatha had become one bit less formidable, by any means! Besides—

Something struck the back of her left hand ever so lightly. She looked down, and her eyebrows rose as she saw the spot of dampness. Another appeared on her sleeve as she watched, and she felt more light impacts on her head.

Told you those clouds were going to rain, didn't I? she told herself tartly. *And you didn't listen, did you? You never do. Honestly, I don't know why I put up with me!*

The rain was falling faster—well, more *thickly*, at any rate. It was still more mist than rain, and she sensed no thunder behind it, but that didn't mean it wasn't going to thoroughly soak anything—or anyone—foolish enough to be caught out in it. Not to mention a specific young lady (of sorts, anyway) who'd managed to get herself caught in an apple orchard the better part of a mile from Hill Guard's snug, tight roofs.

Well, you're not going to get any dryer standing here than you'd get walking back to the castle through it, are you?

The prosaic thought made her chuckle, although she had a gloomily good idea of how Baroness Hanatha would react when she turned up wet, muddy, and bedraggled. Worse, she had a very clear appreciation of how *Tahlmah* was going to react to the same sight.

She started down the orchard's central aisle, suppressing a useless urge to scurry like one of Hill Guard's home farm's chickens. Unless she thought she could somehow run between the raindrops—which seemed, on the face of it, rather unlikely—she was still going to be soaked by the time she got back to the castle. That being the case, there seemed little point in adding breathless and exhausted to the wet, muddy, and bedraggled she was already going to be. Besides, she was wearing those new shoes Tahlmah had insisted she put on this morning, and they'd already rubbed up a blister on her right heel.

The raindrops were thicker and somehow wetter feeling by the time she reached the gate in the orchard's stone wall. She was just reaching for the latch when someone pulled it open from the other side and she slid to a halt in surprise.

"*There* you are!" Sir Trianal Bowmaster, heir-adoptive to Balthar, announced triumphantly. "I thought I might find you here! Hiding from the dance master again, were you?"

"I—" Sharlassa stopped, blushing rosily, and shook her head. "I was *not* hiding from the dance master, Milord!" she said then, a little spurt of laughter bubbling under the words. "Master Tobis is far too kind for me to be that rude to him."

"Really?" Sir Trianal cocked his head, looking at her skeptically. "Are you going to tell me you actually *like* learning to dance? Don't forget, *I* had to learn—from Master Tobis, as a matter of fact—and so did Leeana, and between the two of us, I don't think either of us really enjoyed being taught."

"Really," she told him firmly, and, in fact, it was true. The blister on her heel had her feeling a little less than *eager* about her next lesson with Tobis Yellowshield, but she truly did enjoy them. Unlike altogether too many of the other things she was being forced to learn. "Besides, I'm not scheduled for another lesson with him until after lunch."

"Oho! So you're hiding from Sir Jahlahan and his *etiquette* lesson!"

"I am *not!*" she declared even more forcefully (and mendaciously) than before. "I just . . . went on a walk and lost track of time, Milord."

"Since I am a belted knight, and no true knight would ever doubt a lady's word, I won't go into how . . . likely I find that explanation of your absence, Milady," he told her with a twinkle. "However, I did run into Mistress Tahlmah. She was walking very purposefully along the Great Gallery at the time—heading, I think, to call on the master huntsman to borrow a couple of his bloodhounds."

"Oh, dear!" Sharlassa shook her head, her contrition genuine. So, unfortunately, was the amusement she felt at Sir Trianal's disrespectful but no doubt highly accurate description of her maid.

"Have no fear," Sir Trianal said, touching one hand to his heart and bowing to her. "Being the noble and kindly soul that I am, I assured Mistress Tahlmah that I would take it upon myself to check the orchard just in case. She informed me that she'd already searched—I mean, *checked*—there for you, but I felt it was worth another look. And if we hurry," he straightened, "I think we can probably sneak you back into the Castle before Mistress Tahlmah gathers up her nerve and informs Aunt Hanatha that the fairies have stolen you again."

Sharlassa hung her head, hearing the serious note under his humor and blushing more darkly than before.

"It's not as if you were the first person to ever sneak out for a little time of her—or his—own, you know." She wiggled at the note of amused but genuine sympathy in his tone. "*I've* been known to sneak away on occasion—generally from my tutors, not the arms master," he confessed. "In fact, I'd do the same thing today, and I'm the next best thing to ten years older than you are."

"I know," she sighed, "but I really shouldn't do it. Especially not when Baroness Hanatha is being so kind to me."

"Aunt Hanatha is kind to *everyone*—even me," Sir Trianal told her firmly. "It's the way she is. Although I will confess that she seems especially taken with you." He considered her thoughtfully. "Sometimes I think it's because you remind her of Leanna, but mostly I think it's because she simply likes the person you are. And even if she didn't, she knows how hard this all is for you."

"Milord?" She looked up quickly, startled, and he chuckled.

"You're not the only one who found out his life was going places he hadn't planned on, Milady. I never expected to be Uncle Tellian's heir-adoptive, you know. I knew he and Aunt Hanatha had a kindness for me, and I knew I'd always have a place here at Hill Guard if I needed it, but I always expected that to be as a vassal of whoever Leeana married. Of course, that changed."

His tone was much drier with the last sentence, but he also smiled and shook his head. Sir Trianal, Sharlassa had realized long ago, was not one of those who believed Leeana had disgraced her family or herself. Sharlassa was reasonably certain he was less than fond of war maids in general, but at least he seemed to respect them. She supposed a cynical person would say that was because Leeana's desertion to the war maids had worked out quite well for him, but Sharlassa knew that wasn't the reason for his attitude. She could feel the genuine affection, the love, for his cousin whenever he spoke about her. In fact—

Stop that, she told herself again.

"I do feel a little bit like a duckling trying to become a swan, Milord," she confessed after a moment.

"I know." He smiled again. "And, trust me, it *does* get better . . . eventually. Although—"

A much stronger wind gust blew through the orchard behind a vanguard of rain, drenching Sharlassa's spine, and Sir Trianal broke off.

"A duckling—or a swan—is what you're going to *have* to be if we're going to get you back to the house unsoaked!" he said, looking up at the clouds. He considered them for a moment, then whipped off his doublet and draped it over her shoulders and head.

"Milord, you can't—!" she began.

"Nonsense!" He laughed at her while the strengthening breeze plucked at his fine linen shirt with damp fingers. "I'm sure one of those lessons I evaded when I was younger said that any gentleman was required to give up his cloak or poncho—if he had one—to prevent a fair maid from getting drenched. Unfortunately, I seem to have left the house without either of those, so this will have to do."

"But you'll get soaked, and—"

"In that case, you really should stop arguing with me and get moving so we can get me under a roof before I become soaked to the bone and expire with pneumonia," he said sternly.

She looked at him helplessly for a moment, then laughed.

"Whatever you say, Milord! Whatever you say."

Chapter Six

Rain pattered down on the roofs of Hill Guard castle. It was a little late in the year for the persistent, day-long, soaking rains of spring's first blush, and not quite early enough for the short-lived, torrential afternoon thunderstorms of midsummer, but there was enough water in the air to go around, Bahzell reflected, standing under the overhanging roof which projected over the central keep's massively timbered front door. And probably enough to fill the Bogs knee-deep and send the overflow gushing down the old riverbed to join the water from Chanharsa's tunnel culverts, he thought, regarding the waterfalls streaming like finely beaded curtains from the eaves of that protecting roof. That would be one explanation for the condition in which Baron Tellian's latest guest had arrived at his ancestral keep above the city of Balthar.

Bahzell's lips twitched in amusement as the muddy, soaked-to-the-skin, plainly dressed warrior climbed down from his saddle in Hill Guard's courtyard, for the newcomer bore precious little resemblance to the dandified, arrogant Sir Vaijon of Almerhas he'd first met the better part of ten years ago in Belhadan. The changes were much for the better, in Bahzell's opinion, although he hated to think about how Vaijon's father must have reacted the first time his wandering son returned for a visit. The beautiful, jeweled sword at Vaijon's side was about all that was left of his onetime sartorial splendor, and that sword had been even more profoundly changed than Vaijon himself.

"And aren't you just the drowned rat?" the massive hradani inquired genially as Vaijon climbed the steps towards him while one of Tellian's grooms led his horse in the direction of the stable at a brisk pace.

"Drowned, certainly," Vaijon agreed wryly, reaching out to clasp forearms with him. "The Gullet's hock-deep in a lot of places, and cold, too—somebody forgot to tell Chemalka it's spring, I think—but surely you can find something better than a *rat* to compare me to!"

"Oh, I'm sure I could, if it happened I was so minded," Bahzell replied, returning his clasp firmly.

"Which you aren't. I see." Vaijon nodded, then turned to Brandark, and extended his hand to the Bloody Sword in turn. "You could come to my assistance here, you know."

"I could . . . if it happened I was so minded," Brandark said with a grin, and Vaijon heaved a vast sigh.

"Not bad enough that I'm doomed to spend my life among barbarian hradani, but they have to insult me at every opportunity, as well."

"Aye, it's a hard lot you've drawn, and no mistake," Bahzell's tone was commiserating, but his eyes twinkled and his ears twitched in amusement.

"Yes, it is." Vaijon pushed back the hood of his poncho, showing golden hair which had once been elegantly coiffed but which he now wore in a plain warrior's braid very much like Bahzell's own. The Sothōii-style leather sweatband he'd adopted made him look older and tougher, somehow (not that he wasn't quite tough enough without it, as Bahzell knew even better than most), and the past six years had put laugh lines around his eyes and weathered his complexion to a dark, burnished bronze. At six and a half feet in height, Vaijon was "short" only in comparison to a Horse Stealer like Bahzell, and with his thirty-second birthday just past, he was settling into the prime of his life.

"The bit from Hurgrum to the Gullet wasn't so bad, now that they've got the locks open all the way," he continued. "A lot faster and easier than the *first* time I made that particular trip, at least! But I, for one, will be *delighted* once the tunnel finally breaks through and my poor horse doesn't have to swim all the way to the top of the damned Escarpment whenever there's a little sprinkle! I said as much to Chanharsa when I passed through, too. I even took her a basket of your mother's cookies as a bribe, Bahzell. I was *sure* that would inspire her to greater efforts! But she only laughed at me." He heaved a vast sigh. "I never would've guessed dwarves were just as disrespectful of birth and position as hradani."

"Well, I suppose the least we can be doing is to get you out of the rain now you're here," Bahzell told him. "Tellian was all set to come out and greet you his own self, but I told him as how he should be staying right where he was." The hradani's expression darkened slightly. "I'm not liking that cough of his one bit, and the man's too stubborn to be calling in a healer. Or letting me deal with it, come to that."

"Is he *still* coughing?" Vaijon asked, blue eyes narrowing as he followed the two hradani into the keep and down a flagstoned corridor. It was a sign of how much things had changed in Balthar over the past six or seven years that none of the human armsmen or servants they encountered along the way so much as turned a hair when the unlikely trio passed them. Indeed, most of them smiled and nodded respectfully to Bahzell and his guest.

"Aye, that he is. Mind you, it's not so bad as it was this winter past, but it's easier in my mind I'd be if he could just be shut of it once and for all." Bahzell grimaced, ears flattening slightly. "There's no reason at all, at all, I can see why he *isn't* shut of it, and I'm none so pleased when someone as so many like so little is after being plagued by something like this. No doubt it's naught but my nasty, suspicious mind speaking, and so he's told me plain enough—aye, and more than a mite testy he was about it, too—but I'm thinking it's worn him down more than he's minded to admit even to himself." He shrugged. "Any road, Hanatha was more than happy to be helping me scold him into staying parked by the fire."

"That's ridiculous," Vaijon said testily. "This isn't the time for him to be sick, especially not with something that hangs on this way and won't let go, *wherever* it came from. I know he realizes how much depends on him right now. Why can't he grow up and let you take care of it for him?"

"And aren't you just the feistiest thing?" Bahzell said with a laugh. "Not but what you've a point." He shrugged again. "And I'll not be brokenhearted if it should be you've more success than I at making him see reason. There's times I think he's stubborner than a hradani!"

"Ha! *No one's* stubborner than a hradani, Bahzell! If anyone in the entire world's learned that by now, it's me."

"A bit of the pot and the kettle in that, Vaijon," Brandark pointed out mildly.

"And a damned good thing, too, given the job He and Bahzell have handed me," Vaijon retorted.

"Actually, you might have a point there," Brandark conceded after a moment. "And speaking as someone who always wanted to be a bard, I can't help noticing that there's a wagonload or two of poetic irony in where you've ended up, Vaijon."

"I'm so glad I'm able to keep you amused," Vaijon said.

"Oh, no! Keeping me *amused* is Bahzell's job!" Brandark reassured Vaijon, as they turned a corner and started up the steps to the keep's second floor.

"You just keep laughing, little man," Bahzell told him. "I'm thinking it would be a dreadful pity if such as you were to be suddenly falling down these stairs. And back up them—a time or two—now that I think on it. It's a *fine* bouncing ball you'd make."

Brandark started to reply, then stopped and contented himself with an amused shake of his head as Bahzell opened a door and led him and Vaijon into a well-lit third-floor council chamber. Diamond-paned windows looked out over the gray, rainy courtyard, but a cheerful coal fire crackled in the grate and a huge, steaming teapot sat in the middle of the polished table. The red-gold-haired man seated at the head of the table, closest to the fire, looked up as Vaijon and the hradani entered the chamber.

"Good morning, Vaijon!" Sir Tellian Bowmaster, Baron of Balthar and Lord Warden of the West Riding, said. He rose, holding out his hand, then coughed. The sound wasn't especially harsh, but it was deep in his throat and chest, with a damp, hollow edge, and Vaijon frowned as they clasped forearms in greeting.

"Good morning to you, Milord," he replied, forearms still clasped. "And why haven't you let Bahzell deal with that cough of yours?"

"Well, *that's* coming straight to the point," Tellian observed, arching his eyebrows.

"I've been dealing with hradani too long to beat about the bush, Milord," Vaijon said. "And since, at the moment, you have not one but two champions of Tomanāk right here in your council chamber, it seems to me to be a pretty fair question."

"It's only a cough, Vaijon," Tellian replied, releasing his forearm. "I'm not going to run around panicking just because I don't shake off a winter cough as quickly as I did when I was Trianal's age. And there's no need to be asking a champion—or two champions—to waste Tomanāk's time on something that minor!"

"I don't think He'd mind, Milord," Vaijon said dryly, "and I *know* neither Bahzell nor I would object to spending four or five minutes taking care of it. So perhaps you should balance your laudable determination not to pester Tomanāk over 'something that minor' against the fact that we're both going to be just about insufferable if you *don't* let us take care of it and it gets worse again."

"I think you'd better surrender while the surrendering is good, Uncle," Sir Trianal Bowmaster said, smiling as he crossed the council chamber from his place by the windows and held out his own arm to Vaijon. "I've certainly been suggesting the same thing to you long enough, and so has Aunt Hanatha."

"And why doesn't one of you just go ahead and say 'You're not as young as you used to be and you need looking after, Tellian'?" Tellian demanded acidly.

"Because we're thinking as how it would only be making you stubborner still?" Bahzell suggested in an innocent tone, and despite himself, Tellian laughed.

"Seriously," Vaijon said, "you ought to let us get rid of it for you, Milord. Perhaps it is only a minor inconvenience, but there's no point in your putting up with it, and I agree with Bahzell. There are enough people who wish you ill for something that just keeps hanging on this way to make me unhappy. I'm not trying to encourage you to look for assassins under your bed every night, but we know for a fact that the Dark doesn't much care for you. You're probably right that it's nothing more than a simple cough . . . but you might not be, too, and it would make all of us feel a lot better if it went away. Especially if you're going to be traveling to Sothōfalas with Bahzell and Brandark and this damned rain hangs on the way it looks like doing. The last thing we need is for you to come down with something like you had last winter when you need to be on your toes dealing with Lord Amber Grass and Prince Yurokhas."

Tellian glowered at him for a moment, then sighed and shook his head.

"All right. All right!" He shook his head again. "I yield. I still think you're all worrying like a batch of mother hens, but I can see I'm not going to get any rest until I do it your way."

"And why you couldn't have been realizing that a week ago is a sad puzzle to me," Bahzell told him with a slow smile.

"Probably because I'm getting so old, frail, and senile," Tellian replied darkly, then pointed at the chairs around the table. "And I suppose we should all sit back down before my aged knees collapse and I fall down in a drooling heap."

The others all laughed, although at forty-six, Bahzell was actually a few months older than the baron. On the other hand, he was also a hradani, and hradani routinely lived two hundred years or more, assuming they managed to avoid death by violence. That made him a very young man by his own people's standards. Indeed, he was little more than a stripling, younger even than Trianal of Balthar, by hradani reckoning.

They settled themselves around the conference table and Trianal poured a big, steaming cup of tea and passed it to Vaijon.

"This wouldn't be more of that vile morning moss tea, would it?" the champion asked, sniffing the fragrant steam suspiciously.

"Not in Hill Guard," Tellian reassured him. "Would you like me to drink some first to reassure you?"

"That won't be necessary, Milord," Vaijon said. "Unlike some of the people sitting around this table, I don't think *you'd* deliberately set out to poison an innocent and unsuspecting man."

"You've a way of holding grudges, don't you just?" Bahzell observed. "We told you as how it would relieve your cramps, and so it did, didn't it?"

"That's your story, and you're sticking to it, I see." Vaijon sipped cautiously, then smiled and drank more deeply. "Thank you, Milord," he said. "It's good."

"You're welcome." Tellian leaned back in his chair, covering his mouth as he coughed again, and Trianal poured *him* a cup and slid it across to him. The baron grimaced, but he also drank dutifully, then raised both eyebrows at his nephew. "Satisfied?"

"For now," Trianal replied, and Tellian snorted.

"Well, pour yourself some," he directed sternly. "I wasn't the one running around out in the rain without even a doublet, now was I?"

Trianal smiled and shook his head. But he also poured himself a cup obediently and sipped from it.

"I trust *you're* satisfied now, Uncle?" he asked, and Tellian chuckled.

"For now," he said, drinking some more of his own tea, and then cocked his head at Vaijon.

"Prince Bahnak asked me to give you his greetings," Vaijon

said, responding to the silent invitation to begin. "And Princess Arthanal's sent along that pillowcase she's been embroidering for Baroness Hanatha. I understand this one completes the entire set."

"Your mother's skill with a needle never ceases to amaze me, Bahzell," Tellian said with simple sincerity, "although how she finds the time to use it with everything she and your father have on their plates amazes me even more. Please tell her how much Hanatha and I appreciate the gift... and the thought that went into it, even more."

"I will that," Bahzell assured him. "I'm thinking as how that's not all Father had to be saying, though."

"No, it wasn't," Vaijon agreed. "A messenger came in from Kilthan just before I left Hurgrum. It seems Kilthan's agents are reporting that the Purple Lords are finally waking up, and they don't much like what they're hearing."

"My heart bleeds for them," Tellian said sardonically.

"I don't think anyone's going to waste much sympathy on them, Milord. But Kilthan's of the opinion they might try to do something to scuttle the entire project."

"Like what?" Trianal asked. At twenty-seven, Tellian's nephew was a broad-shouldered, solidly built young man. He was also an inch shorter than Brandark, making him the shortest person in the room, as well as the youngest, but there was nothing hesitant about his manner. "They don't exactly have an army they could send up this way—or not one worth a solitary damn, at any rate." He snorted contemptuously. "And even if they had one, we *are* just a bit too far from their frontiers for that," he added.

"No, they can't get at us with troops, even assuming they had an army used to doing anything more strenuous than terrorizing 'uppity' peasants, but they do have *influence*," his uncle pointed out, never looking away from Vaijon. "That's what Kilthan's thinking about, isn't it?"

"He and Prince Bahnak both," Vaijon confirmed with a nod. "Mind you, I don't think the Purple Lords would be above trying to provoke some sort of more... direct action. I imagine the possibility of using the River Brigands as catspaws has to've crossed their brains, for example. It's the sort of idea that would appeal to them. But I think they're more concerned about behind-the-scenes efforts in Sothōfalas itself, Milord."

"Where Cassan and Yeraghor would just *love* to help them succeed," Tellian said sourly.

"Something along that line, yes." Vaijon nodded again.

"Which would be lending some added point to our visit," Bahzell observed.

"Perhaps. No, probably," Tellian said. "Not that Cassan and Yeraghor need any outside encouragement to do anything they can to break our knees for us."

"From the construction side, I'd say it's really too late for them to stop you, Milord," Brandark put in.

"It's never too late for that, Brandark," Tellian replied. "If the faction that's most worried about Prince Bahnak's power base had its way, the King would lead an army down the Escarpment, burn Hurgrum and the rest of the Confederation to the ground, and take the entire project over in the Crown's name. I suspect at least half of them have to be bright enough to figure out how Kilthan would react to that, even assuming Prince Bahnak didn't hand us our heads—which I rather suspect he would—but that wouldn't stop them from proposing it for a moment. And if they didn't get it, their fallback position would be to insist that King Markhos embargo any trade between the Confederation and the Kingdom. For that matter, some of them are going to argue that the canals and the tunnel are only going to increase the Empire of the Axe's 'already disproportionate influence' in the Kingdom's politics and policy."

"It's not something they'll find simple to be stuffing back into the bottle," Bahzell rumbled, "which isn't to say as how they won't try to do just that. And I'm thinking they've more than enough ways to be causing us grief if it should happen they take it into their heads to be doing it."

"Which is why you and I are going to Sothōfalas," Tellian agreed, then looked back at the window at the steady rain and grimaced. "Not that I'm really looking forward to the trip."

"Ah, but it *could* be worse," Brandark comforted him. "You could be headed in the opposite direction."

"Not a feeble and ancient wreck like myself." Tellian coughed again, quite a bit more dramatically than strictly necessary. "That's a job for a younger—and more waterproof—man."

"You're so good to me, Uncle," Trianal said dryly, and Tellian chuckled and reached across the table to clasp his nephew's shoulder.

"You'll do fine. And you'll have Vaijon along to help out, once we get back from Sothōfalas."

"Isn't that about like saying the tinder will have a spark along to help it out, Milord?" Brandark inquired.

"You're welcome to come along yourself, Brandark," Vaijon invited, but the Bloody Sword shook his head quickly.

"I appreciate the invitation—really, I do—but I'm afraid I don't remember having lost anything on the Ghoul Moor."

The others laughed, although the notion of the upcoming summer's campaign wasn't an especially humorous topic. The Sothōii had been forced to launch periodic campaigns into the Ghoul Moor for as long as anyone could remember. In fact, generations of young Sothōii warriors—like Trianal (and Tellian himself, if it came to that)—had been blooded there. Yet those had all been little more than spoiling attacks, designed to drive the ghouls back from the foot of the Escarpment and remind them to stay clear of the Sothōii's horse herds on the far side of the Hangnysti River. With the approaching completion of the Derm Canal, something more permanent was required.

No one was foolish enough to believe the ghouls could actually be exterminated, although that would have been the preferred solution for anyone who'd ever had the misfortune to meet one of them. But if the entire canal project was to succeed, something had to be done to protect barge traffic on the Hangnysti. Ghouls, unfortunately, were excellent swimmers, and they had objectionable dining habits. It might be just a little difficult to convince bargemen to sail down the river knowing the ghouls—who regarded them as tasty snacks which were tastiest of all while they were still alive—were waiting to greet them.

That was the reason for the joint campaigns Tellian and Bahnak had mounted in the Ghoul Moor over the last two summers. The ghouls' territory stretched over seven hundred miles along the Hangnysti, and there was no hope that anyone could possibly actually control that vast an area. But what they *could* do was to secure the strip along the riverbank itself with a series of blockhouses and forts connected by mounted patrols. Maintaining those blockhouses and garrisons—and especially the patrols—wouldn't come cheap, but the projected earnings of the new trade route would more than cover the expense... assuming King Markhos wasn't convinced by the anti-hradani faction in Sothōfalas to forbid Sothōii participation.

At the moment, there seemed little probability their opponents would be able to persuade him to do anything of the sort, but the possibility couldn't be ruled out. And, in the meantime, the thought of Sothōii cavalry voluntarily cooperating with hradani infantry on *any* endeavor was enough to reduce those opponents to frothing fury. Even many of those who were tentatively in support of the new trade route were... uncomfortable with the notion. After a thousand years of merciless hostility, the concept of an army which combined hradani and Sothōii into a single, unified force was a profoundly unnatural one.

In fact, the first campaign season had gone less than smoothly. The armsmen of the West Riding were deeply loyal to their baron, yet his decision to fight side-by-side with hradani had come hard for many of them. Even those who'd accepted that Bahzell truly was a champion of Tomanāk *and* a wind rider had found it difficult to extend that same acceptance to hradani in general after so many centuries of bloodletting and mutual atrocities. There'd been a great deal of grumbling and more than a little resistance, not all of it from anti-hradani bigots, and Tellian had been forced to lead them himself that first year. And, of course, there were anti-*Sothōii* bigots in plenty on the *hradani* side, just to make the situation still better. Given the obstinacy quotient of Sothōii and hradani, the situation had been rife with potential disasters, and even with Tellian there in person, and with Bahnak's heir, Bahzell's oldest brother Barodahn, personally commanding the hradani contingent (and cracking heads where necessary), things had almost spiraled out of control on more than one occasion.

In the end, it had been the Order of Tomanāk more than anything else which had held things together. The Hurgrum Chapter had earned a high reputation among the Sothōii in the bloody battle to avenge the desecration of the Warm Springs courser herd, and its destruction of Sharnā's influence in Navahk had won it an equally high reputation among the hradani. The respect it enjoyed from human and hradani alike had allowed it to serve as both a unifying force and a buffer between the two factions when tempers flared. It had also led the way once battle was joined, and whatever they might think of one another, the Sothōii and Prince Bahnak's hradani were all fighting men. Where the Order led, they followed, and in the following they learned to respect *one another*, as well.

There were still occasional troublemakers from both sides, of course, although their fellows tended to quash them even more effectively than their officers might have. And the Order of Tomanāk remained a unifying force, as well as the point of the spear. By now, however, the West Riding by and large had at least accepted the concept that fighting with hradani rather than against them was a possibility. The fact that the Hurgrum Chapter was headed by a human, despite its exclusively hradani membership, hadn't been lost on Tellian's armsmen that first summer, either. In fact, the Hurgrum Chapter now boasted almost a dozen *human* members besides Vaijon, although any Sothōii would have flatly denied the possibility of such an arrangement before Tellian had "surrendered" to Bahzell in the Gullet.

Once this summer's campaign began, Vaijon would be personally leading the Order, and over the last half-dozen years, he'd turned into a seasoned and skillful field commander. That was a transition not all knights, even of the Order of Tomanāk, made, and Bahzell was proud of the younger man.

"So you've made up your mind as how Trianal will be after commanding your armsmen this time?" he asked Tellian now, and the baron nodded.

"I've got a feeling you and I are going to be spending more time than either of us might like in Sothōfalas this year, Bahzell," he replied. "Especially me." He grimaced. "Besides, Trianal's more than up to the challenge, and he's senior enough—and old enough now—that I can delegate the job to him without worrying that any of my officers might feel they have to test the limits of his authority." He grinned at his nephew. "And he's still young enough I can downplay just how ticklish the situation in the Ghoul Moor is if I have to in Sothōfalas. After all, if it were really important, or if our alliance with your father was truly shaky, then surely I'd be there myself, wouldn't I?"

"And who was Father thinking about from his side, Vaijon?" Bahzell asked. "Barodahn? Thankhar?"

"Actually, no," Vaijon said. "He's sending Barodahn off to Silver Cavern for a conference with Kilthan and the other clan elders, and Thankhar's busy acting as his eyes and ears with Serman and the Derm Canal work crews. So he's picked someone else—Yurgazh."

Bahzell blinked, ears flattening briefly in surprise, but then his eyes narrowed and he began to nod. Slowly, at first, then faster and more enthusiastically.

Prince Arsham Churnazhson had inherited the throne of Navahk following the death of his father. Despite his own illegitimacy, he'd always been popular with the Navahkan Army, and he'd fought well and hard against Hurgrum and her allies. In the end, he'd surrendered honorably, and while he was unlikely ever to be especially fond of Prince Bahnak or his sons, he'd also never had time for the perversions and cruelty of Churnazh's legitimate sons. Besides that, he was smarter than they'd been, able to recognize the advantages the unification of the northern hradani had brought to all of them. Navahk had gone from starving misery to something which actually approached prosperity; that had done wonders to consolidate the legitimacy of his rule, if not his parentage, in Navahkan eyes, and the completion of the canals and the tunnel was bound to bring his city-state even greater prosperity.

Yurgazh Charkson was cut from much the same cloth as Arsham, and he'd become the Navahkan prince's senior general following the war. In addition, he and Bahzell had formed a wary semi-friendship during Bahzell's days as a political hostage in Navahk, which hadn't hurt his acceptability among Horse Stealers. Yet, like Arsham, he'd distinguished himself in both wars against Hurgrum, as well, which meant he was both popular with the Navahkans and respected by Bahnak's Horse Stealer officers. He had the moral authority to command the allegiance of both, and putting a Bloody Sword in command of the Northern Confederation's half of the Ghoul Moor expedition would constitute another major step in Bahnak's ongoing campaign to truly *unify* the northern hradani.

And letting deputies, however senior, represent both Tellian and Bahnak in the field would go far to suggest that human and hradani cooperation was becoming routine enough it no longer required heads to be knocked together on a wholesale basis.

"He's a canny one, my Da," Bahzell said with a smile. "Almost as canny as someone else as comes to mind." He twitched his ears at Tellian, who snorted.

"It's not canniness on *my* part, if that's what you mean, Bahzell; it's *laziness*. That's why the gods gave us youngsters to send out and do the hard work while we lie about drinking wine and belching."

Chapter Seven

I really hate *this,* Shahana Lillinarafressa thought moodily as the right leaf of Thalar Keep's heavy wooden gates swung open at her approach, and the fact that her own fair-mindedness told her she was being unreasonable only made her mood even worse.

Unfortunately, she didn't have a lot of choice in the matter, and since that was true, she was determined to discharge her duty well. However badly it set her teeth on edge.

Her mail jingled as her horse trotted through the gatehouse entry tunnel, hooves noisy on the pavement, the sound echoing under the circles of the murder holes in the passageway's roof. Then she was out into the sunlight once again, drawing rein in the keep's cobblestoned courtyard. It wasn't much of a keep to someone who'd seen the massive engineering works and fortifications of the Empire of the Axe, but she supposed it was a fairly impressive pile of stone for a relatively minor lord warden of the Sothōii. Poorly designed and laid out by the standards of *competent* fortress engineers, perhaps, not to mention easily dominated by proper siege engines on the nearby high ground and with an equally-easily-mined earth footing instead of solid stone, but impressive for a *Sothōii* keep. Of course, for anyone *else*...

She grimaced mentally as the reflection flashed through her brain. She was being cattish again, she thought, and reminded herself—again—to keep her opinion of Lord Trisu's family seat to herself. However justified it might be.

Stop that! she scolded herself.

Behind her, the combination honor guard and delegation from

Kalatha rode out of the same tunnel, and she sensed the male eyes watching all of them with the combined curiosity and flicker of hostility to which any arm of Lillinara became accustomed, at least in the Kingdom of the Sothōii. The hostility quotient was probably a little higher in this case, she reflected, given her war-maid escort and memories of what had so nearly happened six or seven years ago. However—

"Welcome, Dame Shahana," Sir Altharn Warblade, the senior officer of Thalar Keep's garrison, greeted her with a bow.

Shahana was no knight—no arm was—and the title was yet another thing about her current duty that set those teeth of hers on edge, but she couldn't seem to break the Sothōii of the need to append some sort of title *they* recognized to her name. Even now, she wasn't certain whether that was because they needed that formal label to feel remotely comfortable with any woman who lived her life under arms, or if it was because of her champion's status. Of course, the arms weren't quite like any other deity's champions, but it was probably too much to expect any Sothōii to grasp that point. They were doing their best to be courteous, and given how hard it must be for any new thought to claw its way through their brains, she had no choice but to take it in the spirit in which it was—probably—intended.

"And greetings to you, Sir Alfar," she replied pleasantly, half-bowing in the saddle.

"As always, it's a pleasure to see you," Sir Alfar lied politely. "Will you step down from the saddle and let us see to your horse?"

"With pleasure," Shahana said, swinging down from her mount.

One thing she had to admit was that the Sothōii deserved every bit of their reputation as horse breeders. Her own mare was a case in point, a gift from the man she was here to see. And another of those little irritations with which she had to cope, considering how little she relished having to feel grateful to Lord Warden Trisu for any reason. Sadly, she had little choice from that perspective, since Spring Storm Cloud Rising, the name the Sothōii had inflicted upon the beautiful creature, was undoubtedly the finest horse she'd ever ridden in her life. She'd shortened the splendiferous name to "Stormy," of course—not even the Sothōii routinely used the names they bestowed upon their horses—and she paused to rub the iron gray's satin nose before she handed the reins to the waiting groom. Stormy nosed back affectionately, and Shahana smiled for a moment before she turned back to Warblade.

"We'll take good care of her, Milady," the armsman promised as the groom led the mare away, and Shahana nodded.

"I know," she said, and she did. Despite all the things about the Sothōii which irritated her, there were almost as many things she liked, when she had the patience to admit it to herself, and their near universal dedication to the four-legged wonders they bred was high on the list.

"Then if you'll accompany me," Warblade invited, and she nodded again and fell in at his side as he escorted her into the main keep.

✧ ✧ ✧

Leeana Hanathafressa dismounted from her own gelding as Sir Alfar led Arm Shahana off to her first meeting. She didn't envy the arm—a stubborner, more iron-headed individual than the current Lord Warden of Lorham would have been impossible to imagine—and she wasn't looking forward to her own visit with him, either. But whatever his other failings, Trisu was at least unfailingly (if coldly, disapprovingly, and stiffly) courteous, even to her. The same could not be said for some of his armsmen.

She felt eyes upon her as she came lithely down from the saddle. She knew it wasn't because of her horsemanship, and she suppressed an urge to tug down her chari's hem. It was ridiculous, of course, and one of the reasons she most hated her occasional trips to Thalar Keep, where every single armsman and servant knew exactly who she'd been born to be. The knowledge behind those eyes made her much more aware than usual of just how much thigh the chari showed, and she could imagine only too readily how the minds behind some of those eyes were stripping her the rest of the way naked.

The owners of those eyes would undoubtedly have done the same to any war maid, but there was no point pretending they didn't pay special attention to her. Legally, all war maids were equal before the law, absolved of all previous family affiliation and duties, yet it seemed every living Sothōii knew who *her* father was. That made her an object of special interest to almost everyone... and one of special contempt to those who insisted on thinking of all war maids as unnatural creatures, the best of whom were little better than common harlots and all of whom were dark dishonor to their family names. The thought of successfully bedding *her* held a special attraction for quite a few Sothōii males, and not just because she happened to be young and good looking, and she knew exactly why that was. And what was almost worse, there were countless "proper" Sothōii *women* who undoubtedly figured that was exactly what she deserved after the humiliation and shame she'd inflicted upon her parents.

There'd been a time when her awareness of those watching eyes and the thoughts behind them had embarrassed her more than she would have believed possible; now, it only made her angry. She had no intention of revealing that to her audience, though, however much pleasure it would have done her to rip off a few heads and shove them up their owners' bodily orifices.

The tart thought woke an unexpected sparkle of welcome amusement, and she reached up and patted Boots' neck. The bay brown gelding blew heavily, trying to convince her the journey from Kalatha had worn him to the bone, but she knew better, and she smiled.

"Don't lie to *me*," she told him. "I've known you too long for that."

Boots tossed his head with a snort, recognizing her tone, and she laughed. Yet even as she did, she felt those eyes, and that pissed-off part of her still wanted to go turn some of them black and blue.

"Kitty, kitty, sheathe those claws," a voice murmured very quietly beside her, and she glanced at Garlahna. "*I* know what you're thinking," her best friend said. "For that matter, I'm thinking the same thing, but if you go and start kicking their arses the way they deserve, Mayor Yalith and Balcartha will have a few sharp things to say to you when we get home."

"I don't know what you're talking about," Leeana replied, elevating her nose. "Although I do notice no one's offered to take care of *our* horses for us . . . again."

"As if you'd *let* anyone else take care of Boots!" Garlahna snorted.

"That's not the point. The point is that they didn't *offer*."

Garlahna shrugged, and Leeana reminded herself not to grimace. Her friend was unaware of the finer points of etiquette among the Sothōii aristocracy. As such, she didn't recognize the deeply offensive insult the Kalathan war maids had just been offered. For that matter, *most* war maids wouldn't have recognized it, given the relatively humble origins from which the majority of them sprang, which was probably one reason Trisu's armsmen and grooms took such delight in offering it. *They* knew how they'd just slighted the two of them, and the fact that war maids in general were too stupid to even know they'd been insulted only made it better.

And then there was Leeana herself... the one war maid they could be certain *would* know how profoundly she'd just been insulted.

She found a certain degree of revenge in smiling at the grooms and hostlers standing around with their hands ostentatiously in their pockets as she and Garlahna passed on their way to the stables. It wasn't the kind of smile Sothōii were accustomed to seeing from war maids, and she knew her mother would have been appalled if she could see it. There were advantages to having been raised as the daughter of one of the Kingdom's foremost powerful nobles, however, and she knew exactly how to put the proper cold edge of contempt into an otherwise pleasant expression.

"Thinks her shit doesn't stink," she heard someone mutter in a voice she was perfectly aware she was supposed to hear. She ignored it... except to give her hips a slight swish which would also have appalled her mother.

"One of these days, you're going to get us mobbed," Garlahna told her quietly. "You do know that, don't you?"

Leeana arched an eyebrow at her friend, and Garlahna chuckled. "When it happens, I'm hiding behind you," Garlahna warned, brown eyes gleaming with amusement in the stable's dim light as she and Leeana began unsaddling their horses.

"Coward," Leeana said, smiling back.

"No, just practical; I know my limitations—relatively speaking, of course. Besides, Barlahn doesn't like it when I bring back black eyes from one of these little jaunts with you. I think he thinks it's unladylike."

"*Barlahn?*" Leeana laughed out loud. "He'll just want to hear about what you did to the poor jerk who gave it to you in the first place!"

"I don't know where you get those ridiculous ideas about him," Garlahna said severely, swinging her saddle up onto a tack rack. "He's a very delicate and refined man, you know."

"*Sure* he is. And I know just what part of his 'refined' personality most attracts *you*, too. I *have* seen him swimming, you know!" Leeana rolled her eyes, and Garlahna smacked her lightly on the shoulder.

Leeana racked her own saddle, whisked off Boots' saddle blanket, and began briskly rubbing him down. It was a task she'd performed hundreds, even thousands, of times before, and she flared her nostrils, inhaling the familiar, welcome scents of horseflesh, saddle soap, leather, oil, and hay. Whatever she might think of Trisu's armsmen's standards of courtesy, they kept Thalar Keep's stables in meticulous order, and she was prepared to forgive them quite a bit as long as that was true.

"So, are you going to try to talk to him today, or wait until tomorrow?" Garlahna asked, rubbing down her own horse with considerably less pleasure than Leeana.

"I think Arm Shahana's going to keep him pretty fully occupied today," Leeana replied.

"Besides which, you don't want to talk to him one moment sooner than you have to."

"I didn't say that."

"No, but you were *thinking* it pretty loudly."

"Is it my fault the man's an idiot?" Leeana demanded, shaking her head disgustedly. "I swear, sometimes I wonder what Mayor Yalith is thinking, sending *me* to talk to him about something like this!"

"I'd imagine it has something to do with, oh, I don't know... the fact that you understand 'something like this' better than any of the rest of us?"

Leeana snorted, but she had to concede that Garlahna had probably put her finger on it. There weren't many—in fact, she admitted, there weren't *any*—other war maids with her perspective on the internal workings of the aristocracy and its obligations under the Kingdom's laws and traditions. That made her the logical person to "informally" discuss minor points of contention with Trisu before they turned into formal complaints. Once it reached the complaint stage, someone older and more senior would be sent to handle the matter, but Mayor Yalith had gotten into the habit of using Leeana to keep things from ever getting to that point. Of course, there was the minor fact that the mayor couldn't possibly have found an envoy who would have been more offensive to Trisu's prejudices. Which, Leeana had suspected a time or two, might well be another reason she kept getting selected for these little visits.

I do wish the mayor could find another way to tweak Trisu's nose, she thought moodily, her arm moving rhythmically while she continued to rub Boots down. *Not that I don't sympathize with her. And not that she isn't making a valid point, for that matter. War maids aren't supposed to cater to the prejudices of our male "betters," and sending someone Trisu has to be polite to* despite *himself is one way to underscore that for him. Unfortunately, understanding what she's doing doesn't make it any more pleasant to be her clue stick.*

"I'll talk to him about it tomorrow," she said out loud.

"Try not to do it until after breakfast," Garlahna advised. "That's the most important meal of the day, you know. I'd hate for you to lose your appetite that early."

✧ ✧ ✧

"Welcome, Arm Shahana," Trisu Pickaxe said as Warblade personally ushered Shahana into his spartan, whitewashed office high in Thalar Keep's central tower.

"Thank you, Milord," she replied. As much as she and Trisu grated on one another's nerves, he was always punctiliously polite whenever they met. And he was apparently the only man in all of Lorham who could remember the proper form of address for one of Lillinara's champions.

"May I offer you refreshment?" Trisu continued, waving one hand at the small side table, where a bottle of Dwarvenhame whiskey and two crystal glasses kept company with a moisture-beaded pitcher of beer and a much larger beer stein. At least he'd learned that much about her, she thought.

"That would be most welcome, Milord," she replied with a slight smile, and he personally and expertly poured beer into the stein and handed it to her. She sipped with unfeigned pleasure, since Trisu had one of the better brewmasters she'd ever encountered.

"This is good, Milord," she acknowledged.

"I'm pleased you like it," he replied with a genuine smile. Then he waved her into the chair facing his desk and waited until she sat before seating himself once more. "May I ask to what I owe the pleasure of your visit?"

"Nothing earth-shattering . . . this time, Milord." Shahana smiled thinly. "The Voice knew I had business in Kalatha, and she asked me to stop by and visit you while I was in the vicinity. She wanted me to extend her respects, and to tell you Quaysar expects a very good harvest this year, if the weather holds fair. She hopes to be able to make good on the taxes you so graciously deferred last fall."

"It's good of her to take the trouble to inform me of that," Trisu replied.

He took a sip from his own glass of whiskey, and Shahana wondered if it was to erase the taste of that courteous response from his mouth. Then she scolded herself. No, he didn't like the war maids, and he would have been far happier if Quaysar had lain in someone else's wardenship, but she'd never heard an overtly discourteous word out of him. Bluntness that verged on rudeness, sometimes, for he was a plainspoken, almost painfully honest man who took a certain pride in being that way, but never deliberate discourtesy.

"Please inform the Voice that there's no urgency in making up last year's shortfall," he continued after a moment. "Bad harvests can happen to anyone, but it looks like a good harvest for almost everyone this year if, as you say, the weather holds. That's what I'm hearing from my bailiffs, at any rate, which means we're anticipating a strong income stream, and I realize the Temple has yet to fully recover." He smiled thinly. "Given the way events almost worked out, I fully understand that her treasury is still under considerable pressure."

"Thank you, Milord."

It was a bit difficult for Shahana to get the words out in a normal tone as Trisu reminded her of how close the Quaysar Temple of Lillinara had come to total disaster. He was right about the strain the temple's treasury had been under ever since, although that pressure was finally beginning to ease, thank the Goddess! But the last several years have been hard ones in the wake of Shīgū's devastating attack.

And the real reason you're pissed off by Trisu's "understanding tone" isn't just because he was right all along when he claimed there was something seriously wrong in Quaysar, either. It's because Dame Kaeritha *got the call to straighten that entire mess out instead of* you, *isn't it?*

She didn't much like admitting that. In fact, she was self-honest enough to know she spent as much of her time as she could *not* admitting it. That, unfortunately, didn't make it untrue.

No, it doesn't. But, dammit, we *should have seen what was happening, and the Mother should have sent one of Her arms to deal with it!*

The thought flashed through her mind, and she raised her stein, taking another long swallow of the clean, rich-tasting beer to hide her expression while she dealt with it.

The truth was that Lillinara's arms wouldn't have been remotely as well equipped as Dame Kaeritha had been to deal with the assault on the Quaysar Temple, and Shahana knew it. Arms of the Mother, like Shahana herself, were trained warriors, but Shahana wasn't remotely Kaeritha Seldansdaughter's equal in that respect. Partly that was because of the difference in the deities they served, of course; Tomanāk was the god of *war*, after all! His champions were *primarily* warriors, but that function was secondary for most arms.

Most arms, as Shahana herself had, heard Lillinara's voice early in life and began as arms of the Maiden—students, scholars, and explorers taking their first steps on the road of life, studying and learning in order to prepare themselves for greater responsibilities in the course of time. The majority of them eventually became arms of the Mother, although not all ever made that transition. The ones who didn't tended to become the Church's librarians, researchers, and scribes or sometimes envoys, but they certainly weren't Lillinara's mailed fist. Arms of the Maiden had some training under arms, yet it was minimal, just enough to let them look after themselves in an emergency, because they were supposed to be concentrating on other things.

Arms of the Mother were fully engaged with life. They *were* trained warriors, but their primary function was to nourish. Many of them, too, remained scholars, serving as teachers and educators. Others, like Shahana, were skilled healers and midwives or surgeons in addition to their weapons training. As warriors, they were guardians and protectors, the custodians of the precious fire of life Lillinara shared with her mother Kontifrio. More than one arm of the Mother had died defending that flame, but they were *defenders*, not the spearheads of justice Tomanāk's champions so often were.

And then there were the arms of the Crone. Not all arms of the Mother made that transition, and Shahana sometimes wondered if she had the moral fortitude to make it herself. Arms of the Mother defended life; arms of the Crone were focused on the proper *ending* of life. The healers among them served the hospices which offered care and support for the elderly, the dying. Where those slipping into Isvaria's shadows were given the dignity and comfort they deserved. It took a special bravery to open one's heart to those who must inevitably fade, to embrace the natural tide and ease the final flicker of the flame that the arms of the Mother protected so fiercely, and Shahana wasn't at all certain she had that much courage.

But arms of the Crone weren't just healers. They, too, were warriors, yet their function was not to defend life, but to *avenge* it. An arm of the Mother would seek, far more often than not, to capture a criminal and deliver him to justice, whatever his offense; when Lillinara dispatched an arm of the Crone, it was to slay, not to capture.

And that was why neither an arm of the Mother nor an arm of the Crone would have been remotely as well suited to dealing with Shīgū's attack on Quaysar. However much Shahana might dislike admitting it, that had required a sword with a keener edge than hers. Once Shīgū had replaced the legitimate Voice with her own creature and corrupted the captain of the Quaysar Temple Guard, nothing short of Tomanak Himself and His champions could have pried her loose again without the utter devastation of the temple. For that matter, even Dame Kaeritha and Bahzell Bahnakson had inevitably left broad swaths of destruction in their wake, and the Temple Guard *had* been devastated. Well over two-thirds of its armsmen and war maids had been corrupted to a greater or a lesser extent—many of them knowingly; others without even realizing what was happening—and the survivors' morale had been shattered by the realization of how utterly they'd failed to protect the temple they'd been called upon to serve.

And that was why Shahana had been permanently assigned to Quaysar for the last six and a half years. *Rebuilding* the temple was a task to which arms of the Mother were far better suited, and she and the current Voice—trained healers, both of them—had carried out that rebuilding with slow but steady progress. It helped that the Voice was a native Sothōii . . . and that she'd never been a war maid. Trisu, for example, found it much easier to interact with her than he did even now with Mayor Yalith at Kalatha. For that matter, he found it easier to interact with her than he did with Shahana, who'd been born and raised in the Empire of the Axe.

And he still *gets along better with Dame Kaeritha than he does with* either *of us,* Shahana thought moodily. *Is that because he's more comfortable thinking of her as "just" another warrior? Or is it because, in the end, she realized he was right and the war maids were wrong about what was happening? Does a part of him think of her as his partisan and not simply as an impartial judge sent by Scale Balancer?*

Of course, she admitted, it was also entirely possible that only a champion of Tomanāk *could* have been impartial in a case like this one. Lillinara's arms dealt regularly with prejudice—especially here in the Kingdom of the Sothōii and especially against war maids—and they did have a natural tendency to react defensively first and consider impartiality second.

So the Gods probably knew what They were doing when they sent Dame Kaeritha and not you, she told herself yet again. *Maybe you should just go ahead and accept that They* usually *know what They're doing?*

The familiar tartness of that thought restored much of her humor, and she lowered her stein and smiled at Trisu.

"I'm sure the Voice will appreciate your generosity and understanding," she said. "We're making continued progress in rebuilding, and Quaysar is becoming prosperous again, but there's no point pretending it couldn't very easily have gone the other way."

"I know."

Trisu's gray eyes went cold and distant, looking at something Shahana couldn't see. They stayed that way for several seconds before he shook himself and refocused on her face.

"I know," he repeated. "And the truth is, Arm Shahana, that I blame myself, at least in part."

"You do?" Shahana couldn't quite keep the surprise out of her own voice. As far as she knew, this was the first time Trisu had ever said anything like that. "In fairness, Milord," she said a bit unwillingly, "yours was the only voice raising the alarm. It's scarcely your fault that no one listened to you until Dame Kaeritha came along."

"You think not?" Trisu sat back in his chair, elbows on chair arms, cradling his glass of whiskey in both hands, and smiled in what certainly looked like faint amusement. "I think perhaps you're being overly generous, Milady."

"In what way?" she asked, trying not to bridle at the honorific he'd chosen.

"It's tactful of you and the Voice not to remark upon it, Arm Shahana," he said, still with that faint smile, "but my own attitude, and that of my family, towards the war maids is scarcely a secret. Indeed, I've been known to express myself, ah, somewhat intemperately, I suppose, upon the subject in private conversation from time to time. Nowhere near as intemperately as my Uncle Saeth or my cousin Triahm, perhaps, but still intemperately enough. I won't pretend I don't believe many of my... less than flattering opinions where the war maids are concerned are justified, either. Obviously, you and I aren't going to agree with one another in that regard. However, it's a lord warden's responsibility to discharge his duties as impartially as he possibly can, and I've come to the conclusion that I'd put myself into a position where I wasn't able to do that."

"As nearly as I can tell, Milord," Shahana said a bit stiffly, "you *did* discharge them impartially. It certainly turned out you were the one who was correctly interpreting the situation *and* the provisions of the Kalatha town charter. Whatever anyone may have thought at the time, you were completely within your legal rights."

"Oh, I know I was," he acknowledged with a slightly broader smile, eyes glinting as he recognized how unhappy it made her to acknowledge that point. "But the problem, Milady, is that everyone else knew about my... let's be courteous and call them prejudices where the war maids were concerned. And because they did, there was an automatic assumption that I *wasn't* acting impartially. I put myself in that position by not watching my words more carefully, and I can't quite free myself of the suspicion that Shīgū chose Lorham and Quaysar specifically because I'd allowed myself to be far more outspoken about my feelings than a responsible lord warden would have done. Those opinions of mine were too broadly known, and without Dame Kaeritha's intervention, that would have made Shīgū's lies entirely too plausible."

Shahana blinked. She couldn't help it, because she would never have expected that analysis out of Trisu Pickaxe. It was entirely too insightful to be coming from someone like him.

Only it just did, didn't it? she thought. *And the fact that you would never have expected it probably says more about* you *than it does about him, doesn't it? Damn the man! Now I can't even congratulate myself for overcoming* my *prejudices against him better than he overcomes his against* me!

"Milord," she said, regarding him levelly, "there's probably something in what you say, but perhaps it cuts both ways. I'll concede you've been a bit more... outspoken than I might have wished upon occasion, but so have the war maids. And, for that matter, the Quaysar Temple has been more confrontational than absolutely necessary from time to time. I think you're right that it was the tension between all parties, and the fact that that tension was so widely known, that cleared the way for Shīgū's attempt in the first place. But you weren't the only source of that tension."

"Oh, I never said I was!" Trisu actually chuckled, leaning even further back in his chair. "Milady, it would never do for me to say I was *more* at fault than the war maids! Just think of the consternation *that* would cause among my armsmen and anyone else who knows me! Besides, the entire situation would never have arisen if not for the unnatural and perverse lifestyle the war maids have chosen to embrace, now would it?"

Shahana had just raised her stein for another sip of beer. Now she spluttered into it and lowered the stein again to glare at him as he delivered his last sentence in a tone of perfect, matter-of-fact sincerity, as if he'd simply remarked that the sun was likely to rise in the east tomorrow morning. She started to open her mouth, then paused as their gazes met and she saw the amusement sparkling deep in his eyes. She drew a deep breath and shook her head.

"Milord," she said tartly, "if you're not careful, I'm going to decide you have a sense of humor after all, and then where will you be?"

Chapter Eight

<*Do you think that if I asked Dathgar to just sort of nudge his horse—you know, just hard enough to knock him out of the saddle—he'd stop that racket?*> Walsharno asked rather wistfully in the back of Bahzell's mind.

"Now isn't that a dreadful thing to be asking?" Bahzell replied, quietly enough not even another hradani could have overheard him. "And him doing all he can to while away the leagues and all!"

<*You do realize coursers' ears are even more sensitive than yours, don't you?*> The mental voice was considerably more tart this time, and Bahzell chuckled, glancing ahead to where Brandark rode easily in the saddle, strumming his balalaika.

The musical tastes of individual coursers, he had discovered, varied at least as widely as those of the individual members of the Races of Man, and Walsharno's ran more to stately measures which relied heavily on woodwinds, viols, and cellos. He was *not* a fan of balalaika music, and he had even less taste for the dwarves' latest musical invention. They called it a "banjo," and Brandark was already showing what Walsharno considered a most unhealthy interest in the infernal new device. If he was going to be honest, Bahzell shared his courser brother's reservations where Brandark's new attraction was concerned, but the Bloody Sword's current selection didn't bother him anywhere nearly as badly as it obviously bothered Walsharno. At least he wasn't playing the "Lay of Bahzell Bloody Hand." That was something, Bahzell reflected. And he wasn't *singing*, either, which was even better. In fact, taking everything together, and considering how much worse it could always get, Walsharno shouldn't be complaining at all.

<*I wouldn't* dream *of "complaining." I'm only thinking about helping him have a little accident.*>

"Oh, and isn't that ever so much better? I'm not so sure at all, at all, as how a champion of Tomanāk should be thinking such things."

<*And* you *don't?*>

"Ah, but it's only mortal I am, when all's said," Bahzell replied mournfully. "And I never said as how I'd never the slightest temptation of my own, come to that. The spirit's willing enough, but somehow..."

He shrugged, and Walsharno snorted in amusement. Baron Tellian heard that snort and turned his head, raising one eyebrow quizzically. No wind rider could hear another courser's voice, but all of them got quite adept at reading courser body language.

"Brandark?" the baron asked, gray eyes gleaming appreciatively.

"I'm sure I've no idea at all what it might be you're referring to, Milord," Bahzell replied innocently.

"I thought I'd heard somewhere that champions of Tomanāk weren't supposed to lie," Tellian observed to no one in particular, and Walsharno snorted again, louder than ever. He also tossed his head in an unmistakable nod.

"Traitor," Bahzell said wryly.

<*Nonsense. Is it* my *fault I recognize the truth when I hear it?*>

"It's not really all *that* bad," Tellian said thoughtfully. "And at least he's not singing. That's something."

<*Two minds with but a single thought,*> Walsharno said, and Bahzell chuckled.

"Truth to tell, though I'd not like to be admitting it to him, you understand, the little man's not so bad as all that when he plays. In fact, he's better than most, if it comes down to it."

"Agreed. It just seems...wrong, somehow. Or perhaps the word I really want is frivolous."

Tellian gazed up at the brilliant blue sky and the white drifts of cloud blowing about its polished dome. The day, for a change, was both dry and not too oppressively hot, with a breeze that was just short of brisk blowing out of the north behind them as they headed south along the Balthar-Sothōfalas high road. It was over two hundred leagues from Balthar to King Markhos' capital as the bird might have flown—just under two hundred and sixty for road-bound mortals—and they were roughly halfway to their destination. This particular stretch of road was better maintained than many of the Kingdom's highways, largely because it lay in the West Riding, and both Tellian and his father had made a point of seeing to the proper upkeep of the high roads passing through their riding, but it was still intended for horses and coursers, not heavy foot traffic or freight wagons. Instead of the broad, paved stone of the Empire of the Axe, it had a surface of river gravel, theoretically rolled level and bordered with wide shoulders of firm, hoof-friendly turf. Even in Balthar, the gravel surface left quite a bit to be desired, especially where the ravages of winter had not yet been repaired, but it was wide enough, and Tellian's escort had stretched out a bit, moving towards its western edge to take advantage of the band of shade projected by the trees along that side of the road as the sun moved towards afternoon.

All Sothōii high roads, like most of those in the Empire of the Axe, for that matter, were bordered by carefully planted rows of trees intended to provide windbreaks, shelter, and firewood for travelers forced to bivouac along the way. The penalties for casually felling those trees were stiff, but fallen limbs and branches were another matter, and the road crews thinned and tended them every year when they repaired the ravages of winter. The trees they took down were sawn into convient lengths, with the thicker logs split, and stacked in neat wood piles at semiregular intervals for travelers' convenience. Combined with natural deadfalls, that was enough to keep most travelers from poaching on the living wood for fuel, and over the centuries, the neat rows of saplings had turned into gradually wider and wider belts of towering trees. Some of them were as much as three feet in diameter at the base, and Bahzell could hear the songs of birds and the rapid, drilling tattoo of a woodpecker through the rippling notes of Brandark's balalaika.

Tellian Bowmaster was far less self-important than many a man in his position might have been. In fact, left to his own preferences, he would have made this trip without fanfare, preferably accompanied by only Hathan Shieldarm, his wind brother, and Bahzell, Brandark, and Vaijon. That, unfortunately, was out of the question for one of the Kingdom's four great barons, especially now, and so he was accompanied instead by no less than thirty armsmen and ten pack horses loaded with the camping gear, provisions, and other paraphernalia for a party that size. (An Axeman noble probably would have used wagons; a Sothōii nobleman, painfully familiar with the Kingdom's roads, knew better than to try any such thing.) The armsmen in question wore the boiled leather armor and cuirasses of typical Sothōii light cavalry, and however unassuming Tellian might have preferred to be, the men of his personal guard hadn't been selected at random. They rode easily and comfortably, relaxed in their saddles, but their eyes were busy and alert, watching for any threat even here.

"It makes me feel like a troupe of traveling actors," Tellian grumbled now. "I mean, he's playing *drinking* songs! When he isn't playing something better suited to a brothel, that is. I mean, did he *have* to treat us to 'The Madam's Cross-Eyed Daughter,' of all things? Couldn't he at least play something *serious?*"

"Fair's fair, Milord," Vaijon put in with a grin. "I'd say your armsmen are enjoying the music. Of course, I could always get one of them to ask him for something more serious. Like, oh," he glanced at Bahzell, blue eyes dancing, "what *was* the name of that song... It's on the tip of my tongue. Something Bloody Hand, wasn't it?"

"And if you were to be so foolish as to put any such notion into his head, it's in my mind you'd likely come to a nasty end, my lad."

"It might be an improvement after all, though, Bahzell," Tellian said helpfully.

"That it *wouldn't* be," Bahzell informed him firmly. "Besides, I know it's been a while, but I'm not so sure as how your lads are really all that happy even yet with that verse of his about the 'Battle of the Gullet.' It might just be that if he was after starting in on that one they'd be having a thing or three to say to him about it."

"That was the entire idea, Bahzell," Vaijon explained.

<And a good one, too,> Walsharno said helpfully.

"I heard that!" Brandark called, never turning his head as he rode along in front of them. "And I've been working on another little piece, Vaijon. It's about a human who ends up running a chapter of the Order of Tomanāk full of hradani."

"Oh, it is, is it?" Vaijon grinned. "Go ahead—I'd love to hear it! But if you do, then next time I set out on a trip with you,

I'm bringing along the dancing girls and the troupe of acrobats to help you entertain."

"I've a feeling the lads wouldn't be all that happy about the acrobats, Sir Vaijon," Tarith Shieldarm, the commander of Tellian's escort, said. "But the dancing girls, now—*they* might not be so very bad an idea."

"Yes, they *would* be a bad idea, Tarith," Tellian told him. "Especially when Baroness Hanatha heard about them!"

Tarith laughed, and Bahzell was glad to hear it. Tarith was a first cousin of Hathan Shieldarm, Tellian's wind brother. He and Hathan had both been armsmen in the baron's service when Hathan bonded with Gayrhalan, and Tarith had taken over Tellian's personal guard when Sir Charyn Sabrehand, who'd commanded it for over ten years, finally retired. Before that, though, he'd been Leeana Bowmaster's personal armsman, and he'd taken Leeana's flight to the war maids hard. He and Hathan were both naturally and intensely conservative by inclination, and Tarith had always been one of those Sothōii who thought war maids were "unnatural." He'd been stubbornly unwilling to accept that the young woman he'd watched over literally from her birth—the young woman he loved as if she'd been his own daughter—could have done such a thing. It had turned him dark and bitter for entirely too long, and for years he'd blamed Dame Kaeritha for not stopping Leeana before she could ruin her own and her parents' lives that way.

His expression the first time he'd seen Leeana in chari and yathu on a visit to Hill Guard had been almost physically painful to watch, and he'd quickly turned and disappeared into the barracks. Bahzell had seen the hurt in Leeana's eyes as she'd watched him vanish, but he'd scarcely been the only inhabitant of Balthar to react that way. Still, he did seem to have come to terms with it, by and large, over the last couple of years, and it might just be that some of his prejudices against the "unnatural" war-maid way of life had faded in the process. He still seemed acutely uncomfortable around her on her fleeting visits, as if all the habits of fourteen or fifteen years of watching over her remained steadfastly at war with what she had become. And, like someone else Bahzell could have mentioned (although for rather different reasons), he managed persistently to find reasons he had to be somewhere else during those visits. Yet the *wounded* look had disappeared from his eyes, and taking over Tellian's personal guard had helped.

He'd even learned to admit that he still loved Leeana, no matter what she'd done with her life, Bahzell thought.

<*And about damned time, too,*> Walsharno agreed. <*You two-foots spend an awful lot of time worrying about* other *two-foots' "mistakes"! Think how much wear and tear you could avoid if you only let them do what* they *want with their lives.*>

The courser had a point, Bahzell reflected. Of course, it was different for the coursers with their herd sense. Each courser was an individual, but all of them shared a sort of corporate awareness that left far less room for misunderstandings and hurt feelings than the Races of Man seemed to manage so effortlessly. Not that one courser couldn't develop a lively dislike, even hatred, for another one, but no courser would have questioned Leeana's right to do whatever she chose with her own life.

<*No, we wouldn't have,*> Walsharno agreed. <*And we wouldn't waste so many years of our lives denying our* love *for someone, either,*> he added rather more pointedly. <*No matter who they were or what they'd done.*>

Bahzell looked down at the back of the courser's head for a moment, but Walsharno didn't turn to look back at him. Not even his ears moved as he continued calmly along, and Bahzell turned his attention back to Tellian.

"Surely you're not thinking as how one of your very own personal armsmen would be after running off to the Baroness to be telling her such as that, are you, Milord?" he asked out loud.

"If they wouldn't, *Dathgar* would," Tellian retorted. "Yes, and she'd bribe the traitor with as many apples as he could eat, too!"

Dathgar snorted loudly and shook his head hard enough to set every bell on his ornamental halter chiming, and Bahzell heard Walsharno's mental laugh.

<*Dathgar says he'd hold out for at least a feed bag full of sugar,*> he explained, and Bahzell chuckled as Tellian shook his head in smiling disgust at his companion's treason.

<*I'm glad he finally let you do something about that cough of his,*> Walsharno said more seriously as he and his rider watched Tellian. <*I still don't like the way it was hanging on.*>

I wasn't so very happy about it myself, Bahzell replied silently.

<*No, and you thought the same thing* I *thought about it.*>

The courser's mental voice was sharp, and Bahzell shrugged without replying. Neither he nor Walsharno could quite shake the suspicion that Tellian's "cough" had been entirely too persistent. Bahzell had chosen not to make an issue of it, but he'd also conducted his own quiet yet very thorough investigation. If anyone had been responsible for... helping that cough along, however, he'd failed to find any trace of it among Hill Guard's inhabitants. That wasn't the sort of thing it was easy to hide from a champion of Tomanāk, either, which ought to have put their suspicions to rest.

Ought to.

<It certainly would be convenient for a great many people if something permanent were to happen to him,> Walsharno pointed out, and Bahzell had to agree. On the other hand, they couldn't blame everything that happened on Tellian's enemies. There were such things as a genuine accident or coincidence, after all.

<Of course there are. I'm sure that's the reason you and Vaijon—oh, and the Baroness—gave him so much trouble about that armor *he decided not to wear, too.>*

The irony in Walsharno's mental voice should have withered half the Wind Plain, and Bahzell's ears flicked in acknowledgment. They *had* tried to convince Tellian to take the precaution of wearing his own armor for the trip, only to have him decline. His argument that the extra weight would have been a needless burden for Dathgar had been specious, to say the least, given any courser's strength and stamina... not to mention the fact that Dathgar had agreed with the others, not him. His fallback argument that it was hot, sweaty, and damnably uncomfortable had at least a modicum of plausibility about it, but the real reason was pride.

Now that's being a mite unfair of you, my lad, Bahzell told himself sternly. *Aye, he's prideful enough, and of no mind to look like a man as jumps at shadows, too. But he's a point or three about keeping those as wish him ill from thinking as how they've frightened him, and it may be as how he's wishful to keep his own men from thinking so. Which is even dafter than worrying his head about its weight! There's not a man amongst 'em but knows he's guts enough for four or five. Aye, and wishes he had the sense to go with 'em, as well!*

"—still think the 'Lay of Bahzell Bloody Hand' would be the best choice," Vaijon was saying. "He wouldn't have to *sing*, you know. I'm sure your armsmen all know the words by heart by now, Milord! They could avoid any little verses they didn't care for, and a few rousing choruses as we ride along would have to make the journey seem shorter."

"Aye, that it would," Bahzell agreed genially. "And a mite shorter for some than for others, though we'd not all be reaching the same destination."

"I don't understand why you're so *sensitive* about it, Bahzell," Vaijon teased. "It's not every man whose noble deeds are known to every wandering minstrel in half of Norfressa!"

"Only half?" Brandark turned to look back at them, shaking his head. "I see I really have to get back out on the road!"

"You just go on laughing, the lot of you," Bahzell said. "There's a saying amongst my folk—that as goes around, comes around, and it's in my mind I'll have my day soon enough. Aye, and it's looking forward to it I am."

The others only grinned at him, and he shook his head, then glanced up towards the westering sun. It would be sliding towards the horizon in another three or four hours, he estimated, but the last milestone they'd passed indicated a sizable village or small town lay no more than ten or twelve miles ahead. Personally, he actually preferred making camp on the road, since inn beds tended to be more than a little cramped for someone his height. Sothōii averaged considerably taller than most humans, but they still weren't Horse Stealer hradani, and their furniture simply wasn't sized to fit someone like him. For the others, though—

His thoughts paused, and he felt his ears flattening. For a moment, he wasn't sure what had caught his attention, but then it came to him. The woodpecker had stopped its tattoo . . . and the birds who'd been singing among the trees had stopped. No, they hadn't *all* stopped, only the ones along the *eastern* side of the road.

<Brother—!> he heard Walsharno begin in the depths of his brain, and the courser's head was swinging to the right, as well.

"*Ware right!*" he shouted, and Walsharno was surging forward, swinging to face that silent sweep of trees, moving between them and Tellian as the first venomous arrow shafts came sizzling out from under them.

Something buzzed viciously past Bahzell's ear. Something else struck his breastplate like a mallet and bounced away, ripping the green surcoat of the Order of Tomanāk and scoring a bright line across the polished steel. He heard shouts of alarm, screams, the bark of almost—almost—instant commands from Tarith, and he flung himself from the saddle. He hit the ground already running, followed by Walsharno's bitter, wordless protest, but the courser knew better than to voice his complaint, for whoever had chosen the ambush site had chosen well. Those trees were simply too dense for something Walsharno's size, even with a courser's impossible agility. There were too many places under their branches where a man with a blade could get close enough to use it, and there was no place at all where Walsharno could have made use of his speed and size.

"Come!" Bahzell cried, and a five-foot blade answered his summons, materializing in his right hand even as he charged towards that impenetrable wall of trees. His fingers closed on the familiar, wire-wound hilt, and his left hand found the basket-hilted dagger at his belt.

"Tomanāk!" he heard Vaijon's shout and knew the other champion was no more than a stride or two behind him. More arrows whizzed past him and a human voice cried out—in agonized denial, not pain, this time—but he had no time for that. The shade of the trees reached out to him, and he saw the muted gleam of steel as someone rose out of the shadows before him.

"*Tomanāk!*"

The war cry bellowed out of his own thick throat, and the sword in his hand—a massive, two-handed weapon for any merely human arm—lashed out in a lightning thrust that ended in a gurgling shriek as a foot and more of gory blade drove clean through his victim's chest.

The spasming weight slid off his sword, but another assailant came at him from the left. He engaged the newcomer's saber with his dagger, twisting his wrist, locking the blades together. He drove the human's sword out and to the side as he recovered his main weapon, and more steel rang and clashed beside him as another unfortunate assassin found himself face-to-face with Vaijon of Almerhas.

There were more of them than he'd thought, Bahzell realized, and slammed a knee into his opponent's crotch. The other man saw it coming and twisted, managing to block with his thigh, but he was a foot and a half shorter than Bahzell. The brutal force of the blow lifted him off the ground and knocked him back several feet, and Bahzell saw his face twist in horror as he realized the hradani had gained enough space for his sword arm. He threw his own left arm up in a futile blocking gesture…just in time for that enormous blade to come down, sheer through his forearm, and half-sever his head in a fountain of blood.

Bow strings were still twanging, but not as many of them, and at least a half-dozen more men were coming at Bahzell and Vaijon. Most of them seemed to be armed with the normal Sothōii saber, but others carried shorter, heavier blades, and he saw at least one battleaxe among them. He gave back a step, falling into place with Vaijon on his left, and his own sword came thundering down in a brutal overhead stroke that split a man's head from crown to chin. He kicked the body aside as two more attackers split up, trying to come at him from both flanks at once, but then the one on his right turned with a panicky expression as Brandark came hurtling into the fight. Unlike Vaijon and Bahzell, the Bloody Sword was unarmored, yet that made him no less deadly, and the man who'd turned to face him went down with a high, wailing scream as Brandark opened his belly.

Steel clanged and belled, grunts of effort turned into screams of anguish, and a dozen of Tellian's armsmen surged into the woods on Brandark's heels. No Sothōii would fight on foot if he had any choice at all, and no one would ever confuse them with properly trained infantry when they did. For all their mounted discipline, individualism was the order of the day when they simply *had* to fight on foot. But these Sothōii had profited from exposure to Bahnak of Hurgrum's infantry, and they'd taken the lesson to heart. They hit the woods as an organized unit, driving in under the branches, and they'd brought their light shields with them.

"Tellian! *Tellian!*"

There was something hard and dangerous about the way they shouted their war cries, something with more than the usual Sothōii ferocity behind it, and the sounds of combat were ugly as they slammed into the ambushers. There were no more bows firing now; there was only the desperate clash of steel, screams, and somewhere on the other side of the trees the thunder of hooves as at least some of the attackers got to their horses.

"*Tomanāk!*"

He cut down another opponent. Then another, and they were no longer coming at him. Instead, they were trying desperately to get away, and he felt the Rage, the bloodlust of his people, rising within him. But the Rage had become his servant, not his master, over the years, and he controlled it with the ease of long practice as he, Vaijon, and Brandark hammered forward on their enemies' heels.

Someone on the other side was shouting orders. Bahzell took down yet another of the attackers and chanced a look in the direction of all the noise, and his eyes narrowed as he saw a small knot of archers who still retained their bows. They were clustered around the one doing all the shouting, and the loud fellow was pointing urgently in the direction of the road. The archers raised their bows, taking careful aim at whoever he was pointing out, and Bahzell threw his dagger in a flat, vicious arc.

It was a long throw, especially left-handed, even for Bahzell Bahnakson, but the blade flickered in sunlight and shadow as it flashed straight to its mark. It went home with a grisly, meaty thud, driving quillon-deep in his target's collarbone. Over two inches of bloody steel projected from the man's back, his commands died in a gurgling crimson spray, and the sheer force of the dagger's impact lifted him from his feet and hurled him into two of the archers who'd been listening to him.

That was enough for *all* those archers. Whatever force of will their leader had used to hold them together vanished with his death. They scattered, most of them discarding their bows so they could run faster, and Bahzell smiled in satisfaction through the cold, icy focus of the Rage. An assassin who'd been coming at him saw that smile and tried frantically to brake, but he was too late. Before he could stop, he ran into a steel whirlwind that crashed through his feeble attempt to parry and split his skull.

"Oath to Tomanāk!" someone shouted. "*Oath to Tomanāk!*"

"Damn it!" Brandark grated. "I *hate* it when they do that!"

Bahzell grunted a harsh, unamused laugh, but the Bloody Sword only snarled.

"You think they'd show the least damned bit of interest in letting us surrender if *we* were the ones shouting it?" he demanded as the man he'd been about to skewer threw away his sword and raised his hands.

"Likely not," Bahzell conceded. Another of the ambushers went to his knees, and the Horse Stealer grunted again—this time in disgust—as the gripped the man by the nape of the neck and lifted him back to his feet. His unfortunate captive squealed in pain as he was hauled onto his toes and Bahzell half-threw and half-shoved him back towards the high road.

"I'm thinking you'd best not do one damned thing I could be taking as breaking your oath," he told the would-be assassin, and the man nodded desperately. Another one of the attackers tried to fade into the shadows, only to freeze as Bahzell cocked his head at him.

"You just go on running," the hradani encouraged coldly. "Those as don't come quiet when they've given oath to Tomanāk, why, they're not protected by it, now are they?"

The human stared at him wide-eyed for a moment, then nodded even more violently than Bahzell's first prisoner and started stumbling back towards the high road himself. Vaijon had rounded up a prisoner of his own, and Brandark sent the man who'd surrendered to him hurrying after the others with the Bloody Sword's sword tip prodding him to encourage more speed.

The time compression of combat never ceased to astonish Bahzell, even after all these years. The fight had seemed to last at least an hour, yet the whole thing had taken mere minutes. But they'd been *bloody* minutes, and his jaw tightened and his ears flattened as he came out of the trees and saw the carnage.

Eight or nine of Tellian's armsmen were down on the roadway where the initial volleys of arrows had slashed into them, but men were smaller targets than horses. At least a dozen of their mounts had been hit by arrows intended for their riders, and equine screams of pain tore at his ears with that special heart-rending intensity of wounded horses without the ability to understand why they'd been hurt. Battle-hardened or not, Bahzell had never been able to listen to those screams without hearing the beasts' pleas for someone to explain, someone to make it go away. Here and there armsmen had already cut the throats of mortally wounded horses. It was second nature to any Sothōii—their duty to the horses who served them so loyally—and not one of Tellian Bowmaster's armsmen would have even considered seeing to his own hurts until he'd seen to those of his mount. Nor would he flinch from doing his responsibility to end that uncomprehending agony when he must. It was one of the things Bahzell most liked about them, and—

<Quickly, Brother!>

Bahzell's head snapped up at Walsharno's mental cry. The unbreakable link between them would have told him if the courser had been wounded, and he and Walsharno had learned not to distract one another on those occasions when one or both of them had to enter battle without the other. But now the raw, burning urgency of Walsharno's summons burned through him, and he turned quickly, then froze.

Dathgar was down. The huge bay had been hit by at least four arrows, and there were limits to even a courser's vitality. His coat was saturated with blood, his sides heaved weakly, and bloody froth blew at his nostrils. He tried to raise his head feebly, eyes glazed, and Tellian lay half under him, unconscious, with two snapped-off arrow shafts standing out of his chest. His right leg was twisted, obviously broken where Dathgar's weight had smashed down on it, and Hathan was on his knees beside him, trying desperately to staunch the bleeding, while two more of Tellian's armsmen knelt over Tarith.

"Do you be taking Dathgar!" Bahzell said sharply to Walsharno. The stallion nodded, and Bahzell looked over his shoulder. "Brandark—"

"I'll keep an eye on these bastards," Brandark promised him, brown eyes grim as he glared at the prisoners. "Go!"

It was Bahzell's turn to nod, and Hathan looked up with desperate eyes as the enormous Horse Stealer went down on one knee beside him.

"I can't stop the bleeding!" the wind rider said.

"Aye, I can be seeing that," Bahzell said grimly. Behind him, he sensed Vaijon heading for Tarith, but all of his own attention was focused on the dying man pinned under the dying courser. "Leave him to me," he told Hathan. "You be drawing those arrows out of Dathgar for Walsharno!"

"But—" Hathan began, then chopped himself off. "Of course," he said instead, his voice harsh, and Bahzell touched the shaft of the arrow which had driven into Tellian no more than an inch or two from his heart.

I'm thinking if ever I needed you, I'm needing you now, he thought, his eyes closing briefly as he reached out to that inner link which glowed between him and the god he served like some glittering golden chain or an inextinguishable torch blazing against the dark. *This is a good man—a friend.*

There were no words from Tomanāk this time, only that comforting sense of the god's presence, that feel of two huge hands settling on Bahzell's shoulders. Warmth spread into him out of them, warmth he needed badly as he saw the damage, heard the wet, weak wheeze of the baron's breathing while blood bubbled from his nostrils, and realized Tellian was no more than half a breath, possibly two, from slipping away to Isvaria's table.

But that was as far as he was going, Bahzell told himself with all the grim, iron purpose which had made him a champion of the god of war, and felt Tomanāk's strength fill him as he opened himself once more to the power of his deity.

His eyes opened again, focused and clear with purpose, and blue light crackled around his hands. He laid the palm of his left hand flat on Tellian's feebly moving chest, and that blue light flowed out from it, flooding across the baron like a layer of azure ice. It flickered and glowed, burning more brilliantly than the afternoon sunlight, lighting Bahzell's face from below, embracing Tellian like a shield, and Bahzell reached out with it. He felt Tellian's flickering life force try to sink away from him, and he refused to let it. He locked the grip of his own will upon it, drawing on Tomanāk's power to forbid its extinction, and his right hand gripped that broken arrow shaft and pulled.

The broad-headed arrow ripped out of Tellian's chest with a wet, ghastly sound, making the terrible wound still worse. Blood pumped from rent and torn flesh, and Bahzell reached for the other arrow. This one had driven into the baron's ribs, and bone and cartilage crunched and tore as he wrenched it out of that dying body. He threw it away and his sword reappeared in his bloody hand—reversed, this time—as he summoned it back to him once more. He closed his eyes again, leaning his forehead against the sword's quillons, left hand still pressing against Tellian's almost motionless chest, and reached out to the brilliant presence of his god.

Bahzell Bahnakson had healed many times in the years since he'd first become Tomanāk's champion. He'd faced the challenge of torn flesh, of poison, even of the touch of Krahana herself, and he recognized the smile of hollow-eyed death when he saw it. He recognized it . . . and he threw his own bared-teeth challenge in its face.

The blue light wrapped around his left hand swept up his arm, enveloped his torso, blazed up about him like a forest fire, and he knelt at its heart, eyes closed, emptying himself of everything except the power of Tomanāk and his own fierce, stubborn refusal to let the enemy who had become his friend go. He closed his mind to the picture of Tellian's broken, bloody body. He closed his ears to the baron's failing, gasping effort to breathe. Those things were no longer real, no longer mattered. Instead, he filled himself with the image of Tellian as he *should* be. Of Tellian laughing as they discussed Brandark's music. Tellian frowning thoughtfully as he leaned forward across a map, discussing strategy. Tellian smiling across the breakfast table at Baroness Hanatha, looking up with his heart in his eyes as his disgraced war-maid daughter returned to Hill Guard Castle for her first visit. Tellian sipping whiskey on the first visit any Sothōii baron had ever paid to a hradani warlord as Prince Bahnak welcomed him to Hurgrum. Of Tellian strong and determined and whole once more.

Bahzell forged that image from memories, from hopes, from friendship... from love. He *made* it be, demanded it, rejected any other possibility, and when it had filled him, when there was no room in him for anything else, he gave himself to it. He poured everything he was, everything that made him *who* he was, into that reality, and the levin of Tomanāk's cleansing, healing power ripped through him like a hurricane. It exploded down his arm, erupted around the hand on Tellian's chest, swept outward down that tree-lined high road like a thunderbolt. For an instant—one fleeting moment—Bahzell Bahnakson and Tomanāk were truly one, fused into that eruption of purpose, power, and determination.

It didn't last. It *couldn't* last for longer than one heartbeat, or perhaps two. Yet it lasted long enough, and Bahzell felt Tellian's chest heave convulsively under his palm. The baron sucked in a deep, wracking breath, then coughed convulsively. His faltering, flickering heart surged within his chest, and his eyelids fluttered. Then they rose, gray eyes unfocused, the blood from his nostrils clotting his mustache.

"Dathgar," he whispered, and Bahzell sagged back on his heels, every muscle drained, filled with the joyous, wondering exhaustion of being allowed to be a bearer of life, not death.

Something snorted beside him, and he looked down, then smiled as Dathgar's ears shifted, pricking forward. The hradani looked up, saw the same joyful exhaustion in Walsharno's eyes, and let the hand Walsharno didn't have rest on Dathgar's neck.

"There, now," he told the courser. "Don't you be doing anything hasty. It's work enough Tomanāk and I had putting him back together, so just you bide a bit. Let's not be breaking him all over again getting off of him!"

Chapter Nine

Well, that's *disappointing, and in more ways than one,* Master Varnaythus thought glumly, gazing into his gramerhain as a huge, bloodstained bay courser rolled very, very cautiously off of Tellian Bowmaster.

The courser took three tries to make it back to his feet, and two more coursers moved in on either side, leaning their shoulders against him to help him stay there. It was obvious he needed the help, but he stood there stubbornly, refusing to move until Tellian had been helped back to his feet, as well. The baron was pale, clearly at least as shaky as his courser and just as soaked with blood, but he leaned on Bahzell Bahnakson's arm and reached up to caress the courser's ears.

Dathgar lowered his head, resting his nose gently, gently on his rider's shoulder, and Tellian threw both arms around his neck, leaning into him. It was all very touching, Varnaythus thought with a sour expression, but it would have been ever so much more satisfactory if at least one of them had been standing disconsolately over the other's dead body.

And we came so close to getting both *of them, that's what really pisses me off.* He shook his head. *I'd almost rather have missed them completely than to have come that close and fallen short! Damn it, I thought Salgahn was better than that!*

He wasn't really being fair, and he knew it. He also didn't care. He sat back, arms folded, glowering at the gramerhain as Bahzell left Tellian to Dathgar while he joined Vaijon in seeing to the other wounded. Without Salghan, Arthnar Fire Oar's assassins would never have come as near to successes they had, and he knew it. For that matter, he hadn't *really* expected he and the dog brother would be able to talk the River Brigands' warlord into even making the attempt! It had been worth suggesting to both him and Cassan, though, and no doubt the sizable bag of gold which had passed from the South Riding to Krelik had quite a bit to do with the fact that Arthnar had been willing to run the risk.

Well, that and the fact that he'd been able to hire his killers without their ever realizing who was actually paying them.

That was deft of him, Varnaythus acknowledged grudgingly. *And he thought of that part without even any prompting from Salgahn. Of course,* Cassan *may not think it was all that clever once Bahzell gets around to interrogating his prisoners.*

The wizard had presented Salgahn to Fire Oar as a Sothōii renegade who'd been sufficiently familiar with Tellian's movements and habits to provide the sort of inside information that might make a successful assassination possible. As he'd hoped, that had inspired Arthnar to use Salgahn to organize the attempt itself, but he hadn't expected the twist Arthnar had come up with. Arthnar himself had retained his anonymity as their ultimate employer, since it would have struck any interrogator as highly suspicious, in the unfortunately probable event that any of the assassins were taken alive, if the assassins' ultimate paymaster *hadn't* concealed his identity. But he'd instructed Salgahn to emphasize his Sothōii accent when he recruited them... and to casually "let fall" the fact that he was in the service of an undisclosed Sothōii noble. Salgahn had never actually said he was working for Cassan or Yeraghor, of course, but assuming Tellian followed up on what the surviving would-be assassins could tell him, there wasn't much question who he was going to end up blaming for it. And Cassan could hardly argue that it had been Fire Oar, not him, without facing the embarrassing question of just how he *knew* it had been Fire Oar.

Not too shabby, Varnaythus admitted. *Get paid by someone to be his deniable assassin, then avoid drawing suspicion yourself by arranging things so that the fellow who paid you is the one people are most likely to suspect! I think I may have to revise my estimate of Arthnar's capabilities upward. And however pissed off I am, I also have to admit he came closer to getting Tellian than anyone* else *has! Of course, a lot of that was due to Salgahn. Too bad he won't be around to make any other attempts.* He shook his head.

I'm beginning to understand why the dog brothers are so reluctant to go after Bahzell, given how uniformly fatal their failures have been so far. Who would have thought even Bahzell *could throw a dagger that far and that accurately with his off hand? But, damn it, I really thought* this *time he was going to pull it off!*

The truth was, the wizard thought, blanking his gramerhain with an impatient wave, that if it hadn't been for the presence of not simply one, but no less than three champions of Tomanāk, either Tellian or Dathgar *would* definitely be dead. And if one of Salgahn's men had managed to get an arrow or two into Bahzell or Vaijon—or even Bahzell's Phrobus-damned courser!—Varnaythus would have counted the operation a resounding success, despite the dog brother's spectacular demise.

But they hadn't, and it wasn't, which turned the attempt into an equally resounding failure. Although, now that he thought about it, increasing Tellian's suspicions of Cassan would probably be worthwhile in its own right. After all, it wasn't that the Dark Gods actually needed Cassan to win; they only needed him to destroy the Kingdom's cohesion *trying* to win. In fact, it would actually suit them even better to see the entire Kingdom dissolve into something like that interminable bloodletting in Ferenmoss. Twenty or thirty years of civil war, preferably with enough attention diverted to break up Prince Bahnak's experiment in hradani unity, would be just about perfect from his Lady's perspective.

Well, since you never expected them to succeed in the first place, at least the fact that they didn't hasn't dislocated any of your own plans, he told himself as philosophically as he could. *And you should probably make sure Cassan finds out about this as soon as you can do it without raising any suspicions about just how you learned about Arthnar's failure that quickly. Not that a little delay couldn't be useful.* He smiled unpleasantly. *After all, it'll give you more time to decide exactly how you want to let Cassan know about Arthnar's . . . misdirection. It never hurts to add a bit of salt to the wound when it comes to sowing dissension, now does it?*

✧ ✧ ✧

<So there you are . . . at last,> Walsharno said as Bahzell Bahnakson stepped out of the village inn's back door. A cool, still dawn drifted under the towering oak which shaded the inn, and the hradani stretched hugely, foxlike ears half-flattened while he yawned, as the courser ambled over to greet him.

"And a good morning to you, too," Bahzell said, recovering from his yawn and reaching out to rub Walsharno's nose. "I'm hoping you had a restful evening?"

<*It's a hard, hard life,*> Walsharno said mournfully, raising his head to lip playfully at the hradani's ears. <*Some people get nice, snug roofs overhead, and other people get left out in the freezing cold all night long.*>

"Freezing is it, now?"

Sunlight was already slanting golden shafts through the leaves overhead, promising plenty of warmth to come, and Bahzell chuckled and patted the side of Walsharno's neck.

<*Well, it* could *have been. In fact, it could have been raining or snowing for all* you'd *know about it, and if it had, I still would've been outside in it!*> Walsharno returned with spirit. <*It's not like I would've fitted into that wretched little stable, at any rate!*>

"And no more did I fit into that 'wretched little' bed," Bahzell pointed out. "It's a hard floor that bedchamber has!"

He reached back to knead the small of his back, and someone laughed behind him. He turned his head, looking over his shoulder, and smiled as Hathan Shieldarm joined him and Walsharno.

"Making you feel guilty, is he?" Hathan asked.

"Oh, not so much as all that," Bahzell demurred with a grin. "But not for lack of trying. Is that what you mean?"

<*Tell him a champion of Tomanāk doesn't resort to trickery to get what he wants,*> Walsharno said.

"Now that I won't." Bahzell shook his head with a laugh. "First, because it's a fearful lie it would be, and, second, because he'd not believe a word of it."

Walsharno snorted and shoved hard enough with his nose to stagger even the massive hradani, and Hathan laughed. He obviously didn't need to actually hear what Walsharno had said to make a pretty shrewd guess about its content. He started to say something else, then paused and turned his head, shading his eyes with one hand as another courser—this one an iron gray, smaller (though *no* courser would ever actually be called "small") than Walsharno and obviously at least a few years older—came drifting over.

"Good morning, Gayrhalan," Bahzell said courteously, and the newcomer snorted with a very horselike headshake before he nodded to the hradani.

There'd been a time when Bahzell Bahnakson had not been Gayrhalan's favorite person in the world. Those days were long gone, but Hathan's courser had been well named. "Storm Souled"—that was what Gayrhalan meant—and the gray's temper was as stormy as his name suggested.

Despite which, he whinnied in delight like a child's pony as Hathan reached into his belt pouch and extracted a large lump of maple sugar.

"Greedy!" the Sothōii said as Gayrhalan lipped the sugar delicately from his palm. The courser ignored the charge with lordly hauteur . . . and crunched the sugar loudly.

<*It's nice to see that* some *wind riders actually* appreciate *their brothers,*> Walsharno observed.

"Ha!" Bahzell shook his head. "'Appreciate,' is it, now? More a matter of who's after being under whose hoof, *I'm* thinking!"

"That sort of honest evaluation isn't going to make you any friends, Milord Champion," Hathan said.

"Aye," Bahzell sighed and shook his head again, his expression mournful. "It's a hard lot, this being an honest man. There's never an end to the trouble it can be landing a fellow in! If I'd the least notion then where it would be taking me, I'd not have fallen so easy for himself's little invitation. I mean, when it comes to the sticking point, what's one wee little demon one way or the other compared to a man's spending his whole life long speaking naught but the truth? And me a hradani, to boot."

Hathan laughed. But then he gave Gayrhalan's neck one last pat and turned to face Bahzell fully, and his expression was far more serious than it had been.

"Gayrhalan says Dathgar's strength is coming back nicely. Has Walsharno spoken with him this morning?"

<*Yes, I have,*> Walsharno replied, and from the strength of his mental voice Bahzell knew he was speaking simultaneously to Gayrhalan, as well. <*I think he's almost fully recovered, although I'm none too enthusiastic about putting that to the test just yet.*> He shook his mane and blew heavily. <*He's not so young as he used to be, and I don't think it would hurt a thing for him to have another day or so of rest before we head on to Sothōfalas.*>

Hathan's eyes had narrowed as he listened to Gayrhalan relaying Walsharno's comments. Now he smiled and nodded his head vigorously, but his expression was quizzical.

"I don't know that *I'd* like to be the one suggesting to Dathgar that he might be getting a bit past it," he said, regarding Walsharno with a raised eyebrow. "In fact, I'm pretty sure I wouldn't, even if I were a somewhat younger fellow than him and a champion of Tomanāk. Having said that, though, I agree there's no need to rush getting back on the road. And not just for Dathgar's sake, either."

"Well, I'll not deny it's easier I'd be in my own mind if it so happened we could convince Tellian of the same thing," Bahzell acknowledged. "Mind, champion of Tomanāk or no, I've no mind to be suggesting to *him* as how he's 'getting a bit past it,' either, if it's all the same to you."

"I think that would be an *excellent* thing to avoid doing," Hathan agreed fervently. "In fact, I can't think of anything you could possibly say that would be more likely to inspire him to insist on leaving before breakfast!"

<*There's no need to do anything of the sort.*> Walsharno flipped his ears in the courser equivalent of a shrug when Bahzell and Hathan looked at him. <*We'll just suggest to Dathgar that it would be better for Tellian to rest for another day or two—and, of course, that we don't want anyone telling Tellian that, given how stubborn he is. And then we'll suggest exactly the same thing to* Tellian *about Dathgar.*> He flipped his ears again. <*They'll both jump for it the same way Gayrhalan jumps for sugar.*>

"Sure, and a sad thing it is to see such deceitfulness so early in the morning," Bahzell sighed.

<*Oh?*> Walsharno cocked his head, examining his wind brother with one skeptical eye. <*And do* you *have a better idea?*>

"That I don't," the hradani conceded cheerfully. "And it's no quarrel I have with deceitfulness so long as it's after working, when all's said."

"From your lips to Tomanāk's ears," Hathan said feelingly. "And if convincing the two of them to go easy on each other doesn't work, we can always add Tarith. For that matter, I'm pretty sure we could convince him to hobble around for a day or two—with a properly stoic expression, you understand—to convince Tellian *he* needs the rest!"

"No doubt," Bahzell agreed.

"Good."

Hathan reached up to rub Gayrhalan's nose again for several

seconds, then looked back at Bahzell and Walsharno, and his expression was far more serious than it had been.

"Things were a bit hectic yesterday," he said. "I'm not sure I got around to thanking the two of you for saving Tellian's and Dathgar's lives. If I didn't, I should have." His eyes darkened with emotion. "I knew they were both gone, and all I could think of was telling Hanatha. I think it would have killed her, too, you know."

"I'm thinking she's a stronger woman than that," Bahzell disagreed. "Still and all, it's happier I am we've no need to find out one way or the other."

"The gods know I agree with you there!" Hathan said. "When you pulled those arrows out of his chest, Bahzell . . . I was afraid you were going to finish him off on the spot!" He shook his head. "Of course, I knew even then that we were going to lose him anyway if you couldn't heal him, but still—!"

"I'll not deny it gave *me* a twinge or two," Bahzell admitted. "Yet I couldn't be leaving them where they were, and there was no time at all, at all, for being gentle about it."

"No, and I knew it at the time. For that matter, I had to do the same thing with Dathgar!"

<And a good thing he did, too,> Walsharno said, looking at Gayrhalan. *<Tell him he was my hands, Gayrhalan. Without him, we'd have lost Dathgar for certain.>*

Hathan cocked his head as he listened to the other courser relaying that to him. Then he nodded to Walsharno with a courteous formality.

"It was my honor," he said quietly. "But we were all lucky to have the two of you and Vaijon along! Toragan only knows how many we would've lost without you." His mouth tightened. "For that matter, it was bad enough with all the three of you could do."

"That it was."

Bahzell's ears flattened and his eyes darkened. Not even a champion of Tomanāk could recall someone who'd already crossed the wall between life and death, and seven of Tellian's armsmen had made that journey before he or Vaijon could summon them back. Walsharno had helped with that effort as much as he could, but one thing he and Bahzell had learned over the years since he'd become the very first courser champion of Tomanāk was that there were differences in their healing abilities.

Bahzell wasn't entirely certain why that was so, but they'd

discovered that Walsharno's ability to heal coursers or horses was far stronger than Bahzell's . . . and that *Bahzell's* ability to heal the Races of Man was greater than Walsharno's. They'd discussed the difference often, and they'd come to the conclusion that the difference lay in who—and what—they were. The degree to which any champion of Tomanāk could succeed in a healing depended in large part upon how completely and deeply he could visualize his patient's restoration . . . and how deeply into that patient's soul and innermost being he could reach. Coursers and the Races of Man were simply *different* from one another in some deep and fundamental ways, and that affected how deeply and intimately they could fuse with those they sought to heal, become the essential bridge between the hurt and dying and Tomanāk.

Whatever the reason, Walsharno was plainly better than Bahzell at healing coursers or their smaller equine cousins while Bahzell was better at healing fellow hradani and humans. That was why Bahzell had concentrated on saving Tellian and entrusted Dathgar to Walsharno. It was also why Walsharno had lent his strength to Bahzell and Vaijon, putting all his driving will behind them as they'd plucked as many of the wounded back from death as they could. They'd done all any man could do, and without Walsharno's aid they would have lost still more of them. Bahzell and his wind brother both knew that, and so did Vaijon, yet the hradani also knew it would be a long time before any of them fully forgave themselves for having lost so many.

<Don't be silly,> a deep, rumbling voice said in the back of his brain. *<You did well—all of you. But there are limits to what even my Swords can accomplish.>*

And I'd've done still better if I'd spent less time making bad jokes and more seeing what it was the lot of us were riding into, Bahzell thought grimly.

<Or if I'd taken you by the hand and warned you about it. Or if Tellian had been wearing armor the way he ought *to have been. Or if it had been raining, instead of sunny, and their bow strings had stretched in the wet. Or if an earthquake had swallowed them up or they'd been nibbled to death by tree frogs.>* The voice of Tomanāk Orfro took on a decidedly testy edge, and Bahzell had a mental image of his deity standing there with his hands on his hips and a stern light in his eyes. *<Oh, and while we're on the subject of "if," if Walsharno had been able to maneuver under those*

trees and if the both of you had had wings. *Have I left anything out? Or do the two of you have something else to feel guilty about?*>

Bahzell started to reply, then stopped himself.

<*Better,*> Tomanāk snorted in the spaces of his mind, and the god's voice turned a bit gentler, though its edge didn't disappear entirely. <*Done is done, my Sword. All I've ever asked of you is that you do your best—which you always have—and not even I can undo the past. You know why that is, and I think you might bear that in mind when you consider your own actions and their consequences. I have nothing against remorse when it's merited, Bahzell, but there's something a little childish about blaming yourself for being merely mortal, and that's what you're doing when you go borrowing guilt for things not even a god can change.*>

Bahzell felt a twinge of resentment at being called "childish," but it disappeared as quickly as it had come. After all, Tomanāk was the God of Truth. Which was undoubtedly the very reason the word had stung.

I'll try to be bearing that in mind, he thought a bit tartly. *In the meantime, though, would it be as how you've any more to be telling us?*

<*No,*> Tomanāk replied. <*Too many threads are flowing together here, with far too many possible outcomes. Even if I were tempted to give you more detail, it would be too likely to simply confuse the issue for you—possibly even make you hesitate at a critical moment. I can tell you this, though: you were right about Tellian's cough. I know you never found who was poisoning him, Bahzell, but that's because you couldn't look in the right place.*>

Bahzell frowned for a moment. Then his eyes widened, and he sensed Tomanāk's nod.

<*That was the first sign that the Dark Gods have decided to take an active hand again,*> he confirmed. <*And if the truth be known, Carnadosa's a much shrewder adversary than Sharnā or Krahana, and far closer to sane than Shīgū's ever been. Nor is she so arrogant as to confront us without careful planning and all the support she can muster. Watch yourselves, Bahzell, Walsharno. You can't begin to reckon how dearly Phrobus and all his children would love to see the two of you dead.*>

<*Could you tell us why they've waited this long to try again?*> Walsharno asked.

<*I can't tell you* all *the reasons,*> Tomanāk replied after a moment. <*I will tell you, though, that between the two of you, Kaeritha, and Vaijon, you've done more damage to the Dark Gods' access to this universe than you can imagine.*> Walsharno and Bahzell sensed his fierce satisfaction, his pride in them. <*I suspect none of them would be willing to admit it, especially not to themselves, but they're actually* afraid *of you. That's one of the reasons they've waited, and if they had a choice, they wouldn't cross swords with you—or me—again even now. But they don't have a choice. Those threads I mentioned aren't just flowing together any longer; they're becoming a cascade, gathering power like snowmelt in the East Walls, the sort of flood that washes away mountains, and it could turn in any of dozens of directions. Be warned, My Swords—there are few limits to what they will do to control that direction if they can.*>

And here they've been so shy and hesitant about all they've been doing so far, Bahzell thought in a wondering tone, and Tomanāk chuckled.

<*Fair enough, Bahzell,*> he conceded. <*Fair enough. But rejoice in what you've accomplished so far, the two of you, and rest here until Dathgar and Tellian and Tarith and the others are ready to travel once more. It will take more than a day or two for most of those who wish you ill to discover just how badly yesterday's ambush failed.*>

Bahzell looked at Walsharno as he felt a huge, immaterial hand rest on his shoulder for just an instant. Then it was gone, and as he drew a deep breath he realized the entire conversation had taken place between one heartbeat and the next, without Hathan or Gayrhalan sensing a thing about it.

"Aye, Hathan," he said, resuming the conversation the other wind rider had no idea had ever been interrupted, "it's lucky we were to lose so few. And speaking of luck," he straightened, smiling wickedly, "what say the lot of us go have a word or three with those lads as were giving oath to Tomanāk yesterday? I've the oddest feeling as how it might just be they'll find it in their hearts to be telling us what it is we'd like to know."

Chapter Ten

"Leeana is here, Five Hundred."

Commander of Five Hundred Balcartha Evahnalfressa looked up from the paperwork on her desk, one eyebrow raised as she regarded the youthful war maid currently detailed as her aide. It was a rotating assignment which was usually shared by the newest and most junior members of the Kalatha City Guard . . . much to their trepidation. Most of them thought that things were arranged that way to be sure they were suitably terrified by the Guard's commander before they were released to the general population. In fact, it was so that they got an inside look at how the Guard ran as early in their careers as possible . . . and so that Balcartha had the opportunity to personally evaluate each of them. The Guard wasn't all that enormous, after all. Certainly, it wasn't so big that she couldn't actually know each of her war maids, yet new recruits had a pronounced tendency to hide from their commanding officer in the underbrush, at least until they got their feet under them. Balcartha understood that. She even sympathized with them. Yet she had no intention of allowing them to get away with it, either.

"Leeana, Taraiys?" the five hundred asked in a musing tone, and the girl—she couldn't have been a day over seventeen—blushed rosily. It was a fascinating shade of deep red, Balcartha noted, and Taraiys' blond hair, blue eyes, and very fair complexion made it even more spectacular.

"I beg your pardon, Five Hundred," she said stiffly. "I meant to say that *Seventy-Five* Leeana is here. She says she has an appointment."

"Ah—*that* Leeana," Balcartha murmured, and watched Taraiys' blush turn even darker. For a moment, the five hundred wondered if smoke was actually going to curl up off of the girl's skin. But she didn't quite burst into spontaneous flames, and after a moment, the Guard commander relented and smiled slightly. "As a matter of fact, I've been expecting the Seventy-Five. Please ask her to step into my lair."

"Yes, Five Hundred!" Taraiys actually came to attention and touched her chest with a raised fist in salute, and Balcartha managed not to crack a smile as she solemnly returned it. Then she leaned comfortably back in her swivel chair, legs crossed, propped her elbows on the chair arms, and steepled her fingers under her chin.

"Seventy-Five Leeana, Five Hundred!" Taraiys announced with sharp formality a moment later, opening the door and ushering the considerably taller Leeana through it. Her head barely topped the older war maid's shoulder, and Leanna's jade-green eyes danced with devilish delight as they met the five hundred's over Taraiys' head. Her lips quivered with her womanful struggle to restrain the smile obviously dancing right behind those eyes, but somehow she managed to maintain a suitably solemn demeanor when Balcartha gave her a warning glance.

"Thank you, Taraiys," the five hundred said solemnly. "That will be all, I think."

"Yes, Five Hundred!" Taraiys saluted again and disappeared through the office door with the air of a rabbit escaping down its hole, perhaps half a leap in front of the fox. The door closed behind her, and something suspiciously like a giggle spurted out of Leeana.

"That will be quite enough of that, Seventy-Five Leeana," Balcartha said primly.

"Oh, I beg your pardon, *Five Hundred* Balcartha!" Leeana said earnestly. "Mother! She was so red when you sent her back out I thought you'd set her on fire!" The tall, red-haired young woman shook her head. "What did you *say* to her?"

"That's between her and me." Balcartha smiled and shook her own head. "She does color up spectacularly though, doesn't she?"

"Oh, I think you could certainly say that," Leeana agreed. Then she smiled a bit penitently. "I really shouldn't make fun of her for it though, I suppose. I can produce a pretty spectacular blush of my own, can't I?"

"On the rare occasions when anyone can manage to embarrass you, yes," Balcartha agreed.

"Are you implying that such a low person as myself no longer has the delicacy to feel embarrassment?" Leeana asked innocently, and Balcartha chuckled.

"Something like that . . . these days, at least," she agreed, and Leeana threw up her right hand as if she were acknowledging a touch in a training match.

"I deserved that," she acknowledged. "But she really is awfully young, isn't she?"

"This from the broken-down old grandmother in front of me?" Balcartha raised both eyebrows. "I seem to remember a *fourteen*-year-old who didn't know which end of the dagger to hold when Erlis and Ravlahn first evaluated her. Now, let me see, let me see . . . what *was* her name?"

She gazed up at the ceiling, lips pursed in obvious thought, and Leeana laughed.

"You really are training with live blades today, aren't you, Five Hundred Balcartha?"

"Only against some," Balcartha replied with a twinkle.

As the commander of the Kalatha Guard, she wasn't supposed to have favorites, and she never allowed favoritism to govern her actions, but there was no point pretending she didn't have a special place in her heart for Leeana Hanathafressa. She did remember—vividly—the pampered fourteen-year-old noblewoman who'd fled to Kalatha almost seven years before. Not that Leanna had realized she'd been pampered, and by the standards of her birth rank, she hadn't been. Which hadn't changed the fact that, as Balcartha had just pointed out, she'd been totally unequipped with the skills her new life was going to require of her. Her embarrassment at finding herself clad—more or less—in the traditional chari and yathu had been only too apparent to someone with Balcartha's experience, and unlike most war maids, Leanna hadn't fled to Kalatha to escape an intolerable, all too often abusive family situation. Indeed, she'd escaped to Kalatha no more than hours in front of her pursuing father because of how much she'd *loved* her parents, and she'd been miserably homesick and unhappy at leaving them, however bravely she'd tried to hide it.

Looking at her now, Balcartha could still see that fourteen-year-old inside the poised, confident, athletic young woman who had replaced her. Not the misery or the uncertainty, but the dauntless, uncomplaining spirit which had risen to meet the demands of a life so utterly different from the one to which she had been raised.

Now Leeana smiled at her, and Balcartha unsteepled her fingers to point at the empty chair in front of her desk.

"Sit."

"Yes, Ma'am," Leeana said meekly, and settled obediently into the indicated chair. She also folded her hands neatly in her lap, planted her feet very close together, and sat very straight with a demure, earnestly attentive expression.

"You do realize you're about to draw two extra weeks of patrol duty for being such a smartass, don't you?" Balcartha inquired.

"Oh, I suppose something like that might happen in some other city guard," Leeana replied. "*My* five hundred is far too broad-minded and much too far above the sort of petty-mindedness which would permit that sort of mean-spirited retaliation... Ma'am."

"You just go right on believing that until you see the patrol roster," Balcartha advised her. Then she shook her head. "Although truth be told, and given how much you actually seem to *enjoy* running around out in the grasslands, I suppose I'd better come up with some other way to demonstrate my petty-mindedness. Maybe I should convince the mayor to send you back for another conversation with Lord Warden Trisu."

"Mother forbid!" Leeana leaned back and raised both hands in a gesture of surrender, the dismay in her expression only half-feigned. "I'll be good. I *promise* I'll be good!"

"That bad, was it?" Balcartha swung her chair slowly from side to side. "Didn't Arm Shahana's visit give you any cover? I thought he was on his best behavior when she comes to call on him."

"I suppose he is, really." Leeana cocked her head, and her tone was more serious. "I'd say he's at least *trying*, anyway. Unfortunately—as you and Mayor Yalith are both perfectly well aware—Trisu can't quite seem to forget who my father is." She grimaced. "He's not very good at hiding his conviction that becoming a war maid is about the most disgraceful thing a properly reared young noblewoman could possibly have done. I'm pretty sure he doesn't try very hard, really."

"What do you mean?" Balcartha's chair stopped swinging and her eyes narrowed.

"Oh, I'm not saying he goes out of his way to offer me *insults*,

Balcartha," Leeana said quickly. "On the other hand, you know he doesn't believe in operating under false pretenses, and becoming a war maid isn't some sort of minor faux pas like getting myself caught sleeping with someone else's husband or producing a child whose father I can't name. It's a *seriously* reprehensible thing for anyone to do!"

There was a genuine bite under the humor in her tone, Balcartha noted, continuing to gaze at her intently, and the younger woman shrugged.

"Whatever he may have thought or felt, he was perfectly polite in the way he addressed me, Balcartha. And let's face it, we both know Mayor Yalith chooses me as her envoy to make a specific point to him. I understand that. That doesn't mean I don't get a little tired sometimes of being used as the mayor's hammer, but I *understand* it." She shrugged again. "If putting up with the occasional visit to Trisu is the worst thing the war maids ever ask of me, I'll figure I've been a lot luckier than I deserve."

"I see." Balcartha considered her for another few seconds, then tipped back in her chair once more. "Should I take it, then, that you accomplished whatever it was Yalith sent you there to deal with?"

"I think so." Leeana nodded, but she did not (Balcartha noted) tell her exactly what it was Yalith had sent her to Thalar Keep to do. The younger woman's reticence didn't offend the five hundred. In fact, she approved of it—strongly—and the fact that Leeana wasn't the sort to gossip about any diplomatic missions upon which she might be sent was one of the reasons she tended to get sent on them.

Well, that and the fact that she's smart as a whip, not to mention better educated than at least three-quarters of our war maids, and better informed on the Kingdom's politics than Yalith and me combined. And *equipped with a confidence in her ability to handle even people like Trisu that most war maids twice her age could only envy. The really funny thing is that as smart as she is, I don't think she fully understands even now just how unusual that confidence of hers is.*

Part of it, the five hundred knew, was simply who and what she'd been born. It would have been ridiculous to expect someone like her friend Garlahna, who'd been raised on a farm, to have the same confidence and poise as the only daughter of one of the Kingdom's four most powerful nobles. There was reason in everything, after all. Yet birth alone couldn't explain Leeana Hanathafressa, and neither could the young woman's knife-edged intelligence.

The truth, Balcartha admitted to herself just a bit more grimly, was that the majority of war maids had been damaged—or at least scarred—by whatever it was which had driven them to revolt against all the rules and expectations of "proper conduct" which had been trained into them. Not all of them, of course. There would always be those who simply discovered they wanted something more out of their lives. That they wanted to step beyond the mold and the restrictions, and thank Lillinara for them! But there was no point trying to deny that the war-maid community was a refuge—a place to heal, or even hide—for the majority of women who sought it out.

In a sense, that was true for Leeana, as well, but what *she'd* come to hide from was the proposal of an arranged marriage she'd known her father's political enemies had contrived as a weapon against him. And if she'd had the inevitable regrets, shed the inevitable tears at giving up her family, there'd been nothing damaged or scarred about her. There'd been only that deep, abiding, astounding strength, and over the years, Balcartha had come to have an equally deep and abiding respect for the parents who'd given it to her.

"And did Lord Trisu's grooms offer to take care of Boots for you?" the five hundred asked out loud, her eyes gleaming faintly, and Leeana snorted.

"Lillinara, no!" She shook her head. "How can you even ask such a thing? Any properly bred Sothōii male offer to care for a *war maid's* horse? They were far too busy undressing Garlahna and me with their eyes!"

"Alas, that doesn't seem to happen to *me* anymore," Balcartha said mournfully, running one hand over her gray hair.

"Trust me, I wish it didn't happen to *me*, either!" Leeana said vehemently.

"Oh, hush, child!" Balcartha stopped running her hand over her hair to shake an index finger at the younger woman. "Trust me, the day men *don't* look at you, you'll notice! I know what you'd really like to do is wring their necks, and I'd pay good kormaks to see you do it. For that matter, I'd offer to help if I thought you'd need it! But you're only as young and good-looking as you are once, so go ahead and rub their noses in it. In a properly ladylike way, of course."

"Oh, of course," Leeana agreed, but a faint echo of Taraiys' fiery blush seemed to touch her cheekbones, and Balcartha frowned mentally.

Quite a few war maids, especially the ones who'd fled to the free-towns like Kalatha rather than being born there, took full advantage of the sexual freedom their new lives offered. Some of them took too *much* advantage of it, in Balcartha's opinion, and the behavior of certain war maids she could call to mind didn't help the bigoted stereotype which viewed all war maids as perhaps a half step above common harlots. Or *below* them, perhaps. Of course, it was hard to blame them, after what many of them had endured, and whoever any individual war maid might choose to bed was her concern and hers alone. Whatever else might be true, war maids belonged to themselves, not anyone else, in *all* ways. They'd given up far too much of the rest of their lives to compromise on *that*, however much their "licentious ways" offended the society they'd rejected, and they were perfectly prepared to make their defiance of that society's rules abundantly, one might even have said flagrantly, clear.

Expecting anything else would have been not merely foolish but *wrong*, and as a general rule Balcartha didn't make it her business to worry about what any of *her* war maids did whenever they were off duty. Still, she'd become aware Leeana wasn't one of the ones who took advantage of that particular aspect of her freedom. Or if she did, she was incredibly discreet about it, at any rate. Bacartha had thought for a while that she and Garlahna might decide to pair up, but *that* obviously wasn't the case... especially now that Barlahn Ironsmith had come on the scene! And it wasn't as if someone with Leeana's looks and warm, open personality hadn't attracted plenty of attention, male and female alike, especially over the last few years. But she'd rebuffed all of them—with a smile or a laughing, wicked joke that made it abundantly obvious she was no prude, whatever else might be true, far more often than not. And she clearly had a healthy appreciation for her own attractiveness. Aside from an occasional flash of resentment like her comment about Trisu's armsmen—and the gods knew Balcartha understood *that* well enough!—she never seemed the least... repressed, or unhappy, but still...

"But still" it isn't any of your *business, old woman!* the five hundred scolded herself. *It's up to* her *who she does—or doesn't—sleep with, so just you let* her *worry about it!*

"Well," she said out loud, "I'm glad to hear your mission was a success and you didn't leave any bruised or broken armsmen in your wake."

"Not this time, anyway." Leeana grimaced. "I can't guarantee that won't happen another time, though!"

"Just make sure there's a witness who can honestly testify that he made the first move, and you've got my blessing." Balcartha's tone was light, but there was a genuine note of warning in it, as well, and she waited to continue until Leeana nodded back.

"And now that I've issued my stern injunction, what was it you wanted to see me about?" she asked then.

"Actually, I wanted to talk to you about a furlough," Leeana said, and Balcartha's mental ears pricked.

The younger woman looked as relaxed and comfortable as she'd been from the moment she entered the office, yet there was some subtle change. Some tiny shift in her body language, or perhaps something in her eyes. Balcartha couldn't put a finger on what that "something" was, but that didn't prevent her from knowing it was there.

"A furlough?" she repeated.

"Yes." Leeana shrugged. "It turns out I've been running up unused leave time for quite a while now. In fact, according to Erlis, I've got over three months of it on the books. With your permission, I'd like to use some of that up now."

"Over three *months?*" Balcartha blinked. To have accrued that much unused leave time, Leeana must have pretty much not taken any leave at all for the last couple of years, and the five hundred rebuked herself for not having noticed. Attention to duty and hard work were always praiseworthy qualities and much to be encouraged, but it was important for anyone to save a little time for herself, as well. In fact, it was *as* important as attention to duty, and if she'd realized Leeana was shorting herself on leave to that extent...

"Yes, Ma'am." Leeana made a small, almost apologetic gesture. "It just sort of...piled up."

Those mental ears of Balcartha's twitched again as Leeana's tone registered.

Now why don't I believe it just "piled up"? And if it didn't, why has she been saving it up on purpose?

"I suppose that happens sometimes," she said after a moment, "if not usually to quite that extent. And if it has, then by all means let's get some of it used up. Unless you're planning on letting it go on 'piling up' until you can retire a year or two early!"

"That's not what I had in mind." Leeana grinned and shook her head. "In fact, if the Guard can spare me, I'd like to go ahead and take a month or two of it, starting next month."

"I'm sure we can survive without you for a few weeks," Balcartha said dryly. "May I ask exactly what it is you have in mind to do with all that time?"

"Well..." Leeana shrugged. "Next month is my birthday, and I'd like to go home—to Hill Guard, I mean—for it."

Balcartha's eyes narrowed in sudden understanding.

"That's right. You'll be twenty-one this year, won't you?" she said.

"Yes, I will," Leeana replied, meeting her gaze levelly, and Balcartha nodded slowly.

Twenty-one was the year of majority, the official beginning of adulthood, for a Sothōii noblewoman. For noble*men*, it came two years earlier than that—just another of those little natural advantages which accrued to someone who'd had the good sense to be born male. Among those scandalous war maids, of course, the rules were somewhat different, and unlike Leeana Bowmaster, Leeana *Hanathafressa* had been legally an adult from the moment she completed her probationary period.

Several questions followed one another through Balcartha's mind as she and the younger woman gazed at one another. But the only one who had the right to ask Leeana those questions was Leeana herself, and so—

"I don't see any problem about arranging a couple of months of leave for you," the five hundred said. "You'll have to discuss it with Erlis, of course—make sure she's covered while you're away—but I feel confident we'll manage in your absence somehow."

✧ ✧ ✧

"Leeana! Over here!"

Garlahna's shout cut through the friendly, noisy, dimly lit din of The Green Maiden's common room, and Leeana turned her head, peering through the rather smoky air until she spotted her friend at a corner table. Unlike her, Garlahna had exchanged her chari and yathu for a gown for the evening, and its amber silk clung to her like a second skin. It was interesting, Leeana thought, how the gown actually emphasized Garlahna's undeniably curvaceous figure so much more... emphatically than the far more "revealing" traditional war-maid attire did. It was a point she'd been paying more attention to of late herself, and she admired the embroidery on her friend's deeply plunging bodice.

Of course, some people had more curves to emphasize in the first place, she reflected, although she had to admit she was less challenged in that area herself than she'd once expected to be. It was simply that Garlahna could have challenged *anyone* in that particular competition.

She smiled at the familiar thought as Garlahna waved, beckoning her over. Then she waved back and started working her way through the crowd.

The Green Maiden was always crowded, especially on the evenings like this one, when fresh rain clouds had come swelling up along the western horizon as the sun settled towards evening. It didn't feel like it was going to be one of the Wind Plain's tumultuous thunderstorms, but unless Leeana missed her guess, they were in for a long, steady soaking. In fact, the first drops had already begun to fall, although no one could possibly hear them pattering on the The Green Maiden's roof through the chattering voices, the clatter of tableware, the calls for refilled mugs and glasses, and the preliminary tootling of the three musicians setting up for the evening's entertainment on the tiny stage beside the huge fireplace.

Leeana reached the table Garlahna had snagged and paused to use both hands to slick beads of rainwater off of her bare shoulders and upper arms before she hooked a toe under the unoccupied chair on her side and pulled it out.

"Didn't think you were going to make it before the floodgates opened," Garlahna observed.

"I didn't—quite," Leeana pointed out wryly. "And I've got gate duty tonight. Third watch, in fact." She grimaced. "It ought to be coming down nicely by then."

"And Barlahn and I will be thinking of you with the deepest sympathy as we listen to the rain drumming on the roof and gurgling in the gutters," Garlahna assured her, leaning comfortably against Barlahn Ironsmith's shoulder. It was a well-muscled shoulder, connected to powerful arms and calloused, capable hands, one of which was draped possessively around Garlahna at that very moment. "Assuming we can spare any of our attention from more . . . pressing matters, that is," Garlahna added with a smile.

"Knowing you?" Leeana snorted. "Somehow I don't think I'd better be counting on *you* to come make sure I haven't come down with pneumonia."

"Are you suggesting anything could possibly distract me from my deep and burning concern about my very best friend's well-being on a dark and stormy night like this?"

"I'm suggesting it would take Chemalka's own thunderbolt to get any 'spare attention' out of the two of you!"

"Well, that's only because we're going to be enjoying a few thunderbolts of our own," Garlahna replied, arching her spine ever so slightly to round her bosom provocatively, then batted her eyes in Barlahn's direction.

"Shameless hussy," he remarked comfortably, smiling down at her, and she laughed and patted him on the thigh.

"Yep, and you love it," she told him. "Don't try to pretend differently to *me!*"

"Happen I'm not so likely to be doing that. 'S long as you don't take t' taking me for granted, anywise."

"Trust me, that's not going to happen," she purred, raising her head far enough to plant a kiss on the side of his neck.

"Good." He smiled again, then looked across the table at Leeana. "And a good evening to you, too, Leeana," he said blandly.

"Why don't the two of you just go ahead and get a room here at the inn?" Leeana asked sweetly. "It would save so much time. And I'd be happy to wait to order until you got back."

"I tried, but they were all already taken," Garlahna said mournfully. "Still," she brightened, "I understand Raythas told Shallys she'd only need *her* room for an hour or so." She smiled wickedly at Leeana. "I'm sure Barlahn and I could get it when she's done . . . if you'd care to join us before you go on watch, that is."

"Garlahna, if I thought you were really willing to share Barlahn for even one moment, you might actually manage to embarrass me," Leeana told her with a smile of her own. "Since I know perfectly well what a greedy bitch you are where he's concerned, I'm not really worried."

"Spoilsport!" Garlahna laughed, then looked up as one of The

Green Maiden's servers appeared at the edge of the table. Like quite a few of the other war maids scattered around the common room, the woman had a pipe clasped between her teeth, and smoke curled up from its bowl to join the haze drifting overhead as she cocked an eyebrow at the three of them.

"So are you finally ready to order, Garlahna? Or do you and Barlahn want to sit over here in each other's laps for another hour or so first? Oh, and hi, Leeana."

"Hi, Barthyma." Leeana shook her head and jabbed a thumb in Garlahna's direction. "You know the two of them are lowering the tone of your entire establishment, don't you?"

"I keep telling them to get a room," Barthyma Darhanfressa replied, and raised both eyebrows as Garlahna went into a fit of giggles. "I said something especially funny?" she asked.

"Only to someone like Garlahna," Leeana assured her. "And since I've got the duty in another couple of hours, I'll go ahead and order a beer now, if you don't mind. And is that venison I smell?"

"Shallys' special recipe," Barthyma confirmed.

"Then I'll have that, too. With the buttered potatoes and lima beans. Oh, and don't forget the cornbread! And—"

"And make sure it's a generous portion," Barthyma finished for her with a smile, and shook her head. "Girl, it's a good thing you're as fanatical as you are about those morning runs of yours!"

"I'm just making sure I get to go on enjoying the good things in life," Leeana replied with a smile.

"*Some* of them, at least," Garlahna said. "Personally, I prefer to burn off the pounds without running around barefoot in the misty morn."

Leeana shook her head fondly. Garlahna might miss the occasional morning, but the two of them ran together at least four days a week.

"So, *are* you two going to order?" Barthyma asked the dark-haired war maid, and Barlahn laughed.

"O' course she is. In fact," he smiled down at Garlahna, "I'm thinking you'd best fetch her an extra portion, too." He looked up at Barthyma and winked. "Happen she'll need her strength tonight."

"Mother, take me now!" Barthyma rolled her eyes, and looked back at Leeana. "If it gets any deeper back here, you're going to drown *before* you have to go out in the rain, Leeana. You're always welcome at the bar if you need to escape."

"Thanks," Leeana said wryly, "but I think I'll just stay here and take notes."

"Take notes?" Garlahna sat up a little straighter, brown eyes narrowing slightly. "And the cause of this sudden curiosity of yours would be—?"

"Who said anything about 'curiosity'?" Leeana retorted. "I'm just looking for blackmail material."

"*Blackmail* material?" Garlahna laughed. "You've got to be kidding! I was a *farm girl*, not a 'noblewoman' like *someone* I could mention, before I ran off to the war maids!"

"Oh, I know it wouldn't have any effect on *you*," Leanna shot back. "But Barlahn was a respectable fellow before he took up with you. *He* may still have a reputation to worry about, you know!"

She grinned at her friend, green eyes dancing, but Garlahna gazed back at her with that same speculative air for a heartbeat or two. There was something about Leeana's tone, she thought. And was that the slightest edge of a blush along the other war maid's cheekbones?

Their eyes met for just a moment, and then Garlahna snorted.

"Don't be ridiculous," she said, snuggling comfortably back down beside her freemate. "If Barlahn was going to worry about his 'reputation,' he never would've 'taken up' with *me* in the first place!"

Chapter Eleven

Bahzell leaned one shoulder against the doorframe, arms folded across his chest, and whistled tunelessly as he gazed out from the balcony across the roofs and busy streets of Sothōfalas. They were worth gazing at, although they couldn't hold a candle to Belhadan or Axe Hallow. On the other hand, those were Axeman cities, with dwarvish engineering readily available and located in a far more densely populated land.

Sothōfalas was substantially smaller than Axe Hallow, although it actually covered a greater area than Belhadan, he estimated. But the dwarven sarthnaisks who'd contributed to Belhadan's construction had buried at least half of that city's housing, shops, and warehouses in the solid stone of its mountainous terrain. Sothōfalas sprawled out in every direction from the towering battlements of King Markhos' great fortress of Sothōkarnas, and beyond the rib of granite which had broken the Wind Plain's surface like a breaching whale to serve as Sothōkarnas' foundation, the terrain was flat as a griddle on either side of the Pardahn River.

The Pardahn, yet another of the mighty Spear River's countless tributaries, wasn't all that much of a river, but it did offer the Sothōii capital a reliable source of water. And it was deep enough for barge traffic, he thought, watching a horse-drawn barge creeping towards the city. Hradani eyes were much better than human ones, and Bahzell could easily make out the crossed battleaxe and war hammer of Frahmahn flying from the stumpy flagstaff on the vessel's stern. It was a lengthy haul from Nachfalas to Sothōfalas, but he didn't doubt Cassan was going to show a tidy profit on the barge's cargo.

For now, at least, he told himself with grim satisfaction, and let his eyes sweep back across the steeply pitched, brightly colored roofs of Sothōfalas. They built in stone or brick, the Sothōii, and they burned coal in winter. There wasn't that much wood here on the Wind Plain, and what there was of it was far too precious to be used as a mere building material or fuel. In that respect, they really did have quite a bit in common with the subterranean cities of Dwarvenhame, he reflected. And, even more than his own people, they built thick walls, too, fit to stand the blasts of the far northern winter even at the Wind Plain's altitude and thick enough to shed the sometimes fierce heat of the brief northern summer, as well. There were few exterior windows, however, and all of the larger, more prosperous homes clustered around his present vantage point had obviously been designed with an eye towards defense, even here in the very heart of the Kingdom's capital. It was a reminder that feuds between the great Sothōii clans could be just as bloody as among Bahzell's own people, but it was more than that, as well. Without handy terrain features, the Sothōii had deliberately constructed defensive strong points within their city. At least two-thirds of Sothōfalas' present area lay beyond the old city walls, which had last been extended more than two generations ago . . . and whose maintenance was scarcely the first charge on the Exchequer. That faintly offended Bahzell's sense of the way things ought to be, but stone walls had never been the Sothōii idea of a proper defense, and the capital was far from unguarded. Indeed, if a hostile army ever managed to reach it at all—an almost insuperable challenge, given what Sothōii light cavalry and wind riders would do to any invader here on their home ground—those fortified villas would make Sothōfalas a tougher nut to crack than it might expect, he thought.

Not that the city was any sort of grim, gray fortress. Its streets were as clean and well kept as any Axeman town might boast, and streamers, pennants, and wind-tube banners flew from the towers of Sothōkarnas. The great royal standard which indicated the King was in residence snapped and cracked above its central keep, and every manor in the city appeared to sport the brave banners of whatever noble house had built them, as well. Nor was that the city's only color. The Sothōii didn't favor the bas-relief sculptures and intricate mosaics Axeman architects incorporated into their public buildings, but the walls of Sothōfalas' buildings were bright with painted frescoes and murals. Those on more public buildings tended to reflect each structure's function, but the competition between private homes was often fierce, and mural painters were both highly prized and lucratively paid. From where he stood, he could see artisans touching up at a dozen or so of those murals, apparently repairing the last of the winter's ravages. And the streets themselves were full of pedestrians, carts, and—inevitably—mounted riders. The clatter of hooves, the rattle of cart wheels, the buzz of conversation, the cries of vendors and shouts of children . . . all the vibrant, living noises of the city came to his ears like the music of life.

He'd considered stepping out onto the balcony proper, the better to enjoy its bustling life, but he'd decided against it. He wasn't the hardest person in the Kingdom for people to recognize, and he and his fellow hradani remained less than fully welcome in the eyes of all too many Sothōii. There was no point calling unnecessary attention to his presence here in the city . . . and especially not to the fact that he was an honored guest in this particular house. That was why he'd been careful to remain well back, where—hopefully—none of those who continued to cherish less than warm and welcoming thoughts might spy him.

He'd been careful when he first opened the balcony's glass doors and propped himself here, as well, since the diamond-paned panels looked suspiciously fragile, and he'd had entirely too much experience with furnishings—and buildings—which hadn't really been intended for a hradani who stood nine inches over seven feet to go about leaning on them. He'd tested the strength of the frame with a thoughtful expression before satisfying himself it was truly up to his weight, studiously ignoring the obvious amusement of his two companions while he did so.

<*They're only jealous of your noble stature,*> Walsharno assured him in the back of his brain, speaking from the enormous, spotless stable appended to the mansion. <*We coursers get that sort of thing from the lesser cousins all the time. And, of course, I understand that* some *of us actually get it from our . . . less-well-grown fellow coursers upon occasion, as well.*>

<*Do they now?*> Bahzell responded silently, continuing to whistle. <*And who might it be as hears such a thing from such as, say, Gayrhalan?*>

<*I'm sure* I *wouldn't know,*> Walsharno replied primly, and Bahzell chuckled.

"Dathgar says you and Walsharno are being full of yourselves again," Tellian Bowmaster remarked from behind him. Bahzell stopped whistling and glanced over his shoulder at the baron, ears cocked interrogatively, and Tellian chuckled. "Walsharno's mind voice is a little stronger than other coursers', you know. And, ah, Dathgar's been around longer than he has and developed a bit better 'hearing.' If you two really don't want him eavesdropping, Walsharno's going to have to learn not to shout when the two of you aren't nose-to-nose."

<Shout, *is it?*> Walsharno demanded indignantly. <*It's no more than a . . . firmly voiced discussion!*> There was a brief pause. Then: <*And I don't recall asking for* your *opinion, either, Dathgar!*>

Tellian's eyes twinkled, and he shook his head.

"Dathgar just suggested that perhaps Walsharno thinks it's only a 'firmly voiced discussion' because of the volume you two *normally* need to get through one another's thick skulls."

"I'm thinking you and your four-footed friend need to be finding yourselves another insult," Bahzell said genially. "Mind, I'll not say as how either of us are after having the very thinnest skulls in the whole wide world, but it's in my mind as how someone who's of a truly inventive turn of phrase could be coming up with something a mite fresher."

"We can only do our humble best in Brandark's absence," Tellian replied with an apologetic air.

"Besides," Vaijon put in, looking up from his book in the chair he'd tilted back against one of the handsomely decorated chamber's walls, "we've found the simplest insults are best. You seem to *miss* the more complicated ones every so often."

"Oh! That was a clean hit!" Tellian congratulated, and Vaijon nodded in acknowledgment with a suitably modest expression.

"Aye, so it was," Bahzell agreed, glancing at the younger champion.

Vaijon grinned at him, and the hradani shook his head. His human friend had reverted—partly, at least—to the Vaijon he'd first met in Belhadan. He was never going to attain such heights of magnificence again, thank Tomanāk, but he'd definitely turned his regular attire up a notch for the occasion. The plain woolen surcoat he'd adopted for normal wear had been replaced with one of green silk, glittering with genuine gold bullion, and the spurs on the glistening black boots stretched out before him as he lounged inelegantly on the base of his spine in the comfortable (and expensive) chair gleamed with silver inlay.

"Of course," Bahzell continued, "while I've no choice but to admit it's true as death hradani can be a mite slow noticing as how someone's trying to get through to them, I'm thinking someone as lives in a glass house might be a mite careful how he lobs cobblestones about. It's in my mind as how I recall a young Axeman popinjay as was a bit behind hand himself when it came time to be listening to others."

"Ouch!" Tellian's smile turned into a huge grin, and he shook his head wryly. "I'd say you're playing with fire today, Vaijon!"

"*If* I were minded to be bringing up people who deliberately did their dead level best to shove their fingers into their long, hairy ears to *avoid* hearing someone rather than simply being... too preoccupied to notice someone trying to get their attention, I would undoubtedly respond in kind," Vaijon observed, then sighed. "That would be conduct unbecoming a champion of Tomanāk, however. Besides, it would be taking unfair advantage of someone whose more ancient—uh, excuse me, I meant more *senior*—mental processes have reduced him to bringing up something that happened seven years ago in an effort to divert attention from the sad decay of his own acuity in his declining years."

"Oh ho!" Bahzell laughed. "That's cost you an ally or two, I'm thinking!" He twitched his ears impudently in Tellian's direction, and Vaijon glanced at the baron, who was regarding him with a distinctly beady eye.

"'*Declining* years'?" Tellian repeated. "Are you *sure* that's the way you want to describe someone all of three months older than *I* am? And a hradani, to boot? Unless I'm mistaken, Bahzell is actually considerably younger for his people than you are for ours."

"Perhaps I should re-think that particular, possibly unfortunate choice of words," Vaijon replied. "It does seem to imply I was ascribing Bahzell's less than blindingly fast thought processes to the inevitable deterioration of age, which couldn't have been farther from my intent. After all, it would have been disrespectful for someone as youthful as myself to make such an... indelicate observation about one of my elders. *Either* of my elders."

"If you grab his shoulders, I'll grab his ankles, and I'm sure between the two of us doddering old wrecks, we can toss him off the balcony," Tellian said.

"Tempting as the thought might be, I'm thinking as how it's a nasty mess we'd make in Sir Jerhas' courtyard," Bahzell replied.

"Come to that, there's no need. It's a long journey back to Hill Guard, and no knowing what sort of mischief might be befalling a fellow out on the high road and all. Indeed, we've but to ask, and it's certain I am Dathgar and Walsharno betwixt them could manage to tread on him just a bit."

"I'm sure they could," Tellian said, but his smile had faded. His expression was much more sober as he gazed at both the champions, and Bahzell grimaced slightly.

"It may be as how my brain *is* slowing a mite," he rumbled. "I'd no mind to recall such as that to you, Tellian."

"I know." Tellian shook his head quickly, one hand just brushing his chest where the arrowheads had driven into him. "And I should have listened to the two of you—Tomanāk! The *four* of you!—and gone ahead and worn the damned armor."

<*Eight, actually, but who's counting?*> Walsharno observed, loudly enough Bahzell knew he was making certain Dathgar could hear him and relay to Tellian. <*I make it you, me, Brandark, Vaijon, Hathan, Gayrhalan, Dathgar, and*—especially!—*Baroness Hanatha. Did I leave anyone out, Brother?*>

"No, you didn't," Tellian said before Bahzell could respond. "And I'm *not* looking forward to what Hanatha's going to have to say to me when I get home."

His shudder, Bahzell thought, wasn't entirely feigned, and the hradani didn't blame him. Tellian had written his wife the evening immediately after the attack... and her reply letter had arrived via a courier whose lathered horse spoke eloquently of the urgency with which she'd dispatched it. Bahzell didn't doubt for a moment that she intended to rehash her initial reaction to how close Tellian had come to death the instant she got her hands on him once again. Well, not the very *first* instant; she'd be too busy hugging him until his ribs needed healing all over again before she got around to washing his head for him the way he deserved. But she'd get around to it in time, and take the time to do it properly when she did.

And a good thing it will be, too, the hradani thought, looking at the man who'd become one of his closest friends. *For a man as is one of the canniest, hardest-headed fellows I've yet to meet, that was about as addlepated a decision as ever I've seen.*

He knew he was being at least a little unfair to Tellian, but he didn't really care. Some people were less entitled than others to take chances with their own safety when they *knew* they had enemies who would vastly prefer to see them dead.

And then there's the little matter of that cough of his, the hradani thought grimly, glancing at Vaijon. None of the three champions had shared Tomanāk's confirmation about that with the baron yet, but it was going to have to be addressed eventually. On the other hand, if Wencit of Rūm ran true to form, they ought to be seeing him in Hill Guard sometime in the next two or three months. If dark wizardry was indeed to blame for the baron's "illness," it might be best to have the world's last *white* wizard available for any discussion of how a repeat performance could be avoided.

"I got another letter from her yesterday, you know," Tellian said after a moment, and rolled his eyes.

"Did you now? And should we be taking it she's still a mite put out with you?" Bahzell inquired genially.

"You could put it that way, I suppose. Although, to be fair," Tellian's tone was judicious, "that would be a little like saying the Ice Sisters are a 'mite' chilly. In mid-winter."

Both his companions chuckled at that one, since the Ice Sister Lakes spent three months out of the year under frozen sheets of ice several feet thick. Tellian joined their laughter, but then his expression sobered and he sighed.

"What?" Vaijon asked, and the baron shrugged.

"Hanatha got a letter from Leanna. She's coming home for a visit for her birthday."

"A visit, is it?" Bahzell's ears twitched.

"Yes, and I'm going to be stuck here in Sothōfalas!" Tellian's frustration was plain. "I hardly ever get to see her, and now this!"

He glowered, and Bahzell smiled sympathetically as he heard a father's unhappiness. He had no children of his own—as Tellian had just suggested, he was actually on the young side, by his own people's standards, to even have been thinking about that yet, and champions seldom had the time to even consider parenthood—but he had nieces and nephews in plenty. Some fathers—too many of them, in fact, in Bahzell's opinion—would be less than devastated by missing a visit from a war-maid daughter, but Tellian wasn't one of them, and Bahzell understood the baron's disappointment only too well. In fact...

"And did your lady write how long she'll be visiting?" he asked, and Tellian snorted.

"Not long enough, I'm afraid. Or not for me, anyway, if I end up stuck here, as long as I'm afraid I'm going to. *You* should at least have a chance to see her on your way through to Hurgrum, though."

"Will I, now? That's good to be hearing." Tellian raised an eyebrow at him. "I'm thinking as how by that time she and your lady will have had time enough and to spare to agree with one another about those as don't wear armor when they ought," Bahzell explained with a smile. "Indeed, it's in my mind as how if I'm *truly* lucky, they'll've worn themselves down to a nub without the strength to be starting in on me for having let you be doing something so daft as that. Mind, I'm none too optimistic about it, though. Like as not they'll see me as naught but a setting-up exercise for Hanatha once she's after getting you home again and safely into arm's reach."

"Um," Tellian considered that for a moment, then grimaced. "I'm afraid you may be onto something there. But I'm going to expect you to protect me from her if you are, you know."

"Ah? And would it happen you could explain just why I might be daft enough to do anything of the sort?"

"It's an ancient Wakūo tradition," Tellian assured him.

"Wakūo, is it?" Bahzell cocked his ears and arched one eyebrow, wondering where Tellian was headed. The fierce nomads who dominated the vast, rolling wastelands beyond the Spearmen's Great Eastern Forest had more traditions, customs, and practices (not to mention rituals, ceremonies, and taboos) than even the dwarves. No one—not even the Wakūo themselves, he suspected—could possibly keep *all* of them straight.

"Of course! If a Wakūo warrior saves someone's life, he's responsible for that person for the rest of his own life. And if you don't protect me from Hanatha, you'll be derelict in your duties!"

Vaijon laughed out loud, and Bahzell shook his head as Tellian looked at him guilelessly.

"If it happened as how I was Wakūo—or even as how *you* were Wakūo, come to that—I might be thinking as how you had a point. But as I'm not, and no more are you, and seeing as it happens I'm more than a mite in agreement with her, I'm afraid as how I'll be otherwise occupied at the moment. Probably counting the knotholes in Walsharno's stall. Or something nigh as important as that, leastwise."

"Traitor!"

<*Prudent!*> Walsharno countered with a silent equine laugh. <*A lot more prudent than I ever would have expected out of you, as a matter of fact, Brother*!>

"Now, that's no way for a Sothōii baron to be carrying on," Bahzell chided. "In fact—"

He broke off as the chamber door opened to admit the two men for whom they'd been waiting.

Sir Jerhas Macebearer, Lord Warden of Amber Grass, was in his mid-sixties, white-haired, blue-eyed, and richly dressed, with a luxurious mustache that drooped almost to his chin. He'd never been of more than average height for a Sothōii, and he'd grown slightly stooped with age, but his stride was still firm and powerful, despite the polished ebony cane in his right hand. His shirt was of the finest snow white linen, with its full sleeves gathered into embroidered wristbands; his tabardlike tunic was even more richly embroidered, as befitted the Kingdom of the Sothōii's Prime Councilor; and the intricately worked golden chain of his office flickered with brilliant reflections about his neck. The plain leather scabbard of the businesslike dagger sheathed at his left hip should have struck a jarring note, but instead, it simply looked inevitable.

Prince Yurokhas Silveraxe was over four inches taller than Sir Jerhas, with the same red hair and blue eyes as his older brother, the King. He was five years older than Vaijon, and two inches shorter, yet the two men bore a decided resemblance to one another. Partly, that was because Prince Yurokhas' court tunic was neither the deep blue of royalty nor marked with the simple silver axe of his house. Instead, it was exactly the same shade as Vaijon's and Bahzell's surcoats, and emblazoned with the crossed swords and mace of Tomanāk. Almost more even than that, though, was the fact that Yurokhas, despite his princely rank, believed in keeping himself in training. He was broad-shouldered, powerfully built, and sinewy, and he even *moved* like Vaijon, with an unconscious, almost feline grace.

"Your Highness," Tellian said, rising quickly from his chair and dropping to one knee before Yurokhas.

"Oh, get up, Tellian!" the prince said testily. "We both have better things to do than to waste time with you crawling around on the floor. Besides, I've heard about that little *adventure* you got yourself into on the way here!" Blue eyes scrutinized Tellian closely as the baron rose obediently. "Hanatha's going to have your hide, and my only regret is that I won't be there to watch her take it. What in Fiendark's Furies did you think you were *doing?*"

"Always so tactful, so *diplomatic*," Tellian murmured, and Yurokhas cracked a laugh.

"I'll give you 'diplomatic' if you ever let anything like that happen again!" The prince reached out, resting one hand on each of Tellian's shoulders, and looked deep into his eyes. "There's too damned much going on for you to let people go poking arrows into you, damn it! And that doesn't even consider how *I'll* feel if you let something like that happen to you again."

His voice softened on the final sentence, and he gave Tellian a gentle shake. The baron smiled crookedly and shrugged.

"Nobody seems to believe this," he said a bit plaintively, "but I genuinely didn't expect anyone to go 'poking arrows' into me. I suppose the event demonstrates that I *should* have, but I didn't actively set out to help . . . parties unknown finish me off, you know. That could have happened to anyone."

Yurokhas snorted with panache.

"You were doing pretty well there, until that last sentence," he told the older man. "You aren't just 'anyone,' and things like that aren't supposed to happen to one of the Kingdom's barons. Especially not when it's one of the *other* barons who's behind it!"

"Your Highness." Sir Jerhas spoke quietly, but his tone carried an edge of admonition, and he shook an index finger at the prince when Yurokhas looked at him.

"I'll dissemble all you want me to in public, Jerhas," Yurokhas replied unrepentantly. "In private, though, I'm not going to pretend we don't all know who was really behind this. Or that his holdings don't lie somewhere roughly, oh, *south* of here!"

"As for that, Your Highness," Bahzell rumbled, "while I'll not say as how he didn't have a finger in the pie somewhere, there's not a one of the fellows as surrendered to us who'd a word to say at all, at all, about Baron Cassan."

Sir Jerhas rolled his eyes and puffed his mustache disapprovingly as Bahzell mentioned Cassan's name, although he didn't waste his time denying that the Baron of Frahmahn could possibly have been involved in the assault on his fellow baron. Yurokhas, on the other hand, didn't even try to disguise his skepticism.

"I'm not one to question one of His champions in the normal

order of things, Prince Bahzell," he said, reaching out to clasp forearms with Bahzell. "Especially not when the champion in question's accomplished all you have. But I find it very difficult to believe anything like this could have happened to Tellian without Cassan being involved in it *somewhere*."

"Aye, and so he may've been," Bahzell acknowledged. "And I'll not deny I'd find more than a mite of pleasure in seeing him take the tumble he's more than earned. But for all that, it's a rare man as is willing to try to lie to one of Himself's champions, and I've yet to meet the one as can actually do it! So if it were to happen as you called me to testify, it's no choice I'd have but to swear under oath as not one of them so much as mentioned Cassan by name. In fact, it's in my mind as how whoever did buy their swords for this was never a Sothōii at all."

"What?" Yurokhas' skepticism was clearer than ever, and even Sir Jerhas' eyes widened at Bahzell's assertion.

"I'll not say it didn't surprise me, as well," the hradani confessed. "But the more I thought on it, the more it came to me as how there's more folk than I can count betwixt here and Bortalik as might just feel the kormaks slipping from their fingers these days. There's not a Purple Lord ever born, for instance, as wouldn't cut his own mother's throat to stop such as the Baron and my Da and old Kilthan are about. And Vaijon"—he flipped his ears at the human champion as he spoke—"and I questioned each of them separately, and more than one time apiece. They'd a mortal lot to say in hopes of avoiding a nasty end on someone's rope, yet the thing that struck me strongest was every one of them laid to it as how the 'armsman' as paid for Tellian's death 'let slip' as how he was in the service of a Sothōii lord. Now, I'm naught but a simple hradani, when all's said, yet it's in my mind as how a clumsy fellow might let such as that slip out once or twice, but it's a true work of art to be 'accidentally' telling every single one of the men as you're sending out to kill the second- or third-ranking noble of the entire Kingdom as how it was one of the Kingdom's *other* nobles hired them."

Yurokhas' eyes narrowed, and Sir Jerhas frowned. The Prime Councilor had been chosen for his office in part because Amber Grass lay in the North Riding, which was traditionally neutral in the struggle between Cassan and Tellian. Following the King's dismissal of Garthmahn Ironhelm, he'd needed an obviously "neutral" choice, and there were those who'd been inclined to think that was the only reason he'd settled on Sir Jerhas. The new Prime Councilor was a bluff sort of fellow, with little time to waste on things like book learning. He was not, to put it mildly, broadly respected as a scholar, and he wasn't above being flattered and cajoled by someone who approached him the right way. But he was also personally incorruptible, highly experienced, and one of the shrewdest negotiators Bahzell had ever encountered. Despite his impatience with formal learning and erudition, there was nothing at all wrong with the brain behind those blue eyes of his. And for all of his efforts to dissuade Yurokhas from flinging Cassan's name about, there was no more doubt in his mind than in the prince's about where Tellian's most dangerous enemies were to be found.

"A truly clever conspirator might expect us to think exactly that, Prince Bahzell," he pointed out after a moment.

"Aye, and so he might." Bahzell nodded calmly. "Yet truth be told, Sir Jerhas, Cassan's not so clever as all that."

The Prime Councilor looked as skeptical as Yurokhas had a moment before, and Bahzell chuckled coldly.

"Don't you be forgetting who my Da is! If you're minded to watch a *clever* conspirator at his trade, you'll not do better than him. Ruthless, yes—I'll grant Cassan that. And crooked-minded as Sharnā. But it's only the power he was born with and the black-hearted greed of him makes him truly dangerous. It's that as gives him so many others to be hiding behind and using. Aye, and throwing away as soon as ever it suits his needs." The huge hradani's expression was grim. "I've no use at all, at all, for a man as sets out to betray not only his oaths but all of those as have a right to look to him for justice and protection, and that's a frame as fits Cassan like a glove. But it's in my mind he's not nearly so clever as he's thinking he is, and it's that will bring him down in the end."

Sir Jerhas grimaced. Clearly, he wasn't precisely overjoyed to hear Bahzell predicting Cassan's ultimate downfall, and in many ways, the hradani couldn't blame him. Bringing Cassan down, however satisfying, and however obvious the rogue baron's guilt might become, would be a deadly dangerous business. The ties of personal loyalty ran deep among Sothōii; that was one of their greatest strengths. Yet it was one of their greatest *weaknesses*, as well, for many a lord warden and armsman would consider himself bound by his personal oath of fealty, no matter how great the guilt of the one to whom he'd given it. Cassan and Yeraghor of Ersok had far too many retainers who were likely to feel exactly that way, even in an open confrontation with the Crown, and it hadn't been that many years since the Sothōii's most recent "Time of Troubles."

Which, after all, went a long way towards explaining how cautious King Markhos and his Prime Councilor had to be in their dealings with the emerging alliance of Tellian, Bahnak, and Kilthandahknarthas.

"You may well be right," Yurokhas growled. "In fact, I hope you *are*, because the bastard can't be 'brought down' too soon for me!"

The prince's sincerity was obvious, and Sir Jerhas' grimace became a genuine wince.

"I'd like to see him a foot or so shorter, myself, Your Highness," Tellian observed mildly. "In fact, at the moment, with all due respect for Bahzell and Vaijon's opinion as to who hired this particular lot of assassins, I probably have even more motivation than you do. Having said that, however, I'm not so certain your brother would thank you for saying that where anyone else might hear you. For that matter, I don't think you're doing Sir Jerhas' peace of mind any great favor even now."

Yurokhas looked at him for a moment, then gave himself a shake and barked another laugh.

"You're right, of course, Brother," he said, addressing Tellian not simply as one wind rider to another but as the long-ago youth who'd been fostered by Tellian's father in Balthar. "I never was exactly noted for my patience, was I?"

"No, not so much," Tellian agreed in a judicious tone. Then he chuckled and smacked the prince gently on the shoulder. "On the other hand, much as I would never have admitted it to you when you were a scrubby young terror, all elbows and knees, Your Highness, you're not exactly the most thick-witted fellow I've ever known, either."

"Spare my blushes," Yurokhas snorted with a smile, and Bahzell wondered how many other Sothōii—if any—could have spoken to the prince that way.

Yurokhas stood for a moment, looking back and forth between Sir Jerhas, Tellian, and Bahzell, then gave himself another shake and drew a deep breath.

"Well," he said briskly, "now that I've had the opportunity to get all that out of my system, I suppose it's time we got down to business."

"By all means, Your Highness," Sir Jerhas said, bowing his guests towards the large, polished table set to catch the breeze billowing the silk hangings as it swept in off the balcony.

It would, perhaps, have been unfair to call the Prime Councilor's expression relieved at the prince's willingness to step back from his anger at Cassan, but it would have been headed in the right direction, Bahzell thought as he settled somewhat gingerly into his own chair. It creaked alarmingly under him, but it didn't collapse.

Immediately, at least.

"Should I assume the fact that you came along for the trip indicates you and Tellian have settled your plans for the summer well enough to discuss them with me, Sir Vaijon?" Yurokhas asked once they were all seated, and Vaijon shrugged slightly.

"Mostly, Your Highness," he agreed. "To be honest, I couldn't actually have told you the *real* reason for my decision to accompany Bahzell and the Baron this time." He smiled crookedly. "Tomanāk has a tendency to send us where He needs us without necessarily explaining it all to us ahead of time. Unless I'm badly mistaken, though, this time around it was more to send another healer than another sword."

"And I'm grateful for it," Yurokhas said quietly. "But you do have a campaign plan?"

"We do." Vaijon nodded. "Or the skeleton of one, at any rate. Baron Tellian and I still have to work out the exact number of armsmen he can make available."

"Under Trianal?" Yurokhas asked, glancing at Tellian, who nodded.

"I really wish you wouldn't risk him quite so readily, Milord," Sir Jerhas said. Tellian looked at him, and the Prime Councilor shrugged. "I understand your thinking, and I won't say you're wrong, but the lad's not even married yet." Sir Jerhas shook his head. "It was difficult enough getting the Council to settle the succession on him in the first place." There might have been a faint flicker of distaste in his eyes for the circumstances which had made that Council decision necessary, but no trace of it touched his voice as he continued. "If something happens to him before he produces an heir of his own, all of that work will have been for nothing in the end."

"I appreciate that," Tellian replied after a moment. His tone was also level, and he held Sir Jerhas' gaze with his own for just a moment before he continued. "I appreciate it, and I've pointed out to him that it's past time he be thinking about that. Hanatha... has some thoughts on the subject, as well. I think they're very *good* thoughts, as a matter of fact, but the truth is that there's no wife officially on the horizon for him yet, and in the meantime, someone needs to lead my armsmen and lords warden when *I* can't. Besides, he's already demonstrated his ability. He's not simply my heir; he's also one of my two or three best field commanders."

Sir Jerhas nodded in unhappy acknowledgment. Not necessarily agreement, Bahzell thought, but in acceptance. No one needed to explain to the Prime Councilor how important it was for any baron's heir, especially an heir-adoptive like Trianal, to prove his mettle in the eyes of the fighting men sworn to his service. Tellian *couldn't* keep Trianal home if he himself wasn't to take the field, not without some of his retainers questioning his own confidence in the youngster's capabilities.

That much, Sir Jerhas understood perfectly. However little he might like the thought of exposing Trianal—and, through him, the security of the West Riding's succession—to that sort of danger, it came with the young man's position and duties. But Bahzell also suspected the Prime Councilor was less than delighted with Tellian's failure to *demand* Trianal settle down and choose a wife. Or, for that matter, to select a bride *for* him. That was the way it was supposed to work among the great Sothōii houses, after all. Yet Tellian's tone made it obvious that whatever "thoughts" Hanatha might be having, he had no intention of forcing the issue any time soon, despite the near-disastrous consequences of his own... lack of marital resolution.

More than one of King Markhos' nobles blamed Tellian's soft-heartedness for the fact that Balthar had ever required an heir-adoptive. In their opinion, Tellian should never have settled for a single girl child in the first place! No one blamed Baroness Hanatha for the riding accident which had left her unable to bear additional children, but her barrenness would have constituted a perfectly acceptable cause for him to set her aside and remarry. Indeed, given who he was and how much depended upon Balthar's succession, it had been his *duty* to remarry. No one could have faulted him for it, nor would any dishonor have attached to Hanatha, under the circumstances, and two or three healthy sons would have obviated the entire mess that disgraceful hoyden Leeana had left in her wake when she scandalized the entire Kingdom by running off to the war maids.

Bahzell was reasonably confident Sir Jerhas tended to agree with those critics. He'd never said so, not in so many words, and the hradani was certain he never would. Yet there was no escaping the Prime Councilor's basic conservatism, and he would vastly have preferred for Trianal to be settled in a nice, stable, carefully arranged marriage—preferably one which constituted a solid political alliance—rather than see yet another Baron of Balthar sliding off into Tellian and Hanatha's mushy-minded romanticism. That sort of thing might make for good bard's tales, but it was also the sort of thing that gave prime councilors sleepless nights.

"Well, I'll want to discuss exactly what you and Tellian—and Prince Bahzell's father, of course—have in mind for the campaign," Yurokhas told Vaijon. "My brother's going to want a report as soon as I can put one together for him."

"Of course, Your Highness." Vaijon gave Yurokhas a polite half-bow across the table.

All of them understood that Yurokhas was the Crown's true go-between. Sir Jerhas' presence made it abundantly clear King Markhos continued to support both the Derm Canal and Tellian's increasingly close relationship with Prince Bahnak's Confederation, but Sir Jerhas was only his Prime Councilor. In a pinch—as Sir Jerhas understood perfectly well—he could be dismissed, banished back to Amber Grass in official disgrace, if it became politically expedient to do so. In fact, Bahzell suspected the old man would probably prefer to return to his own estates. Life would certainly be simpler then, and he wouldn't have to worry quite as much about whether any of Cassan's assassins might be looking *his* way, as well as Tellian's.

Yet Markhos himself could have only the slightest personal contact with Bahzell or any other hradani envoy. The delicate balance of factions and attitudes among his own nobility precluded anything closer, and probably would for years to come. It was inconvenient, but there was no point pretending it could be any other way. Yurokhas, on the other hand, was not only a wind rider—like Bahzell—and a devout, well-known follower of Tomanāk—also like Bahzell—but Tellian of Balthar's foster brother, as well. If there was a single high-ranking member of the Sothōii nobility who could afford the "contamination" of hobnobbing with Bahzell while simultaneously staying in close touch with Tellian and the King, that person was Prince Yurokhas. One or two of King Markhos' nobles might be sufficiently irate over Tellian's unforgivable actions to regard Yurokhas' ongoing relationship with him with distaste, even anger, but the prince was far too wellborn for anyone to actually *say* so. And in the meantime, everyone maintained the fiction that Yurokhas' association with Tellian—and Bahzell—had nothing at all to do with canals, Axemen, hradani kingdoms, or any of the rest of that appalling business. Nobody *believed* it for a moment, perhaps, but no one dared admit that.

"Should I assume you'll be taking the Order into the field, as well?" Yurokhas asked Vaijon now.

"I will." Vaijon's smile was crooked. "We're no longer at the point of our lads needing to keep the Baron's armsmen and Prince Bahnak's warriors from each other's throats, but Hurthang tells me we'd probably have something like a mutiny on our hands if we tried to keep them home!" He shook his head. "There are just some things you can't seem to get a hradani to do, and staying home from something like this is one of them."

"I've come to the shocking conclusion that Sothōii and hradani are even more alike than Wencit's always insisted they are," Yurokhas said wryly. "In fact—"

"No," Tellian said firmly. Yurokhas looked at him, and the baron snorted. "You are *not* invited, Yurokhas. Norandhor may mean you aren't the King's heir any longer, but if anything were to happen to *you*, it would be just as bad—probably worse!—than having something happen to Trianal. Can you *imagine* how Cassan and his lot would react if you managed to get yourself killed on the Ghoul Moor fighting alongside hradani as part of this entire plan they're opposing as a threat to the Kingdom's very existence?!"

"His Lordship is entirely correct, Your Highness," Sir Jerhas said with unwonted, decidedly frosty formality. "The very possibility is out of the question!"

Yurokhas looked back and forth between them for a moment, then shrugged.

"Well," he said mildly, "if that's the way you both feel about it, I suppose that's all there is to be said about it. Which means we should probably turn to the rest of the reason for your visit.

I assume you have a progress report on the canals and the tunnel, Tellian?"

"I do," Tellian replied, regarding the prince's apparent meekness with an air of pronounced suspicion.

"Then I suppose we should go ahead and get started on that," Yurokhas said equably, and Bahzell hid a smile. He might not yet know Yurokhas as well as Tellian did, but he'd come to know him well enough to understand the baron's skepticism perfectly.

And to profoundly doubt that the matter of where Prince Yurokhas was going to spend the summer was remotely close to resolved.

Chapter Twelve

"Lovely!" Baroness Myacha breathed, looking down at the sparkling amethyst glory displayed on the swatch of black velvet.

The cloth—and the exquisitely cut gem on it—had been arranged on the polished mahogany table in the exact center of a shaft of golden sunlight, and sun reflections danced in eyes that were almost exactly the same shade as the stone. Neither the placement of the cloth nor the choice of the gem had been anything remotely like random, and Master Talthar Sheafbearer (who bore very little resemblance to a wizard named Varnaythus) smiled broadly behind his trader's carefully bland expression as Borandas Daggeraxe, Baron Halthan, winced ever so slightly.

"It is quite a nice stone, Milady," Talthar acknowledged after a moment, "although I fear it's a bit overlarge for a lady's delicate hand."

"Oh, I quite agree," the dark-haired baroness replied. "But set into a proper pendant, in silver, perhaps, not gold, I think..."

Talthar decided to let himself meet Baron Borandas' eyes. Borandas gazed back at him for a heartbeat or so, then smiled wryly in acknowledgment of his inevitable defeat.

"Do you truly want it, my love?" he asked, and Talthar's mental ears pricked at the baron's gently teasing, undeniably tender tone.

"Yes," Myacha sighed, looking up with a slight smile. "On the other hand, I fear Master Sheafbearer has far too good a notion of his wares' worth! I have entirely too many furbelows and pretty toys to justify paying him what I have no doubt he would demand from you, Milord."

She actually sounded as if she meant it, Talthar noted, and that was interesting, too. Myacha was barely half Borandas' age. She was also his second wife, two years younger than Borandas' eldest son, Thorandas, and when their marriage had been arranged by Myacha's father three years earlier, the near-universal opinion had been that Borandas was buying himself a sweet, toothsome morsel to warm his bed and flatter his ego as he moved into his sixties. In fact, that had been Talthar's opinion until perhaps thirty or forty seconds ago.

I tend to forget sometimes how much . . . detail and nuance you can lose relying solely upon scrying spells and the gramerhain, he thought. *I should have paid more attention and not relied so heavily on Court gossip, I suppose. Of course, having to worry about that bastard Brayahs didn't make it any simpler in this case.*

His professional merchant's expression hid his inner frown as readily as it had hidden his smile, which was just as well. Thoughts of Brayahs Daggeraxe, the son of Borandas' deceased uncle, tended to have that effect upon him. Having any mage that closely related to one of the Kingdom's barons would have been bad enough, but Brayahs was considerably more strongly talented than the majority of his fellows. He was not simply a wind walker and a healer, but (if the rumors were true) had the gift of foresight, as well. And to make Talthar's unhappiness complete, he was a mind-speaker, to boot, and one who'd come to his mage powers late. That mind-speakery of his made him particularly good at sniffing out any use of wizardry in his vicinity, and the fact that he'd been a man grown before his mage talents awoke meant he'd also been trained as a knight before he became a mage. After which he'd gone on and added the martial arts training of a master mishuk to his repertoire. His weapon (and weaponless) skills would have been more than enough to make him particularly resilient to assassination attempts, and successfully ambushing any wind walker, even one without those skills, was no easy achievement at the best of times.

All of which meant that while it wouldn't necessarily be *impossible* to assassinate him, it would be extraordinarily difficult to do it in any way that didn't require the obvious use of sorcery or some other less-than-natural agency which would draw all sorts of unwanted attention. Talthar was perfectly prepared to have Brayahs murdered—indeed, he was looking forward to it—and he was more than willing to use whatever was required to make that happen, but he couldn't afford any moves in that direction at this point. The last thing he needed was to focus the attention of other magi on the North Riding before he had his hooks firmly into Borandas or his heir.

Time enough for that later, he reminded himself now. *Patience and cunning are just as important as—and more reliable than—brute power, especially at a time like this. Once all the pieces are in place he'll have to go, but let's not joggle our own elbow just because we find his continued existence inconvenient as hell.*

All of which was true enough, although "inconvenient" was a pale description of the situation. The one good thing about Brayahs' birth and ability was that King Markhos had enlisted him as one of the Crown magi who served as his investigators and agents. That made him even more dangerous, in some ways, but it also meant he'd been called to Sothōfalas for the summer session of the Great Council, which would keep him busy for at least a month or two. His talents—and his influence with his cousin—were the real reason Talthar had deferred his first visit to Halthan until he could be certain the mage would be somewhere else. And why it had taken him over six months to prepare the ground properly for this first approach at all.

"Oh, I'm certain the Baron and I could come to a reasonable agreement, Milady," he said out loud, allowing a very slight flicker of amusement into his eyes in response to Borandas' smile.

"Why do I have the feeling that your idea of 'reasonable' and my own aren't going to be precisely the same, Master Sheafbearer?" the baron responded, and Talthar permitted himself a chuckle.

"Because you, Milord Baron, are a shrewd, hardheaded bargainer, while I, alas, am an equally shrewd, clutch-fisted trader. Nonetheless, when such a fair lady is involved, it's likely—well, possible, at any rate—that even such as I may find myself giving at least a modest amount of ground."

"You, Master Sheafbearer," Baroness Myacha told him with a smile of her own, "are a very dangerous man. Milord," she looked at Borandas, "I forbid you to pay this man what this stone is truly worth."

"A shrewd blow, Milady!" Talthar congratulated her. "Not that I would ever have expected the Baron to willingly part with this gem's true worth." He sighed heavily. "Unfortunately, that state of affairs is one any master trader is unhappily accustomed to confronting." He sighed again, his expression mournful. "In order to make our way in the world at all, we become accustomed to being regularly out-bargained by our customers!"

"I trust you'll forgive me for asking you this, Master Sheafbearer," Baron Borandas said a bit tartly, "but would it happen that your mother was particularly well acquainted with Hirahim?"

"*Borandas!*" Myacha laughed and smacked him across the knuckles with her hand-painted fan.

"Actually, Milord Baron," Talthar allowed with a smile, "when I was a mere lad, my father did remark once or twice upon how little like the rest of the family I looked."

"I'm not surprised," Borandas said, then drew a deep breath. "Very well, I already know this is going to hurt. Why don't you go ahead and name your starting point. And in the meantime, my love," he looked at Myacha with a warm smile of his own, "would you be so kind as to ring for Trelsan and request beverages. And perhaps a plate of sandwiches, as well." He looked back at Talthar with a challenging glint in his blue eyes. "I believe we might be here long enough to require the sustenance before we're done."

✧ ✧ ✧

Much later that evening, Talthar Sheafbearer carefully locked the door of his bedchamber on the second floor of The Halthan Arms, the most prestigious—and expensive—inn in Borandas' capital city, behind him. It was a large, luxuriously furnished chamber, as befitted a merchant of his obvious wealth, but that wasn't the reason he looked around it for several moments with careful, intent eyes. Then he drew a deep breath and closed those eyes, reaching out with other senses and trained abilities. He extended his feelers delicately, carefully, with all the hair-trigger sensitivity of a nervous cat, searching for the aura he'd learned to associate with Brayahs Daggeraxe. Brayahs wasn't scheduled to visit his cousin for at least the next couple of weeks, but Phrobus knew schedules were subject to change, and if that accursed mage was anywhere close to Halthan...

After the better part of five minutes, Talthar drew a deep breath and opened his eyes once more, this time with an expression of satisfaction. He crossed briskly to the chamber's window and carefully closed the drapes before he set the hard-sided leather case in his right hand in the center of the table placed in front of the window. There was nothing particularly remarkable about that case—any gem-trader would have carried something very like it—and he drew a finely wrought key from where it had nestled inside his tunic on a silver chain and used it to unlock the case. He returned the key to its normal place, opened the case, and reached into it for the fist-sized lump of almost-clear quartz stowed away at its very bottom. The quartz was no more remarkable than the case itself, aside from the fact that it was an extraordinarily plebeian piece of rock for a gem merchant of Talthar's obvious wealth to carry about with him.

Except, of course, for the fact that it wasn't quartz at all.

He laid the gramerhain on the table, then closed the case and set it aside. He wasn't entirely happy about what he was going to do next, but there were limits in all things. He could have continued to hold the glamour which disguised him while using the gramerhain, but the combination of the glamour and the scrying spell he was about to use would have required him to expend considerably more energy. After all, scrying spells were intended to provide True Sight, so in many ways the two workings would be diametrically opposed to one another. Worse than the drain upon his own powers, however, that opposition would produce a far stronger, brighter signature and make him even more vulnerable to detection by any other wizard—or mage, damn it—in the vicinity. Besides, the glamour was a relatively low-energy construct tied into the diamond stud in his left ear, and artifact-bound spells were not only harder to detect but could be activated (or *re*activated) very quickly.

He knew all of that, and none of it made him any happier. Nor did it make the decision any less inevitable, unfortunately, and so he drew a deep breath, touched the stud with his index finger, and murmured a single word in Old Kontovaran.

Talthar Sheafbearer seemed to waver like a reflection in moving water. And then, between one breath and another, he vanished, replaced by Master Varnaythus.

Varnaythus exhaled, then smiled mirthlessly as he caught his slightly blurry reflection in the chamber's mirror. Talthar was no more remarkable looking than Varnaythus himself, but he *was* an inch or two taller, at least ten years older, and fair-haired where Varnaythus' hair was a nondescript brown. Neither of them would ever stand out in a crowd, but neither would either ever be mistaken for the other, which was rather the point.

He'd seriously considered creating yet another persona for his activities here in the North Riding, but he'd decided against it in the end. Cassan and Yeraghor both knew him as Talthar. While they had every reason in the world to keep "Talthar's" existence a secret, they knew what he looked like, and as Varnaythus was able to burrow deeper and deeper into the North Riding it might become important for Talthar to be able to function as a known go-between for the various conspirators he intended to put into play and keep there. Bringing in yet someone else he'd have to remember to be would only complicate things still further, and unlike some of his fellow wizards, Varnaythus had never delighted in complexity for its own sake. Nor had he ever been foolish enough to confuse mere complexity with subtlety, which was probably one of the reasons he'd been so much more successful—and longer-lived—than some of those selfsame fellow wizards.

He smiled again, more naturally, at the thought, then seated himself at the table and drew the gramerhain towards him. He cradled his hands around it, gazing down into its depths, and spoke the quiet command that woke a gradually strengthening glitter deep in its clear, flawless depths. The flicker of light grew stronger, glowing up from the table to light his face from below, throwing his eye sockets into shadow. Had the window's drapes been open and had anyone happened to glance in the inn's direction, they would have seen an improbably clear, bright brilliance flooding out into the night. Fortunately, the drapes weren't open, and so no one disturbed him as the brilliance flared up, brighter than ever, and then coalesced, settling back into the gramerhain. It flowed together, darkening steadily, until it became the closed-eyed face of Magister Malahk Sahrdohr in Sothōfalas, more than three hundred and fifty leagues from Halthan.

It took Sahrdohr almost three full minutes to become aware of him and activate his own gramerhain. Then the eyes of his image opened as he settled into the working from his own end, and he arched an eyebrow.

"I expected you two hours ago," he pointed out mildly.

"I'm aware of that." Varnaythus' tone was just a bit testy. "You may remember, however, that there are a few additional difficulties from this end?"

"True," Sahrdohr responded, apparently oblivious to his superior's testiness. "On the other hand, you only have to worry about *one* mage. A powerful one, I'll grant, but still only one. By my current count, there are at least three dozen of the bastards here in Sothōfalas... including the one *you're* worried about. Which means I'm just a little more likely to be detected by one of them than you are."

"Really?" Varnaythus smiled thinly. "Your wards are that inferior, are they?"

Sahrdohr's eyes gleamed. He was obviously pleased by his ability to get a rise out of Varnaythus, but he also bent his head in acknowledgment of the other wizard's point. His own chamber in Sothōfalas had been carefully shielded and warded with every detection-deflecting glamour the Council of Carnadosa had been able to devise. As far as they'd been able to determine—so far, at least—those glamours ought to baffle even a mage. There was no way to be certain of that, however, and putting them in place required a series of workings which had to be accomplished in a very precise order and over several days' time. There was no way Varnaythus could possibly have erected matching wards here in Halthan.

"So now that I *have* contacted you," Varnaythus continued in a brisker tone which accepted both Sahrdohr's point and his unspoken concession, "is there anything interesting to report from your end?"

"I'm not sure, really." Sahrdohr shrugged. "Bahzell and Tellian are still here; according to my sources, Bahzell, at least, will be heading back to Balthar sometime in the next two or three days. Vaijon's already left, probably to get the summer campaign into the Ghoul Moor properly underway. The only really interesting thing about that side of things"—the younger wizard smiled—"is that Yurokhas went with him."

"Ah?" Varnaythus arched an eyebrow and pursed his lips. "That *is* interesting," he acknowledged after a few moments' thought. "Are you suggesting Yurokhas is going to be involved in Tellian and Bahnak's campaign?"

"According to my sources, Yurokhas is most definitely *not* going to be involved," Sahrdohr replied. "One of Sir Jerhas' senior clerks told me—confidentially, of course—that His Majesty was very firm about that and that His Highness was very meek and dutiful about accepting the King's instructions."

"Of course he was."

Varnaythus shook his head. Prince Yurokhas was almost certainly the only person in the entire Kingdom of the Sothõii who would meekly and obediently accept his monarch's instructions . . . and then cheerfully go and do exactly what he'd intended to do all along. It wasn't something for the faint of heart, even in Yurokhas' case, but by now he'd had years of practice. More than enough of them to accustom King Markhos to the notion that it was going to go on happening. In fact, it had gotten even worse since Crown Prince Norandhor's birth four years ago, when Yurokhas had suddenly become *second* in line for the crown. He'd always chafed against the restrictions imposed by his place as Markhos' heir, and now that he'd become so much less irreplaceable . . .

"That could work out quite well, couldn't it?" Varnaythus continued. "Assuming that campaign goes as well as I'm sure we all hope it will, at any rate."

"That's true. Such a tragic possibility for any good, loyal Sothõii." Sahrdohr allowed himself a suitably mournful expression for a moment, then shrugged. "Of course, we still have a long way to go before we can convince Cassan to take advantage of the opportunity at his end, and unless we can move against both of them simultaneously—"

He grimaced, and Varnaythus nodded. Eliminating *one* of the royal brothers would be a less than optimal outcome. In fact, it might well prove disastrous, depending upon the circumstances under which that elimination occurred.

"That's a worthwhile point," he acknowledged, "but if this was going to be easy, They wouldn't have needed us, would they? They could have gone on trusting it to idiots like Jerghar or Dahlaha."

"Agreed."

"I take it the numbers Tellian provided to Shaftmaster confirmed what we'd expected?" Varnaythus asked, changing the subject.

"Unfortunately." There was no amusement in Sahrdohr's grimace this time. "I'm not senior enough to have sat in on any of the meetings myself, but I was able to get my hands on a true copy of Sir Whalandys' notes courtesy of my capture spell. I'll transfer a copy to you at the end of our conversation, but I don't think you'll be any happier with them than I was. Assuming Kilthandahknarthas' estimates are accurate—and when was the last time one of his estimates *wasn't* accurate?—Tellian Bowmaster is about to become the richest Sothõii noble in history. Phrobus only knows how much Bahnak is going to make out of it, but the Exchequer's share of Tellian's income alone is going to add somewhere between ten and twelve percent to its annual revenues. And that's from its *direct* share of his income; it doesn't even count all of the indirect revenues the Crown is going to generate off of the increased trade."

Varnaythus' jaw clenched. He'd known the numbers were going to be bad, but he'd continued to hope they wouldn't be quite that bad. Unfortunately, the wizard lords of Carnadosa weren't very good when it came to estimating trade revenues and opportunities. The economy they'd rebuilt in Kontovar depended upon totally different means of manufacture and transport, and the truth was that he'd been slow to fully recognize the implications of the Derm Canal. As it was, he'd come to suspect Kilthandahknarthas was being deliberately *conservative* in the estimates he was sharing with his partners in the project, which suggested all sorts of unpleasant possibilities if it couldn't be stopped after all. On the other hand...

"The Purple Lords aren't going to like that at all, are they?" he said thoughtfully.

"I think that would be putting it rather conservatively, actually." Sahrdohr's irony came through the link quite well, Varnaythus thought. "This is going to literally ruin at least a dozen of their major trading houses. In fact, it's probably going to be a lot worse than that, especially if the Spearmen come on board with Kilthandahknarthas and Tellian as enthusiastically as I expect they will. If Bortalik Bay suddenly isn't the only—or even the best—gateway to the Spear, the consequences will be devastating for them."

"Yes, and they'll resent it, won't they?" Varnaythus' eyes gleamed. "And while they're resenting it, who are they going to *blame* for it?"

"Ah?" It was Sahrdohr's turn to pause, eyebrows rising in speculation. He sat that way for perhaps fifteen seconds, then nodded. "Yes, that *would* have unfortunate repercussions for any sense of loyalty they might feel for their neighbors to the north, wouldn't it?"

"Which might make them more open to conversations with their neighbors to the *south*, don't you think?" Varnaythus almost purred.

"I suspect it might," Sahrdohr agreed. "Of course, that doesn't change our instructions, does it?"

"No, but it might not be a bad point for me to include in my next report."

The two wizards' gazes met in shared understanding. There was very little chance they would be ordered to cease their efforts to strangle the entire project before birth, but it never hurt to have a fallback position ready. Pointing out the potential benefits—especially when that potential was as large as it might well prove in this instance—which could still accrue if they failed in their mission could well contribute to their own continued existence if worse came to worst.

"I think that would be a very good idea," Sahrdohr said, and Varnaythus snorted in amusement.

"And may I ask how your mission in Halthan is faring so far?" the magister asked after a moment.

"Reasonably well," Varnaythus replied. "I think we need to look more closely at Baroness Myacha, though. She's not the bedchamber trophy we thought she was. Worse, I think she has a brain that works, and she seems to be unfortunately... resilient."

"Another one with a latent Gift?"

"Possibly. Quite possibly." Varnaythus shrugged. "We'll have to see what we can do about tracking back on her pedigree, but I wouldn't be a bit surprised if she has at least a touch of it. It runs in too damned many of the old families to make me happy."

"You think she has the True Sight?" Sahrdohr's unhappiness with that thought was obvious.

"If she does, it's completely untrained, and without training, the worst likely outcome would be for her to be vaguely uncomfortable around me without being able to put her finger on why. I didn't see any sign of that this afternoon, although that doesn't prove anything." Varnaythus grimaced. "I'll just have to add her to the list of people in this accursed barony that I need to avoid as much as possible. It would help if Borandas weren't as besotted with her as he obviously is, though."

"Wonderful." Sahrdohr shook his head with a disgusted expression.

"Oh, it's not *that* bad. Potentially inconvenient, I agree, but as I say, I'm not that concerned about her realizing Talthar is a glamour."

"No, but what if she should find herself feeling 'vaguely uncomfortable' around him and happen to discuss that with her husband's cousin the mage?" Sahrdohr challenged. "And what if her husband's cousin the mage has already figured out she could have a touch of the Gift herself?"

"Which is the reason I'm going to do my best to avoid her," Varnaythus pointed out in an oblique acknowledgment of the magister's point.

The magi had made it a matter of high priority to collect every scrap of information they could on the art, and that unmitigated pain in the arse Wencit of Rūm had made it an equally high priority to answer their questions and hand over the not inconsiderable personal library he'd managed to salvage from the wreckage of Kontovar. As a result, they were far better informed about wizardry than their Carnadosan opponents were about the powers of magi, which meant Master Brayahs was probably as conversant with the symptoms of a latent Gift for the art as Varnaythus himself.

"In the meantime," he went on in a determinedly brisk tone, "the rest of my visit here seems to have gone quite well. It's remarkable how gems of high quality open doors, isn't it?"

Sahrdohr snorted. Given the possibilities of the art, "Talthar's" wares could have been still better, but it was unwise to draw too much attention. His stones were of just about the highest quality anyone could reasonably expect a single trader outside Dwarvenhame to possess; anything more than that might well have drawn the very questions they were so eager to avoid.

"And our friend Bronzehelm? Is he as . . . suitable as we'd hoped?"

"I believe so." Varnaythus leaned back in his chair, steepling his fingers under his chin. "He's more devoted and loyal to Borandas than we'd estimated—quite a bit more, to be honest. But he's nowhere near so resilient as Baroness Myacha seems to be. I think we're going to have to be as careful to avoid using the art to . . . shape him appropriately as I was afraid we were, but I also think he's going to be even more amenable to suggestion with the appropriate enhancements."

Sahrdohr's smile would have done credit to a shark, and Varnaythus smiled back. Sir Dahlnar Bronzehelm was Baron Borandas' seneschal, responsible for the management and administration of the baron's household here in Halthan. He was also one of Borandas' closest confidants, and he'd been with the baron for the better part of thirty years. Very few people could be better placed to subtly shape Borandas' views, which didn't even consider how valuable a listening post within the North Riding he could become. It would have been far more convenient if they'd been able to use the art to . . . modify his existing loyalties and views, but there was too much chance of a mage noticing that sort of tampering. Especially if the mage in question was so inconsiderate as to be both a healer and a mind-speaker. Fortunately, there were drugs which could produce the same effect, albeit more slowly and gradually. Even better, that slow and gradual process was virtually indistinguishable from the fashion in which anyone's opinions might naturally come to change over time. There was some risk, of course—nothing could completely avoid that when one was was forced to deal with a mage—yet the probability that even as strongly gifted a mage as Brayahs would notice their meddling would be far, far lower than the chance of his detecting the art.

"And Thorandas?" Sahrdohr asked.

"I haven't had an opportunity to come within reach of him yet," Varnaythus admitted. "Hopefully I'll manage that before 'Talthar' is scheduled to leave. In the meantime, though, judging from what I've been able to pick up about him from the more open minds here in Halthan, I'd say our original impressions are probably fairly accurate. Borandas clearly relies heavily on his advice—that was obvious from the way his aura peaked each time I mentioned Thorandas' name. I think it's safe to say he trusts his son's judgment in most ways, if not all."

"That fits pretty well with everything I've heard about them here in the Palace," Sahrdohr agreed. "And I had an opportunity to drop his name into a conversation with Shaftmaster day before yesterday, which led to a couple of interesting tidbits. For one thing, Sir Whalandys made it pretty clear that most people think Thorandas is a sharper blade than his father... and that Baron Borandas realizes it."

"Really?" Varnaythus cocked his head thoughtfully. "That's helpful, especially if Cassan's right about Thorandas' attitude towards the hradani. He has to be as well aware as his father that at the moment the North Riding holds the balance between Tellian and Cassan on the Great Council. The question is how he's likely to react when he realizes just how thoroughly this Derm Canal is going to scramble all of the traditional balances of power here on the Wind Plain. If he's as prejudiced against the hradani as Cassan and Yeraghor think, that's bound to play a role in his evaluation of the new... realities, shall we say? And *that's* going to have an effect on the advice he gives his father about it, now isn't it?"

"Exactly." Sahrdohr's smile was even thinner than before. "And if Sir Dahlnar starts giving the same advice?"

"Especially if he comes slowly and gradually to share Thorandas' concerns, yes." Varnaythus nodded. "Not too quickly, though. Borandas may not be the very smartest man in the entire Kingdom, but he's not exactly a fool, either. He's going to think twice—more likely three or four times—before he steps into any sort of arrangement with Cassan. For that matter, Thorandas isn't going to be in any hurry to forget how badly Cassan burned his fingers last time he and Tellian squared off."

"No, but I've had a thought about that."

"What sort of thought?" Varnaythus' tone was a bit cautious, and Sahrdohr chuckled.

"It's not *that* inventive," the magister assured his superior. "But that's the second interesting tidbit I got from our good Chancellor. According to Shaftmaster, Thorandas is in the market for a wife. In fact, Sir Whalandys approves of that; he thinks it's past time Thorandas settled down and started breeding heirs of his own. Unfortunately—from my esteemed superior's perspective, at any rate—Sir Thorandas seems rather taken with Shairnayith Axehammer."

"He does?" Varnaythus' eyes narrowed, and Sahrdohr leaned back and raised both hands.

"That's what Shaftmaster seems to believe, at any rate, and he's not very happy about the notion."

"I can see why he might not be, given how enthusiastically he's been supporting Tellian at Court," Varnaythus observed in a tone of considerable understatement. Then he frowned. "I can see why he might not be," he repeated, "but I didn't pick up a hint of anything of the sort from Cassan the last time I was in Toramos."

"Maybe he isn't aware of Thorandas' thinking," Sahrdohr suggested.

"*Cassan?*" Varnaythus barked a laugh. "Trust me, if Shaftmaster's right and Thorandas really is looking in Shairnayith's direction, Cassan knows about it, all right. He'd never miss something like that, especially where Shairnayith is concerned! In fact," his eyes narrowed again, "that could be the problem. He dotes on the girl, after all, and it could be that he's perfectly aware of the opportunity and simply chooses to ignore it. If he'd been in any rush to marry her off, they could have managed it long ago, I'm sure. There have to have been plenty of other offers for her by now, at any rate. She's—what, twenty-two?—for Carnadosa's sake! Do you seriously think nobody's even so much as tested the water where a prize like her is concerned?"

"Maybe there've been quite a few offers and he simply hasn't thought any of them were worth accepting," Sahrdohr pointed out. "She's his older daughter, after all. As you say, that makes her the kind of prize that doesn't come along often. That's a political token a man like Cassan isn't going to be in a hurry to use too soon!"

"That's true enough," Varnaythus acknowledged. "But she's a deep one herself, and the Lady knows she worships the ground her father walks on. The possibility of a direct marriage alliance between the Axehammers and the Daggeraxes?" The wizard snorted. "She'd have to recognize the potential advantages Cassan could wring out of that! And short of Yurokhas himself—and Fiendark knows Yurokhas would *never* marry an Axehammer—where's she going to find a better marriage than to the North Riding's heir?"

"Agreed. On the other hand, the consequences would be fairly obvious to just about everyone," Sahrdohr pointed out, "and the Great Council would have to approve the marriage."

"If Borandas approved it, he, Cassan, and Yeraghor between them would have a clear majority."

"And would Markhos be foolish enough to let it go through, anyway?" Sahrdohr challenged. "*He'd* have to assent, too."

"If he were around to do the assenting," Varnaythus pointed out in turn, his voice soft. "If he wasn't—if the Great Council happened to be acting as regent to a minor heir—then that wouldn't matter, would it?"

"No," the magister said slowly.

"So if Cassan and Yeraghor were to decide this marriage would be a good idea, and if Thorandas is as receptive to the notion as your good friend the Chancellor seems to be suggesting, then we might just have found another argument to help sway Cassan to our thinking about the best way to deal with the Crown's unfortunate support for Tellian's little project, mightn't we?"

The two wizards gazed at each other through their linked gramerhains and slowly, slowly smiled.

Chapter Thirteen

The membership of the council of war no longer struck its participants as bizarre, although there *were* moments when any one of them was likely to feel as if he'd fallen into some sort of fever dream. On the other hand, those moments were no longer as common as they had been, and they were becoming steadily less frequent.

Not that anyone expected they were ever going to disappear entirely.

"Well, I suppose we should get started," Sir Vaijon Almerhas said, looking around the spacious wooden table.

That table sat in one of the stout stone buildings which had blossomed along the new, Axeman-style high road between the Escarpment and the equally new Lake Hurgrum over the past few years. They were obviously of dwarvish design and construction, their stones laid without mortar yet cut so precisely it would have required a sledgehammer to drive a knife blade into any single joint. One of the by-products of enjoying the services of Silver Cavern's strongest sarthnaisks, Vaijon reflected, was that Chanharsa could turn (and *had* turned) several thousand cubic yards of rock into perfectly uniform, impossibly precisely "cut" stone blocks without so much as turning a hair. Driving the tunnel clear up through the Escarpment had provided them with what was literally a small mountain of building material, and hradani and dwarvish work crews had made good use of it.

These buildings had been constructed specifically to serve as the central military base for the Ghoul Moor campaigns, however, which meant they had very lofty ceilings for any dwarvish designed structure. Sothōii tended to be tall, and Vaijon was taller even than most of them, but even he tended to feel a bit undersized when he looked up at the meeting chamber's twelve-foot ceilings and nine-foot doorframes. Rooms sized for Horse Stealer hradani had that effect on most people. Of course, *heating* them could be a tad difficult, especially in a north Norfressan winter, as Vaijon had discovered over the past several years. Fortunately, the dwarves who'd designed these buildings had pronounced opinions on things like comfortable winter temperatures and they'd built heating ducts into the concrete foundations when they poured them. In fact, they'd gone even further and used some of the water power tapped from the lake to drive fans that circulated heated air through ceiling ducts, as well.

Which was one reason he had Sermandahknarthas building the Order of Tomanāk its own properly spacious—and comfortably heated—hall back in Hurgrum, as well. With luck, they'd have it finished before first snowfall and he'd finally spend a winter in Hurgrum without icicles hanging from the tip of his nose.

At the moment, however, brilliant sunlight spilled down from a sky like polished lapis lazuli, dancing on the enormous lake's sapphire water, and the chamber's windows were open to admit a cooling breeze. Distant shouts drifted in with the breeze as construction crews continued their unending labors, and he could hear a leather-lunged hradani sergeant counting cadence from the drill square beside the nearest block of barracks. Bhanak Karathson's Hurgrumese had learned the value of discipline, training, and drill and used it well. Now they were teaching it to the rest of the Northern Hradani, and if the new Confederate Army remained short of the smooth, polished perfection of the Royal and Imperial Army's demonstration drill teams, Vaijon would have been perfectly willing to match its battalions against any regular Axeman field force. They were certainly better than any *non*-Axeman infantry he'd ever seen, and he found that a very comforting thought just at the moment.

Although he was the second youngest person present, Vaijon was, by common consent, the council's moderator. In no small part, that was because his background was probably the closest of that of any of its members' to something approaching true neutrality. An Axeman by birth, he came from outside the millennium-long hatred and mutual bloodletting of Sothōii and hradani, and as a champion of Tomanāk by training and choice, he served the Judge of Princes. As such, he and the members of his chapter of the Order of Tomanāk were sworn to strict neutrality in any confrontation between princes or kingdoms so long as the God of War's code was not transgressed.

More than that, he commanded the one force which could tell any of the proposed expedition's other commanders they had no authority over it. And while the Hurgrum Chapter of the Order was going to provide the smallest single component of the campaign's field force, it was also the most disciplined and highly trained. For the last couple of campaigns, it had been used as often as not as what Prince Bahnak had referred to as the expeditionary forces' "fire brigade," and no one in his right mind would care to get on its bad side. That reflection brought Vaijon a sense of satisfaction he occasionally found a bit difficult to prevent from sliding over into complacent pride, and as he considered the other senior officers gathered about the table, he reminded himself (in a mental voice which sounded remarkably like Bahzell Bahnakson's) to not get too full of himself. All of those other officers were at least as experienced as he was, at least where campaigns and battlefield maneuvers were concerned, and there were some dauntingly powerful personalities seated around that table. Some fairly prickly ones, for that matter... which was one reason he had no intention of mentioning that another reason Prince Bahnak and Baron Tellian had selected him for this particular assignment was that he'd developed something of a talent for herding cats over the last few years.

Hurthang Marahgson, Bahzell's fourth cousin and the senior member of the Hurgrum Chapter, sat directly across from Vaijon. Hurthang stood "only" two inches over seven feet, but he was quite possibly even stronger than Bahzell. And while the symbols of Tomanāk might be a crossed mace and sword, Hurthang disdained such puny weapons in favor of the great, two-handed daggered axe from which Clan Iron Axe took its name. Of course, he normally wielded it *one*-handed, which Vaijon found just a bit flamboyant even for a Horse Stealer. At the moment, however, Hurthang looked a little uncomfortable (although only someone who knew him as well as Vaijon did was likely to notice it) in his resplendently embroidered, finely woven green surcoat. By choice, Hurthang preferred attire as practical and plain as his cousin Bahzell's, but his wife Farmah had spent much of the winter working on that surcoat for this very meeting, and a warrior who could have—and had—glared unawed into the very teeth of death had been powerless to resist the calm insistence of the mother of his child.

General Yurgazh Charkson sat to Hurthang's right, and his expression and body language were a bit on the stiff side, Vaijon judged. Hopefully, that stiffness was only temporary, and Vaijon suspected it had more to do with the unanticipated nature of his elevation than to anything else. Yurgazh had worked well as one of Prince Barodahn's subordinate commanders the previous year, and he was a known quantity to everyone else seated around the table. Still, of all those present he was the closest to a "self-made man," a former free-sword mercenary who'd fought his way to his present rank and position through sheer guts, ability, determination, and—even in Churnazh of Navahk's service—integrity. The remarkable thing, really, wasn't that he'd won the trust of his former adversaries following Navahk's surrender, but that he'd survived under Churnazh.

Prince Arsham Churnazhson, seated beside Yurgazh, looked like a man who wasn't entirely happy to be there. On the other hand, he didn't look like someone who was *un*happy to be there, either. There were greater depths to Arsham than Vaijon had anticipated before Navahk's defeat, and while it seemed evident that defeat still stung, Navahk's new prince was a practical man. And a prudent one, which was the only reason he'd survived Prince Churnazh's reign. Certainly his paternity didn't explain that survival, at any rate!

Arsham was still referred to by his own people as "the Bastard," but however odd it might have seemed to an Axeman, the appellation had always been a title of respect in Navahk. A title, indeed, which specifically separated him from his father's reputation for tyranny . . . and one which could only have made Churnazh even more suspicious of him.

Among hradani, more than any of the other Races of Man, rape was an unforgivable crime. Hradani women, with their immunity to the Rage, had provided most of what little stability and order hradani society had managed to cling to for too many centuries for that particular outrage to be tolerated. Those in a position of power might get away with it—for a time—but no known rapist could ever hope to command the true loyalty of any hradani city-state or clan. Yet also among hradani, unlike too few of the other Races of Man, rape imposed no stigma upon its victim... or upon any child born of it. For that matter, children in general were unspeakably precious to hradani, with their low fertility rates, and they were often too busy rejoicing in any child's birth to worry over minor details like establishing its precise paternity. So while there was enormous shame in Churnazh's rape of Arsham's mother, there was no shame in Arsham's birth, and the fact that his mother descended in a collateral branch from the previous ruling family of Navahk gave him a claim to the throne in the eyes of his subjects which neither his late, unlamented father nor his fortunately deceased half-brothers could ever have enjoyed.

Of course, that same claim had been one of the reasons Arsham had been very, very careful never to dabble in politics during his father's lifetime. He'd spent his time with the army, instead, which had posed potential problems of its own, given how Churnazh himself had used the army to slaughter his way to power. That was one reason Arsham had always preferred field commands which kept him well away from Navahk, and his father had been perfectly happy to keep him there. He'd still managed to become dangerously popular with his troops, yet he'd also made it abundantly clear—to his father, at least; his half brothers had been less inclined to believe it—that he had absolutely no interest in the throne of Navahk. The fact that he'd been Churnazh's best field commander had probably helped his father's willingness to let him keep his head, Vaijon thought. And then there'd been the minor fact that his mother and his legitimately born older sister had been comfortably housed in Navahk... where they stood hostage for his good conduct, not to mention dissuading him from seeking vengeance upon his mother's rapist. That was something Churnazh had carefully never discussed with him openly, but Arsham had never been a fool, and it wasn't as if Churnazh hadn't made examples of far too many of his enemies' families in the course of his reign.

Now Arsham found himself upon that throne he'd never sought, after all, with his mother restored to a place of honor in Navahk, and that could never have happened without Navahk's defeat. More, he sat upon the throne of a Navahk more prosperous than it had ever dreamed of being, as a member of the Council of Princes Bahnak of Hurgrum had created as what was effectively the Royal Council of the Northern Confederation. He was far too intelligent to believe for a moment that he could ever have risen to such a position under other circumstances. Besides, unlike his father, Arsham's word meant something, and he'd sworn fealty to Bahnak and the great charter Bahnak had drawn up for the Confederation. Whether it rankled or not, that was the end of the matter as far as his loyalty was concerned; if anyone could be confident of that, a champion of Tomanāk was that anyone.

Sir Trianal Bowmaster sat to Hurthang's left. Trianal was the only person at that table younger than Vaijon, yet he sat back comfortably, his expression and his body language equally relaxed among the presence of those who had once been his sworn enemies. He still hadn't overcome quite all the attitudes his conservative mother had instilled in him as a child, but Tellian had been stretching his heir's thought processes for the better part of ten years now, and it was starting to show. The thought amused Vaijon, particularly given the way his own thought processes had required a little "stretching" once upon a time. And how much more . . . vigorously that stretching had been achieved, for that matter.

Sir Yarran Battlecrow sat at Trianal's elbow. A grizzled, competent warrior who was now well into middle age (or possibly even a little further than that, although Vaijon wasn't going to be foolish enough to suggest anything of the sort where he might hear of it), Yarran had been "loaned" to the expedition at Trianal's request by Sir Festian Wrathson, Lord Warden of Glanharrow. The commander of Lord Festian's scouts, Sir Yarran would perform the same function for Trianal, and the comfortable, confident relationship between him and his youthful overlord was easy to see.

Gorsandahknarthas zoi'Felahkandarnas sat beside Sir Yarran, in a chair which was considerably higher than that of anyone else seated around the table. Gorsan wasn't there as a member of the war council per se, but as the supervisor of the entire Derm Canal project, his interest in the summer campaign was obvious, and he had a better grasp than anyone else present of how well—and how readily—their troops could be kept in supply. The tall (for an Axeman, at any rate), black-haired human in well-worn mail seated beside Gorsan, on the other hand, *was* a member of the war council in good standing. Rianthus of Sindor was normally the commander of Kilthandahknarthas' personal security force, but this summer the ex-major in the Royal and Imperial Mounted Infantry had been detailed to command the relatively small force of Dwarvenhame infantry which would provide close security for the dwarvish combat engineers who'd been attached to the field force.

And then, finally, between Rianthus and Vaijon, there was the fellow who most definitely was *not* a member of the council of war, although no one was likely to mention that to him. Exactly how Tellian—or, for that matter, King Markhos—expected even a champion of Tomanāk to keep Prince Yurokhas out of the inevitable fighting was more than Vaijon was prepared to guess. He intended to do his best, but it wasn't going to be a simple little task like, oh, slaying a demon or two.

His lips twitched at the thought, and he gave himself a mental shake as all those other eyes looked back at him.

"I thought we might begin," he said, "by considering our logistics for the summer."

Yurgazh looked a little wary in the wake of that comment, but he wasn't entirely alone in that. In fact, his weren't even the wariest eyes present. Pre-Confederation Bloody Sword concepts of military logistics had been rudimentary, at best, yet Vaijon had come to the conclusion that they'd still been better developed than those of the their neighbors atop the Wind Plain. Sothōii who'd served with Axeman armies, like Sir Kelthys Lancebearer, another of Tellian's cousins, tended to have a sounder appreciation than their fellows for the importance of forethought and organization when it came to supplying troops in the field, but even they were inclined to leave such matters up to their Axeman allies. For the most part, however, Sothōii armies were far more likely to improvise as they went along, with occasionally disastrous consequences. Fortunately, that was beginning to change—for this lot of Sothōii, at any rate—in the wake of the last couple of years' campaigns. They'd discovered that keeping their troops well fed, well armed, and well supplied with fodder was a significant force multiplier, but they still had the look of someone expected to converse in a foreign language (and dreading it).

I wonder if they think there's going to be a quiz after the meeting? Vaijon thought sardonically, reflecting on how Sir Charrow, his own mentor in Belhadan, would have done just that to *him*. Then he scolded himself. Of course Sir Charrow would have! He was, after all, a knight of the Order of Tomanāk, and the Order believed in training its members thoroughly, which meant he'd been given the opportunity for a much sounder grounding in such matters than any of these officers—with the possible exception of Rianthus—ever could have gotten in the normal order of things.

And you even paid attention to those *lessons, didn't you, Vaijon?* he reflected.

"Gorsan?" he invited out loud, and the engineer shrugged.

"I'm sure Rianthus actually has a better appreciation of the nuts and bolts than I do," the dwarf said, "but I can say the canal head is almost thirty leagues further east than it was at this point last year. That's going to shorten how far we'll have to haul supplies by wagon between Derm and the Hangnysti by ninety miles or so, and Prince Bahnak spent the winter building more barges here at Hurgrum. We'll have almost twice the cargo capacity we had last year once we do get those supplies to the Hangnysti to barge them down to you. And that other project we discussed a few months ago"—he looked around the table—"is looking a lot more practical than I really thought it would."

Several of the others stirred slightly, eyebrows rising in expressions which ran the gamut from satisfaction to skepticism. Prince Yurokhas' expression was firmly at the skeptical end of the spectrum, and Vaijon hid a smile as he saw it. For all the prince's enthusiasm for the Derm Canal, he continued to cherish strong reservations about the practicality of Bahzell's latest brainstorm. Not that Vaijon was even tempted to fault Yurokhas for his doubts, for the prince had never visited Dwarvenhame as Bahzell (and Vaijon, for that matter) had. As such, he had no real concept of the sheer tonnage of high-quality steel, not simply iron, Dwarvenhame's water-powered blast furnaces and "convertors" could produce. Nor had he ever seen heavy wagonloads of ore, coal, limestone, coke, or manufactured goods moving along ribbons of steel rails. Given the far more limited—and vastly more expensive—quantities of iron Baron Yeraghor's East Riding foundries and smithies produced, it was no wonder Yurokhas continued to consider the notion that anyone could possibly produce enough *steel* to lay a track of rails literally dozens of miles long across the terrain between the canal head and the Hangnysti more than a little ridiculous. And even assuming that was possible, no one accustomed to the Kingdom's atrocious roads could be expected to grasp how much more efficient draft animals became when they hauled their loads along smooth steel rails instead of lurching laboriously from one mudhole to the next.

Which is fair enough, Vaijon reflected. *The* dwarves *hadn't really considered the possibility of using rails anywhere except inside their mountains until Bahzell suggested it to them.* He snorted silently in amusement. *I guess it took someone who was too ignorant of all the reasons it wouldn't work to come up with the idea in the first place! And I wonder what kind of effect it's going to have on the entire Empire by the time Kilthan and the others are done with it?*

That was actually, he realized, a very good question. Even Axeman roads often left a bit to be desired, especially in winter weather or heavy rain. Dwarvenhame freight wagons were far better sprung and more efficient than anyone else's, yet according to Kilthan's experts, a draft team could pull twice or even as much as three times the load in one of the "rail carts" than the same team could manage in even a dwarven wagon. That was why they used them to move the massive loads their foundries required, after all. So if Dwarvenhame truly did begin extending "rail ways"—or would they end up calling them "rail roads," instead, Vaijon wondered?—alongside the existing Axeman high roads, what effect was that going to have on the Empire's internal economy?

"According to my latest messages from Silver Cavern, the first shipments of rails should be arriving at the canal head in a few more days," Gorsan continued, "We've already surveyed the route, and I've had work gangs grading the worst stretches for the last couple of weeks." He grimaced. "I can't say I'm happy about having to divert work crews from the canal, but Prince Bahnak's promised us additional manpower to make up for it, and I expect we can have the tracks down by, oh, the end of next month or the middle of the month after. Once we do, and coupled with the extra river barges, we'll be able to keep your forces supplied a lot more easily, without the bottlenecks we had last year. And"—this time his grimace segued into a grin—"it'll be a lot less expensive than it was last year, too!"

"Well, Uncle Tellian will certainly be in favor of both of those," Trianal remarked with an answering smile. Then his expression became more thoughtful. "On the other hand, I can't help wondering. If this 'rail way' is going to be as efficient as it sounds like it is, are we wasting unnecessary effort building the canal in the first place?"

"Oh, no, Milord!" Gorsan shook his head emphatically. "Draft teams can pull much heavier loads along rails, that's true, but there's really no comparison between how much freight we can can haul overland and how much we can manage using barges. A single barge can carry as much as three or four hundred tons of cargo at a time, and that's a lot more than you could put into any rail cart! This is going to allow us to move larger quantities of supplies much more rapidly for your army, and it may well help a lot—on a smaller scale, at least—in places where even canals simply aren't practical, but it's nowhere close to being a substitute for *this* canal. Not with the amounts of freight we're talking about moving once everything is finished and running properly."

"I see." Trianal nodded.

His voice was both satisfied and courteous, yet Vaijon's mental ears pricked as something about the younger man's tone registered. Then, as he glanced at the expressions of the others seated around the table, he felt an ungrudging sense of respect.

He didn't ask that for himself. *He asked it for the* others, *to make sure no one else was going to start questioning exactly why we're about to go out and get altogether too many of our people hurt or even killed this summer. I wonder if that was Tellian's idea or he came up with it on his own? A year ago I'd've bet it was Tellian's, but now...*

"And the new arbalests?" he inquired out loud, turning his attention to Rianthus after giving Trianal the very slightest of approving nods.

"They should be arriving along with the first shipment of rails," Rianthus answered. "And Kilthan tells me they're considering a version for merely human archers, as well," he added with a wry smile.

A chorus of chuckles greeted that remark, and they were actually louder from the Sothōii side of the table than from the hradani side, Vaijon noted. That was good, although he rather doubted the Sothōii in general were going to be quite as cheerful about the new weapons as "his" Sothōii were. Given how much of the Sothōii cavalry's invincibility depended upon the deadly accuracy and speed of their mounted archers, it would have been unreasonable to expect them to happily greet the notion of infantry missile troops whose weapons were not only longer ranged and harder hitting than their own bows but fired far more rapidly than anyone else's crossbows—even *medium* crossbows, far less arbalests—possibly could, to boot.

The very idea was going to deeply offend the more hidebound of the Sothōii traditionalists (and right offhand, Vaijon couldn't think of anyone who could possibly be more hidebound than a Sothōii traditionalist), and the thought that those weapons were going to be in the hands of *hradani* was only going to make it worse. Of course, if they'd been paying attention for the last, oh, twenty years or so, they would have realized Prince Bahnak's Horse Stealers were already fielding heavy crossbowmen with preposterous rates of fire. But the new arbalests Silver Cavern had designed expressly for Bahnak (and for which they had charged him a pretty copper, Vaijon knew) had heavier pulls than even a Horse Stealer's arm could span with a simple goat's foot. Their built-in integral cocking levers were geared and cammed to provide their users with a heavy mechanical advantage, which allowed for a pull many times as powerful as any bow's could possibly be. Not to mention the fact that once spanned, an arbalest could be held that way far longer than any archer could hold a fully drawn bow, which gave the crossbowman time to aim carefully. Indeed, one of Kilthan's artisans had actually figured out how to fit them with sights for even greater accuracy.

They were big enough (and heavy enough) to constitute two-man weapons for anyone but a hradani, and they still couldn't match a horse archer's rate of fire. A trained Sothōii could fire as many as fifteen aimed shafts in a minute, whereas even a Horse Stealer with one of the new arbalests could manage no more than six. But hradani crossbowmen were *foot* archers, and trained marksmen firing from their own feet were always going to be more accurate than even the most highly skilled mounted archer firing from the back of a moving horse.

On the other hand, human crossbowmen aren't going to be able to handle the weight of pull our *lads can, even with the new design,* Vaijon thought cheerfully. *There* is *a limit to how much mechanical advantage you can give any cocking lever if you're going to span the thing with a single pull! I doubt any of Trianal's fellows are going to complain about having that kind of fire support against the ghouls, though.*

"Actually," Rianthus continued with a sly smile, "one of Kilthan's bright young engineers claims to have come up with a still better idea. He thinks he may be able to design an arbalest that can be loaded with more than one quarrel at a time."

"Of course he can!" Trianal snorted. "No doubt they'll be able to fire five or six with each shot!"

"Oh, no!" Rianthus looked at him with becoming solemnity. "That would be *wasteful*, Milord! What they're talking about is just an arrangement that would automatically put another quarrel onto the string every time the arbalest is spanned without the archer having to individually load it."

"Ah, that's *much* better!"

Trianal rolled his eyes, and Sir Yarran smiled under his mustache and shook his head. Vaijon chuckled as well, although given what he'd seen out of the dwarves, he was less confident than the Sothōii that Rianthus was simply pulling their legs.

"Even without the new, magical, multishot arbalest," he said dryly, "I think the ghouls are going to be exceedingly unhappy when they run into several hundred quarrels at a time."

"That they will, Sir Vaijon," Sir Yarran said with undisguised satisfaction. Unlike the other Sothōii sitting around the table, he'd personally experienced Horse Stealer arbalests from the receiving end, and he hadn't enjoyed it a bit. The others lacked that particular target's-eye insight, but he and Trianal had both seen it from the firing side in the previous campaigns into the Ghoul Moor. "And I hope no one will take this wrongly, but it occurs to me that there's no one in this whole wide world I'd sooner see unhappy."

"Oh, I don't think anyone's going to argue with you about that, Sir Yarran," Yurgazh said. He and Yarran had met for the first time less than a week earlier, yet it was obvious they were kindred spirits in many ways. Now, as he smiled nastily at the Sothōii scout, much of his earlier stiffness vanished. "Myself, I was born and raised in Tralth." His smile remained, but his eyes turned much grimmer. "We had more experience than I like to remember with ghouls—aye, and trolls, come to that—spilling across our frontier." He shook his head. "There's more than a few Bloody Swords who think burning the entire Ghoul Moor to the ground is a wonderful idea, canal routes or no canal routes!"

"I think we can all agree with that, General," Prince Yurokhas said. Yurgazh looked at him, and the prince shrugged. "We may have the river between us and the Ghoul Moor proper, but we've lost more horses and cattle—and children—to them than any of *us* like to remember, either." He shook his head, his expression as grim as Yurgazh's eyes. "I don't think there's a single Sothōii, however... ambivalent he may be about your Confederation, who won't lift a mug in Hurgrum's direction the day the last ghoul's head goes up on a pike somewhere."

"Aye?" Prince Arsham's deep voice was rough-edged, even a little rasping, from too many orders on too many battlefields. He gazed at the brother of the Sothōii king for several thoughtful seconds, then smiled slowly. "Good," he said. "To speak honestly, Your Highness, there are times I'm less confident than Prince Bahnak about how all of this is likely to work out in the end, but it's good to know there's at least *one* thing we can all agree to."

"There are those on top of the Wind Plain who undoubtedly cherish even more doubts than you do, Your Highness." There wasn't a trace of irony in Yurokhas' voice as he returned the honorific to Arsham. "And that doesn't even consider the ones who're actively opposed to everything your people and Baron Tellian are trying to accomplish here."

He looked around the council table at the faces which had suddenly smoothed of all expression at the waters they'd unexpectedly drifted into, and he smiled grimly.

"There are limits to what even a king can do in the face of entrenched hatred... and stupidity," he said. "I'm sure you and Prince Bahnak have discovered the same thing from your side. But that doesn't keep it from *being* stupidity, and there comes a time when it *must* be changed. That's my view, at any rate. And"—he met Arsham's gaze levelly—"my brother's, as well."

Arsham's eyes flickered and his ears folded back ever so slightly. That was all he allowed to show, but Vaijon drew a deep, unobtrusive breath and felt others around the table doing the same. However candidly and openly Yurokhas might have discussed the canal project and even the entire future of human-hradani relations with Tellian and Bahzell, he'd been careful to avoid anything which might have been construed as an unconditional statement of support in King Markhos' name. There'd never been any doubt about where Yurokhas' own sympathies lay, but everyone had always understood why the *King* couldn't be that open... assuming, of course, that he'd ever truly been as supportive as his younger brother. But now—

I wonder if he was actually authorized to say that? Vaijon wondered. *But surely he wouldn't have said it* without *Markhos' approval! I know a lot of people dimiss him as impulsive or even reckless, but I also know that reputation's a mask, a façade he's built just as carefully as Bahzell's built that "country bumpkin" disguise of his. Even so, though . . .*

He looked at Yurokhas, one eyebrow arched, and the prince looked back at him and then nodded, ever so slightly.

Tomanāk, that was *an official statement. To a very select group, perhaps, but that was Markhos himself speaking to Arsham—and to Bahnak, for that matter! I wonder if delivering that was the real reason the King let him come along as an "observer" in the first place?*

"Well," the champion heard his voice say into the silence which had greeted Yurokhas' comment, "speaking as someone who's had a little experience with stupidity of his own, I can say of my own knowledge that it *is* possible to . . . reshape it once someone finds the appropriate hammer. Of course, it takes a heavier hammer for some of us than for others."

Another rumble of amusement—this one more than a little relieved-sounding—greeted his wry tone, and he smiled.

"In the meantime, unfortunately," he continued, "according to both Prince Bahnak's and Kilthan's sources, somebody seems to have found a big enough hammer to get through to the River Brigands and the Purple Lords." He grimaced. "At this point, we don't know exactly what they're likely to do about it, but I think we can take it for granted that anything they *can* do, they *will* do. In a lot of ways, we probably need to be more concerned about the Brigands than the Purple Lords, simply because they're so much closer. At the same time, though, however Arthnar may feel about the canal in general, I can't see him actively trying to interfere with *our* operations, given the Brigands' own history with the ghouls."

Heads nodded, and he shrugged.

"We'll be keeping an eye on him, of course, and on the Purple Lords, but I don't expect either of them to have much short-term effect on us here. So, having said that, let's take a look at where we are and where we want to be by the end of the summer. Hurthang?"

The Horse Stealer nodded and rose. He walked around to the

large easel set up at the foot of the table and flipped back the cover to show the large-scale map of the Ghoul Moor it had concealed.

"As you can see," Vaijon said, "we've marked last year's gains in green. We lost a little ground over the winter down in the southwest, farthest from the river, and we need to regain that first."

Hurthang drew his dagger and used it as a pointer, indicating the area in question, and Vaijon gave everyone a moment to absorb the lines on the map. Then he continued.

"Hopefully, we can clean that up in the next week or two. Prince Bahnak would like to get it taken care of before the new arbalests arrive. After that, we'll turn to expanding the depth of the corridor along its southern edge, pushing back from the river. As you can see, there are at least half a dozen ghoul villages in the area we're talking about." Hurthang's dagger indicated the crimson symbols of the villages in question. "Two of them in particular are going to be hard to get at because of the terrain, so we're thinking—"

Chapter Fourteen

“I’ll not want to hear as how you’ve taken any foolish chances once I’ve gone,” Bahzell Bahnakson said sternly, frowning down at Tellian Bowmaster with his mighty arms folded across his chest. “There’s healers in plenty here in Sothōfalas, but never a champion, and there’s limits in all things.”

“I’ve been putting on my own boots every morning for quite some time now.” Tellian’s tone was mild, but there was a certain sharpness in his gray eyes. “And what happened on the way here made your point for you quite nicely, Bahzell. Don’t pound it into the ground.”

“It’s not the *ground* I’m after trying to pound it into,” Bahzell replied with a twinkle. “Still and all,” he continued before Tellian could fire back, “I’ll grant you’ve a point of your own. And it’s not as if you’ll be gallivanting around the city where just anyone as wishes you ill can be getting at you.”

“Oh, no,” Tellian agreed cuttingly. “I’ll be hiding in my apartments—when I haven’t crawled under the bed, that is. Is there anything else you’d like to remind me about before you go? Like coming in out of the rain? Eating all of my vegetables? Wait! I know—reminding me to wipe the drool off my senile old chin?”

“If I’d not come so close to losing you, I’d not give you so hard a time,” Bahzell said in a much gentler tone. “I’ll not say another word about foolishness, but this I will say. Whoever it was as was truly behind the lads who tried for you, they’ve proven as how you *can* be killed.” He looked very levelly into Tellian’s eyes. “It was only Norfram’s luck you weren’t, and had one of those arrows been after hitting you betwixt the eyes rather than in the chest, there's not a thing in all the world even Vaijon and I could have done about it. That's a scare I'm not wishful to be having again, nor one as Hanatha should have. You've those who love you, Tellian Bowmaster, and there's not a one of us doesn't know how many others would sooner see you dead than sit down to dinner. They've come close enough to be thinking as how next time they might succeed, and if it should happen they do, there's too much chance as how all you've set your hand to would be dying with you. It's not in my mind to badger or pester, and well I know there's no way at all, at all, we could wrap you up in cotton wool. But that's not to say you can't be taking a *little* caution, and you'll do me the favor of thinking about those of us who do love you."

Tellian's eyes softened, but then he shook his head with a snort.

"Of course I will, you big . . . lummox. Now go before you make me break down and bawl into my beer."

"Now *that* I'd pay money to see," Brandark remarked to no one in particular, and Tellian shot him a quick grin.

"Don't start saving your kormaks anytime soon. I suspect I'll be able to bear up under my embarrassment with manly fortitude."

"And after you went and got my hopes up." The Bloody Sword shook his head, ears half-flattened mournfully.

"Blame your overgrown friend. And"—the baron glanced out the open window at the early afternoon sunlight—"you're wasting daylight."

"Such a way with words you have," Bahzell said, and unfolded his arms to clasp forearms. "I've your letters to Hanatha and Leanna," he added, touching his belt pouch, "and I'll tell them as how you were whole and healthy when last I saw you. Stay that way."

"Yes, Poppa," Tellian sighed, gripping the hradani's massive forearm.

"Good."

Bahzell gave his arm one final squeeze, then he and Brandark turned and headed for the stables where Walsharno and Brandark's warhorse awaited them. Hathan Shieldarm and his cousin Tarith were waiting as well, and Hathan arched his eyebrows.

"Took it with his usual becoming humility, did he?"

"Not so much as anyone would have been noticing," Bahzell told his fellow wind rider dryly.

"I wouldn't want to say I told you so, but—"

Hathan shrugged eloquently, and both hradani laughed. Then they sobered, and Bahzell turned to Tarith.

"I know it grates on him, Tarith, and I've no doubt at all as how he'll snap and fret if it should be you sit on him too tight. But I'm thinking whoever it was tried last time won't be minded to give over."

"I know, Milord." Tarith's shrug was heavier than Hathan's, but his expression was determined. "And I'll bear what you had to say about poisons in mind, as well. I won't deny I'd feel happier with you here to do the sitting on him, but I know you can't. For that matter, if you tried, he'd *really* pitch a fit! He's not going to like it if he finds out about it, but I've arranged for one of the Court magi with the healing talent to 'just happen' to run into him every two or three days." Tellian's armsman smiled. "If anyone's managing to get any poison into him, she'll pick it up."

"And just who's going to pick *you* up—or the pieces of you, at any rate—if the Baron should discover this little plan of yours?" Brandark asked interestedly.

"She's a very good healer, Lord Brandark," Tarith said without so much as cracking a smile, "and she's promised to repair any damage I might suffer."

"Good man!" Bahzell clapped Tarith on the shoulder, then looked past the cousins to where Walsharno stood, ears cocked, beside Brandark's mount. The warhorse looked like a pony in the courser's shadow, and Walsharno tossed his head impatiently.

<They'll take the best care of him he'll let them take, Brother,> the courser told him. *<And while you're so busy worrying about people who might try to kill* him, *you might want to spare little thought for the number of people who'd cheerfully kill* you *if the opportunity should come their way.>*

Bahzell started to reply, then stopped himself. Walsharno had a point, after all, and the courser would undoubtedly be unscrupulous enough to use Bahzell's own words to Tellian against him if he tried to pretend otherwise. Under the circumstances, discretion would undoubtedly be the better part of valor, he decided.

"I'm thinking we should be on the road," he said out loud, instead, and heard Walsharno's silent laugh in the back of his mind.

✧ ✧ ✧

"Well, at least we're rid of Bahzell." Malahk Sahrdohr's tone was almost as sour as his expression. "That should simplify things a bit. For now, at least. Somehow I have the feeling he'll be back."

"He is rather like the bad kormak, isn't he?" Master Varnaythus replied. The older wizard sat well back in the comfortable leather chair, feet propped on the ottoman in front of him, nursing a moisture-beaded tankard of ale. He took a deep, appreciative sip, although he really preferred wine or whiskey as a rule, then looked back up at Sahrdohr. "In a way, I rather admire him, you know."

"*Admire* him?" Sahrdohr blinked. "He and his father—his whole damned family—have been nothing but a massive pain in the arse for years now!"

"And your point is?" Varnaythus arched one eyebrow across the small table at the younger, taller man. "There's nothing wrong with admiring an adversary, Malahk." He waved the forefinger of his free hand gently. "In fact, it's far better to admit you admire—or at least respect—an enemy than it is to denigrate him the way Cassan does. Think about it. Cassan gives lip service to the fact that Tellian is a dangerous opponent, but under the surface he lets his hatred turn into contempt. He doesn't really *respect* him because he's too busy hating to waste time and effort dispassionately evaluating him, and that's one of the reasons Tellian's been able to to accomplish so much. Respecting an adversary's capabilities is the first step to taking them effectively into consideration in your own plans."

Sahrdohr started to reply quickly, then stopped and obviously reconsidered what he'd been about to say. After a moment, he nodded, albeit more than a little grudgingly.

"All right, that's fair," he said. "In fact, I'll go further and admit it's *wise*. And having all three of Scale Balancer's champions out of Sothōfalas should make actually killing Tellian a lot easier if we can get another shot at him. But Bahzell's clearly Their more important target, and we didn't even come close to killing *him* when we had the chance."

"No, and I'm not going to be anywhere within thirty or forty leagues of him when we *do* try to kill him, if it's all the same to you," Varnaythus said dryly. "That's what demons, devils, ghouls, trolls, and dog brothers are for, thank you very much. When the time comes, of course. And the good thing about it is that we can use anything that comes to hand against *him* without worrying about drawing attention to our plans for the Sothōii in general. No one's going to be a bit surprised if any of Them or Their allies want to kill one of Tomanāk's champions, after all. And *that*, my friend, means we can delegate that particular little task to one of Their other servants. I don't know if we're going to manage to get him onto the Ghoul Moor to enjoy our little surprise along with Vaijon and the others, of course. In some ways, that could work out for the best, but that really irritating talent of his for surviving could cause that whole arm of the operation to come up short, instead. And I'm just *delighted* to leave it up to Krashnark's servants... *especially* if Bahzell's going to put in an appearance. After all," he smiled thinly at his companion, "we're wizards. We do the subtle, sophisticated work and leave that crude heavy lifting to those better suited to it."

Sahrdohr gazed at him for several moments, then leaned back in his own chair, took a large bite from the pretzel in his left hand, and washed it down with a healthy swig of beer.

"You know," he said after he'd swallowed, "I hadn't thought of it quite that way, but you're right, Master Varnaythus."

"Of course I am." Varnaythus treated himself to another swallow of ale. "That's why I'm in charge. And it's also the reason, young Malahk, that I've *survived* long enough to be in charge. You might want to write that down somewhere."

✧ ✧ ✧

"Prince Bahzell!"

Bahzell turned in the saddle as Walsharno halted under him. He and the courser both looked back the way they'd come, and the hradani frowned as a man made his way down the stone-slab sidewalk towards him. The newcomer was a tallish man, like most Sothōii, with auburn hair just starting to gray and a neatly trimmed spade beard. He wore his hair in a warrior's braid and there was a saber at his side, but he wasn't dressed like an armsman, and he certainly wasn't dressed like a noble. In fact, he wore a blue tunic badged with the white scepter of Semkirk, the god of wisdom... and magi.

<Do you have any idea who this fellow might be?> Walsharno inquired.

"No more than what you see yourself," Bahzell replied.

"He might be a really cleverly disguised assassin," Brandark suggested cheerfully, and Bahzell gave him a disgusted look. "I'm just saying it's possible," the Bloody Sword said mildly. "I never said it was *likely*."

<If it wouldn't hurt the lesser cousin, I'd step on him.>

"As to that, he'll have to be dismounting sometime."

<*True. And I'm a patient fellow. I can wait.*>

"Why do I have the feeling you and Walsharno were talking about me?" Brandark asked.

"I'm thinking that's because I've the look of a man with a bellyache."

"My, you *are* in a sour mood today."

"Now," Bahzell agreed with a pleasant smile, and Brandark chuckled.

The Bloody Sword opened his mouth, but before he could say anything else, the stranger had caught up with them. Bahzell looked down at him for a moment, then courteously dismounted. He still towered a foot and more taller than the newcomer, but at least the fellow wouldn't have to crane his neck staring up at him.

"And how might I be helping you?" he inquired.

"Your pardon, Milord." The other man gave him a small but polite bow. "I'd hoped to catch you before you left Sir Jerhas' townhouse, but I was delayed along the way, so I cut through the side streets to make up for lost time. My name is Brayahs—Brayahs Daggeraxe—and I have a message for you from Mistress Zarantha."

"Ah! Then you'd be Baron Halthan's cousin, I'm thinking?"

"I have that honor," Daggeraxe acknowledged with another half-bow. If he was surprised at Bahzell's identification, it didn't show. "And I was one of Mistress Zarantha's mentors at the Axe Hallow mage academy. She's stayed in touch over the years, and she's always spoken most warmly of you."

"Aye, she would." Bahzell shook his head with a smile. "She's always been one as thinks the best of others, whether they're after deserving it or not, hasn't she just?"

"Actually, I've always found her rather hardheaded and careful about who she chooses to trust, Milord," Daggeraxe said dryly.

"Oh, no, Master Brayahs!" Brandark said cheerfully, swinging down from the saddle and inserting himself into the conversation. "You must be thinking about someone else. Why, Mistress Zarantha even trusts *me*!"

"And I'm sure you've never given her cause to do anything of the sort." Daggeraxe shook his head. "Shocking."

"I'd not go quite so far as all that," Bahzell said, looking down at Brandark, "but I will say there's times a man needs to be reminding himself just why it is he puts up with some people."

Brandark grinned impudently at him, and Daggeraxe chuckled. But then his expression turned more serious and he looked around. He'd overtaken them several blocks from the Prime Councilor's home, on a broad street fronted by busy shops, eateries, sidewalk stalls, and taverns.

"I truly regret not having caught up with you sooner, Milord," he said.

"Well, seeing as how no one was supposed to know—officially—as how I was even here in the first place, I'm thinking you didn't do so very poorly as all that. Still," Bahzell glanced around in turn, "I'll allow as this isn't the very most private place in all the world."

"There's a park another two blocks down this street," Daggeraxe said. "Earlier in the day it's usually fairly crowded—it's one of the city's larger parks, and there's room to hack a horse or even take a turn in a carriage, if you're truly fashionable. Most of the city exquisites should have taken themselves off for the day by now, though."

<If he really was a cleverly disguised assassin, that would be a wonderful way to get us off into a quiet corner,> Walsharno observed in the back of Bahzell's brain. Bahzell looked up at him with something very like a glower, and the courser tossed his head. *<I'm just saying it's possible,>* he said in a very passable imitation of Brandark's voice. *<I never said it was* likely.>

"A park sounds just fine, Master Brayahs," Bahzell said. "Another two blocks, you were saying?"

✧ ✧ ✧

Bahzell could see why the park to which Daggeraxe guided them might be popular. It was quite old, surrounded by gray stone walls mottled with lichen, with paths of carefully raked gravel threading their way under ancient trees just starting to come into full leaf. Broader paths—more like promenades than roads—wound through the park's gently rolling spaciousness, and a large fountain at its heart splashed around an inevitable equestrian statue. Groundskeepers were at work as the three of them—and Walsharno—passed through the open gate in the stone wall. They looked up, and their eyes widened as they saw the hradani. Most of them stiffened automatically, as well, but Bahzell and Brandark had grown accustomed to that response, and the Horse Stealer watched at least some of them relax as they took in the sword and mace on his surcoat, added to them to Walsharno, and realized who he had to be.

Not, he noted sourly, that most of them relaxed very *noticeably*.

Daggeraxe led them in a comfortable, ambling stroll along one of the main promenades with Walsharno walking at Bahzell's shoulder.

"Most of Zarantha's message isn't really all that confidential, Milord," the mage said. "Private, but not something that needs to be kept secret from those who might not have your best interests at heart, shall we say."

Bahzell cocked his ears politely, and Daggeraxe chuckled a bit sourly.

"As a mage—especially a Crown mage—I'm officially neutral in Baron Tellian's spat with Baron Cassan and Baron Yeraghor, Milord. And as a Daggeraxe and a loyal supporter of the North Riding's interests, as well, of course. For that matter, to be completely honest, I think my cousin may be showing the better part of wisdom to steer clear of that entire dogfight. If I *were* to pick a side, though, I think I'd probably favor Tellian, on the theory that you can tell more about a man from the enemies he makes than from the company he keeps. I think the quality of Tellian's enemies speaks well of him. But however neutral I may be where the Kingdom's internal politics are concerned, Zarantha is a friend and you're her brother as far as Clan Jâshân and Clan Hûrâka are concerned."

"That's after being more than good enough for me, Master Brayahs," Bahzell said.

"I'm glad to hear that. And while we're being honest with each other, I suppose I should admit that it's probably just as well I didn't catch you at Sir Jerhas' after all." The mage grimaced. "I doubt very much that any of Baron Tellian's enemies would believe for a moment that I'm only passing on a friend's message like any other mage might do. The last thing my cousin needs is to have my actions suggest he's choosing a side after all."

Daggeraxe arched an eyebrow, and Bahzell nodded.

"I can be seeing that."

"Well," Daggeraxe said more briskly, "about that message. First, she asked me to tell you Tothas is doing well and that he's about to become a father for the second time. According to the healer, it will be a girl this time."

"Will it now?" Bahzell grinned broadly. "It's good money I'd give to see him sitting with a babe on his knee! Especially a girl child. She'll have his heart in one grubby little fist before she's as much as walking!"

"Ha!" Brandark shook his head. "What makes you think she'll wait that long? She'll have him under her thumb before she's even *born*!"

"Likely you've the right of that," Bahzell agreed, still smiling, and looked back at Daggeraxe. "It's grateful I'll be if you'd be good enough to be telling Zarantha as how Brandark and I are both wishing Tothas and Tarenka well. Aye, and I'll be thinking on a proper birth gift."

"*You*?" Brandark hooted a laugh. "More like your sister Marglyth, you mean. Or maybe even your mother!"

Bahzell ignored him, and Daggeraxe's lips twitched as he resolutely did the same.

"In addition," the mage continued, "Zarantha says to tell you her academy is sufficiently well established now that Tothas is confident it can provide for its security out of its own resources. She asked me to tell you she can never thank you or the Order of Tomanāk enough for having protected them until that was true, and that she's informed Sir Yorhus of the same thing. I have the impression, however, that Sir Yorhus—he's the commander of the Order's detachment at the academy, is he?" Bahzell nodded and Daggeraxe shrugged. "As I say, I have the impression Sir Yorhus is rather less confident they can do without his presence."

"You're probably right," Brandark said. "On the other hand, Sir Yorhus would probably feel that way if they had the entire Spearman army camped around the academy!"

"Aye, you've a point there," Bahzell agreed with a wry smile. "It's an amazing amount of good Tothas has done with him, but he's still Sir Yorhus, when all's said." He glanced at Daggeraxe. "Sir Yorhus is a good man, Master Brayahs, but he's . . . a way about him. A man of *enthusiasms*, as you might say."

"A man who won't pull his detachment out of Jâshân without a direct order from Sir Terrian countersigned by all three of the commandery's senior officers, you mean!" Brandark snorted.

"Now he's not so bad as all that these days," Bahzell replied repressively. "I'll just be sending him a letter of my own and see how things go from there."

"Right. You'd better go ahead and send a letter to Terrian in Axe Hallow while you're at it. At least you can save a little time that way."

"I'll ask you to be ignoring him, Master Brayahs," Bahzell said. "It's little he can help it, being born a Bloody Sword and all. You were saying about the rest of Zarantha's message?"

"Well, this is where we start getting into the bits you'd probably not want to become public knowledge."

Daggeraxe glanced around casually. None of the groundskeepers were close enough to overhear anything that might be said, and the mage gestured for them to stop at a stone bench under one of the trees.

"She wanted me to tell you," he continued, once he'd seated himself on the bench, "that the Purple Lords have figured out what your father and Baron Tellian have in mind."

He paused, one eyebrow raised, and Bahzell flicked his ears.

"Aye, we've other reports that say the same," he acknowledged. "Not that we've any clear idea just yet how it might be as they're inclined to react."

"I think you may have one now, Milord." Daggeraxe's tone was much grimmer than it had been. "And truth to tell, the fact that the Purple Lords are among Tellian's enemies is one of the things that speaks most loudly in his favor, as far as I'm concerned. I spent three months in Bortalik just after I'd completed my training. It seemed like three *years*, and not just because the Purple Lords are so full of themselves, either. I'm sure Zarantha's told you about her suspicions where the Purple Lords are concerned?"

He looked a question at Bahzell, and the hradani nodded.

"I assumed she must have, given that you and Brandark are the only reason she managed to get home alive *despite* the Purple Lords."

"As to that, Wencit did have more than a mite to do with it," Bahzell said mildly. "And we'd never any actual proof as how the Purple Lords were behind it their very own selves."

"Trust me, Milord," Daggeraxe said even more grimly. "Precognition is one of *my* minor talents, too. In fact, my talent's at least a bit stronger than Zarantha's in that regard. I know how it works, so I would have been inclined to trust her foresight about the Purple Lords and the mysterious death of every Spearman mage before she came along under any circumstances. But one of my other talents is what we call aura reading."

"Aura reading?" Brandark repeated, ears cocking intently. "Of living creatures or objects?"

"I see you've been doing some research, Lord Brandark," Daggeraxe said. "But the answer to your question is neither. Oh, I have some sensitivity to the auras of people—including four-footed ones, Milord Courser," he added, nodding courteously to Walsharno. "But mostly I read the auras of *places*. I'm what we call in the academies a 'sniffer.' It's a talent which is often useful for someone investigating a crime, for example, because a powerful sniffer can actually read the motives and emotions of people who have passed through a given place. It's not infallible, and our readings are always subject to a degree of interpretation. For that matter, if there's been a lot of traffic through the spot, the overlays of so many auras can make it impossible for us to be very specific at all, so it's not something we can present in court before a judge or jury, but it's frequently helpful in directing the investigator's attention towards likely motives and suspects."

"I can see where such as that would be an uncomfortable thing for someone as found himself stuck amongst the Purple Lords," Bahzell rumbled.

"Oh, it was, but not for the reasons you're thinking, perhaps. You see, like my precognition, it's a minor talent for me, not a strongly refined one. But it's not emotions and motives I sense when I read a place's aura, Milord; it's sorcery. I'm a wizard-sniffer, and the stink of wizardry is heavy in Bortalik."

Bahzell's face stiffened and his ears flattened. He and Brandark looked at one another for a moment, then back at Daggeraxe.

"It's certain of that you are?" the Horse Stealer asked.

"That there's wizardry in Bortalik? Oh, yes, Milord! Not that I could get any of the city officials to take my word for it. After all, there are no Purple Lord magi, are there? And at that time, there were no Spearman magi, either. So I could scarcely expect them to take the word of a visiting Sothōii for it, now could I? But that's another reason I'm confident Zarantha's right about who's been helping Spearman magi die before they ever came into their abilities."

"You're convinced she's right that those deaths were unnatural? They didn't simply fail to survive their 'mage crisis'?"

"Lord Brandark, the severity of mage crisis is directly proportional to the power of the mage's talents. The more powerful the talent, the more of them the mage might possess, the more severe the crisis. But the truth is that the majority of magi have only one or two talents, and many of them are far from powerful. In fact, there are far more 'magi' than most people ever suspect running about, most of them with talents too weak to train effectively, and many of them never even realize they're talented at all. For someone like that, 'mage crisis' might seem no worse than a particularly protracted case of the flu, with the sort of fever dreams you might expect to experience with a high fever." Daggeraxe shook his head. "No, Milord. Zarantha was absolutely right about that. There should have been at least a handful of magi who survived their crises on their own but whose talents were still powerful enough to be recognized after the fact. The only explanation for why there never were is that someone made certain they *didn't* survive. And who would have a greater interest in that than someone dabbling in wizardry?"

"I'm thinking you've the right of it," Bahzell said after a moment. "Mind you, I'm also thinking as how it's a tempting thing to be finding 'proof' someone I've so little fondness for is after being blacker than black."

"That's the way a champion of Tomanāk is supposed to think, Milord." Daggeraxe smiled thinly. "I'm only a mage, and I know what I sensed in Bortalik. If I never have to go back to that city again, it will still be a lifetime too soon!"

"What a pity we missed the opportunity to tour the city on our last visit to the Purple Lords, Bahzell," Brandark said lightly. "You could have slaughtered another couple of dozen landlords before you set it on fire!"

Bahzell snorted and twitched his ears at the Bloody Sword, then looked back at the Daggeraxe.

"I'm thinking we've gone a bit astray, Master Brayahs?"

"Yes, we have." The mage smiled apologetically. "Whatever *my* experiences in Bortalik may have been all those years ago, Duke Caswal's factor's experiences there are much more recent, and the Duke specifically asked Zarantha to pass them on to you. She tells me a written letter is on its way, giving more detail, but her father wanted you to have what you might call the high points of his factor's account of his last trip downriver to Bortalik as soon as possible. In fact, he's specifically asked you to pass them on to *your* father, to Kilthandahknarthas, and to Baron Tellian."

"Ah?" Bahzell cocked his ears, and Daggeraxe smiled mirthlessly.

"Duke Caswal's never been particularly popular with the Purple

Lords. He's too independent-minded to suit them at the best of times, and he hasn't made any secret about his suspicion that 'parties unknown' among the Purple Lords—no doubt acting without the knowledge of any Purple Lord *official*, of course—were directly responsible for what almost happened to Zarantha. What *would* have happened to her without the two of you and Wencit. That's put him on the bad side of Bortalik, and they've punished him for it often enough, so his factor wasn't exactly surprised when they decided to call him in and threaten him with retaliation if Duke Caswal didn't toe the line this time. For that matter, Zarantha says, her father's of the opinion the Purple Lords are aware of *your* connection with Jâshân. They don't pay a great deal of attention to what happens here in the Kingdom, but they appear to have at least determined who the prime movers behind the Derm Canal project are, and you *have* been a little more visible than most folk up this way. That song about you is quite popular among the crews of Axeman merchant vessels—and especially, for some reason, apparently, among the crews of Marfang Island merchant ships. They seem to take a particular pleasure out of singing it where Purple Lord ears are likely to hear it, so it wouldn't be too hard for even a Purple Lord to put you, Zarantha, and your father together."

Bahzell managed not to glare at Brandark, but it was hard when the Bloody Sword pursed his lips, looked intently up into the branches of the tree under which they stood, and whistled tunelessly.

<*I am going to step on him this time,*> Walsharno said.

Aye, well, I'm not so minded as usual to be stopping you this time, and that's a fact, Bahzell replied.

"So they've decided as how if any Spearman's likely to be encouraging the canal, Caswal would," he said out loud, and Daggeraxe nodded.

"That's the Duke's conclusion, at any rate. And they were quite clear about their intentions, as well. Anyone who dares to trade directly with the Axemen courtesy of your canal will be embargoed in Bortalik. All traffic *upriver* to that noble will be cut off."

"A bit of cutting off their own noses to spite their faces in that, don't you think?" Brandark put in with a grin. "It seems to me that would be most likely to encourage the offender to switch *all* of his trade to the new route."

"No doubt it would," Daggeraxe acknowledged. "There were also some suggestions—less explicit ones, of course—that the new route was likely to find itself seriously beset with piracy and accidents of navigation, however. Which, as they pointed out to Caswal's factor, would probably have an unfortunate effect on insurance rates. And, finally, there was a *very* explicit threat that they'll seize any Spearman monies invested in Bortalik or any other Purple Lord trading venture if the investors take advantage of the new route. And, of course, at the same time, all debts of any Spearman foolish enough to do such a thing will be immediately called by his creditors."

Brandark's grin disappeared, and Daggeraxe nodded.

"Given how much a typical Spearman noble already owes the Purple Lords, that could turn into a very potent threat, indeed. And if I were someone like Duke Caswal, I wouldn't much care for that business about piracy and 'accidents,' either," Daggeraxe said. "As I say, Prince Bahzell, I understand why my cousin has no desire to mix in Baron Tellian's quarrel with Baron Cassan, and I have no intention of doing anything which might drag him—or even *seem* to drag him—into it. But speaking purely for myself and on behalf of a very dear friend and her father, I think it might be wise for you to look very closely at any . . . connection between Cassan, the River Brigands, and the Purple Lords. And if I were you," the mage's expression was grim, "I wouldn't be so very surprised to find a wizard or two buried somewhere in the mix, as well."

Chapter Fifteen

Leeana Hanathafressa tried to analyze her feelings as she watched the familiar towers and turrets rising steadily against the horizon from Hill Guard Castle's perch on the swell of granite overlooking Balthar. Boots moved sweetly and steadily under her, and she watched his mobile ears swiveling, pricking higher with anticipation. There wasn't much doubt about *his* mood, she thought fondly, reaching down to rest one hand on his shoulder. This was the land where he'd been foaled and raised, gentled to saddle, lived half his life, and first become her horse, and he felt that homecoming in his bones just as surely as she did.

Yet there was a difference between them, and she felt it looming before her even as Hill Guard drew closer and closer, for Boots could be certain of his welcome. He might have had the ill fortune to belong to Hill Guard's ne'er-do-well disgrace of a daughter, but that wasn't *his* fault. No one would look askance at him, or find themselves feeling awkward and out of balance trying to deal with what that same daughter had become.

She felt it again, that yearning for the place where she, too, had been born and lived almost two-thirds of her life. For the familiar fields, the familiar faces, the welcome which had once been hers without stint or limit. She supposed everyone experienced at least some of that sense of loss, of never being able to return to who and what they'd once been. But for any war maid, the old cliché about not being able to go home again had a special poignancy.

Oh, stop that! she told herself. *No, it's not like it used to be, and it never will be again. But think about someone like Raythas.*

The last thing she'd ever want is to "go home again"! Unless she took two or three of us along to geld that bastard brother of hers, at least.

Her jaw clenched with remembered fury as she remembered the night Raythas Talafressa had gotten drunk enough to tell her seventy-five why *she'd* run away to the war maids, and there were hundreds of others who could have told the same tale or worse. Not that those who lifted their noses at the war maids from the security of their own lives ever thought about the sorts of things that drove women into choosing that escape. After all, those weren't the sorts of things nice people talked about, far less wanted to admit happened.

At least you do *want to go home... and at least Mother and Father are glad to see you when you do, whatever the other citizens of your hometown may think. That's something most of the others will never have, so why don't you just take a deep breath and* deal *with it?*

It was a conversation she'd had with herself every time she'd come home for one of her brief, infrequent visits, and that irritated her far more than she would ever have admitted to another soul. It wasn't the sort of conversation a strong, competent person ought to have to have more than one time before she dealt with it once and for all, and she hadn't. In fact, she might as well admit that she was nowhere near as strong and competent as she wanted to pretend, since there was a very simple reason her visits had been so few and so brief. And, no, whatever she might choose to tell herself, it *wasn't* because her mother's long and frequent (and her father's shorter, but even more frequent) letters had let her keep up on events in Balthar and Hill Guard without making the long, wearisome ride between there and Kalatha.

It was because she was afraid of those visits. Because it hurt her to see what she saw all too often in the eyes of the people who'd once thought of themselves as hers. She might long to be here, and this might be the place she would always think of as home at the very center of her being, but it *wasn't* her home any longer. She'd thrown that away, however good her reason for doing so might have been, and for all the calm demeanor she showed her father's subjects when she visited, that deeply buried center of her being ached for all she'd lost. Not the power, not the wealth, but the *belonging*. That sense of knowing precisely who and what she was because her bone and blood were part of the soil on which Hill Guard stood, of the generation upon generation of Bowmasters who had been laid to rest in Bowmaster earth, stood guard over the people of Balthar and the West Riding, and died in their defense. She could stand the scorn of others, let the contempt of strangers roll off the unbowed shoulders of her soul without even a wince, but here it cut too deep, for these people had been *hers.* And so she'd visited no more than a dozen times in the years since she'd fled this place, and each of those visits had been brief and fleeting because, whether anyone else ever guessed it or not, she'd fled all over again at the end of each of them.

But not this time. No, this time she meant to stand her ground, and that was the reason she was having what she thought of as The Conversation with herself yet again. And the reason she'd *been* having it ever since she'd left Kalatha.

Of course, this time you're having The Conversation as a distraction, too, aren't you? Because you've finally found something—or gotten around to it, anyway—that makes you even more nervous than having run off to the war maids in the first place! Don't want to think about that, *do you?*

Her mouth quirked, and she gave Boots' shoulder another pat as she admitted that to herself, but it was true. She'd promised herself this day more than six years ago. That should have given her plenty of time to come to grips with all its implications, yet the butterflies dancing in her middle suggested that she hadn't. There was excitement and anticipation in that dance, but there was also apprehension—possibly even fear, as difficult as she found it to admit that to herself—and she found herself wondering yet again how her parents were going to react to *this* decision.

Assuming it works out the way you plan for it to, she told herself. *It may not, you know. And* then *how will you handle it?*

She'd made a point of reminding herself of that possibility regularly, especially over the last couple of years, just in case. On the other hand, there had been those clues, however hard certain parties had labored to conceal them. There were times she'd been frustratingly certain it was all her own imagination . . . and other times she'd been absolutely positive it wasn't. And then there'd been that peculiar, almost vibrating feeling that had tingled in her bones. She was prepared to admit at least some of that—possibly quite a lot of it, if she was going to be honest—had been no more than her own imagination and hope and desire speaking to her, yet not all of it had been. She was convinced of that. The problem of course was that what *she* was feeling might not have a great deal of bearing on anyone *else's* feelings.

She snorted at the thought, but she also squared her shoulders and pressed with her heels, asking Boots for a little more speed. The gelding happily complied, and Leeana Hanathafressa reminded herself that whatever else might be true, she wasn't accustomed to failing once she'd set her mind to something.

Especially not when it was something as important as this.

✧ ✧ ✧

Sharlassa stood leaning on the battlements of Hill Guard's main gate tower, shading her eyes as she peered down the long approach road. No one had asked her to take up her lookout post, and she supposed she should feel at least vaguely guilty about having done it, although no one had actually *told* her she was supposed to be in Sir Jahlahan's office for another deadly dull session of etiquette lessons instead. Fortunately, the seneschal's schedule was erratic enough to make arranging lesson times too far in advance difficult, and so this particular block of *her* time had simply been left unassigned in hopes Sir Jahlahan would find the opportunity to give her a little extra polish. Was it her fault no one had informed her he'd been able to find that opportunity before she took herself unobtrusively off to her present position? Of course it wasn't!

She told herself that very firmly, resolutely suppressing the small inner voice which tried to point out that *before* taking herself unobtrusively off to her present position she'd suggested to Tahlmah that she was going for a walk in the formal gardens instead. She hadn't quite come out and *said* so, of course; that would have been deceitful. Yet whenever that irritating inner voice reached a volume where she could no longer entirely ignore it, she was forced to concede that what she *had* said had certainly amounted to . . . misdirection.

On the other hand, it wasn't exactly as if she were trying to hide her present location. Anyone looking out from one of the taller towers behind her could easily see her standing here in the sunlight if they happened to look in the right direction. Oh, Tahlmah would probably have gone to the gardens looking for her there *first* if Sir Jahlahan had found time to tutor Sharlassa, but her maid was an experienced Sharlassa-hunter. How long could it possibly take her to realize she was looking in the wrong spot and search elsewhere?

Besides, Sharlassa had a special reason for being here this afternoon, although the event she was waiting for was running behind schedule. That was scarcely a surprise. There were always delays on any journey. And while she was guiltily aware she was violating at least the spirit of the letter's request, that request hadn't actually been made to *her*, now had it? And even if it had—

Her thoughts broke off as she saw the handsome brown bay gelding with black legs and white stockings start up the approach road from Balthar. She watched it for a handful of seconds, then turned towards the stair and started down it at a pace just a bit too rapid to be called ladylike.

✧ ✧ ✧

The main gate tower loomed above Leeana as Boots trotted up the last hundred yards of the approach road.

The trip through Balthar itself had been about as bad as it had every other time she'd come home to visit. She'd been tempted, actually, in a craven sort of way, to circle around the city completely this time and approach Hill Guard from behind, despite the hours it would have added to her travel time. She didn't like admitting, even to herself, how much more the reaction she drew here in Balthar bothered her than did getting the same sort of reaction from anyone else, and she *refused* to admit it to anyone else. And so she'd ridden calmly and steadily through the very heart of the city where she'd grown up, erect and yet relaxed in the saddle, head high, looking about her with precisely the correct degree of interest for someone visiting home after yet another lengthy absence. It had been too much to hope she simply wouldn't be recognized—she had too much of the Bowmaster look, and even those who'd never seen her with their own eyes had to have had the overgrown, disgraced war maid described to them in glowing detail—but at least a handful of people had actually looked happy to see her. There'd even been a few waves of welcome, and she'd acknowledged those with smiles and nods, even a few waves of her own, while resolutely ignoring the scowls and frowns coming back at her from far too many other faces.

At least the people of Balthar were too polite to actually throw things at war maids, she thought. They probably wouldn't have thrown anything even at war maids who weren't the daughters (whatever the law might say) of their baron. Knowing how Baron Tellian and Baroness Hanatha would have reacted to anyone who'd dared to publicly revile Leeana (however thoroughly she might deserve it) undoubtedly reinforced their restraint in her own case, but she was fairly certain they probably wouldn't have done that to any other war maids, either.

Probably.

There was always a flow of traffic in and out of Hill Guard, and there were always gate guards to watch it. She'd expressly asked her parents not to tell any one outside the immediate family she was coming or to wait to greet her at the gate themselves. That would only have made it even worse, once word got back to the rest of Balthar, she thought glumly. That didn't mean she looked forward to how the gate guards were going to react when they spotted her coming at them with no advance warning, though, and she found herself watching them much more warily than she ever had when she'd been Leeana Bowmaster. She saw them stiffen as they saw her in turn and recognized her and Boots, and she was close enough to see their faces fade almost instantly into total nonexpression. She knew two of those armsmen well—or she had, once, at any rate—and fresh hurt spiked as she saw the completely neutral countenances which had replaced the broad smiles which once would have greeted her. Still, it was better than—

"Leeana!"

Boots' ears twitched at the sudden, clear-voiced, *happy* greeting, and Leeana drew rein and looked up sharply. An attractive, auburn-haired young woman with eyes as green as her own leaned out of one of the lower archer's slits, waving energetically.

"Leeana!" she repeated, and Leeana felt her lips quiver with a stillborn smile. Obviously at least one of Hill Guard's inhabitants had missed that bit about not greeting her. Or maybe the other young woman had simply figured the request didn't apply to someone who wasn't a member of the family? Either way, she suddenly realized how glad she was that someone had ignored it.

"I'll be down to meet you as soon as I can find the way," Sharlassa Dragonclaw continued. "Don't you *dare* go away until I get there!"

"Well, if you insist," Leeana replied a bit more mildly.

"I do," Sharlassa said firmly, and disappeared back into the stonework of Leeana's ancestral home.

It took Sharlassa a little longer than it would have taken Leeana to make the same trip, but then Leeana had been *raised* in Hill Guard whereas Sharlassa was undoubtedly still learning its interior geography. Besides, Sharlassa probably didn't plunge headlong down stairs and through doors the way a teenaged Leeana once had.

While she waited, Leeana swung down from the saddle, looped her reins over her left arm, and stood beside Boots, leaning companionably against the gelding's strong shoulder. Three of the four gate guards seemed a little uncomfortable, obviously unsure of exactly how they ought to react to her. Fortunately, Sergeant Barek Irongrip, the guard detachment's commander, was one of the armsmen she'd known since childhood.

"Good afternoon . . . Ma'am," the sergeant said after a moment with a smile which was almost natural. It wasn't *quite* natural, of course, but it was genuinely warm, Leeana noted gratefully, even if Irongrip was clearly trapped between the way he would have addressed any other war maid and the way he would once have addressed *her*.

"Good afternoon, Sergeant," she replied, addressing him with the formality of his rank, instead of using his given name, as once *she* would have. She owed him that, especially in front of his detachment.

"Her Ladyship said you'd be arriving today," Irongrip continued. "She didn't say how long you'd be staying, though."

Well, so much for not warning them I was coming, Leanna thought philosophically. *I wonder if I really ever expected Mother not to? But at least she and Father didn't send a drum-and-fife band to meet me on the front doorstep!*

"Probably for a little longer this time," she said out loud. He started to say something else, then stopped with a smile of acknowledgment, and Leanna hid a somewhat tarter smile of her own. Had he been about to express pleasure that she'd be there longer and stopped himself because of other listening ears? Or was she doing him a disservice because of her own hypersensitivity? Or—

"Welcome home, Leeana!"

Leeana looked up quickly as Sharlassa finally appeared out of the great, stony arch of the gate tunnel. There was no doubting the warmth of the younger woman's smile, or the genuine welcome in her greeting, and something inside Leeana seemed to melt—or thaw, at least—as Sharlassa used the word "home." It was a tiny thing, she thought, wondering why tears insisted on prickling behind her eyes, but—

"Thank you, Milady," she replied.

Sharlassa's nostrils flared at the honorific. She started to say something quickly, then visibly stopped herself, and Leeana regarded her levelly. Understanding flickered in Sharlassa's eyes as their gazes met, and she smiled, instead.

"I know you're accustomed to seeing to Boots yourself," she said, "but I think I should probably take you straight to the Baroness. Sergeant Irongrip will see to it he's taken care of, won't you, Sergeant?"

"Course I will, Milady. Happy to." The sergeant saluted Sharlassa, not Leeana, but he looked directly at the war maid who'd once been heiress conveyant to Hill Guard as he spoke, and the smile behind his last two words was genuine.

"Thank you, Sergeant," Leeana said, and turned to unbuckle her saddlebags and sling them over one shoulder. She unstrapped her blanket roll from behind the cantle and tucked it under her arm as well, suppressing a sudden, inappropriate urge to giggle as she reflected on the fact that everything she needed for a two-month stay had been packed into those bags or rolled up inside that blanket. Once upon a time, it would have required a freight wagon to haul everything a lady of her exalted station required for a visit like this one. She couldn't deny that she missed some of those luxuries, often quite badly, but travel was certainly more convenient this way. At least for someone who had to travel without the hordes of servants who would also have been packed into that freight wagon along with the luggage, at any rate. Of course, back in that same once upon a time, those servants would have leapt to relieve her of her baggage rather than let such a nobly born personage soil her dainty hands carrying it herself.

So there is *a downside to your more humble status, too, isn't there?* she asked herself. *You just don't want to admit how much you miss some of the priviliges of an effete, pampered noblewoman, do you?*

Sharlassa started to reach for the blanket roll to help her carry it, but a glance from Leanna stopped her. She grimaced ever so slightly, but she also lowered her hand while Leanna got her baggage settled comfortably.

"At your service, Milady," she said, then, nodding to the other young woman, and the two of them headed down the gate tunnel and into the castle grounds proper.

"It's good to see you again," Sharlassa said quietly as they emerged into the cobbled forecourt. "I know your mother's really been looking forward to this visit, too."

"It's good to see you, too, Milady," Leeana replied, smiling warmly as Sharlassa said "your mother" and not "Baroness Hanatha." She considered the younger woman thoughtfully for a moment, then cocked an eyebrow. "Have you grown again since the last time I saw you?"

"No." Sharlassa shook her head with something suspiciously like a giggle, and turned her head to look up at the far taller Leeana. "I wish I had! I feel like a dwarf—or even a halfling—around here most of the time. But it's just the ridiculous heels they make me wear."

She grimaced, and Leeana chuckled. Sharlassa Dragonclaw was scarcely as short as her comment might have suggested, although it was understandable enough that she might feel that way, especially walking beside Leeana. There was no denying that at a mere five feet four inches, Sharlassa was on the petite side for a Sothōii woman, whereas Leanna, who'd inherited her height from her father, was tall—very tall—for *any* woman, even among the Sothōii. In fact, she stood six feet three, a full inch taller than Brandark Brandarkson . . . and almost a full *foot* taller than Sharlassa.

Just as well you *don't have to wear heels anymore*, she told herself. *Mother! You'd tower over* everyone *then, wouldn't you? Or over everyone who wasn't a hradani, at any rate!*

"I never much cared for them myself, either, Milady," she said out loud. "And I avoided wearing them whenever I could get away with it."

"So do I," Sharlassa said with feeling. "But they keep catching me and making me put them back on. Personally, I think Mama told Tahlmah to make sure I wear them. Which is pretty unfair, when you come down to it, since *she* doesn't wear them at home!"

"Part of the training, I suppose," Leeana commiserated, and Sharlassa sighed in heartfelt agreement.

It was odd how her and Sharlassa's lives had moved in opposite directions, Leeana thought, and felt a strong surge of affection, as well as sympathy, for the younger woman. She'd given up the sort of life most young women could only have envied when she became a war maid, and that had been even harder than she'd expected it to be, yet she suspected Sharlassa was finding the transition in her own life equally difficult. In fact, she was probably finding it even *more* difficult, when it came down to it.

They'd crossed the forecourt while they were speaking, and Leeana followed Sharlassa down the awning-shaded, stone-slab walk fronting the neatly kept barracks as they headed for the gate into the inner bailey. Sharlassa seemed a little uncomfortable at having Leeana drop back to follow a half-pace behind her, but it was only proper, just as Leeana's use of "Milady" was only proper. Whatever she might once have been, Leeana Hanathafressa was a guest in Hill Guard Castle . . . and a guest of House Bowmaster, not its daughter.

Nobody actually stopped and stared as they passed, but Leeana was aware of scores of watching eyes, and she wondered what sorts of comparisons some of those eyes' owners were making between her and Sharlassa when they saw her striding along in her supple leather trousers, plain linen shirt, and sleeveless leather doublet at the younger woman's elbow, an identical short sword riding at each hip and a dagger sheathed horizontally at the back of her belt. At least she wasn't in chari and yathu, and she tried not to feel too much like a coward for having avoided that traditional garb for this visit . . . so far, at least, she reminded herself wryly. She'd have plenty of time to outrage everyone before she left.

And it's not as if you don't genuinely prefer trousers when you ride, she scolded herself. *You only wear the chari—and the yathu—to Thalar to make a point to Trisu and his idiots. No need to rub anyone's nose in it here.*

They ascended the steps up into the great keep with Leeana following one stairstep below Sharlassa. Which, given the difference in their heights, meant the top of her head was only a few inches higher than Sharlassa's all the way up. Then they stepped through the great double doors and crossed the vast, cool entry hall where the banners of Bowmaster and Balthar hung from the beams far overhead, with servants bowing to Sharlassa as they passed, and started up the inner stair towards the family's private quarters. Sharlassa waited until they'd climbed halfway to the first landing, then stopped and looked at Leeana.

"And now that we're inside," she said, pitching her voice to reach only Leeana's ears, "I'd better not hear another 'Milady' pass your lips." Leeana started to smile, but the smile faded as Sharlassa glared at her with what looked like true anger. "I understand the rules," the younger woman said, "and I suppose I actually appreciate them. But I'm *not* your lady and this *is* your home and *I'm* a visitor in it, not you!" Her eyes softened and she shook her head, reaching out to lay one hand on Leeana's elbow. "I'm sure I can't really imagine how difficult it is for you to come home on a visit, Leeana. I know it has to be hard, though. Please don't make it any harder on yourself—or on me—than it has to be."

She may not have gotten any taller, but she has *grown*, Leeana thought, reflecting on the confidence and assurance in that scold. *Of course, she's wrong... but she's right, too.*

"All right, Sharlassa," she said. "At least when we're in private."

"Good." Sharlassa gave her elbow a little shake, then smiled. "In that case, I believe your mother is waiting in the solarium."

✧ ✧ ✧

"Look who I found, Milady!" Sharlassa announced as she opened the solarium door and waved Leeana through it.

Hanatha Bowmaster was tall, although not remotely as tall as her daughter, and her back was straight as she leaned on her cane, despite the right leg which had been crippled so many years before. But there were streaks of silver in her long, black hair, Leeana realized. Streaks which hadn't been there before, still tiny enough she might not have noticed if their flicker hadn't caught the sunlight pouring in through the solarium's windows. And there were lines in her face which hadn't been there before Leeana ran away from home. But her eyes—those green eyes, exactly like her daughter's—lit with delight as she saw Leeana at Sharlassa's shoulder.

"Leeana!" Hanatha started towards her, but Leeana dropped her saddlebags and blanket and crossed the solarium in three long strides before her mother could move. Her arms went around Hanatha in a crushing hug, and she felt a pang as she realized how much taller she'd become. Her cheek pressed the top of her mother's head, exactly as Hanatha's cheek had once pressed hers, and she felt those pesky tears burning in her eyes once more.

"Oh, it's so *good* to see you, love!" her mother half-whispered, and then gasped as Leeana's arms tightened even further. "Mind the ribs!" she scolded. "Your father already broke them once!"

"Sorry." Leeana's voice was husky, and she cleared her throat as she released her mother and stood back. She held Hanatha at arm's length, hands on her upper arms, and smiled a bit mistily into her eyes. "Did he really?" she asked after a moment. "Break them, I mean?"

"Yes, he did, love." Her mother reached up to touch her cheek. "The morning you were born."

Leeana swallowed hard, looking back into her mother's face for a moment, and then nodded.

"Well," she said in a more normal voice, "I'll try not to follow in his footsteps—in that regard, at least. But it's wonderful to see you, too." She gave Hanatha's arms a brief squeeze, then stepped back. "Your letters are wonderful, but it's just—"

She broke off and shrugged, and it was Hanatha's turn to nod.

"I know," she agreed. "I know. But you're here now, and that's what really matters." She looked past Leeana to where Sharlassa stood just inside the door, smiling at them both. "Somehow I have the feeling someone is playing truant again," the baroness observed, raising one forefinger in an admonishing gesture. "Under the circumstances, however, I'm inclined to let it pass... this time."

"Thank you, Milady," Sharlassa replied meekly... and dimpled.

"Well, since you are playing truant, and since we have a guest, why don't you ask someone to send up a light tea for the three of us?"

"Of course, Milady," Sharlassa agreed, turning back towards the door, and Hanatha waved her daughter towards the window seat along the solarium's western wall.

Leeana started to stoop and pick up her saddlebags, but Hanatha shook her head.

"Time enough for that later," she said, shooing her daughter towards the window seat. "I don't doubt that war maid code of yours is going to demand you carry them to your chamber yourself instead of relying upon the labor of some hapless servant like a properly decadent aristocrat, but there's no rush. Besides, much as I've come to love Sharlassa, the girl is unnaturally neat." She shook her head. "You can't imagine how much I've missed having a proper teenager's clutter around the place!"

"Was I really that bad?" Leeana smiled. "I *tried* to keep it out of your sight in my room, you know."

"Yes, you *were* that bad," Hanatha said firmly.

She settled into a comfortable chair, facing the window seat, and studied her daughter intently for several seconds. Then she nodded.

"It suits you," she said simply.

"I beg your pardon?" Leeana arched an eyebrow, and her mother snorted.

"Leeana, I practically had to rope and tie you to get you into a gown before you ran off to the war maids. And while it's probably highly improper of me to say this, I always actually sympathized with you a lot more than you knew. But this"—a wave of her hand gestured at Leeana's trousers, shirt, and doublet—"suits you far better. And at least it's not as scandalous as that chari and yathu—if I got it right—of yours!"

The words could have been biting, but instead they were almost teasing, and Hanatha's eyes flickered with what certainly looked like genuine amusement.

"I hope they aren't *too* scandalous for you, Mother," Leeana said after a moment in a rather more serious tone, and Hanatha shrugged.

"I won't pretend I wouldn't really rather not have you showing your belly button to all the world, my dear," she said dryly. "And it would probably be as well for me to keep my opinion of other aspects of traditional war maid attire to myself, as well. For that matter, I strongly suspect you never want to hear your *father's* reaction to the first time he ever saw you in it."

She rolled her eyes, but then her expression sobered.

"Nonetheless, Leeana, it's part of who you are and who you've become, and I expect you to wear those scandalous, overly revealing, appalling garments with style, grace, and composure." She squared her shoulders, resting her folded hands atop the cane braced upright before her. "I doubt you can truly understand, even now, how terribly it hurt when you ran away to the war maids, but most of that hurt of mine was about what I knew it was going to cost you. No mother wants to see her daughter pay that kind of price, especially for something which was never her fault in the first place. But what it's taken me quite a long time to fully understand from your letters and those fleeting visits of yours is how much you've *gained* from it. You were always a falcon fighting its jesses, even when you didn't know it yourself. Now you're free to fly, and I want you to fly high, love. Stretch those wings and soar."

Leeana looked back at her, then swallowed hard.

"Thank you, Mother," she half-whispered.

"You're welcome. Although, judging from your track record, you probably really don't need a great deal of encouragement. I wouldn't precisely want to call you *headstrong*, of course—although, now that I think about it, I can't come up with a more appropriate adjective—but I have this strange suspicion that a young woman who ran away to become a war maid at fourteen isn't very likely to start settling for anyone else's foolish restrictions at this late date. In fact, you're extraordinarily like your father in that respect. Although it's to be hoped you're at least a *little* smarter."

Hanatha's last sentence came out with a certain tartness, and Leeana's eyebrows rose.

"I know that tone, Mother," she said, settling back in the window seat as Sharlassa came back from her errand and sat facing her and Hanatha both. "I admit it's been a while since I've heard it, but I *do* know it. So what is it that Father's been up to that you didn't include in your letters?"

Chapter Sixteen

Chemalka wasn't cooperating, Sir Trianal Bowmaster reflected. Or not yet, at least, he amended. There was still time for Her to straighten this mess out, and he sent an urgent mental appeal to Her to get on with it. Who knew? It might even do some good, despite Her well-earned reputation for completely ignoring the requests of mere mortals.

The thought was rather less amusing than it might have been, and the night-black stallion under him stamped one rear hoof as it caught its rider's mood. The warhorse blew heavily, tossing its head, and Trianal shook his own head mentally. Anyone who knew Windy (otherwise known as Nightwind Blowing) well wouldn't have any problem reading his rider's mood from the stallion's body language. Not that it was very likely Trianal was the only one thinking what he was thinking at the moment.

"Never did like fog, Milord," Sir Yarran Battlecrow said conversationally. Trianal turned his head, and the older knight smiled crookedly at him. "Seems like you and I have been here before, doesn't it, Milord?"

"I was just thinking that myself," Trianal admitted, remembering the very first battle he'd ever commanded... and how comforting Sir Yarran had been to him that time, too. Windy had been under his saddle that time, as well, now that he thought about it. "But at least there's no damned swamp for them to be hiding in!"

"Don't know as how fog's that much of an improvement," Sir Yarran said philosophically, easing himself in the saddle and glancing back over his shoulder at the waiting light cavalry.

"Leastwise, it wouldn't be if we were the ones who had to go in after the bastards."

"I'd just as soon *no one* had to go in after them blind," Trianal said a bit testily. "And in visibility like this, we *are* going to have to go in amongst them if everything goes according to plan. Won't *that* be fun?"

Sir Yarran made a sound of unhappy agreement and craned his neck, peering up in hopes of discovering that the sun had suddenly decided to rise in the heavens and burn away the ground fog. Instead, all he saw was more fog—cold, damp, thick... and thoroughly unseasonable.

He lowered his gaze to the dripping branches of the scrub trees among which the members of Trianal's command group had parked themselves. They were farther out in front of the main body than Sir Yarran really liked. In fact, it made his spine itch uncomfortably, although his concern was far more about something happening to Trianal than it was about anything happening to him personally. And, under normal circumstances and against another foe, he wouldn't have been worried as much about Trianal as he was, either. But ghouls were blindingly, incredibly fast, and despite their size, the damned things moved like ghosts. Then there was that keen sense of smell of theirs. It was said a ghoul could sniff out spilled blood more than a league away. Yarrow found that difficult to believe, yet he was prepared to admit their sense of smell matched that of the finest hunting hound he'd ever seen. Which meant it was entirely possible one of them had already scented the Sothōii's presence, in which case the gods only knew how many of them might be flitting around in the mist just out of sight right this moment. And if one of them took it into whatever passed for a ghoul's mind to launch an attack on the cavalry force's youthful commander...

Stop that, he told himself firmly. *It's not going to happen. And even if it does, there isn't much you can do about it unless you want the lad to go hide somewhere in the rear ranks, and you know how well* that *suggestion would work!*

"'Fraid you're probably right about the bows in this stuff, Milord," he said glumly, after a moment. "Still and all, it'll take their javelins out of it, too."

"You *are* determined to find a bright side, aren't you?" Trianal's tone was sour, but he gave Sir Yarran a smile to go with it. Then he sobered and turned to one of his aides. "Head back along the column, Garthian. Tell them it's going to be lance and saber, not bows. And"—he held up a restraining hand as the courier started to turn his horse's head back towards the rear—"tell them anyone I see charging ahead without somebody to cover his flanks is going to wish he'd never been born . . . assuming he survives long enough for me to rip his head off, at any rate. Clear?"

"As crystal, Milord!" Garthian replied with a broad smile.

"Then go. And keep your voice down while you're passing the word."

"Aye, Sir!" Garthian slapped his chest in acknowledgment, turned his horse, and went briskly cantering back along the mounted column.

"Think Yurgazh and Sir Vaijon will hold to the schedule, Milord?" Yarran asked more quietly as the spattering thud of muddy hoofbeats faded.

"I'm sure they will," Tellian replied. "Trust me, Yarran," he turned and looked into his henchman's eyes levelly, "one thing they *aren't* going to do is leave us hanging out here in the fog by ourselves."

✧ ✧ ✧

"Don't suppose you could have a word with Scale Balancer about this fog, Sir Vaijon?" Yurgazh Charkson grumbled, waving one hand in front of his face like a man trying to brush away a fly. It made him look a little silly, Vaijon thought, not that he intended to say anything about it.

"I'm afraid weather is Chemalka's jurisdiction, not Tomanāk's," he replied.

"Pity," the Bloody Sword general half-grunted. He started to add something more—probably something fairly biting, Vaijon thought—but he stopped himself, and the champion smiled crookedly.

Yurgazh was one of the hradani who still had remarkably little use for any gods, Light or Dark, Vaijon reflected. From what he'd learned of the hradani's struggle to survive for the last twelve centuries, Vaijon couldn't really blame them for holding to the opinion that no gods had done them any favors during the process. Tomanāk had always had a certain grudging acceptance among them as the one God of Light a warrior could truly respect, although (much as it dismayed him to admit it) Krashnark had enjoyed almost as much respect. The balance had tipped in Tomanāk's favor when He revealed the truth about the Rage to all hradani through Bahzell, but it probably would have been demanding a bit too much to have expected all hradani everywhere to immediately embrace the Gods of Light after so many centuries.

Not that he could disagree with Yurgazh's fervent desire that *some* god would take it upon himself or herself to dispel the unexpected fog. If there'd been some way to get word to Trianal, Vaijon would have been tempted to suggest they call off the attack entirely until the weather had cleared. Unfortunately, there wasn't any way to get word to the Sothōii—not without risking having any courier go astray and probably ride smack into the enemy, in this fog—which meant they were committed.

And wasn't that going to be fun?

Ghouls were nothing anyone in his right mind, even a hradani, wanted to engage in hand-to-hand combat. They were constructs from the Wizard Wars which had doomed Kontovar, and no one seemed to know how any of them had made the journey to Norfressa. They weren't the only... less than desirable echoes of the Fall which had washed up in Norfressa, unfortunately. In fact, until very recently, no Sothōii had made much of a distinction between ghouls and hradani, and in some ways—especially considering the way in which arcanely enslaved hradani had served as the Carnadosans' shock troops during the Wizard Wars—it wasn't that hard to understand. But even the Sothōii, at their worst, had recognized that ghouls were far more dangerous than the hradani, and not simply because they had even more objectionable personal habits.

Unlike hradani, with their low fertility rates, ghouls had been specifically designed to reproduce quickly and mature rapidly, which meant even a relatively small infestation of them could grow to frightening size with dismaying speed. They weren't precisely what anyone might call fastidious eaters, either, and any given band or village of ghouls had no friends, even among their fellow ghouls.

Physically, ghouls resembled trolls. They were a bit shorter—few of them stood much over eight and a half feet in height—and more lightly built, but their frames were deceptively powerful and their reflexes were unbelievably swift. According to Wencit of Rūm, who certainly ought to know, that speed had been arcanely engineered into them along with their reproduction rate, and they paid for it with ravenous appetites and shortened lifespans. It was unusual for any ghoul to attain as much as forty years of age, and most of them died before they were thirty-five, which was no more than half the lifespan of a troll. They were almost as hard to kill as a troll, though, and like trolls, they recovered with almost unbelievable speed from any wound which didn't kill them outright. Indeed, they healed much faster even than hradani; it wasn't unheard of for a troll's or a ghoul's blood-spouting wound to close itself and actually begin healing in the course of the same battle in which it had been inflicted. The only way to be certain of killing one of them was to take its head; otherwise, what a warrior might have been certain was a corpse was all too likely to recover and rip *his* head off from behind.

What made ghouls even worse than trolls was threefold. First, their greater speed made them far more dangerous in a fight, far more difficult to outrun, and far more difficult to run *down* if they tried to evade. Second, unlike trolls, ghouls used weapons other than their own admittedly efficient talons and fangs. They were *crude* weapons, fashioned out of stone and wood, not iron or steel, but a chipped flint javelin head could kill a man just as dead as one forged from the finest Dwarvenhame steel, and the sawlike obsidian teeth which fringed their wooden war clubs might be fragile, but they were also razor-sharp. And third, and worst of all, they were *smart.*

The one true blessing about trolls was that they were stupid, little more than mobile appetites. That had its downsides, since it meant they were unlikely to recognize times when discretion was the better part of valor, but it also meant every small band of trolls operated entirely on its own. The idea of cooperating with anyone outside the immediate family group simply didn't occur to them.

Ghouls understood the advantages of cooperation. Like trolls, they were egg layers, and—also like trolls—they were carnivores. The one good thing about their intelligence (from anyone else's perspective, at least) was that they understood the value of raising their own meat animals, and as long as there was sufficient chicken, mutton, goat, or beef from their own flocks and herds, they were content to stay home. Unfortunately, it took a lot of meat to keep a village of ghouls fed. Even their willingness to eat their own eggs—or their own young—often failed to keep their populations down to something their herds could support, and when that happened, they went raiding.

And since they were prepared to eat their own young, they saw no reason they shouldn't eat anyone else's, as well. Which, coupled with the fact that—like the trolls from which, according to Wencit, they'd been bred—they preferred their food living, pretty much explained why they were not preferred neighbors.

Both the hradani and the Sothōii had tried at one time or another to sweep the Ghoul Moor clear and exterminate them once and for all. Unfortunately, a single female could produce literally scores of eggs in her lifetime, which was the reason even a handful of trolls or ghouls could grow to astounding numbers in an astonishingly short time. Even worse, both Troll Garth and the Ghoul Moor backed up against Barren Fell, and Barren Fell was terrible terrain to follow them into. Hilly, uneven, heavily overgrown, it offered ideal hiding places or spots from which they could ambush pursuers. And, worse yet, directly on the far side of Barren Fell lay the Forest of the Sharmi. No one in his right mind went into the Sharmi, and upon occasion things much worse than any troll or ghoul came *out* of the Sharmi. At least twice, the Sothōii had believed they'd actually finished the ghouls off, only to have them reemerge from the Sharmi and Barren Fell to reclaim the Ghoul Moor once again.

There was a reason the River Brigands confined themselves almost entirely to their settlements and towns close to the shores of the Spear and the Lake of Storms. There was also a reason Bloody Swords near the fringes of Troll Garth lived in palisaded towns, not on individual farmsteads, and always posted sentries at night. And there was a reason Prince Bahnak and Baron Tellian had decided the best they could hope for was to clear a strip along the Hangnysti and secure it with fortified camps and patrols.

But to do even that, they had to clear out the ghoul villages in that area, and that was always hard, dangerous, and ugly. Ghouls matured physically quickly, but there were always dozens of their young—for the life of him, Vaijon simply could not apply the word "children" to them—in any village. Ranging in size from twenty or thirty pounds up to as much as a hundred, they were just as vicious as their fully grown parents, but killing them bothered him far more than it did to kill a full adult. Unfortunately, there was no way to convince any ghoul—cub or adult—to surrender.

The only two approaches to any other living creature which they seemed to grasp were to attack and devour or to run away, and running away was usually their second choice.

Tomanāk, he thought now wryly, *I know I just told Yurgazh the weather was up to Chemalka, but if You could see Your way to giving Her a nudge and getting this fog out of here, I'd appreciate it.*

There was no direct reply, although he did think he might sense someone else's rueful amusement in the back of his brain. Not that he'd really expected a reply. A champion of Tomanāk didn't count on his deity to lead him about by the hand.

"Well," he sighed finally, pulling his dwarf-made watch from his belt pouch and consulting its face, "it's about time, Yurgazh."

"Lovely," Yurgazh grunted, and glanced over his shoulder.

Vaijon and the twenty or so human members of the Hurgrum Chapter who were present were the only mounted troops in Yurgazh's entire force. Now the Bloody Sword turned to look at those motionless, waiting ranks of infantry with the fog drifting about them and shook his head.

"All right, lads," he told his officers. "You see the Phrobus-damned fog as well as I do. So it's going to be cold steel instead of arrows." No one said a word, but no one had to. Although the majority of Bloody Swords continued to feel archery was an effete and possibly even immoral way for a proper warrior to settle a quarrel, none of them looked forward to letting a ghoul into sword range. "Keep your ranks, keep those damned shields up, and keep your heads," Yurgazh continued in that same pre-battle growl, raising his voice to reach the companies closest to hand. "We want as many kills as we can get here so we won't have to kill 'em later, but I'd just as soon take as many of *you* home afterward as I can. Keep that in mind."

Something almost like a chuckle rolled along the waiting lines of infantry, and he smiled.

"In that case, let's summon the Rage and be about it!" He glanced at the bugler beside him. "Sound it," he said flatly.

✧ ✧ ✧

"Hear that, Milord?" Sir Yarran said sharply as the clear, rapid notes came soaring through the fog, faint with distance, and Trianal nodded.

"I told you they wouldn't leave us hanging about by ourselves, didn't I?"

"That you did, Milord."

Trianal flashed the older man a smile, then looked at his own bugler.

"Be ready," he said.

✧ ✧ ✧

Vaijon moved forward behind the double line of infantry Yurgazh had deployed to lead his attack.

No one was going to confuse Confederation troops with the Royal and Imperial Army, but hradani tactics had improved immensely under Bahnak Karathson's influence. Yurgazh had placed two of his battalions in a line five hundred men wide and two ranks deep while his other two battalions followed in platoon columns, prepared to deploy to either flank or to reinforce the front line. Vaijon and the double handful of mounted Sothōii members of the Order of Tomanāk rode between the columns, followed by fifty dismounted brothers—*and one* sister; *let's not forget that,* Vaijon thought just a bit sourly, deliberately not glancing back at Sharkah Bahnaksdaughter—all ready to counterattack any unexpected break in the hradani lines. Not that any such break was likely to occur.

There were two schools of thought about the best way to attack a ghoul village. One was to sneak up on it as unobtrusively as possible and attack with the advantage of surprise. The other was to let it know you were coming in order to draw its defenders out into the open in one spot so you knew where they all were. Of course, in either approach the idea was to kill as many of them with bows or crossbows as you possibly could before you ever got to the hand-to-hand part of the business, which wasn't going to happen this time, but the principle remained the same even for those stupid enough to take ghouls on without archery support. Over the last couple of years, Vaijon had had the opportunity to see both approaches tried, and he'd decided that—given steady troops who could be expected to hold their formation—drawing them out was better than the sorts of ambushes and nasty little fights which were likely to accompany a surprise attack that went charging in among a village's crude stone and notched-log buildings.

Now he heard the yelping voices of ghouls, calling to one another, sounding the alarm from the other side of the dim, misty fog. Their intelligence on exactly how many ghouls they were about to confront was less complete than he would have liked—intelligence was *usually* less complete than one might like where ghouls were concerned—but it was unlikely there were more than a few hundred of them. This was one of the villages they'd cleaned out (and burned) last year, and not even ghouls would have had time to repopulate it with an entire new generation. On the other hand, it was an ideal location for a village, with reliable water and plenty of pasture land near at hand, which made it exactly the sort of place which would attract any roving band looking for a place to settle. From the number and volume of the yelps coming out of the fog, it sounded like the band in question might well have been larger than they'd anticipated.

"Watch your front!" Yurgazh's voice bellowed. There was something different about its timbre—something Vaijon recognized instantly after all these years. It was the voice of a hradani who'd given himself to the Rage, deliberately summoned the ancient curse of his people to serve his will.

Vaijon still didn't know whether he more envied or pitied the hradani for the Rage. He'd seen it in action too many times not to recognize the strength and focus and absolute clarity it bestowed upon someone who had knowingly summoned it, and no fighting man could possibly fail to understand what an enormous advantage it was in combat. But by now he'd seen too many instances of the *old* Rage, the Rage which had come without summons—often even without warning—and reduced its victim to a berserk, blood-maddened killer who could be stopped only by killing *him* instead. It happened far less often than it had since Tomanāk and Bahzell had told the hradani they could master it rather than be mastered *by* it, but it was still far too common. Much as he might envy the power and absolute, unstoppable determination of the new Rage, the price the hradani had paid for it had been terrible almost beyond belief, and they were not yet done paying it.

His thoughts broke off as the first wave of ghouls came loping out of the fog towards them. Most of them yelped louder, waving their war clubs and their spears, when they saw the hradani. A handful—smarter, or perhaps simply more cautious—turned and fled back the way they'd come, but the ones who didn't flee hurled themselves towards their enemies with all the blinding speed of their kind.

"Axes! *Axes!*"

The bull-throated war cry of clan Iron Axe went up from the

lead battalion, but no one rushed to meet the ghouls. Once upon a time, they would have, but that had been when the Rage was their master, not their servant... and before Bahnak had taught their warriors to be *soldiers,* men who understood discipline was far more valuable than simple individual skill and strength. Now they drew the Rage's focus, that ice-cold, distilled purpose, about them, holding their ranks, advancing at a steady walk rather than charging furiously as so many individuals.

The ghouls attacked with less concern about formations than even pre-Bahnak hradani would have shown. They were smart enough to recognize the advantages in working and fighting together, yet the notion of actually thinking through their tactics seemed to elude them... which was just as well, given their sheer size, speed, and strength. There were very few foes who could match hradani for size and strength; ghouls *over*matched them. A foot and more taller than all but the tallest Horse Stealer, they towered over the shorter Bloody Swords, with an enormous advantage in reach and sheer physical power. And they were faster, faster even than a hradani riding the Rage. They hit the front line of Yurgazh's infantry as individuals, but only in the sense that an avalanche was built of *individual* boulders.

"Axes! Axes!"

Howls of pure ghoulish fury answered the war cry, and then the outriders of that avalanche were upon the hradani. Stone-tipped javelins—javelins longer and heavier than many humans' two-handed thrusting spears—soared over the front rank, seeking targets beyond, and one of the Order's horses screamed in agony and went down. But only a handful of them were thrown; the others came thrusting for flesh with deadly speed.

Stone shattered on stout shield faces as the infantry closed up the way Bahnak—and Vaijon—had taught them. Their huge, rectangular shields—boiled leather over heavy multi-ply layers of seasoned wood and rimmed in iron, modeled on the tower shields of the Axeman army but even larger—were a moving fortress wall, covering them from shoulder to knee. They were big enough to help cover the man to their left, as well, leaving an opening between adjacent shields just wide enough for them to wield their own weapons. The ghouls flung themselves against that shield wall, snarling and slavering in their rage, and yelps of fury became howls of anguish as steel blades licked out from the wall's battlements, driving into flesh and bone with ghastly, wet crunching sounds.

Some of the ghouls went down, snapping and twisting, clutching at their own wounds and yet still lashing out at any hradani they could reach. Others hewed at the shields, scoring their surfaces, splintering the stone heads of their spears or the stone teeth of their war clubs. They were so strong, so powerful—and struck so quickly—that even Horse Stealer hradani riding the Rage were staggered by the raw impact of their blows, and here and there, a hradani went down as well. There were no screams of pain from them—not from hradani in the Rage—and even as they went down, they struck back. Vaijon saw one of them on his back, covering himself under his shield, as he drove a sword blade up and completely through the body of the ghoul leaping on top of the shield to claw and tear. The ghoul twisted and raised its snout to howl in agony just in time for one of the downed hradani's shieldmates to lop its head from its shoulders. It pitched over, and someone in the second rank grabbed the fallen man's harness and heaved him to his feet.

The stink of blood and riven bowels rose in the distinctive stench of battle, but the hradani drove onward, moving forward with steady, merciless precision. Many of those who'd gone down came back to their feet, like the one Vaijon had watched, as their companions advanced. Some had been merely stunned, bowled over or lightly wounded, and they moved forward to regain their places in the formation. Others, with more serious injuries, were turned back by sergeants and corporals when they tried to do the same thing. Not all of them were able to rise, even with the Rage pulsing in their veins, and parties of designated and trained corpsmen (another innovation of Prince Bahnak's) followed the front line, checking for signs of life and moving the more seriously wounded back from the fighting.

Part of Vaijon wanted desperately to fling himself from the saddle and minister to those wounded warriors himself, but he couldn't do that yet. The battle was still to be fought, and he couldn't turn away from that.

Many of the ghouls had shattered and broken their weapons against the shield wall. Most of those who had went loping back towards the village, perhaps in retreat but more probably to find fresh spears and clubs. Others, though, flung themselves bodily on the hradani's shields, seizing them in razor-sharp, curved talons, trying to wrench them aside, batter them down so that they could lunge across them with their fangs. Some of them were so strong they actually managed to drag even Horse Stealer hradani forward, out of formation, shaking them by their shields the way a terrier might shake a rat. A handful of other ghouls turned on the exposed hradani, ripping at them from behind, yet the rest of the infantry line drove forward, taking the ghouls from the side or behind in turn. Another handful of ghouls hurled themselves into the openings where hradani had been pulled out of position, but only to meet the unshaken shield wall of Yurgazh's *second* line and the avenging swords driving in from either flank as the first line cut them down.

Specially detailed squads followed behind the second line, decapitating downed ghouls. Quite a few of those theoretically dead ghouls showed a dangerous degree of fight when the cleanup squads closed in on them, but they were no match for their disciplined, organized, and uninjured enemies. The foggy morning was hideous with grunts, gasps, screams, blows, the thud of clubs on shields and flesh, the sounds of steel driving through sinew and bone, and a fresh wave of ghouls—this one more organized than the first—came sweeping out of the mist.

"*Axes!*"

The war cry went up to meet them, and now a fresh shout of "*Bone Fists!*" roared up from the second line to join it. Screams of pure, wordless fury answered, and a new, better organized torrent of ghouls crashed into the shield wall.

The new attack hit hard enough to actually stop the hradani in their tracks. They hunkered down behind their shields, bending their helmeted heads as if against the blast of a hurricane, and put all their strength, all their Rage, into simply holding their ground as that flood of squealing, yelping flesh and muscle hammered into them. For a moment Vaijon thought even a line of hradani was going to break, and at least a dozen men went down—none of them to rise *this* time, as throats were ripped out or they were dragged out of position into that whirlwind of war clubs and spears and rending claws—yet they held. They held, and the thick, powerful voice of Yurgazh Charkson of the Navahkan Bloody Swords rose over all that hideous clamor.

"By the right flank . . . *advance!*" he thundered, and the battalion at the right end of his line responded instantly.

"Stone Daggers—*at the charge!*" its commander bellowed, and the column slammed forward like Tomanāk's own mace, hooking in from the flank to drive into the ghouls who had coalesced in front of Yurgazh's battle line.

The ghouls shrieked as that hammer blow crunched into them. They'd been so focused on the foes in front of them that they'd never seen the flank attack coming, and simple surprise would have been enough to rock them back on their heels. But there was more than surprise in that attack—there was razor-edged steel, there was fury... and there was the Rage.

The charging column ground over the ghouls in front of it, cutting them down, trampling them underfoot, driving them before it, and panic replaced the ghouls' savage determination. They began to fall back, and once the first of them gave ground, it became a retreat... and then a rout. They went pounding back the way they'd come, and the charging battalion started after them.

"*Halt!*" Yurgazh bellowed, and in what would have startled any pre-Bahnak hradani commander more than anything else which had happened, the column obeyed instantly.

"Stone Daggers, form front!" he continued. "Iron Axes, take the flank!"

The Iron Axe battalion which had taken the initial brunt opened its ranks, allowing the Raven Talon battalion of the second line to pass through it while the Stone Daggers formed a new front rank. The Iron Axes filed to the right, settling into column formation to replace the Stone Daggers, and Vaijon's mouth tightened as he realized at least twenty or thirty of them were down, wounded or dead. That was what happened when even hradani had to fight ghouls hand-to-hand, yet with the fog negating archery...

"Advance!" Yurgazh commanded, and the hradani moved forward once again, closing in on the village where, hopefully, they would discover the bulk of the ghouls had already been dealt with.

And where we may discover nothing of the sort, instead, Vaijon thought grimly. *House-to-house is going to be really ugly if we haven't, too. Unfortunately, there's only one way to find out. And at least our lads are better suited for this kind of work than Trianal's Sothōii are.*

It no longer even occurred to him to think of the hradani around him as anything except "our lads," and the Hurgrum Chapter of the Order of Tomanāk moved forward with him as they followed.

A bugle call sounded from somewhere in the mist ahead of them—a cavalry call, not an infantry one—and he heard fresh yelps and snarls and the sound of human war cries, faint with distance but growing in intensity as the first wave of fleeing ghouls encountered the waiting Sothōii.

"At least they'll be broken when they run into Trianal's lot," a voice said beside him, and he turned his head and looked at Yurgazh. The Bloody Sword general shook his head, his expression a strange alloy of battle fever, determination, and the icy control of the Rage. "I'd as soon not be taking this kind of knock myself, you understand," he continued with a crooked smile, "but better us than the horse boys. Not their kind of fight, I don't think."

"No," Vaijon agreed, "but they'll do their bit. In fact"—another bugle call sounded through the fog—"it sounds like they're doing it right now."

"Never doubted it," Yurgazh said simply. "And now, if you'll excuse me, I've a battle to see to and a village to burn."

He jerked his head at his bugler, his standardbearer, and his runners, and the entire command group went forward at a trot behind his infantry.

Chapter Seventeen

“Beg pardon, Milady.”

Baroness Hanatha looked up from her cup of tea as the armsman stepped respectfully into the small breakfast parlor. She normally breakfasted alone when Tellian was away, but since Leeana had returned home to visit, she’d eaten with the two younger women each morning.

“Yes, Mardor?” she said.

“Beg pardon, Milady, but the Sergeant sent me to tell you there’s a courser arrived here at the castle.”

“A courser?” Hanatha repeated, lowering her teacup and raising both eyebrows in surprise.

“Yes, Milady. A mare. A big one, and she looks pretty . . . well, banged up, if you’ll pardon my saying so.”

“She’s been *hurt?*” Hanatha set down her cup with a snap, starting to climb urgently out of her chair. Her haste betrayed her so that she stumbled on her weakened leg, and Leeana came swiftly to her own feet, reaching for her mother’s elbow.

“Oh, no, Milady!” The armsman shook his head quickly, his expression apologetic as Leanna caught the baroness’ weight and steadied her. “I’m sorry. I meant she’s been hurt bad sometime *before*, not now. She’s lost an eye and an ear, and she’s scarred pretty bad, too.”

Hanatha’s eyes widened. Leeana still looked confused, but her mother nodded crisply to the armsman.

“Where is she?” she asked.

“Well, Milady, Sergeant Warblade didn’t want to leave her

standing at the gate, nor she didn't look like she was any too fond of that notion, her own self. So the Sergeant passed her through and she found her own way to the stables right smart. When I passed, she had her nose down in a bag of oats and seemed like she was doing pretty well."

"I see." Hanatha straightened and picked up her cane, then looked at Leeana and Sharlassa. "Ladies, it sounds as if we have a visitor who's come quite some way. I believe that as dutiful hostesses we ought to go and welcome her to Hill Guard, don't you?"

✧ ✧ ✧

Leeana was unprepared for the sight which greeted her as she followed her mother and Sharlassa into Hill Guard Castle's spacious, meticulously neat stable yard.

His stables were the pride of any Sothōii noble—or, for that matter, of any reasonably prosperous Sothōii yeoman—and Hill Guard's had been rebuilt completely little more than fifteen years earlier. Faced with marble, made of fired brick with thick heat- and cold-shedding walls, well ventilated and heated against the winter's chill, and supplied with piped-in water, they'd also been made much loftier than most, which was fortunate, since they were currently home to no less than three coursers. The well drained, freshly washed-down brick stable yard was just rough enough to provide a horse or courser with secure footing, and a large fountain at its center jetted water high into the air before it came tumbling back down into a circular marble catch basin in a musical smother of foam.

That much was as familiar to Leeana as the palm of her own hand, but the huge chestnut mare standing beside the fountain, just finishing off the oats the stablemaster had offered her on her arrival, was something else. The distinctive Sothōii warhorses stood about fifteen hands in height, and the largest draft horse Leeana had ever seen stood no more than seventeen hands, or about five feet eight at the withers. Her father's courser companion, Dathgar, on the other hand, stood twenty-one hands and two inches, a foot and a half taller than that, yet the mare in the stable yard was enormous even by courser standards. Courser mares averaged somewhat smaller than courser stallions, but *this* mare didn't seem to have heard about that. She must stand almost a full hand taller even than Dathgar. Indeed, the only courser Leanna had ever seen who would have been taller than her was

Bahzell Bahnakson's Walsharno, who stood the next best thing to twenty-*five* hands.

Yet it wasn't just the mare's size that took the eye. Her confirmation was breathtaking. No Sothōii could look at her and not see the perfect proportions, the perfect muscle balance, the fine shape of that proud head. Toragan Himself could not have crafted a more magnificent creature... which made her disfigurement all the more shocking. A line of startling white marred her coat's smoothness, marking the scar where some long-ago claw or fang had ripped her flesh from the point of her left hip forward almost to her shoulder. Another ugly scar ran downward along her right knee and cannon, and a dozen other patches of white marked where other wounds—long healed, but obviously terrible—flawed her coat. Her right ear was only a stump, and her maimed right eye socket was empty.

Whatever "unseemly choices" Leeana Hanathafressa might have made in her life, she was a Sothōii to her toenails, and her stomach twisted around her recent breakfast as she saw those scars, those long-ago wounds. They were more than simply confirmation of the terrible damage this courser had suffered; they were a desecration... and they were unforgivable.

Yet even as she thought that, the mare raised her head, turning it sideways so that she could focus her remaining golden eye on the newcomers. No, not on all the newcomers, Leeana realized—on *her*.

"This is an unexpected pleasure, Milady," Hanatha said, leaning on her cane as she swept an abbreviated curtsy to the courser. "Welcome to Hill Guard, Gayrfressa."

Leeana's eyebrows shot up. Of course! She ought to have recognized who this courser had to be from those scars, from that missing ear and eye. Who could it have been but Gayrfressa, one of the only seven adults of the Warm Springs herd to survive Krahana's attack... and Walsharno's sister? And a worthy sister she was, Leeana reflected, trying to imagine what it must have taken for those seven surviving mares—*none* of the stallions had lived—to fight free of Krahana's shardohn demons with the handful of foals they'd managed to save. And Gayrfressa had been the youngest, and the most savagely wounded and maimed, of them all. "Daughter of the Wind," her name meant in Old Kontovaran, and the north wind itself should be proud to call her its own,

Leeana thought, her own eyes burning as that big, intelligent eye considered her.

Gayrfressa gazed at Leeana for another moment, then glided across the stable yard towards Hanatha. She moved with the impossible grace which no one who'd never seen a courser move would have believed was possible in something so massive and powerful. She stopped directly before the baroness, head turned aside so she could see her, and then leaned forward to just touch Hanatha's hair with her nose. She exhaled gently, then raised her own head once again, and Hanatha smiled up at the huge creature towering over her.

"You're most welcome, Milady," she said, "but I fear Dathgar and Gayrhalan are both stuck in Sothōfalas with Tellian and Hathan, and Walsharno is somewhere between there and here at the moment, so we have no one to translate for us."

Gayrfressa snorted and shook her head in obvious amusement. Then she looked away from Hanatha at Leeana once more, and the baroness cocked her own head. She looked at her daughter for a moment and then shrugged.

"I think Gayrfressa's business may be with you, love," she said.

"With me?" Leeana's voice sounded entirely too much like a teenager's on the pronoun for her own satisfaction, and her mother chuckled.

"Well, she's not being discourteous, but she's also not looking at *me* at the moment, now is she? May I ask if I'm correct, Milady?"

Gayrfressa looked back at Hanatha and then tossed her head in clear, unambiguous agreement. The baroness shrugged.

"There you have it, Leeana. I would suggest that since Gayrfressa has clearly come quite some distance, it would only be courteous for you to see to the quality of our hospitality." The baroness let her eyes sweep the watching stablehands and raised her voice ever so slightly. "In this, you act for me and for your father," she said. "I'm certain you'll be able to find any assistance you might require."

"I—" Leeana changed what she'd been about to say and bent her head in a respectful bow. "Of course, Milady."

"Good." Hanatha let her gaze circle the stable yard one last time, then held out her free hand to Sharlassa. "Come with me, my dear. I'm sure some of that tea is still left. Until later, Milady."

She gave Gayrfressa another one of those half-curtsies, and

then she and Sharlassa departed, leaving Leeana nose-to-nose with the towering courser.

✧ ✧ ✧

"Well, this is the first time I've had *this* problem in years," Leeana murmured wryly as she stepped up onto the stool.

She'd already checked and picked out Gayrfressa's feet, noting in passing that it was time the courser was reshod. Now it was time to work down the mare's coat with the dandy brush, starting at the poll, which posed a slight problem, since the top of Gayrfressa's head was over ten feet off the ground. That was quite a reach, even for an overgrown war maid, hence the stool.

Gayrfressa made an amused sound as Leeana lifted her mane to the far side to get it out of the way and began working the dandy brush down her neck. Coursers, like horses, spent a great deal of their time in the wild grooming one another, and they were cleverer about it than horses because of their greater intelligence. Nonetheless, they didn't have hands, and on the occasions when an uncompanioned courser came calling on the two-footed inhabitants of the Wind Plain, simple courtesy required those who did have hands to groom them properly and completely. Of course, Gayrfressa wasn't leading a stabled existence, so it wouldn't do to give her the complete rubbing down with body brush and scrubbing cloth Leanna gave Boots each day. Horses—or coursers—exposed to the elements needed a little grease and oil in their coat. On the other hand, Gayrfressa was a lot of mare to groom at all.

"Oh, I don't know as it was all that long ago . . . Ma'am."

Leeana looked over her shoulder and Doram Greenslope smiled at her. Greenslope had served in Hill Guard's stables at least since the creation of the world. As a senior undergroom, he'd taught Tellian himself how to ride, and he'd become stablemaster years before Leeana was born. He'd taught *her* how to ride, as well, and schooled her rigorously in the care, treatment, respect, and courtesy to which any horse was entitled. Along the way, he'd also pulled a rambunctious girl child out from under various horses when she'd gone darting into their stalls, helped set the left arm one of those horses had broken, and—at least once that she could remember—hauled her out of the stable yard fountain after the gelding a six-year-old Leeana had been enthusiastically riding bareback decided to stop unexpectedly for a drink.

Now he stepped up beside her with a polite bob of his snow-white head to Gayrfressa.

"I seem to remember someone needing a *ladder* to groom Dathgar," he went on to Leeana. "Yesterday, that was, or maybe the day before."

"Trust me, it was longer than that, Doram," Leeana said, moving the dandy brush in long, sweeping strokes to break loose the sweat and dust clinging to Gayrfressa's coat. The courser's remaining ear moved and her eye half-closed in pleasure, and Leeana smiled. But then her smile dimmed, as she looked back at the stablemaster. "It was a lifetime ago," she said softly.

"Ah, now, that's a weighty thing, a lifetime," Doram replied. "So far, mine's been a mite better than three of yours... Ma'am." He smiled. "And I'm planning on being around for quite a few more years, you understand, so maybe a lifetime's just a bit longer than it might be seeming to someone your age."

"Maybe." She shook her head, her eyes going back to the steadily moving brush. "But you can measure lifetimes in more than just years. There's what you do with them, too."

"And you've gone and used yours up already?" The irony in the stablemaster's voice pulled her gaze back around to him, and it was his turn to shake his head. "Seems to me you've time enough to be doing just about anything you choose to with your life... Leeana."

Tears blurred her vision for a moment. It was the first time in her life Doram Greenslope had ever addressed her simply by her name. No honorific, no "ma'am," simply "Leeana." He never would have dreamed of doing such a thing when she'd been heiress conveyant to Balthar... and how many "properly reared" Sothōii men would ever have called a *war maid* by her name at all, she wondered?

"Was a time," Greenslope continued, looking back up at Gayrfressa and reaching up to stroke the white blaze running down the mare's forehead, "when you just about lived in this stable. Learned a lot about you when you did, and nothing I've ever seen or heard's changed who you were. *What* you were, maybe, but what's inside... that's harder to change. Might be you've made some decisions I'd sooner a daughter of mine not make, but I'm one as spends a lot of time around horses—and coursers—and their riders, young Leeana. Could be I've heard a thing or two passing between a certain wind rider I might name and his courser, or between him and his wind brother while they were seeing to their coursers together. And it might just be, you know," he turned his head, meeting Leeana's eyes levelly, "I've heard a story about why a certain young lady ran away from home that's not so much like the ones I hear in town."

"I—"

The dandy brush stopped moving, and Leeana felt a mortified blush sweeping over her face as her throat closed and she literally could not speak. She stared into Greenslope's eyes, and the stablemaster did something he hadn't done since she was ten years old. He reached up one gnarled, work-hardened hand and laid it ever so gently against her cheek.

"I'd not want my daughter to make that decision, lass," he said quietly, "but my heart would fair bust with pride if she did. And I don't think any lass as had the heart and courage and the love to make it is going to do anything with her life that could ever cause shame to those as love her."

Tears welled in Leeana's eyes, and he smiled crookedly, then smacked her cheek lightly with his palm and turned away.

"I'll just go and see to the manger in Her Ladyship's stall," he said, and walked away whistling.

✧ ✧ ✧

"You look . . . better," Hanatha said, regarding her daughter across the table.

Tahlmah Bronzebow had successfully corralled Sharlassa before she could escape at the end of lunch and hauled her off for a session with Sir Jahlahan, leaving Hanatha and Leeana to sit in companionable silence. Now Leeana swirled her glass of lemonade, listening to the gentle clink of a few precious pieces of ice from the spacious Hill Guard icehouse. It was a scandalous luxury, of course, and one she hadn't sampled in at least six years.

"I feel better," she admitted, looking up from the glass to meet her mother's gaze. "I hadn't really talked with Doram in too long."

"Ah." Hanatha smiled faintly. "I wondered if he might take the opportunity to offer you some sage advice."

"Sage advice?" Leeana tilted her head, looking at her mother quizzically, and Hanatha chuckled.

"Doram Greenslope's been a fixture of Hill Guard since before your father was born, my dear. And I don't suppose any Sothōii with a working brain—which *does* describe your father . . . most of the time, at least—picks a fool to supervise his stables, do you? Over the years, Doram's found a way to give quite a few bits and pieces of sage advice to various inhabitants of this castle. Including various inhabitants who happen to be sitting across the table from each other at this very moment." Her green eyes warmed. "I'd be lying if I said I hadn't hoped he might have a few gems to share with *you*, love."

"Well, he did," Leeana acknowledged, feeling her eyes prickle afresh with memory. "And you might want to mention to Father that just because no one else can hear Dathgar when Dathgar talks to him, that doesn't mean no one can hear *him* when he talks to *Dathgar*."

"So Doram knows the real reason you ran away?" If Hanatha felt any distress over the discovery, she hid it well, Leeana thought.

"He didn't come straight out and say 'I know you ran away to avoid that proposed betrothal to Rulth Blackhill, well-known philanderer, lecher, and rapist,'" Leeana said dryly, "but I think he had most of it figured out."

"Including the bit about running away to prevent your father's political enemies from using you as a weapon against him?" Hanatha asked softly.

"Maybe." Leeana looked back down into her lemonade again and inhaled deeply. "No, not maybe. He *knows*; I'm pretty certain of it."

"Good," Hanatha said in that same soft voice, and Leeana looked back up quickly.

"Mother—" she began, but Hanatha's headshake cut her off.

"Leeana, there's no one in the entire Kingdom who can see lightning or hear thunder who hasn't figured out by now that the dearest desire of Cassan Axehammer's heart is to see your father ruined and—preferably—dead," she said calmly. "The lines have been drawn for longer than you've been alive, and the political battlefield's changed—changed pretty significantly—since you became a war maid. To be honest, part of that is *because* you became a war maid, which cleared the way for your father to formally adopt Trianal as his heir. I suppose it's unfair, but removing you from the succession and settling it firmly on a *male* heir took the wind out of Cassan's sails where that whole flank attack was concerned. And then Bahzell had the sheer effrontery to save the survivors of Gayrfressa's herd from Krahana, after which he and Kaeritha—with the help of your father and a few other wind riders and coursers—settled that situation in Quaysar and Trianal and Lord Warden Festian settled Cassan's hash in that little campaign of his to ruin Glanharrow. And as if that weren't enough, there's this whole new canal project and tunnel your father's concocted with Kilthandahknarthas and Brandark!"

She paused to take a sip of her own lemonade, then smiled crookedly.

"Darling, if any of us had been able to read the future and know what was going to happen in Warm Springs and in Quaysar, and what Trianal and Sir Yarran were going to do to Lord Saratic's armsmen, there would never have been any *need* for you to 'run away' to the war maids. I regret that more than I could ever tell you, in many ways. I regret what it's cost you, and I regret the last seven years that it's cost your father and me because it was so painful for you to come visit us here."

Leeana started to protest, but her mother shook her head and raised her hand.

"Leeana, I've loved you more than life itself from the day your heart began to beat beneath mine, and so has your father," Hanatha said quietly. "And, I'm sorry to tell you this, but you really can't lie or pretend very well to me. Not when I can look in your eyes, hear what your voice is trying to hide. I know exactly why you've stayed away for so many years. Perhaps I should have said something about it at the time, but to be honest, I thought it wouldn't hurt to let you do a little more growing up before you came home to deal with the kinds of looks and attitudes you're likely to deal with here in Balthar. You were always strong, love, but sometimes it takes a while to grow the armor we need, and you needed the time away from here to grow yours.

"Now I think you have, because when I look at you now all I see is the strength, not the pain. I don't doubt there's still hurt in there, because I don't see how it could be any other way, but you've got the strength—and the armor—to watch it bounce off instead of cutting you to the quick. Enough that maybe you'll realize Doram isn't the only one of your old friends who's missed you. And I'm not surprised Doram's kept your father's confidence and not broken a few tankards over loudmouthed heads down at the Crimson Arrow when they started talking about the barony's 'disgraced daughter.' I'm sure he *wanted* to, but he'd never dream of revealing anything he learned in confidence... or by accident, especially if it might hurt the family, however badly his heart might have wanted to tell certain idiots what really happened. And, truth to tell, it was probably a good thing he did, at least for the first few years. But now?"

She shook her head again.

"Now I don't think your father's worst enemies could make any capital at all out of the fact that you 'fled' to the war maids to prevent Cassan and his cronies from using a forced betrothal to you as a weapon against him. And the fact that you're a war maid, shocking and appalling as that must be to any decent-minded person"—Hanatha's irony was withering—"doesn't worry either of us a single solitary damn." Leeana's eyes widened, because Hanatha never swore even the mildest of oaths, but her mother only smiled. "Time and events have moved on, love, and hard as that decision was for you at the time, it simply doesn't matter now. I don't care who Doram might choose to share his interpretation of the truth with. In fact, I hope he shares it with everyone in Balthar!"

It was a day for revelations, Leeana thought, feeling the glass of lemonade cold in her fingers. First Doram and now her mother.

Should've known better than to think you could fool her, *nitwit,* she told herself. *Your skull always was made out of glass where she was concerned. But I wonder if—?*

"I... I don't think he has to," she said out loud. "Oh, it matters to me that *he* knows, and it matters more than I could ever say that you understand why I stayed away. But you're right, I think—probably more right than I would've realized before this moment. I have grown the armor I need; I just hadn't realized I have." She smiled, and if it was a bit lopsided, that smile, it was also warm and loving. "I don't need Doram to convince anyone else I did the right thing as long as *I* know I did and as long as I know *you* believe I did. We despicable war maids are used to standing up for ourselves, you know."

"So I've heard," Hanatha said with a smile of her own. "But even the hardiest of warriors can occasionally use an ally, and Doram could be a very useful one. No one's ever dared to denigrate you openly in front of your father or me, but I'm pretty sure quite a few people who might have done just that—your Aunt Gayarla comes to mind—have refrained only because they felt we would have defended you out of mushy-minded love, no matter what you'd done. Oh, admittedly becoming a war maid wasn't a minor social faux pas like, say, *murder*," her smile flashed suddenly into a grin, "but it was undoubtedly the same thing. Just a pair of parents unable to accept what a totally self-centered, spoiled ingrate of a child they'd raised. But Doram has a rather different perspective on you and the family, and anyone who knows him knows he's about as stubborn and independent-minded as they come. He could go a long way toward defanging some of the resentment and anger I know a great many in Balthar feel where you're concerned. Of course, quite a few of those people are going to be extremely reluctant to admit they've been wrong for the last half-dozen years or so, so they probably won't. It's much more comfortable to cling to your bigotry than it is to admit you've been wrong to feel it in the first place, you know."

"I do know. You only have to look at how some of them still feel about hradani," Leeana agreed and snorted just a bit more harshly than she'd intended to.

"True."

Hanatha sat back in her chair, regarding her daughter thoughtfully, then cocked her head.

"Odd you should mention hradani, love," she said.

"Odd?" Leeana's tone sounded a bit forced to her own ear. "Odd how, Mother?"

"Well, it's just that the only *other* person no one ever dared to denigrate you in front of—I mean, aside from your father and me, who love you, of course—was Prince Bahzell."

"Oh?" Leeana swore with silent, vicious venom as her voice cracked on the single syllable, and her mother smiled again, with an odd gentleness this time.

"Yes. Well, I imagine that would only be to be expected, now that I think about it. He *is* a champion of Tomanāk, after all. He recognizes justice—and injustice—when he sees it, and he did know the true reason you'd run away. And on top of all that, there are those scandalous liberties the hradani allow their own womenfolk, so naturally he'd be more blind than a proper Sothōii to how the war maids violate every conceivable canon of respectable female behavior. No doubt that's why he was always so quick to defend you."

"He was?" The question was forced out of Leeana against her will, and her mother's smile grew broader.

"Actually, now that I think about it, it wasn't so much the way in which he sprang to your defense as the way he simply *looked* at whoever might have made the unfortunate comment. It's most entertaining to see a strong man's knees quiver under a mere glance, you know. No," her tone turned thoughtful, "I don't believe he ever actually had to *say* a single word."

"He... always seemed to understand," Leeana said slowly. "Before I ran away, I mean. He... gave me some very good advice." She smiled at her mother a bit mistily. "If I'd listened to him, I never would've run."

"No, you wouldn't have," Hanatha agreed. "And that would have been a very wonderful thing... from my perspective. But from yours?" She shook her head. "Your father is one Sothōii noble in a thousand, Leeana. You would have grown up freer, less confined, than any other young woman of your station in the Kingdom. And you would never have become all you can be, because there still would have been limits, barriers, not even he could have removed for you. And"—Hanatha Bowmaster's eyes stabbed suddenly into her daughter's—"you would never truly have been free to follow your heart wherever it leads you."

Silence hovered, so still the buzzing of a bee in the flowers of the open window's planter box could be clearly heard. Then Leeana very carefully and precisely set down her glass and looked at her mother.

"You've guessed?" Her tone made the question a statement, and Hanatha nodded gently.

"I told you, you've never really been able to hide your feelings from me, sweetheart. I guessed long ago, before you ever fled to Kalatha, in fact. For that matter, I've always suspected it might have been one of the reasons you ran."

"I..." Leeana inhaled deeply. "I think, perhaps, it was. At least a little," she admitted.

"That made me very angry with him, for a while," Hanatha said in the tone of someone making an admission in return. "I thought how silly it was—how *stupid*—for me to have lost my only daughter over a schoolroom miss's infatuation. How ridiculous it was for you to have ruined your life at fourteen for something that could never happen. But I don't know if *he* ever realized it at all." She paused, frowning, then shook her head. "No, that's not really quite right. I don't know if he ever *allowed* himself to realize it at all. You're very young, you know," she smiled faintly, "and you were considerably younger then."

"Maybe I'm not as much of a war maid as I thought I was." Leeana's voice was a mixture of wry admission, frustration, and anxiety. "Somehow I never really envisioned us having this particular conversation, Mother. And . . . and I'm afraid."

"Afraid?" Hanatha asked gently. "*My* daughter, afraid? Ridiculous. A slight case of nerves I'll allow, but not fear. Not in someone who will always be a daughter of the House of Bowmaster, whatever that silly war maid charter may say!"

Leeana surprised herself with a gurgle of laughter, and her mother leaned forward, reaching across the table to stretch out an index finger and wipe away the single tear Leeana hadn't realized had trickled down her cheek.

"Better!" Hanatha said.

"Maybe so, Mother, but it doesn't get me any closer to a solution to my problem, now does it?"

"Leeana Hanathafressa, are you going to sit there and tell me—as your *father's* daughter, as well as mine—that you came all the way home to Hill Guard for your *twenty-first* birthday, without a plan of campaign? Please! I know you far better than that."

"But, you really wouldn't . . . I mean, you and Father won't . . . ?"

"Six and a half years ago, possibly I would have," Hanatha admitted. "For that matter, *four* years ago I might have. But now? Today? Today you've earned the right in my heart, as well as under the law, to make this decision without deferring to anyone except your *own* heart. I'd love you and accept and respect any decision you might make, even if I felt it was a mistake which would bring you more heartache than you could possibly imagine. Fortunately, I don't think you are making a mistake, and I've had every one of those years you were away to watch him any time your name was mentioned."

"Then you truly won't be distressed?"

"Have you become hard of hearing as a war maid, dear?"

"No! No, I haven't," Leeana assured her with another, freer laugh.

"Good, because I was beginning to think you must have!"

The two of them sat in silence for the better part of two minutes, then Hanatha picked up her own glass of lemonade, sipped, and set it back down once more.

"I trust you do have a plan of campaign," she told her daughter with a composed expression, "because I'm quite sure he's spent the last seven years going over every reason it would be totally unsuitable, unacceptable, wrong, and diplomatically disastrous. I wouldn't be a bit surprised by now if he's managed, with that excess of nobility I've noticed he tries very hard to hide, to decide he never actually felt any of those things in the first place. In fact, he's probably done almost as good a job of it—no, maybe even a *better* job of it—than Trianal's done where Sharlassa is concerned."

"Trianal and *Sharlassa?*" Leeana's eyes widened.

"Of course, Leeana!" Hanatha shook her head. "She's a dear, sweet child, but that isn't the only reason I've been so happy to have her staying here at Hill Guard while we polish her education in all those things *you* managed to run away from. And she, of course, thinks she's far too poorly born to be a suitable match for Trianal, while he thinks she's too young—Lillinara, all of seven years younger than him!—for him to be thinking about 'robbing the cradle' or using his position as your father's heir to 'pressure' her into accepting his advances." The baroness rolled her eyes. "There are times I feel surrounded by nothing but noble, selfless, utterly frustrating blockheads."

"Oh, my!" Leeana laughed, leaning back in her own chair. "It really would be a perfect match, wouldn't it? And it would take all of the traditional political alliance-building out of the equation when it comes time to find Trianal a wife. Even better, no one on the Council could possibly object if Father and Sir Jahsak both approve of it. And you *know* Sir Jahsak would always support Trianal as his father-in-law!"

"You see? You truly are your father's daughter. Leaving aside the undoubted political and tactical advantages, however, *I* think it would be a good idea because whether they realize it yet or not, they're both in love with each other. Which, oddly enough, brings me back to you, my dear."

"It does? How?" Leeana's voice was wary, and her mother snorted.

"You *have* been listening to me for the last, oh, half hour or so, haven't you? Trianal and Sharlassa? You and . . . someone else? You wouldn't happen to see any parallels emerging here, would you?"

"Well, yes, actually," Leeana admitted.

"Well then. Do you want my advice or not?"

"Of course I do," Leeana said, mostly honestly, and Hanatha smiled.

"I'm afraid you're going to have to be direct, love," she said.

"Possibly *very* direct, because I think you can trust him to come up with at least a thousand perfectly plausible reasons why it would all be a dreadful mistake and somehow a betrayal of your father's hospitality and friendship. Not to mention a political disaster." She cocked her head thoughtfully for a moment, then shrugged. "Actually, the 'political disaster' idea is probably his best argument against it, so if I were you, I'd take steps to avoid or neutralize it as early as possible. I understand war maids can be shamelessly forward in matters like this. Is that true, my dear?"

"I've . . . heard it said, yes, Mother," Leeana replied primly.

"Good. A frontal attack, that's the ticket. A surprise assault," Hanatha's eyes gleamed with what Leeana realized was genuine humor, possibly even delight. "An ambush, before he can get his defenses erected." She gave her daughter another very direct look. "Was that approximately what you had in mind?"

"Something very much along those lines, actually, Mother," Leeana admitted, feeling the blush heating her cheekbones.

Her mother considered her for several moments, then smiled.

"Good," she said again. "And now that that's settled, my dear, would you care for a little more lemonade?"

Chapter Eighteen

<No, she hasn't *told me why she's here.>* Walsharno's long-suffering mental voice didn't sound particularly surprised, Bahzell noted. *<She* never *tells me why she does things. Why should she? I'm only her older brother. Only a champion of Tomanāk. Why in the world should she worry about telling* me *why she does things? I can tell you this much, though—she's got some kind of secret that has her just absolutely* delighted *with herself!>*

"Well," Bahzell replied, his own tone rather more pacific and consoling than his companion's as Walsharno moved smoothly up the approach road towards Hill Guard, "I'm not so very surprised as all that, I suppose. I'm thinking there's never a sister been born as didn't think her brother was after poking his nose where it didn't belong. Not a one of *mine* ever did, any road."

<I'm a courser,> Walsharno pointed out. *<We're* supposed *to poke our noses into each other's business! It's one of the traits we share with the lesser cousins.>*

"And mighty handy I'm sure you find that when it's time to be pestering Gayrfressa," Bahzell observed shrewdly. "And not so much when it's time for her to be pestering you."

<You're supposed to be on my *side, you know, Brother.>*

"Ah, but himself wouldn't be so very pleased if I were to take it into my head to be starting to lie just because the truth's one as you're not so very fond of."

"My mother," Brandark remarked to no one in particular from where he rode at Bahzell's side, "always told me it was impolite to have a conversation in which not everyone present had the opportunity to participate."

"Did she, now?" Bahzell looked down at the Bloody Sword with a smile.

"Yes, she did." Brandark tilted his head back to look back up at his towering companion. "Of course, now that I think about it, I believe she also mentioned something about Horse Stealers' ideas about politeness and manners in general being just a little backward."

<*Tell him I'd be perfectly willing to include him in the conversation if I could only figure out how to hammer a thought into his brain,*> Walsharno said tartly. <*Of course, first I'd have to* find *it!*>

"Now, that I won't," Bahzell told his companion, smiling at Walsharno's mobile ears. "If it's an insult you're mindful to give him, then I'm thinking you should figure out how to do it yourself and not be dragging me into it. I've insults enough for him of my very own."

"Oh, you do, do you?" Brandark's eyes glinted. "Well, I've got some for you that I'd considered trotting out, but I thought better of it."

"*You* thought better of it?" Bahzell flattened his ears, regarding the Bloody Sword incredulously.

"Yes, I did," Brandark said virtuously. "I was inspired by something Vaijon pointed out to me before he left with Yurokhas, actually."

"Aye?" Bahzell's eyes narrowed in suspicion. "And what would that have been?"

"He simply pointed out that it's both unjust and unfair to challenge an unarmed man to a duel."

"Did he now?" Bahzell glanced up at the curtain wall and towers beginning to loom before them and his expression turned speculative. "I'm wondering how high someone would bounce if someone else was to be tossing him off the main keep's battlements?"

"Lady Hanatha would be very upset with you for making such a mess in the courtyard," Brandark said severely.

"Aye, there's that," Bahzell acknowledged. "Still and all, I'm thinking she'd likely consider why it might be I'd gone and done it, and she *does* know you. Taken altogether, I've no doubt she'd be willing enough to forgive me as long as I promised to be cleaning up the mess my own self."

Brandark laughed, conceding the round, then cocked his head inquisitively.

"Still, I have to admit the two of you have managed to pique my curiosity. Should I assume Gayrfressa's been up to something?"

"In a manner of speaking." Bahzell shrugged. "I've no more idea why than Walsharno, you understand, but she's taken it into that head of hers to be paying us a visit."

"She has?" Brandark reached up and rubbed the tip of his truncated ear thoughtfully. "All the way from Warm Springs."

"Aye. I thought as how I'd caught just a trace of her yesterday, but it wasn't until this morning Walsharno and I were sure of it." Bahzell flipped his ears. "Not that she's said a thing at all, at all, about why it might be she's here."

"She's always struck me as fairly independent-minded for a courser," Brandark observed.

<"Fairly *independent-minded*"?> Walsharno repeated, and tossed his head with a superb snort. <*Well, I suppose that's accurate enough. Just like saying "It snows a little on the Wind Plain each winter!"*>

Bahzell chuckled, but Brandark and Walsharno had a point. A very good one, in fact. Gayrfressa was a courser, with the innate sense of corporate identity they all shared. Individuals, yes, all of them were that. But they were constantly aware of themselves as a component of their herd, as well. Yet Gayrfressa had... not less of that awareness, but a stronger sense of her individuality to set against it. She was far more likely to go her own way than any other courser mare Bahzell had ever met, and he certainly knew her well enough to realize that.

Any wind rider became accustomed to the shapes and patterns of courser personalities, yet Bahzell was even more aware of them than most. When he'd healed the survivors of the Warm Springs courser herd, a part of him had... *merged* with them. That was the only way he could describe it, and none of the other wind riders he'd discussed it with—and it wasn't something he discussed even with many of them—had ever heard of it happening before. As nearly as he could tell, he'd acquired the herd sense—the awareness of every other member of the herd, whenever he was within a few leagues' distance—which set courser herd stallions apart from all other coursers. And his link with Gayrfressa was stronger and richer than with any other member of the herd, perhaps because she was Walsharno's sister, or perhaps because she was the first of the survivors he'd healed.

<And perhaps because she loves you so dearly,> Walsharno murmured in the back of his brain, and Bahzell sent back a wordless surge of affection.

It was true enough, he thought, and it worked both ways. Besides—he chuckled at the thought—Gayrfressa was probably the only creature on earth who was even stubborner than Walsharno.

<Probably the only four-footed *creature, at any rate,>* Walsharno observed dryly.

<And aren't you just the most humorous fellow this morning?> Bahzell replied, and heard Walsharno's silent laughter in his brain.

"I'll allow as that's a fair enough way to describe her," he told Brandark out loud. "Still, I'm thinking there might be just a mite more to it than usual this time. She's not given Walsharno so much as a hint as to why she's come, and it's pikestaff plain she's something on her mind. Aye, and it's something as has her amused clean down to her hoofs."

"Chesmirsa!" Brandark rolled his eyes. "Something a *courser* thinks is funny? I wonder—if I start running now, do you think I can get out of range in time?"

<No,> Walsharno said as the gate tower's shadow reached out to claim them and the gate guard came to attention. *<Not if* Gayrfressa *thinks it's funny.>*

✧ ✧ ✧

Bahzell swung down from Walsharno's saddle in the stable yard. Over the years, he'd actually learned to do that gracefully, despite both Walsharno's height and the traditional Horse Stealer lack of familiarity with horses large enough to bear their weight. In fact, he looked quite *improbably* graceful for someone his size, if the truth be known.

He reached up to pat Walsharno on the shoulder, and the stallion bent his lordly head to lip his companion's hair affectionately, as Doram Greenslope came out to personally greet them.

"Welcome home, Prince Bahzell! Walsharno!" the stablemaster said, crossing the stable yard to bow respectfully to Walsharno. "And to you, too, Lord Brandark."

"It's glad we are to be here, Doram," the hradani replied, and it was true. In fact, in many ways, Hill Guard—Sothōii fortress or no—was at least as much his home—and Walsharno's—now as ever Hurgrum had been. And wasn't that the gods' own joke on hradani and Sothōii alike?

"We've visitors," Greenslope continued as he beckoned two of the stable hands forward to take the pack horses' leads from Brandark and see to the Bloody Sword's warhorse.

"Aye, so Walsharno and I had guessed," Bahzell rumbled, turning towards the stables as Gayrfressa appeared.

The big chestnut mare crossed the bricks towards him with that smooth, gliding courser's gait, her head turned to the right so that her single remaining eye could see where she was going. The hradani felt a familiar pang as he saw the scars not even a champion of Tomanāk had been able to erase, and her eye—the same amber-gold as Walsharno's—softened with shared memory as he felt his regret. But it was his memory she shared, and not his regret. That had always astounded him, yet it was true. The loss of her eye, of half her vision, was... inconvenient, as far as Gayrfressa was concerned, although Bahzell would have found it far worse than that if their positions had been reversed. Unlike any other hradani ever born, he'd actually *shared* a courser's vision, the ability to see a world totally different from that of the Races of Man. Like the horses from which they had sprung, coursers possessed very nearly a three-hundred-sixty-degree view of their world. They saw distances differently, colors were even more vivid in many ways, and they were accustomed to seeing everything about them with a panoramic clarity that was difficult to imagine and impossible to adequately describe. They *knew* what was happening around them at virtually every moment.

And Gayrfressa had lost that. Any courser—or horse—had a tendency to flinch when something or someone managed to get into its blind spot, for those blind spots were small, and they were unaccustomed to having that happen. Yet half of Gayrfressa's world had gone black on the day a shardohn's claw ripped through her right eye socket. That would have been more than enough to turn a lesser creature into a nervous, perpetually wary, and cautious being, but not Gayrfressa. The absolute boldness of her mighty heart refused to back down even from the loss of half her world, and he sensed her gentle amusement at his own reaction to her fearlessness. Because, he knew, she genuinely didn't see it that way. It was simply the way it was, and all she had ever asked of the world was to meet it on her feet.

"And good day to you, lass," he rumbled, reaching up to wrap one arm around her neck as she rested her jaw on his shoulder. He couldn't hear her mental voice the way he could hear Walsharno's, but he didn't have to. She was there, in the back of his brain, and the depths of his heart, glowing with that same dauntless spirit—older and more seasoned, now, but still the same—he'd sensed on the dreadful day they'd met.

<*And for me, too,*> Walsharno said, loudly enough for Bahzell to hear him as clearly as Gayrfressa. The stallion leaned forward, nibbling gently at the base of his sister's neck in greeting, and her remaining ear relaxed in response to the grooming caress. Then she raised her head and touched noses with him.

"And who might be seeing after Sharnofressa and Gayrhodan while you're off gallivanting about?" Bahzell asked teasingly, and Gayrfressa snorted.

She remained a bachelor, without the permanent mate most coursers found by the time they were her age, but she'd done her bit to help rebuild the Warm Springs herd. Her daughter Sharnofressa—"Daughter of the Sun," in Old Kontovaran—was four and a half years old, one of the almost unheard-of palominos who were born so seldom to the coursers, and her son Gayrhodan—"Born of the Wind"—was almost two, and bidding to become the spitting image of his Uncle Walsharno. Coursers matured slightly more slowly than horses, but Sharnofressa had been on her own for some time now, and Gayrhodan was certainly old enough to be trusted to the rest of the herd's care—and surveillance—while his mother was away.

<*She says Gayrhodan probably hasn't even noticed that she's gone yet,*> Walsharno told Bahzell dryly. <*I can't decide whether she's more pleased by his independence or irritated by it.*>

"Not so much unlike us two-foots, after all, aren't you just?" Bahzell said, reaching up to the side of her neck again. "And would it happen you're minded to tell us now what it is as we owe the honor of your presence to?"

Gayrfressa looked at him for a moment, then snorted and shook her head in the gesture of negation the coursers had learned from their two-footed companions. He gazed back up at her, ears cocked, then shook his own head. If she wasn't, she wasn't, and there was nothing he could do about it. Besides—

"Hello, Prince Bahzell," another voice said, and he froze.

For just a moment, he stood very, very still. Then he turned, and it would have taken someone who knew him well to recognize the wariness in the set of his ears, the intensity of his gaze.

"And good day to you, Mistress Leeana," he said.

✧ ✧ ✧

<*Gayrfressa knew she was there, you realize,*> Walsharno murmured from the stable as Bahzell made his way up the exterior stair towards the quarters he'd been assigned in Hill Guard's East Tower. East Tower had been his home for almost seven years now, and his feet knew the way without any need for directions from his brain. Which was just as well, since his brain had other things to be thinking about just now.

"Sure and I'm not so clear what you're meaning," he said to his distant companion, and heard Walsharno's gentle laughter in the back of that overly occupied brain of his.

<*Brother, your secret is safe with me, but it's scarcely a secret* from *me,*> Walsharno told him. <*And surely, despite how hard you've tried, it can't be a secret from* you, *either, now can it?*>

"I'm not—"

Bahzell stopped, standing on the stair, turning away from the tower to look at the setting sun, and drew a deep, lung-swelling breath.

"It's not something as could happen, Brother," he said softly.

<*Why not?*> Walsharno's tone was honestly curious…and deeply loving. Clearly, the courser didn't understand all the innumerable reasons why it couldn't happen, but then coursers had discovered over the centuries that quite a few things the Races of Man did didn't make a great deal of sense to them.

"Taking first things first," Bahzell said considerably more tartly, "I'm after being hradani, and she's after being human—aye, and Sothōii, to boot! I'm thinking it wouldn't be more than half—no more than two-thirds, at worst—of all the Sothōii warriors in the world as would be hunting my ears. And after that, she's after being Tellian and Hanatha's daughter. A fine thing it would be if such as me—and twice her age and more, come to that—was to be breaking their trust that way! Aye, and her the daughter of the Lord Warden of the West Riding! Wouldn't *that* just make such as Cassan and Yeraghor sit up and start sharpening those daggers all over again."

<*I thought the war maids made up their own minds about things like this,*> Walsharno said. There was no irony in the stallion's

tone, only simple thoughtfulness. <*And doesn't their charter absolve them of any relationship to their birth families? I never really understood exactly how that bit is supposed to work—it has to be a two-foot thing—but how could anyone be offended or upset because of her relationship to Tellian and Hanatha if she doesn't have one anymore? Legally, I mean?*>

"There's matters of law, and then there's matters of custom, and finally there's matters of the heart." Bahzell's voice was softer than it had been. "Whatever the law might be saying, there's those as would use *custom* against Tellian quicker than spit, if such as me was to be wedding such as she. And I've no interest at all, at all, in what the law might be saying, either, Walsharno. Charter or no, that lass will be the daughter of their hearts until Isvaria takes them both, and I'll not break those hearts. There's better for her than me, and safer, too."

He shook his head, ears flattened.

"I doubt the thought's ever so much as brushed her mind—and if it did, it was never aught but a young lass's imaginings when she'd grief and worry enough for a dozen lasses twice her age! Aye, and when she'd done no more than turn to an older and a wiser head for counsel." His lips tightened, remembering a conversation atop another tower of this very castle. "I'd no business thinking what I was thinking then, and a fine fellow I'd be to be taking advantage of a lass so young who'd done naught but cry on my shoulder, so to speak. And that was all it was after being, Walsharno. Naught but a lass in pain and a foolish hradani thinking things he'd no business thinking, with her so young. Aye, and I *knew* she was too young for me to be thinking any such! And for all it's true my skull's a bit thicker than most, it's not so thick as to think she'd any deeper thought of me than that... and well she shouldn't have. No." He shook his head again. "No, there's things as can be and things as can't, and all the wishes in the world can't turn the one into the other, Brother."

<*I think you're wrong,*> Walsharno told him gently, <*but coursers don't think the same way two-foots do. Perhaps this is simply one of those things we don't understand very well. But whether you're willing to admit it even to yourself or not, this choice of yours is heavy on your heart, Brother.*>

"Oh, aye," Bahzell half-whispered. "It is that. Yet it is what it is, and I'll not shame her by trying to make it something it isn't."

Walsharno made no reply to that—not in words—but his loving support poured through Bahzell, and the hradani leaned against it as he might have leaned physically against the stallion's tall, warm side, taking comfort from it. He stood there for several more minutes, unmoving, then shook himself and continued up the stair.

"Welcome home, Milord!" Tala Varlonsdaughter had obviously been awaiting his arrival, and she greeted him with an enormous smile as she opened the tower door. "We've missed you!"

"Ah, and I you!" Bahzell replied, smiling almost naturally at her and sweeping her into a warm embrace. He picked her up and bussed her firmly on the cheek, and she laughed and swatted him.

"None of that, now!" she told him. "I'm a respectable old woman, I'll have you know!"

"Aye," he sighed in deep, mock regret, shaking his head as he set her back on her feet. "And a sad disappointment that's been to me over the years!"

She laughed again, smiling up at him fondly, and he remembered the terrified Navahkan "housekeeper" who'd helped him smuggle Farmah to safety despite her awareness of what would have happened to her had Churnazh caught the brutalized young maid trying to escape. Her own son was long dead, but as the head of his household here in Hill Guard, she'd become almost a second mother to him, and clearly a foster mother to every single member of the Hurgrum Chapter of the Order of Tomanāk when they came to call. She took far better care of him—and Brandark—than they deserved, he thought fondly, and that didn't even consider her *cooking*!

"And did Lady Hanatha feed you, Milord?" she asked now, eyeing him shrewdly.

"That she did," he admitted, choosing not to mention the fact that he'd eaten rather less than usual. The food had been excellent, as always, but the red-haired young woman sitting across the table from him had tightened his stomach and turned the tasty meal into something very like sawdust in his mouth.

"I'm thinking it's time and past time I was in bed," he continued, smiling down at her, and she smiled back, ears half-cocked.

"No doubt you're right, Milord," she agreed, and tilted her head to one side. "Now that you mention it, you do look tired—and why shouldn't you, after riding all day to get here?" She made shooing motions towards the internal stair to his bedchamber, waving both hands. "Go! I'm sure you'll feel better in the morning."

"No doubt you've the right of it," he said, nodding to her, and headed for the stairs.

Brandark had excused himself after dinner and taken himself off to Balthar, where, no doubt, he was even then making the rounds of his favorite inns and taverns with his balalaika. It was unlikely he'd be back much before dawn—if then—and Bahzell's lips twitched with amusement at the thought while he climbed the stairs. With his luck, Brandark would have composed a new verse to "The Lay of Bahzell Bloody Hand" by morning to "suitably" chronicle Tellian's attempted assassination. He hadn't added anything new to that accursed ditty in almost a year, after all, and nothing that good could last forever.

He chuckled to himself as he reached the landing, opened the door, stepped through it . . . and froze.

"Hello, Bahzell," Leeana Hanathafressa said. "I've been waiting for you."

Bahzell stood in the open doorway, head bent slightly—as it had to be to clear doorframes even in a Sothōii castle—and stared at her. She sat crosslegged on the foot of his bed in the leather breeches and doublet that couldn't make her look even remotely masculine, however hard they tried, and cocked her own head slightly.

"Are you going to just stand there all night?" she asked gently, and he shook himself, stepped very slowly into the room, and closed the door behind him.

"Better," she said with a small smile. "Why don't you have a seat?"

She pointed at one of the chairs Baron Tellian had had manufactured to a hradani's stature, and Bahzell sank into it, his eyes still fixed upon her. She looked back at him, one elegant eyebrow raised, and he shook himself.

"Lass—" he began, then corrected himself. "Mistress Leeana, I'm thinking as how you shouldn't be here," he said.

"No?" She considered him with a thoughtful eye, then shrugged. "Why not?" she asked simply.

"Why not?!" He stared at her for a moment. "Because—"

He broke off, and her smile grew a bit broader. Amusement danced in her green eyes, and yet that smile had an edge of tenderness that sang in his heart. It was a song he had no business listening to, however. He told himself that firmly, and his nostrils flared as he drew a deep breath of resolution. But she spoke before he could.

"Bahzell," she said, "I'll be twenty-one in two days. That's legal age even for a Sothōii noblewoman, far less a war maid! In case it's escaped your attention, that means I'm old enough to make my own mind up about where I ought or ought not to be."

"Then I'm thinking you've gone daft," Bahzell said with a certain asperity. "Or it might be as how what I'm really looking for is run clean mad!"

It came out sternly, rumbling up out of his massive chest, and he furrowed his brow, frowning at her with the ferocious sort of look which had turned strong men's knees to water more times than he could count.

She laughed.

"Oh, no, Bahzell!" she shook her head. "I promise you, I've never been less daft in my entire life!"

"But—"

"No." She said the single word gently, cutting him off, and shook her head again. "No. I'm not going anywhere, Milord Champion. Not from something I've waited for this long. And not unless you tell me—on a champion's oath—that that's what you *truly* want. Not what you think you *should* want, but what you *do* want."

He opened his mouth . . . and froze.

He sat that way for several moments, then drew a deep breath, and his ears half-flattened as he looked at her.

"It's not about wants, lass," he said then, very softly. "It's about right and about wrong. And it's ashamed of myself I should be—and am—for what it is I'm thinking now."

"Why?" she asked quietly. His eyebrows rose, but she went on in that same quiet tone. "I asked Dame Kaeritha one time about champions of Tomanāk and about celibacy." The faintest of blushes colored her cheekbones, but her green gaze never wavered. "And I remember one of the things she said to me, practically word for word. She said 'All of the Gods of Light celebrate life, and I can't think of anything much more "life-affirming" than the embracing of a loving, shared physical relationship.' Was she wrong about that?"

Bahzell looked into those eyes for a long moment.

"No," he said finally. "But it's not so simple as all that, and well you know it. Like it or no, you're still your father's daughter, and human, while I'm not. And for all you may be of 'legal age,' you're less than half my own."

"And?" She raised an eyebrow at him, and for just a moment he had the absurd impression that *she* was the older of them. His eyes widened in consternation, and she laughed deep in her throat. "Bahzell, first, I was born and raised as a Sothōii noblewoman, the daughter of a baron. You do remember what that means? The betrothal that was proposed for me when I was less than fifteen years old to Rulth Blackhill . . . who was four years older then than you are *now?*" She snorted. "You were right, Father never would have approved it, but the *Council* would have, and I can't even begin to count the number of other fathers who *would* have approved it—or a marriage with an even greater differential than that, for that matter! So you're not going to shock any Sothōii by pointing out the difference in our *ages*."

"It's not *Sothōii* as I'm thinking of," he said. "No, and before you've said it, it's not your war maids, either. It's myself, lass. I'm too old for such as you."

"You're going to have to do better than *that*, Bahzell," she said, and he'd never heard such mingled laughter and tenderness in a voice. "How long do hradani live?" she asked him.

"That's neither here nor there." He heard an edge of something very like desperation creeping into his own voice and gave himself a mental shake. "It's not so very likely a champion of Tomanāk is to live to die of old age, any road," he told her, rallying gamely.

"And that should keep one of His champions from ever opening his life to love?" Leeana asked him gently. "Are His champions that cowardly, Bahzell? That unwilling to embrace the life they're supposed to defend for everyone? Or are they supposed to defend it only for everyone *else?*"

"I—" He paused, then raised his right hand, holding it out to her palm uppermost. "It's not the thought of *my* dying before *you* as scares me, lass," he said very, very quietly, "though well it should be. Aye, and it's shamed I am that it isn't."

"You shouldn't be," she said softly. "And you still haven't answered my question. How long *do* hradani live?" He looked at her, stubbornly—or perhaps desperately—silent, and she shrugged. "Two hundred years, that's how long," she told him, "and humans, even Sothōii, seldom live as long as *one* hundred. So when it comes down to it, love, *you're* younger than I am."

A strange, fiery icicle went through him as she called him "love," but he shook his head.

"That's not the way of it," he said.

"Then Dame Kaeritha was still a child when you met her?" Leeana challenged. His ears flattened at the question, and her green eyes glinted. "Thirty years old she was, I believe. And how long had she been a champion of Tomanāk? I believe she was all of two years older than I am now when He accepted her service as one of His swords, wasn't she? And she'd been *training* for the Order for almost three years before that! Is the War God in the habit of taking the oaths of *children*, Bahzell?"

He stared at her, trying to find an answer to her unscrupulous question, and she smiled again. Then she rose, unfolding from the foot of his bed with the hard-trained grace of a war maid. She stood in front of him, so tall for a human woman, yet so delicate and petite—almost tiny—beside a Horse Stealer hradani, and the champion who'd glared unawed in the face of demons, monsters, creatures of the undead, and even an avatar of a Dark God himself felt himself tremble like a child.

"Before I ran away to the war maids, Bahzell, you told me any man with his wits about him should realize it was best to have someone who could help when life threw problems at him. And that he ought to be smart enough to want a wife with brains at least as good as his own. I don't know about the brains, and because of the charter, I can't offer you a wife the law would ever recognize, but this I *can* offer you: a heart that loves you. A heart that loves *you*, Bahzell Bahnakson, not some romantic, imagined champion out of song and story. You *are* the kind of champion the songs and stories search for, but that's not the man I love. That's *what* the man I love is, not *who* he is. Who he is is a man as gentle as he is strong. A man who tries to hide the size of his heart from the world . . . and fails miserably, because he can never—ever—turn away from someone else's distress. A man who treated a frightened girl as his equal. Who gave her the respect of listening—really listening—to what she had to say and who took the time to understand why she was frightened. A man, Bahzell. Not a hero, not a champion, not a warrior anointed by the gods . . . just a man. A *good* man. A loving man. A man who stands by his friends, his word, and his duty and who I know no power on earth or in hell could ever cause to betray my trust and my love. That's who I love, Bahzell Bahnakson. Can you honestly tell me that he doesn't love *me?*"

Silence hovered between them, and then he closed his eyes, his foxlike ears flat against his skull.

"No." The whispered word was drawn out of him, so low even a hradani's hearing might have missed its fluttering ghost. "No, I can't be telling you that, and may all the gods there be forgive me for it."

"Why?" She moved closer, standing directly in front of him, and cupped his face between her hands. His eyes opened again, and she smiled into them, her voice gentle. "There's nothing to forgive, my love."

"Lass, lass—" He felt himself falling into those green eyes of hers, and he raised his right hand again, this time to touch her cheek with birdwing delicacy. "I'm hradani, Leeana, and you're human. It's not so many children we hradani have, but it's more than ever human and hradani could. And if it should happen as we did, there's never a grandchild you'd ever see, for the mix of human and hradani is barren."

"You're not the only one who ever discussed that with Wencit, Bahzell," she told him, leaning closer until their foreheads touched. "I've always known that. And I don't care."

He made a sound of mingled protest and disbelief, and she shook her head, her forehead still against his.

"I didn't say it didn't matter," she said softly. "I said I didn't *care*, because I would wed you—*will* wed you, before every god there is, whatever the charter may say about war maid marriages before the *law*—knowing we would *never* have a child. If we did, I would raise that child with you with love and happiness, and I would treasure every moment with him. But I'm a war maid, Bahzell, and war maids know there's more to life than bearing children, however wonderful it may be to know that particular joy. Well, there's more to life, more to being a man, a lover, and a husband—than simply *siring* children, too. If the gods see fit to give us that gift, it will fill me with more joy than I could ever describe, but whatever you may think of my age, I'm no longer a child myself. Young, yes; I'll give you that. But I know what truly matters to me. I've spent more hours than you could imagine thinking about this, and I've made my choice. I want *you*, just Bahzell Bahnakson, and that will be enough. If we're granted children, then my heart will overflow... but only because you've already filled it to the brim."

She straightened enough to kiss his forehead gently, then stepped back again, standing between him and the bed while she unlatched her doublet and slid it from her shoulders. She smiled at the almost frightened look in his eyes and tossed it into another of the chairs. She raised her arms and stretched, arching her spine with luxurious, feline grace, green eyes gleaming with wicked, challenging tenderness at his expression before she put her hands on her flaring hips, cocked her head, and looked directly into his eyes.

"So, tell me, Milord Champion," she said, her voice husky and soft and warm and teasing all at the same time, "are you really going to be so churlish as to throw me out of your room at such a late and lonely hour? Or are you going to prove a champion of Tomanāk can be wise enough to recognize the inevitable and surrender gracefully?"

Chapter Nineteen

"Good morning, Tala!" Brandark sang out, clattering down the stone steps to the second floor chamber which had been established as the tower's inhabitants' dining chamber. "I could smell that omelette all the way up—"

The Bloody Sword halted abruptly as he came through the arched stone doorway. Bahzell sat in his usual place at the head of the table, but seated at his right hand, red hair loose over her shoulders and shining like flame in the sunlight pouring in through the archer's slit, sat Leeana Hanathafressa, nursing a steaming cup of tea in both hands.

She wore a loose linen shirt and soft trousers of a deep, grassy green, bloused and tucked into the tops of her riding boots. The hilt of a throwing knife showed above the sewn-in sheath in her right boot, and a pair of scabbarded short swords stood propped upright against the stone wall under the slit. Now she looked up at Brandark through the wisp of steam rising from her tea and arched one eyebrow. He stood frozen, even his facile brain obviously slithering in confusion, and she glanced at Bahzell.

"That's odd," she said with a lurking smile. "I don't believe I've ever heard him when he didn't have something smart to say. In fact, now I come to think about it, up until this moment, I didn't think it was possible for that to happen!"

"No?" Bahzell rumbled a deep-chested laugh, his brown eyes sparkling as they met hers. "I can't say as how I'd ever *hoped* it might be possible. Mind you, I'm thinking it makes for a morning a sight more restful than most mornings are around here."

Brandark gave himself a shake and stepped fully into the room. He looked back and forth between them for a moment, then smiled and swept them a deep, graceful bow not even one of Saramantha's elven overlords could have bettered. When he straightened, the normal sardonic humor had vanished from his expression.

"I find myself . . . deeply happy for you both," he said simply. "I see now what Gayrfressa's secret was, I think . . . and why she was so pleased by it. May your lives be long, may your love be deep, and may every day bring you as much joy as I see in your eyes *this* day."

Leeana's eyes softened, and she blinked quickly. Then she set down her teacup, stood, walked around the table, and hugged him tight.

"Thank you," she said quietly. "I'm sure there will be others who don't see it quite that way, but I don't care about them. I *do* care about about how you feel. A brother's blessing is always a joy."

"Aye, little man," Bahzell agreed, smiling from his chair. "But don't you be expecting *me* to come and hug such as you and get your fancy waistcoat all damp and teary!"

"It's fortunate Leeana has enough poetry in her soul for both of you," Brandark replied, standing back and resting his hands on Leeana's shoulders while he looked into her eyes. He studied them for several seconds, then nodded and squeezed her shoulders once, firmly. "You've chosen an . . . interesting road, Leeana. I'm happy for Bahzell's sake, but the bard in me is already itching to write the ballads *this* is going to inspire!"

"Bahzell tried to warn me about that, too." Leeana smiled. "But we war maids are just natural troublemakers at heart. Surely you've heard that about us?"

"I believe I have heard something to that effect, yes," he said dryly, and she chuckled.

"If you've got the name for it anyway, you might as well take advantage of it. Now come sit down! I hadn't realized just how good a cook Tala really is, and it would be a crime to let that omelette get cold."

"I agree entirely." Brandark swept her another bow, this one less deep and touched with more of his usual insouciance, and followed her back to the table. He sat across from her and served himself a generous portion of the bacon, cheese, onion, and mushroom-stuffed omelette, then collected one of Tala's patented sourdough rolls to keep it company.

"May I assume I'm the first to be informed—in a manner of speaking—about the, um, change in your status, as it were?" he asked as he spread butter across the roll and took a largish bite.

"Well," Leeana said judiciously, leaning back in her chair and crossing one booted ankle elegantly over her knee, "aside from Gayrfressa, Walsharno, Tala—who saw me sneaking up to Bahzell's room last night and kept her mouth shut about it, Lillinara bless her—and, of course, Mother. That makes you, let me see, *sixth*, I think."

"I only make that fifth," Brandark said, after counting carefully on his fingers, and cocked his ears inquisitively at her.

"Well, that's because I had to fit *Bahzell* in there somewhere," she told him demurely, and he chuckled.

"He can be a bit . . . obtuse sometimes, can't he? Have I ever told you how hard he worked at never hearing Tomanāk at all?"

"As to that, I'm thinking that ditty of yours has done damage enough without adding more to it," Bahzell told him.

"I suppose that as a special observation of this day's significance I *could* go ahead and exercise that exquisite sense of tact and discretion which is so much a part of my naturally sensitive nature."

"Aye, and be keeping your 'naturally sensitive' arms unbroken, in the way of it," Bahzell agreed, and Brandark chuckled. Then his expression sobered a bit.

"I'm truly happy for you both, happier than I know how to tell you, but I wonder if you've given any thought to exactly how you intend to go about letting other people know about this?"

"We plan on discussing it with Mother after breakfast," Leeana said serenely. "Not that I'm particularly worried about how she'll react." She smiled faintly. "It's certainly not going to come as a *surprise* to her, at any rate. And I've already written Father, telling him what I had in mind." She cocked her head, gazing not at Brandark, but at Bahzell. "I sent it off two days ago, in fact."

"And did you now?" Bahzell rumbled, twitching his ears in her direction. "Never thought as how you might be being just a mite premature?"

"Oh, I had confidence in my . . . powers of persuasion," she murmured, and Brandark took a hasty swig from his tankard of ale.

"Well, as to that," Bahzell replied judiciously, "it might be you had a point, after all."

"I thought so, at any rate." Her eyes laughed at him before she looked back at Brandark. "Aside from Mother and Father, there isn't anyone we *have* to tell about it. Another of those advantages of being a shameless war maid. On the other hand, neither Bahzell nor I have any intention of hiding from anyone." Her green eyes hardened ever so slightly. "I'm sure some bigots are going to have... strong opinions on the matter. If any of them cares to bring his opinion to my attention, I'll be delighted to *discuss* it with him."

Brandark winced.

"You know," he said after a moment, "you don't really look very much like her, but you remind me a great deal of Kaeritha in some ways."

"Why, thank you, Lord Brandark!" Leeana dimpled. "I've always greatly admired Dame Kaeritha. I think it's that streak of what she calls 'peasant practicality.'"

"Exactly what I was thinking," Brandark acknowledged. "In fact—"

He broke off as Tala bustled in with a fresh pot of tea for Leeana in one hand and a basket of fresh, hot rolls in the other.

"Out late again last night, I see, Lord Brandark," the housekeeper said severely. "Drinking, no doubt!"

"When I wasn't dicing, wenching, or slitting purses," he agreed cheerfully, lifting his tankard in salute, and she set down the basket of rolls so she could swat him with her freed hand.

"Exactly what I would have expected!" she told him roundly, and he heaved a huge sigh.

"It's so sad when everyone sees straight through my façade of respectability," he mourned.

"Respectability, is it?" Bahzell snorted. "Not the very word *I'd've* chosen, I'm thinking!"

"But that's because you've known me so long. I ought to at least be able to fool some totally unsuspecting, innocent stranger, don't you think?"

Bahzell gave him a speaking glance, and Brandark tucked the rest of his original roll into his mouth so he could snag one of the newly arrived ones as a replacement, and began spreading fresh butter with a lavish hand.

"You wouldn't happen to have any of those fig preserves left, would you, Mistress Tala?" he asked wheedlingly.

"I'm down to just the two jars," she said, waving an index finger under his prominent nose, "and the *last* time you asked that, it cost me a jar and a half!"

"Is it *my* fault you make such excellent preserves?" He looked at her innocently. "You should take it as the most sincere possible compliment!"

"Oh, should I, now?" The housekeeper planted her hands on her hips to give him her very best glower, but he only looked back at her with that same innocent expression.

"Oh, all right!" she told him finally. "But only the one jar, mind! I'm saving the other."

"Whatever you say," he agreed meekly, and she laughed.

"Promises are easy, Milord, but don't think you can turn me up sweet enough for me to be taking my eye off of my pantry when you're around!"

✧ ✧ ✧

After breakfast, Leeana and Bahzell left the tower and walked along the curtain wall towards the keep. The keep's early-morning shadow lay deep and cool across the battlements, and Bahzell gazed down into the courtyard with a pensive expression.

"Second thoughts?" a gently teasing voice asked, and he turned quickly to smile at Leeana.

"Now, that I don't have," he told her. "Mind, I've no doubt I *should*, but it's a rare, determined wench you are, Leeana Hanathafressa! And"—his voice softened—"it's never happier I've been."

"Good. See to it you stay that way." She tucked her hand into his elbow and laid her head against his upper arm. It felt odd not to tower over a man, but it felt . . . good, too. Of course, that might have something to do with the man in question, she reflected warmly, storing up the memory of the night just past like the treasure it was. A gentle and considerate man, her Bahzell, in more ways than one.

Sentries manned Hill Guard's walls at all times, and she saw the armsman at the angle between the curtain wall and the keep jerk upright as he glanced in their direction. The sentry's eyes widened, and then he snapped to attention. It would have taken a very tall human—even for a Sothōii—to fix his eyes above Bahzell Bahnakson's head without straining his neck, and so the armsman locked his gaze on the center of the Horse Stealer's massive chest.

"Good . . . morning, Milord Champion," he said.

"And a good morning to you, as well," Bahzell rumbled back. It couldn't have been a more pleasant response, yet there was a little something in its timbre. Something that snapped the sentry's eyes to Leeana, as well. He colored, then cleared his throat and bobbed his head.

"Give you good morning, Mistress Leeana."

It came out in a commendably normal voice, only a bit more gruff than it might have been, and she smiled at him.

"Thank you," she said, then looked up into the cool morning sky, her hair flying like red silk on the breeze that laughed its way across the castle and danced with the banners. "And the same to you. It *is* a beautiful morning, isn't it?"

"Aye . . . Mistress." The armsman returned her smile. "It is that. And"—he let his eyes meet hers, then Bahzell's—"more beautiful for some than for others, I'm thinking."

"Why, yes, it is," she told him with a fleeting dimple.

He bent his head respectfully and stepped back out of their way, and Leeana laughed softly as they passed on into the keep proper.

"There!" she told her towering lover. "That wasn't so bad, was it?"

"Now that it wasn't," he replied, looking down at her, "and it's a fair start we've made, I suppose, in a manner of speaking. Your Da's no more than another fifteen or twenty score armsmen here in Hill Guard and Balthar. Why, I've no doubt we'll have dealt with all of them by lunch!"

✧ ✧ ✧

"I'm sorry, Leeana." Sharlassa looked back and forth between her and Bahzell, obviously afire with curiosity. "Baroness Hanatha isn't here. She finished breakfast early and said she was going riding." The younger woman grimaced. "She invited me to join her, but Master Tobis is expecting me this morning."

"I see." Leeana smiled at her resigned tone, remembering her own lessons with the dance master. "Do you think we could catch her at the stable, or is she already out and about?"

"I think you could probably catch her," Sharlassa replied. "She hasn't been gone long, and she said she had something to discuss with Master Greenslope before she left."

"Well, love," Leanna glanced up at Bahzell, "do we want to wait for her here, or go beard her in Doram's den?"

"There's a cowardly part of me says as how we ought best hide right here," Bahzell admitted, "but I've not seen Walsharno at all, at all this morning, and I'm thinking Gayrfressa is after having a 'told you so' or three for me, as well."

"My thinking, as well," Leeana said, and chuckled at Sharlassa's expression. It was obvious the younger woman was simply *dying* to ask the dozens of questions dancing through her mind, and Leeana shook her head at her.

"Wish me joy, Sharlassa," she said. "Wish *both* of us joy."

"Oh, I do. I *do!*" Sharlassa clapped her hands in obvious delight. "I wondered if—that is, I mean—what I meant to say was—"

She paused, her expression flustered, and Leeana reached out to lay a hand briefly on her shoulder.

"I *know* what you meant to say. And thank you. Now I think we'd better go find Mother."

"Oh. *Oh!*" Sharlassa's eyes widened suddenly. "Does she—I mean, had you—?"

"I believe I can safely say Mother is the one person in Hill Guard this news is *least* likely to surprise," Leeana reassured her, and Sharlassa heaved a deep sigh of relief.

"Oh, good," she said, and then blushed brightly as Leeana laughed and Bahzell rumbled a chuckle.

"I'm thinking we'd best be off to the stables before this poor lass is after catching fire and burns to the ground in front of us," he said, and Sharlassa's blush burned even hotter for a moment before she shook her head and looked back up at him with a laugh of her own.

"Better," he told her then, and extended his arm once again to Leeana.

"Milady?" he invited, and she snorted as she tucked her hand back into his elbow.

"Not anymore," she reminded him.

"Ah, but there's ladies, and then there's *ladies*," he told her, "and war maid or no, it's *my lady* you are now, Leeana Hanathafressa."

Her eyes softened. Then she nodded to Sharlassa, and the two of them were gone.

✧ ✧ ✧

"—and after the farrier finishes with the two-year-olds, we'll want him to see to Gayrfressa," Baroness Hanatha said, her cane hanging by its lanyard from her wrist as she leaned back against the dark gray mare saddled and waiting for her. Despite her damaged right leg, she rode at least three times a week, and Mist Under the Moon (less formally known as "Misty") was her favorite mount. Now Misty waited patiently while Hanatha and Doram Greenslope spoke.

"Aye, Milady," Greenslope agreed. "Mistress Leeana pointed that out to me already, she did."

"I'm sure she did." Hanatha smiled warmly at the stablemaster. "And I'm sure you'd have seen to it without my saying a word. I do try to be a proper hostess, though, Doram!"

"Aye, so you do, Milady." Greenslope smiled back at her, then stooped slightly, making a stirrup of his hands. She balanced on her weakened leg, lifting the toe of her left riding boot to his waiting hands. Her bad leg prevented her from getting her foot high enough for a regular stirrup, but the stablemaster's strong boost as she straightened her good leg sent her more than high enough to settle into position on Misty's back, and Greenslope shook his head as he gazed up at her.

"Always does my heart good to see you up there, Milady," he said simply. "That it surely does!"

"I'm glad. It *feels* good, too," she told him, and touched Misty with her heel, turning towards the stable yard's gate and the pair of armsmen already mounted and waiting to escort her on her morning's ride. But even as the mare moved forward, she saw the armsmen stiffen in their saddles, looking at something she couldn't see yet. She drew rein, and then felt her eyebrows rise as Bahzell Bahnakson and her daughter stepped through the gate together.

Very together, she thought. She doubted she could have defined any single aspect of their body language—of the way they moved, their subtle awareness of one another in time and space—but it was more than enough, especially to a mother's eye, and she felt her lips twitch as Bahzell caught sight of her and his shoulders straightened ever so slightly.

The two of them crossed the stable yard to her, Leeana looking up and Bahzell looking more or less across at her, and she shook her head.

"Why do I have the feeling the two of you have something to tell me?" she demanded, frowning ferociously.

"Well, as to that—" Bahzell began, but Leeana poked him none too gently in the ribs.

"Perhaps because of a certain discussion you and I had a few days ago, Mother," she observed sweetly, and Hanatha laughed.

"If I get down from the saddle," she told her daughter, "then this vast lummox of yours is going to have to help me get back into it. You *do* understand that, don't you? I'm not as young and . . . nimble as you are, my love!"

"I feel confident he'd be happy to assist you," Leeana assured her, and took Misty's bridle as Bahzell stepped forward to help Hanatha down from the saddle she'd so recently climbed into. It was rather like what Hanatha imagined one of the dwarves' "elevators" must feel like. Those huge hands lifted her effortlessly down from the saddle, and despite her weakened leg, she knew she was no featherweight.

Bahzell set her smoothly on her feet, and she clasped both hands on her cane, leaning on it as she considered the two of them. She couldn't see them, but she felt certain at least a dozen pair of eyes must have been peeking out of the stable's shadows behind her, watching her. And she *knew* her waiting armsmen were soaking up every detail from behind those disciplined faces of theirs. She hadn't contemplated "discovering" what Leeana had been up to quite this publicly, but Hanatha Whitesaddle had never been a coward, and Hanatha Bowmaster hadn't changed in that respect.

"Knowing you, Bahzell," she said after a moment, aware of all those watching eyes and deliberately pitching her voice *just* loudly enough to be certain they could hear without being obvious about it, "I feel confident you've come to apologize to me for abusing Tellian's and my hospitality."

The hradani started to say something, but she raised her left hand and waved it in a shushing motion.

"Give me leave to finish, Milord Champion," she said sternly, and waited until he'd subsided. "Good," she said then. "As I say, I feel sure you've come to apologize. And before you do, I forbid it. Leeana is a war maid, and war maids make their own decisions and live their own lives. And even if that weren't true, I know where her heart lies, and I have no qualms whatsoever about the man to whom she's given it." She looked directly into his eyes. "There may be some among the Sothōii—and possibly among your own people, as well—who *will* have qualms over this. None of them will be named 'Bowmaster,' however."

She spoke clearly and calmly, although she felt her lips twitch again most inappropriately as Leeana arched one politely incredulous eyebrow and silently mouthed the words "Not even Aunt Gayala?" at her. Bahzell glanced down at the crown of his undutiful lover's head as if he'd been able to read her mind, then looked back at Hanatha.

"It's my best I'll do to see as how you've never any cause to feel such," he told her.

"I'm certain you will . . . and that I won't," she told him, reaching up to lay her hand on his chest as she sensed Walsharno and Gayrfressa moving into the yard behind her. "I know too much of what lives in here," she said, pressing his chest lightly, "to worry about that, Bahzell. And since Leeana will always be my daughter, whatever the war maids' charter may say, I trust you won't mind if I find myself claiming you as a son, as well?"

"Oh, it's in my mind that won't be so very hard a thing to stand," he replied, putting one of his hands over hers for a moment.

"And as far as that goes—" Leeana began, then broke off suddenly, and Bahzell looked down at her again, much more sharply this time, as his link with Gayrfressa tingled abruptly. Hanatha looked at her daughter, as well, but her expression was confused, wondering what had interrupted Leeana in midsentence.

<*Well,*> Walsharno said philosophically in the back of Bahzell's mind, <*now we know why she came calling, don't we?*>

Bahzell nodded slowly, but his eyes never left Leeana as she stepped forward, reaching up towards Gayrfressa's cheek. She looked no larger than a child beside the massive courser, but the chestnut mare's remaining eye glowed as she gazed down at the human standing in front of her.

<*I'd no notion courser mares ever bonded,*> Bahzell replied silently to Walsharno, and the stallion tossed his head in a curious mixture of pride and resignation.

<*As far as I know, they don't,*> he said dryly. <*No one's ever said they* couldn't, *you understand, but it just . . . doesn't happen. Until now, of course.*>

"Leeana?" Hanatha reached towards her daughter, but Bahzell intercepted her hand just before she touched Leeana. The baroness looked at him in surprise, and he gave her a wry smile.

"She's a mite distracted, just now," he said.

"Distracted?" Hanatha repeated, and he chuckled.

"Aye, that she is." He shook his head again, watching Leeana reach up to Gayrfressa as the mare dropped her nose to blow gently against her hair. "It seems as how your daughter's not the only young lady minded to set tradition on its ear this fine morning," he told her.

Hanatha stared at him, and then, slowly, understanding dawned in those green eyes so much like Leeana's, and she drew a deep breath.

"Oh, my," she said.

"Aye." Bahzell flipped his ears at her. "You're more like to know than I, being a Sothōii born and all, but it's in my mind that there's not been a wind *sister* before, has there now?"

Chapter Twenty

"Well, that's marvelous," Master Varnaythus said sourly, leaning back in his comfortable chair in the windowless room.

Malahk Sahrdohr sat across from him, eyeing the images in the gramerhain on the desk between them with an equally sour expression. Two coursers, a red roan and a chesnut with a white star, forged steadily through the Wind Plain's tall, blowing grass towards the Escarpment. They moved side-by-side, in the smooth, unique four-beat "trot" of their kind, moving like echoes of one another and so close together their riders could hold hands as they went.

It was all too revoltingly romantic and touching for words, Varnaythus thought, grumpily watching the loose ends of Leeana Hanathafressa's red-gold braid dance on the breeze.

"Surely it doesn't make much difference, in the end," Sahrdohr said after a moment. He sounded rather more hopeful than positive, Varnaythus noted.

"I'm not prepared to say that *anything* 'doesn't make much difference' where Bahzell is concerned." Varnaythus' tone was no happier than it had been, and he glowered at the younger wizard, although he couldn't really blame any of his current lack of joy on his associate. "And it particularly bothers me that none of Them suggested anything like this might be going to happen."

"More evidence it really isn't going to matter," Sahrdohr suggested with a shrug.

"Or more evidence They didn't see it *coming*."

"What?" Sahrdohr straightened in his chair, frowning. "Of course They must've seen it coming, if it's one of the cusp points!"

"Why?" Varnaythus asked bluntly, and then chuckled sourly as Sahrdohr stared incredulously at him. "Don't tell me you think They're infallible!"

Sahrdohr's incredulous expression segued from astonishment to apprehension to complete blankness in a heartbeat, and Varnaythus' chuckle turned into a humorless laugh.

"Of course They're fallible, Malahk! We wouldn't be sitting here in Norfressa if They were *in*fallible, because They'd have won in Kontovar twelve hundred years ago! Of course, the other side is fallible, too, or *Wencit of Rūm* would still be sitting in Trōfrōlantha." He shrugged. "It's a fair balance, I suppose, though I've never been all that fond of the concept of fair. And if either side truly was infallible, They wouldn't need us mortals to help things along, which has worked out pretty well for me personally... so far, at least. But don't wed yourself to the idea that They always know what They're doing. Or that They even know what all the cusp points are. Both sides manage to hide at least some of the more critical threads from each other. That's how They blindsided Wencit and the Ottovarans in Kontovar, but it also means the other side can blindside Them."

It would have been hard to say whether Sahrdohr looked more unhappy or more worried by Varnaythus' frankness, but he gave a grudging nod.

"Still," he said after a moment, "I can't see this leading to any fundamental advantage for them. So Bahzell's found a lover—so what? If anything, it makes him *more* vulnerable, not less, especially if anything... unfortunate were to happen to Mistress Leeana. And she's already legally out of the succession, so even if they were to have a child someday—and you know how likely *that* is—it won't make any difference in the West Riding. For that matter, Bahzell's so far down the succession from his father that it wouldn't make any difference in Hurgrum, either!"

"Granted." Varnaythus nodded. "And granted that it's going to be more grist for the mill of really traditional Sothōii like Cassan and Yeraghor. In fact, it'll be interesting to see which outrages them the most in the end. They've been disgusted over Leeana's becoming a war maid in the first place, but now they get the chance to be even more disgusted and revolted by the notion of a hradani 'polluting' one of the most highly born Sothōii ladies imaginable. Of course, it would be more than a bit inconsistent of them to be pissed off over both those things at once, but little things like consistency never hamper your true bigot's outrage, now do they?" He pursed his lips while he considered it for several seconds, then snorted. "Knowing Cassan, I imagine they'll come down on the side of its being no better than bestiality, in the end. After all, what else could you expect out of an unnatural bitch like a war maid?"

"Ummmmm." Sahrdohr frowned thoughtfully. "You may have a point there, especially if we handle it properly—get behind it and push judiciously in the proper direction."

"I'm perfectly willing to push all you want, but I'm not going to let myself be distracted from the main object. And if the chance comes along to kill either of them, I intend to take it." Varnaythus showed his teeth in an expression no one would ever have mistaken for a smile. "Bahzell's on our list anyway, and you're right about the way this makes him more vulnerable. Champions of Tomanāk should be smarter than to offer up hostages to fortune this way. And any nasty little accident which befell Mistress Leeana would have a salutary effect on Tellian, too, for that matter. Using this to foment more unhappiness among the bigots might be useful, but if she's considerate enough to wander into our sights at an opportune moment, I'll take the opening in a heartbeat."

"Do you think there might be a way we could use her as bait?" Sahrdohr thought out loud. "Grab her and use her to suck Bahzell into a place and time of our choosing?"

"Oh, there might be 'a way,'" Varnaythus said, "but I wouldn't hold my breath looking for it, if I were you. We're talking about a war maid. *And* a wind rider, now. Not exactly the easiest person in the world to capture and use for 'bait'! Especially not when the war maid in question is as good with her hands as Mistress Leeana, and the courser who's adopted her is Walsharno's sister. You *do* remember what Gayrfressa did to the shardohns who attacked her herd, don't you?"

"Of course I do," Sahrdohr replied a bit irritably. "Not even a courser is immortal, though. Arthnar's men would've killed Dathgar if Bahzell and Walsharno hadn't been there. For that matter, they could've gotten *Walsharno* if they hadn't been so focused on Tellian! So it doesn't really matter how dangerous Gayrfressa might be if we can get enough arrows into her first. And the same goes for Leeana, for that matter."

"True." Varnaythus nodded. "That's why I'm perfectly willing to kill her if the opportunity presents itself. But trying to take her alive?" He grimaced. "*That* would require getting just a bit closer to her than bow range, and I'd suggest you ask the dog brothers how many of them would be eager to take on that particular commission. Personally, I'm willing to bet none of them would. Not without a damned substantial bonus, at any rate." He chuckled mirthlessly. "For that matter, I'm sure they remember what happened the *first* time they went after someone close to the Bloody Hand—and he wasn't even a champion then! Does the name 'Zarantha' ring any bells with you, by any chance?"

"You're probably right," Sahrdohr conceded with a sigh. He frowned again, absently this time, and sat staring into space for several seconds. Then he shrugged and refocused on Varnaythus.

"I assume we do want to pass this information on to Cassan and Yeraghor as soon as we can?"

"Of course we do. Master Talthar will turn up in Toramos to discuss it with the good duke in a day or three." Varnaythus shrugged. "I'll even do a little of that judicious pushing we discussed, although he probably won't need that much to throw three kinds of fit over it. Especially when I report on Tellian's antics here in Sothōfalas at the same time."

"No, he isn't going to be happy about that, is he?" This time Sahrdohr's smile was almost beatific. "Particularly not with my own esteemed superior's contribution."

Varnaythus returned his subordinate's smile. Sir Whalandys Shaftmaster and Sir Jerhas Macebearer had finally talked King Markhos into officially sanctioning Tellian of Balthar's Derm Canal project. *All* of the Derm Canal project, including not only the Gullet Tunnel but the open challenge to the Purple Lords' monopoly of the Spear River, as well.

Macebearer had been supportive from the outset, although his acute awareness of the potential political price had prevented him from openly and officially endorsing it. His advice to the King on the subject was hardly likely to come as a surprise to anyone, however, whereas Shaftmaster had been far more dubious initially. Unfortunately, the fact that everyone—including King Markhos—knew the Chancellor had originally cherished such powerful doubts only made his conversion into a supporter an even weightier argument in the canal's favor.

Of course, Shaftmaster's original reservations had stemmed from more than one factor. First and foremost, he'd doubted that such a monumental project was possible, even for dwarven engineers. As the Chancellor of the Exchequer, he'd been only too well aware of the enormous economic advantage for the entire Kingdom if it *could* be done, but he'd been far from convinced it could. And as the son of one of Tellian of Balthar's lord wardens, he'd probably been even more aware of the advantages for his father's holding of Green Cove, squarely on the most direct route from the Gullet Tunnel to Sothōfalas. But he'd also been aware of the political risks inherent in endorsing it too loudly, specifically because of his family's links to the West Riding and just how wealthy Green Cove stood to become if it succeeded. The last thing any Chancellor of the Exchequer needed was to be accused of using his position for personal or family profit, especially in the Kingdom of the Sothōii, where political exchanges were still known to turn into personal combat upon occasion. Quite aside from any considerations of physical survival, a chancellor whose personal honor and honesty had been brought into question would become far less effective as a minister of the Crown.

And on top of any political factors, there'd been the fact that he'd been about as thoroughly prejudiced against the hradani as anyone could have been. In fact, up until three or four years ago, he'd belonged to the court faction most concerned by the threat of a unified hradani realm, and it was no secret that he'd quietly approved of Sir Mathian Redhelm's attempt to prevent that from happening, which had put him in direct opposition to Tellian's actions. That had led to a certain tension between him and Sir Shandahr Shaftmaster, his father... not to mention Tellian himself. In fact, that tension was one of the things which had made him acceptable at the Exchequer (at least initially) as far as Cassan and his partisans had been concerned, and he'd frankly doubted that anyone as primitive and barbaric as hradani could possibly hold up their end of the proposed construction schedule even if the dwarves could actually design the thing in the first place.

Unfortunately, while he might have been prejudiced, he wasn't stupid, and his attitude had shifted steadily from one of acid skepticism to one of enthusiastic support. The numbers had been too persuasive for him to ignore, and the steady—indeed, astonishing—rate at which the construction had progressed, coupled with the success of the expeditions Tellian and Bahnak had launched into the Ghoul Moor, had dealt his contempt for the hradani a death blow. He still didn't like them—or the idea of an actual alliance with them—but he'd been forced to admit the same things which had made them formidable foes could make them equally formidable allies. Besides, he was a realist. Unlike Cassan, who might continue to dream fondly of the way the Northern Confederation must inevitably disintegrate upon Bahnak's death, Shaftmaster recognized that Bahnak had built better than that. The Confederation was here to stay, whether he liked it or not, and since it was, he preferred to be on good terms with it and to bind its future economic interests to those of the Kingdom in any way he could. People were far less likely to attack people whose prosperity was intimately linked to their own, after all. A point, Varnaythus thought glumly, which wasn't lost on Kilthan, Bahnak, or Tellian, either.

That realism and pragmatism of Shaftmaster's were the reasons he'd finally come out and firmly supported Macebearer and Prince Yurokhas in urging the King to issue a formal Crown charter for the canal. And with his three most trusted and powerful advisers in agreement, it was hardly surprising Markhos had agreed. Indeed, it had taken them so long to bring him around only because he'd recognized just how thorny and sensitive the issue was with certain of his *other* advisers. That recognition was probably the reason he still hadn't made his approval of the charter official; he wasn't going to do that until the Great Council's official fall session, when anyone who wanted to object would have to look him in the eye to do it. That sort of defiance took a hardy soul, Varnaythus thought sourly. There wasn't likely to be a lot of it, and once he *did* make the charter official, the canal and all of its traffic would come under royal protection, which would assure the Crown of a tidy new source of income... and make any effort to sabotage it an act of treason.

Cassan wasn't going to like that one little bit.

"Do you think this will finally move him off dead center on the assassination issue?" Sahrdohr asked after a moment, and Varnaythus grimaced again, even more sourly than before.

"If anything will," he replied. "It's been an uphill fight to get him to even consider it, though. I think part of it is that he'd genuinely convinced himself he was 'too honorable' a fellow to violate his oath of fealty." The wizard rolled his eyes. "But I suspect most of it was that he was too well aware of how the Kingdom could disintegrate back into the Time of Troubles. As long as he thought he could game the situation to get what he wanted without that, he didn't have any desire to face Tellian and the wind riders across a battlefield. He isn't anywhere near as smart as he thinks he is, but he's not *that* stupid! And he *is* smart enough to recognize that unless he takes some sort of drastic action—probably before the fall session, given Markhos' intention to announce Tellian's charter then—he's done. There won't be any way he can 'game' anything after the Crown for all intents and purposes gives Tellian its full backing. I imagine his 'man of honor' image will fly out the window pretty quickly as soon as he realizes that. And if it doesn't occur to him on his own, Master Talthar will certainly find a way to point it out to him. A clever fellow, Master Talthar."

He smiled thinly at Sahrdohr, and the younger wizard chuckled.

"So, actually, this"—he jutted his chin at the images and the gramerhain—"is more likely to work in our favor than against us."

"Probably," Varnaythus agreed. "I don't plan on betting anything particularly valuable on it, though. Carnadosa knows I've been . . . unpleasantly disillusioned every *other* time I've thought Bahzell was going down or that we'd finally gained a decisive advantage! Still, at the moment I don't see any way it's likely to *hurt* us any."

It was a somewhat less than ringing declaration of confidence, and he knew it. It was about as far as he was prepared to go, however, and he glowered down at the gramerhain for another few moments, then shrugged and passed his hand over it. The light in its heart flared once, then vanished, and he looked at Sahrdohr.

"I suppose we should start thinking about the most effective way for Master Talthar to present this unfortunate information to his good friend Duke Cassan, don't you?"

✧ ✧ ✧

"I'm thinking I must look a right idiot," Bahzell Bahnakson remarked as he and Leanna rode along the eastern bank of the Balthar River. "Or so I would if it happened as anyone was watching, any road."

He sounded remarkably unperturbed by the possibility, Leeana noted, and smiled across at him.

"I faithfully promise to turn loose of your hand and look suitably dour the instant anyone turns up," she told him.

<*Not that it's going to fool anyone,*> Walsharno remarked. <*Even a courser only has to look at the two of you to know your brains have turned into mush. Any* two-foot *is going to decide you need to be locked up in a nice, safe room somewhere where you can't hurt yourselves!*>

<*And who asked* your *opinion?*> another, less deep mental voice inquired tartly, and Bahzell chuckled. He supposed he shouldn't have been surprised he was able to hear Gayrfressa now that she'd bonded with Leeana. It was unheard of—impossible!—of course, but the two of them—well, the *four* of them, now—had never done anything *else* the way they were supposed to, now had they? It seemed likely to him and to Walsharno that his own version of the coursers' herd sense had a lot to do with it . . . but that neat, comforting explanation didn't account for Leeana's ability to hear Walsharno.

<*You really* are *full of yourself, aren't you?*> Walsharno observed in a teasing tone, regarding his sister fondly. He'd deliberately taken a position to her left, where she could see him with her single eye, and now he tossed his mane at her. Then he snorted profoundly. <*Newly bonded coursers are* always *full of themselves, I suppose. Why, even* I *was for the first, oh, twenty minutes or so.*>

<*But you got over it, I see,*> Gayrfressa replied sarcastically.

"I see this is going to be a lively relationship," Leeana said dryly, yet there was an undertone, a softness, to the words. An undertone Bahzell remembered only too well from the day a courser named Walsharno had opened his heart to one of his people's most bitter traditional enemies.

"Never another minute of privacy will you have," he told her, flattening his ears and grinning at her. "Natter away at the drop of a hat, they will. And there's never a courser born as isn't positive his brother shouldn't be let out on his own without a keeper. I've little doubt Gayrfressa's after being one more chip off the old block, when all's said."

<*There must be* some *reason I like you so much,*> Gayrfressa mused. <*Probably I'll be able to remember what it was, if you give me a day or two.*>

"Be nice," Leeana said mildly. "He's mine now, and I don't want you picking on him without my permission."

<As *long as you don't go putting unreasonable restrictions on it,*> Gayrfressa replied.

"I'm going to be very strict." Leeana's tone was much more severe than it had been. "You're absolutely forbidden to pick on him on any day of the week that doesn't have a letter 'y' in it. Is that understood?"

<*Coursers can't read, you know,*> Walsharno pointed out.

<*Perhaps* you *can't read, Brother,*> Gayrfressa said sweetly. <*I, however, have spent the last few winters learning to do just that.*>

"Have you, now?" Bahzell looked across at her, and she turned her head to meet his gaze.

<*Actually, Walsharno, as usual, is only partly correct,*> she told him. <Most *coursers never learn to read. For one thing, our eyes don't seem to focus properly for it.*> Bahzell felt the unspoken allusion to her lost eye behind the words, but there was no trace of self-pity, and his heart filled with fresh pride in her. <*Quite a few of us have, over the years, though. Of course,* writing *is just a bit more difficult for us!*>

<*Showoff,*> Walsharno teased, nipping her very gently on the shoulder, and she snorted in amusement.

"If anyone had ever told me I might be riding along on a courser, having a conversation like this one, I would have told him he was mad," Leeana said. She shook her head, green eyes soft. "I don't know what I might have done to deserve it, but whatever it was, it couldn't have been enough."

"There's never a wind rider I've met as doesn't feel exactly the same thing, lass," Bahzell told her. "And I'm thinking the truth is there's nothing we *could* have done to be 'deserving' it. It's a gift we're given, not something as we could ever have earned."

<*It works both ways, Brother,*> Walsharno said quietly, his mental voice very serious. <*The joy you take from our bond is no greater than the joy I take from it. It can't be.*>

Gayrfressa tossed her head in agreement, and Bahzell found himself nodding back to her. Leeana looked down at the big mare's single ear, then leaned forward to stroke Gayrfressa's neck.

"I feel the same," she said. "And yet I can't help worrying about Boots."

<*Worrying?*> Gayrfressa repeated.

"He's not just my horse, Sister," Leeana said slowly. "He's my friend, too, and he has been for a long time."

<*And?*>

"And I saw him watching from the paddock as we rode away,"

Leeana said even more slowly. "Don't misunderstand me, please, but he deserves better than for me simply to ride out of his life, even on you."

<*Of course he does,*> Gayrfressa said, turning her head to the left until she could see her rider. <*Did you think I wanted you to do anything of the sort?*> She shook her mane, her ear half-flattened. <*The lesser cousins aren't as intelligent as we are, Sister, but that doesn't mean they aren't* wise. *And it doesn't mean we don't love them as much as you two-foots do, or that their hearts aren't just as deep as ours. A courser needs less looking after than one of the lesser cousins, but I would be very angry with you if you didn't give Boots stable space right along with me. Besides,*> her tone lightened and Leeana heard a silent laugh, <*it will do you good to spend a little time on one of the lesser cousins on a regular basis. In fact, it's a pity Bahzell can't do the same. It would make him appreciate Walsharno more.*>

<*True, too true,*> Walsharno agreed. <*Of course, it would crush the poor lesser cousin. Oh, the burdens I bear!*>

"Thank you, dearheart," Leeana said softly, patting Gayrfressa's shoulder. "I don't know for certain about *his* heart, but it would've broken mine to simply walk away from him."

"Then I'm thinking it's—"

Bahzell's voice broke off in midsentence, and the coursers stopped in perfect unison, as someone else joined the discussion. *Two* someone elses, in fact.

Tomanāk Orfro, God of War and Judge of Princes, appeared before them with the tall, wind-blown grass stirring about his boots. Ten feet tall, he stood—tall enough to put even coursers into perspective—with his sword across his back and his mace at his belt, but Bahzell had become accustomed to that on those occasions when he met his deity face-to-face. It was the midnight-haired woman at his side, who'd appeared as silently and effortlessly as Tomanāk himself, who managed to take even Bahzell Bahnakson aback.

She was taller than any mortal woman, although still rather shorter than Tomanāk, with a regal, womanly beauty, and she regarded Bahzell, Leeana, and the coursers with sapphire eyes deeper than the sea. Her gown glowed and flowed, gleaming somehow with a deep, cool silver luminance even in the bright sunlight, and a beautifully carved ivory moon hung between her rich breasts from a chain of wrought silver set with plaques of opal.

"Bahzell," Tomanāk said that in that earthquake voice that seemed to take the Wind Plain by the scruff of the neck and shake it with gentle power. Bahzell nodded back to him, and Tomanāk smiled. But then the god's smile faded.

"This is a day long awaited, my Sword," he said.

"Is it now?" Bahzell inquired politely when Tomanāk paused.

"It is. Although, like so much about you mortals, it isn't quite what we'd expected." The god cocked his head at Gayrfressa, who simply looked back at him, meeting his gaze with her single eye. "An interesting development, Wind Daughter," Tomanāk said to her. "But great heart knows great heart."

"Yes, it does," another voice agreed. It was as powerful as Tomanāk's own, that voice, but as different as wind from earth, and it sang, for it wasn't a single voice. It was three, combined, flowing together in perfect a cappella harmony, and Bahzell suddenly wished Brandark could have been there. One of those voices was a high, sweet soprano, sparkling with youth and the joy of beginnings, yet almost cool and deeply focused. The second was deeper and richer, blurring the line between mezzo soprano and contralto, confident and strong, reaching out as if to embrace and strengthen everyone within its reach. And the third . . . the third was softer—sadder perhaps, or perhaps more weary. There was a hardness in that third voice, a coldness, and yet it, too, reached out as if to offer solace and comfort and acceptance at the end of day.

"Great heart always knows great heart when they meet," those voices sang now, and those sapphire eyes moved from Gayrfressa to Leeana. "Yet not all hearts, for all their greatness, have the courage to reach beyond themselves as yours has, Daughter."

"My heart had good teachers, Mother," Leeana replied, meeting that bottomless blue gaze as fearlessly as ever Bahzell had met Tomanāk's.

"Yes, it did," Lillinara Orfressa acknowledged. "Would that all of my daughters had mothers fit to give their wings such strength."

"It wasn't only Mother, Milady," Leeana said. "I love her dearly, but anything I am today isn't her work alone."

"No. No, it isn't. And despite what even many of my followers believe, it isn't true that men find no favor in my eyes, Daughter. Not even in the full dark of the moon, when the taste of justice burns hottest on my tongue. Man and woman were always meant for one another, and my heart is filled with joy when they find one another—when they *know* one another as your mother has known your father through all the years of joy and pain . . . and as you know Bahzell."

Those deep, dark eyes moved to Bahzell as she spoke, and the hradani felt their weight. He felt them measuring and evaluating, weighing and trying, testing strengths and weaknesses not even Tomanāk had touched so directly. He met them steadily, shoulders squared, and slowly, slowly she nodded.

"You are all my brother has said, Bahzell, son of Arthanal. I see why he thinks so highly of you . . . and so do I."

"I'm naught but what you see before you, Lady," he replied.

"Perhaps not, but what I see before me is quite enough." She smiled. "Many men can die obedient to their sworn word, or for justice, or to defend the weak, but not all of them do it out of love."

"And not all of them are called upon to give up so much for love," Tomanāk rumbled. Bahzell and Leeana both looked at him, and he smiled at them. That smile was warm, yet there were shadows in it, and in his eyes.

"Grief awaits you, children," he told them softly. "Love is mortal kind's greatest and most painful treasure. When another's happiness is more important to you than your own, the time must always come when darkness shadows the light and the joy you've taken from and given to one another. It will be so with you."

"Grief is part of life, Milord," Leeana said, reaching out to reclaim Bahzell's hand. "That's why you gave us love, so we could cope with the grief."

"An interesting theory," Tomanāk told her with a smile. "Yet the truth is that love surpasses us in ways no mortal can fully understand. You are full of surprises, you mortals—so weak in so many ways, and yet so strong *because* of your weaknesses. So easily drawn to the shadow, so many of you . . . and such blazing torches against the Dark." He shook his head. "The courage you show in facing every day of your mortal lives puts the courage of any god or goddess to shame, Leeana Hanathafressa. Did you know that?"

"No." It was her turn to shake her head. "We only do our best, Milord."

"Which is the most anyone, god or mortal, could ask of you," he agreed. "And which is also the only thing you and Bahzell—or Walsharno and Gayrfressa—know how to give."

None of the mortals knew how to respond to that. They only looked back at him, and he smiled. Then his smile faded, and he reached out one enormous hand to touch first Bahzell's head, and then Leeana's. They felt the power to shatter worlds singing in his fingers, yet that mighty hand was as gentle as a bird's wing, and his eyes were gentler yet.

"I have no desire to embarrass any of you, my children, and great hearts that you are, it *does* embarrass you when anyone sings your praises. That's why you're so much more comfortable turning deep emotion aside with jokes and insults. But what you give to all about you is the reason Lillinara and I have come to you today."

"The reason?" Bahzell repeated in an unwontedly humble voice.

"The war maids' charter denies you something both you and Leeana long for, my Sword, whether you would admit it even to yourselves or not. Your parents, your friends, will recognize that the 'freemating' to which the law restricts a war maid is a true marriage, one of heart and soul and not simply of the flesh. Yet both of you know not everyone will share or accept that truth. Not even a god can change the heart of someone who hates or denigrates with blind, unreasoning bigotry. But *we* know, Lillinara and I, and whatever the law of mortals may say, we are not bound by charters or legal codes or custom."

"Great heart knows great heart, I said," Lillinara sang, "and so do we. So tell us, my children, do you truly take one another as man and wife? Will you cleave to one another through times of joy and times of sorrow? Will you love, protect, care for one another? Will you share your lives in the face of all this world's tempests and bring one another at the end of everything into the still, sweet calm of your love?"

"Aye, that I will, Lady," Bahzell replied, raising Leeana's hand to his lips.

"And I," Leeana replied, equally firmly, turning to smile not at the goddess but into Bahzell's eyes.

"Then hold out your left hands," Tomanāk said.

Bahzell released Leeana's hand and they both extended their left arms.

"Blood of blood," Tomanāk rumbled.

"Bone of bone," Lillinara sang.

"Flesh of flesh," Tomanāk pronounced.

"Heart of heart," his sister said.

"And soul of soul," their voices mingled in a duet fit to set the heavens trembling or send mountains dancing, a song that echoed from the stars themselves. "Be two who are one. Give, share, love, and know the joy such love deserves."

Light gathered about the extended wrists—a cloud of blue touched with the argent of moonlight and burnished with gold. It enveloped Bahzell's and Leeana's arms, flashing higher and brighter, and then, with a silent explosion, it vanished and they gazed at the bracelets upon their wrists. The traditional cuff-style marriage bracelets of a Sothōii wife and husband, but different. They gleamed not with the gold of which such bracelets were made, at least among the wealthy, nor with the rubies with which such bracelets were set. No, these were of silver and set with opals in a gleaming circle about the full moon of the Mother between the crossed sword and mace of Tomanāk. More than that, they were broader and made in a single, unbroken piece, without any opening, as if they had been forged about their wearers' wrists, and even in the bright daylight of the Wind Plain, they gleamed faintly in blue and silver.

Bahzell and Leeana stared down at them, then raised their eyes to Tomanāk and Lillinara once more, and Tomanāk smiled at them.

"We promise they won't glow when you don't want them to," he said. "When you're creeping around in the shrubbery, for example." His smile grew broader, then faded into an expression of sober pleasure. "And I know the two of you needed no outward symbol of your love for one another. But when we find ourselves as proud of someone as we are of you, we reserve the right to give them that outward symbol, whether they need it or not. Wear them with joy, my children."

Bahzell and Leeana nodded, unable for once to speak, and Lillinara cocked her head.

"And now, Leeana, I have a gift to celebrate your wedding."

"Lady?" Leeana looked puzzled.

"I think it will bring you joy, Leeana, but it isn't really for you. Or not directly, at least," Lillinara continued. "Not even a goddess can make things as if they'd never happened. But that doesn't mean we can't take steps... Gayrfressa."

The mare twitched, her surprise obvious, and her ear pricked forward as she gazed up at the deity.

<*Yes, Lady?*> Even her mental voice seemed less brash than usual, and Lillinara smiled at her.

"You are as worthy a daughter as Leeana," the goddess said. "And, like her, you would never ask any special favor for yourself. And that is why I give both of you this gift on the day of her wedding and to celebrate the day of your bonding with her."

She reached out, touching Gayrfressa's forehead, and silver light blazed up, blindingly bright in the daylight. The courser's head tossed—in surprise, not fear or hurt—and then the light flashed once and was gone.

Bahzell's ears flattened as Gayrfressa turned her head, looking at him, and her incredulous joy flooded into him through his herd sense. The mutilated socket of her right eye had been filled once again—not with an eye, but with a glittering blue and silver star. It glowed, almost like Wencit of Rūm's wildfire eyes but without the shifting rainbow hue of Wencit's gaze, and delight roared through Gayrfressa's heart like the proud, joyous strength of the wind for which she was named as the vision which had been ripped from her was restored.

"You've always seen more than most, Daughter," Lillinara told her gently. "Now you'll be able to see what others see, as well. And perhaps," the goddess smiled almost impishly, and delight chuckled and rippled through the glorious harmony of her voices, "you'll see just a little more *clearly* than they while you're about it."

She stepped back, beside Tomanāk, and the two deities gazed at the four mortals before them for a long, silent moment. Then, in unison, they bent their heads in a bow of farewell and vanished.

Human, hradani, and coursers looked at one another, bemused, shaken, joyous, and somehow deeply rested and refreshed, and the voices of god and goddess whispered in the backs of their brains.

"Love each other, children. Love each other always as much as you do now, for yours is a song this world will long remember, and love is what will take you there, and give you strength, and bring you home to us in the end."

Chapter Twenty-One

✣✣✣✣✣✣✣✣✣✣✣✣✣✣✣✣✣✣✣✣✣✣✣✣

"Now *that's* impressive," Leeana observed the next morning as Gayrfressa and Walsharno rounded a last bend and emerged in a clearing in the middle of a forest of towering pines.

"Aye, that it is," Bahzell replied, and it wasn't the simple agreement it might have been. Unlike his wife—and, oh, but that word tasted good in his thoughts!—he'd seen the plans, although the last time he'd actually been here, there'd been nothing to see but trees. He'd known exactly what to expect... and his expectations had fallen well short of the reality anyway.

The pine forest about them covered a stretch of gently rolling hills on either side of the Balthar River. Anywhere except atop the Wind Plain, they probably wouldn't have been dignified with the name of "hills" at all. But they were high enough to be noticeable, heaved up by whatever long-ago cataclysm had diverted the Balthar from the Gullet, and they sloped steadily downhill to the southeast until they met the Bogs that diversion had created. The trees themselves were enormous, rising out of a gauzy layer of early mist the sun had yet to burn away, but they'd been cleared and the stumps had been rooted out from an area at least five hundred yards across.

That clearing wasn't what had evoked Leeana's comment, however. No, what she was looking at was the gaping hole at its center. That hole was a rectangle, sixty-five feet by thirty feet, sloping gently but inevitably downward into the lantern-lit depths at a three-degree angle. The last few yards, where it passed through clay and soil, were lined with brick and concrete, but beyond that it was bored out of smoothly polished stone, and a constant, gentle pressure blew out of it to greet them as they approached it.

"Why is there so much breeze coming out of it?" she asked.

"You'll have to ask that of Serman, if it's a complete answer you want," Bahzell said wryly. "It's often enough he's tried to explain it to *me*, but I'll not pretend I actually *understand* it. As nearly as I've been able to lay hands on it, even air is after having its own weight, and the thicker it is, the more it's after weighing. And the air at the foot of the Escarpment is just a mite thicker than it is up here where you Sothōii are after living. So the weight as presses down on all that air down below is after squeezing it up through the tunnel."

Leeana looked at him as if she suspected him of making sport of her, and Walsharno snorted.

<*I was there when Serman explained it to him.* All *the times Serman explained it to him,*> the courser told her. <*He got it pretty much straight. Of course, Serman is one of those two-foots who can't seem to explain anything without numbers.* Lots *of numbers.*>

<*Which must have been dreadfully confusing for someone who can't even read,*> Gayrfressa observed to no one in particular. Walsharno ignored her rather pointedly, and the mare tossed her head in the equine equivalent of a laugh.

They'd continued towards the opening while they spoke, and now they halted as the score or so of hradani and dwarves laboring to build the brick housing which would protect the upper end of the tunnel from wind and weather—and especially from ice and snow, given Wind Plain winters—when it was finished looked up and saw them.

"Prince Bahzell!" one of the hradani called, laying aside his trowel and walking across to greet them. He wiped his powerful, calloused hands on his canvas work apron, then reached up far enough—it was a stretch, even for a Horse Stealer hradani—to clasp forearms with Bahzell. "Sure, and you might have warned us as you were coming," he said with the informality of a member of Bahzell's own clan.

"So I might, if I'd been minded to," Bahzell agreed cheerfully. "But it was in my mind as how I might surprise you and your lads lazing around up here if it so happened you weren't expecting me, Harshan!"

"Lazing around, is it?" Harshan grinned up at him. "Not so likely with Serman cracking the whip!"

"And a true terror he is." Bahzell's foxlike ears twitched with amusement. "Given the choice, I'd sooner face dog brothers than a dwarf with a schedule to meet!"

"You'd not find yourself alone in that," Harshan said with feeling. His eyes drifted sideways to Leeana, and they might have widened just a bit over the gleaming bracelets clasped around her and Bahzell's wrists, but he simply nodded courteously to her, then cocked an eyebrow at Bahzell. "And this lady would be?"

"Leeana Hanathafressa," Bahzell replied. "My wife."

It was the first time he'd said those two words out loud, and they tasted even better that way than they had in the privacy of his own thoughts.

Harshan's ears flattened and he pursed his lips as if to whistle in astonishment, then visibly thought better of it.

"Congratulations, Your Highness," he said, addressing Bahzell with atypical formality, and bowed deeply. "And to you, Milady," he added, bowing to Leeana in turn. "May you be having many years together, and may your joy grow greater with each of them."

"Thank you," she responded a bit wryly. "But I'm no 'milady,' I'm afraid. War maids don't have much use for titles."

"Well, that's as may be," Harshan said in a more normal tone, his ears coming fully upright again, and smiled at her. "Happens hradani don't much bother ourselves with such as that. You've wed Prince Bahzell, and that's enough and more than enough for the likes of me. It's not a thought as we'd like to be going to his head, but we're a mite fond of him in Hurgrum, and if you're his lady, then you're after being *our* lady, as well. Which isn't to be saying I'd not give good kormaks to see him explaining to his lady mother how it was he came to get himself married with nary a word to her at all, at all, as to how he meant to. I've no doubt she'll be pleased to see *you*, Milady, but I'm thinking there's a word or three as might just be singeing someone else's ears."

"I've no doubt of that," Bahzell sighed philosophically. "But in the meantime, we'd best be moving along smartly if we're to reach Hurgrum before nightfall."

"Aye, so you had," Harshan agreed, and bowed to Leeana again. "He can be a mite slow sometimes, Milady, but a sharp rap to the skull usually gets his attention. Mind you use something besides your hand, now, though! I've heard as how broken knuckles take time to heal."

"I'll remember that!" Leeana promised as Gayrfressa and Walsharno started forward once more.

The other workers looked up from the courses of masonry they were laying to nod or wave as they passed. Some of them called out greetings of their own, and then the coursers were into the steadily descending tunnel, and Leeana looked about her in amazement as Gayrfressa's freshly shod hooves clattered on the stone floor.

"We heard rumors about this in Kalatha," she said, "but I never could have imagined something like *this!* How long *is* the tunnel, Bahzell?"

"Just more than a league and a half," Bahzell replied, and found himself looking at the tunnel through fresh eyes in the face of her amazement. "The tunnel head is after being the best part of five miles back from the Escarpment's edge, and it climbs a mite over three feet in every hundred. I'd thought as how it would be shorter, but old Kilthan and Serman wanted a shallower grade, and as Chanharsa was after doing all the hard work, we let them have their way."

"I can see why some of Father's critics thought he was out of his mind to even contemplate this." Leeana shook her head. "Even seeing it, it's hard to believe it's real!"

"Oh, it's real enough to be going on with, lass!" Bahzell chuckled. "And it's a mite hard for someone as grew up in Hurgrum to believe, as well. Though not so hard, in some ways, as having a lake lapping up against the edge of town!"

Leeana nodded, but she was still looking at the tunnel as if trying to take in its reality. She asked Gayrfressa to move closer to one of the square channels cut into the tunnel's floor, and the mare obliged. Gayrfressa was clearly doing her best to look unimpressed, taking the enormity of the engineering project in stride, but Bahzell's ears twitched with gentle amusement as he sensed her true reaction. She was just as taken aback by its sheer scale as Leeana.

Leeana peered down into the channel, then looked back at Bahzell. It was dim in the tunnel, with the entrance shrinking steadily into a brightly lit dot behind them. The light level was low enough for the gleam from Gayrfressa's right eye socket to be clearly visible, but the lanterns and regularly spaced air shafts gave more than enough illumination for a hradani's eyes to see Leeana's raised eyebrows.

"There's two of the biggest waterwheels ever you've seen down yonder ahead of us," he told her, "and when all's finished, it's them as will move the wagons up and down the tunnel."

"How?" Leeana asked wonderingly, and he snorted.

"Would it happen you've seen one of the dwarves' 'bicycles'?"

"Not really," Leeana admitted. "I've seen drawings of them in some of Father's books, though."

"And were those drawings good enough to be showing you the chain as drives the back wheel for them?"

"Yes," she said slowly. "Surely you don't mean—?"

"That I do," he said wryly. "Mind, it's a cable they're using, and not a chain, but I'd not have believed even dwarves would come up with such. It's trees I've seen—and not saplings!—less thick than it is, and they'll have one of them in each channel, when they're done. And each of them the better part of nine miles long, to boot."

Leeana pursed her lips in an unconscious echo of Harshan and shook her head.

"It's a mite much when it comes at you all in one go," Bahzell said cheerfully, "but if there's one thing I've found, it's that dealing with such as Kilthan has a way of stretching a man's mind. And it's a sound enough idea, once you've had time to be looking at all the edges and angles." He shrugged. "Even as gentle as this slope is," he waved one hand at the tunnel about them, "a wicked hard task it would be for horse or mule or even ox to be dragging freight wagons up it. Or down it, come to that, when the weight's against them. It's not too very close together you'd want to be hooking wagons to any cable, even one as stout as Kilthan's, but each of them will move a sight faster than any team could. And any wagon as is cleared to be passing through the tunnel in the first place will be fitted with an emergency brake as will stop it dead if the cable breaks."

"And how long would it take them to repair the cable if it *did* break?" Leeana asked shrewdly, and he chuckled.

"Aye, you've put your hand on the meat of it, haven't you just? But Kilthan's an answer for that, too. Either cable can run in either direction, so if it happens as one of them breaks, the other can still be moving wagons up and down at half the rate while repairs are made. And if it should happen as both of them break—which, I'll have you to understand, Kilthan swears is a thing as could *never* happen to something *his* engineers had the designing of—wagons could still be moving with teams, after all. Not such big wagons, and not with such heavy loads, but enough to be keeping the tunnel open. And it's not the entire cable they'd have to replace, either. It's made in sections as can be spliced in or cut out, and not a one of them is more than a hundred feet long, so it's likely enough they'd have it fixed almost as quick as Kilthan's after claiming."

"Well," Leeana said after a moment, "I'd always heard dwarves had a way with stonework and machinery. To be honest, though, I always thought the tales had to have grown in the telling. Apparently I was wrong."

"As to that, I'm thinking as how one day you'd best come with me on a visit to Kilthan in Silver Cavern. I'll not call this a minor undertaking, lass, but the Dwarvenhame Tunnel, now—that's after being an *impressive* little trip."

✧ ✧ ✧

Even the long, northern summer's day had drawn to a close by the time Bahzell and Leeana reached Hurgrum. The western horizon was a pile of blue cloud against a sea of copper coals as the sun disappeared at last, and lanterns and streetlamps gleamed along the embankment which had been erected to protect the city of Hurgrum from the rippling blue waters of the lake of the same name. They glowed against the gathering dark like lost stars, their reflections dancing on the nighttime mirror of the lake, and the sound of gentle wind and moving water filled the world.

The Hangnysti River had been dammed well downstream from the city, but the water it had impounded stretched at least five miles above Bahnak's capital, as well, and Kilthandahknarthas' engineers had designed and constructed the embankment along the lake's western shore—over six miles long, thirty feet wide, and twenty feet high—not simply to protect the city but to serve as the foundation and base for the huge docks and the warehouses they would serve when the Derm Canal was finished, as well. Not that there wasn't already quite a lot of traffic on the lake. As they approached the roadway along the crest of the dam, Bahzell, Leanna, and the coursers had seen the sails and running lights of work boats and barges of bricks and mortar and other construction supplies moving north, up the lake towards the Balthar, while still others moved south, laden with supplies for the Ghoul Moor expedition.

Now, as they rode out across the dam itself, Leeana shook her head in fresh bemusement. That dam was broad enough for two of the enormous freight wagons to pass abreast along its top, and it was a single, seamless-looking expanse of gleaming white stone.

"More of the dwarves' 'concrete'?" she asked Bahzell, and he laughed. She cocked her head at him, and he shook his own head.

"No, that it's not," he said wryly. "Mind you, it's what I was after expecting when Da first showed me the plans. But Kilthan and Serman were of the opinion as how that wouldn't be strong enough. It's stone, lass. Solid stone, top to bottom."

"What?" Leeana blinked, then turned in the saddle, surveying the bridge. It had to be at least a mile in length, she thought, and it rose the better part of thirty feet above the land behind it—closer to forty, where it crossed the riverbed.

"Stone," she repeated carefully, turning back to Bahzell, and he flicked his ears at her.

"Stone," he agreed. She still looked skeptical, and he shrugged. "The bedrock's not so very far down hereabouts, which comes as no surprise to those as spend their lives plowing the rocks and finding places to be sticking seeds between them." He grimaced. "It's not such wonderful crops we Horse Stealers manage to grow, Leeana, and not for want of trying. There's things the Axemen can be teaching us where that's concerned, and Father's teachers from amongst them showing our farmers how it's done, but it's never farmland like Landria's or Fradonia's you'll see in Hurgrum. Still and all, there's some good in almost anything, I'm thinking, and it wasn't so very deep a trench Serman had to be digging before he hit rock. He ran it clear across the river valley, and after he'd finished, and after he'd built a wooden form betwixt one side and the other, my folk and his were after spending a full year entire filling it with gravel and crushed rock. A mortal a lot of sweat it took us, but once we'd done, why, Chanharsa and two more sarthnaisks told all that loose rock as how it was one solid piece, and it decided as how it'd best take their word for it. It's as solid as the East Walls themselves this dam is, lass."

Leeana drew a deep breath, thinking very carefully about what he'd just said, then exhaled.

"You know, Father had more than a handful of dwarves in the West Riding when he hired them to make his new maps. I didn't see much of them, but they seemed pleasant enough. Polite. Yet

I always had the feeling that, despite their courtesy, they were looking down their noses a bit at Hill Guard and Balthar. Now I suppose I see why."

"Were they now?" Bahzell smiled at her. "Well, I'm thinking you've probably the right of it. Still and all, for all their way with rock and metal and earth, they've not the least notion of woodworking, farming, or horses. And it's in my mind as how most of the world is after offending their notion of neatness and order. They've a way of burrowing through rock and stone and bidding it do as they say, but I'm thinking they've less skill when it comes time to deal with things as they can't command."

Leeana nodded, but her expression was still bemused, almost awed, as they continued across the mighty dam. Stout stone bridges crossed the thundering spillways, and the spray rising chill and damp from below only drove home yet again the audacious scale of the project Prince Bahnak and his allies had undertaken.

The coursers' hooves thudded on heavy wooden timbers as they crossed the drawbridge spanning the barge locks built into the Hurgrum end of the dam. One of the supply barges destined for Trianal's expedition had just passed through them and headed downriver, and the water level in the lock chamber was thirty feet lower than in the lake above it. There were two sets of locks, actually—cavernous affairs with canyonlike sides, extending well out into the new lake—and once the entire route from Derm to the Spear was open, each set of locks would pass four or five barges at a time.

Bahzell had been home often enough to see all of the mammoth construction as a work in progress, yet he'd been away long enough between visits to be constantly surprised by how much things had changed during his absences. Now, as he and Leeana rode along the top of the embankment (sarthnaisk work, like the dam itself), he found himself looking down on Hurgrum from above, seeing the new houses spreading out far beyond the original city wall as the town in which he'd been raised expanded by leaps and bounds. It was hard for him to imagine, even now, what was going to happen to Hurgrum's size and wealth when it became the essential anchor and transfer point for all of the trade which would pass through those new docks and spacious warehouses. Despite the way Bahnak's capital had already grown, some of his fellow Horse Stealers obviously found their prince's predictions difficult to credit, but Bahzell had seen the Purple Lords' capital of Bortalik. He knew firsthand how much wealth passed through that city every year, just as he knew his father had actually understated his own predictions because none of his people would have believed the numbers he and Kilthan and Tellian were truly projecting.

<*He's an impressive man, your father,*> Walsharno said quietly as he and Gayrfressa started down one of the several ramps leading from the embankment's crest into the city proper.

"Aye, so he is," Bahzell agreed. "And a patient one, too."

"Really?" Leeana gave him a crooked smile. "Is that the truth? Or are you just trying to encourage me before I meet the rest of your family?"

"Well, as to that," Bahzell gave her a smile of his own, "no doubt you've heard as how any father is after getting wiser and wiser as his son gets older?" She nodded, and he chuckled. "I'll not say *my* Da's gotten one bit wiser as I've grown older, but this I will say—he's gotten a sight more *patient* than ever I realized he was when I was after finding every way as how I could *try* his patience." He shook his head, his smile turning into a grin. "It's a rare wonder, I'm thinking, that ever I had the chance to finish growing up at all!"

<*Really?*> Walsharno's ears flicked in amusement. <*I wasn't under the impression that you* were *particularly* "grown up"*!*>

Bahzell laughed, but then his ears pricked as a hradani woman—tall, even for a Horse Stealer—in the green surcoat of the Order of Tomanāk rose from the bench under one of the streetlamps at the ramp's foot.

"So, here you are . . . at last," she observed, folding her arms and looking up at him. "Taking your own sweet time about it, were you?"

"And it's a joy as ever to be seeing you, too, Sharkah," Bahzell replied mildly. He dismounted and cocked his ears at his older sister. "And would it happen as there's a reason you're biding here in the dark?"

"Oh, it's not so dark as all that yet," Sharkah replied, and opened her arms to him. He embraced her, hugging her tightly, and tall as she was, her head scarcely topped his shoulder as she hugged him back. There was nothing fragile about that hug, though, and ribs less substantial than Bahzell's might not have survived it.

She gave him one last squeeze, then stepped back with a smile.

"As for how it happens I've been sitting here this last hour or so," she said, "Harshan decided as how it might not be so very bad an idea to use one of Baron Tellian's pigeons to give Da and Mother a wee bit of warning. Not"—she added innocently—"that I've the least idea at all, at all, what that warning might have been, of course."

"And you a servant of Tomanāk." Bahzell shook his head. "It's amazed I am that himself hasn't fetched you a smart rap for such a fearsome lie as that!"

"I've no doubt he was too busy clouting someone else about the head and ears to be bothering with such as me," she told him, and cocked her head with a quizzical smile as Leeana swung down from Gayrfressa's saddle beside Bahzell.

"And this—" Bahzell began, but Sharkah snorted a laugh.

"You've no need to be telling me that, little brother! I told you Harshan'd sent word ahead. And even if he'd done no such thing, I've eyes in my head, you know!"

Bahzell's ears pricked, but then he looked down, following his sister's gaze, and shook his head. The bracelets about his and Leeana's wrists had begun to glow—softly, at first, but steadily brightening, the opals shining like bright, tiny moons in the gathering evening.

"So you're the woman as was daft enough to take *him* on," Sharkah said, reaching out to Leeana. "It's glad I am *someone* was, but truth to tell, I'm wondering if you truly looked before you leapt!"

"Oh, I looked more carefully than you might think," Leeana replied. "And to be honest, I think I did *fairly* well out of it."

She smiled as Sharkah clasped arms with her. Leeana Hanathafressa had never met the woman who could make her feel petite . . . until now. But Sharkah Bahanksdaughter managed it quite handily. She was at least eight or nine inches taller than Leeana, and broad-shouldered for a woman even in proportion to her height. The hand-and-a-half sword sheathed across her back was nowhere near the size and weight of Bahzell's massive blade, but Leeana suspected most Sothōii men would find it uncomfortably heavy even as a two-handed weapon.

Sharkah, obviously, did not.

"I've met your Da," Sharkah said, releasing her forearm. "You've the look of him. And although I'm thinking he might not be wishful of admitting it to you, he was fair bursting with pride when he spoke of you." Her teeth flashed in a white smile under the street lamp. "It might be as how he was of the mind that one scapegrace daughter might appreciate another!"

"I believe I may have heard a *little* something about you, too," Leeana acknowledged. "Something about stubbornness and sword oaths, I think."

"I've no least idea what it possibly could be as you're talking about," Sharkah said, and then raised an eyebrow at Bahzell as he stepped back a full pace from her.

"Pay me no mind," he told her. "It's just stepping clear of the lightning bolt I am."

Sharkah laughed, then looked back at Leeana.

"I'm thinking we'll deal well together, you and I, Sister," she said, "and anyone as could get this fellow"—she jabbed a thumb in Bahzell's direction—"into harness will be coming as a welcome surprise to Mother and Da. So why don't we just be taking you off to meet the family?"

Chapter Twenty-Two

"She's a likely lass," Bahnak Karathson allowed, looking across the hall at his newest daughter-in-law. "Mind," he smiled a slow smile as his youngest son, "I'm thinking as how the ears might take some getting used to."

"Do you, now?" Bahzell asked mildly, his own ears flattening ever so slightly. He glanced across the hall at Leeana—totally surrounded by his sisters (*all* his sisters) and his mother—and then looked back at his father. "It's fond of her ears I am," he said in that same, mild tone.

"Aye?" His father raised his eyebrows and took a long, slow considering sip of ale, then set the tankard back on the table and gave Bahzell another smile, this one warmer and broader. "Well, that's all any man could be saying, isn't it then? And the only thing as matters, when all's said. I've not forgotten how your grandfather argued and shouted—aye, and threatened to disown me entire, more than once—when I'd the questionable taste to be falling in love with your mother. A stubborn man, your grandfather, but a wise one, too, when all was said. He came to love your mother like his very own daughter by birth, and it's in my mind as how a son should learn from his father's wisdom. So if it's all the same to you, Bahzell, I'll just be skipping over the stubborn bit and allow right now as how it's a rare, beautiful wife you've found, and one it's pikestaff plain has wit and wisdom enough for three . . . even allowing as how her taste in husbands might be just a wee bit odd."

Bahzell gazed at his father steadily for a handful of heartbeats, then twitched his ears in solemn agreement.

"She is that, all of it," he said softly, turning his head to look in her direction once more as she went off in a peal of laughter at something his youngest sister Adalah had said.

At twenty-five, Adalah came closest to Leeana in age of any of his siblings, but she wasn't yet out of the schoolroom, given the difference in hradani and human lifespans, and it seemed fairly evident she was in the process of developing a deep schoolgirl's admiration for her new, exotic, red-haired, *human* sister-in-law. It rather reminded him of the way Sharkah had reacted when she first met Kaeritha Seldansdaughter, although he doubted Adalah would be particularly tempted to take up the sword. Like his immediately younger sister Halah—and most *unlike* Sharkah—she was more inclined towards the domestic lifestyle.

"I'll admit, it's more than a little hesitant I was at her age," he admitted quietly to his father. "She's naught but a girl, by our people's way of thinking."

"A well grown 'girl,' for such a wee little thing," his brother Tormach said dryly. He was only twelve years older than Bahzell himself, and his . . . admiration for Leeana was evident.

Bahzell cocked an eyebrow at him, and Tormach colored quickly.

"I've no doubt as how your brother meant only to be saying she's a way about her as makes you think she's older than her years," Bahnak said blandly, and Tormach's face burned still hotter. He looked helplessly at Bahzell for a long moment, then shook his head.

"I meant nothing of the sort, Bahzell," he admitted, "and it's your pardon I beg. Aye, Father's the right of it—I'd not believe she was a year less than forty, to see how she carries herself and the confidence of her—but that's not what I meant, and it's a wonderful muddy taste that boot in my mouth is after having."

"Well." Bahzell considered him thoughtfully, then snorted and reached for his own tankard. "It's not so very irked I can be, given the same thought's spent quite a bit of time working its way through my own brain. And that was part of the problem, as well. It's years I've spent amongst the Sothōii now. I'm after knowing how quick humans grow into their lives, yet still any time I so much as looked in her direction I'd come all over guilty at the thought of 'robbing the cradle.'"

"And you such an ancient graybeard yourself," Bahnak observed in a marveling tone.

"You've no need to be rubbing it in, Da," Bahzell replied, and his father laughed. But then his expression sobered.

"If ever I'd doubted that there's more to adulthood than years, Kaeritha and Vaijon—aye, and Baron Tellian and Sir Trianal, come to that—would have cured me long since, Bahzell. Leeana is one as will keep you on the straight path, standing beside you, lending you her shoulder when you're after needing it, and it's plainer than plain as how the two of you were made to be one. It's proud I am you had the good sense not to let the difference in your ages be standing betwixt you."

He met his son's gaze levelly, and Bahzell nodded slowly, reading the other part of his father's message in the shadow deep within Bahnak's eyes. Even if Leeana lived a very long time for any human woman, he himself would be little past middle age for a hradani when he lost her. Yet it wasn't how long he'd have to miss her that mattered. What *mattered* was how long they'd have together, the life they would share. The memory of that would keep his heart warm to the end of his own days, happen what would. And, he reminded himself a bit more briskly, he *was* a champion of Tomanāk, and as Tomanāk himself had told him on that long-ago day, few of the war god's champions died in bed.

"I'll not be calling it good sense myself, Da," he said quietly. "It might be that's not so very bad a way to put it, but it was the heart of her that took me by the throat, and there was no turning away from her, come what would and sense or no sense."

"Aye?" His father reached across and squeezed his shoulder firmly. "Well, that's not so bad a way to be starting a life together, either, now I think about it. Not so bad a way at all."

✧ ✧ ✧

"Bahzell, it's good to see you!"

Vaijon stood, reaching out to clasp forearms as Bahzell, Tormach, and their father walked into the council chamber. Trianal of Balthar and Arsham of Navahk rose a heartbeat later, and Bahzell smiled as he gripped Vaijon's arm firmly.

"And the same to be seeing you," he said, but his smile faded slightly as he studied Vaijon's expression. There were lines of fatigue in that face, and he looked at least two or three years older than the last time Bahzell had seen him. The Horse Stealer glanced at Trianal and saw an echo of Vaijon's weariness in the Sothōii's face, as well.

"And Brandark?" Vaijon asked, leaning to one side as if to look around the three massive Horse Stealers and spot the Bloody Sword.

"As to that, I'm thinking he'll be along in a day or three," Bahzell replied, and snorted. "We'd some letters from Tellian to Kilthan, and the little man allowed as how he'd just be taking them on to Silver Cavern to collect Kilthan's response before he was joining us here. He'd some business of his own he wanted to discuss with Kilthan, and he'd some strange notion of giving Leeana and me a mite of privacy on the ride from Balthar."

"Did he now?" Vaijon chuckled. "Brandark as an exquisite soul of tact. The mind boggles."

"Oh, he's not so bad as all that," Bahzell replied, and glanced at Trianal. He'd been more than a little worried about how Trianal might react, given the younger man's original attitude towards hradani in general, but Trianal only smiled at him and extended his own arm, in turn.

"So Leeana finally caught you!" His smile turned into a grin. "I'd wondered how long she was going to wait."

"And was it every living soul in Hill Guard—except myself, of course—as knew what was in her mind?" Bahzell asked a bit aggrievedly.

"Oh, no," Trianal reassured him. "I'm pretty sure at least three of the undergrooms never suspected a thing. Of course, that was probably only because she paid us so few visits over the last few years." Bahzell snorted, and Trianal squeezed his forearm firmly. "The truth is she and I did discuss it—well, discuss *around* it, I suppose—in some of our letters, Bahzell. I doubt she realized how much she'd let slip, but there was enough for me to be happy for her. And for you, of course, although speaking as her cousin and someone who was fostered in her father's household, I have to warn you that you're going to find your hands full the first time you manage to do something that truly pisses her off. And you *will*, you know. She comes by that hair coloring honestly!"

"Bahzell is a champion of Tomanāk," Vaijon pointed out, looking down his nose at Trianal, "and as all the world knows, champions of Tomanāk are wily tacticians, skilled strategists, and complete strangers to fear. The first time Leeana picks up something to throw at him, Bahzell will demonstrate all of those championlike qualities and run. Quickly."

Everyone but Arsham chuckled, and even the Navahkan smiled.

"It's an approach as has served *me* well on more than one occasion," Bahnak observed after a moment, then shook his head. "Still and all, I'm thinking we'd best get to it."

He waved at the chairs around the council table, and all of them settled into place. Arsham and Tormach got their pipes lit and drawing nicely, and Bahnak lifted the moisture-beaded pitcher and poured ale into all of their tankards with his own hand. They sat for a moment, gazing out the council chamber windows at a fine, misty rain filtering down across the broad blue waters of the lake, and then Bahnak inhaled deeply.

"It's glad I am to be seeing the lot of you," he nodded particularly to Arsham, "but it's not so glad I was to be reading your reports." He shook his head, ears half-flattened, and Vaijon sighed.

"I wasn't exactly delighted to be writing them, Your Highness," he said, and glanced at Bahzell. "Have you had a chance to read them since you got here?"

"Aye. That's to say as how I've skimmed them all, but it's more attention I paid to the last two or three of them." Bahzell shook his head. "No one but a fool—and I'm thinking there's none of them around this table—would have been thinking it was going to be all sunny skies and fair weather once we'd got this deep into the Ghoul Moor. Still, having said that, it's in my mind none of us were expecting this."

"It's not really as bad as it could be," Trianal pointed out. He took a pull at his tankard, then sat back in his chair, his expression serious. "It's not as if our casualties have gone soaring—yet, at least. Not compared to what they could've been under the circumstances, at any rate. But I admit *I* didn't see it coming, and I've studied everything I could get my hands on about previous expeditions into the Ghoul Moor. This is something new, and those casualties of ours *are* going to climb if it continues and we're not very, very careful."

"It's buried I've been—if you'll be so good as to excuse the phrase—in Silver Cavern, my own self." Tormach's tone was half-apologetic. "I've not been back more than a day or so, and I've not read those reports as Bahzell has. But I'm thinking this hasn't been going on for so very long?"

He looked back and forth between Vaijon and Trianal, and Vaijon shrugged.

"Actually, I think it may have started before we ever noticed," he admitted. "The first engagement or two, it was more the weather than anything else that made problems. And the weather still *is* making problems, for that matter. But looking back, we should have noticed even then that there seemed to be an awful lot of ghouls in those villages. Especially the first one, given that we'd cleared and burned it to the ground *last* year."

"I've been reading Yurgazh's reports, as well, Sir Vaijon," Arsham put in, "and I don't see any reason you should have thought anything of the sort on the basis of what you knew then." The Bloody Sword prince shook his head. "I know Yurgazh thinks all of you let yourselves miss it because of your 'contempt' for ghouls, but I think you're being too hard on yourselves."

"You may be right, Your Highness," Vaijon said after a moment, "but whether we should have spotted it then or not, we've damned well spotted it *now!* And it was only by the grace of Tomanāk—not to mention Yurgazh's good sense—that it didn't cost us a lot more than it did, too."

"That's true enough," Trianal agreed with feeling, and grimaced. "I wish certain Sothōii nobles and armsmen whose names I won't mention could see what a solid line of hradani infantry is really like! There wouldn't be any more stupid talk about riding down the Escarpment and 'dealing' with your folk once and for all!"

"Well, as for that," Bahnak said with a slow smile, "it's not hurt a thing, a thing, for some of our own hotheads to've been seeing why it is no man in his right mind's any desire at all to find out the hard way what your 'wee little pony-riders' can be doing to them as might be foolish enough to poke their noses where they've not been invited!"

Arsham snorted in agreement, and Trianal acknowledged Bahnak's point with a wave of his tankard. Then the young Sothōii shrugged.

"True enough," he repeated, "but it really was Yurgazh's steadiness and those Dwarvenhame arbalests that saved all our necks, Your Highness." He shook his head. "I never thought there were that many ghouls in the world, and when they came boiling up out of that valley..."

His brown eyes went cold with memory of how the sudden, unbelievable tide of ghouls had flooded up over the hill when his own men had dismounted to water their mounts. They'd swarmed his pickets right under, then charged directly towards the rest of his command, screaming their bestial war cries and waving their weapons of stone and wood like some furious, hungry sea. Only three of the men on picket duty had survived, but at least they'd given enough warning for the majority of his men to scramble back into the saddle before the ghouls hit them. That was *all* they'd managed to do, though, and it was only the gods' own luck that Yurgazh's scouts had seen the attack uncoiling from the other side of the valley.

There'd been no time for the Sothōii to uncase or string their bows. It had been all saber and lance, yet Trianal had dared not sound the retreat. Not only had he still had men on the ground, dismounted, hideously vulnerable to the ghouls if their mounted comrades left them unprotected, but the enemy was too fast. They couldn't keep pace with his superb warhorses over a long course, but even the finest horses took time to accelerate. The ghouls certainly *could* have caught his troopers before they managed to pull away, and the nightmare creatures were tall enough and strong enough to pluck any Sothōii armsman from his saddle as easily as Trianal himself might have plucked an apple, if they took him from behind.

The situation had been headed towards the desperate when Yurgazh had brought his infantry across the valley at a dead run. The Navahkan general had halted to give the enemy a single, murderous volley of arbalest bolts at point-blank range before ordering the charge, and then his battalions had crunched into the ghouls' backs like Tomanāk's mace.

Trianal suspected the ghouls had been too focused on his own horsemen even to realize Yurgazh was approaching their town from the other side. Their shock and surprise when the hradani suddenly poured fire into them and then charged into their rear had been obvious, at any rate. Yet even then, they hadn't reacted the way ghouls were *supposed* to react. They'd neither fled in yelping panic nor turned and fought in the grip of their own ferocity. Instead, they'd run away—run away as a *body*, in something closer to an actual formation than he'd ever seen out of any ghouls, and in clear obedience to some sort of pre-battle plan—and his own cavalry had been too disordered to pursue immediately.

"They're better organized than they've ever been before," he said flatly, "and this is the first time I've ever heard of ghouls doing anything that could be described as actually *planning* an attack."

"And it's certain you are that's what they were doing?" Bahzell asked, ears half-flattened and eyes narrowed and concentration. "It's not that I'd doubt your judgment, Trianal, but it's often enough I've seen what looked as how it was a planned response when it was after being nothing of the sort."

"Yes, and it's often enough I've been *part* of a response like that," Arsham put it dryly. "Just because your troops are operating like a mob—the way certain Bloody Swords I could mention had a way of operating, once upon a time—doesn't mean they can't get lucky and simply catch the other side unawares."

"I'm certain," Trianal said, and raised an eyebrow at Vaijon, who nodded firmly in agreement. The Sothōii looked back at the hradani. "It might not have been the very best plan in all the world, and they obviously didn't have enough scouts out to watch their own backs while they concentrated on ambushing my men, but it was planned, all right. And so was the way they broke off. I lost thirty-seven men, dead or wounded. Yurgazh lost another eight, and even with his arbalests, we accounted for less than two hundred ghouls." He shook his head. "That's not an exchange rate we can sustain, and it's a lot worse rate than we've ever had before. Worse, there must've been a good three or four hundred of them still on their feet when they ran for it. How often have we seen that many of them simply take to their heels when they've got an enemy in reach?"

Bahzell nodded slowly, cradling his tankard between his hands on the tabletop while he considered what Trianal had said.

"And not a one of their young did you see?" he asked after a moment.

"No, and that was another strange thing," Vaijon replied. He looked more worried than Bahzell was accustomed to seeing him, and his blue eyes were distinctly unhappy. "I'll admit, it . . . bothers me when their young come at us, but it bothers me even more when we take one of their villages and there are *no* young—or females—in it. That's another reason I'm sure Trianal's right about their having planned the entire 'battle.' They had to have sent their young and their females away ahead of time, which means a couple of things I don't like to think about."

"Ah?" Bahzell's tilted ears invited him to continue, and Vaijon shrugged.

"First, they're trying to protect their young, and they've never worried about that before. Everyone knows ghouls don't care about that—Tomanāk, they *eat* their own young! But this time, they'd sent them away, which can only mean they were deliberately protecting them from us.

"Second, they knew we were coming far enough in advance to send them off before we ever got there. How? We were over twenty miles away before we made our night approach march, and we'd been moving in the other direction for two days. We'd even bivouaced 'for the night,' in case any stray ghouls were wandering around in our neighborhood, before we turned the men out for the attack. So either they spotted us on the way in and managed to organize the removal of all their females and their young—and you know how hard it is for even a ghoul to catch *one* of their young, Bahzell, much less round up *all* of them—on the fly, or else they decided to evacuate their 'noncombatants' ahead of time simply because we were in the vicinity. I don't know which would be more unnatural coming out of a ghoul: the ability to respond that quickly and flexibly, or the forethought to evacuate just as a precaution!"

"Vaijon is right," Trianal put in, and his expression was even more frankly worried than Vaijon's had been. "And that's part and parcel of the way they broke off, too." He shook his head. "I think it's obvious they let themselves get too focused on my prong of the attack—probably because of our horses—and didn't realize Yurgazh was there until he hit them, but when they did realize he was there, they *immediately* turned and ran."

"So they're fighting smarter," Arsham murmured, and Trianal nodded.

"Fighting smarter and in greater numbers than they ought to be," Vaijon expanded. "There shouldn't have been that many males in a village that small, and they didn't have anywhere near enough food animals to support them there for very long. If I didn't know it was impossible—and given what's been happening lately, I *don't* know it's impossible—I'd say some sort of ghoul... warlord, for want of a better term, is managing to impose some kind of discipline on them. It's as if they'd deliberately pulled all of the 'noncombatants' out of the area and transferred in more fighting strength, instead."

"Now, that's a thought I'm not so very happy to hear," Bahzell murmured.

"Nor I," his father agreed, frowning as he scratched the tip of one ear thoughtfully. "And no more will Kilthan or Baron Tellian, come to that."

"They'd have to be able to mass in substantially greater numbers before they could hope to actually defeat us in battle," Vaijon said. "Their tactics are getting better, but 'better' is a purely relative term when you're starting from what we normally see out of ghouls. I'm not saying they won't continue to improve, and they've already moved well beyond their usual scream-and-leap approach. But until they get a lot better than anything they've shown us yet, they'd still need a crushing numerical advantage before they could realistically threaten a field force the size of ours.

"Unfortunately, they can *hurt* us a lot worse than we'd anticipated, whether they can actually beat us or not . . . and we don't know what kind of numbers they'll eventually be able to assemble. Given what we saw in this instance, I'm inclined to think whatever ghoul military genius is managing to coordinate them may well be able to concentrate even more of them next time. And even if he can't, as Trianal says, we can't sustain that kind of exchange rate over the entire summer's campaign."

"No, and if it should happen as how there truly is a 'military genius' on the other side, I'm thinking he's not so very likely to be letting us cordon off the Hangnysti from the rest of the Ghoul Moor," Bahnak observed sourly.

"I think it's certainly going to be harder to clear the riverbank and keep it that way, at any rate," Trianal said grimly.

"Yurgazh's report makes it clear he's of the same opinion, Sir Trianal," Arsham said.

"Well, then." Bahnak's chair creaked as he leaned back and tipped it up on its back legs while he surveyed the others. "I'm thinking we'd best not let it come to that."

"And would it happen you've a notion as to how we might accomplish that, Da?" Bahzell inquired, and his father snorted harshly.

"It's in my mind we'd best nip in there quick and hard," he said. "It's a rare strange 'military genius' as is able to exercise his genius if it should so happen someone's been and disconnected his head from his neck. So I'm thinking it's time and past time as we saw to that little thing."

"I could agree with that, Your Highness," Arsham said dryly.

"Good."

Bahnak let his chair's front legs come back to the floor and leaned forward over the table, folding his arms on its top.

"Trianal, your uncle's after being stuck fast in Sothōfalas, and well I know it. Would it happen as how you could be calling out more of his armsmen of your own authority and get his approval after?"

"Within limits." Despite his youth, there was no hesitation in Trianal's response. "I can call up the Riding's first levy, as long as I don't keep them in the field for more than sixty days. Any longer than that, or calling for the general levy, would require the Crown's authorization, which we might or might not get, given the balance on the Great Council." He smiled fleetingly. "And, of course, I'd better be able to give Uncle Tellian a *very* good reason for why I did it when he asks!"

"And the first levy would be giving you, what?"

"If I call up all of it?" Trianal shrugged. "About another eight thousand men."

Bahnak nodded, his eyes distant for a moment as if he were doing sums in his head. Then he turned to Arsham.

"It's checking with Gurlahn I'll have to be, but it's in my mind as we could put that many more—or it might be even ten thousand more—of our own into the field without pulling too many hands out of the fields or off the canal."

Arsham looked a bit dubious, but he didn't challenge Bahnak's numbers. Gurlahn Karathson, Bahnak's only living brother, had been Hurgrum's chief of staff for over thirty years. If Bahnak was being overly optimistic, Gurlahn would lose no time in bringing him back to reality.

Bahnak's ears flicked in amusement, as if he'd read Arsham's mind.

"It might be as we won't be coming up with quite so many as all that," he continued, "but I'm thinking as how another sixteen thousand men might just come as a bit of a nasty surprise to yon 'military genius.'"

"Hit them with a bigger offensive than they've seen out of us yet?" Vaijon murmured. "Enough bigger to punch through anything they could pull together to stop us?"

"I'll not be going so far as all that," Bahnak said grimly. "We've too little idea of exactly what's been after changing. But, aye, it's in my mind to cut a broader swath than we'd first intended. I know we'd planned on taking the rest of the summer to be clearing the river line, and I'll not pretend I won't begrudge the kormaks to pay for so many more men. But I'll not be frittering away anyone's men at this nasty rate if it should happen there's a way to avoid it, and I'm thinking this is most likely the best way to do that. It's go in hard and fast we will, and take the ground of our choosing, and if it should so happen our 'military genius' is minded to be doing anything about it, then it's fighting on *our* terms he'll find himself."

Bahnak Karathson, Prince of Hurgrum and of the Northern Confederation of Hradani, flattened his ears and showed his teeth as he let his gaze circle the council chamber.

"And any ghoul as chooses to cross swords with the likes of hradani infantry and Sothōii cavalry on ground of their own choosing... well, I'm thinking he won't be making so very many *more* mistakes."

Chapter Twenty-Three

Varnaythus of Kontovar stood in his carefully concealed, thoroughly warded working area, hidden at the very heart of Sothofalas, and looked about himself at the bookshelves, scrolls, and instruments of his profession. Lamps burned in the corners of the scrupulously neat, meticulously organized chamber, and he allowed himself to contemplate the level of skill, training, and raw power it represented. He'd vanquished more foes and taken more lives than even he could remember as the price of amassing that skill and power. Over the many years of his life, he'd defeated more than a dozen rivals for his position on the Council in duels arcane, adding the spoils of *their* libraries and *their* research to his own, and among the handful of wizards who might truly be counted his peers, he was respected and feared as a subtle, dangerous foe—a master not simply of the art but of craftiness and guile—it was best not to challenge. Yet somehow tonight's contemplation of his place of power, the very core of his strength and the unassailable proof of his skill and cunning, failed to provide the sense of assurance, of being the controller and manipulator of others' fates rather than the victim of his own, that it normally imparted.

As one of the handful of wizards powerful enough to claim a seat on the Council of Carnadosa itself, he was . . . unaccustomed to feeling such acute anxiety. Very few beings capable of entering the mortal plane of existence frightened him. Wencit of Rūm came rather forcibly to mind as an exception, of course. Although, to be fair, *fear* might not be precisely the right word for what he felt in Wencit's case. Perhaps self-honesty might be a better term, since there was no doubt in his mind what would happen if he and Wencit should ever meet, and he was in no hurry to embrace that experience, but he was scarcely alone in that. And while he was being fair about things, he wouldn't have cared to face one of Tomanāk's or Isvaria's champions without a handy escape route carefully planned for and laid out in advance, either. There was such a thing as prudence, after all. Demons could be a nasty handful, too, although even the brightest of them were thankfully stupid and easily diverted into attacking a properly prepared glamour. One wouldn't care to try to *fight* one, perhaps, but if one had taken the elementary precaution of preparing ahead of time, *evading* even the most powerful demon was scarcely what one might call difficult. On the other hand, he could remember at least two practitioners of the art who *hadn't* prepared properly ahead of time, but those were rather . . . messy memories upon which he tried not to dwell.

Yet even allowing for all of the prudence and preparation in the world, he hadn't lived as long and accomplished as much as he had without becoming inured to terrors which would have turned the bowels of even the most courageous to water. The art, at the high level at which he practiced it, was for neither the weak hearted nor the weak willed, and now he gathered that will—the will of a wizard lord of Kontovar—about himself before he spoke the final word of his current spell.

A brilliant flash enveloped the working chamber. Had there been any witnesses, they would have been painfully blinded for long, purple-and-red minutes. Even if they'd been warned in time to close their eyes, they would have blinked on tears once they opened them again, and the skins of those particularly sensitive to the art would have prickled and burned as if they'd injudiciously exposed themselves to too much sunlight. But once their eyes started working again, they would have seen that the working space at the very heart of the chamber was empty.

✧ ✧ ✧

It was night on the Ghoul Moor.

The moon drifted overhead, floating in and out of star-spangled cloud rifts, and a cool breeze sent tree branches curtsying in the darkness. Yet there was no darkness in the clearing, where bonfires roared and crackled in snapping showers of sparks at either end of the treeless space. There *had* been trees here once, and not so very long ago, but they'd been felled with stone axes and hewn into massive, sap-oozing timbers. Their branches, leaves, and twigs had helped fuel those bonfires, but the timbers had been cut and notched, laid up to form a massive, open-air dais for the trio of hulking thrones set upon it.

A shape sat in each of those thrones. Roughly man-shaped, each of them hideous in its own fashion, they loomed monstrous in the dancing, seething firelight. The smallest would have stood at least ten feet tall, had it risen from its throne; the largest was half again that huge, and glaring crimson eyes—pupilless and touched with a poison-green sheen—glowed like lava in the firelight.

One of them was covered in shaggy, rank hair, thick and snarled with knots. It had huge, six-fingered hands, the fingers tipped with scimitar-shaped claws longer than most daggers, a snouted face with foot-long, boarlike tusks, and a misshapen skull crowned with a six-foot spread of needle-pointed, bulllike horns. Another was hairless, with a thick, plated hide, an extra set of arms, and legs half again as long as they ought to have been. Each plate was crested with its own jagged, two-inch stalagmite of horn, and it wore the head of some nightmare-designed hunting cat with a direcat's fangs that glittered with the same venomous green luminance dancing in its eyes. But the third—the largest of the three, seated on the central throne—dwarfed that cat-headed horror, for it was an even more nightmarish parody of a hradani. Its hands were enormous, even for something its size, and armed with claws that put its horned companion's talons to shame. Crawling patterns which might have been tattoos, but were not, moved constantly across its skin in the firelight, like a nest of mating serpents, and that same pestilential green clung to it, wavering about it in a foul, deadly nimbus. It sat there, naked and hairy, blood running down either forearm and painting its massively muscled chest in shining red as it raised the tattered torso of a ghoul and ripped huge, dripping chunks of flesh—chunks larger than a grown man's head—from it with sawlike teeth.

The ground before the dais was littered with gnawed and splintered bones, and the clearing beyond was packed with other ghouls. The creatures crouched on their knees, bending forward, faces pressed to the ground as they prostrated themselves worshipfully, and something like a wordless, animallike hymn rose from them. The hairy, horned-headed creature rose, striding to the edge of the dais, and raised a clawed hand. It pointed to one of the kneeling ghouls, and the indicated creature looked up, eyes huge, then squealed as three of its neighbors seized it and dragged it forward. The captive twisted and fought wildly, but strong and fast as ghouls might be, its captors were just as strong, just as fast. And terrified as it might be of its fate, its fellows were even more terrified of *their* fates if they should allow it to escape.

They didn't.

They reached the edge of the dais, the waiting monster reached down with one misshapen hand, and its selected victim gave one last, squealing shriek as that hand closed about its throat and lifted it effortlessly into the air. The ghoul squirmed and twisted frantically, its own claws raking uselessly at the hand which had plucked it from the ground. They opened gaping wounds in those strangling fingers, that massive wrist, but those wounds closed again as quickly as they were torn, and the horned creature only roared with hideous, hooting laughter and tightened its grip. Something crunched noisily, the ghoul's struggles ended abruptly, and the creature returned to its throne, pulled one of the dead ghoul's arms from its socket with casual, appalling strength and a hideous sucking, tearing sound, and began to feed upon its fresh meal.

A light flashed suddenly on the dais, like some lost lightning bolt. It was less brilliant than the one which had filled Varnaythus' working chamber in that self-same instant in far-distant Sothōfalas, well over four hundred leagues to the north. Yet it was bright enough to dazzle eyes no one had warned, and an edge of fresher, sharper fear added itself to the ghouls' worshiping chant.

The creature which had just begun to feed paused, then grunted contemptuously at the diminutive human figure that stepped out of that glittering billiance, and resumed its interrupted chewing. Its cat-headed fellow only leaned back with disinterested red eyes, resting one set of forearms on the arms of its crude throne while it picked bits of ghoul from between its own fangs with the clawed hand at the end of one of its upper arms. But the biggest, hradani-shaped creature tossed aside what was left of the ghoul it had been devouring and glared at the newcomer.

"You're late," it rumbled. Granite boulders screaming their agony as they were crushed in an iron vise might have sounded like that voice, and the stink of death, decay, and blood blew on its words, washing around the human before it.

"No," Varnaythus replied. His merely mortal voice seemed small and frail after that sound of pulverized stone, but he gazed calmly up at the monster before him, and no witness could have guessed how hard it was for him to appear unshaken. "No, I'm not. This is precisely the time I told you I'd be here."

"Do you call me *liar?*"

The creature's roar shook the night like a terrier shaking a rat, and it half-rose from its throne, yet Varnaythus stood his ground.

"That wasn't what I said. I said this is the time I told you to expect me here. That happens to be the truth. Whether you were mistaken, misspoke, or lied is more than I can say. And, frankly, of very little interest to me."

The huge, obscene parody of a hradani glared at him, and the ghouls who filled the clearing went silent, trembling in terror, but Varnaythus simply stood there, arms folded before him, hands tucked into the full sleeves of his robe, and waited. Tension crackled in the night, and then, after a long, breathless moment, the creature sank back onto its throne.

"You said you would have word for us," it rumbled. "Give it and be gone."

"Very well."

Varnaythus inclined his head, but only very slightly. It was a carefully metered gesture of respect from one who was at the very least an equal, and the glare in the creature's eyes glowed hot, a brighter, deadlier green flaming through the lava for just an instant. Yet that was all that happened, and the wizard inhaled deeply, despite the stench filling the air, as he raised his head once more.

Both demons and devils were drawn from other universes, ones in which the Dark had triumphed over the Light and such abominations roamed free, yet they were very different from one another. There were other, even more powerful servants who couldn't be brought across the chasm between universes, for the Gods of Light forbade it, and those other servants were too powerful to creep across unobserved. Sharnā's greater servants approached that limit, but not so nearly as Krashnark's. His devils might be physically less imposing than demons, yet they blazed with so much power it was even more difficult for them to elude the Gods of Light's vigilance. They were far, far more intelligent than Sharnā's creatures, as well, and appearances could be deceiving even where simple physical strength was concerned. The creature in front of him—Anshakar—could have matched any demon strength for strength, and its mere presence warped reality in subtle, distorting ways. The very air about it seemed to shimmer and waver, as if it were water covered by a thin skim of polluted oil, and that distortion could have ruinous consequences for any spell directed at it. More than that, demons were bound by their summoners; they were controlled, not controllers. But unlike a demon, Anshakar could not have cared less that Varnaythus knew his true name, for—also unlike a demon—no mortal could summon him against his will, and Anshakar's name had no power over him, except in the voice of Him whom he called Master. He could not be bound, he could not be commanded, and his wrath could not be appeased by any mortal ever born.

That was the reason no wizard in his right mind ever even *attempted* to summon a devil. If it deigned to respond at all, it was usually only to discover who'd had the audacity to disturb it before it devoured that unfortunate individual... usually while the meal was still alive, since its soul was tastier that way. Occasionally—*occasionally*—it might actually choose not to destroy its summoner, but only when the reason it had been summoned was more entertaining than dismembering a wizard, and very few things were more entertaining for a devil than dismembering *anyone*.

But Anshakar and his companions hadn't been summoned; they'd been *sent*, by Krashnark Phrofro, the one being they had no choice but to obey. Every devil in existence, wherever it might dwell, came from a universe which had fallen into Krashnark's power as His personal fief, and every one of them owed Him a fealty no other god—certainly no mere mortal—could challenge or overcome.

That was one of the reasons for the burning hatred between Him and His twin, Sharnā. There were many times as many demons as devils, but Sharnā lacked the power to command those more powerful beings, and a single devil was more than a match for any score of demons. There had been confrontations, upon occasion, between Sharnā and Krashnark, mostly in the closing stages of the conquest of universes which had fallen to the Dark. The infighting at moments like that tended to be vicious beyond belief as Phrobus' children battled to rip the choicest bits of power from the toppling wreckage. Yet unless one of Their siblings chose to league with Sharnā (which They rarely did; They had no desire to make Krashnark an enemy for Sharnā's sake), those confrontations had always... ended badly for Him and His demons.

Varnaythus didn't know all the details of those other universes, and he often suspected that what he *did* know—what he'd been allowed to discover—had been carefully shaped and limited by the Dark Gods. They didn't want Their mortal servants in this universe knowing too much about the weaknesses, the potential vulnerabilities, They might have revealed in another. But he also suspected that one reason Krashnark's devils were so loyal and obedient to Him was also the reason they were more powerful; Krashnark had taken at least a partial page from the God of Light. He had a far more direct relationship with His greater servants than the other Dark Gods, deliberately choosing to have fewer of them than He might have, but making those He *did* have His champions, as surely as Bahzell Bahnakson was Tomanāk's champion. Not in the same way, for even the greatest of His servants was still His slave, as well, yet He allowed them a greater degree of autonomy—and access to far more power—than any of His siblings (except Carnadosa) or even His mother would ever dream of permitting.

"I have fresh information, Anshakar," the wizard said now, feeling the malevolent will behind those green-shot red eyes beating upon him as he made himself meet their weight steadily. "My art has learned of certain events which couldn't be predicted when They sent you forth upon this mission."

"*They?*" Anshakar snarled. The blast of his foul breath rippled the fabric of Varnaythus' robe, like a gale howling up out of some opened tomb. "There is no *'they'* who can command *me*, Wizard! I come at my Master's bidding—no one else's!"

"True," Varnaythus conceded calmly. "Yet He's commanded you to cooperate with my Lady in this mission, has he not? And told you that His Father has given Her primary direction of it."

He held the devil's gaze until Anshakar spat on the dais and snarled something which was probably an affirmative. The dais' surface smoked and sizzled where the spittle struck, and a reek of brimstone rose from it.

"My Lady has enjoined me to remember that this portion of the mission is yours," Varnaythus continued, "and I have no desire to attempt to give you commands or require you to do anything other than that which Lord Krashnark has instructed you to do. Yet, by the same token, the overall coordination of the mission falls to me, and that requires me to share information with you as it comes to my hand. Now, are you prepared to hear it?"

Anshakar reclaimed the shredded, oozing torso from where it had fallen and took another huge bite from it. His jaws worked, an icicle of gore dangling from them, and he nodded curtly.

"Speak and be gone," he snarled through his mouthful.

"Very well. I'm not yet certain, but it seems likely that rather than the single champion of Tomanāk you were expected to face, there will be three."

The creatures seated on either side of Anshakar—Zûrâk and Kimazh—looked up abruptly, but Anshakar only waved the shredded torso dismissively.

"And you think this is going to change *my* plans?"

His laugh boomed, and the crouching ghouls shuddered in bestial, ecstatic terror at the sound. The whimpering moan of their fear rose at Varnaythus' back, but the wizard only shrugged.

"I think it's information you should have so that you can take it into consideration," he replied, and Anshakar laughed again.

"You mean you think it's information I should run and hide from, as you would!" the devil grunted.

"I admit *I* have no pressing desire to meet the Bloody Hand face-to-face," Varnaythus said frankly. "His record of success is formidable, and I doubt Walsharno's presence would make him any *easier* to defeat. On the other hand, as you yourself pointed out, I'm a wizard, not a warrior. My strengths lie in other areas than direct confrontation with champions, and they aren't as great as yours to begin with."

"Your strengths are *nothing*," Anshakar sneered. "You and your precious 'Lady' are so proud of your little magics, your puny spells. *This* is strength!"

He held up what was left of his meal in one hand and closed his fist upon it. There was a ghastly crunching sound as bones pulverized and crushed, and then the entire mangled lump exploded in lurid green fire that roared up into the night, like a meteor homesick for the heavens. It lasted less than a heartbeat, and when he opened that fist again, a few stinking flakes of ash drifted to the dais on the night wind.

"I have drunk the blood of more champions than you could

count, Wizard. Champions of Isvaria, of Lillinara and Semkirk . . . and of your precious, terrifying *Tomanāk*, as well. I personally slew the *last* champion of Tomanāk in all my universe! His head is mounted on the wall above my throne and his precious sword is in my treasure chamber! You think I should *fear* this Bahzell?"

"How you respond to my information is your own affair," Varnaythus replied, although it was evident to him that both Zûrâk and Kimazh were less than delighted by the prospect of confronting Bahzell Bahnakson and Walsharno. "It was my responsibility to see you had it. I've done that. And, as is also my responsibility, may I ask before I leave if there happens to be any other information you wish me to seek out for you?"

Anshakar glared at him, but he also sat back in his crude throne, thinking.

"Can you tell me when this terrifying champion of Tomanāk will come to end my miserable existence?" he asked after a handful of seconds.

"Not at this moment," Varnaythus acknowledged. Fresh contempt guttered in Anshakar's eyes, and the wizard cocked his head. "I know where he is and what his general plans are, but not even the best scrying spell can reveal things which have yet to be decided. If you wish, I can continue to monitor him and send you word when he actually leaves Hurgrum to join their army here in the Ghoul Moor. Should I do so?"

Anshakar waved one clawed hand in a brusque gesture of agreement, and Varnaythus inclined his head ever so slightly again.

"Very well, my art and my agents are at your disposal in that much. I would, however, remind you of the importance of *timing* in this matter. They've made it clear They wish your presence here to remain unsuspected until all the other parts of Their plan are prepared and ready."

"My Master made that plain enough, *Wizard*. Just as He made it plain"—Anshakar glared at him—"that He would have little patience with any delays on *your* part. We are here, these miserable ghouls are prepared, and I thirst for the blood of yet another champion. It's been too long since the last one. I advise you not to waste my time or my Master's, or when this is done, you will answer to me." He bared his fangs. "No matter where you may hide, in any universe, I can find you, Wizard, and if I do, you'll take little joy from our meeting."

"I never waste Their time, Anshakar," Varnaythus said coldly, "and you might find me somewhat more formidable than you think, here in my own world. Nor do I think Milady would look kindly upon any attempt on your part to damage one of Her servants without Her permission." He smiled thinly. "I readily acknowledge that you could destroy *me* whenever you chose, but I doubt even you would wish to face *Her* afterward."

A deep, rumbling growl grated up out of Anshakar's chest, and Varnaythus allowed his smile to grow a bit broader.

"And with that, Anshakar, I bid you farewell," he said. "I have other errands to run if I'm to have all of those other parts of Their plan in readiness soon enough to make you happy."

"Go. *Go!*" Anshakar snarled, and Varnaythus spoke the word of command and vanished once more.

Chapter Twenty-Four

"Are you sure you don't want me to sound out the Great Council and the Manthâlyr about this, Father?" Sir Seralk Axehammer asked. "If the rumors we're hearing are even remotely accurate, don't we need to be taking a strong position against approval of Tellian's madness?"

Cassan of Frahmahn looked up from his plate and frowned thoughtfully as he contemplated his only son and heir across the breakfast table. Physically, Seralk was very similar to his father, with the same tall, powerful build and gray eyes, although he had his mother's dark hair. The resemblance was even closer where their attitudes were concerned, and despite his youth—he was not yet twenty-three years old—Seralk fully shared his father's loathing for the entire Bowmaster clan. He was, however, younger and more impetuous than Cassan. Indeed, he was impetuous enough that he and Sir Trianal Bowmaster had come within less than one hour of meeting one another in a highly unlawful personal combat which would almost certainly have been fatal for one of them. Fortunately (or unfortunately, depending upon what the outcome might have been), they'd been in Sothōfalas at the time, and Sir Jerhas Macebearer had gotten word of the impending combat in time to have both young men arrested for conspiring to violate the King's Peace during the Great Council's session. Before releasing them, he'd extracted a binding oath from both of them—before witnesses—to stay clear of one another for at least two full years. That had prevented a repetition of the challenge Seralk had issued, but it had also poured fresh oil on the fire of his hatred for Trianal and his uncle, which was one reason Cassan had taken such pains to keep him completely separated from his own . . . deeper plans.

There were other reasons, as well, of course.

"And who on the Council would you be sounding out?" Cassan asked after a moment. "In addition to my own sources, I mean."

Seralk snorted.

"Father, I don't begin to have your sources on the Council itself," he conceded. "But, you know, even the hoariest Councilor tends to have an heir or two floating around. For that matter, even members of the Manthâlyr do, although I'll admit few of *them* are going to run in the same circles I do. And while you may not have noticed, *some* fathers have a tendency to share their thoughts with those heirs of theirs."

"Actually, I have noticed that, now that you mention it. Sloppy of them, but understandable, I suppose," Cassan said, and heard something like a chuckle from his right, where his daughter Shairnayith had finished her meal and sat lingering with a fresh cup of hot chocolate. "Not that the Manthâlyr matters all that much."

He grimaced in distaste. The Manthâlyr, the ancient and traditional assembly of the Kingdom's commoners, had no real authority where the formulation of the Crown's policy was concerned, although he supposed a wise monarch at least *listened* to them. The Manthâlyr did have the authority to vote to withhold any Crown tax on any free city or town—or free yeomen, for that matter—if the Crown *didn't* listen to its members, after all. And, he conceded sourly, it was far more likely to weigh in in favor of Tellian's insanity than against it, given the heavy representation of merchants and bankers in the Manthâlyr's membership. The more far-sighted artisans and craftsmen might be wise enough to see what a flood of Axeman-made goods was likely to do to their own livelihoods, but the moneycounters wouldn't care about that.

If this works out the way Yeraghor and I hope, perhaps it's time we look into reducing the Manthâlyr's authority still further, he thought. *We'd have to be careful how we went about it, but if Tellian succeeds, there'll be no stopping it from gaining still* more *power when Markhos hands the entire Kingdom over to the bankers and loan sharks! And it's not like* Tellian *would mind. He probably thinks that abortion of a "Parliament" they *have sitting in Axe Hallow or that "Dwarfmeet" in Dwarvenhame are good ideas!*

He brushed the thought aside and made himself smile dryly at his own heir.

"So what you actually have in mind is to take yourself off to Sothōfalas to wallow in dissipation with at least a dozen other equally dissipated young blades while peering at them through a drink-induced haze in an effort to pick their brains between goblets of wine in hopes their fathers may have been foolish enough to tell any of them what they were truly thinking. Do I have that approximately correct?"

"Actually, no, Father," Seralk replied. "I was thinking more of doing that between tankards of ale."

"Ah! Thank you for the clarification. That's a *much* better idea!"

Shairnayith laughed out loud. Seralk grinned and raised his own chocolate cup to his father in a gesture of surrender, and Cassan smiled more broadly back at him. There was nothing at all wrong with his son's brain when it wasn't being hampered by his ingrained hostility for all things Bowmaster. It was, perhaps, unfortunate that he was also young enough to make keeping a rein on that hostility such a chancy proposition. Yet that certainly didn't mean Seralk's proposal didn't have much to recommend it, and behind his smile, the baron's brain was busy.

Actually, he reflected, Seralk's idea was shrewder than it might have appeared at first glance. The gods knew young men's tongues wagged freely, and fathers—or *some* fathers, at any rate—sometimes did forget that unfortunate fact when it came to sharing information with their heirs, so it was likely a certain amount of discreet pumping would extract valuable information. Of course, Cassan's sources were so much better than Seralk could possibly know that he was unlikely to discover anything of which Cassan wasn't already aware. For example, he couldn't know that "the rumors" weren't simply "remotely correct." In fact, those sources of Cassan's had positively confirmed that the worst had already come to pass, although there was no way *Seralk* could know that at this point. And the proposal also had the virtue of being exactly what Cassan's opponents would have expected out of his son. Given the nature of Cassan's actual plans, having Seralk visibly pursuing a totally unrelated strategy might have a great deal to recommend it, if only as an exercise in misdirection.

On the other hand, it could also turn out to be a serious mistake if those actual plans of Cassan's went awry.

As Cassan's only son and the legal heir to the Barony of Frahmahn and the Lord Wardenship of the South Riding, Seralk was too important to risk casually. That was the real reason Cassan had kept him totally separated from his discussions with Yeraghor, Arthnar Sabrehand, and Talthar Sheafbearer. Seralk might share his hatred for Tellian of Balthar and his anger over King Markhos' current policies, but his son could honestly testify that he'd never had any part in any actions anyone could construe as even remotely treasonous. And if Cassan's more ominous suspicions about just how it was that Sheafbearer managed so persistently to come up with information he shouldn't have been able to get should turn out to be accurate, Seralk's ignorance would also protect him against any charges of associating with wizards.

If he became too obviously active in his father's *open* efforts to influence the Council, however, it might become difficult to convince their enemies he wasn't involved in *all* of Cassan's plots and machinations... including the ones which were far from open. Of course, if the honesty and integrity of the accursed magi could actually be trusted, they'd be able to testify that Seralk wasn't, although people being people, it was unlikely those enemies of Cassan's would be willing to take the magi's word for it.

The baron's inward frown deepened, although no one could have suspected that from his merely thoughtful expression.

Despite his concerns about Seralk's youthful impetuosity, he knew the young man was far from a fool. It was unlikely he'd press too hard or do anything outstandingly foolish, but he *did* represent the succession. As long as he personally wasn't associated with any plots some pettifogging law master might consider illegal, the House of Axehammer's ultimate position was secure. No king was going to attaint the heir of one of the Kingdom's barons for treason unless he could prove conclusively to all of his *other* barons and lords warden that the heir in question had truly been guilty. Not unless he actually *wanted* to bring about a fresh Time of Troubles. Still...

"That might not be so very bad an idea at that, despite who had it," he said finally. "I know you're going to be out drinking and carousing with them anyway, so we might as well get some good out of all the money you'll be wasting on beer and ale."

"I'll try to stay sober, or at least to avoid sliding down under the table until I've pumped their drink-addled minds clean, Father," his son promised with a gleam in his eye.

"Good. And considering the fact that you've inherited my hard head where drink is concerned, you'll probably even succeed... mostly. But"—Cassan's teasing tone sobered—"remember not to be too obvious about it." The baron raised one hand. "I trust you not to be heavy-handed, Seralk, but there are going to be a lot of eyes on you, including quite a few I'm sure you'll never see. Given how... difficult things have been at court for the last few years, we don't want to give any of Tellian's friends something they could use to suggest you're trying to actively oppose the King on this. Disagreement with Macebearer's or Shaftmaster's advice to the Crown is one thing, and no one could expect anyone of our house *not* to be in active opposition to Tellian of Balthar, but any suggestion of opposition to the *King* could hurt our position in Sothōfalas badly. Especially if any of those friends of Tellian could manage to convince him we were planning anything more... forceful than arguing against those mistaken advisors of his within the Council."

"I understand, Father," Seralk said seriously, "but you've always said being forewarned is the first step in being forearmed."

"That's because I'm a wise and insightful sort of fellow," his father informed him with another smile. "And it probably wouldn't hurt anything for you to agree with any of your fellow young hellions if *they* have anything less than flattering to say about Tellian or that bastard Bahzell." The smile turned into a grimace. "And it's fine for you to steer the exchange so they say as many unflattering things as possible, as long as you can do it without being obvious. Just be sure someone else *starts* the exchange. You need to bolster that reputation of yours for being the exact opposite of a hothead, especially since that... unfinished business with Trianal last year." Cassan gave him a moderately stern look. "I understand the provocation, but sticking two or three feet of steel through someone isn't always the most discreet possible way to remove the problem. Especially if you break the King's Peace in the process."

"Yes, Father."

Seralk inclined his head in a respectful nod, then finished his cup of chocolate and set it back on the table empty.

"And now, Father, if I may be excused, I have to finish packing if I want to get out of here before lunch."

"Of course you're excused." Cassan made a shooing gesture with both hands, and Seralk laughed as he pushed back his chair. "Just don't forget to tell your mother goodbye!"

"Oh, I'm far too smart to do anything *that* stupid!" Seralk informed him, then gave him a more formal bow before he straightened, gave Shairnayith a smile, and headed purposefully out of the dining room.

"He'll do fine, Father," Shairnayith said, and Cassan raised an eyebrow at her. Unlike Cassan's younger daughter, Lynaya, who was virtually a female duplicate of her father, Shairnayith had her mother's brown eyes, dark hair, and petite stature. Outward appearances aside, however, she was much more like Cassan where it counted, and now those brown eyes regarded him thoughtfully. "Of course, I have to wonder exactly what it was you weren't telling him about."

"Not telling him about?" Cassan asked innocently.

"Father, I've never known you when you didn't have at least a dozen irons in the fire at the same moment, but you've been remarkably . . . quiescent in the last year or so. Since I happen to know you're not at all happy with what's been happening in Sothōfalas, that suggests you're keeping some of those irons of yours carefully out of sight. That discussion we had about Thorandas Daggeraxe suggests exactly the same thing to me. And the fact that you're not discussing any of those irons with Seralk before you send him off to Sothōfalas suggests you're deliberately keeping him clear of them. I, on the other hand, am merely a daughter. As such, there's no reason I shouldn't give my imagination free rein trying to ferret out what it might be you're not discussing with him. Especially"—her brown eyes looked directly into his gray gaze—"given how directly they're likely to affect my own life."

Cassan's expression sobered. He looked back at her for several seconds, then inhaled deeply and nodded.

"You're right," he acknowledged. "At the same time, I know you'll understand there are many things going on right now that I can't discuss with you or anyone."

"Of course I do," she said quietly. "I know exactly the stakes you're playing for, Father. I don't need to know all the details of how you plan to play the game, and I understand the reasons for holding your cards close to your tunic. I even understand that not telling me everything is one way of protecting me . . . exactly as you're doing with Seralk. But I hope you understand why I want to know anything you can and want to tell me. You're my father, and I love you. Even if it weren't my responsibility to do whatever I can in our house's service, my own heart would command me to assist you and your plans any way I can."

"I know," he said quietly, reaching across the table to cover one of her hands with his. He squeezed it gently, and felt the same pang at the heart of him that he'd felt the very first time he considered the information Talthar had brought back from Halthan.

He couldn't pretend he hadn't already been aware of Thorandas Daggeraxe's interest in Shairnayith's hand. And it was indisputable that Shairnayith, at twenty-four, ought to have been married years before. Yet she was the daughter and child of his heart. More than that, of all three of his children, she—more even than Seralk—understood the intricate, complex, sometimes deadly nature of the unending contest between the Kingdom's great houses. There were times when he wished she, not Seralk, might have been his heir. The very idea was impossible, of course, and Shairnayith would probably have been vehemently opposed to it even if it hadn't been. She was nothing at all like Tellian's depraved, debased daughter, thank all the gods! The very thought of the most nobly born of Sothōii noblewomen actually coupling with one of those hradani *animals* was enough to make Cassan spew. If anything in the world had been wanting to confirm the weakness, corruption, and degeneracy of the entire House of Bowmaster, Talthar's information that Leeana "Hanathafressa" had deliberately set out to bring a *hradani* to her bed would have provided it! Better—*far* better!—that she should have coupled with one of Tellian's wolfhounds! That sort of insult to all Sothōii could be washed away only in blood, and one way or another, Cassan of Frahmahn would see that blood spilled. But unlike Tellian, he knew he would never have to blush for *his* daughter's conduct, whatever else happened, and he felt a fresh flood of warmth as he looked at her.

Yet that very warmth explained why he'd taken no action for so long where Thorandas' indirectly expressed interest in her was concerned. He didn't want to give her up, didn't want her to move away from him. The long, weary leagues between Toramos and Halthan would separate them, take away that closeness forever, and the very thought was enough to fill him with gloom. None of which meant he wasn't going to have to do it anyway. That was what he'd discussed with her earlier that week.

"The truth is," he told her now, releasing her hand and sitting back in his chair, "that several things are coming together at this moment. I have . . . reason to believe Tellian's actions are inspiring opposition from outside the Kingdom, as well as in. I know I don't have to explain to *you* why the Purple Lords and the River Brigands would both be opposed to this insane plan of his, and I'm afraid my sources indicate some of them are seriously contemplating some sort of . . . direct action here in the Kingdom in an effort to make certain it comes to nothing in the end."

Shairnayith nodded seriously. She probably suspected—no, she almost *certainly* suspected—that he was carefully tailoring what he told her. She was far less impulsive than Seralk, yet many of the same considerations applied when it came to protecting her by limiting what she actually knew. And everything he'd just told her was the absolute truth; it simply left out his own increasingly risky part in that opposition to Tellian's plans.

"No one could possibly predict where that sort of opposition might end, or how it might be expressed," he continued. "Unfortunately, I believe it's quite probable that it could lead to serious instability here in the Kingdom. That's one of the things Tellian and the idiots supporting him have completely overlooked. The sheer scope of the threat he poses to those outside elements' prosperity—especially to the Purple Lords', and the gods know a Purple Lord will stop at *nothing* where money's involved!—is almost bound to bring about interference here on the Wind Plain. The kind of interference that could well have disastrous consequences for the entire Kingdom! And however much I might fear the effect of their actions, I can't pretend Tellian isn't offering sufficient provocation for them to justify almost anything they might choose to do in response. But does he recognize that, or *care* about it if he does? No, of course he doesn't!" He grimaced angrily. "He doesn't give a single solitary damn that he's embroiling us far more directly in the Axemen's quarrels with both the Purple Lords and the Spearmen, which can hardly be in the Kingdom's long-term interest!"

He shook his head in unfeigned disgust at the way Tellian was subordinating the Sothōii's interests to those of outsiders. He was honest enough to admit he probably would have been less disgusted if his own interests and influence weren't going to be so severely damaged if Tellian succeeded, but that didn't make anything he'd just said untrue.

"In the worst case," he said more somberly, "we could find ourselves in a situation which literally threatens to tear the Kingdom apart, possibly even send us back to the Time of Troubles." He watched her eyes darken and nodded grimly. "And, frankly, that's even more likely to happen because of how evenly matched Tellian and I are on the Great Council. You've read enough history to know what happens when opposing factions are so evenly balanced that neither seems likely to be able to achieve its ends through politics and compromise, and that's exactly what I'm afraid we're looking at. Obviously, Yeraghor supports me, but the wind riders support Tellian. That makes the North Riding critical, and that, I'm afraid, is the reason I've mentioned Thorandas' request to you."

Shairnayith looked at him, then sighed. Despite how well he knew her and how much he loved her—or perhaps *because* of how much he loved her—he couldn't read her emotions from her expression this time, and he wished desperately that he could.

"Father," she said after a moment, her voice low, "I've always known that when the time came I'd marry for 'reasons of state.' You did, when you married Mother, and it would have been foolish for me to think even for a moment that it could be any different in my case. For that matter, we only have to look at the West Riding to see what happens when people with the responsibilities we have marry to please themselves and let Phrobus take the rest of the Kingdom."

She hadn't yet heard about Leeana and that bastard Bahzell, he knew, but she didn't need to. The effects of Tellian and Hanatha's selfish refusal to provide a clear succession before Leeana obliged everyone by running off to the war maids like the whore she'd turned out to be was quite bad enough. Her nostrils flared with genuine anger and contempt as she thought about it, and her eyes hardened. But then she raised them to meet his gaze again, and they softened once more.

"I know you don't want to 'marry me off,' Father. I know why you don't. And to be completely honest, there's a huge part of me that never wants to leave Toramos, move away from home... away from you. For that matter," she smiled crookedly, "you've established a high standard for any future husband. I had to conclude some time ago, when I looked around and surveyed the possibilities, that I wasn't going to find a husband of my own who was *your* equal, but that doesn't keep me from wishing I could.

"I don't really know Thorandas." She shrugged. "Oh, I've spoken with him several times at balls in Sothōfalas, and I've encountered him from time to time when you've taken me to court, but I can't say I've ever had the opportunity to actually become acquainted with him. On the other hand, how many noblewomen truly know their husbands before their wedding nights? From what I *do* know about him, he seems a likely enough man. I won't pretend I haven't had my own share of dreams and fantasies about dashing, handsome young men battling one another for my hand, but that's what happens in bad ballads and worse novels, not in real life. And what young woman in her right mind could object to marrying the heir to one of the ridings? Especially when it would unite two of them not just politically but by blood?

"You don't need my consent to approve my betrothal to Thorandas." Her smile warmed. "I can't deny I'm pleased you *did* discuss it with me, even though the decision is ultimately yours. But I'm hardly *surprised* you did, however some other father might have acted in your place, and if you were concerned I might object to it, don't be." She drew another deep breath. "I imagine every young woman feels nervous, even a little frightened, when the time finally comes for her to leave her home and go make another one with someone else. I know *I* feel that way, at any rate! But I understand the reasons, and I'm sure that in time, Thorandas and I will build a life together just as you and Mother have."

Cassan's eyes prickled as he looked across the table at her, and pride in her filled his heart. Yet he couldn't help hoping Shairnayith and Thorandas' lives together would be more complete than his own with her mother. Indeed, despite his disgust and contempt for Tellian, there was a tiny corner of his own heart which had never quite been able to stop envying him, as well, when he thought about the closeness which had kept him from setting Hanatha aside. Stupid, willful, and selfish of him, yes; it had been all of those things and worse, just as it had been the stuff of those bad ballads and worse novels of Shairnayith. Yet still that tiny piece of him envied the two of them for having something he himself had never had. Felytha Blackhill had wed a much younger Cassan Axehammer for the same sort of "reasons of state" Shairnayith faced, but there'd never been anything of fire or passion—or love—between them, and unlike her brother Rulth, she'd always hated the "great game." She was far too intelligent and properly reared to ever let that hatred show, and Cassan doubted that even their children were aware of just how bitterly unhappy she'd been over the years as he waged his fierce, unremitting war against Tellian of Balthar. And however unhappy she'd been, she'd never shirked for a moment on her responsibilities to her house, her husband, or her position.

"Watching you leave Toramos will break my heart," he told his daughter softly, "but you're right. I've always known the time would come when I'd have to let you go, and perhaps I've been selfish not to have done it sooner. Yet the truth is that Thorandas is probably the only match I could make which could possibly be worthy of you."

"I'm less concerned with worthiness than I am with binding our house more closely to the Daggeraxes for the good of them both... and for the Kingdom as a whole, as well," Shairnayith replied.

"I've never doubted that for a moment, but I hope you'll forgive a father for trying his best to find his daughter the husband she deserves... and the position for which she's so well fitted."

Shairnayith smiled and made a tiny waving away gesture with her right hand. Then she straightened and pushed her chair back from the table.

"I'm sure you're actually thinking about all sorts of other things right now, Father." She shook one finger at him teasingly, her voice and manner almost—*almost*—normal. "I know you too well to think anything else could be possible! But with your permission, I think I'll leave you to your plans and machinations while I go for a ride to think about what we've discussed this morning."

"Of course, my dear," he agreed. "Just be sure you take your armsmen along."

"And here I was, planning on sneaking away without them." She sighed and shook her head. "Very well. Since you insist."

"Such a dutiful daughter," he said, a deep, gentle note underlying the humor in his voice, and she bent to kiss him lightly on the cheek before she rustled out of the room in the whisper of her skirts.

He sat looking after her for a long, still while. Then he took another sip from his chocolate cup and made a face as he discovered how it had cooled.

He put the cup back down, rose, and crossed to one of the dining room's windows, gazing out it with his hands clasped behind him while he considered his children, their places in the

Kingdom, and the dangerous decision which had made itself as Talthar brought him the latest news from Sothōfalas.

His gray eyes turned bleak and hard, and his jaw clenched. He'd tried *so* hard to avoid crossing that final line in his conflict with Tellian, yet now Tellian and Yurokhas had left him no choice. They'd convinced Markhos not simply to allow their accursed canal, but actually to grant it a Crown charter! That was intolerable. Even if Shairnayith's marriage to Thorandas Daggeraxe were to bring the North Riding into alignment with the South Riding and the East Riding on the Great Council, the success of Tellian's project would permanently tilt the balance of power towards Balthar. It could be no other way when the floods of wealth Shaftmaster was predicting at the Exchequer began to flood into the West Riding and the Kingdom. Tellian's position as the gatekeeper of that wealth would inevitably establish him in an unchallengeable position as the Kingdom's most powerful noble, and if that happened, Cassan's power base would be destroyed. Worse, he told himself, it would mean Tellian's obscene alliance with the bestial hradani would succeed, and that was unacceptable. He'd rather see the Wind Plain inundated by ghouls and trolls than see those horse-stealing *bastards* actually accepted as Sothōii allies—as *equals*—after everything they'd done to balk his own plans at every step of the way!

No. He shook his head, eyes like gray flint. No, it was the only way, and it wasn't simply Tellian and Yurokhas who were to blame. The gods knew he would never have raised his hand against his King if his King hadn't driven him to it! If he hadn't *proven* how unworthy of his crown he was. But Markhos had—worse, he'd broken faith with countless generations of Sothōii who'd known the enemy when they saw it. All he'd had to do was to say no, to refuse to lend his approval to Tellian's insanity, but he'd refused to do that. He'd taken his stand with the enemies of the Kingdom, not those who had its best interests at heart, and in doing that, he'd left Cassan no choice, no option.

If Crown Prince Norandhor should suddenly inherit his father's crown, the Kingdom would be looking at a regency at least sixteen years long. And if the North Riding aligned itself with Cassan and Yeraghor on the Great Council and neither Markhos nor Yurokhas were there to oppose them, then *they* would name the Crown Prince's regent . . . and that regent would *not* be someone named Tellian Bowmaster.

Talthar's right, damn him, Cassan thought bitterly. *I know he's after more than just all the kormaks he's had from me. The man has plans of his own, and I don't trust him as far as I could throw a warhorse. But I also know he's here, where I can keep an eye on him once the dust clears. If I can't keep him under control with that starting advantage, then I'll* deserve *whatever happens to me! And even if that weren't true, he's still right. I have to* act, *and act* now, *before Markhos officially promulgates his charter for Tellian at the fall Council session. And I have no choice but to make sure he and Yurokhas both die.*

Something inside him flickered rebelliously at the thought, but he suppressed it sternly. The die was cast; now it was simply a matter of arranging things as carefully as possible. As he'd suggested to Shairnayith, there were outsiders who would do almost anything to see Tellian's canal fail. The trick would be to make certain any suspicion within the Kingdom fell upon those outsiders, instead of Cassan.

And if Talthar's right and Yurokhas means to continue ignoring his brother's summons home and stays right where he is on the Ghoul Moor, his *death can probably be made into an accident—and one* Tellian *will be blamed for, since it's his expedition Yurokhas is accompanying.* He smiled thinly at the thought. *Having him "killed accidentally in battle" will decouple his death from Markhos', too, now that I think about it. Just a dreadful, tragic coincidence... and one which would never have happened—just as those "outsiders" would never have had any motive to murder the King—if not for Tellian's perverted alliance with the hradani and Dwarvenhame!*

The smile grew broader and colder as he contemplated the possibilities. If he was going to be forced to do this thing, then he would do it as well and as effectively as it could be done.

And he knew just how to go about doing that.

He turned from the window, crossed to the table, and tugged on the embroidered silken bell rope. No more than two or three seconds passed before the door from the pantry into the dining room opened and one of the under-butlers stepped through it with a bow.

"May we clear away now, Milord?" he inquired.

"You may," Cassan replied brusquely. "But first, send word to Sergeant Warshoc. Tell him I want to see him in my office as soon as possible."

Chapter Twenty-Five

"Excuse me, Sir Dahlnar, but you have a visitor."

Sir Dahlnar Bronzehelm frowned as he looked up from yet another of the endless documents on his desk. But the frown disappeared as he recognized the well-dressed man standing behind the smiling clerk in his office's doorway.

"Master Talthar!" Bronzehelm stood, the last of his frown turning into a smile. "I didn't expect to see you again so soon."

"I didn't expect to *be* here again so soon," Talthar Sheafbearer replied. "Obviously, circumstances changed."

"Probably because kormaks were involved somewhere," Bronzehelm said shrewdly, and nodded dismissal to the clerk as he waved Sheafbearer into the office proper and pointed at the comfortable chair in front of his desk. His visitor seated himself, and Bronzehelm sank into his own swivel chair and tipped it back.

"There *are* kormaks involved, aren't there?" he said.

"Well, I *did* just happen to find myself in possession of a particularly nice set of rubies I thought Baroness Myacha might like," Sheafbearer acknowledged with a charmingly modest smile. "That's what brought me back here so unexpectedly."

"I see. Well, it pleases me immensely—speaking purely as Baron Borandas' seneschal and the protector of his private purse, you understand—to inform you that you've missed her. She and the Baron won't be back from Leehollow for at least another three days."

"Oh." Sheafbearer grimaced, but then he shrugged. "I suppose that's what I get for not checking to see whether or not they'd be here."

"I'm sure it wouldn't bankrupt a merchant of your deep pockets to spend a day or two in an inn here in Halthan while you wait for them. In fact, I think that would be a marvelous idea. At least someone here in the barony would recapture some of the disgusting amount of hard currency you've been sucking out of the Baron's treasury ever since that first visit of yours."

"I'm sure I don't have the least idea what you're talking about."

"Oh, of course not!" Sheafbearer rolled his eyes. "And I suppose it's pure happenstance that you keep turning up here with such spectacular pieces which just happen to be perfectly suited to the Baroness' coloring?"

"Well, perhaps not *pure* happenstance," Sheafbearer conceded, and Bronzehelm laughed.

A few of Dahlnar Bronzehelm's clerks and assistants had been surprised by how quickly and thoroughly the seneschal had warmed to Master Talthar. It wasn't that they didn't understand how charming the gem merchant was, for he was unfailingly courteous even to the most lowly bureaucrat, and he radiated an amiable, easy-going warmth that was rare indeed. No doubt that natural geniality of his helped to explain his obvious success as a merchant, yet no one who'd spent more than a very short time in his company could have doubted that however useful his charm might be to him, it was also completely genuine. Nor was Sir Dahlnar a cold and distant personality, either. In fact, all of his clerks were devoted to him, for he was a naturally warm and generous man himself, and one who always appreciated wit and humor when he encountered them. So it surprised no one that he and Master Talthar should find themselves kindred sorts.

But for all his own warmth, Sir Dahlnar was also shrewd and conscientious, well aware of the implications of his position as Borandas Daggeraxe's seneschal. Any number of people had attempted to take advantage of him, use him as a way to influence the baron or to profit from him over the years; none had ever succeeded. Yet Master Talthar, a merchant who was obviously making a great deal of money here in Halthan, had quickly—almost effortlessly—become a visitor Sir Dahlnar's clerks automatically escorted to his office whenever he arrived.

Of course, it was also true that however many kormaks might

be spilling into Master Talthar's purse, his wares were worth every copper he'd ever been paid. In fact, on those occasions when Sir Dahlnar had been able to convince Baron Borandas to let him serve as his agent rather than dealing with the merchant directly, he'd driven a hard, hard bargain, however much he might like Master Talthar. Indeed, the price of Talthar's gems in *those* cases had been low enough the merchant might well have actually taken a loss on the final price. And no one could have been more disinterested in the North Riding's politics than Master Talthar. He kept himself informed upon them, but that was only to be expected from a shrewd and prosperous Axeman merchant who frequently carried a not-so-small fortune in gems about with him. Yet aside from the sort of information any merchant might have found useful, he paid them no particular heed, and he'd certainly never used his own contacts with Baron Borandas to try to influence him in any way.

If anyone had looked more closely, they might have begun to realize that rather than Talthar cultivating Bronzehelm, it was the seneschal who'd cultivated a relationship with the merchant, at which point things would have started to make much more sense. Bronzehelm had always had a shrewd eye for worthwhile sources of information, an ability to recognize observers who were both intelligent and insightful, and for all Master Talthar's dry humor and warmth, that described the gem dealer quite well. The quality of his wares meant he dealt with many of the wealthy and powerful, in the Empire of the Axe and even in the Empire of the Spear, not just the Kingdom. He obviously knew quite an extraordinary number of people, and he had factors or at least contacts in what appeared to be every major marketplace from Bortalik Bay to Sothōfalas to Belhadan. Indeed, in his more modest fashion, his network of connections clearly echoed that of the great trading houses, like Clan Harkanath itself.

He paid the same attention to politics and attitudes elsewhere that he did here in the North Riding, for the same reasons, and he was perfectly willing to share his observations with Bronzehelm. He refused to violate any personal confidences, which only made the seneschal respect both his judgment and his character even more highly, but that didn't detract from the value and clarity of his analysis.

"I hope you'll forgive me for this, Talthar," Bronzehelm said now, "but I know damned well it's not 'happenstance'!" He shook his head. "I see how you've become so immoderately wealthy, given that eye of yours."

"Rubies *do* go well with her hair, don't they?" Sheafbearer observed, and Bronzehelm snorted. "On the other hand, however good my *eye* might be, I don't seem to have a very good sense of *timing*, do I?" The merchant grimaced. "I seem to've devel oped a positive talent for visiting Halthan while the Baron and his lady are away!"

"I suppose so." Bronzehelm nodded. "On the other hand, given how expensive it is whenever you *don't* miss them, I'm not going to pretend I'm brokenhearted by it."

"The Baron truly does love to surprise her, doesn't he?"

"Yes, he does, bless him. And every time he does, Her Ladyship scolds him for 'wasting money' on her... and then *you* come along and convince him to do it all over again."

"Nonsense. I don't convince him to do a thing, and you know it." Sheafbearer waved a finger at the seneschal across his desk. "I simply *assist* him in doing exactly what he would have freely chosen to do without any prompting from me at all."

"I suppose that's one way to describe it," Bronzehelm said dryly, and Talthar chuckled.

"Well, I'm not going to get rich trying to sell *you* anything, now am I?" He shook his head, surveying the plainly dressed seneschal. Bronzehelm was always neatly, even impeccably, attired, yet he obviously had no taste for the rings and neck chains many a Sothōii noble favored.

"I'm sure I'll be able to restrain my tears of sympathy," Bronzehelm said even more dryly. "In light of how rich you're getting off of certain *other* parties here in Halthan, that is."

"Such heartlessness," Sheafbearer sighed. Then he brightened. "On the other hand, I might actually have something to tempt you with this time."

"You can *try*, anyway," Bronzehelm told him.

"All right, I will."

Sheafbearer unlocked the sturdy gem case he carried with him everywhere. He reached into it and rummaged about for a moment before he brought out a remarkably plain golden ring, its band set with a single modest-sized (though very well-cut) emerald. He held it in the palm of his left hand for a moment, stroking the emerald with the tip of his right index finger as if it were a small, friendly animal, then offered it to Bronzehelm.

"I think this might be plain enough even for you," he said, extending it across the desk.

"Really?" Bronzehelm reached for it, and the merchant dropped it into his hand. "I'll admit, I've never been partial to the more gaudy—"

The ring's emerald flashed brightly, just once, and Sir Dahlnar Bronzehelm froze, sightless brown eyes locked to the small golden circlet on his palm.

✧ ✧ ✧

Master Varnaythus smiled at the abruptly motionless seneschal of the North Riding. There was an undeniable edge of nervousness in that smile, yet any anxiety was more than compensated for by sheer satisfaction.

Bronzehelm had worked out even better than Varnaythus had anticipated. His susceptibility to the rather exotic "herbs" the wizard's art had unobtrusively introduced into his diet was even more pronounced than Varnaythus had allowed himself to hope. It often worked out that way, however. Intelligent people accustomed to thinking clearly and concisely seemed to have less inherent resistance once someone managed to begin suggesting things to them with the proper... pharmaceutical enhancements. That very clarity and concision could be marshalled against them, put to work in the service of justifying and rationalizing the ideas others had inserted into their thoughts.

It was just as well Bronzehelm *was* more susceptible to them, though, Varnaythus thought, his smile fading, given how much more rapidly he'd found himself forced to act in the seneschal's case. He hadn't anticipated that Markhos would decide to come out so unambiguously in Tellian's favor so soon, and he'd hoped for at least another two or three months—possibly even the full length of the summer—to "adjust" Bronzehelm's thinking, if only to keep anyone from wondering about the rapidity with which it had shifted.

Unfortunately, Thorandas had been more eager to seek Shairnayith's hand than Varnaythus had expected. Then Markhos had reached a formal decision in Tellian's case, and, finally, there was Anshakar and his fellows. Varnaythus had always had his doubts about introducing them into the Ghoul Moor quite so soon, given how... tenuous his control over them was bound to be. Yet they'd needed to get the ghouls organized early in Tellian and Bahnak's current campaign, and only Krashnark's devils could have hoped to accomplish *that*. And he didn't like the change in emphasis which had crept into his instructions from his own Lady.

He didn't know if it was Her idea or if it had been "suggested" by Her father, and he couldn't really quibble with the logic behind it, but it was unlike Her to change plans in midstream. And it was at least partly his own fault for emphasizing the advantages of recreating the Time of Troubles here in the Kingdom, he supposed. He'd intended it as a fallback position, an alternative prize he could offer in the interests of his personal survival if the plan to eliminate Bahzell failed (as such plans had a demonstrated tendency to do). Unfortunately, those advantages had been as evident to Her and the other Dark Gods as they were to him, and They'd decided They wanted both possibilities followed up. Indeed, They'd *demanded* that both strategies be pursued, all of which meant things were moving faster than Varnaythus might have preferred. Not that there was any point in expecting his Mistress or Her siblings to sympathize with him. They didn't care how inconvenient or worrisome Their servants might find their lives as long as they produced the desired result, after all.

And it doesn't help that I have to figure out how to avoid that bastard Brayahs while I'm about it, he thought sourly. *The truth is, Dahlnar, my friend, that I'd love to have more opportunities to work directly on the Baron, if I weren't so worried that his darling wife or his cousin the mage might notice it. Unfortunately, that's out of the question, which leaves me with you. And I need to pick moments when dear, sweet Brayahs is away if I want a little quality time even with* you. . . .

Working around the mage wasn't the only challenge Varnaythus faced, despite Bronzehelm's susceptibility, and some of those additional challenges were more worrisome than others. Especially since he'd come to the conclusion that Baroness Myacha was profoundly opposed to Thorandas' marriage to Shairnayith. He'd expected her to be less than enthusiastic about the proposal, yet the strength of her opposition had taken him by surprise, and he'd been a bit surprised by the shrewdness of her insight into the political realities—and potential liabilities—behind it. Fortunately, perhaps, that very shrewdness had led her to doubt anything would come of Thorandas' ambitions in that direction, given Borandas' long-standing policies and the North Riding's traditional neutrality between Cassan and Tellian, so she'd been willing to bide her time. There'd be plenty of time for her to advise against the match if it should begin to seem likely, and the bad news was that despite her youth, Baron Borandas clearly valued her advice and took it seriously.

The *good* news was that she seemed to be determined to avoid even the appearance of "meddling" in his decisions. If Varnaythus had her analyzed properly, that determination sprang not from any lack of strong opinions but from an adamant resolve that no one was going to think of Borandas as some feeble-witted old man who could be manipulated through his marriage bed. She would give her advice, if it was asked for, but she was unlikely to press her views strongly *unless* they were asked for. That was all to the good, but it also meant that if she saw him about to do something she feared could seriously hurt him, she might very well abandon that restraint.

That made Bronzehelm even more important, because Myacha respected him so deeply. She knew how long he'd served her husband, how devoted he was to Borandas, and she'd had ample evidence of his intelligence, as well. She also knew how deeply she herself disliked Cassan, and Yeraghor of Ersok was scarcely among her favorite people, either. So if Bronzehelm spoke strongly and positively in favor of the marriage, she was likely to remind herself of how easily emotions could overrule reason and decide she was too prejudiced to render the sort of objective judgment the seneschal was likely to provide.

Unfortunately, things had moved so quickly Varnaythus hadn't yet been able to prime Bronzehelm properly, which had required him to return to Halthan several weeks sooner than he'd intended. He'd been lucky to find a window when Borandas, Myacha, and Brayahs were all absent, but he wasn't at all happy about sitting here in the seneschal's office in the middle of the day with Bronzehelm staring fixedly at a ring while "Master Talthar" whispered in his ear. It was unlikely, to say the least, that any of the seneschal's well-trained clerks were going to intrude upon them, but "unlikely" wasn't remotely the same thing as "certain," and while Varnaythus had prepared an escape strategy which would take him safely out of harm's way, a teleportation spell wasn't exactly unobtrusive.

Disappearing in a blinding flash of light would draw all sorts of undesirable attention. Worse, it would absolutely confirm to Baron Cassan that his fellow conspirator was a wizard. To this point, Cassan could honestly say he didn't *know* "Talthar" was a practitioner of the art, and not even a mage or a champion of Tomanāk could prove he did. It was entirely possible, now that he'd finally agreed Markhos and Yurokhas had to die, that not even that discovery would have changed his mind. It was also possible it *would,* though, and if that happened, if the entire strategy came apart and They decided it was *Varnaythus*' fault...

You've got better things to do than sit around worrying about other *things you can't change anyway,* he told himself tartly. *And the sooner you get started, the less likely you are to still be sitting here when someone* does *walk in.*

He sat back in his chair, cleared his throat, and spoke a single word in a language which hadn't been openly spoken in Norfressa in over twelve centuries. Bronzehelm's unseeing eyes lifted from the emerald, tracking obediently to Varnaythus' face, and the wizard smiled.

The best part was that there was no magic at all involved in what he was about to do. There *couldn't* be, since any wizard would have been able to detect any command or compulsion which had been implanted by the art if he'd looked close enough. Varnaythus couldn't be positive whether or not a mage like Brayahs could have done the same thing, yet it seemed likely. He would have preferred to be more certain about that, but although he'd learned more about the magi in his years here on the Wind Plain than any of his colleagues on the Council of Carnadosa ever had, he still couldn't be sure about that particular point. He supposed he ought to get around to jotting down all the bits and pieces he'd picked up about the mage talent and make certain the information was available to the rest of the Council, as well. In fact, he'd been meaning to do that for some time now. Still, there were arguments *against* making it available, now weren't there? One never knew when it might be...advantageous for one of one's colleagues to suffer a mischief, and from what he'd already discovered, magi were quite likely to turn into mischiefs of a rather permanent variety under the wrong—or the right—set of circumstances.

Especially if one had somehow failed—purely inadvertently, of course!—to warn one's colleagues about what they were about to walk into.

For the moment, though, what mattered was that Bronzehelm's trance had nothing at all to do with the art except for the activating word Varnaythus had imprinted not on *him*, but on the ring in his hand. It was the drugs and the trance which had rendered his mind open and pliable, ready to accept whatever Varnaythus offered as his own thoughts and conclusions. Speaking of which—

"If it should happen that Cassan chooses to accept Thorandas' offer for his daughter," Varnaythus said quietly but clearly, "it would offer many significant advantages to the North Riding. First, it would create a strong political and family alliance in the center of the Kingdom. Second, it would serve notice to Tellian that he can no longer take the North Riding's neutrality on the Council for granted—that he'd have to be more conciliatory, more open to accommodations with Borandas than he's been in the past. Third, it would create a united bloc on the Council to serve as a counterweight for the power and wealth Tellian is bound to amass if this canal project of his actually succeeds. Let's face it, Dahlnar, if it does succeed, he'll inevitably become the dominant member of the Council. He doesn't necessarily have to have any designs on tyranny or control of the Crown's policies, either. In fact, it would be perfectly natural for him to try to shape them into something more acceptable to him, even if he has the best of motives and truly believes what he wants is the best policy for the Kingdom as a whole, and without that counterweight to hold him in check, he'd be bound to succeed. And, of course, if he *does* have designs on controlling the Crown for his own benefit, a counterweight would become absolutely necessary to protect the other ridings' interests. Fourth, it's likely Markhos himself will recognize the need for such a counterweight at some time in the future, once he realizes how Tellian's success has skewed the traditional balance of political power in Sothōfalas, at which point Borandas' ability to play a moderating role on *Cassan's* demands and ambitions would clearly be in the Crown's—and the Kingdom's—best interests. Fifth, given the growing closeness between Tellian, Dwarvenhame, and the hradani, a firm alliance of nobles who recognize that the Kingdom's interests and those of the Axemen may not always be identical would best serve—"

✧ ✧ ✧

The better part of twenty minutes later, Varnaythus drew a deep breath of relief as he came to the end of his points.

He paused for a moment, running back over them in his own mind. One of the things any wizard acquired early was a perfect memory, since no wizard who failed to acquire one was likely to survive long enough to master the art. It only took a moment for him to be certain he'd covered all of them, and he nodded in satisfaction. He could rely on Bronzehelm's own intelligence to nurture the points he'd made, find all the reasons they made sense, and the fact that most of them *did* make sense in many ways would only help that process along.

But he wasn't quite finished yet. Bronzehelm was no fool, and it would be disastrous if he ever realized he couldn't account for entire blocks of time during his visits with his good friend Master Talthar. It was tempting to simply direct him to dismiss the possibility out of hand, and if Varnaythus had been particularly stupid, he might have done just that. The entire purpose of suggesting things to him in this fashion, however, was to avoid exactly that sort of brute force approach. It wouldn't have been difficult to direct him to manufacture memories of a lengthy, witty conversation before he was released from his trance, and he certainly had both the imagination and the intelligence to do just that, but there were drawbacks to that approach, as well. In particular, returning him to a similar trance—which Varnaythus' research suggested quite a few magi ought to be able to do—would allow any reasonably adroit practitioner to peel away the false memories. And that could all too easily prompt a deeper, more aggressive probe which might well reveal the way in which his judgment and opinions had been tampered with.

Which was why Varnaythus had absolutely no intention of implanting false memories of any sort. There was a certain degree of risk in what he proposed to do instead, of course, but it was a very minor one. The working itself was relatively low-powered, and it was focused in an artifact—the ring in Bronzehelm's hand—and not upon the seneschal himself at all. A very, very faint residue of the art would cling to him for the next several days, but even Varnaythus would have found it extraordinarily difficult to detect, and that assumed he'd have some reason to look for it in the first place.

He drew another breath and very carefully shaped another single word in that long-forgotten language, and the ring's emerald flared again. The flash was much brighter this time, and Bronzehelm's eyes flickered. They never closed, yet they moved rapidly from side to side as a sleeper's might have in the midst of some detailed dream. The ring's brilliance endured for only a very few moments, but Varnaythus was more than content. The glamour he'd worked into that stone didn't touch Bronzehelm's *mind* at all; it simply projected an extraordinarily vivid reality through the seneschal's eyes and ears. The images he saw, the sounds he heard, were manufactured, perhaps, but he truly *did* see and hear them, and so the memories of them were *true* memories, with none of the telltale tags of the art to betray them to any suspicious mage who might examine them.

The emerald gave one last flicker of light, then went blank once again, and Dahlnar Bronzehelm's sharp, alert eyes snapped back into focus on his guest's face.

✧ ✧ ✧

"Well, Talthar, it's been a pleasant visit, as always," the seneschal said. "And I thank you for sharing your observations with me. I'm afraid I have several more appointments this afternoon, but would you be free to join Milady and me for supper this evening?"

"I'd enjoy that very much, Milord," Master Talthar said. "I'll have to make an early evening of it, though, I'm afraid." He smiled wryly. "Since I've missed my opportunity to seduce Baron Borandas out of more of those kormaks of his, I'm going to have to seek other prey—I mean, be on the road early tomorrow."

"Oh, of course." The seneschal smiled, then flipped the ring he was still holding across to the merchant. "And I'm sorry you couldn't convince me to buy this one to defray your expenses. I told you I'd be a hard sell, though, didn't I?"

"Yes, you did," Master Talthar agreed with another smile, but then he cocked his head and regarded the seneschal shrewdly. "I knew *you'd* be a hard sell, of course, Milord. That's one reason I accepted your supper invitation. After all," his smile grew broader, "*Lady* Bronzehelm is a much easier sell, now isn't she?"

Chapter Twenty-Six

<*You two-foots are an interesting breed,*> Gayrfressa remarked as she moved steadily through the pine trees in the coursers' ground-eating gait. The breeze blowing through the trees was cool, scented with the resinous, spicy smell of pine needles and just kissed with the damp breath of the Balthar River, and the road to Kalatha and Leeana's return to duty lay before them. The head of the Gullet Tunnel, on the other hand, lay far enough behind for the voices and noise of the construction gangs to be lost in the distance, and the sound of bird song and the breeze sighing through the needles only made the vast silence of the world seem even greater and more perfect.

"What do you mean, 'interesting'?" Leeana asked, glad for the distraction from her inner thoughts.

<*I mean the way each of you thinks you're your very own isolated island,*> the mare explained.

She shifted smoothly to her right to skirt a particularly dense clump of trees, and Leeana could taste her quiet, ongoing delight at having had the vision of her right eye returned to her. Nor was that the only thing Leanna could sense, and the expansion of her own world was an unending thing of marvel and wonder... one she was coming to suspect would *always* be unending.

Leeana Hanathafressa had spent a goodly part of her life in the saddle. She knew the union, the understanding and ability to anticipate, which grew between a rider and her horse, yet never had she and her mount *fused* the way she had with Gayrfressa. She shared the feel of the mare's mighty muscles, the play and stretch of tendons, knew Gayrfressa shared her own sense of balance and supple strength in turn, and the tiniest shift, the most subtle movement, blended into a symphony of balanced grace and motion. She savored the sharper, stronger, and ever so much more informative scent of everything about them—not simply the sharp pungency of pine trees, but of moss, water, rock, and earth, as well—as they spoke constantly, almost unconsciously to the huge mare. Those things didn't come to her through her own senses, and yet the bond between her and Gayrfressa carried their meaning, their import, and their ever shifting texture to her in a constantly flowing, ever-changing tapestry that moved with Gayrfressa through her world.

"Well," she said out loud, inhaling deeply and savoring the duality of her own merely human sense of smell as it mingled with Gayrfressa's while the courser carried her from shadow to dappled sunlight and back again, "we aren't born with your herd sense, either. We can't speak mind-to-mind with each other the way you can. I think it's inevitable we feel isolated from one another in ways you don't."

<And that's why you think no one could possibly understand why you're so sad and worried about leaving him behind, is it?>

Gayrfressa's tone was suddenly much gentler, and Leeana felt an unexpected stinging in her eyes. The mare, she'd discovered, was fully capable of calling Bahzell by name, yet she seldom did. Leeana wasn't certain yet why that was, but she suspected Gayrfressa truly did think of him as her herd stallion on some deep, inner level. Courser social dynamics were quite different from those of normal horses. Their herds tended to be larger—considerably larger—than the single-stallion-and-his-harem which was the norm for horses, for one thing. And, for another, coursers lived far longer, and most of them mated for life; the herd stallion was simply the lord of the herd, their baron, not the sire of all their offspring. The members of his herd thought of him that way, without the romantic or sexual overtones which would have colored their thoughts about their own mates, and that seemed to be the way Gayrfressa thought of Bahzell.

At the same time, there *was* something else, as well, an additional bond between her and Bahzell. Of course, Gayrfressa had never taken a life mate. That was unusual (but not unheard of) among courser mares, although coursers who bonded with wind riders never life-mated, aside from a handful—like Walsharno, for example—who'd lost their life mates *before* they took a rider. No one—not even the coursers, so far as Leeana could tell—knew whether they never life-mated because on some deep, deep level they were *waiting* for their rider, or if they never life-mated because they *had* bonded with a rider. In Gayrfressa's case, though, there was that "something else." Was it because of the way Bahzell had healed her so long ago?

And did it matter? Was Leeana worrying about it to keep from thinking about the question Gayrfressa had just asked her?

"I . . . didn't want to sound like I was crying on your shoulder," she said after a moment. "Or maybe I mean I didn't want to sound petulant and spoiled. It's not as if I didn't know he was a champion of Tomanāk. And I was raised a Bowmaster—we're supposed to understand about things like responsibility and duty. And we're *not* supposed to whine when responsibility or duty require something from us."

<*I didn't notice anyone doing any whining,*> Gayrfressa pointed out a bit tartly.

"No?" Leeana chuckled. To her dismay, the chuckle sounded a little watery, and she blinked her eyes quickly. "Well, maybe that's because I was afraid that if I *started* whining I wouldn't be able to stop!"

Gayrfressa snorted and tossed her head, and Leeana felt the mare's gently amused understanding almost as if a comforting arm had been laid around her shoulders. But then—

<*It's not just being separated from him when you're both still busy learning about each other,*> the courser pointed out. <*Not that you don't both seem to* enjoy *the learning, of course!*>

Leeana felt her cheekbones heat. Coursers were even more devastatingly frank about certain matters than war maids, and she expected it was going to take her some time to grow accustomed to Gayrfressa's amused perspective on her relationship with Bahzell.

<*I don't understand why you worry about that at all,*> Gayrfressa said calmly. <*I mean, it's not as if he didn't understand how to—*>

"We'll . . . talk about that later, all right?" Leeana interrupted a bit hastily. "That's one of those areas where two-foots and coursers need to . . . take a little time deciding how—or if—to talk about it at all."

<*Well, if you say so,*> Gayrfressa agreed equably, but not so

serenely that Leeana didn't taste the mare's bubbling amusement. <*But it's* not *as if he doesn't understand how to, is it?*> she continued, and Leeana laughed and shook her head.

"Yes, he certainly *does* 'understand how to,'" she admitted, and it was true. She was still growing accustomed to the notion that by Horse Stealer hradani standards she was a tiny, delicate little thing, and at first Bahzell had clearly been afraid he might inadvertently break her. Once she'd disabused him of that notion, however, it had turned out that he "understood how to" even more thoroughly than she'd ever allowed herself to hope he might. Which, she was forced to admit, was indeed one of the reasons she was so unhappy at riding steadily away from him on this beautiful, cool morning.

<*And so it should be,*> Gayrfressa told her. <*But it's* only *one reason. And the other reason is that you're* worried *about him, not just unhappy about leaving him behind.*>

"Yes," Leeana admitted. "I'm worried about all of the others, too, really—especially Trianal and Brandark. But I'm discovering I'm more selfish than I thought I was."

<*That's another two-foot attitude. It's not selfish to worry about your other half, Leeana. And that's what he is: your other two-foot half. Not worrying about what might happen to him would be like trying not to worry about what might happen to your right forehoof!*>

Gayrfressa was right, Leeana realized, yet it was difficult for her to admit it. War maid or not, she was the daughter, granddaughter, and great-granddaughter of baronesses. Generations of her mothers and grandmothers had sent husbands and fathers and sons and brothers off to war, obedient to that drumbeat of responsibility and duty.

And too many of us never saw them come home again, she thought. *Maybe that's my real problem. He's so much larger than life—a god-touched champion, the most deadly man I've ever known . . . and the gentlest. He's all of those things and more, even if he is a blanket-stealer in the middle of the night, grumpy in the morning, impossibly stubborn, and impossibly determined to do the "right thing," however maddening it may be for the people who love him! But despite all that, I know he's not really immortal. I know he won't necessarily be coming home again just because of how much I love him, how much I* need *that "other two-foot half" of mine. And the truth is, that terrifies me. The thought of losing him, of feeling some cold, empty hole where he used to be . . . I'm not sure I'd truly have the courage to face that. Not that I'll ever admit it to* him; *not after he tried to use that very argument to convince me I was making a terrible mistake!*

She snorted in sudden amusement of her own, and felt Gayrfressa's encouragement and affection in the back of her brain.

"I think you're good for me," she told the mare, breathing the resinous air deep once again. "You help me 'put things in perspective,' as Mother always used to say. Usually," she admitted with a thoughtful air, "about the time I started feeling most sorry for myself, now that I think about it."

<*So two-foot mothers do that, too, do they?*>

"Oh, yes!" Leeana said fervently.

<*Good.*>

The ground sloped downward in front of them, and Leeana automatically adjusted her seat and balance as Gayrfressa started down the slope.

<*I'm glad you spent so much time learning to ride the lesser cousins,*> the mare remarked. <*Walsharno didn't have that advantage when* he *climbed into the saddle the first time. I got to watch, you know.*> The mare tossed her head again, this time with a whinny of laughing memory. <*He fell off a lot.*>

"He hadn't had much opportunity to practice, you know," Leeana said a bit primly.

<*Of course he hadn't! Which of the lesser cousins could have carried him?*> Gayrfressa inquired pragmatically. <*Doesn't change the fact that he looked like a bag of feed in the beginning . . . when he wasn't bouncing along the ground behind Walsharno, at least.*>

"I suppose not," Leeana agreed, lips twitching on the edge of a smile. "He's made up for it since, though," she added, remembering Bahzell's graceful seat . . . and other things about him.

<*Yes, he has.*> Gayrfressa's mental voice carried a possessive pride, and Leeana leaned forward to pat the courser's shoulder. <*In fact,*> the mare continued, her voice turning more serious, <*he's learned quite a few things* you're *going to have to learn.*>

"Such as?"

There might have been the very thinnest edge of pique in Leeana's two-word question. She was a Sothōii, after all. The suggestion that her equestrian skills might be wanting in any respect came perilously close to insult.

<*How to fight from the saddle,*> Gayrfressa replied with a tart snort. <*Nobody ever taught you a* thing *about that, now did they?*>

"Well, no," Leeana admitted after a slightly huffy moment, then shrugged. "Properly reared young noblewomen aren't supposed to even think about something as unladylike as actually *fighting*." She grimaced as she remembered a long-ago morning in Kalatha when Ravlahn Thregafressa had invited a very young Leeana Hanathafressa to "attack her" with a practice knife. It hadn't been a very . . . impressive attack.

"If I'd had the good taste to be born a boy, they *would* have taught me to fight mounted before I ever got to Kalatha," she continued. "Except, of course, that if I'd had the good taste to be born a boy I wouldn't ever ever have had to run away to Kalatha. Which I did. Have to run away to Kalatha, I mean." She paused, trying to straighten that out in her own mind, then shrugged again. "But after I got to Kalatha, there wasn't anyone to teach me. War maids mostly fight on their own feet, you know. We're not very cavalry oriented."

<*No, you're not,*> Gayrfressa agreed in a tone of distinct disapproval.

"It wouldn't be fair to expect anything else," Leeana pointed out. "Not given where most of us come from. Garlahna, for example. Or Raythas. Or even Erlis. They may be Sothōii, but nobody was throwing *them* into a saddle when they were two years old, you know!"

<*I suppose not,*> Gayrfressa conceded. <*Not that that explains why they couldn't have learned later!*>

"I suppose not." Leeana used Gayrfressa's own words deliberately, accompanied by a snort of purely human dimensions. "Although," she continued more thoughtfully, "I really wouldn't be too surprised to find out the war maids decided years and years ago that they weren't going to put mounted troops into the field because of how much they expected all the menfolk would carry on if they did. They may have decided that was one toe they didn't need to step on."

<*Well,* you're *going to have to learn how to do it.*> Gayrfressa said in a no-argument sort of way.

"Fine," Leeana replied, a bit surprised by the firmness of Gayrfressa's tone.

<*And you're going to have to get rid of those silly short swords*

when you do it, too,> Gayrfressa continued. <*How do you expect to reach anyone with something like that from my saddle? And we* have to *get you a bow. You* do *know how to shoot a bow, don't you?*>

"From my own two feet, yes." Leeana frowned down at Gayrfressa's single ear. "That's not the same as using a horse bow though, you know!"

<*Oh,* don't *I know?*> Gayrfressa shook her head in profound disgust. <*It took* years *for Walsharno to convince* him *to learn to use a bow properly. If you can call the way he uses one even today "properly," that is!*>

"There are some advantages to that arbalest of his," Leeana pointed out.

<*Not from a courser's saddle, there aren't, and a wind rider doesn't have any business fighting from anywhere else!*>

Something clicked in Leeana's brain, and she cocked her head, still looking down at Gayrfressa's ear.

"I don't think it's going to be very easy for Balcartha to integrate a single wind rider into the Kalatha Guard," she said slowly.

Gayrfressa didn't reply, but she turned her head far enough she could look back at her rider, and the set of her ear was not encouraging.

"I *am* a member of the Guard," Leeana told her firmly. "And my current term of enlistment won't be up for another two years."

Still nothing... aside from a slightly flatter ear.

"I'm a seventy-five, Gayrfressa. I can't just walk away from the rest of my platoon, you know, and none of *them* are wind riders!"

<*And none of them are my wind sister, either,*> Gayrfressa pointed out stubbornly. <*Your place is in my saddle when you have to fight—not down there running around on those two ridiculous little feet of yours where I can't keep an eye on you!*>

"But—" Leeana began a bit hotly, then clamped her teeth tightly on what she'd been about to say as she tasted the anxiety behind Gayrfressa's obstinacy. And the mare had a point, she admitted to herself a moment later. She was the daughter of one wind rider and the wife, now, of another. She'd always known—or thought she had, at any rate—how completely and intimately a wind rider and his courser merged, both in and out of combat. It had been natural enough for her to think she understood, at any rate, beginning from the standpoint of the many years she'd spent learning to become one with a horse like Boots. Yet she'd already realized she'd never truly grasped the totality of a wind rider's bond before Gayrfressa had entered her life. Not even a marvelous horse like Boots could have taught her that... or what would happen to a rider who lost his courser.

Or to a courser who lost his—or *her*—rider.

It wasn't something any Sothōii liked to think about, and the coursers' longer lives meant it didn't happen as often as a rider lost a horse, but it *did* happen. More often, it was the rider who survived, if only because human lives were a bit longer, on average, even than a courser's. But it also happened because coursers were bigger targets... and because they couldn't be armored as well as a human. Leeana had met a handful of wind riders who'd lost their coursers, and she'd sensed the gaping wounds which had been left at the heart of them, but not until now—not until she'd felt the richness of Gayrfressa's mind and voice in the depths of her own mind—did she truly grasp how terrible those wounds had actually been.

It wasn't unusual for a rider to end his own life if he lost his courser, despite the Sothōii's cultural prohibition on suicide... and coursers had no such prohibition.

"Dearheart," she said quietly, after a moment, "I don't know how we're going to deal with this. We're going to have to—I understand that now—but I don't have any idea how." She leaned forward in the saddle, running her hand gently over the scar reaching to Gayrfressa's shoulder, feeling the hard, ridged line of it under the mare's chestnut coat and shivering deep in her bones as she remembered how Gayrfressa had received it. "That's one reason you were talking about islands, wasn't it?"

<*Partly,*> Gayrfressa admitted after a moment, her voice as quiet as Leeana's own. <*I'm not sure I realized that when I started, though.*> She snorted again, more gently than before. <*I was actually thinking about how silly it was of you to feel like you were "leaving him behind" when he rides with you in your heart every moment, no matter where you are.*> Leeana felt her eyes prickle afresh and stroked Gayrfressa's shoulder again. <*Still, I think you're right—I was thinking about this, too. I understand you have obligations to the other two-foots, Sister. I know you assumed them before we'd ever even met, and I don't expect you to shirk them. But surely the war maids can understand how our bond changes things?*>

"War maids certainly ought to understand changes if anyone can," Leeana agreed feelingly. "Unfortunately, they haven't had any experience with war maid *wind riders.* No one has!"

<*I know war maids fight on their own feet, but you can be far more dangerous on my back than on foot,*> Gayrfressa said in an almost hopeful tone. <*Think how much faster you can move! That alone would be a huge advantage, wouldn't it?*>

"Sometimes, at least. On the other hand, you're not exactly built for creeping about in the grass, now are you?" Leeana teased gently. "That's where war maids spend a lot of their time, you know," she added more seriously. "And however effective a wind rider might be, *one* wind rider by herself is hardly going to constitute what you might call a concentrated striking force, is she?"

<*No, but—*>

It was Gayrfressa's turn to cut herself off, and Leeana nodded. "I understand," she repeated. "Now I really do understand, dearheart. And we *will* work it out somehow, I promise. I don't have a clue *how* yet, but I'm sure something will come to me." She chuckled a bit sourly. "I already knew I was going to have to explain the wedding bracelet, given the Charter's position on war maid marriages. I don't suppose there's any good reason why we can't go ahead and add this to the situation, as well." Her chuckle turned into a laugh. "By this time, Balcartha and Mayor Yalith ought to be used to my making problems for them. If they aren't, it's not for lack of trying on my part, anyway!"

She felt Gayrfressa's silent chortle of agreement meld with her own, and her heart eased. They *would* find a way to work it out. She didn't know how, but she was certain something would come to her, and—

Gayrfressa turned a bend and came to a sudden halt as the trail which would become a proper road—and an *Axeman* road, at that—someday soon abruptly disappeared. It didn't peter out or fade. It didn't even end, really. It simply . . . *stopped*, cut off as if by a blade, and the thick carpet of pine needles from years past spread out before them unmarred and unmarked.

Leeana stiffened in the saddle, her head coming up and her eyes widening as her own astonishment merged with Gayrfressa's. She opened her mouth, although she didn't actually know what she intended to say. But before she could begin on whatever she might have been going to say, she saw the red-haired woman seated on that carpet of needles, leaning back against the tallest, thickest pine tree she'd ever seen in her life. And that was just as strange as the disappearance of the trail, because the woman hadn't been there when Gayrfressa stopped. For that matter, Leeana felt certain—or *thought* she did, at any rate—that not even the *tree* had been there when Gayrfressa stopped.

She shook her head, but the surprises weren't quite finished yet.

The woman at the base of the pine tree wore plate armor. Reflected light curtsied across its burnished surface like rippling water as the cool breeze tossed the pine trees and let shafts of sunlight burn golden through the canopy. She wore a surcoat over it, and for some reason, Leeana wasn't certain of the surcoat's color. It seemed to be black, but perhaps it was actually only the darkest cobalt blue she'd ever seen or imagined. Or perhaps it was a blend of colors from a midnight summer sky no mortal eye had ever beheld or envisioned. Leeana didn't know about that, but the device on the breast of that surcoat was a white scroll. It was picked out in gold bullion and tiny, brilliant sapphires and rubies, that scroll, with silver skulls for winding knobs, and bound with a spray of periwinkle, the five-lobed flowers wrought in showers of dark amethyst. The woman wasn't especially tall by Sothōii standards. Indeed, she was several inches shorter than Leeana... which meant she was also shorter than the huge, double-bitted axe leaning against the same pine tree.

The woman seemed unaware of their presence, her attention concentrated on the mountain lynx stretched across her lap. It lay on its back, totally limp, all four paws in the air as she rubbed its belly and smiled down at it. A helmet sat beside her, and her hair—a darker and even more glorious red than Leeana's—was bound with a diadem of woven gold and silver badged with more of those amethyst-leaved blossoms of periwinkle.

Courser and rider stood motionless, frozen, trying to understand why the world about them seemed so different, and then the woman looked up, and Leeana's throat tightened as midnight-blue eyes looked straight into her soul.

The woman gazed at them for several endless seconds, then clucked her tongue gently at the lynx across her lap. The cat—it was enormous, probably close to seventy pounds—yawned and stretched, then gave itself a shake, rolled off her lap, and stood. It looked up at her, then butted her right vambrace gently and affectionately before it glanced at Leeana. It regarded her for a moment, supremely unimpressed by her or even by Gayrfressa, then gathered its haunches under it, leapt lightly away from the red-haired woman . . . and vanished into thin air in mid-leap.

Leeana blinked, but before she could speak or otherwise react, the woman had risen, coming to her feet as if the armor she wore was no more encumbering than a war maid's chari and yathu. She stood gazing up at Leeana, and somehow, despite Gayrfressa's towering height, it seemed as if *Leeana* was gazing up at *her*.

"Give you good morning, daughters," the woman said, and a strange shiver, like a flicker of lightning touched with ice and silver, went through Leeana. She knew she would never be able to describe that voice to anyone, for the words which might have captured it had never been forged. It was woven of beauty, joy, sorrow, celebration—of tears and terror, of memories lost and dreams never forgotten. It was freighted with welcome and burnished with farewell, and wrapped about it, flowing through it, were peace and completion.

Leeana never remembered moving, but suddenly she was on her feet, standing at Gayrfressa's shoulder, left hand raised against the mare's warm chestnut coat, and the woman smiled at them both.

"Lady," Leeana heard her own voice say, and inclined her head, for she knew the woman before her now.

Isvaria Orfressa, firstborn of Orr and Kontifrio, goddess of death, completion, and memory and second only to Tomanāk himself among Orr's children in power. A quiet terror rippled through Leeana Hanathafressa as she found herself face-to-face with the very personification of death in a quiet, sunny pine wood she knew now was somehow outside the world in which she'd always lived. Yet there was no dread in that terror, no *fear*, only the awareness that she gazed upon the ending which must come to every living thing.

"I haven't come for you, Leeana," that awesome, indescribable voice said gently. It sang in Leeana's blood and bone, murmured from the roots of mountains and sent endless, quiet echoes rolling across the heavens. "Nor for you, Gayrfressa." Isvaria smiled at both of them. "Not yet, not today. Someday I will, and gather you to me as I gather all my worthy dead, and, oh, but the two of you *will* be worthy when that day comes! I'll know you, and I'll come for you, and you will find a place prepared for you at my table."

Leeana inhaled deeply, feeling the power of life racing through her with the air filling her lungs, the blood pumping through her veins, and knew that in some strange way she had never been as alive as in this moment when she stood face-to-face with death Herself and saw in Isvaria's face not terror or despair but only... welcome.

"But that day is not today," Isvaria told them. "No, today I've come for another purpose entirely."

"Another purpose, Lady?" Leeana was astounded by the levelness of her own tone, and Isvaria shook her head, her smile broader and warmer.

"You're very like your husband, Leeana—and you like your brother, Gayrfressa. In this universe, or in any other, all any of you will ever ask is to meet whatever comes upon your feet."

"I don't know about that, Lady," Leeana replied, more aware in that moment of how young she truly was than she'd been in years.

"Perhaps not, but I do—*we* do," Isvaria told her. Then her smile faded, and she reached out and touched Leeana's cheek ever so gently. That touch was as light as spider silk, gentle as a breeze, yet Leeana felt the power to shatter worlds in the cool, smooth fingers touching her skin so lightly. "We know, just as we know you, and we've waited for you as long as we have for Bahzell and Walsharno."

"I don't understand," Leeana said, and felt Gayrfressa with her in her mind.

"Of course you don't." Isvaria cocked her head, those bottomless eyes studying Leeana's face. "And I'm sure it's a bit overwhelming, even for someone as redoubtable as you and Gayrfressa, to encounter so many deities in such a brief period of time." She smiled again. "Time is a mortal concept, you know—one we've been forced to come to know and share... and abide by, but one that would never have occurred to us, left to our own devices. In that respect, you mortals are mightier than any god or goddess. And in the end, just as you created time, you'll transcend it, and in the transcending you'll heal or damn us all."

Leeana swallowed, and Isvaria shook her head quickly.

"I haven't come to lay the burden of all eternity upon you and demand you take it up today, Leeana!"

"Then may I ask why you *have* come, Lady?"

"Yes, *very* like Bahzell," Isvaria murmured. Then she stood back slightly, folded her arms, and looked at the two of them levelly.

"My daughters, both of you have roles to play in a struggle which began before time itself. Has Bahzell told you what my brother Tomanāk explained to him about the nature of time and the war between Light and Dark?"

"He's . . . tried, Lady," Leeana said after a moment. "He said there are many universes, each of them as real as our own yet separate. Some are very like ours, others are very different, but Light and Dark are at war in all of them. He said that everyone—*all* of us—exist in all those universes, or many of them at least, and that we're the ones who determine who finally wins in each of them. And that, in the end, the final confrontation between Light and Dark will be settled by how many of those universes each side controls when the last one falls."

"Not a bad explanation at all," Isvaria told her. "But not quite complete. Did he tell you not even a goddess can know exactly what future, what chain of events and decisions, any single mortal in any single one of those universes will experience?"

Leeana nodded, and Isvaria nodded back very seriously.

"That, my daughters, is where mortals' freedom to choose—and ability to fail—enters the equation. In the end, it all depends upon you and your choices. Oh, chance can play its role, as well, but over the entire spectrum of universes, chance cancels out and choice and courage and fear and greed and love and selfishness and cruelty and mercy—all those things which make you mortals what you are—come into their own.

"Yet the great pattern, the warp and woof of reality—*those* we deities can see clearly. Those are what guide and draw our own efforts to protect this strand as it works its way through the loom of history, or to snip that one short. It's there, at those moments, that our champions—and those who love them, Leeana Hanathafressa and Gayrfressa, daughter of Mathygan and Yorthandro—take their stands in the very teeth of evil to fight—and all too often to die—in defense of the Light. And no being, no mortal and no god, can know for certain whether they'll triumph or fail before that very moment. My daughters, I know no better than you whether or not this world in which you live, this universe which is all you know, will stand or fall at the end of time. That decision rests in your hands. Not in mine, not in my brothers' or my sisters'—in *yours*."

Leeana swallowed, and Isvaria touched her face once more.

"You're fit to carry that burden, Leeana, whether you realize it or not . . . and you will. In every universe, in every time, when the moment arrives, you will. And if the Dark triumphs, it will *never* be because you failed the Light in that moment of need. But I tell you this, as well—if the Light triumphs in this universe of yours, it will triumph through you and Bahzell."

Leeana's eyes went huge, and the fingers touching her face cupped her cheek gently.

"Power and possibilities, outcomes and events, swirl so thickly about you that even a goddess can see only dimly. And we can take advantage of that dimness, we deities, and . . . manipulate it so that our enemies are even blinder than we. Not always, not in all places. We must choose our times, pick those events where it becomes most crucial for our enemies to guess rather than to know. Your life, and Bahzell's, are one of those times. We can't tell you what will happen, or even what you must do, because by the very act of telling you we would affect the outcome. But in every future I see, you come to me, Leeana. And you, Gayrfressa. You come to my table, in all your thousands of choices, and I welcome you. You come through pain, and you come through sorrow, and you come through loss, and you do not always come in triumph. But you come to me unbroken and as you are now, upon your feet and *never* your knees, and the light of you *shines*, my daughters."

Leeana stared into the eyes of the Goddess of Death, and those eyes touched something inside her. There was a . . . flicker. A dancing current or a flaring candle flame. She couldn't put a name to the sensation, not really, yet she knew it would always be there. She might lose it, from time to time, and it would be no armor against fear, uncertainty, doubt . . . but it would always return to her, as well, and under that fear and uncertainty and doubt there would be this assurance, this promise, from the power to which all life returned in the fullness of time.

"I know it's a heavy weight to bear," Isvaria told her, "but you're fit to bear it, both of you, and love will take you to places the Dark can never come. I do not name you my champions, but I do name you the daughters I've called you—*my* daughters. Whether you come to me early, or you come to me late, I *will* be waiting for you, and I will gather you as my own."

Leeana stood gazing into those eyes, feeling the iron fidelity of that promise, for an eternity. It lasted forever . . . and took no longer than the flicker between the beats of a hummingbird's wings.

And then the pine woods were empty once again, except for her and Gayrfressa.

She blinked, shaking her head, feeling as if she were awakening from a dream and yet with every memory perfectly formed, and felt Gayrfressa's matching bemusement. Perhaps it *had* been only a dream, she thought, but then she felt something in her hand and looked down.

It was a sprig of periwinkle, its stem wrought of silver, its tiny flowers exquisitely formed in chips of sapphire. Periwinkle, the flower of memory . . . and of Isvaria Orfressa, the keeper of that memory.

Chapter Twenty-Seven

"So you think I should actually listen to this fool?" Arthnar Sabrehand, Fire Oar and Fleet Captain of the River Brigands, demanded.

He took another long pull from his battered tankard, adam's apple bobbing, then smacked the tankard down on the expensive, exquisitely inlaid table—a piece of Saramanthan work worth more than most men would ever see in a lifetime, which had somehow failed to make it across the Lake of Storms to its intended Sothōii purchaser some years earlier. It had been hard used over those years, but its pedigree still showed through all the casual scratches, gouges and chips, like an old and weary soldier not yet ready to quit despite wounds and too many harsh campaigns. A fresh spill of ale dribbled down the tankard's side to make yet another ring on the tabletop, another stain on the soldier's shield, and the Fire Oar glowered across it at the man he knew as Talthar.

"*I* haven't seen any evidence the man can find his arse with both hands!" The River Brigand chieftain belched and wiped his mouth with the back of his hand. "So far, Tellian and that bastard Bahnak—oh, and let's not forget *Bahzell*—have pinned his ears back every time he's crossed swords with them. And don't even get me *started* on the frigging dwarf!"

Arthnar's table manners might leave a little to be desired, Varnaythus reflected, and his shaggy mane of oily black hair and the bushy beard that went with it were an accurate hint that he wasn't the sort of fellow you'd care to invite home as a house guest. Not unless you *wanted* to see your house burned to the ground, at any rate. But he did have a way of coming straight to the point. Which was probably only to be expected of the man who'd cut his way to the office of Fleet Captain, Fire Oar of the River Brigands, almost twenty years ago . . . and stayed on the Captain's Thwart ever since. *Becoming* Fleet Captain and winning the title of Fire Oar hadn't necessarily required much in the way of brains—ruthlessness, a ready sword, a naturally devious nature, and the ability to buy support with promises of plunder had been more than enough for that. *Staying* Fleet Captain, though . . . that took some doing.

And for all his contempt for Cassan, it's largely his . . . understanding with him that's allowed Arthnar to stay in his position, the wizard reflected. *He's actually managed to convince his council of captains that it makes more sense to charge tolls on traffic crossing the Lake of Storms than it does to raid. Cassan doesn't care; he simply passes the cost of the toll—it would never do to call it* "tribute," *after all—along to his customers and blames it on the Purple Lords and the threat of the River Brigands without ever mentioning that he's actually paying them off. And Arthnar's even managed to negotiate a subsidy from the Purple Lords for letting* their *trade pass unhindered, as well!*

Of course, what neither Cassan nor the Purple Lords (nor the majority of Arthnar's own followers) knew was that a little discreet help from Sharnā, the dog brothers, and Carnadosa—in the person of one Master Varnaythus, although Arthnar knew him as Talthar Sheafbearer—had also played their part in the Fleet Captain's successful longevity. Unfortunately, no one could ever accuse Arthnar of an excess of piety. He was perfectly prepared to work with the Dark Gods, but it was purely business as far as he was concerned, and he'd been more careful than most about staying out of their clutches. He was willing to use them, but he never forgot for one moment that they hadn't been so happy to help him over the years out of the goodness of their hearts. He was ready enough to help them achieve their goals as long as that helped him achieve *his*, yet that didn't mean he was stupid enough to *trust* them, and he was adamantly opposed to allowing himself to simply be used by them.

But even the wiliest fish ends up in the boat eventually, if the hook's been properly set, Varnaythus reminded himself. *If he has no objection to using Them, then They certainly have no objection to using* him. *And nothing They've said to me suggests They're especially concerned about whether or not this particular fish survives in the process.*

Given the man's personality, Varnaythus was privately rooting for "not," although it would never do to suggest anything of the sort to Arthnar.

"I think whether or not you should listen to him depends entirely on how happy you'll be to see Kilthandahknarthas sailing cheerfully by your ports on the Lake of Storms and Bahnak of Hurgrum and Tellian of Balthar maintaining patrols all the way down the Hangnysti to the lake," he said after a moment, and shrugged. "Somehow I think Tellian and Kilthan are going to be less than willing to maintain the sort of... relationship you've had with Cassan. House Harkanath has hired entire armies in its time to deal with bandits, and I rather doubt Kilthan's going to regard you and your fellow captains as anything other than bandits who happen to float to work. I suppose you might be able to count on increasing your subsidy from the Purple Lords as long as they think they could use you to bottleneck the Axemen's trade down the Spear from the lake, but how long will they realistically be able to do that before Bahnak and Tellian burn Krelik and Palan to the ground?"

"They won't find that so easy as kicking a bunch of ghouls' arses!" Arthnar snapped, glaring at the wizard, and Varnaythus shrugged again.

"Possibly not, but I don't think either of them is the sort to be dissuaded just because a task looks a little difficult. Neither one of them would be where they are right now if they thought that way. And with Kilthan and the rest of Silver Cavern ready to cover their expenses and ship all the weapons, armor, and food they need through their brand-new canal, well—"

He shrugged a third time, and Arthnar gritted his teeth. Master Talthar was correct, of course, he thought sulfuriously. He knew exactly how Tellian would react to the sort of arrangement he had with Cassan. The Baron of Balthar, for all the surprising flexibility he'd displayed over the last few years, was a Sothōii of the old school where his personal honor was concerned. And then there was Bahnak, as pragmatic and ruthless a hradani warlord as had ever lived, and one likely to reflect that a single sharp military campaign or two would ultimately cost him far less than years of extorted "tolls." And none of that even considered Kilthandahknarthas, who was quite probably the most ruthless—not to mention the *wealthiest*—of the three and, as Talthar had just pointed out, had a short way with bandits. But still...

"From all I've heard and all my agents have been able to discover," he growled after a moment, "they've practically finished their damned canal—*and* their tunnel—already!" He hawked up a gob of phlegm and spat it noisily into the battered spittoon beside his chair, then glowered at his visitor with profound disgust. "So to hear you tell it, no matter how it works out, I'm screwed. That being the case, why should I risk a single pimple on my arse for that idiot Cassan?"

A reasonable question, Varnaythus conceded silently. *Not that I have any intention of admitting that to you.*

"Because there's one way you might be able to not simply maintain your current arrangement but make an even better profit off of it," he said instead.

"Aye?" Arthnar arched a skeptical eyebrow. "And how might that miracle be brought to pass?"

His tone was a bit less abrasive than it had been, and Varnaythus could almost literally see the thoughts working through the brain behind the Fire Oar's brown eyes. Cassan might go out of his way to avoid any official knowledge of Varnaythus' true nature, but Arthnar knew perfectly well that "Master Talthar" was a wizard. He probably *didn't* know he was a Carnadosan, as well. In fact, Varnaythus had been at some pains to convince him that Talthar was actually a renegade Spearman in the service of the Purple Lords, although he frankly doubted Arthnar would've cared a copper kormak even if he'd known "Master Talthar" had been dispatched from Trōfrōlantha itself. On the other hand, he did know at least a little bit about the... special abilities Master Talthar could bring to the table, since he'd made use of them himself in the past.

"It's all a question of who *controls* the new route," Varnaythus told him now. "I think you're right; it's progressed too far for anyone to stop it now. And I don't think my... employers to the south, shall we say, are going to be happy about that." He held out his right hand above the table, palm down, and waggled it from side to side. "In fact, I think they're going to be very *un*happy, but I believe I'd be able to endure their sorrow if it happened I'd been able to make even better arrangements for myself somewhere else." He smiled at Arthnar. "And by the strangest coincidence, I believe I may have found a way to do just that."

"Have you now?" Arthnar sat back, running the fingers of his right hand through his beard and considering his guest speculatively.

"If it should happen that Tellian and Bahnak's expedition into the Ghoul Moor suffered a sufficiently unfortunate accident, it might well put the entire project back for several years." Varnaythus' smile grew thinner and more sharklike. "I doubt even that would manage to *stop* it in the long term, but it would probably be the best-case outcome from my employers'—my *current* employers', I mean—perspective, and I've made certain arrangements which may actually be enough to bring it about. I'd say the chances are at least close to even, in fact, although I'd never be foolish enough to promise they'll succeed. If they do, however, I'm sure everyone will be happy to maintain our existing relationships. On the other hand," he waggled his hand again, "my arrangements may not succeed, which is why I think Baron Cassan's plan has something to recommend it. If something should . . . happen to King Markhos and Prince Yurokhas—something tragic and unfortunate, you understand—and *if* Baron Cassan had been able to reach an understanding with Baron Borandas before that happened, then it's almost certain either Cassan or, more likely, Yeraghor would end up being named Crown Prince Norandhor's—I'm sorry, *King* Norandhor's—regent. And if that should happen, then the Crown would step in and demand control of the entire canal."

"And you actually think that might *happen?*" Arthnar gave a crack of scornful laughter. "Yeraghor and Cassan might—*might!*—be able to force *Tellian* to surrender his stake in in it if they control the Great Council, but Bahnak and Kilthan?" The Fire Oar shook his head. "Either one of them alone would tell those two pissants to pound sand! Both of them *together* would invite them to bring their damned army down the Escarpment and try to enforce that little 'demand' of theirs!"

"Really?" Varnaythus cocked his head. "You think Bahnak would risk the destruction of everything he and his father have spent their entire lives building? Because that's what any Sothōii army would really have in mind if it came down the Escarpment, and Bahnak would know that as well as you and I do. And then there's Kilthan. Do you think the King Emperor would thank the head of one of the Empire's trading houses for embroiling the Axemen in a war with the Empire's most important ally over a *trade route?*"

Arthnar looked suddenly more thoughtful, and Varnaythus leaned back in his chair and rested his forearm comfortably on the table.

"Bahnak might," the Fire Oar said after a moment. "He's hradani, and he's stubborn, and with all the northern clans united at his back, he'd probably figure—rightly, I think—that he'd have a damned good chance at beating the horse boys, especially with someone like Cassan commanding them in the field. But I hadn't thought about the King Emperor. He *wouldn't* thank Kilthan for dragging the Empire into that kind of a position, would he?"

"I think that's probably putting it mildly," Varnaythus agreed. "And if Kilthan wound up advising Bahnak to accept the Crown decree in return for a smaller but still quite tasty slice of the pie, Bahnak's probably a practical enough fellow to take the advice. After all, it's going to be a very large pie, isn't it? Large enough that Kilthan, Bahnak, the Sothōii—and you—could all carve off bigger chunks than you've ever seen before. It's not that Cassan has any objection to Axeman merchants being able to trade directly with the Spearmen without having to go through the Purple Lords, you know. It's not even that he has any objection to the Axemen making money hand over fist. He only objects to all of the profit from that money going into *Tellian's* purse instead of his own. And he's a reasonable man. All of you could make quite a comfortable profit off of the trade, and it would still be far cheaper for the Axemen—and the Spearmen, for that matter—than the existing arrangement."

Arthnar nodded, slowly at first, and then more rapidly. It wasn't a nod of *agreement*, Varnaythus knew, but it *was* one of understanding.

The Fire Oar took another thoughtful swallow of ale, then gave the wizard a very sharp look, indeed.

"Assuming all of this was going to work half as well as Cassan seems to be expecting, why does he need me? I'd sooner not go wading around in a Sothōii swamp. They tend to be full of snakes with horse bows and lots of nasty, pointy arrows. And that notion of something unfortunate happening to Markhos and Yurokhas . . . why do I have the feeling Cassan thinks *I* might be stupid enough to provide it?"

"It's not so much that he needs *you* to provide it," Varnaythus said, "as that he needs someone besides *himself* to provide it. He can scarcely assassinate the King and the Prince and then expect to be named regent, now can he?"

"And there's some reason you think the Sothōii wouldn't burn Krelik and Palan even flatter than Bahnak and Tellian if it happened they thought I'd had anything to do with killing their King?" Arthnar snorted harshly. "No, thank you, Master Talthar. There are simpler and less messy ways of committing suicide!"

"I didn't say he needed it to be *you*," Varnaythus said patiently. "But it does have to be someone from outside the Kingdom. Actually, he's thinking in terms of a double feint, as it were."

"Overly clever idiots always make me nervous," Arthnar grunted, and Varnaythus nodded in agreement.

"Oh, you're right about that," he said. "But what Cassan really needs from you is for you to act as . . . a broker, or perhaps an expediter. Very much the way you did in that attempt on Tellian earlier this summer."

Their eyes met across the table, and Varnaythus smiled faintly.

"I'm afraid Cassan was just a bit miffed when he realized how cleverly you'd managed to suggest *he* was the one behind the attack. Personally, I rather enjoyed the irony, since he *was* the one who'd paid for it, after all. He didn't quite see it that way, though." The wizard shrugged. "But after he'd thought about it for a while, it suggested another possibility to him. He wants you to recruit the manpower he's going to need—hire as many Spearman mercenaries as you can in the time you have, and see who you can pick up from the Border Kingdoms, as well. But you could still fill out the numbers with your own River Brigands . . . as long as none of them know *you're* the one hiring them."

"And who would actually be hiring them? Officially, I mean?" Arthnar's eyes had narrowed and he was frowning intensely.

"Why, the Purple Lords, of course!" Varnaythus smiled more broadly. "Obviously, they've decided the King is going to support Tellian after all, and they've taken steps to prevent the destruction—the *total* destruction, when you come down to it—of their trade monopoly. Not hard to understand why they might feel that way, given that their entire economy *depends* on that monopoly, now is it? Of course, after Cassan—the new Regent, I mean, whoever he happens to be—discovers who was behind it, the knowledge will only make him even more determined to push the canal through and see that it operates under the Crown's aegis as a way to crush the Purple Lords completely."

"That *might* work." Arthnar stroked his beard again, brown eyes half-shut while the brain behind them raced through the possibilities. "Assuming he could actually sell the notion that the Purple Lords were behind it, of course. And," the Fire Oar added grudgingly, "it would actually make a kind of sense, I suppose. But you said he was thinking about a *double* feint."

"Oh, indeed I did." This time Varnaythus' smile was positively beatific. "That's why we have to put this entire operation together so quickly. Tellian's placed his hunting lodge at Chergor at the King's disposal, and Markhos will be taking himself off to spend some time there in another few weeks. After how hectic the spring session's been in Sothōfalas, he wants to keep things as simple as possible, too, so he's taking only his personal guard and a handful of his senior advisors, like Macebearer and Shaftmaster. He's planning on staying there for quite some time, hiding from all those damned courtiers, so we'll know where to find him for—oh, at least two months or so. And, of course, Chergor's in the *West* Riding, now isn't it?"

"Yes, it is," Arthnar acknowledged slowly.

"Well, at this moment Tellian and the others believe Markhos is going to approve their operation and grant the canal a Crown charter on their terms. It's all supposed to be a secret, of course, but you know how secrets have a way of leaking at court. Especially when someone makes it his business to get behind the effort and *encourage* the leaks. I'm afraid, however, that Cassan's come into possession of a draft charter—one in the handwriting of the *King's* personal secretary, not the Prime Councilor's—which actually happens to establish exactly the sort of arrangement I was just discussing with you a few moments ago. Now, clearly Tellian would be horribly upset to discover the King had reached that decision when the good Baron had been confidently expecting to get everything *he* wanted. Why, he might actually be upset enough to decide to murder the King—and blame it on the Purple Lords, of course—and to substitute a forged charter more in line with all of those rumors. In fact, it *might* turn out he'd planted those rumors himself expressly so he *could* substitute that forgery of his and have people accept it. And as part of his despicable plot, he generously offered to loan his hunting lodge to the King in order to get him into a comfortable spot to be assassinated. It might be a little risky of him to have it all happen on his own lands, but he'd know he could control the situation there . . . and he'd undoubtedly be counting on how his long friendship with Prince Yurokhas—and Yurokhas' known antipathy for Cassan—would lead Yurokhas to accept his version of what happened. Under the King's will, Yurokhas would become Norandhor's regent, so if Tellian was able to convince Yurokhas the Purple Lords—or even, perhaps, *Baron Cassan*—had been behind it, he'd undoubtedly get everything he wanted all along."

"No one who actually knows Tellian would believe that for a moment," Arthnar said, but his tone was thoughtful, not an objection.

"Perhaps not, but how many people *do* actually know him?" Varnaythus riposted. "And the gods know ambition can make a man do strange things. For that matter, Tellian's used up a huge amount of his credit with the more conservative lords warden over this business with Bahnak and his friendship with Prince Bahzell. *None* of the conservatives are happy with that, and they're going to be even less happy when the word finally leaks out to the Kingdom as a whole that Tellian's daughter is actually *sleeping* with Bahzell!"

"She's *what?*" Arthnar blinked in astonishment, and Varnaythus allowed himself a laugh.

"That's exactly what she's doing, and when the real conservatives find out, they're probably going to think she should've gone ahead and bedded a donkey instead. It certainly wouldn't have been any *worse*, by their way of thinking, and given the way diehard Sothōii think, the insult and 'perversion' involved in *that* is far more likely to generate disgust and revulsion than any mere matter of high treason and murder! And the political infighting in Sothōfalas this year's been the bitterest anyone can remember, Arthnar. Tellian's opponents are going to be more than ready to believe the worst, especially if believing it—however ridiculous it might be—lets them knock him out of the saddle. For that matter, given the nastiness of the fight, even some of Tellian's supporters are likely to find themselves wondering how far he might be willing to go to win, especially given that charter Cassan will 'find.' After all, if he's discovered that the King's been playing him along all the while—that he's actually decided to support Cassan and only *pretended* to be favoring Tellian to put him off guard—who knows how he might have reacted? All of that's going to be running through the backs of their brains, whether they think it's *likely* or not. However you look at it, tensions are going to run high, suspicion is going to be everywhere, and fingers are going to be pointing in every imaginable direction while people look for enemies and try to square old accounts. If the North Riding throws its support to Cassan and Yeraghor on the Great Council, that should be enough to carry the day at least long enough to get one of them named Regent. And once one of them is named Regent, Tellian is done."

Arthnar sat back in his own chair, tugging at his beard while he thought hard. He stayed that way for the better part of three minutes, then refocused his gaze on Varnaythus.

"That all sounds well and good, and it might even work. But I'm not prepared to just write Tellian off. He's too tough a customer, and much as I might like to see his head on a pike somewhere, I'm not stupid enough to underestimate him. There's not an ounce of give in him, and if someone starts accusing him of murdering the King, he's not going to sit back and take it."

"He might, if the alternative were a return to the Time of Troubles," Varnaythus pointed out. "Especially if Cassan and Yeraghor were to officially declare that since there's no real proof he was behind it, they personally were prepared to take his word that he wasn't. With the understanding, of course, that if he raises a ruckus they'll decide *not* to take his word."

"He might, and if pigs had wings they '*might*' be pigeons!" Arthnar snorted. "More likely, though, he'd call out his armsmen and cut a swath clear across the South Riding on his way to the *East* Riding!"

"He might," Varnaythus replied, deliberately reusing the same two words. "If he was alive, of course."

"Excuse me? Was there some part of this master plan you'd forgotten to mention to me?" Arthnar demanded caustically.

"Well, ideally, Baron Cassan will become aware—belatedly, I'm afraid—that a large body of mercenaries has crossed part of the South Riding on its way towards Chergor. One of the mercenaries in question will have fallen into his hands, perhaps. Or possibly the poor fellow fell off his horse and broke his neck, and Cassan's armsmen found some incriminating document in his saddlebag. At any rate, Cassan will discover that this body of mercenaries is headed towards Chergor, apparently in the Purple Lords' pay, although that could turn out to be purely a clever bit of camouflage on the part of someone else, like, oh, Baron Tellian. Knowing His Majesty is at Chergor, Cassan will immediately call out his own armsmen and ride in pursuit to attempt to rescue the King. He'll send a warning to Balthar, too, of course—the fact that he and Tellian have their differences couldn't possibly be allowed to stand in the way of protecting the King! Unfortunately, it's a long way from Toramos to Balthar, so it's most unlikely his messenger will be able to get there in time.

"Meanwhile, Cassan will ride hell-for-leather for Chergor in person. Hopefully, despite his heroic efforts, he'll arrive just too late, and the mercenaries will have killed everyone at Chergor, including Baron Tellian, who—in this version, of course—will have fallen fighting desperately in the King's defense against the Purple Lords' assassins. Should that have happened, Cassan will do his level best to take at least some of the assassins alive to be interogated before magi and prove *he* had nothing to do with the plot. If, however, Cassan is unlucky enough to arrive before that moment, or if it should happen the King's guard manages to fight off the mercenaries, then Cassan will discover that *Tellian* was actually behind it. And when he summons Tellian to surrender to give an account of this tragic assassination to the Great Council, Tellian will refuse and be killed by the loyal armsmen trying to take him into custody. Of course, the King will have to already be dead before that happens to make everything work out properly, but I'm sure Cassan can handle a little creative rearrangement of the chronology if he has to.

"As far as Baron Cassan is concerned, either of those outcomes is quite acceptable, although he'd obviously prefer the first one. If Tellian doesn't happen to be at Chergor—he hasn't been home to Balthar in quite some time, and it's entirely possible he'll be off on a visit at the critical moment—then Cassan would be forced to fall back on the charter in his possession to prove—or at least strongly suggest—Tellian's involvement. Obviously, it would be far more convenient if he didn't have to do that."

"And Yurokhas and Trianal?"

"I think it's entirely possible both of them might end up dead even before the King, given the little surprise I've arranged on the Ghoul Moor." Varnaythus smiled unpleasantly. "It's a remarkably *nasty* surprise, if I do say so myself. And on top of that, I understand Baron Cassan has sent a rather skilled specialist of his own—a man who's very good with an arbalest *or* a horse bow—to attend to the Prince. I'm sure that if the opportunity presents itself, Sir Trianal will receive the same treatment."

"There are an awful lot of separate moving parts to this strategy of Cassan's," Arthnar observed. From his tone—and from the look in the narrowed eyes gazing at Varnaythus—an unbiased witness might have concluded that the Fire Oar was less than convinced Cassan had come up with the idea all on his own. "Any one of them, or *all* of them, could come apart."

"That's possible," Varnaythus conceded. "I think it's highly unlikely *all* of them would fail, however. They might, and I won't pretend that couldn't happen, but how much worse off would you be if it did?"

"You mean if King Markhos, and Baron Tellian, and Prince Yurokhas, and Bahnak, and Bahzell, and Kilthan, and the gods only know who else, all survive and every one of them wants my blood for helping Cassan try to kill them?" Arthnar asked acidly.

"That would require them to know that, though," Varnaythus pointed out. "It's the Purple Lords hiring the mercenaries, if I recall properly."

"And you think Markhos and his magi wouldn't be able to get the truth out of Cassan?" Arthnar's tone had gone beyond acid to derisive, and Varnaythus allowed himself a chuckle.

It was a remarkably *cold* chuckle, the Fire Oar noticed.

"I'm afraid Baron Cassan knows too much about my own business in the Kingdom," he said. "I won't bore you with all the minor details," he waved his right hand in a brushing away gesture, "but let's say it could be . . . *inconvenient* for me if he were to be properly interrogated by the King's investigators."

"You seem remarkably unconcerned about the possibility," Arthnar said slowly, and Varnaythus shrugged.

"Let's just say I've taken certain precautions to make certain that doesn't happen. Of course, I might still find it expedient to take a short vacation someplace besides the Wind Plain—just for a year or two, perhaps, while things quiet down again. I was thinking about Krelik, as a matter of fact. I'm sure a Fleet Captain of your stature could find some minor service a man of my talents might perform to repay you for your hospitality."

"Oh, I imagine I could," Arthnar agreed after a moment. "If I really thought about it for a while, I mean."

And he smiled.

Chapter Twenty-Eight

"She did *what?*"

Mayor Yalith Tamilthfressa stared back and forth between Commander of Five Hundred Balcartha Evahnalfressa and the young, red-haired woman in her office in disbelief. Balcartha looked back at her for a moment, then glanced at her younger companion.

"Warned you she wasn't going to take it well," she said dryly.

"*Take* it well?!" Yalith's stupefaction was turning rapidly into something else as the initial shock wore off, and she glared at the five hundred. "Lillinara, Balcartha! Is that all you've got to say?!"

"Honestly?" Balcartha shrugged. "No. I'm afraid my initial reaction was rather like your own, but I've had a little longer—like, oh, twenty minutes? Possibly as much as an entire half-hour?—to think about it."

"You have, have you?" Yalith gave her a dirty look. "In that case, I'd be overjoyed to hear what conclusions you've reached!"

"Well, basically, there are two of them," Balcartha replied. "First, Leeana has a right—the same right every war maid has—to decide for herself what to do with her life. And, secondly, there's not one damned thing anyone can do to change any of it." She shrugged again, smiling crookedly. "That being the case, I decided there wasn't any point getting myself all worked up about it."

"Oh, that's *incredibly* useful!" Yalith said scathingly, and turned to Leeana. "Gods, girl, haven't you done enough crazy things in your life without dumping *this* on us?! Do you have any idea at all how someone like Trisu or the other hard-line conservatives is going to react? Oh, and let's not forget Baron Cassan!"

"Now, that's unfair, Yalith," Balcartha said in a rather firmer tone, regarding her old friend sternly.

"Unfair? *Unfair?*" Yalith stared at her. "Who said it was *fair?* It's *not* fair. I never said it was! But that doesn't change any of the repercussions that're going to be coming our way as soon as the anti-war-maid bigots hear about this!" She looked back at Leeana, her expression marginally less thunderous, and shook her head. "Balcartha's right, your decisions are your own, but you know they're going to splash all over the rest of us, don't you? Bad enough that we 'let' the daughter of one of the Kingdom's barons run away to join us when she wasn't even fifteen years old. But now, now that we've finished 'corrupting' her and teaching her to wallow in the gods only know what sort of perversions, she's decided to take a *hradani* lover?"

"And become a wind rider, to boot," Balcartha added helpfully.

"*Don't!*" Yalith whirled back to Balcartha to shake an index finger under her nose. The five hundred looked down at it, deliberately crossing her eyes in the process, and Yalith glared at her. "Balcartha, you are *not* making this one bit better!" she snapped.

"Of course I am," Balcartha replied calmly. "Someone has to interject a note of calm—or at least levity—into the proceedings, Yalith, and Leeana's far too junior to go around throttling the mayor just because she's spluttering and hissing like a demented teakettle."

Yalith's jaw dropped. She stared at the five hundred, as if unable to believe her own ears, and Balcartha snorted.

"Better," she said, and shook her head gently at her old friend. "Now take a deep breath, Yalith, and sit back down. I'll admit Leeana and Gayrfressa and—Lillinara help us all—Bahzell have . . . put us in an awkward situation, shall we say? But war maids are supposed to be accustomed to dealing with awkward situations, aren't we? And the one thing none of us can afford is to let it appear for one moment that *we* have any qualms about Leeana's right to do exactly what she's done. And"—she added a bit more sternly as the mayor settled slowly back into the chair behind her desk—"she *does* have the right to do exactly what she's done, and you know it."

Yalith looked back at her for several seconds. Then she shook herself, sank slowly back into her chair, drew the deep breath Balcartha had commanded her to, and looked back at Leeana.

"She's right."

It would have been grossly inaccurate to describe the mayor's tone as remotely cheerful. Indeed, the word that came most readily to mind was "resigned," Leeana thought. But Yalith only pinched the bridge of her nose and shook her head.

"She's right," the mayor repeated, "but I'm right, too, Leeana. I can't even imagine what all of the repercussions of this are going to be, but you *know* there are going to be a lot of them, don't you?"

"Of course I do," Leeana replied steadily. "And I never intended for things to get as . . . out of hand as they have, I suppose. Or to 'splash' on Kalatha." She shook her own head, her expression wry. "To be honest, Mayor Yalith, I didn't really expect anyone besides possibly my closest friends to even know anything about it at all! But then, well—"

She extended her left wrist, and wonder replaced the exasperated worry in Yalith's eyes as the wedding bracelet glowed. The silvery luminescence was soft at first, yet it grew quickly stronger, spreading up Leeana's arm, radiating in the office's shadows, sending ripples of moonlight across the ceiling and down the walls, and the mayor drew another, even deeper breath.

"Who am I to argue with the Mother Herself?" she murmured, and Balcartha chuckled gently.

"My very own thought when Leeana showed it to me. And, if I'm going to be honest, one of the reasons I'm taking this as calmly as I am." The five hundred folded her arms across her chest and twitched her shoulders. "If Lillinara and Tomanāk both decide to turn up and pronounce Leeana and Bahzell man and wife, who is *anyone* to argue with Them? This isn't a matter of what the Charter says or doesn't say, Yalith—not anymore. Not if the gods Themselves decide to change the rules!"

"And who's going to believe that's really what happened?" Yalith tipped back in her chair, her eyes regaining their normal shrewdness. "I'm not saying you're not right, Balcartha, but you and I—and, eventually, I suppose everyone here in Kalatha—have seen or will see Leeana's bracelet. That's almost six thousand whole people!" She grimaced. "We're not even the biggest *war maid* town, you know, much less anything most people would think of as the big city. How many of the *rest* of the Kingdom's subjects do you think are going to be ready to take a bunch of war maids' word for something like this *without* seeing that bracelet for themselves with their very own eyes?"

"About the same number who're ready to take a war maid's word for *anything*," Balcartha retorted. "Give me a minute to take my boots off and I'll count up the exact total for you."

"Exactly." Yalith nodded. "And now we add Gayrfressa to the rest of it." She shook her head. "I admit my initial reaction was hardly what I'd call calm and reasoned, Leeana, but you do understand that rumor and exaggeration and outright lies—especially from people who don't like war maids anyway—are going to spread like a thunderstorm, don't you? And that no one who hasn't seen that bracelet or you on Gayrfressa's back with her—or *his*, damn it—own eyes is going to believe for a moment that the gods really and truly approved of all this. In fact, most of those people who don't like war maids—which, I remind you, is just about everybody in the entire Kingdom—are going to be absolutely convinced we made up the entire blasphemous lie as a way to excuse your unnatural relationship with a hradani even if they *do* see the proof with their own eyes. Not to mention the way the people who think all war maids are basically whores at heart are going to take the fact that you're actually sleeping with a *hradani* as proof of how thoroughly depraved and degenerate we *all* are!"

"I know," Leeana sighed. "But, in a lot of ways, Mayor Yalith, this is just my original decision to become a war maid all over again, really, isn't it?" She grimaced. "I do seem to be more of a lightning rod than anyone else, and I have to admit I'm a little frightened when I think about that. I mean, look at everything that's already happened to *Bahzell*! I'm not too sure Norfressa's going to survive adding my ability to attract stray lightning bolts to his!"

"It's certainly going to be interesting to watch, anyway," Balcartha said dryly. "From a safe distance, at least. Not that I don't think you have a point," she continued when Leeana and Yalith both looked at her. "On the other hand, I doubt the gods chose the two of you for those 'stray lightning bolts' at random, Leeana."

"You may be right," Leeana acknowledged, thinking about midnight eyes in a grove of pines beyond the world's edge and a glittering gold and sapphire sprig of periwinkle hidden in Gayrfressa's saddlebag. "Not that it's going to make the experience any less . . . exciting."

"And not just for *you*," Yalith said sourly. Then she laughed. "But

Balcartha's got a point, too. I may wish you hadn't done it, I may be nervous as hell about where all this is going to end, but one thing I'm *not* is stupid enough to argue with the gods Themselves. They obviously approve of your choice, Leeana, and to be honest—and speaking for myself, not as Mayor of Kalatha—from what I've seen of Prince Bahzell, I do, too." She smiled. "I admit it would take me a while to get used to the ears, but, hradani or not, I don't think there could possibly be a better *man* on the entire Wind Plain."

"Thank you," Leeana said softly.

"You're welcome—in a cranky, harassed, exasperated, preoccupied, worried sort of way."

The mayor gave her another smile, then shook herself.

"All right, Balcartha. Have you had time to think about what this means for Leeana's duties with the Guard?"

"Not really," Balcartha admitted. "It's obviously going to change them, of course. I may not be able to hear Gayrfressa's voice when she talks to Leeana, but, trust me—one look at her body language, and I knew better than to even *mention* the fact that there's no such thing as war maid cavalry! I doubt we've got more than a couple of hundred mounted war maids in the entire Kingdom, and aside from the thirty or forty of them serving with the Quaysar Guard, most of them are couriers, not cavalry troopers. I'm going to have to come up with some way to work around that. Still," she looked consideringly at Leeana, "aside from this mildly irritating propensity of hers to run off and get married to hradani and bring coursers home with her and otherwise set the entire Kingdom by its collective ears without mentioning her plans to anyone, Seventy-Five Leeana's always seemed to have her head screwed on properly. I'm sure we'll come up with something."

"Good luck," Yalith said feelingly, and looked back at Leeana. "I don't even want to think about what kind of... housing arrangements you're going to have to make for Gayrfressa, either. Nobody in Kalatha has the kind of stables Baron Tellian could have provided, anyway—I know that much!"

"I've already thought about that, Mayor," Leeana replied. "To be honest, Gayrfressa doesn't really like stables all that much. She and I talked it over, and we think the best bet's going to be to move me to the old guesthouse, assuming you and Five Hundred Balcartha approve." She made a face. "I know it's huge for a single war maid, but I'd have to spend enough time fixing the holes in the roof—and the floor—that I doubt anyone's going to think of it as special treatment, and it backs up against the edge of town and all those open fields down to the river. And I could patch up the old stable to give her cover against bad weather. For that matter, once I got it into semi-habitable condition, I'd probably move Boots to it from the city livery."

"So you're keeping him, too?"

"Of course I am. And I'm going to be riding him regularly, as well." Leeana smiled. "Gayrfressa would insist on that even if I didn't want to."

"That's good to know," Yalith said. She thought about it for several moments and then shrugged. "No one's using that old wreck, anyway. In fact, I was thinking about having it torn down before it collapsed of its own weight. So if you and Gayrfressa want it instead, I don't see any problem. Balcartha?"

"There's always been provision for active-duty Guard officers to live off-post under special circumstances." Balcartha shrugged back at her. "I don't see a problem, either. And I rather suspect that Seventy-Five Leeana's platoon may well see fit to help her with those repairs she was talking about."

"Ma'am, I don't want to—"

"Oh, hush, Leeana! No one said anything about *telling* them to do it! The problem would come in if I tried to *stop* them from doing it, and you know it."

Leeana subsided, and Balcartha nodded in satisfaction.

"All right, I think we can take that as settled. Mayor?"

"As far as I'm concerned, you can," Yalith assured her. "Of course, it's probably the *only* part of it that's anywhere near 'settled'!"

"One day at a time," Balcartha said philosophically. "One day at a time."

She stood for a moment longer, head cocked and arms still crossed, lips pursed as she obviously ran over a mental checklist. Then, suddenly, she chuckled richly.

"What now?" Yalith asked warily, and Balcartha smiled broadly.

"Oh, I was just thinking. You're probably right about how the rumors are going to fly, and how our critics are going to react to all this, but that's nothing—a mere bagatelle!—compared to what Leeana's going to have to deal with right here in Kalatha itself."

"I beg your pardon?" Leeana's tone was even warier than the mayor's had been, and Balcartha laughed.

"Oh, yes, Leeana! I promise you I intend to be right there to see it when it happens, too!"

"When *what* happens?" Leeana demanded.

"Why, when you have to explain this to *Garlahna* and she starts pumping you for all the juicy details about Bahzell!" Balcartha told her. "After all those years when you gave her grief over her, ah . . . *energetic* love life while you weren't sleeping with *anybody?*" The five hundred snorted. "Trust me, girl—you are *never* going to live this down where *she's* concerned!"

✧ ✧ ✧

There were, Brayahs Daggeraxe acknowledged, advantages to being a wind walker.

For one thing, he could get away from all of the exquisitely polite, venomous backbiting and intrigue of court quickly when the time came.

He stood on the east tower of Sothōkarnas, looking back across the city of Sothōfalas and the blue ribbon of the Pardahn River, wending its way towards the distant Spear. The barge traffic was thicker and denser than it had been earlier in the year, he thought, and his mouth twitched wryly as he thought about how much thicker it was likely to become in the next few years if things worked out the way he was fairly certain they were about to. At the very least, those "things" were going to get very . . . interesting, and Sothōii were by nature conservative. "Interesting" had never been their favorite word, not with its implications of change and unpredictability, which, after all, was why peope like Tellian Bowmaster made so many of their neighbors so acutely uneasy.

He snorted in harsh amusement at the thought and inhaled a deep, cleansing breath. Summer was moving steadily towards fall, and it was hot, even here on the lofty Wind Plain. There was scarcely a breath of breeze to ease the heat this afternoon—not down here at his current level, at any rate—and he listened to the cries of the birds hovering almost motionless in the updrafts above the mighty fortress. Those cries were distant yet crystal clear over the less distinct stir and murmur of the city.

The noise of the horses and armsmen gathered in Sothōkarnas' main courtyard was rather closer to hand, and the crisp rasp of commands came to him as Sir Frahdar Swordshank, King Markhos' personal armsman and the captain of his forty-man detachment of the Royal Guard, chivied along his armsmen's final preparations. Brayahs knew other eyes—hundreds of them, at the very least—were watching the same scene. It would scarcely do to admit it, but he rather suspected the owners of most of those eyes had already ordered their own escorts to assemble as soon as the King had been good enough to take himself out of the way. It didn't need a mage to sense the palpable aura of impatience hovering like fog over Sothōkarnas, at any rate, and Brayahs wondered if perhaps—just perhaps, unworthy though the suspicion might be—His Majesty wasn't deliberately dawdling just a bit in order to tweak his loyal courtiers' impatience. Markhos Silveraxe wasn't the sort to pitch tantrums. Indeed, there were those who considered him rather cold and bloodless for a proper Sothōii king. Most people thought that was better than someone whose fiery temper led him into missteps, as his grandfather had demonstrated on more than one occasion, but Brayahs had been able to observe him from closer range than most for the past few years. There was a far sharper temper below the King's surface than he'd seen fit to let most people see . . . and he was far more subtle about it than those same people were ever likely to guess.

He probably is *deliberately making the lot of them wait,* the mage thought now. *He knows exactly how they're all dancing with impatience to get home to their own estates and their own affairs. It would never do for him to say so openly, of course—just as it would* never *do for any of* them *to admit it, but he knows. And there's no way he'd pass up this opportunity to whack them by making them pretend they aren't champing at the bit . . . not if he's one half as tired of all this quarreling and snapping and veiled innuendo as I am, at any rate. And the gods know he's had to put up with even more of it than I have. On the other hand, he's not a mage. He doesn't have to hold his personal shields every minute of the day just to keep these idiots from driving him mad with their incessant, babbling, calculating, manipulating, dishonest, self-seeking, devious—*

He chopped off the catalog of adjectives and inhaled again, even more deeply than before. Thank Semkirk mind speech wasn't one of his major talents! Just the emotional aura that went with the steadily intensifying power struggle had been bad enough without having the participants' actual *thoughts* spilling over into his brain!

Be nice, he told himself. *It's not as if they're deliberately radiating all that garbage at you. In fact, Semkirk knows they'd be just deliriously happy to have you somewhere else entirely! The mere thought that you might be perching in a corner somewhere and surveying the contents of their muddy little minds is one reason they get so . . . apprehensive whenever they notice you walking by. And,* he admitted more grudgingly, *you know it's inevitable that people who don't have mage talents are going to worry about the intrusiveness of anyone who* does *have them.*

Of course it was. And the fact that everyone knew the King relied heavily on magi as royal agents and investigators only made any good, devious-minded conspirator even more nervous. And the gods knew they'd been more devious than usual this summer!

He snorted at the thought and rested his forearms atop one of the battlements' crenelations and cushioned his chin on them as he gazed moodily down at the assembling armsmen and considered what that meant for his own family and the North Riding in general.

His thoughts, not surprisingly, were not happy ones.

It was scarcely astonishing that his cousin Borandas had chosen to send his heir to represent him for the summer session of the Great Council rather than attending in person. He'd done that for the last two or three years, in fact, and the truly important decisions were usually made at the fall session. Borandas always attended that session in person, and sending Thorandas to deal with the normally more routine business of the summer session was undoubtedly good training for him, not to mention making sure the North Riding's heir knew *exactly* what was happening in the capital if he should suddenly inherit the title. But this session had been far less "routine" than normal, and Brayahs rather wished Borandas hadn't delegated it to his son this year. Or perhaps not. Brayahs loved his cousin, and he respected him as both his baron and a man, but there was no point pretending Borandas of Halthan was as needle-witted as Tellian of Balthar or Cassan of Frahmahn. Of course, he wasn't as devious, ambitious, and unscrupulous as Cassan, either. That had to be considered a plus for those living under his governance in the North Riding, although a bit more deviousness on his part might have stood the Kingdom as a whole in rather better stead at a moment like this one.

Brayahs didn't really like admitting that, yet it was true. And while he generally applauded his cousin's determination to remain neutral in the struggle between Tellian and Cassan, Borandas' willingness to delegate to Thorandas had started to worry him. He had to agree that Thorandas was better suited than his father, by both nature and inclination, to holding his own in the snake pit of factions here in Sothōfalas. Unfortunately, either Borandas had changed his policy where the North Riding's neutrality was concerned without mentioning it to Brayahs, or else Thorandas had begun changing it for him.

You don't know what messages Borandas may have sent him, Brayahs Daggeraxe, he told himself sternly. *And no law or custom requires Borandas to keep* you *informed about his policies, either—not after you swore mage oath, and* especially *not since His Majesty tapped you as one of his court magi. It's entirely possible he's gotten more concerned over Tellian's growing ascendancy than he's mentioned to you, and who could blame him if he has? It can't be comfortable for any of the other barons to reflect on how that new trade route's going to pour kormaks into Tellian's purse like water. For that matter, it's enough to make* you *nervous . . . and you actually* like *Tellian!*

All of that was true enough, yet Brayahs knew his cousin's profound distrust for Cassan Axehammer. Borandas might be concerned by Tellian's expanding powerbase, but Brayahs rather doubted he believed for a moment that Tellian had any designs on seizing outright control of the Kingdom's policies, whereas anyone who'd ever met Cassan knew exactly what *he* had in mind.

The problem was that fear of Tellian—not to mention that deep, bred-in-the-bone conservatism of Sothōii in general—had pushed those who feared his new trade route, his new closeness to the Axemen and Kilthandahknarthas of Silver Cavern, and (above all) his friendship for the hated and feared hradani into ever more vociferous opposition to him. The rumors of increasing hostility on the part of the Purple Lords didn't help matters where Tellian's critics were concerned, either. And for all its centuries-long alliance with the Empire of the Axe, more than one Sothōii noble feared that Tellian's plans were going to bind the Kingdom *too* tightly to the Axemen, turn them into some sort of hapless appendage of the Empire and subordinate their interests to those of their Axeman "friends."

So, yes, there was enormous scope for completely reasonable anxiety over Tellian's plans and ambitions. Brayahs understood that, even sympathized with it, but Thorandas was clearly fishing in those troubled waters, and that worried the mage. In fact, it worried him a lot.

No doubt Thorandas was seeking every advantage he could

find for the North Riding, and Brayahs trusted his loyalty to the Crown, yet there was no denying that his prejudices against the hradani had produced a simmering hostility towards Tellian's efforts even before the entire Derm Canal project had ever been proposed. And this business of offering for Shairnayith Axehammer's hand . . . that worried Brayahs. It was a perfectly suitable match in almost every way—indeed, it would have been difficult for Thorandas to find an equally suitable one, given the girl's birth and his own position—and the mere fact of a marriage connection didn't automatically promise a union of policies, as well. That wouldn't keep it from giving the *appearance* of one, however, and it *would* inevitably make Thorandas more . . . susceptible to Cassan's advice.

Brayahs wasn't the only one thinking those thoughts, either. He'd seen it in quite a few of the lords warden, and of the more perceptive members the Manthâlyr, as well. Everyone knew the true power in the Kingdom rested with the Great Council, but no monarch could simply ignore the Kraithâlyr or Manthâlyr, and if the minor nobility and the commoners seated in those bodies decided Cassan was regaining his influence in the Great Council—or, even worse, successfully forging an alliance that pitted all three other ridings against the West Riding—the implications could be profound. Surely Borandas had to be aware of the dangers inherent in presenting that sort of appearance! For that matter, Brayahs *knew* Borandas was—or had been, the last time they'd discussed it, at any rate. So what could have possessed him to allow Thorandas to offer for the girl?

The mage sighed heavily, feeling the hot sun across his shoulders, listening to those birds, and worried. He'd also come to a decision, however. He'd deliberately resolved to stop discussing Borandas' policies with him when King Markhos summoned him to serve at court, but he was going to have to break that resolve. At the very least, he had to reassure himself that Borandas was accurately informed on what had been happening here in Sothōfalas. He didn't like to even consider the possibility that Thorandas might have been . . . shading his own messages to his father, but he'd seen too many painful examples of what ambition or political expediency could do to simply set the thought aside.

At least we've got some time, he told himself encouragingly as a trumpet rang out and the King came striding across the courtyard to his waiting horse at last. *Whatever Cassan and Yeraghor may be up to, they aren't going to get a lot actually accomplished with the Council, the Conclave, and the Manthâlyr all adjourned for the summer! And as soon as His Majesty disappears up the road to Chergor, every one of those Councilors, lords warden, and delegates is going to vanish in clouds of dust of his very own. Cassan'll play hell trying to coordinate anything complicated over the rest of the summer, and that should give me at least a month or two to figure out exactly what Borandas' real policy is.*

He watched Markhos climb into the saddle. Then a bugle sounded and his armsmen surrounded him, with Tellian of Balthar riding on his left and Sir Jerhas Macebearer riding on his right, and swept out of Sothōkarnas' gates in a clatter of steel-shod hooves. Brayahs straightened and nodded in satisfaction as the last armsman passed under the great stone arch into the dark gullet of the gate tunnel. With the King's departure from Sothōkarnas, he was officially released from his own attendance here at court, and that was where the advantages of being a wind walker came into their own.

He closed his eyes, turning his face up to the sun, seeing its redness through his eyelids, and sought his own center. He found it quickly, with the ease of long training and years of practice, and a sense of calm purpose and focus settled over him. It didn't magically erase his concerns about his cousin and the Kingdom, but it set them to one side, placed them in a sort of mental pigeonhole until he needed them once again, in order to free his mind for other things.

His nostrils flared as he pictured the familiar towers and walls of Star Tower Castle, tall and proud, standing guard over the city of Halthan. He'd grown up in those towers, those walls, and he smiled as he felt them calling to him, beckoning him home.

He fixed the image in his mind, locking it there until it was more real than the bird cries coming down from above, or the sun on his face, or the distant, murmuring, thousand-tongued multivoice of Sothōfalas. He took that image in his mental grasp and heard the wind rising at his back. The wind only he could hear, only he could feel, summoned by his talent, sweeping around him in an invisible, silent cyclone. It wrapped itself about him, plucking at his hair and garments with a thousand tiny, laughing hands, and he smiled again, released his grip on Sothōkarnas, and stepped from everyday reality into the laughter of the wind.

Chapter Twenty-Nine

"I don't like this one bit," Brandark Brandarkson said quietly, sitting in the saddle and peering into the misty rain. His cap's jaunty feather drooped under its own sodden weight, and a thin, persistent stream of droplets dripped from its end. "I know it rains more down here, close to the river, than it does up on top of the Wind Plain this time of year, but this is just plain wrong."

"Aye, it is that," Bahzell acknowledged grimly.

The Horse Stealer stood leaning against Walsharno's shoulder, his oilskin poncho gleaming with wet, and the courser's ears moved restlessly as both of them strained to sense and identify what instinct told them was out there somewhere. Bahzell's ears were almost as busy, but Brandark's were half-flattened, and his warhorse stamped uneasily as it sensed its rider's mood. The Bloody Sword had returned to Hurgrum from Dwarvenhame six days before, bearing with him greetings, letters, a fresh supply of books for his library, and a brand new specimen of the dwarves' latest musical invention. He'd been welcomed warmly on his arrival (despite his new instrument), yet he clearly didn't care for what he'd heard—and seen—since then. He'd come ahead with Bahzell to join Yurgazh and the field force on the Ghoul Moor while Trianal personally returned to Balthar to raise the riding's first levy. The additional Sothōii should be arriving in the next few days, and Vaijon would be close behind them with Bahnak's infantry reinforcements, but summer or no summer, there was a cold, ugly feel to the air. A sense of something building, of a malevolent force biding its time and assembling its strength before it struck.

The expeditionary force had encamped along the bank of the Hangnysti while it awaited its reinforcements. Its dwarven engineers had laid out, and human and hradani fatigue parties had constructed, field fortifications that would have done the King Emperor himself proud, and the small army should have been secure against anything the Ghoul Moor had ever produced. Yet every man in it knew no one had ever seen or heard of ghouls acting as their enemy was acting now, and that left them feeling unanchored despite their fortified camp. Off balance. It wasn't *fear*, but it was uncertainty, made all the worse because ghouls had always been so predictable before.

And the weather wasn't helping, Bahzell thought. Brandark was right about that. The wet, sloppy mud and rain was more like what one would have expected in late fall or even early winter, not this time of year. It would have been enough to depress anyone's spirits at any time; coming now, in what was supposed to be high summer, the effect was even more pronounced. And the eerie emptiness around them, the lack of activity from the ghouls who should have been swarming about their fortifications, trying to pounce on scouting parties, gibbering and hooting their challenges from the weather's concealment, only made that even worse. Yurgazh and Sir Yarran were undoubtedly right about the need to patrol aggressively—as much to keep the men focused as to seek contact with the enemy—but those patrols persistently found nothing. It was almost as if the ghouls knew about their army's expected reinforcements and were deliberately *waiting* for them to arrive before offering battle, and wasn't that a cheery thought?

Well, it was your own stiff neck got you out in the muck and the mud today, he told himself sardonically. *There's more than a mite could be said for sitting snug with a fire on a day like this, but could you be doing the smart thing?* He snorted mentally. *Of course you couldn't! And if you and Walsharno were after being so bent on wading about out amongst the weeds and the rain just to see for yourself as how there's never a ghoul stirring, of course the little man had to be coming along with you, didn't he just?*

"I wouldn't want to say this kind of weather was deliberately *designed* to make horse bows less effective," the Bloody Sword continued now, "but it does rather have that effect, doesn't it?"

"Aye," Bahzell grunted even more disgustedly.

Bows were less susceptible to rain than some people thought, but even a Sothōii's well-waxed and resined bowstring lost power when it was thoroughly saturated. Fletching tended to warp and even come completely unglued, for that matter, which did bad things to accuracy. Because of that, the Sothōii rode with their bows unbent, strings tucked into their ponchos' inner pockets to keep them dry, and their quivers capped to protect their arrows. That meant they were going to be slower—much slower—getting those bows into action than they might have been otherwise. Even worse, these blowing, misty curtains of rain reduced visibility badly, and *that* meant they were likely to have less warning before they needed those unbent, unstrung bows.

It wasn't quite as bad for the hradani's Dwarvenhame arbalests, with their steel bowstaves and wire "strings" and their quarrels' wooden slot-and-groove stabilizing vanes, but even they found their effective range reduced in this sort of weather, simply because of the visibility. And given that even a Dwarvenhame arbalest was slower-firing than a horse bow, their front ranks were likely to have time for no more than a single volley before they were forced to sling their missile weapons and bring their shields and swords into action.

It could have been worse, of course. For example, they could have faced a hard, driving rain rather than this billowing grayness. But it was quite bad enough, even if Brandark hadn't been right about the unseasonable nature of it. This was the third straight day, with no end in sight, and the sense of being closed in, half-blinded, was enough to make a man's skin itch.

<*Especially when both of us know* something*'s on the other side of it,*> Walsharno murmured in the back of his brain. <*And Vaijon, too.*>

<*Well, it's not as if it was after being the first time we've smelled such as that,*> Bahzell replied silently. <*Mind, it's happy I'll be to have Vaijon along this time, but there's times I wish as how himself could be telling us just a* mite *more before we've stepped full into it.*>

<*I wish that, too, Bahzell,*> a far deeper voice said. <*Sending those who trust you and who have proven you can trust* them, *even to the death, into battle without all the knowledge you possess . . . that's a hard thing, my Swords, even for a god. Perhaps* especially *for a god.*>

Most people, perhaps, might have flinched just a bit when a

god's voice rolled through their brains with no warning at all. Bahzell and Walsharno, however, had become accustomed to it over the years, and the hradani's ears didn't even twitch in surprise.

Anymore, at least.

<*As to that, it's no god I am,*> he said, <*yet I can see as how it could eat on a man.*>

There was no recrimination in his tone, only acceptance of the way it must be, and he felt a vast, immaterial hand rest lightly on his shoulder.

<*I don't think you have anything to worry about today,*> Tomanāk's voice rumbled in his mind. <*I can't be certain of that, however. You're right that there's something ugly, something powerful, behind this rain, yet my nephews and nieces have prevented me from seeing as clearly as I might otherwise. What I do see is bad enough, though.*> The voice was deeper, grimmer. <*When it comes, my Swords, it will demand all that all of you have to offer . . . and perhaps even that will be less than enough this time. I know you'll give all I could possibly ask of you, yet the Dark has planned better this time, and I see too far and too deeply to see* clearly. *There are too many possibilities, too many strands weaving together, for me to see any one of them unambiguously, and this time battle is fully joined beyond the edges of your universe, as well as within it.*>

Bahzell's ears flattened and he turned his head far enough to meet Walsharno's eye, remembering a cold, windy night in the Empire of the Spear when Tomanāk had explained to him why the gods dared not contend openly with one another, strength to strength, lest their unleashed power destroy the very reality for which they fought.

<*No, Bahzell,*> Tomanāk said. <*We do not contend* in *your universe, nor for this universe alone. We meet* between *them, beyond their fringes, and it's less a matter of sheer strength than of . . . leverage, perhaps. Balance. The proper grips and counters.*>

It was evident Tomanāk was seeking the best way to describe something in terms a mortal might grasp.

<*When a mishuk grapples with another mishuk, the outcome depends far less on who has the most powerful muscles, the longer reach, than on who has the superior* technique,> Tomanāk continued. <*All of those other factors matter, but in the end, he who's more skilled—and experienced—has the greatest advantage. Yet in the struggle between Light and Dark, there are still more*

factors which must be taken into consideration. There's a tide, a current—a flow—to the seas of possibility and the current of history. Deities see that flow far more clearly than mortals, and with that clarity we can assist the mortals who must contend with it, yet we ourselves can never lay hand upon it and shape it as we will. For us, much of the struggle lies in not simply what we can perceive but what we can prevent the other *side from perceiving. And when too many strands, too many possible outcomes, flow together, it becomes harder for us to see clearly ourselves . . . and easier for the other side to blind us to critical possibilities.*>

Bahzell gave a slow mental nod and sensed Walsharno's understanding along with his own.

<*For the last twelve centuries of your universe,*> Tomanāk continued in the voice of someone choosing his words with exquisite care, <*events have been spiraling through the echoes of the last great clash which doomed Kontovar and gave birth to most of the evils which have afflicted Norfressa since. It took far too many of your years for those echoes to be damped, but now they have, and they're poised to rebound. There are literally uncountable variations on* how *they may rebound, but there are really only two basic outcomes. Either the Light will hold its ground, strike back, and reverse the verdict of Kontovar, or else the Dark will conquer all. One way or the other, my Swords, the decision will be reached in your time. If you fail, if you fall in your current struggle, the Dark triumphs; if you succeed today, then it will only be to face another and still sterner test in the uncertain mists of your future, but that other test* will *come to you. All I can tell you is that you have the strength—the strength of will, of heart, of mind and courage—to meet Evil sword-to-sword. You have my trust, and my confidence, and you have the power of your own belief in what's right and your willingness to fight—and die—for it. That, my children, is all anyone, god or mortal, can ask of anyone else or demand of themselves, and I know—I* know, *if I know nothing else in all the universes that may ever be—that you* will *give it. And when you do, I will stand beside you and give you of my strength. There's no shame in defeat, my Swords; there is shame only in surrender, and that is something neither of you, nor Vaijon, know how to do.*>

Neither hradani nor courser said anything. They simply reached back to their deity, feeling the bonds between them, the interweaving of their very essences with Tomanāk's, and that was enough.

Bahzell never knew exactly how long the entire conversation had lasted, although he was confident the interval had been far briefer for Brandark than it had for him and for Walsharno. He inhaled deeply, nostrils flaring, as Tomanāk withdrew once more, and then he turned to look at his friend.

"Well, I'm thinking we've splashed about mud enough for one day," he said.

"Really?" Brandark cocked his ears. "Odd, I didn't think it was *my* idea to go out and squelch around all day."

"No more it was," Bahzell agreed. "Still and all, I'm thinking that was because it's so very rare for you to be having an idea at all."

"Given the handicap under which you labor, that actually wasn't such a bad effort," Brandark said judiciously. "Not very subtle, a little heavy-handed, but overall, and bearing in mind it had to work its way through a *Horse Stealer's* so-called sense of humor..."

He shrugged, and Bahzell chuckled and swung back up into Walsharno's saddle.

"Such a small, nasty attitude," he said, shaking his head. "I'll not be making any comments about lack of size and the smallness of brains that might be coming along with it. But I *will* mention as how I've just this morning taken delivery of a brand-new bottle of thirty-year whiskey—the Silver Cavern Granservan Grand Reserve, as it happens—courtesy of old Kilthan. If it should so happen you could be minding that silver tongue of yours—aye, and leaving that curst 'banjo' of yours in its case!—it's pleased I'd be to share it with you while I've the writing of a letter to Leeana."

"Granservan Grand Reserve?" Brandark's ears perked up instantly, and he squared his shoulders and gathered up his reins. "Well, if *that's* the case, why are we still standing here?"

✧ ✧ ✧

"It's good to see you home, Brayahs," Baroness Myacha said, smiling as her husband's cousin entered the sunny breakfast chamber. "It does Borandas' heart good whenever you can find time—and whenever the King lets you go long enough—to visit us."

"Well, it's kind of you to say so, at any rate," Brayahs Daggeraxe said, crossing to the table to kiss the back of the hand she held out to him. The sunlight spilling in through the windows lit a dancing sparkle in her amethyst eyes, and he smiled back at her as he straightened. "Still, I remember the occasional conversation he and I had when I was only a lad. There's not so very much difference between forty-seven and fifty-eight, but there was a *world* of difference between eight and nineteen!" He shook his head. "Frankly, I'm amazed sometimes that I got to grow up after all."

"That's a terrible thing to say!"

There was an extra edge of something like gratitude in Myacha's laugh, for Brayahs was one of the very few people who could remind her of the difference between her own age and her husband's without ever making her wonder if there was a buried edge of malice in it. Of course, it was tactful of him not to mention that she was eighteen years younger than *he* was, as well, she supposed.

On the other hand, she thought, her humor fading, he was one of the even fewer people—especially *male* people—who'd never been tempted to dismiss her intelligence because of her youth. Even her "son" Thorandas seemed to want to pat her on the head sometimes, as if even he couldn't quite get past the notion that her primary function was simply to warm his father's bed and adorn the baron's arm suitably on social occasions. To be fair, she believed Thorandas honestly *tried* not to think of her in those terms, but he didn't always succeed. And if her opinion happened to differ from his, he was far more likely to fall back into the thought patterns of a traditional Sothōii noble*man* rather than considering the possibility that she might actually be right and *he* might actually be wrong.

Stop that, she told herself sternly. *You know how hard it must be on him to have a stepmother two years younger than he is! Under the circumstances, he does remarkably well. Even if he* is *being especially stupid at the moment.*

Brayahs cocked an eyebrow at her, his expression speculative, but she only shook her head and waved him into his chair across the table from her. His breakfast materialized before him with the silent, smiling efficiency of Star Tower Castle's servants, and he began spreading butter onto a scone while he regarded her through the faint wisp of steam rising from his cup of hot tea.

"And where is my esteemed cousin, if I might ask?" he inquired.

"He finished breakfast early and asked me to wait and keep you company," Myacha replied, sipping from her own cup of hot chocolate. "He had an appointment with Sir Dahlnar this morning. They're still catching up on the reports Thorandas brought home from Sothōfalas."

"I see." Brayahs finished buttering, took a bite of the scone, and rolled his eyes in bliss. "Semkirk, I miss Mistress Shahlana's baking! I tried to get her to run away and live in sin with me in Sothōfalas, you know."

Myacha choked on a sip of chocolate. She set the cup down hastily, mopping her lips and glaring at him, and he smiled unrepentantly. Trelsan Partisan had been Star Tower's butler for better than thirty years, and his wife had been the castle's housekeeper almost as long. She was a woman of immense dignity and ability as a manager and organizer, but she'd started as a cook, and she still loved to bake. Of course, she was also at least fifteen years older than Brayahs, and she and her husband—who doted upon her—both tended to regard House Daggeraxe's mage as the rapscallion teenager they remembered entirely too well.

"If you did manage to get Shahlana to leave Star Tower, I'm sure Borandas would put a price on your head!" Myacha said severely. "And rightly so, too. If that didn't constitute an act of high treason, I can't think of anything that would!"

"Oh, come now! Surely that's being at least a little too severe. Remember, I've just spent the last three months in Sothōfalas, Milady!" Brayahs grimaced only half-humorously. "I've had a chance to see *real* treason being contemplated there."

"Oh?" Myacha cocked her head, amethyst eyes narrowing, and Brayahs kicked himself mentally. He did know how sharp a blade she was. He should have known she'd pick up on that.

In fact, I wonder if I actually wanted *her to? Not exactly the most subtle possible way to ask her about Thorandas, I suppose, but then, I'm a Sothōii. We're not* supposed *to be subtle.*

"Sorry," he said out loud, and bought a moment by taking another bite of scone, chewing, and swallowing. He washed the mouthful down with another sip of tea and smiled a bit crookedly at her. "It's just that the summer session of the Council was a lot worse than usual this year."

"Tellian and his canal, I suppose?" Myacha shook her head, her eyes darkening despite the sunlight.

"And Cassan and Yeraghor's plans for strangling it in its cradle," Brayahs agreed. He shrugged. "I suppose I understand their position—*I'd* certainly be worried if I were a baron and one of the other barons was about to gain such a decisive advantage. Especially if I'd gone as far out of my way to piss him off as

Cassandras where Tellian is concerned. I mean, it may be unreasonable of me, but I'd think trying to have someone murdered might constitute a legitimate reason for him to be less than fond of the fellow who did it."

It was a mark of his comfort with Myacha—and of his respect for her—that he permitted himself to speak to her so frankly, and she rewarded him with a faint—very faint—smile. It was brief-lived, though.

"Borandas says Thorandas' reports suggest the King is going to grant Tellian his charter," she said, her tone making the statement a question, and he nodded.

"That was the rumor running around court," he confirmed. "And my own reading of the situation suggests it was probably accurate. It makes too much sense from the perspective of the Kingdom as a whole for Markhos not to approve it, frankly. And, for that matter, there isn't any way he could stop the canal portions of it even if he wanted to, since they run across *hradani* lands and then down the Hangnysti without ever going near the Wind Plain. Bahnak of Hurgrum is going to drive this project through, one way or the other, so it only makes sense for the King to give it his blessings and participate in it. If nothing else, that should put him in the best position to have at least some influence on how the whole thing operates. Not to mention providing a very nice addition to the Crown's revenues!"

"I can see where that would make sense," Myacha said after a moment. "Thorandas seems less convinced it will be good for the North Riding, though." Brayahs looked a question at her, and she shrugged. "You know he's never been happy about Tellian's dealings with the hradani in the first place, Brayahs! Part of that's hardheaded pragmatism and the memory of how much blood we've shed on hradani swords over the centuries, but another part of it—and a bigger one, to be honest—is plain old-fashioned bigotry." The baroness smiled with an edge of unhappy humor. "He's been fairly careful about how he's allowed himself to phrase it in front of me, but these rumors about Leeana Bowmaster and Prince Bahzell haven't exactly made him deliriously happy, you know."

"No, I can believe that." Brayahs grimaced and reached for his fork. He cut a neat forkful from the omelette before him and chewed slowly, remembering his conversation with Bahzell Bahnakson and Brandark Brandarkson in Sothōfalas. A mage learned to trust his instincts where another's character was concerned, and even if he hadn't, he was talking about a champion of Tomanāk, after all.

"That's not the only reason he's worried about Tellian, though," Myacha continued. "And from a logical perspective, I have to admit he's got a point. Tellian's already the most powerful and influential member of the Great Council. If he succeeds in getting his charter, his ascendancy's only going to become greater. And as the West Riding becomes more dominant—"

"—all the *other* ridings lose ground, whether they've done anything specifically to piss him off like Cassan or not," Brayahs concluded for her.

"Exactly." Myacha picked up a jeweled butter knife and toyed with it, the cut gems sparkling in the sunlight. "As I say, he has a point. But I'm still—"

She cut herself off abruptly, and Brayahs looked at her speculatively. He didn't need his mage talents to sense her unhappiness. Nor was he unaware of the reason she'd stopped so suddenly, and he felt a surge of sympathy for her position. Much as she had to know Borandas loved her, there was still an inevitable awkwardness whenever she might find herself in disagreement with her husband's son.

"The North Riding's policy is for Borandas to determine," he said, after a moment, "and Thorandas is his logical advisor, not to mention his heir. For that matter, I'm officially in the King's service now, and that means I have a tendency to look at these things from the Crown's perspective. Borandas would have to take that into consideration when the time came to think about any advice I might have for him. Having said that, however," he looked directly into her eyes, "I can't escape the feeling that having *Cassan* in a position of ascendancy would be far worse for the Kingdom—*and* the North Riding—than having someone like Tellian there."

"I know. I know." Myacha put down the butter knife and reached for her chocolate cup again, but she didn't drink from it. She only held it cradled between her palms, as if for warmth, and her expression was worried. "And I think Borandas feels the same way. In fact, up until a few weeks ago, I was *certain* he did. To be honest, I'm *still* certain he felt that way . . . then."

"Oh?"

Brayahs wanted desperately to push for more information, but he wasn't about to ask her to violate her husband's confidence, so he kept his voice as close to merely politely interested as he could. Unfortunately, Myacha knew *him* as well as he knew *her*, and she laughed harshly.

"Borandas has asked my opinion, and I've given it to him," she said. "In most ways, that's that, as far as I'm concerned. But... but he doesn't seem truly at ease in his own mind over this, Brayahs. I think... I think his instincts and his reason aren't in full agreement. And I think this betrothal between Thorandas and Shairnayith Axehammer worries him more than he's prepared to admit even to himself."

"I haven't spoken to him about any of this myself, yet," Brayahs said slowly. "I know he's going to want my impressions of the summer session, and I'll give them to him, of course. But he *is* Baron Halthan. When it comes down to it, the decision's his, and in fairness, I don't remember the last time I saw him make a hasty judgment when it was something this important. I may not always have agreed with his logic, or even the decision he ultimately reached, but he's a good man, your husband, Myacha. He takes his responsibilities seriously."

"I know." Myacha blinked, her amethyst eyes bright with unshed tears, and inhaled deeply. "I know. But... there's something *odd* going on, Brayahs. Something that... worries me."

"Odd?" Brayahs repeated. That wasn't a word he was accustomed to hearing from Myacha. Nor was the youthful baroness in the habit of jumping at shadows or seeing "odd" things that weren't actually there. "What do you mean, 'odd'?"

"It's just..."

Myacha stared down into her cup for several seconds. Brayahs could almost physically feel her tension across the table, although he couldn't begin to put his mental finger on its cause. It was certainly more than any simple concern over her husband's peace of mind, however; that much was obvious.

"I'm worried about Sir Dahlnar," she said finally.

"About *Dahlnar*?"

Sheer surprise at the sudden shift in direction startled the question out of Brayahs, and her eyes lifted from the inside of her cup to his face. He looked back at her for a second or two, then shook himself.

"I'm sorry. You just... surprised me." He smiled wryly. "Dahlnar Bronzehelm has to be one of the most levelheaded men I've ever known."

"I agree," she said softly. "But something's... changed, Brayahs. Last winter, even earlier this spring, he was consistently urging Borandas to be wary of Cassan. And Yeraghor, of course, but mostly of Cassan. In fact, I remember Borandas saying to me that Sir Dahlnar had told him Cassan had to be growing desperate over Tellian's growing successes, and that desperate men made dangerous allies."

"I can believe that," Brayahs said. In fact, he could almost hear Bronzehelm saying those very words, just as he'd given similarly astute advice so often in the past.

"Well, he's changed his mind," Myacha said flatly. "He's actually in favor of Thorandas' betrothal, despite how closely that's going to bind the North Riding to the South. And he completely agrees with Thorandas' concerns over Tellian's growing power base. In fact, I think he's even more concerned about it than Thorandas is, and he's entirely ready to support Cassan—tactically at least—as a means of slowing Tellian down."

Brayahs blinked in astonishment. That sort of shift in position, especially in such a brief period, was *very* unlike Dahlnar Bronzehelm. The seneschal was almost maddeningly deliberate and analytical. That was exactly what made him so valuable to Borandas. So unless he'd become aware of something *Brayahs* had seen no indication at all of from Sothōfalas, why would he have—?

"You're not suggesting Cassan's influenced him," he said, and it wasn't a question.

"No, of course not." Myacha tossed her head impatiently. "If there's one thing in the world I've *never* worried about, it's Sir Dahlnar's integrity. In fact, that's what concerns me so now. It's not as if any of this—except, possibly, Leeana's relationship with Bahzell—came at him suddenly and without warning. And, unlike Thorandas, he'd never allow his... prejudices to color his advice on such an important question. I'm not saying *Thorandas* does that on purpose; I'm only saying Sir Dahlnar would consciously make sure he *didn't* do it. And yet he's completely changed his position on cooperating with Cassan and Yeraghor."

"Well, it's always possible he's actually been inclining in that direction gradually for quite a while," Brayahs pointed out. "He's not the sort to give radically different advice without having spent the time to consider it carefully first."

"No, he isn't... even if that does seem to be exactly what he's done."

Myacha set her cup down very precisely on its saucer, folded her hands on the edge of the table, and leaned over them towards Brayahs.

"It's not just the change in his position that concerns me," she said very, very quietly. "It's that... it's that when I look at him, there's something... *wrong*." Her expression was frustrated, and she gave her shoulders an impatient shake. "It's like... like he's casting two shadows, Brayahs. I know that doesn't make any sense, and it doesn't really describe what I feel like I'm seeing, but it's the closest I can come. It's just... wrong," she repeated.

Brayahs sat very still, his own expression blank, as only a master mage's expression could be, yet a sudden, cold tingle went through him.

The magi of Norfressa, the Order of Semkirk, knew far more about the art of wizardry than anyone outside the Order probably even imagined. Among other things, the Axe Hallow Academy was the keeper of the entire library Wencit of Rūm had managed to save out of the wreck of Kontovar. No mage could use wizardry, of course. Indeed, the mage talents and wizardry were mutually exclusive, and that was one thing which had made the Axe Hallow Academy and the Council of Semkirk the logical keepers and protectors of Wencit's manuscripts and notes.

As long as the object was to keep them out of the hands of other *wizards*, at least.

Brayahs had wondered, on occasion, why Wencit had never attempted to reconstitute the White Council of Ottovar here in Norfressa. Oh, immediately after the Fall, in the face of the refugees' hatred and distrust of anything smacking of wizardry—aside from Wencit himself, perhaps—the decision against training a new generation of wizards had undoubtedly made sense. But that had been twelve hundred years ago, and Brayahs knew of his own personal knowledge that the "art" was far from extinct among the descendants of those long-ago refugees. Surely Wencit had to have at least considered the possibility of rebuilding the White Council, training wizards to support him against the threat of Kontovar and the Council of Carnadosa!

Yet he'd never made a single move in that direction. Instead, he'd devoted himself to building and training the Council of Semkirk, as if he, too, had concluded that wizardry was simply too dangerous. That if the Empire of Ottovar, with all its power and all the legacy of Ottavar the Great and Gwynytha the Wise, had been unable to prevent its abuse in Kontovar, then *no one* could. He didn't want to create a new generation of wizards; he wanted to exterminate the art of wizardry entirely, and in the magi he'd found a counterweight, possibly even the weapon which ultimately, in the fullness of time, would accomplish that extermination.

Whatever his thinking, he'd seen to it that the Council of Semkirk had all the information he could give it about wizards and wizardry, and Brayahs Daggeraxe was a wizard sniffer. He probably knew more about the art of wizardry than any other nonwizard ever born, and that was why Baroness Myacha's words had sent that chill through him.

Myacha was no mage. He was certain of that, and, for that matter, no mage would have perceived what she seemed to be describing the way that she'd just described it. But someone with the Gift, someone who with the proper training, the proper awareness, could have become a wizard herself, might well have the True Sight. And someone who had the True Sight might describe a glamour, or an enchantment, or even—if they were sensitive enough—simply the residue of an arcane working, in exactly that way.

Chapter Thirty

"It's amazing how much easier the tunnel made this," Trianal Bowmaster said, shaking his head bemusedly. He sat at a plainly made table of unvarnished planks with Bahzell, Vaijon, Prince Arsham, Yurgazh Charkson, and Tharanalalknarthas zoi'Harkanath, who'd accompanied him on the last leg of his journey from Hurgrum, while unseasonal rain pattered noisily on the roof and distant thunder grumbled somewhere to the south. Sir Yarran was absent, occupied with settling in the troops Trianal had just brought in from the West Riding... which included at least one wind rider Trianal would have much preferred to leave behind.

"The weather was miserable all the way down," he continued, "but getting troops down the Escarpment in some sort of order is a whole lot simpler this way."

"So long as you've got permission to use it, at any rate," Arsham said dryly, and Trianal chuckled.

"Works both ways, Your Highness. With all due respect, I doubt if even hradani could fight their way through the tunnel with an entire Sothōii army waiting at the other end for them," he pointed out, and it was Arsham's turn to laugh.

"And speaking of weather," Trianal said, glancing at Tharanalalknarthas, "I have to say that this"—he waved at the rough but sturdily constructed walls of the building in which they sat and the coal-fired iron stove in one corner—"is a lot more pleasant than sleeping in another wet bivouac."

"I wish we had walls and a solid roof for everyone, Milord," Tharanal replied. "We never planned on a force this large last winter, when we were allocating construction materials and crews for the expedition."

"Believe me, no apologies are necessary," Trianal assured him. "We may not have a *solid* roof for everyone, but at least we've got everyone under canvas. Trust me," he grimaced wryly, "Sothōii armsmen will take that as a major improvement over what we usually get in the field."

Laughter rumbled around the table, but Trianal had a point, Bahzell reflected. Tharanal had traveled along with Trianal for the express purpose of coordinating the supply of their suddenly larger field force, and while sheltering in tents and under tarpaulins was hardly pleasant in this sort of weather, it really was better than most Sothōii armies could have anticipated. Or hradani ones, for that matter. His father had made huge improvements in the Northern Confederation's quartermaster's corps (in fact, he'd *created* the quartermaster's corps and hired dwarvish advisors to help establish its duties and training), yet it was still decidedly on the bare-bones side. Not even Bahnak of Hurgrum could have reorganized all of his supply arrangements for an army which had suddenly more than tripled its anticipated size.

"As to that," Arsham said after a moment, "I'm in agreement with Sir Trianal, Tharanal. I am a little nervous about how long we can keep the force provisioned now that it's concentrated, though."

"*That* part shouldn't be a problem." Tharanal shrugged. "I'm not saying it won't cost a pretty penny, but most of the actual food's coming directly from the Confederation, not over the rails from the canal head. It's just a matter of getting it onto enough barges and the barges down the river, and Prince Bahnak's building even more hulls in Hurgrum. To be honest, it's likely to be a bigger problem once you break camp and begin your campaign. As long as you stay fairly close to the river, we'll be able to supply you easily enough, but we don't have the draft animals or the wagons to haul provisions any great distance overland, especially in this kind of weather."

There was no laughter in response to *that* remark, Bahzell noticed. Ghouls didn't bother with things like roads, and the Ghoul Moor had been so thoroughly soaked over the last few weeks that the wheels of even Dwarvenhame wagons would sink to their hubs in trackless mud in very short order. Transporting the necessary quantities of food and fodder for the Sothōii's horses would quickly overwhelm the limited number of pack animals they had, as well, and no army could support itself by foraging on the Ghoul Moor. Small foraging parties would be all too likely to be swarmed under by ghouls, and there wasn't all that much to forage *for*, anyway.

"Hopefully, that won't be an issue," Vaijon said, glancing across the table again at Yurgazh, who'd actually carried out most of the planning while he awaited the reinforcements' arrival. "We're not planning on getting more than a day or two's march from the river. We'll issue each man five days' rations before we head inland; with what the mule train can carry, that should give us at least eight days before food becomes a problem. Fodder's going to be more of an issue, actually, but we're late enough into the summer that we can graze the horses for at least some of what we're going to need."

"As to that," Bahzell rumbled with a sort of wry resignation, "it's in my mind as how feeding all our people's likely the least of our worries."

"Oh?" Arsham cocked his ears at him.

Theoretically, the Bloody Sword prince had come down by barge solely to attend this conference. He was supposed to be returning to Hurgrum the next day, although Bahzell entertained a few doubts about just how rigorously Arsham intended to hew to his official schedule. The same thing was true of another prince the Horse Stealer could think of, for that matter.

"Is that simply a prediction based on experience, or do you have a specific reason for thinking that?" Arsham continued. "The sort of specific reason that, oh, a champion of Tomanāk might have, for instance?"

"I'll not be saying as how it's anywhere near to 'specific' as I might be wishing," Bahzell replied. "Mind, we've every one of us more experience than we'd like as to how what can go wrong does, yet it's something nasty Walsharno and I have been smelling this last two weeks."

"And me," Vaijon put in grimly. Bahzell cocked an ear at him, and the younger man shrugged. "It's stronger down here on the Ghoul Moor, Bahzell, but I've been feeling it all the way from Hurgrum. I don't know what it is, but I do know we're not going to like it very much when we meet it."

"And this is supposed to be a surprise?" Trianal asked, looking back and forth between the two champions with a raised eyebrow.

In that moment, despite the difference in their coloration and ages, he looked very like his uncle, Bahzell thought.

"I'm sure there have been other summers as rainy as this one," Trianal continued dryly. "The only problem is that no one I've been able to ask about it can remember when those other summers might have been. That includes your father and anyone else in Hurgrum, Bahzell, so some of those memories go back the better part of two centuries." He snorted. "Anyone—or anything—who can arrange to dump this much rain on our heads is pretty likely to come under the heading of 'something nasty,' don't you think?"

"Aye, you've a point there," Bahzell acknowledged.

"What worries me more," Yurgazh said frankly, "is why somebody or something that can actually control the weather has waited this long to do anything except rain on us." The Bloody Sword general shook his head, ears half-flattened. "I guess it's possible rain is *all* it can produce, but I'm not very inclined to base our planning on that. And if it can do more than rain, why wait until we've reinforced before it starts doing it? Why not take us earlier, when we had less than a third this much strength?"

"I'd like to think it was because the presence of two champions of Tomanāk gave it pause," Vaijon said frankly, grinning tightly at Bahzell. "And I don't know *what* whoever or whatever it is might be capable of, Yurgazh, but I take your point. You're wondering if it's just been waiting until we offered it a bigger, juicier mouthful, aren't you?"

"Aye," Yurgazh said, and shrugged. "Mind you, I know it sounds a bit foolish, given that we're talking about ghouls, but this entire campaign's been . . . wrong for an expedition against ghouls." His expression was grim. "I'm no champion, and the gods know I'm no wizard, but I've got a hradani's nose, and it smells the stink of wizardry."

Eyes met around the table. All of them—including Trianal, now—knew what dark wizardry had done to the hradani in Kontovar during the Fall. Knew how the Council of Carnadosa had enslaved every hradani who fell into its grasp. Knew how the Carnadosans had driven them against the forces of the Empire of Ottovar, using them as unwilling, ravening sword fodder to overwhelm the last defenders of the White Council . . . and leaving them with the curse of the Rage.

"I'm thinking you've the right of that, Yurgazh," Bahzell said after a moment. "But wizardry's not the only stink *my* nose is after smelling. There's more—and worse, I'm thinking—behind that stink."

"Wonderful!" Trianal shook his head. "I don't suppose you've managed to get hold of Wencit to ask *him* about it, have you?"

"Now that I haven't," Bahzell replied. "Mind, he's not in easy fellow for a letter to be catching up with. And he's a way of coming and going as suits himself best, but I'll not deny it's easier I'd be in my own mind if he and those eyes of his were to be walking in that door"—he twitched his head in the direction of the blockhouse's door—"this very moment."

"Not even Wencit of Rūm can be everywhere," Vaijon pointed out. "I'm not saying I wouldn't be just as happy to see him as you would, Bahzell, but he's usually got enough on his plate to keep at least a dozen white wizards busy, and there's only one of him. Besides, unless I'm mistaken, you and Walsharno and I are the champions around here, aren't we?"

"That we are." Bahzell nodded with a slow smile. "And while I'd not want any of our lads to be getting their heads swelled, it's not so very bad a little army we have here. Betwixt Trianal's cavalry, Yurgazh's infantry, and the Order, I'm thinking whatever might be minded to make us that 'juicier mouthful' of yours is like to find itself just a bit of a bellyache before all's said and done."

"Good," Trianal said and looked at Yurgazh and Prince Arsham. "I'd like to give my lot a day or two to rest the horses before we move out. The day after tomorrow, you think?"

"Yes," Yurgazh said without even glancing at Arsham, and the Navahkan prince smiled slightly. His general had been hinting—loudly—that a prince with no heir of his own body had no business wandering about the Ghoul Moor, especially under circumstances like this. He had a point, too, and Arsham knew it. Nor was the prince in question about to overrule his own hand-picked general's orders or dispositions. In fact, he fully intended to climb into a barge headed back up the Hangnysti sometime soon. Like within the next two or three days.

Probably.

"Tell me, Sir Trianal," he asked, his smile growing broader as he looked across the table at the young Sothōii, "just how exactly did Prince Yurokhas happen to accompany you all the way from Hurgrum? I thought you'd managed to convince him to go home."

"I thought *Prince Bahnak* had managed to convince him," Trianal said rather sourly. "Tomanāk knows the King's going to be just a bit upset if his brother manages to get himself killed in what's essentially a freelance operation against ghouls." He shook his head. "I don't know that King Markhos actually *ordered* him to join the rest of the Chergor hunting party, but I'm pretty sure it was a most emphatic suggestion. Of course," his expression turned even more sour, "you can see how well that seems to have worked, Your Highness."

"And an odd thing it is that you're here to be seeing it," Bahzell remarked, gazing at Arsham, "as it's in my mind as how my Da most likely said something along those selfsame lines to another prince I might be mentioning."

"I don't have the least idea what you're talking about, Prince Bahzell."

Arsham didn't waste any particular effort trying to convince his audience he wasn't lying, but he did do it with a certain flair, Bahzell conceded. The Horse Stealer opened his mouth, but Arsham held up his right hand and shook his head.

"I promise I'll go home the instant you manage to convince Yurokhas to do the same thing." His eyes glinted with challenge, and Bahzell felt his own lips twitch on the edge of an unwilling smile. Then Arsham's expression turned more sober. "I know you and Yurgazh are both right, Bahzell. The last thing any of us need is for me to get myself killed doing something even hradani would consider stupid. Well, I don't intend to do anything of the sort, but I do want to see what it is we're up against with my own eyes. It's not that I don't have complete faith in Yurgazh," he rested his left hand lightly on his general's shoulder, "and I don't have any intention of trying to interfere in his management of the army or of any battles. But I think you and he and Vaijon are right that something a damn sight worse than ghouls is roaming around down here, and there's no way of knowing it will *stay* here. If it moves north, up the river, to hit the Confederation, I want the best idea I can get of what it really is."

"I might be pointing out that before ever it's able to move north, up the river, it's the lot of us here to deal with, first," Bahzell said mildly. "And if it happened as how I was so underhanded as to be using logic, I might be pointing out that if it should happen it *can* deal with us first, then it might just be any ideas you might have wouldn't be doing so very much good—seeing as how you'd most likely be dead and all, I mean."

"Then it's probably just as well a champion of Tomanāk wouldn't stoop to such low tactics," Arsham replied, and Bahzell shook his head.

He'd always rather liked Arsham, even when he'd been a political hostage in Navahk, although he'd never really gotten to know him before Churnazh's defeat. And he'd understood why Arsham had to have mixed feelings, at the very least, where his own family was concerned. Yet any lingering resentment the Navahkan prince might feel at having been defeated by Hurgrum had vanished—for the moment, at least—at the prospect of action, and Bahzell found himself liking the other man even more because of it. Which probably said something he'd rather not think about too deeply where his own mental processes were concerned, since both of them knew Arsham was actually being an idiot.

But it was a very *hradani* sort of an idiot, Bahzell reflected.

"You know," Trianal said thoughtfully, "since it's obvious Prince Arsham has no intention of being reasonable about this, it may not be an entirely bad thing. From my perspective, I mean."

"And would you be so very kind as to explain that?" Bahzell cocked his ears at the young Sothōii. "Seeing as how *I've* yet to see a single good thing about the entire notion, and all, I mean."

"Well, if he's serious about staying out of the fighting and just observing," Trianal bent a moderately ferocious glare on Arsham, "he may be able to sit on Prince Yurokhas at the same time." Trianal looked at Vaijon. "I'm thinking that *if* they stay, they both promise to stay with the Order and out from underfoot, and Prince Arsham sets the example for Yurokhas by doing exactly that."

"And exactly how was it that you intended to make either one of us promise you anything of the sort?" Arsham inquired, cocking his head. "I ask only in the spirit of honest curiosity, you understand."

"Actually, it's fairly simple." Trianal smiled, looking even more like his uncle. "Unless you both do promise, we'll just sit here in camp letting the barges bring food down to us for however long it takes. I'm sure Yurgazh and Sir Yarran could always find the extra training time useful. Of course, that means you'd have to explain to Prince Bahnak and Prince Yurokhas would have to explain to King Markhos exactly why it was that a force this size stood idle for the remainder of the campaigning season. I'm fairly certain neither of them would want *my* ears over it."

✧ ✧ ✧

Darnas Warshoe muttered unhappily to himself as he carted another bale of fodder ashore.

Hradani were never going to be anything but a scourge to be eradicated—in that much, Warshoe was in complete agreement with his baron—but he had to admit the supply arrangements for this expedition were better than anything he'd ever seen back in the days when he'd been an officer in the Royal Army. Of course, most of that was probably thanks to the damned dwarves who were propping up Bahnak and the rest of his bloodthirsty scum, yet there was no point pretending it wasn't so. And Warshoe had never minded getting his hands dirty (in more ways than one) when it came to getting the job done. For that matter, his current employment as little more than hired labor was an admirable cover for his actual reason for being here. And little though he might care for unloading cargo in the rain, at least Tharanalalknarthas had seen to it that his work crews had snug, covered quarters aboard the barges.

No, the reason for his current unhappiness had nothing to do with his cover or its demands. It was more . . . fundamental than that.

He swung the bale down from his shoulder and into the lean-to riverside warehouse where it would be out of the wet, and stood for a moment under the same roof, surrounded by the scents of rain, riverwater, and dry hay as he massaged the small of his back and gazed out into the gauzy veils of mist while he thought.

It had sounded forthright enough when Baron Cassan described his mission to him. Not without risk, but risk was part of the job, as far as Warshoe was concerned. And a part of him was looking forward to the opportunity to correct his failure seven years ago when Sir Trianal Bowmaster had been so disobliging as to move at just the very wrong instant. Darnas Warshoe didn't miss very many arbalest shots, and he'd always taken that failure a bit personally. Assassinating Prince Yurokhas didn't bother him, either. His loyalty to the Sothōii crown had disappeared along with his commission, and if Baron Cassan wanted the Prince dead, that was reason enough for Warshoe. Nor had he objected to the Baron's insistence that the two of them had to die in the course of an open battle with the ghouls. Battlefields provided admirable cover for an assassin plying his trade, after all.

But there was something in the air, something Baron Cassan hadn't warned him about. He didn't know what it was, yet the sensitive cat whiskers of a successful assassin quivered incessantly.

It was just his nerves, he told himself. Only a perfectly understandable anxiety over the scale of this assignment. That was all it was.

He told himself that very firmly...and he never believed it at all.

✧ ✧ ✧

"It's going well," Malahk Sahrdohr said with undisguised satisfaction.

With the court's removal from Sothōfalas, Sahrdohr was able to move about the city more freely. Unlike the Prime Councilor, the Chancellor of the Exchequer had remained in the capital where he could stay in touch with the manifold details of his responsibilities. Sahrdohr had responsibilities enough of his own in his disguise as one of Whalandys Shaftmaster's senior clerks, but even the Exchequer's tempo had dropped with the King's departure. "Mahrahk Firearrow" had much more free time than he'd had earlier in the year, and the exodus of everyone who'd possibly been able to get out of Sothōfalas had reduced the sheer congestion enough to make it far easier for him to drop out of sight without some busybody's noticing. At the moment, he and Master Varnaythus sat once again in Varnaythus' warded working chamber, watching the senior wizard's gramerhain.

"It *appears* to be going well," Varnaythus corrected him, but even his tone was more judicious than disagreeing, the voice of a conscientious man refusing to succumb to overconfidence.

"I think it's more than just appearances," Sahrdohr said, respectfully but firmly, and raised his left hand, ticking off points on its fingers with his right index finger as he made them.

"Arthnar's men are on their way—they've already passed through Nachfalas without anyone noticing and linked up with those horses someone 'stole' from Cassan's herds," he said, and Varnaythus nodded.

The Fire Oar's assassins weren't the very best quality armsmen he'd ever seen, but they were tough, individually competent, and about as unscrupulous as they came. Even better, Arthnar had managed to retain an entire mercenary company of Spearmen who'd been too eager for work to worry much over what their new employer wanted them to do. That company provided better than two-thirds of his total manpower, under its own officers, which gave it a much greater degree of cohesion and experience working as a unit than Varnaythus had allowed himself to hope for when he'd hatched the original plan. They'd passed through Nachfalas in groups of no more than a half dozen, small enough not to draw attention to themselves...especially when Baron Cassan had taken some pains to see to it that they wouldn't. Now they'd reassembled with their "stolen" mounts and were on their way to Chergor, and Arthnar's hiring agents had successfully convinced them they'd been hired by the Purple Lords, exactly as planned.

"Second," Sahrdohr ticked off his next point, "Bahzell, Walsharno, Vaijon, Trianal, and Yurokhas are all on the Ghoul Moor where Anshakar and the others can get at them. And just as an added attraction, Prince Arsham's with them, as well." The younger wizard smiled coldly. "Killing him's likely to destabilize the succession in Navahk, and that can't help the stability of this Northern Confederation of Bahnak's. *And*, if we're lucky, we might even get Tharanalalknarthas, too, which would be a much heavier blow to Kilthan than he'd want to admit to anyone."

Varnaythus nodded again. Anshakar and his two companions were already cautiously moving their massed army of ghouls into position. Even the three of them found controlling that many ghouls difficult, but they were managing the task quite nicely, between their own more-than-natural powers and the sheer terror they'd instilled in their new worshippers.

"Third, Borandas has clearly decided to support Cassan."

"That might be putting it a bit too strongly," Varnaythus pointed out. Sahrdohr cocked an eyebrow at him, and the older wizard shrugged. "I admit he's decided to support Thorandas' marriage to Shairnayith, and that's a major plus. But we still can't be positive which way he's going to jump when Cassan makes his move. Thorandas and Bronzehelm are both primed to push him into jumping Cassan's way, but even the two of them together may not be able to overcome his common sense at the critical moment, and I'd be happier if we could keep a closer eye on Halthan." He grimaced. "I'm not happy having Brayahs back home to muck things up, especially when I can't be certain he won't pick up on our scrying spells."

"Granted." Sahrdohr nodded. "But the mere fact that Borandas has agreed to the betrothal ties him to Cassan in everyone else's eyes, and all the indications are that Tellian's partisans are already taking that into their calculations. If the entire Kingdom looks like going up in flames, who's going to believe his shift wasn't orchestrated ahead of time as part of whatever Cassan's up to, however hard he denies it?" the younger wizard shook his head. "No, if Arthnar's men pull this off, Borandas isn't going to have much choice but to back his son's new father-in-law, especially if Tellian and his faction are saddled with responsibility for the King's assassination. Brayahs would have a hard time undoing *that* even if he figured out that you've been meddling with Bronzehelm's mind."

He paused, eyebrow still arched, until Varnaythus nodded back to him. The older wizard remained uneasy over the possibility that Brayahs might realize someone was using wizardry to manipulate the Great Council's members. If he did come to that conclusion, the logical thing for him to do, as one of the King's trusted mage investigators, would be to warn Markhos, and the fact that he was a wind walker made him just the man to do it. The last thing they needed was for the King and his personal guard to take additional precautions or even withdraw entirely from Chergor to the safety of Balthar. Fortunately, Varnaythus had learned and deduced enough about mage talents to construct a trap spell barrier around Chergor which he was reasonably confident would kill even a wind walker if he tried to cross it. *Un*fortunately, he was *only* reasonably confident, since there'd never been any opportunity to test the underlying theory upon which it was based.

"Fourth," Sahrdohr went on after a moment, continuing his count, "Tellian is going to be at Chergor when Arthnar's men attack after all." He smiled unpleasantly. "I really thought he'd spend longer at home with his wife after being away so much of the summer. It's a pity that attentiveness to duty of his isn't going to be better rewarded."

He contemplated the four extended fingers of his left hand for a moment longer, then leaned back in his comfortable chair and raised both hands, palm uppermost.

"I'll admit it's unlikely we're going to run the board and succeed *everywhere*," he said, "but we really only have to succeed partially to accomplish what They sent us here to do. And there's still all that marvelous potential where the Purple Lords are concerned, after Kilthan and his canal cut off their entire economy at the knees!" He shook his head. "Even granting all the things that can still go wrong, the odds are heavily on our side, Varnaythus."

"And if someone on the other side knows what They're doing—or what They have *us* doing, at any rate?" Varnaythus challenged.

"If Tomanāk or any of the others realized what was happening, They'd have already taken steps to stop us," Sahrdohr said confidently. "Because, frankly, by this point, I don't see anything They *could* do to prevent our basic strategy from biting Them right on the arse. There just isn't enough time for anyone on the other side to adjust their positions enough to stop us before we actually hit them."

"Probably not," Varnaythus conceded. "On the other hand, I suspect Jerghar, Paratha, and Dahlaha thought that right up to the last minute the *last* time, too. I know we don't have people running off in all directions at once the way *those* three managed, but that doesn't mean it can't still come apart on us."

"No," Sahrdohr agreed. "But in a worst-case situation, there's still the karsalhain." He shrugged. "Coming out into the open with the art may be a last resort, but at least we can still *guarantee* that Markhos, Tellian, and everyone else in Chergor dies, whatever else happens. It won't be as neat, and it won't be as precisely targeted as we wanted, but it may actually work out even better, especially if Borandas and the wind riders decide Cassan was behind it. They won't have any choice but to move against him if they think he's been hobnobbing with Carnadosans, Varnaythus, and *Yeraghor* won't have any choice but to *back* him, because they've been joined at the hip for so long no one would believe he hadn't known exactly what Cassan was up to all along. That gives us a brand-new Time of Troubles, and there's no telling how many fish we could land out of waters *that* troubled!"

Varnaythus was forced to nod again, although he dearly hoped to avoid using the karsalhain. Someone like Wencit of Rūm was entirely too likely to be able to track that sort of working back to its caster. It would probably take him quite a while, but one thing wild wizards had plenty of was time, and if he did succeed, the result could be decidedly fatal for the caster in question.

At least you haven't done a single thing to attract Wencit's attention back to the Wind Plain yet, he reminded himself. *And Sahrdohr's right; the karsalhain is* definitely *a "last resort"... and one it doesn't look like we're going to need. Not when not a single one of them so much as suspects what's coming at them.*

✧ ✧ ✧

"Shahana?"

Shahana Lillinarafressa sat up in bed and rubbed her eyes. It was pitch black outside the windows of her austerely appointed sleeping chamber in the Quaysar Temple, but the chamber itself was filled with gentle, silvery illumination. There might not be any moon in the heavens over Quaysar, but there was one—or at least the light of one—in Shahana's bedroom, flowing from the dark-haired, dark-eyed woman standing in her doorway. The Quaysar Voice was slender and quite tall, and she kept herself physically fit, yet she was also in her forties, and her hair was just touched with the first strands of frost.

"Yes?" Shahana rubbed her eyes again, grateful that the Voice had decided to call the Mother's light rather than carry a lit lamp with her. Being awakened in the middle of the night was bad enough without having bright light blasting into her darkness-accustomed eyes.

"I'm sorry to disturb you." The Voice smiled crookedly as if she'd been able to read Shahana's thoughts. Which, the arm conceded, she might very well have managed to do. Some of the Voices *could* read thoughts, after all.

"I assume you wouldn't have if it hadn't been necessary," Shahana said.

"No, I wouldn't," the Voice agreed. "You have to leave for Kalatha. Now, I'm afraid."

"Now?" Shahana repeated. "You mean as in *right* now, in the middle of the night?" Her tone made it clear she wasn't complaining, merely making certain she'd understood correctly, and the Voice nodded. "May I ask *why* I'm leaving for Kalatha?"

"You can ask, but I can't tell you," the Voice said wryly, and this time the arm's eyebrows rose in surprise. "I would if I knew," the Voice continued, "but I'm afraid She didn't tell me, either." She shrugged. "I got the impression it has something to do with young Leeana and that whole business about her marrying Bahzell, but it was *only* an impression, Shahana. I wouldn't depend too heavily on it, if I were you."

"It's not like Her to be quite that vague," Shahana said, and the Voice snorted.

"I've been listening to Her for over twelve years now, Shahana, and I've discovered She's *never* vague. When she seems to've been, it usually turns out we simply didn't know enough about what was going on—then—to realize She was actually being quite specific. Unfortunately, in this case, I don't have a clue what She has in mind."

"Well," Shahana said philosophically, climbing out of bed and reaching for her clothing, "I suppose we'll just have to find out, won't we?"

Chapter Thirty-One

"Good afternoon, Master Brayahs," the armsman in the crimson and silver of House Daggeraxe said.

"Good afternoon, Sergeant. I'd like to see Baron Borandas, please."

The sergeant outside the closed door considered Brayahs Daggeraxe thoughtfully. There'd been a time when Brayahs had been one of Borandas' most trusted advisers, and the sergeant knew he was still extremely close to the baron and his baroness. But he also knew Brayahs had been chosen as one of the King's magi, with his oath given to the Crown first and Halthar second, and that imposed certain constraints.

"Your pardon, Master Brayahs," the sergeant said, "but the Baron is conferring with Sir Dahlnar. Perhaps it would be better if you came back later."

"I realize he's meeting with Sir Dahlnar," Brayahs replied, returning his regard steadily. "In fact, I really need to speak to both of them. Please announce me and ask if they can see me now."

The sergeant stood thinking for another moment, then made his decision. Baron Borandas valued judgment in his armsmen, and he expected his senior noncoms to use that judgment.

"Wait here, please," he said. He turned, knocked once on the closed door, and then opened it and stepped through, leaving Brayahs with the rest of his three-man detachment in the hallway.

He was gone for only a few seconds before the door opened once again.

"The Baron says he'll be most pleased to see you, Master Brayahs," the sergeant said with a respectful bow.

"Thank you, Sergeant."

Brayahs returned the bow and stepped past the armsman into Borandas Daggeraxe's personal office. It was on the fourth floor of the spire-like tower from which Star Tower Castle took its name, and its opened windows looked out over the castle's courtyard and the green fields beyond. A cool breeze blew through them, setting the curtains dancing in a flicker of sunlight, and Borandas stood behind his desk, holding out his right hand to his cousin with a broad smile.

"Brayahs!" he clasped forearms with the mage, squeezing firmly. "I'm sorry I missed you yesterday."

"I know you've been busy conferring with Thorandas and Sir Dahlnar," Brayahs replied as he returned the clasp. "And, to be honest, I had some thinking of my own to do."

"Oh?" Borandas released his arm and stepped back, waving towards one of the unoccupied chairs in front of his desk. Sir Dahlnar nodded to Brayahs with a friendly smile, offering his own hand, and Brayahs reached out to take it. He clasped Bronzehelm's forearm firmly, looking deep into the other man's eyes, and his nostrils flared. He held Sir Dahlnar's arm for an extra moment or two, then released it and sank into his own chair.

"And what were you thinking about?" Borandas inquired. He leaned back in his own chair, clasping his hands behind his head, and regarded his cousin a bit quizzically. "I don't seem to remember you taking very long to think things over when you were younger, Brayahs!"

"Life was simpler when I was a runny-nosed brat pestering my grownup cousin," Brayahs replied. "When you have so many fewer thoughts in your head, it doesn't take as long to sort through them, you know."

"I've heard that," Borandas agreed, but his eyes also narrowed slightly, as if he'd caught a trace of something unexpected in his cousin's expression or manner, and he lowered his hands, sitting upright once more. "And now that you've sorted through the ones currently rattling around in your head, what conclusions have you reached?"

"I've reached the conclusion that I have to take advantage of our kinship," Brayahs said in a tone which had grown suddenly far more somber.

"Meaning what?" Borandas' expression turned warier, and Brayahs drew a deep breath.

"Borandas, I've been the King's man for three years now. In all that time, I've never approached you *as* the King's man or in any way questioned any of the policies you've chosen to pursue here in the North Riding. And I have no instructions from His Majesty to do that now. Coming here this morning is my own decision, but I ask you as my kinsman and my Baron to hear me."

Borandas looked at him silently, and the sounds of birds from beyond the open windows were clear and distinct in the stillness. Seconds trickled away, but then, finally, he nodded.

"Speak." His voice was cooler, more formal, but he sat regarding his cousin levelly, and Brayahs glanced at Bronzehelm for just a moment. Then he squared his shoulders and faced the baron.

"You know I'm a mage. In fact, you know what my mage talents are." He paused, and Borandas nodded again, slowly, his eyes suddenly very intent. "Then you'll understand I know what I'm talking about when I tell you wizardry has been at work here in Halthan," Brayahs said softly.

"*What?*" Borandas snapped fully upright in his chair, leaning forward, staring at him. Bronzehelm looked at him, as well, equally shocked, and Brayahs nodded.

"How?" the baron demanded. "Where?"

"I can't say exactly how, or what the spell may have been," the mage replied. "You know the *limitations* of my talents, as well. But I can tell you where it was cast."

"Then tell me!" Borandas more than half-snapped, and Brayahs looked at him sadly.

"There," he said... and pointed at Sir Dahlnar Bronzehelm.

✧ ✧ ✧

"Are you *certain* about this, Brayahs?"

Borandas Daggeraxe's face was twenty years older than it had been a half hour earlier, his eyes haunted, and Brayahs nodded unhappily.

"I'm afraid I am, and I wish I weren't. But not as much as I wish I knew what the spell was supposed to do and how in Semkirk's name anyone got into a position to cast it in the first place." Brayahs' jaw clenched. "And not as much as I wish that whoever the bastard is, he'd picked someone besides Dahlnar to cast it on!"

Myacha sat beside her husband, holding his left hand, her amethyst eyes huge and dark. Despite everything, she'd hoped desperately that the suspicion she'd awakened in Brayahs' mind had been groundless.

"I wish that, too," the baron said now, his voice grim and harsh. He shook his head. "It's not Dahlnar's fault. I know that as well as the gods themselves do! But how can I ever trust him again now that he's been . . . tampered with?"

"We're not *positive* he has been," Brayahs said, remembering the look in Bronzehelm's eyes as he'd been gently but firmly escorted from Borandas' office by no less than five Halthan armsmen. The seneschal's shock had been only too evident, and there'd been a sort of ineffable horror *under* the shock. Yet there'd been no resistance. In fact, he'd been the first to suggest that Borandas had no choice but to confine him to his own quarters until they could determine what had been done to him . . . and by whom.

"Come now!" Borandas said even more harshly. "You detected the stench of wizardry both on him and in his office!"

"But what I smelled hadn't been cast directly upon him," Brayahs pointed out. "He was *present* when it was worked, and he obviously doesn't remember it, but I'm detecting no indication *he's* been arcanely altered. And you saw his eyes as well as I did, Borandas. He's more horrified by the possibility that he's been forced to betray your confidence than *you* could ever be."

"Of course he is!" Borandas scowled. "He's not just my seneschal—he's my *friend*, and he would never have betrayed me in any way if the choice had been his! Do you think I don't realize that?!"

"No, I'm sure you do," Brayahs replied. "And I think it's evident he *has* been influenced—unknowingly and against his will—whether it was done arcanely or not. There are many ways that could have been done by someone who'd managed to gain access to him and worked his way into his confidence, and not all of them require wizardry. If it was done without using sorcery, I think a good mind-healer could almost certainly find and repair the damage, now that he knows there's something there to look for. And if it *was* done using sorcery, then I think once the Council of Semkirk gets word to Wencit, he'll be able to undo whatever it was." He smiled sadly at his cousin. "Dahlnar's too good a man for us to allow this—whatever 'this' *is*—to take him away from you forever, Borandas. I promise we'll do everything we can to give him back to you and to himself."

The baron continued to stare searchingly into Brayahs' face for a dozen more heartbeats, and then he slowly relaxed—a little—and sucked in a deep, deep breath.

"Thank you," he said quietly, and turned his head to smile at his wife when Myacha squeezed his hand in both of hers.

"You're welcome," Brayahs said, "but we still have to decide what to do about this."

"'We'?" Borandas repeated, arching one eyebrow, and Brayahs shrugged.

"*You* have to decide what to do here in Halthan, and what the North Riding as a whole is going to do about it, Milord," he said much more formally. "As the King's man, I already know what *I* have to do."

Borandas grimaced, but he also nodded, and turned back to Myacha.

"I should've listened to you, love," he said, and his expression tightened once more. "And now I have to decide how far I can trust Thorandas, as well."

His voice hardened with the last sentence, and Myacha's eyes went dark with distress.

"You don't know that whatever's happened has anything at all to do with Thorandas," she said quickly.

"No?" He looked into those eyes for several seconds, then shrugged. "You're right, I don't *know* anything of the sort, but given how radically Dahlnar's advice changed—and how strongly he supported Thorandas' positions after it *did* change—I have no choice but to consider the possibility that Thorandas was the one behind it, now do I?"

She stared back at him, unshed tears gleaming. Then one of those tears broke loose, trickling down her cheek, and she shook her head.

"For what it's worth, I agree you have to consider the possibility, Milord," Brayahs said with that same formality. "At the same time, I would respectfully point out to you that *Thorandas'* positions haven't changed anywhere near so radically as Dahlnar's, and I've seldom met a man more aware of the dangers of wizardry than your son." He shook his head. "I don't see any more reason for his position on *that* to have changed than for it to have changed on anything else."

"If not him, then who?" Borandas demanded bitterly.

"I have my own candidate in mind," Brayahs replied in a grim voice. "The problem is that I can't be sure how much my own prejudices are shaping my suspicions at this point."

"You're thinking about Cassan." Borandas' voice was even grimmer than his cousin's, and the mage nodded.

"The gods know he's demonstrated there are very few things he'd be prepared to stop short of, Milord, and he has to have been growing steadily more desperate. If Tellian gains the Crown's full-blooded support for his present policies—and everything I've seen and heard in Sothōfalas suggests he will, if he hasn't already—any chance Cassan might ever have had of regaining the ground he's lost will be gone forever. I have no idea what that's likely to do to a man like him, but I think it's certainly possible he'd be willing to resort even to wizardry as a means of getting what he wants."

"And Dahlnar's convincing me to support Thorandas' betrothal to his daughter would *be* what he wants, wouldn't it?"

"It would certainly be a long step in that direction, at any rate," Brayahs agreed. "But there are those who oppose Tellian's plans for reasons that have nothing to do with *Cassan's* ambitions, and I've always thought Thorandas was one of them. So I think it's entirely possible—and far more probable—that he's simply taken advantage of Thorandas' existing opposition to Tellian. Your son loves you, Borandas," he said much more gently. "He always has, and I've seen nothing to suggest that's changed in any way. It's far more likely he's being used without even being aware of it than that he would not only betray your trust but resort to the sort of dark sorcery that tampers with another man's mind."

"He's right, Borandas," Myacha said softly. "You *know* he's right."

"I know I *want* him to be right," the baron whispered. "And that's the problem. I want him to be right so desperately that I dare not assume he *is*. Not until the truth's *proven* one way or the other. And how will Thorandas feel when he realizes I've considered even the possibility that he might have committed treason against me? And against the *Crown*, if he truly has resorted to wizardry?"

"He'll realize you had no choice, Milord," Brayahs told him.

"I pray you're right," Borandas said.

"I believe I am. And, with your permission," the mage stood, "I need to be on my way. His Majesty has to be informed that someone's using sorcery in an effort to manipulate the Kingdom's great nobles."

"What will—?"

Borandas broke off, unable to complete the question, and Brayahs smiled at him a bit sadly.

"What will I tell him, Milord?" He moved his right hand in a tossing away gesture. "I'll tell him I've detected the residue of sorcery on your seneschal and adviser, that Sir Dahlnar's advice to you has changed dramatically over the last month or two, and how that advice has shifted. From that point, the decision of how to proceed will be his, but if he asks me, I'll advise the dispatch of a team of mage investigators to Halthan to determine how far all of this might extend. My own talents don't include truth-reading, but at least two of his Crown magi do have that talent. If *he* sends them here to investigate and they interview Thorandas, they'll know the truth about any involvement of his in this affair. Personally, I think they'll find he knew nothing about it—that he'll be as horrified and infuriated by it as you and Dahlnar. And"—he looked into his cousin's eyes—"the questions will be posed by the Crown, and by the magi, Milord... not by his father."

Borandas looked back at him for a moment, then blinked suspiciously shining eyes and nodded choppily.

"Thank you." His voice was a bit hoarse, and he cleared his throat hard. "Thank you," he repeated, and managed a smile. "And on that note, I know you must be going. May the gods go with you."

✧ ✧ ✧

Fifteen minutes later, Brayahs stood atop the Star Tower, looking down on the courtyard so far below and remembering that final afternoon on Sothōkarnas' battlements.

He believed every word he said to his cousin, yet he also knew that, like Borandas, he desperately *wanted* Thorandas to be innocent of treason. And if he wasn't, if he paid a traitor's price, then Brayahs would never be able to forget *he* was the one who'd uncovered that treason and led to his cousin's death.

No, if he is *a traitor, that was* his *decision, not yours*, the mage told himself. *And whatever comes of this, none of it can change* your *duty. So it's time you stopped worrying about things you can't change and got on with doing what you know you have to.*

He shook himself and inhaled deeply.

Fortunately, he knew exactly where Baron Tellian's hunting lodge at Chergor was, and he'd been there several times before. It was always easier to wind walk to a known *place* than to an individual who might be almost anywhere, and it was easier still if the wind walker had been to that place before, for that gave him an anchor that let him make the journey in a single stride rather than a lengthy series of shorter stages.

Tellian's lodge had been built in the Forest of Chergor, backed up on the hills in the angle where the upper Ice Sister Lakes drained into the Spear, by his grandfather, who'd wanted a place to hide from what he'd considered the oppressive crowding of Balthar... which had been little more than two-thirds the size of the present city. As part of his escape from civilization (or what had passed for it atop the Wind Plain sixty years ago), he'd opted for a consciously rustic building plan that was deliberately designed to accommodate a minimum of servants during his visits there. Of course, "minimum" was an elastic term, and no Sothōii noble would expect it to apply to stable space, so the lodge consisted of a large, ornamental brick wall around an open courtyard, stables spacious enough to accommodate at least fifty horses, a large chalet-style main building for himself and his guests, and a second, much simpler chalet with room enough for forty or fifty armsmen and retainers. The buildings inside the courtyard were all built of wood which had been cut right on the site, but he'd employed a small army of carvers and woodworkers to sculpt the eaves and overhangs into fantastic, whimsical shapes. An only slightly smaller army of glaziers had been brought in to provide his lady baronness with stained glass windows for her attic solarium in the main lodge, and the veranda along its front wall was large enough to provide picnic space for half a troop of cavalry.

The protected reserve of forest land around the lodge held game in plenty, and it was about as quiet an isolated a spot as a monarch seeking a patch of calm after a tempestuous Council session could have asked for. That was good; it would give the King and his closest advisors time to think carefully about Brayahs' news without the inevitable rumors and panicky speculation which would have flown about Sothōfalas within hours of his arrival. And it was also the sort of place which left an impression on those who visited it. That was always a good thing for a wind walker, and he settled into the proper trance, reaching out to that anchor while the winds of his talent rose about him.

There. Talent, memory, and focus snapped into place, becoming one, and he stepped into the winds no one else could even perceive. They whirled him away like a spray of autumn leaves, sweeping him into the space between worlds. He'd never been able to explain that space to anyone other than another wind walker. It was shot with the roar of his personal wind, sharp-tasting like the aftermath of a lightning bolt, crackling and alive with energy that seemed to seethe and dance on his skin in cascades of sparks. It was—

Something was wrong!

The winds faltered, then shifted, their steady roar turning suddenly into an insane howl. The energy dancing on his skin changed in a heartbeat from a crackling, comforting cocoon into a furnace, fanned by those berserk winds, hissing and popping as it consumed him. Agony crashed through him—agony such as he'd never felt, the like of which no wind walker had ever described—and he thought he screamed, although no mage had ever been able to decide if a merely human voice could even function in a place like this, and that hideous shriek of the winds would have drowned it anyway.

A trap.

Somehow, the thought fought its way through the red tides of anguish, forcing itself upon him. He had no idea how it could have been done. Indeed, everything he'd ever learned about his own talent told him it *couldn't* be done. Yet even in his torment, he knew, but what could he—?

He reached out. Somehow, without even knowing what he was doing, Brayahs Daggeraxe drew upon what had made him a mage so many years before. He felt himself fraying, dissolving, coming apart in the maw of that furnace fury, and somehow he held on. He clung to what he was, to the duty which made him *who* he was, and fastened his invisible hands desperately upon the winds. They ripped at his palms—*his* winds no longer, but demons, lashing him with even more terrible torrents of pain—yet he clenched his teeth, refusing to let go, and then, in a way he would never be able to describe even to himself, he wrenched sideways.

He lost his focus. That had never happened. He'd never imagined it *could* happen, and panic choked him, more terrible even than the pain, as he felt himself spinning sideways, lurching into a darkness he'd never seen before. It was lashed with lightning—a bottomless night filled with the crash of thunder, his winds a tempest, howling like some ravening beast—and he screamed again as he felt that searing lightning ripping away everything he'd ever known or been.

Blackness claimed him.

Chapter Thirty-Two

Boots moved steadily and sweetly, cantering across the parched, golden grass of late summer while Gayrfressa paced him with the peculiar, ground-eating gait of her kind. The gelding was well aware of the courser's presence. In fact, he had a distinct tendency to act more like a friendly kitten than a warhorse of mature years in her presence, frisking around her as if he were a child's pony, and she regarded his antics with a fond, sometimes exasperated patience.

<*Of course I do,*> Gayrfressa said now, turning her head slightly to better regard Leeana as she caught her rider's amused thoughts. <*The lesser cousins have great hearts. It's not their fault no wizards fooled about with* their *ancestors, now is it?*>

"No, it's not," Leeana agreed. The coursers were remarkably comfortable with the notion that they—like the halflings—were the product of arcane meddling. Of course, in their case it had been a deliberate manipulation, all of whose consequences, including the unintended ones, had been highly beneficial—one wrought by the White Council to make those ancestors stronger, more powerful, and far more intelligent. The halflings hadn't enjoyed that deliberate design process. They represented an accident, a completely unintended consequence and byproduct of the most destructive war in Orfressa's history, and neither they nor any of the other Races of Man were quite able to forget that.

<*I don't really know why they should,*> Gayrfressa said reasonably. <*What is, is; trying to "forget it" can't* change *it. And it's not as if the halflings are the only "accident!" What about the magi?*

Or, for that matter, what about the hradani and the Rage? And if what Wencit once told him and Brandark is true, even the elves *are the result of "arcane meddling." Although it* was *deliberate in their case, as well, I suppose.>* The courser tossed her head in amusement. *<I don't understand why you two-foots worry about it so much!>*

"I didn't say I *do* worry about it," Leeana pointed out. "I think the halflings do mainly because of the way most of the other Races of Man are . . . prejudiced against them, I suppose. And I have to point out that what was done to the hradani wasn't exactly 'accidental.' Or done by wizards who gave a single solitary damn about what happened to their victims, for that matter." Her tone had darkened. "And they've paid for the Rage they have now with over twelve hundred years of pure, unmitigated hell."

<True.> Gayrfressa sounded more subdued than usual for a moment, although Leeana doubted it would last. *<I didn't mean to make light of what's happened to other people, Sister.>*

"I know you didn't, dearheart." Leeana smiled at her. "I think, though, that you coursers probably got the best deal out of all those . . . tinkered-with species. And I'm glad you did."

<So am I.> Gayrfressa moved closer, the blue star of her restored right eye gleaming as she reached out to touch Leeana's left shoulder ever so gently with her nose. *<If we hadn't been "tinkered with," then you and I would never have met, would we?>*

"Not something I like to think about, either," Leeana told her softly.

She looked into Gayrfressa's glowing eye for a moment, then turned her head, surveying the endless sea of grass about them. The year had turned unexpectedly dry over the last several weeks, almost as if Chemalka had decided to send the normal rain away to somewhere else, and those tall, wind-nodding waves of grass were browner and dryer than was usual, even for this late in the summer. They shimmered and stirred endlessly under the gentle breeze, entrapping and bewildering the unwary eye.

The Wind Plain was always an easy place for the incautious to get lost, but Leeana knew the area about Kalatha even more intimately than she'd known the land around Balthar. She knew the swells of the ground, the scattered, individual colonies of aspens and birch, the greener lines of tiny streams and seasonal watercourses. She knew where the springs were, and where to find the best spots to camp in all that trackless vastness. And she knew her sky, where the sun was at any given time of day and how to find her way about by its guidance or by the clear, sparkling stars that blazed down through the Wind Plain's thin, crystalline air like Silendros' own diadem. She didn't really have to think about it to know where she was in relationship to Kalatha . . . or to realize it was about time they turned for home.

She rather regretted that, and she knew Boots would, too. She made it a point to ride the gelding at least three times a week, and he spent his days in an open field, bounded by the river, with ready access to field shelter. Gayrfressa shared the same field with him, although unlike Boots, she was as adroit at opening the gate in the fence around it as any two-foot and came and went as she willed. The manager of the city livery stable had helped erect the shelters in return for permission to put a half-dozen other horses whose owners preferred to keep them at grass into the field with Boots, which gave him plenty of company. With the extra horses to play with, he was self-exercised enough to keep him fit, but Leeana didn't ride him only to exercise him. He needed the time with her, just as she needed it with him, and in an odd sort of way, the hours she spent on Gayrfressa's back only made riding him even more enjoyable. Her bond with Gayrfressa was so deep they truly were one creature; with Boots she had to work at that kind of fusion, and that made her appreciate it even more deeply.

"Time to head back," she said more than a little regretfully. "I've got the duty tonight, and I owe him a good grooming."

<*Handy to have around, you two-foots, when it comes to things like that,*> Gayrfressa observed with a deep, silent chuckle.

"'Handy,' is it?" Leeana retorted, wincing at the deliberate pun, and Gayrfressa tossed her head in an equine shrug. "I'll figure out a way to make you pay for that one."

<*I see why Brandark feels so unappreciated around him,*> the courser said mournfully, and Leeana laughed.

"Well, either way, we need to be getting back to town," she pointed out, and reined Boots around.

The gelding clearly understood what she had in mind . . . and equally clearly was in no hurry to get back to his field. Playing tag with the other horses was all very well, but he was enjoying himself too much to end his afternoon with his rider any sooner than he had to. Leeana smiled down at his ears as he tossed his head, sidestepping and expressing his reluctance with an eloquence which needed no words.

"Sorry, love," she told him, reaching down to pat him on the shoulder. "Erlis is going to be irked if I don't get back on time today."

<*I think everybody in Kalatha is "irked" at the moment,*> Gayrfressa put in. <*Or perhaps the word I really want is* worried. On edge? *Or is there another two-foot word that comes closer?*>

"I think either of them comes close enough," Leeana replied after a moment. "It would help if *Shahana* knew why she was here!"

Gayrfressa blew heavily in agreement. The arm had arrived in Kalatha the day before, accompanied by a twenty-man—and woman—mounted platoon from the rebuilt Quaysar Temple Guard. Their appearance had taken the entire town by surprise and sparked more than a little anxiety, especially when Shahana couldn't explain why Lillinara had chosen to send them in the first place. Leeana's husband had had rather more practice at being moved about in response to divine direction than most, and even she found the arm's arrival . . . disconcerting. For those without her own secondhand experience, Gayrfressa's "worried" probably came a lot closer than "disconcerted."

"At least if it's worrying us, I'm sure it's worrying Trisu even more," she said with a slow grin. "And anything that worries *him* is worthwhile, as far as I'm concerned!"

<*Isn't that just a little petty of you?*>

"Of course not! It's a *lot* petty of me, and that only makes it even more enjoyable from my perspective. It's a two-foot thing."

<*You wish,*> Gayrfressa told her. <*The truth is—*>

She broke off suddenly and stopped in mid-stride. Her head snapped up, her remaining ear pointing sharply as she turned to her left, and her nostrils flared.

"What?" Leeana demanded, halting Boots instantly.

<*Smoke.* Grass *smoke.*>

Gayrfressa's mental voice was brittle with tension, and Leeana's spine stiffened with matching alarm. The tall, browning grass was rustling tinder, more than dry enough to feed the rolling maelstrom of a prairie fire, and the breeze would push any fire directly towards Kalatha. Every child of the Wind Plain knew what that could mean, and while a courser might outrun the holocaust's outriders, all too many of its creatures couldn't.

"Where? Can you tell how far away?"

<*Close . . .* too *close,*> Gayrfressa replied, but there was a new note in her mental voice. The alarm was colored by another emotion—surprise. Or perhaps confusion.

"What is it?" Leeana asked, frowning as she tasted her four-footed sister's perplexity.

<*Why didn't I scent it on the way out?*> Gayrfressa asked, her ear shifting, and her head rose higher as she sniffed the breeze even more deeply.

"Probably because it hadn't caught yet," Leeana replied.

<*And did* you *hear any thunderstorms or lightning strikes to set it* after *we passed?*> Gayrfressa demanded.

"Well . . . no," Leeana admitted.

<*Neither did I. I think we'd better look into this, Sister.*>

"So do I. You're the one with the keen sense of smell, though."

Gayrfressa snorted in agreement and took the lead, forging steadily through the grass that was shoulder-high on Boots.

They'd gone only a short distance before Leeana's merely human nose began to catch the sharp, acrid scent. The gelding noticed it too, and he snorted uneasily. She felt the sudden tension in his muscles as he recognized the threat, and her own pulse quickened, yet there were only wisps of the odor, not the kind of overpowering wave that would have rolled along the breath of a true grass fire. That had to be a good thing, she told herself. Whatever had caused it, the burning or smoldering grass producing that hint of smoke was almost certainly limited enough that she and Gayrfressa could deal with it before it turned into the kind of fiery tempest that wreaked such havoc.

<*There!*>

Gayrfressa's head rose again, her nose pointing sharply, and Leeana squinted, trying to see whatever the mare had seen.

"Where?" she asked after a moment.

<*You can't* see *it?*>

Gayrfressa sounded astonished, and Leeana shook her head. The courser brought her head around to look at her for a moment, then turned back in the direction she'd been staring, and Leeana felt a fresh stab of surprise come from her.

<I *can't see it, either . . . if I close my right eye,*> Gayrfressa said slowly, and something tingled along Leeana's nerves as she remembered Lillinara telling them both that Gayrfressa would see more clearly than most.

"What is it?" she asked after a moment, and Gayrfressa snorted softly.

<*I have no idea,*> she admitted. <*It's like... almost like the kind of glow I saw when he healed the rest of the Warm Springs herd, but it's...* wrong. *Like it's been... broken or* twisted *somehow.*>

For some reason, Gayrfressa's "explanation" wasn't making her feel any calmer, Leeana reflected.

"And where are you seeing it?" She was surprised by the levelness of her own tone.

<*There's a hollow up ahead.*> Gayrfressa sounded as positive as if she'd actually seen that hollow before, Leeana noted. <*Whatever it is, it's coming from something in the hollow.*>

"Then let's go see what it is."

Gayrfressa tossed her head in agreement, and they moved ahead once again, more warily than before. They'd gone perhaps two hundred yards when Leeana saw thin, twisting tendrils of smoke rising ahead of them. She clucked to Boots, pressing gently with her heels to request more speed, and despite his own nervousness, the gelding moved quickly from a fast walk to a trot.

They crested one of the low, almost imperceptible swells of the Wind Plain and stopped suddenly.

An auburn-haired man lay facedown before them, and the grass around him was blackened char and powdery ash. Leeana couldn't understand why whatever had consumed that ten- or twelve-foot circle of grass hadn't spread further, but she spared a moment to give silent thanks that it hadn't. Yet even as she realized how lucky they'd been in at least that respect, her brain seemed to be racing off in a dozen directions at once as she tried to find some explanation for how he'd gotten there in the first place. There was no sign of a horse or anything else—the grass around the hollow stood straight and unbroken, with no trace of how he could have gotten here on foot, even if he'd had no horse. It was as if he'd fallen out of the heavens, and his clothing was almost as scorched-looking as the grass upon which he lay. And then there was that "glow" only Gayrfressa seemed able to see....

Logic told her she wasn't going to like the answers to all the questions ripping through her thoughts, but there'd be time to worry about them later. There were more urgent things to deal with at the moment, and she was out of the saddle, dropping the reins to leave Boots ground-hitched, almost before the gelding had stopped. Gayrfressa delicately placed one huge forehoof on the reins to make certain he'd stay there, and Leeana gave the courser a brief smile of thanks as she passed her sister on her way down into the hollow.

Thank the Mother I'm wearing boots! she thought, feeling the heat radiating upward from the charred area around the unconscious man. There was a lot of that heat, enough to make the toughened soles of her feet tingle when she stepped out into it, even through her boots, underlining the mystery of why no fire had spread from it. Then she reached him and went down on one knee, extending her hand to touch the side of his neck.

A pulse fluttered against her fingertips. It was weak, racing, but at least it was there, and she exhaled a long breath of gratitude. Then she gritted her teeth and rolled him over onto his back as gently as she could.

His hands were badly seared, blistered everywhere and with deep, angry wounds burned into their tissue, and her stomach knotted as she saw the damage. Burned scraps of skin and flesh hung in tatters around those deeper wounds, weeping serum. It looked as if he'd closed his grip on a white-hot iron, she thought sickly, wondering if he'd ever be able to use those fingers again. His face was burned, as well, although not as badly, and she smelled singed, burned hair. But then her eyes widened as she saw the white scepter on the scorched shoulder of his dark blue tunic.

"A *mage!*" she said sharply. "He's a mage, Gayrfressa!"

<A mage? All the way out here? Where did he come from? How did he get here?>

"Your guess is as good as mine."

Leeana sat back on her heels, staring down at the brutally injured man, then looked back up at Gayrfressa.

"We need help, and I don't want to move him without a healer. Mother only knows how badly hurt he may be inside!" She rose and reached into her belt pouch for the pad of paper an officer of the city guard carried everywhere. "I think I'm going to have to stay here to keep an eye on him, Gayrfressa." She found her stubby pencil and began writing quickly. "You're going to have to give this to Erlis or Balcartha or—*no!*"

She shook her head sharply, discarding the note she'd already started and scribbling a different one in its place.

"Give it to Arm Shahana," she said instead, choosing not to

think too deeply about the possible implications of their discovery and the arm's mysterious arrival from Quaysar.

She felt Gayrfressa's thoughts matching her own, but the courser said nothing as she finished her hasty note and tucked it into Gayrfressa's ornamental halter. The huge mare took long enough to press her nose to Leeana's raised hand and blow heavily. Then she turned, whirling away, and vanished with the blinding speed only a courser could produce.

Leeana watched her go, then got her canteen from Boots' saddle and went back to her knees beside the injured mage. Perhaps she could get him to drink a little, and if she couldn't, she could at least cleanse those hands of his.

✧ ✧ ✧

Shahana Lillinarafressa stiffened shaky knees and straightened, looking down at the still-unconscious man in the Kalatha infirmary. She felt as if she'd just completed a ten-mile run, but his breathing was stronger, and his hands looked far better than they had. Despite which, she was far from certain he'd ever be able to use them again, despite all she'd been able to do. It had always struck her as ironic, possibly even unfair, that champions of Tomanāk, the God of *War*, could heal so much more completely than an arm of the Mother. Of course, not even Tomanāk's champions could heal the way one of *Kontifrio's* priestesses could, but at the moment they didn't *have* a priestess of Kontifrio.

No, you don't. And try feeling grateful for the fact that the Mother's at least allowed you to save this man's life *rather than whining over the fact that someone else got a shinier toy than you did!*

"That's the best I can do, at least for now," she said.

"And it's an awful lot better than anything *I* could have done," the senior Kalathan healer told her fervently.

"Granted," Five Hundred Balcartha agreed, standing out of the way to one side, frowning down at the injured man. "Granted, and I'm as grateful as the next woman we had you here to save him, Milady. But what in Lillinara's name *happened* to him? And what was he doing out in the middle of the Wind Plain all by himself?"

"I have no idea," Shahana said frankly, settling gratefully onto the stool the healer pulled over to the side of the bed for her. "Leeana's obviously right that he's a mage, so I'm going to make a wild guess here and suggest that whatever happened to him has to have had something to do with his mage talent. But I've never heard of anything the magi do that could have produced *this*." She gestured at the still-raw ruins of his terribly damaged hands and the fresh, livid scars of the lesser burns she *had* been able to heal completely, crawling up both of his forearms. "It's like he was holding onto some kind of burning rope!"

Balcartha nodded unhappily. It was her job, as Kalatha's senior military officer, to recognize and deal with potential threats, and all of her instincts were insisting that "potential threat" was exactly what this man represented. Yet she had no clue as to why that might be.

"I could wish—" she began, then closed her mouth with a click as the injured man's eyelids fluttered. They rose, and his face twisted as muscles which had been slack in unconsciousness tightened in reaction to the pain of awareness. He sucked in a deep, hissing breath, and then, with startling suddenness, his slate-gray eyes snapped into focus.

He looked up at the five hundred for an instant, then tried to push himself up, only to gasp in anguish and fall back as his hands' injured strength failed him.

"Gently, Master Mage!" Shahana said. "You're safe now. I give you my word."

His head turned, his gaze moving to the arm's face. He stared at her for an instant, and something flickered in those gray eyes. He let himself settle fully back onto the mattress, yet the tension within him only seemed to grow.

"You're in Kalatha," Balcartha told him. "One of my officers found you out in the grass. We brought you back to the infirmary, and the Arm here"—she touched Shahana's shoulder—"did what she could for you. But what in the names of all the gods were you *doing* out there?"

The mage looked at her for a long moment, then licked cracked and blistered lips... and told her.

✧ ✧ ✧

Trisu of Lorham swept into Thalar Keep's great hall like a windstorm to greet his unexpected guests. There were three of them: Shahana Lillinarafressa, Balcartha Evahnalfressa, and the young woman he couldn't—simply could not, however hard he tried—think of as anyone except Leeana Bowmaster. At least this time she was in trousers, shirt, and doublet instead of that scandalous attire she normally danced around in, flaunting her body at every male eye like the worst, cheapest sort of strumpet. Not that the sight of the wedding bracelet on her left wrist was much of an improvement, especially given the rumors about just who it was she was supposedly "married" to!

Still, he reminded himself, there were certain standards of courtesy, even with war maids. Although exactly how one went about *politely* greeting this particular covey of guests was beyond him. "Ladies" was out of the question, and most of the terms one normally applied to war maids scarcely came under the heading of polite at the best of times.

He opened his mouth to begin, but Arm Shahana raised her hand before he could speak.

"We apologize for breaking in on you so discourteously, My Lord," she said quickly, and his eyes narrowed as he recognized the tension in her eyes and the harshness of her voice. "Unfortunately, what brings us here leaves little time for courtesy."

"Indeed?" He looked back and forth between her and the other two women, and his stomach tightened as he saw the matching tension in the two war maids, the coiled tautness of their muscles. He thought about several things he might have said and discarded all of them.

"May I know what *does* bring you here, Milady?" he asked instead.

"Treason, Milord," she said flatly, and his narrowed eyes widened abruptly. He darted a look at the older war maid's face and saw the flat, hard agreement in her expression.

"In that case," he said after a moment, "please join me in my office—all three of you—where we can speak freely."

✧ ✧ ✧

Leeana sat in the wooden chair beside the narrow, converted archer's slit that formed one of Trisu's office windows. She and Balcartha had let Shahana carry the burden of recounting Master Brayahs' story to Trisu. In fact, she'd deliberately kept her mouth closed lest she put up the lord warden's back, although she'd responded as concisely and completely as she could when he'd fired a half-dozen questions in her direction. And to his credit, they'd been clear, concise questions . . . and he'd completely ignored the fact that she was a war maid—and her father's daughter—as he concentrated on her answers. She couldn't help thinking it was a pity it took something like this to get past his automatic prejudices, but it was obvious his brain was working, and he'd wasted far less time grasping the essentials than she would have expected out of most people.

"So we don't know for certain *what's* happening," he said now. "Except, of course," his face tightened, "that we know for damned sure—pardon my language, Milady," he glanced apologetically at Shahana, "—that sorcery's involved in it somewhere!"

"Actually, Milord, we *do* know one other thing," Shahana said. He raised an eyebrow invitingly, and she shrugged. "Whatever's happening, and whoever's behind it, they took steps to prevent Master Brayahs from reaching the King at Chergor when he learned of it."

Trisu's jaw tightened and he gave a jerky nod.

"Fair enough, Milady. And it follows from that that if they wanted to prevent *him* from reaching the King, presumably they don't want anyone *else* doing it, either."

"They don't want anyone else doing it *in time*, Milord," Leeana heard someone else say with her voice, and Trisu's gray eyes flicked to her. She met them levelly, then shrugged. "There wouldn't have been any point in stopping a single mage—or anyone else—if they don't have a plan already in place and operating," she said flatly. "I don't know what that plan might be, but I do know we're the only people in the entire Kingdom who know they're planning *anything*."

"An excellent point... Milady," he replied after a moment. "And since we are, then clearly it's our responsibility to do something about it. The question is what we *can* do."

"How many armsmen could you ride with within the hour, Milord?" Shahana asked.

"Perhaps twenty-five—thirty, at the most," Trisu said. "It would take several hours to summon more than that."

"And I have twenty of the Temple Guard at Kalatha." Shahana shook her head, her face tight with worry. "Fifty isn't a huge force—especially when there may be wizardry involved."

"But fifty is fifty better than none, Milady," Trisu countered. "And Lorham's the closest wardenship."

"I have a suggestion," Leeana said after a moment. All of them looked at her, and she shrugged again. "War maids weigh less than most armsmen, Milord, and as you say, it's not a long trip from here to Chergor. Your armsmen's horses could carry double that far, and Kalatha could probably provide another twenty or thirty mounts. They won't be as good as the ones under your or the Arm's armsmen, but they'll be a lot better than none. Split the difference in numbers and call it twenty-five, and that gets you from fifty to a *hundred* and fifty."

Trisu's eyes hardened in instant, automatic rejection, and his mouth opened. But then he paused, mouth still open, looking at her. Silence hovered for at least ten seconds before he drew a deep breath and nodded.

"You're right," he said, and Leeana saw her own surprise at his response mirrored in Balcartha's eyes. He obviously saw it, too, and he flashed his teeth in something which bore at least a passing resemblance to a genuine smile.

"At this moment, what I care about are swords and hands to wield them," he said. "I'll worry about whether or not they're 'proper' hands later."

"Good, Milord," Shahana said. "But we're going to need at least two other horses." Trisu cocked his head at her. "We've got to send word to Balthar and to Sothōfalas," she said.

"Agreed." He looked at her for another long moment, then inhaled sharply. "To Balthar and Sothōfalas . . . but not to Toramos." The silence crackled with sudden tension, and he smiled even more mirthlessly than before. "If I'm being unjust to Baron Cassan, I can always apologize later. For now, we all have more important things to worry about. And *my* loyalty and *my* oaths are to the Crown and"—he met Leeana's eyes very levelly—"to the Baron of Balthar."

"Well said," Shahana said quietly. "But even if yours is the closest wardenship, it's going to take time for us to get there."

"True," Trisu acknowledged. "And that's why at least one of us won't be riding with the rest of us." Shahana frowned, and he raised his hand, pointing at Leeana. "If you have a wind rider, Milady, you don't hold him—or her—back when speed is of the essence."

Chapter Thirty-Three

Master Varnaythus took another sip of truly excellent wine and leaned back, glass in hand, to contemplate the images in the heart of his gramerhain. Malahk Sahrdohr had joined him in his working chamber once more, finished at last with his assumed identity as Mahrahk Firearrow. Today was the day their plans came to fruition . . . or didn't. Either way, "Firearrow's" utility would be limited in the aftermath.

"Arthnar's men are only five miles from Chergor," Sahrdohr reported, looking up from his own gramerhain, and Varnaythus smiled.

There was anticipation in that smile, and more than a trace of relief. Keeping all the necessary balls in the air simultaneously had been more taxing than he'd anticipated, even for a juggler as skilled he was, but he'd managed to pull it off after all. In fact, everything was coming together—down on the Ghoul Moor, as well as here on the Wind Plain—literally simultaneously. That was a piece of work his Lady was going to appreciate, given all the scores of things that could have gone wrong along the way.

His own stone showed Trianal Bowmaster's army, moving steadily down the course of the Hangnysti River . . . towards a rendezvous with a rather nastier handful than they anticipated, he thought smugly. It wouldn't be so very many hours before they were finding out about that, and in the meantime, things were shaping up very nicely farther to the north.

Shaping up despite the fact that something damned nearly did *go wrong,* he reminded himself. *I don't know what it was, but that miserable busybody Brayahs must've twigged to* something. *Bastard.* He grimaced. *I wonder if it was something Myacha noticed?*

He didn't know, and it was possible he never would, given the fact that Brayahs was dead and wouldn't be around to do any explaining. It seemed likely, though, for the more Varnaythus had studied the baroness, the more he'd come to the conclusion that she was very strongly Gifted indeed. With the proper training—and attitude—she probably could have found her own place on the Council of Carnadosa. So it was quite probable she *had* noticed something and pointed Brayahs at it.

Not that it mattered. Oh, if Brayahs had somehow figured out what had happened—and convinced Borandas of it—his plan for enlisting the North Riding as Cassan's ally had probably been knocked on the head. That would be inconvenient, although it might not matter all that much in the long run. In fact, he'd realized once he'd had time to think it over, it could even work out better than the vicious political fight to name Cassan or Yeraghor regent he'd anticipated. It might even lead to open civil war between the factions . . . assuming either Tellian or Trianal survived to lead *their* faction, at any rate. And his smile was thin as he contemplated how unlikely *that* was.

Well, I know Tellian, *at least, isn't going to be around much longer, one way or the other*, he reminded himself. *And the odds aren't looking very good for poor Trianal at the moment, either. In fact, it could be that if Brayahs and Myacha have convinced Borandas of the truth*, he *might end up taking over for Tellian, and he's nowhere near the soldier Tellian was. The wind riders would still side with him, though, and with his . . . limited talent leading one side and Cassan and Yeraghor leading the other, any Sothōii civil war could go on forever. It might even turn into something like that neverending mess in Ferenmoss!* He smiled almost blissfully at the thought, then shook regretfully free of it. *But the really important thing is that whatever Brayahs might have figured out or suspected, he didn't get to the King or Tellian to warn them.*

That was the one thing which might still have defeated that prong of their strategy. No matter what happened with Arthnar's assassins or Cassan's men, Markhos and Tellian and everyone with them would still die . . . as long as they remained at Chergor. Nothing this side of direct divine intervention could prevent that, and the theory behind his trap spell had obviously been correct.

He'd felt the moment when it discharged, blotting Brayahs—or *some* wind walker, at any rate—out of existence when he tried to reach Chergor.

And that's *worth knowing, too*, he reflected. *It's about time we started getting a handle on how to deal with the Phrobus-damned magi! And now that I know it worked, I suppose I'm going to have to go ahead and share my research with the rest of the Council after all. Pity. I hate to give up the edge over the others, but the Lady wouldn't approve of my holding it back if we're as close to a major cusp point as I think we are. Then again, with my notes as a starting point, maybe we can come up with a way to just* kill *all the bastards and be done with it!*

He smiled at the thought, sipped more wine, and returned his attention to the gramerhain before him. His viewpoint shifted and swooped about dizzyingly, but he was accustomed to that, and his smile went cold and cruel as he found Anshakar, Zûrâk, and Kimazh haranguing their army while shamans pounded their massive drums and no less than fifty thousand yammering, leaping, bounding ghouls salivated for their promised prey.

Not long, he thought. *No, not long at all now.*

✧ ✧ ✧

Sir Tellian Bowmaster leaned back in the comfortable chair, contemplating the chessboard while he considered how best to respond to his opponent's move.

Markhos Silveraxe, King of the Sothōii, had all the fierce drive to win one might have expected in the scion of a warrior dynasty, and quite a few of his courtiers, Tellian knew, would have made sure that winning was exactly what the King accomplished. The more adroit would have contrived to lose in a fashion which disguised their intentions, but all too many of them would simply and cheerfully have thrown the game and then gushed fulsome compliments on Markhos' skill which both they and the King would have known were as insincere as their desire to win had been.

And the King would have accepted the victory, smiling as if he were completely unaware of what they'd done. But behind his smile he would have marked them down for what they were... and he would never have fully trusted them again. Markhos was not a perfect monarch—few monarchs were—but susceptibility to sycophancy had never been one of his failings.

Tellian's problem at the moment, however, was that although

he was generally a better player than the King, this time the only options available to him were as unpalatable as they were limited. It was really unfair of Markhos to have departed from his normally aggressive, straightforward tactics and set the trap which had just cost Tellian both his king's castle and his queen's bishop *and* left his own king in check. Of course, it was his own fault he hadn't seen it coming, and he rather suspected that his reaction when he realized what he'd stumbled into would have handily quelled any suspicion the King might have cherished about his own determination to win.

"You are going to move sometime this afternoon, I trust, Milord?" the King said now, and smiled as Tellian looked up at him sharply. Markhos' sleek mustache was less bushy than Tellian's, and the King stroked it with a thoughtful fingertip. "It's not that I'm trying to rush you, you understand," he continued, "but I believe supper will be served in only another two or three hours."

"Your forbearance is deeply appreciated, Sire." Tellian's tone was . . . dry, to say the least. "Somehow, though, I suspect you're not in all that great a hurry, though."

"No?" The king arched an eyebrow. "And why would that be?"

"Because you have me well and truly in a hole, and you're enjoying every moment of it."

"Nonsense," Markhos replied in a remarkably insincere tone, and Tellian smiled. "Well, perhaps just a bit," the King conceded, holding up his thumb and index finger four inches or so apart. "I have lost the occasional game to you in the past. Of course," his smile faded and his gaze sharpened, "I'm not precisely alone in that, am I? I really do hope this whole canal business isn't going to turn out as ugly as it has the potential to become."

"Your Majesty—" Tellian began, but the King's raised hand stopped him in midsentence.

"I'm not suggesting I'm going to change my mind, Milord," he said. "And you don't have to bring in Yurokhas to see to it that I don't. Not that his support would do you all that much good at the moment. I'm just a *bit* irked with him, given his . . . disinclination to obey my instructions to join me here instead of running around with that heir of yours on the Ghoul Moor." Markhos smiled thinly. "But I'm not irked enough to change my mind about your charter. You don't even have to get Jerhas in here for that, because the simple truth is that your entire proposal makes far too much sense for me *not* to support it. Yet that doesn't blind me to how Cassan and Yeraghor are going to react—or to the fact that they're hardly going to be alone when they do."

"Your Majesty, I'm truly sorry my long-standing... disagreement with Cassan should have such implications for the Kingdom as a whole," Tellian said. "I'm sure my 'unnatural' suggestion that we might actually try coexisting with the hradani would have infuriated someone else if *he* hadn't been available, but there's no denying the bad blood between us is like a forge bellows where his reaction to it is concerned. And I'd be lying if I didn't admit there's enough 'bad blood' from my side for the thought of just how infuriated he truly is—and how badly this is going to *hurt* him—to give me a certain sense of satisfaction." The baron met his monarch's gaze levelly as he made that admission. "But even so, if he'd been willing to meet me even a fraction of the way, I would have been more than prepared to set aside a portion of my own increased revenues to compensate him for what I expect him to lose in trade through Nachfalas. It would have stuck in my throat like a fish bone, but I would have done it."

"I know you would have." It was Markhos' turn to sit back, laying his forearms along the armrests of his chair. "And for the sake of his father's memory, I wish he'd been willing to accept the offer. Unfortunately, Yurokhas was right; Cassan's mind simply doesn't work that way."

There was more than a hint of anger in the King's voice, Tellian reflected, and wondered again how much of Markhos' willingness to support his own proposals stemmed from the King's memories of Cassan's... incautious efforts to control him in his early days upon the throne. There were those—Tellian among them, to be honest—who were of the opinion that Yurokhas had been gifted with a significantly sharper brain than his royal brother, but there was nothing wrong with the head in which Markhos' brain resided. In point of fact, it was remarkably level, that head, and if he was slow and methodical—maddeningly so, upon occasion—when it came to making up his mind, there was nothing hesitant about him once he had.

"I don't suppose there's ever a major policy choice in any kingdom where the great nobles' rivalries don't factor into the decision process, Your Majesty," the baron said after a moment. "And I suppose it would be unfair—or at least unrealistic—to believe there wouldn't be rivalries between them, no matter what else might be true or how sincere they were in their disagreements. It doesn't necessarily need avarice and ambition to breed conflict . . . or hatred, for that matter. Which isn't to suggest all three of them don't play a role in this particular rivalry. I think Cassan and I would've detested each other even if we'd both been born peasants, but having the two of us as barons can't have been easy for you."

"Oh, you're right about that, Milord," Markhos agreed with a knife-thin smile. "There've been times I've actually found myself wishing one of you would just go ahead and kill the other one off, to be perfectly honest. Of the two, I'd have preferred for you to be the one still standing, although given Cassan's . . . devious nature, I'm not sure I would've been prepared to place a wager either way. But at least if one of you'd won, I'd have had a *few* moments of peace after the state funeral!"

Tellian snorted, although he knew the King was as well aware as he was of Cassan's efforts to accomplish precisely that end. Not that Markhos could ever officially admit anything of the sort without absolute, irrefutable proof—unless, of course, he *wanted* to bring back the Time of Troubles.

On the other hand, his extension of a royal charter is a pretty clear inclination of what he actually knows, whether he can admit *it or not. Shaftmaster's revenue estimates and Macebearer's arguments in favor of our increased influence with the Spearmen are all very well, but there's a part of him that shares the real conservatives' suspicions of Bahnak and the hradani. Come to that, it's his* responsibility *to share those suspicions, given all the bloodshed lying between us and them. Despite which, I doubt anyone in the entire Kingdom's going to miss the subtext of his proclamation or doubt for a minute that he sided with Bahnak, Kilthan, and me at least in part because it lets him hammer Cassan the way the bastard* deserves *to be hammered.*

And, for that matter, I should probably admit there's a nasty, vindictive side of me *that bought into the entire idea so enthusiastically because I knew* exactly *what it was going to do to Cassan if we pulled it off.*

Fortunately, for all his keen intelligence, Tellian Bowmaster was given to neither second thoughts nor self-deception. He knew *precisely* what was going to happen to his most bitter rival's political and economic power, and he was looking forward to it. None of which kept him from truly regretting the way in which their decades-long struggle had overflowed onto the Kingdom as a whole and the King in particular.

"Well, Your Majesty," he said, reaching for his surviving bishop and interposing it between his king and Markhos' queen, "we may not have killed each other off—yet—but there's a pretty good chance sheer apoplexy will carry him off when he finds out about your decision!"

The King laughed. There might have been just an edge of sourness in that laugh, but it was genuine. And probably owed something to the fact that the move of Tellian's bishop allowed him to exchange one of his knights for the baron's remaining castle.

"I *would* like to see his reaction," the King admitted, setting the captured castle to one side. "Unfortunately, not even a king can have everything."

✧ ✧ ✧

The sheer, wild exhilaration filled her mind and heart with a fiery intoxication.

The fiercest gallop upon the back of the fleetest warhorse ever bred paled to insignificance. Perhaps—*perhaps*—a warhorse might have touched, ever so briefly, that headlong, booming, drumroll speed, but it could never have sustained it, never maintained it for more than the barest handful of minutes. Yet the mighty muscles continued to stretch and play, the matchless heart thundered not simply with exertion but with the untamed, unquenchable power of a courser's dauntless will, and Gayrfressa's link to the energy which formed and sustained the entire universe burned like a coil of lightning. It poured that energy into her, and her hooves spurned the earth not for mere minutes, but for *hours*.

Leeana Hanathafressa was part of those booming hooves, shared those straining muscles, tasted that energy and felt it pour through her. She was submerged within the wild rush of speed, feeling it as Gayrfressa felt it even as she felt the wind of their passage whipping at her braided hair, bringing tears to her eyes. It was the first time since their bonding that Gayrfressa had truly loosed the incomparable speed and endurance of her kind. They'd touched *moments* of such swiftness, yet until this moment, not even Leeana—a wind rider herself, wife and daughter of wind riders—had truly grasped what it would be like. Now she knew... and as she rode the tornado named Gayrfressa, she and her hoofed sister merged on an even deeper, even more complete level.

Dimly, in the back of her mind where her own thoughts resided separately from this driving charge across the Wind Plain, she understood that part of the magic was her own love of running. Her delight in the speed of her merely human feet, of the deep breaths pulsing in and out of her lungs, of the steady, elevated beat of her heart. She knew that love for herself, and so she truly shared Gayrfressa's passion to outrace the wind and give herself to the thunder of her hooves—to gallop until even *she* could gallop no more. And as that thought wended its way through her own mind, she felt Gayrfressa touch it with her and sensed the mare's agreement, exalted and joyous despite the gravity of their mission.

She raised her head, green eyes slitted against the wind, gazing ahead. Few creatures on earth could match a courser's sense of direction. Gayrfressa knew exactly where they were headed, and she burned her way across open fields, vaulted dry stream beds and small creeks, slowed just enough to maintain her footing as she forged across a broader watercourse, carrying both of them arrow-straight toward their goal. Leeana knew the land around Chergor well, if not so intimately as the terrain around Kalatha, yet she could never have picked out the shortest path to her father's hunting lodge as Gayrfressa had. She wondered how the courser had done it, yet that was something not even Gayrfressa could have explained to her. The huge chestnut mare simply knew where her destination lay, and no power on earth could have deflected her from her course.

Now Leeana blinked on tears, and her heart rose as she recognized known landmarks. They were no more than a quarter-hour from their goal, the way a courser galloped, and she lowered her head once more, lying forward along Gayrfressa's neck, cheeks whipped by the courser's mane, and laid her palms against her sister's shoulders and the bunchy, explosive power of her muscles. She flattened herself, molded herself to the courser, and they and the wind were one.

✧ ✧ ✧

Tellian stroked his beard, looking down upon a chessboard which had done nothing but grow progressively (and inevitably) worse from his perspective.

"Mate in three, I believe," the King said genially, and the baron snorted.

"I believe you're correct, Your Majesty. And in the interests of moving on to allow you to do something more worthwhile with your time—"

He reached out and tipped his king over, conceding the game.

"I won't pretend I'm not savoring this moment," Markhos told him with a smile, beginning to reset the pieces. "Of course, I'm sure you would never be so undutiful as to point out that I'd need to do this no more than . . . oh, another couple of hundred times to pull even with you."

"I don't think it's quite *that* bad, Your Majesty," Tellian corrected with a smile of his own. "It couldn't be more than a few *score* games—certainly not *hundreds*."

"You're making it ever so much better, Milord." Markhos' blue eyes glinted with amusement.

"It's not that I don't—"

Tellian cut off abruptly, jerking upright in his chair. The King looked up quickly, his eyebrows rising in surprise, but the baron didn't even see him. His eyes were unfocused, his expression that of a man listening to a voice only he could hear. And as King Markhos watched, that expression transformed itself from one of sheer astonishment to something far, far darker.

✧ ✧ ✧

The ornamental wall barely topped the fruit trees Baroness Hanatha had planted along the its foot as Gayrfressa slowed her hurtling pace at last. The trees of Chergor Forest rose beyond the lodge, climbing the gently rolling hills between its eastern wall (such as it was) and the northernmost reaches of the Spear River. Leeana had always loved the vast, leafy hunting preserve, and the graceful, airy architecture of the timbered lodge itself, with its leaded windows, breezy verandas, and steeply pitched roof had offered a far younger Leeana a wonderful contrast from the grim, indomitable battlements and turrets of Hill Guard Castle. But as she watched that low, purely decorative wall show itself above the apple trees, she found herself wishing that it was twice as tall and three times as thick.

<*At least Dathgar and Gayrhalan heard me,*> Gayrfressa pointed out, and Leeana nodded.

"I know, dearheart," she agreed, catching the glint of a lookout's polished steel helmet from the top of that damnably low wall. "I know. But I wish—"

She cut herself off with a grimace. She knew how *she* wanted the King's Guard to react, but there was no sign they were doing anything of the sort.

I don't suppose I should be all that surprised they aren't, either, when all they have to go on is the word of a war maid, even if she is a wind rider, she thought.

<*From what Dathgar's had to say, I don't think that's the only reason they're not already headed for Balthar,*> Gayrfressa said grimly in the back of her brain. <*I wish you two-foots were just a* little *more like us, sometimes!*>

"Unfortunately, we're not," Leeana replied even more grimly. "We don't always think of the rest of the herd first, and you can always count on *someone* to argue, no matter how sensible your suggestion might be. And," she conceded unwillingly, "this has all come at them completely unexpected. It's not too surprising that there might be a certain amount of... disagreement on the best way to respond, I suppose."

Gayrfressa snorted, slowing still further to the fast, smooth walk of a courser as the two of them approached the open gate in the outer wall. It wasn't much more of a gate than the wall was of a wall, Leeana reflected. It had seemed much more substantial when she'd been younger, and she wished fervently that her childhood memories could have changed the reality.

A knot of men stood waiting as the courser swept through the gateway, ducking her lordly head to clear its intricately carved and painted lintel, and came to a graceful stop. Even she was sweating heavily after her driving run, but she stood tall and proud as Leeana swung quickly down from the saddle and bowed deeply to the red-haired man at the center of the small cluster.

One or two of his companions—predictably—looked more than a little contemptuous as she gave her monarch a "man's" greeting, though just how they expected her to *curtsy* in riding breeches was beyond her.

"Your Majesty," she said. "I apologize for intruding without an invitation."

"Indeed?" Markhos' tone was cool but courteous, and she raised her head to meet his eyes. "Given the news your companion sent ahead and the message you bear, invitations would seem to be the least of our concerns."

"I'm afraid so, Your Majesty," she agreed, and reached into her belt pouch. One of the armsmen at the King's back stiffened as her hand disappeared into the pouch, but he relaxed again—slightly—as it emerged again with nothing more threatening than a piece of paper. "From Lord Warden Lorham, Your Majesty," she said quietly.

The King accepted the hastily written message with a small nod, broke the seal, and scanned it rapidly. Then he handed it to Sir Jerhas Macebearer. The Prime Councilor read it as quickly as the King had, his face tightening, then passed it across to Tellian, in turn. Leeana watched from the corner of her eye as her father read it, but she'd never moved her own gaze from King Markhos'. The King's blue eyes were intent, narrowed with concentration as he looked back at her measuringly.

"It would seem Lord Lorham confirms everything your courser already relayed to Baron Tellian's brother," he said, ignoring—as law and custom alike demanded—the fact that "Baron Tellian" was also her father. "He says, however, that you were the one who found Master Brayahs?"

"That's so, Your Majesty," Leeana confirmed. "Gayrfressa"—she reached up to lay one hand on the mare's shoulder—"smelled the smoke, and we went to investigate." She shrugged ever so slightly. "We found him, but it was Arm Shahana who healed him. I think he might very well have died without her, and he would never have regained consciousness in time to warn us if she hadn't been there."

"How *fortunate* she was there, then," a slender, golden-haired man of perhaps thirty-five said. He was richly dressed and an inch or so shorter than Leeana herself, and his tone, as he stressed the adverb, was nicely seasoned with a courtier's venom.

"I agree," her father said in a very different voice, and the blond-haired fellow's blue eyes flashed as they locked with Tellian's. That flash might have been anger, Leeana thought, but it could also have been . . . satisfaction.

"My Lords." King Markhos said the two words quietly, and the two men looked at him instantly. "Master Brayahs is a valued servant of the Crown, Lord Golden Hill," the King continued softly. "Anything which preserves him for future service to the Kingdom is, indeed, fortunate."

"Most certainly, Your Majesty," Golden Hill replied.

Markhos held his eye a moment longer, then shifted his attention equally to Macebearer, Tellian, and a man Leeana recognized as Sir Frahdar Swordshank, the commander of his personal guard. Swordshank had just finished reading Trisu's note for himself, and he passed it to another of his officers as he returned his monarch's gaze.

"Suggestions?" the King inquired.

Tellian started to reply, then stopped and looked at Swordshank. The Guard commander looked back at him, and the baron gestured for him to speak first. No one could have called that gesture discourteous, but there was an undeniable curtness to it.

"My opinion remains the same, Sire," Swordshank said. He twitched his head in the direction of Trisu's note. "We know very little, other than that Master Brayahs believes sorcery has been at play in Halthan and that it's apparently been used to influence Baron Borandas' seneschal."

"Forgive me, Sir Frahdar," Sir Jerhas said a bit tartly, "but we also know sorcery came within a hairsbreadth of *killing* Master Brayahs when he attempted to wind walk to us here to warn us of what he'd discovered!"

"You're correct, of course, Milord." Swordshank gave the Prime Councilor a respectful half-bow. "The question, however, is whether that sorcery reacted to his attempt to reach this particular *place* or to his attempt to reach *His Majesty*, wherever he might have been."

"In either case, it was obviously intended to prevent him from warning the King," Tellian pointed out in what struck Leeana as an oddly neutral tone.

"Granted," Swordshank said, giving the baron the same abbreviated bow. "But we have no way of knowing what else might be afoot." His gaze lingered for just a moment on Tellian's before he looked back at the King. "I think we must assume Lord Trisu's fear that this is a part of some larger and more complex plot is accurate, Sire. That being the case, I would greatly prefer to keep you here, safely inside these walls, until Lord Trisu and Arm Shahana arrive to bolster our strength. With only forty men, I fear we might find ourselves hard-pressed to protect you properly if we should meet an organized attack in the open. Especially if that attack might be supported by sorcery."

"Surely your armsmen should be able to protect His Majesty long enough to get him to safety at Hill Guard!" Sir Jerhas retorted sharply.

"With all due respect, Sir Jerhas," Golden Hill said, "no one can predict where even a stray arrow may strike, far less one which might be aimed at a crowned head. Indeed," he looked sharply at Tellian, "Baron Tellian himself can testify to that, given his experience earlier this year." He returned his gaze to Macebearer. "Here, at least, His Majesty is within a wall, protected from that hazard. Once Sir Frahdar has been reinforced by Lord Trisu's armsmen, we would be far better placed to move His Majesty safely to some place of greater security."

He'd managed to avoid mentioning Arm Shahana, the Quaysar Temple Guard detachment, or Kalatha's war maids quite handily, Leeana observed. That was the first thing she noticed; then she saw the way her father's nostrils had flared ever so slightly and the tiny, almost invisible muscle tic at the corner of his right eye. She'd seen that tic only rarely as a child, but she'd known to brace herself whenever it put in an appearance, and she wondered exactly what had brought it on this time. Then she realized it had been Golden Hill's last five words.

<*'Some place of greater security' than* Hill Guard, *is it?*> she snapped silently to Gayrfressa, and the mare tossed her head.

<*That's what Dathgar was suggesting,*> she agreed. <*I don't understand why, though. He's* my *King, too, even if he does have only two feet! I say let's take him someplace we can protect him properly!*>

<*They're afraid* Father *might be behind it,*> Leeana told her flatly. The courser's single ear pricked in astonishment, and Leeana reminded herself not to look up at her. <*I haven't seen Swordshank since I ran away to Kalatha, and I'd never actually spoken to him even then, but I'll bet you he's not one of the war maids' greater admirers. And if this Golden Hill is who I think he is, he's one of the King's gentlemen-in-waiting... who just happens to be one of Baron Yeraghor's lords warden from the East Riding. I'd say it's crossed Swordshank's mind that Father might be the one trying to influence Borandas. The idea's ridiculous, but in all fairness, it's his job to worry about even ridiculous things where the King's safety is concerned. And if he* is *wondering about Father's possible involvement, having me turn up with a warning may only have made him even more suspicious. That's what Golden Hill's playing on, and it wouldn't surprise me very much if* he's *actually party to whatever's happening!*>

<*You truly think so?*> The notion clearly distressed Gayrfressa, and Leeana leaned her shoulders comfortingly back against the mare.

<*I don't have any evidence of that except for the fact that he's from the East Riding,*> she admitted, <*and the fact that he's casting aspersions on Father isn't exactly calculated to help me look at him less suspiciously. But that's obviously what he's suggesting, whatever his motives are, and Father can't argue against it too strongly without making anyone else who might be inclined to wonder about his own motives—like Swordshank—wonder even harder.*>

"I agree His Majesty's safety has to be our paramount concern," Tellian said. His tone was still neutral, but the chipped-flint anger under the neutrality was painfully evident to his daughter. "However, Chergor was never intended as a place to be seriously defended. Its wall's unlikely to do more than inconvenience a determined assailant, and even if it weren't, we have too few men to man it adequately."

"But if there's a wizard involved, and if he's using his accursed sorcery to spy upon us," another of the King's gentlemen-in-waiting said, "he'll be able to steer any attackers directly to us, wherever we might be. This is the only place Lord Trisu knows to find us, on the other hand. If we leave, he may never make contact with us—in time, at any rate."

"Exactly." Golden Hill looked earnestly at King Markhos. "Your Majesty, Lord Trisu did precisely what he ought to have done. He sent his message to you here by his swiftest courier, so that your personal guard might be forewarned. But according to his letter, he also sent couriers to Balthar and Sothōfalas. The instant those couriers reach their destinations, scores of additional armsmen will be sent directly here. In the meantime, Lord Trisu will arrive to reinforce us. Surely the wisest course is to wait until he does and *then* determine where—if anywhere—it would be wiser for Your Majesty to go."

Leeana Hanathafressa was no mage, but as she looked around the faces of the men gathered about her father and her King, she needed no mage talent to realize what the decision was going to be.

Chapter Thirty-Four

"Fiendark fly away with them!"

Varnaythus looked up from his gramerhain quickly, eyes narrowing. Sahrdohr was glaring into his own stone, and his earlier smile had turned into a snarl of fury.

"What?" the senior wizard asked sharply, and Sahrdohr raised his head to look at him, gray eyes fiery.

"I don't think your trap spell killed that bastard Brayahs after all," he grated.

"What?" Varnaythus' eyes narrowed further into mere slits. "Why not?"

"Because that bitch daughter of Tellian's just arrived at Chergor on her damned courser, *that's* why!" Sahrdohr snarled.

"*What?!*"

Varnaythus wasn't normally the sort who repeated himself, but he did this time. And then he snatched himself up out of his chair and took two explosive strides to look over Sahrdohr's shoulder. The images in someone else's gramerhain were never as clear for any wizard as the ones in his own, but Varnaythus could make out enough to see the huge chestnut mare standing in the hunting lodge's courtyard and the tall, slim young woman who'd arrived upon her back. He leaned closer, craning his neck as if listening, then scowled darkly.

"What the hell is causing that racket?" he demanded harshly. "Can *you* hear what they're saying?"

"Not very well," Sahrdohr replied in a distinctly unhappy tone. "Something's affecting the scrying. It's almost like a counter glamour, but not quite." His expression was as disgusted as it was angry. "If I had to guess—and that's *all* the hell I can do at this point—it's that damned wedding bracelet of hers. Carnadosa only knows what sort of effect an artifact like *that's* going to have on fine-control spells like this! But whatever it is, it's not fully effective. Vision isn't too bad, and at least a little sound is getting through. I can read their lips if they turn their heads the right way, and even with all that background noise, I can actually catch at least a little of what they're saying. That's how I heard one of them mention Brayahs by name . . . which leads me to suspect he's nowhere near as dead as we'd prefer."

"Damn." Varnaythus spoke almost mildly, but his eyes were ugly. "How in all of Krahana's hells did he manage to survive?"

"If it's any consolation, I'd guess he didn't survive by much," Sahrdohr replied, waving one hand at the gramerhain. "A courser can carry double farther and faster than any regular horse. If he hadn't been banged up pretty badly, he'd damned well have come along with her, if only to make sure they *believed* her when she got there. As it is, I think at least some of the King's companions—like Golden Hill, for example—are feeling just a little suspicious of friend Tellian at the moment." He produced something much more like a smile. "The fact that *his* disgraced and degenerate daughter 'just happened' to end up as the messenger seems to be putting their backs up. Looks like a lot of them are thinking about all the ways *they* could have arranged for something like this to work to their benefit."

"Thank Carnadosa for ambition," Varnaythus replied with sour fervor, his brow furrowed while he thought hard. Then he crossed back to his own chair, waved his hand over his gramerhain, and muttered a word of command.

The images of Bahzell, Vaijon, Trianal, and their marching army vanished, replaced by Arthnar Fire Oar's mercenaries. They were riding hard, if not so hard as he might have wished, given Sahrdohr's news, and his lips tightened.

"Did the war maids send her all by herself, or are they following her with reinforcements?"

"I can't say for certain," Sahrdohr replied. "From the bits and pieces I've been able to actually hear, I think they probably have. I'm backtracking along the shortest route from Kalatha to Chergor, though, and I haven't found anyone yet. I think—"

He broke off, leaning more intently over his gramerhain, then grunted unhappily.

"They did send more," he said sourly. "I've got what looks like seventy-five or a hundred horses, most of them carrying double, and they're making good time despite the weight."

"*How* good?" Varnaythus demanded.

"They're probably four hours out. More probably five." Sahrdohr shook his head. "To be that close behind her, they must have gotten themselves assembled right on her heels."

"Horses?" Varnaythus looked up again. "Where the hell did they find that many mounted war maids?"

"They aren't all war maids." Sahrdohr grimaced. "It looks like a third of them are Trisu of Lorham's armsmen. And another third are in the colors of the Quaysar Temple Guard. In fact, one of them looks an awful lot like that busybody Shahana."

"Wonderful." Varnaythus suppressed a strong desire to spit on the floor and looked back at his own gramerhain.

"Well," he said flatly after a moment, "Arthnar's cutthroats aren't more than a couple of hours from Chergor right this minute, and Cassan isn't more than another two hours behind them. So they should both reach their target before Trisu and Shahana can interfere."

"Phrobus, what a mess!" Sahrdohr muttered.

"It should still work," Varnaythus countered. "As long as Tellian doesn't manage to convince the King's armsmen to pull out in the next hour and a half, at least. 'Captain' Trâram has enough men to overwhelm Markhos' party even without Cassan, and Cassan has more than twice as many men as he does. They should be finished and done by the time Trisu and Shahana get there."

The wizard knew he sounded as if he were trying to convince himself of his own argument, because that was precisely what he was doing. Still, that didn't make it untrue. Erkân Trâram, the commander of Arthnar's assassins, had the next best thing to two hundred and fifty men under his command, better than four times the strength of the King's bodyguards. Courtiers, gentlemen-in-waiting, and their servants added perhaps another twenty swords to the defenders' strength, but none of the King's guests had brought armor with them. So it was entirely possible Trâram would sweep over them in his initial rush, despite the rudimentary wall around the hunting lodge. And if *he* failed, Cassan would be arriving on his heels with better than *five* hundred armsmen. Finding himself forced to dispatch the King himself would be a less than optimal solution from Cassan's viewpoint, but it would work just fine from Varnaythus'. In fact, having Trisu and Shahana arrive while Cassan was still in the process of completing the assassination would be even better. Outnumbered though Trisu's force was, at least some of them would escape with their own version of what had happened, and the probability of a Sothōii civil war would rise sharply if *that* happened.

"And if they *do* convince them to run for it before Trâram gets there?"

It was technically a question, though Sardohr's tone made it a statement, and Varnyathus bared his teeth at him.

"As soon as they start to ride out of that lodge, I trigger the kairsalhain," he confirmed grimly. "It won't be as clean as we wanted, and I know it'll warn them *someone* was willing to use the art, but it looks like Brayahs has already done that, curse him! And at least it'll also be *final*, by Carnadosa's ebon eyes!"

✧ ✧ ✧

Cassan Axehammer looked up at the cloudless blue sky, squinting at the sun. Summer might be trending into autumn, but he had at least another ten, possibly even eleven hours of daylight, he reflected. That was good—in fact, it was almost perfect.

Ahead of him, Sir Garman Stoneblade, his senior armsman, raised his hand to signal another halt. Cassan started to override the command, but stopped himself. They'd been in the saddle for almot two weeks now, pursuing the "unknown horsemen" who'd chosen to make their way across his riding without permission. The journey had been a long, hard ride, even for Sothōii cavalry troopers, but they'd been making up ground steadily. He'd taken that into consideration when he timed his "discovery" of Arthnar's mercenaries—it would never have done to actually catch them short of their objective—yet timing was even more critical now. They had to catch the killers in the act, or at least run them to earth before they could escape. Yet even so, Stoneblade was right to rest the horses periodically; they had at least two more hours of hard riding ahead of them, and the last thing they needed was to arrive with their mounts too exhausted to accomplish their mission.

Which wouldn't be a problem if I had a few damned wind riders I could actually trust, the baron thought bitterly.

There were far fewer wind riders among his vassals and armsmen than most of the other barons—and especially that bastard Tellian!—could claim. That had always been a sore point, one more coal in the fire of his resentment and ambition. Yet there were times it could be an advantage, as well, he reminded himself, and the truth was that this was one of those times, whether he liked it or not. No courser was any man's vassal. They might bond to someone who was, and share their rider's fealty at secondhand, as it were, but they themselves owed obedience only to their herd stallions . . . and the herd stallions owed obedience only to the Crown. He couldn't have brought a wind rider on *this* mission even if he'd had one to bring.

Speaking of which . . .

He shared a quick, meaningful glance with Tarmahk Dirkson, his personal armsman, then trotted over to Stoneblade before he dismounted and gestured for Sir Kalanndros Horsemaster to join them. Both of his captains were typical Sothōii: tall for humans, with fair hair and blue eyes. Stoneblade was twelve years Horsemaster's senior, and his beard was going gray, although it was hard to see against that blond background. Horsemaster was a bit rangier than Stoneblade and perhaps a bit more ruthless. Both were highly competent, or they wouldn't have held their positions, but Stoneblade had the better eye when it came to suiting tactics to terrain.

"Yes, Milord?" Horsemaster said as he drew rein beside Cassan and Stoneblade and swung down from the saddle himself.

"I have a bad feeling about this," Cassan growled.

"Milord?" It was Stoneblade this time, and his eyes were hooded but thoughtful as he gazed at his baron.

"All we had to go on when we first realized an organized band of horsemen was crossing the Riding was the messenger from Nachfalas," Cassan replied. He saw no reason to confuse the issue by mentioning that the messenger who'd brought word of the "unknown mercenary company" which had filtered through Nachfalas had been sent on his own orders. "I'd have been a lot happier if we'd had enough warning to actually intercept them south of Toramos, but there's no point crying over spilt milk, and at least our scouts cut their trail while it was still reasonably fresh. Still, all we've had since then were tracks—tracks where there shouldn't have been any, from people who sure as hell hadn't asked permission to trespass on our lands. But now—" He shrugged. "Do you realize where these people—whoever they are—seem to be headed?"

"Into the West Riding, Milord," Horsemaster said a bit delicately, and it was obvious from their expressions that neither Horsemaster nor Stoneblade had been especially enthusiastic about the notion of crossing the border into the riding of their baron's most bitter enemy.

Which they'd done late that morning... with no more permission than the mysterious riders they were pursuing. Neither man was familiar with the lay of the land in Tellian Bowmaster's riding, but the border markers had been clear to see even before they crossed the high road midway between Magdalas and the Spear River, and they felt far from home and dangerously exposed. The only good news, as far as they were concerned, was that whoever they were following had made a point of avoiding villages and towns, picking a route across the vast, empty Wind Plain where no human eye would note their passing. It was one more sign they were up to no good, but Cassan's captains were clearly happy to be avoiding those watchful eyes in their wake.

"West Riding!" Cassan spat on the ground. "If it was only the West Riding, I'd be overjoyed to let that bastard Tellian worry about it! He'd probably try to lay responsibility for whatever they're up to on me, of course, but I could live with that. Unfortunately, I think I know *where* in the West Riding they're headed." Both men looked at him, and he coughed out a harsh laugh. "Chergor," he told them. "They're headed for Tellian's hunting lodge at Chergor... and the King."

The armsmen stiffened abruptly, eyes wide. They stared at him for a moment, then, in unison, shared a quick glance before they turned back to their liege.

"Are you certain, Milord?" Stoneblade asked urgently.

"Certain? How could any man be *certain* about something like this?" Cassan shot back. "But I've been to Chergor. I recognize the terrain, and these bastards we're following are headed directly towards it, allowing for staying out of sight of the locals. What else could pull a force this size together from out-kingdom and then send it almost five hundred leagues from Nachfalas? It's awfully small for an *invasion force*, now isn't it? But King Markhos won't have more than two- or threescore armsmen with him, and these bastards have to have at least twice that many men!"

"Milord, if you're right—and I'm afraid you are," Stoneblade said, "we must send a courier ahead immediately! And another to Sothōfalas and"—the senior captain braced himself visibly—"to Hill Guard."

"Do *you* know the shortest route to Chergor from here?" Cassan challenged. "I don't, and I've *been* there before!" He shook his head. "No, you're right about sending a messenger to the capital, but even if our horses were fresh enough to send a courier around them, I couldn't give him the directions he'd need to even *find* the lodge, far less beat them to it. Our only real hope is to push the pace as hard as we can, make up as much distance as possible. We may be able to catch them short of Chergor, and if we can't, they'll be our surest guide to it. Even if we don't catch them before they reach it, we can hope to arrive close on their heels."

Stoneblade's expression was as unhappy as it was worried, but there was no disputing Cassan's logic. Not about Chergor, at any rate. The older armsman opened his mouth, but before he could find the proper way to frame the suggestion, Cassan cut him off harshly.

"As for sending word to Hill Guard, it couldn't possibly get there in time to do any good. We're far closer to Chergor than Balthar. Besides," his voice turned even harsher, "I have an ugly suspicion about just how the King comes to be spending his vacation in such a conveniently isolated spot—in the *West Riding*—when a band of assassins 'just happens' to have set out to attack him."

Both captains' eyes widened. It was clear they thought their baron's bitter enmity toward Baron Tellian was behind his suspicions, but neither was prepared to argue the point. Especially since it would take at least three times as long for any courier just to reach Balthar—or Sothōfalas, for that matter—as it would take *them* to reach Chergor.

"Of course, Milord," Stoneblade said after a moment.

"I know the horses all need this rest," Cassan continued, "but we're going to have to push on harder as soon as it's over. I think it would be wise for you to go have a word with all of our troop leaders, Garman. Tell them what I think is happening here so they understand how vital it is that we move as quickly as possible from here on out."

"Of course, Milord!"

Stoneblade slapped his breastplate in salute and headed off purposefully, his expression grim. Horsemaster started to follow him, but Cassan gripped the younger armsman's elbow before he could.

"Milord?"

"A word more, Kalanndros," the baron said quietly. The captain cocked his head slightly, eyebrows rising, and Cassan smiled grimly. "There's another reason I didn't want to send a courier to Balthar," he said in that same quiet tone. "My agents in Nachfalas actually gave me a little more information than I was willing to share with you and Garman . . . until I realized where they're headed, at least. Now I think you need to know it."

He paused, waiting.

"What sort of . . . information, Milord?" Horsemaster asked finally.

"Information suggesting these people were met by one of Baron Tellian's spies," Cassan said flatly. "To be honest, that's the reason I pulled this many men together before I went looking for them in the first place. I was afraid they were up to some mischief in the South Riding, something Tellian could deny responsibility for because the men who carried it out it had obviously come from out-kingdom. But now that I've realized where they're really headed, I have to wonder if there wasn't a much darker reason than I'd suspected for why they met with one of his agents before setting out."

Horsemaster's expression was suddenly intensely wary, and Cassan smiled without a trace of humor.

"If this *is* an assassination attempt and Tellian's behind it, there's only one reason he would have recruited them from outside the Kingdom and had them enter the Wind Plain at Nachfalas and come at Chergor across my lands. He's not just setting up a way to hide his hand—he's obviously hoping to saddle *me* with responsibility for whatever they're about to do. And if he's been as clever about it as he usually is, they probably truly believe I'm the one who hired them!"

Horsemaster nodded slowly, his eyes narrow, and Cassan shrugged.

"Obviously, I don't have any sort of proof he's the one who set this all up. For that matter, I might even be wrong to think he is." The concession was perfunctory at best, Horsemaster noted. "The gods know this canal business offers enough of a threat to the interests of the Spearmen and the Purple Lords for *them* to want to wreck it even more badly than I do! But the point is that if it *is* Tellian, and if whoever he used as his agent hired them in *my* name, the consequences could be . . . serious."

Horsemaster's nod was far more emphatic this time.

"So I think it would be best, when we overtake them, that there be no survivors," Cassan said flatly, and gave another shrug. "Men who hire their swords for assassinations are scum, anyway. If we're fortunate, we'll catch them short of Chergor and finish the business then."

"And if we don't, Milord?" Horsemaster asked softly.

"Well, that will depend on whether or not they've had any opportunity to talk to anyone on the other side, won't it? Someone who might actually believe their lies and think I'm the one who hired them."

Cassan's tone was completely neutral, but understanding flickered in Horsemaster's blue eyes. Understanding of what his baron had just said and perhaps—*perhaps*—just a trace of what he *hadn't* said.

"That would be... unfortunate, Milord," he said.

"Yes, it would, wouldn't it?" Cassan replied.

"I'll see to it, Milord," Horsemaster said, and if he was unhappy about the possibilities, there was no sign of it in his level gaze.

"Good."

Cassan released the other man's elbow and watched him walk across to his own company. Someone's armor and weapons harness creaked behind him, and he looked over his shoulder.

"All well, Milord?" Dirkson asked softly, and the baron nodded.

Dirkson was younger than Darnas Warshoe, but they were very much cut from the same cloth, and the armsman nodded back to his patron. Then he glanced over his shoulder at the six handpicked armsmen of his personal squad. Aside from Cassan and Dirkson himself, they were the only ones who knew the baron's full plan, and if the thought of regicide bothered any of them, there was no sign of it.

"Won't hurt a thing for Sir Kalanndros' lads to be busy cutting inconvenient throats, Milord," Dirkson said, touching the hilt of his own saber, and his eyes were cold. "Lots of confusion and people running and shouting."

"Best of all if we get there just too late," Cassan told him in an even softer tone. "But if we don't, remember to make sure the dagger's in Tellian's hand. Or the hand of one of his allies, at least."

"Oh, aye, I'll do that little thing, Milord," Dirkson promised with an icy smile. "A cold, *dead* hand... and I'll make sure it's dead myself."

✧ ✧ ✧

Erkân Trâram drank deeply from his canteen, then looked around the small circle of intent faces gathered about him.

"All right, lads," he said. "It's time we were about it."

That circle of faces tightened, but no one argued. It was far too late for second thoughts, even if they'd been inclined to entertain them, and they weren't. All of them recognized the risk inherent in their task, especially if anyone escaped to set wind riders on their trail. Their horses were good, even by Sothōii standards, but *no one's* horses were that good. Still, if things went according to plan, there'd be no survivors *to* escape, which ought to give them at least several hours—possibly even a day or two—of head start on any pursuit. Besides, they weren't going to escape overland; river barges were waiting just below the point at which the Ice Sisters' outflow reached the Spear to bear them back to Nachfalas more swiftly than even a wind rider could cover the distance. If they reached the barges, the only real concern would be one of those blasted magi who could throw their thoughts over vast distances, or one of the "wind walkers." Nothing else would be able to get word to Nachfalas in time to prevent them from escaping back down the Escarpment and disappearing into the Kingdom of the River Brigands and the Empire of the Spear once more.

Or that was the plan, anyway.

"Somar," Trâram looked at his senior lieutenant, Somar Lararк. Like Trâram himself, Lararк was a veteran of the Spearman Army, although it had been some years since either of them had been that reputably employed.

"Yes, Sir?" Lararк responded with the discipline Trâram had carried over from his army days.

"Go ahead and circle around to the other side. Take Gûrân with you and send him back once you're in place. I know it doesn't look like much," he twitched his head in the direction of the hunting lodge hidden by the half mile or so of woodland between them and it, "but the Sothōii don't pick Royal Guardsmen out of a helmet at random. We're going to lose some of the lads no matter what else happens, so let's take time to do this right."

"Yes, Sir," Lararк said again, and nodded to Sergeant Gûrân Selmar, the company's senior noncom. The two of them moved off towards Lararк's command, and Trâram looked at his other subordinates.

"Go," he said flatly.

They nodded and filtered off through the trees, leaving Trâram with his bugler and his small command group. He stood there, listening to birdsong and the scolding chatter of an outraged squirrel. The light was dim and green as it filtered through that dense leaf canopy, like being at the bottom of a lake, and it was cool under the trees. He drew a deep breath, smelling the leaf mold, the moss, the deep scent of earth and growing things. Of life.

There were times when even a man like Erkân Trâram had qualms about the choices he'd made in his own life. When he felt himself at the center of a leaf-whispering, breezy pool of living energy and thought about all the lives he'd ended. All the blood he'd spilled for more paymasters than he could any longer count. But those times were few and far between, and he'd long since learned how to banish them when they insisted upon intruding.

Bards and poets could rhapsodize about noble conflict, about honor and the warrior's call to duty under his liege lord's banner in time of war. But the skills of a warrior weren't worth a copper kormak in time of peace, and there wasn't always a war when he needed one. A man had to make his way in the world with the talents he had, and Erkân Trâram's talent was for killing.

And with what you're earning for this *one, you may finally be able to retire, after all,* he told himself.

Besides, it wasn't as if Markhos Silveraxe was *his* king, now was it?

Chapter Thirty-Five

Leeana forced herself to sit calmly on the hunting lodge's deep, roofed veranda.

What she really wanted to do was to stand up, pace vigorously, and spend several minutes screaming at Sir Frahdar Swordshank. She would, however, cheerfully have traded the screaming time for the opportunity to remove Lord Warden Golden Hill's handsome, sleekly groomed head instead.

Slowly, preferably. One inch at a time.

It seemed evident that whatever anyone else might think, King Markhos cherished no suspicions about her father's fidelity. For that matter, she wasn't at all certain Swordshank truly worried about Tellian's loyalty. But it was Swordshank's job to consider all possibilities, and the truth was that they knew far too little about what was happening. Given what they did know, the decision to stand fast or to seek a place of greater safety could have been argued either way, and the King wasn't in the practice of capriciously overriding the skilled and experienced armsman he'd chosen to command his personal guard even before he'd attained his majority and assumed the Crown in his own right. The choice Swordshank had made might frustrate and worry her, and she might be convinced it was the wrong one, but she wasn't *angry* at him for it. Not once she'd had a chance to think about it from his perspective and cool down a bit, at any rate.

But Golden Hill, now . . . him she could *definitely* be angry with. Even now, she knew, he was standing attentively with the knot of unarmored courtiers and servants surrounding the King in the lodge's great room as the final line of defense. And while he was standing there, sword in hand and expression of noble purpose firmly fixed, he was undoubtedly continuing to drop the occasional, carefully honed, poisonous word to undermine her father. Nor was Baron Tellian in any position to parry his attacks at the moment.

Unlike any of the other courtiers, he and Hathan had brought their armor with them. Leeana knew that was solely because of his promise to her mother after the ambush had come so close to killing him last spring. Golden Hill (predictably) had commented on how "fortunate" it was that Tellian—and, of course, his closest and most trusted companion (it would never do to call him a henchman)—"happened" to be in full armor at a moment when the King might be exposed to the threat of assassination. *Obviously* he'd meant only that it was fortunate that the defenders should have been reinforced by two such formidable wind riders! He'd *never* meant to imply that it might keep the two of *them* safe in the sort of confused, desperate melee which might break out under such circumstances! Why, that might have suggested that they'd suspected their armor might actually be needed, and nothing could have been further from his intent!

At least a few of those barbed words had to be coming her way, as well. And, unfortunately, Golden Hill wasn't the only one of the King's courtiers who clearly wished that if someone was going to warn the King about a potential plot, the warning might at least have come from someone with a modicum of respectability.

All of that was quite enough to make anyone seethe with anger, yet she knew those reasons were almost superficial.

No, the true reason for the fury bubbling away just beneath her outward semblance of calm was the fact that, unlike her father, *she* didn't have armor . . . and she remained far from anything someone might have called a trained wind rider. Which was why she was sitting on this veranda with a strung bow beside her, a quiver of arrows over her shoulder, and a war maid's short swords at her side while her father, Hathan, their coursers, and Gayrfressa waited to take the battle to any attackers.

<*I should be with* you . . . *and Father!*> she raged silently to her hoofed sister.

<*Not yet, Sister,*> Gayrfressa replied far more gently, raising her head and looking back over her shoulder at Leeana from her own place in the hunting lodge's central courtyard. <*Not until you've*

learned to fight from the saddle, not simply ride. I love you too much to risk you when you haven't been trained to defend yourself properly from my back. And you don't even have armor!>

Leeana felt her jaw tighten and forced herself to relax it, shocked by the spike of anger she felt at *Gayrfressa*, of all people!

<*You're not mad at me,*> Gayrfressa told her with something almost like a tender laugh. <*Not really. You're mad at hearing the voice of reason telling you what you don't want to hear, and it happens to be mine. And the* reason *you're angry is that you feel as if you're somehow at fault for sitting there "safely" while your father, Hathan, Dathgar, and Gayrhalan are all out here with me. But you're not really all that "safe" where you are, you know. You're simply safer there than you would be out here until we get you properly trained. And while I admit you have a* much *better starting point than* he *did when Walsharno first took him in hand, that's going to take a while.*>

Leeana was forced to nod, and Gayrfressa shook her head in a mane-flipping gesture, then turned back to the closed gate, standing between the two stallions and their heavily armored riders. Neither her father nor Hathan had thought to bring lances with them, unfortunately. Instead, they had their horse bows strung, which would be more effective from a courser's saddle than a sword—in the beginning, at least—unless their enemies were far better armored than anyone anticipated. Yet what gnawed at Leeana's heart was the knowledge that Gayrfressa had no bow-armed rider, because Leeana hadn't yet acquired that proficiency. And that meant that while the two armored wind riders might be able to stay out of weapons reach of an opponent, Gayrfressa would have no choice but to close so that she might use those weapons with which nature had endowed her.

And unlike the stallions, she was unbarded.

Stop that, she told herself firmly. *You can't change it by worrying about it, and Gayrfressa knows what you're feeling even if you don't actually* say *a thing to her. The last thing you need to be doing at this moment is to* distract *her!*

A wordless ripple of love reached back to her, and she drew a deep breath as she reached back.

✧ ✧ ✧

Gûrân Selmar came out of the undergrowth as silently as a puff of breeze, and Erkân Trâram looked up from the mossy boulder upon which he sat.

"Lieutenant Larark's in position, Sir," the sergeant said, and Trâram grimaced.

"Should I assume you took a close look at that lodge on your way back?" he asked the veteran noncom, and Selmar chuckled grimly.

"Aye, Sir. I did that." He shrugged. "'Pears to be pretty much the way it was described, Captain. The wall's nothing much—can't be more than twelve, thirteen feet tall, and it looks like it's only a couple of courses of brick." He shrugged again. "Don't see how it could have any kind of fighting step, and the ropes and grapnels should go over it clean and easy. The only thing that bothers me is the gate."

"The gate?" Trâram's eyes narrowed. "What about it?"

"No tougher or heavier than any of the rest of that 'wall' of theirs, Sir. The thing is, though, it's closed up tight. Seems to me the reasonable thing for them to do would be to leave it open."

Trâram's face tightened.

"*I'd* think so," he acknowledged. "Our information didn't suggest anything one way or the other about it, but still..."

He and Selmar looked at one another for several moments. Then the captain shrugged.

"Well, either way, they've only got forty or fifty men in there. But if that gate's closed because they've figured out somehow that we're coming, I think we should just *leave* it closed. Go tell Lieutenant Râsâl—I want him and his men on the west wall with me rather than trying to rush the gate."

"Yes, Sir."

Selmar disappeared into the undergrowth once more, and Trâram drew a deep breath. The closed gate might mean nothing at all, although that seemed unlikely. The next most likely possibility was that someone inside the lodge's ornamental wall had caught sight of one or more of his men skulking about in the bushes getting into position. He wouldn't have believed that could happen—his men were better than that—but anyone could make mistakes, however good they were, and sometimes the other side simply got lucky.

And then there was the *least* likely probability—that someone had betrayed their operation to the Sothōii. In that case, that gate might be closed to conceal the fact that King Markhos was somewhere else entirely... having left a hundred or so of his elite cavalry packed in the hunting lodge's courtyard, waiting to come thundering out as soon as anyone was sufficiently injudicious as to disturb them.

You're jumping at shadows, Erkân, he told himself. *Jumping at shadows. If there'd been that much traffic in or out of that lodge, you'd have seen signs of it along the road, and you didn't, did you? No, the only realistic worst case is that someone did spot one of the boys.*

That would be bad enough, yet it was a chance he was prepared to accept. Without the element of surprise, his casualties would climb sharply, but the defenders simply didn't have enough manpower. The harsh truth was that he could afford far higher losses than the King's bodyguards possibly could, and given how much they were being paid for this one—

The staccato cry of a southern bird who had no business on the Wind Plain sounded clearly through the cool, green woods, and Erkân Trâram drew his sword and looked through the thin screen of branches at the top of that ornamental wall Selmar had described.

"*Now!*" he bellowed.

✧ ✧ ✧

Leeana came to her feet with a dancer's grace, and somehow the strung bow had appeared in her left hand. For just a moment, she wasn't certain what had snatched her out of her chair. Then she realized—*she* hadn't heard that single shouted word; *Gayrfressa* had.

She turned to her left, facing the direction from which the command—and it *had* to be a command—had come, and her right hand drew an arrow from her quiver. Somewhere deep under the surface of her thoughts, she recalled her first morning at Kalatha and her hopeless performance as an archer under Erlis and Ravlahn's evaluating examination. She'd come a long way since that day, and despite the bigger muscles with which an unfair nature had gifted male arms, there weren't a great many men who could have pulled the bow she'd mastered in the intervening years. She nocked the arrow, her brain ticking with the cool precision of a Dwarvenhame pocket watch, and felt the alert, tingling readiness purring through her nerves and sinews. Despite her years of hard, sometimes brutal training, she'd never faced an enemy when lives were in the balance, and she was vaguely astonished that what she felt most strongly at the moment was an overwhelming focus and purpose, not fear.

Well, a small inner voice told her almost whimsically, *there's always time for that.*

✧ ✧ ✧

Trâram's shout brought his entire company to its feet. Whistles shrilled and other voices shouted their own orders, galvanized by his command, and the attack rolled forward.

The approaches were most open on the western side of the lodge, which was why Trâram himself commanded that prong of the assault. The dense greenery of the Forest of Chergor swept up to within little more than thirty or forty feet of the lodge's other walls; here, on the west, the approach lay through the more open and orderly lines of an apple orchard. The apple trees' leaves and ripening fruit provided a wind-tousled screen, concealing most of his men's approach from any observer who might be perched awkwardly atop that purely decorative wall, but they were still far more exposed coming through the orchard. On the other hand, the orchard was much more open than the forest's tangles, which allowed him not only to move more quickly, but also to maintain a tighter formation.

A bugle blared from somewhere inside the lodge before his men had moved ten yards, and he grimaced at the confirmation that the defenders had indeed had at least some inkling they were under threat. He'd never personally fought Sothōii before, but the deadly reputation of the Wind Plain's horse archers told him the next few minutes were going to be ugly.

Still, he'd seen ugly before, and he'd taken the job.

✧ ✧ ✧

The corner of Leeana's eye noticed the three coursers turning away from the gate they'd been facing. They moved smoothly to the right, where the southernmost wall was screened from the main courtyard by the stables, taking up a position from which they could reach either the gate or the wall, as need required. Between the stables and the wall, there was—or had been—a small riding ring, but the white-painted fencing around it had been demolished to clear fighting room behind the stables, and she felt a flicker of Gayrfressa's grim satisfaction as she trotted to one end of that open space between Dathgar and Gayrhalan.

It was a vague recognition, at the back of her mind, for her own eyes were fixed on the western wall as the first grappling hooks soared up over the masonry. Iron teeth clattered, dug into the mortar between the bricks, and there were dozens of them.

She raised her bow, the watch ticking in her head a bit harder and faster, picturing the men who must even now be swarming up the knotted ropes attached to those grapnels. Men coming to kill her King.

Men coming for *her* to kill instead.

She drew and loosed with smooth, flashing speed, hands and muscles moving before she'd even realized what she'd seen. The range was less than fifty yards, and the man who'd drawn her attention had just transferred from the climbing rope. He flung his arms across the top of the wall to heave himself up and over... and disappeared without even a scream as her arrow tore through the base of his throat, just above the collarbone.

Something quivered deep inside her, like a momentary flash of nausea, as she realized she'd just killed another human being. It wasn't like taking a hare or an antelope, yet there wasn't the degree of shock she'd expected, either. Perhaps there simply wasn't time to allow herself that distraction. Perhaps it would come back to haunt her later. But for now there was only that clear, clean focus, and she nocked another arrow even as a score of other heads topped the wall.

More bowstrings sang and snapped—dozens of them—along the northern, western, and eastern walls. There'd been no time to construct any sort of fighting step from which those archers might have engaged attackers short of the walls themselves, just as there was too little space for mounted troops to fight effectively within them. No Sothōii cavalryman was ever truly comfortable fighting on foot, but the Royal Guard was rather more flexible than most, and Swordshank had left his troopers' mounts in the lodge's capacious stables rather than pack its interior with a congested mass, unable to maneuver. Instead, he'd positioned his dismounted armsmen carefully around the main lodge, placed where they could simultaneously guard its entrances and cover the walls where the sightlines were clear enough for archery. But most of the southern wall, encumbered by the stables, was impossible to see—or sweep with arrowfire—from the central courtyard. That was why he'd demolished the riding ring... and the reason Tellian and Hathan had moved to cover that vulnerability the instant they were confident the attackers were coming over the walls rather than attempting to storm the gate.

Of course, the attack on the walls could always be a diversion to draw our attention away from the gate before they smash it open, that preposterously calm voice remarked inside Leeana Hanathafressa's skull as she loosed a second arrow and another body collapsed.

This time the corpse sprawled across the top of the wall until the next man up the rope shoved it out of his way. There were screams now, she noticed, nocking another arrow, yet the attack never faltered. Whatever else these men might be, they weren't cowards, and their experience showed in the speed and ferocity of their assault. Clearly they recognized their numerical advantage... and that their best hope of success and survival lay in swamping the defense. There could be only so many bows inside the lodge, and the arithmetic was coldly pragmatic. Spread the defenders as thinly as possible by attacking from all points of the compass simultaneously, then throw the greatest possible number of bodies over each wall as rapidly as possible. King Markhos' armsmen might wound or kill many of them; the trick was to get the survivors across more quickly than they could be killed. Every one of them who got a sword close enough to threaten one of Swordshank's armsmen would take that armsman's bow out of play...and make it easier still for the men behind them to get over the walls, in turn.

The man who'd swarmed up behind Leeana's second victim seemed to embrace his predecessor's body. For an instant, she thought she'd only wounded her second target; then she realized the newcomer was using his companion's corpse as a shield, putting it between him and the incoming arrows while he rolled across the wall and let himself drop. An arrow plunged into the shielding body. Then another. Someone else's arrow slashed past him, shattering against the wall's inner brickwork, as he pushed the dead man clear and plummeted, and Leeana dropped her own point of aim. He landed in a controlled tumble, coming back to his feet quickly, and she loosed.

The attackers were more heavily armored than most Sothōii. They wore chain or scale armor, rather than light cavalry's leather armor, and at least some of them had cuirasses, as well. Someone's arrow hit a steel breastplate and skipped off harmlessly, but the man springing back upright in front of Leeana Hanathafressa's pitiless green eyes didn't have one, and the needle-sharp tip of her arrow's awl-like pile head drove between the links of his mail.

The armor might slow it, might rob it of much of its power, but it couldn't *stop* it at that short range, and he cried out, clutching at the shaft quivering in his chest before he crashed back to earth. He lay twisting and jerking in agony, and Leeana swung away from him, seeking another target.

There were more than enough of them, for there were more grappling hooks than there were royal armsmen, and more and more of the attackers made it across the walls while the defenders were occupied picking off their companions. And just as the attackers had planned, every man who made it to the ground inside instantly became a greater threat than those still swarming up the ropes. He *had* to be dealt with, and that diverted the defenders' fire from the walls themselves. Leeana loosed again, and then again, killing one target and watching her arrow glance off the other's steel plate. She had no time for a follow-up shot against that assassin; he was coming straight at her, and she dropped her bow, shed her protective finger tab, and swept out both of her short swords.

The man wore an open-faced helmet, and he was close enough now for her to see his eyes, see his sudden savage smile, as he realized the single defender dancing towards the head of the veranda's steps was unarmored. His sword was much heavier—and at least a foot longer than hers—as well, and she had no shield. He bounded forward, three or four others following at his heels, and Leeana sensed his eagerness to cut her down and be on about the mission which had brought him here. His own armor and helmet gave him an enormous edge, and he drove straight up the steps towards her with a veteran's ruthless determination to capitalize on that advantage.

It was a mistake.

Leeana was taller than most men—over half a foot taller than him—with more than enough reach to offset the greater length of his sword, and war maid training was actually harder, harsher, and more demanding than that of most professional armsmen. It had to be, for they needed that razor edge of lethality, because unlike Leeana, the majority of war maids were *smaller* than the men they were likely to confront in combat. Leeana wasn't, but she'd trained to the same hard, unforgiving standard as her smaller sisters, and her own sword technique had been adopted directly from Dame Kaeritha Seldansdaughter. She hadn't trained in it for as many years as Kaeritha, but very few swordsmen—and even fewer swords*women*—had been mentored by a champion of Tomanāk and then polished under the unrelenting eye of Erlis Rahnafressa and Ravlahn Thregafressa since she was fourteen years old.

The assassin's eyes widened in astonishment as Leeana's left-hand blade engaged his longer sword, twisting elegantly about it, binding it and carrying it out and to the side. It was a very *brief* astonishment, however—his eyes hadn't finished widening before the razor-edged steel in her *right* hand licked out through the opening she'd created, precise as a surgeon's scalpel, and sliced effortlessly through his throat.

He went down with a bubbling scream, the sudden geyser of his life's blood splashing Leeana's arm, and his tumbling body tripped the man behind him. The second assassin managed not to fall, but he was off-center, fighting for balance, as Leeana lunged and recovered in a single, supple flash that left another slashed throat spouting blood in its wake.

It had taken perhaps three heartbeats, and the men following on her victims' heels paused in what might have been consternation. The two bodies before Leeana encumbered the steps up to the high veranda. There *might* be space enough for two of them to come up simultaneously, but they were far more likely to get in one another's way or stumble over their unfortunate companions, and no one was inclined to share their fate.

Yet neither were they inclined to abandon the effort, and more and more of the King's armsmen had been forced to abandon their bows as the tide of attackers swept over the walls. The courtyard was carpeted with bodies—there had to be at least thirty or forty of them—and the gods only knew how many more had fallen backward off the wall, but at least that number had made it into sword range of the archers. They'd charged straight towards the central lodge, forcing the guardsmen to intercept them and stop picking off their fellows as they swarmed across the wall.

Now half a dozen of them flowed across the body-strewn ground to join the men glaring up at Leeana, and her heart sank as they began to spread. There was only the single set of steps, and the veranda was high enough to be an awkward, climbing scramble from any other approach. The wooden railing along its edge was open, without any sort of upright pickets to bar anyone willing to make the climb, however, and she could be in only one spot at a time.

She drew a deep breath, forcing herself to focus on only the next few moments, and stepped back slightly from the head of the steps.

✧ ✧ ✧

Tellian of Balthar dropped his bow.

He and Hathan had dropped at least a dozen attackers as they scaled the wall, yet there'd never been any hope of actually *holding* it with only two bows, for the attackers had redoubled their efforts when they realized there were only two archers on the southern side of the lodge's perimeter. They'd swarmed up the ropes, vaulted across the top of the wall, and dropped exultantly to the ground at its foot, with only a tithe of the casualties their companions had suffered elsewhere.

Exultation became something else as they found themselves face-to-face with two wind riders and a one-eared chestnut mare with an eye of unnatural blue flame.

Dathgar, Gayrhalan, and Gayrfressa had swept from east to west along the southern wall while Tellian and Hathan drove arrows into the attackers' faces. Now they wheeled, facing back to the east, and the space between the solid block of stables and the lodge's outer wall was no more than seventy feet across. With the riding ring's demolition, it was also smooth and obstruction-free, like a corridor between two sheer walls.

With three coursers at one end of it.

The men coming over that wall could not have been more badly positioned to receive a cavalry charge. They were in no particular formation, without the tight frontage and pikes or halberds which might have fended off even regular cavalry, far less coursers, and the space in which they were trapped was just long enough for those coursers to spring off their hocks and accelerate towards them with preposterous speed.

As Leeana had already realized, whatever else Erkân Trâram's men might be, there were precious few cowards among them. Most of the men who'd already made it to the ground drew their swords. Some flung themselves forward, trying desperately to somehow get under the coursers to gut or hamstring them. Others pressed as close to the outer wall as they could, trying to stay out of the coursers' path and come at them from behind once they'd passed. A handful sprang towards the back of the stables, prying frantically at closed and barred doors, and another handful, closest to the eastern end of the confined space, boiled around that edge of the stables, funneling past it to join their fellows in the main courtyard. And then—

"*Balthar!*" Tellian bellowed, leaning low from his saddle, and red spray flew as his saber removed an assassin's right hand.

The man's sword spun away, still clenched in his severed hand, and Dathgar trumpeted a high, piercing echo of his rider's war cry. Another assassin screamed as steel-shod hooves bigger than his own head crushed the life from him, and the baron swept along the inner face of the wall, while Hathan and Gayrhalan took the back side of the stables. The other wind rider always took Tellian's left flank in battle, for he was left-handed, and his own saber flashed crimson as his courser thundered forward.

Gayrhalan's herd stallion had known what he was about when he christened the iron gray "Storm Souled." He'd never been noted for the gentleness of his temper, but unlike Dathgar, he sounded no trumpet call of defiance; he was too busy crushing a shrieking mercenary's shoulder into ruin between battleaxe jaws. His victim squealed desperately as the courser jerked him off his feet, snapping him in midair like a greyhound with a rabbit, without even breaking stride. Then the body was tossed aside to bounce brokenly off the stable wall, even as Gayrhalan put his barded shoulder into a fresh victim, knocking him off his feet to sprawl directly in front of Gayrfressa.

The mare had neither rider nor barding, but she was actually larger than either of the stallions, and mere men in armor held no terror for someone who'd trampled demons in defense of her herd when she was only a filly. More than that, coursers weren't horses. Even the most superbly trained warhorse was far less lethal than a creature half again as large, as intelligent as any of the Races of Man, and as thoroughly trained as any mishuk in a combat technique the coursers had spent a millennium perfecting.

Her left forehoof—shod in steel and broader than a dinner plate—came down on the assassin Gayrhalan had toppled with the brutal efficiency of a water-driven Dwarvenhame drop hammer. Her target didn't scream, and even as he died, she was thundering forward with the stallions, taking her next victim. She trampled him underfoot, jaws reaching past him, closing on a fourth enemy, and not in Gayrhalan's shoulder-crushing grip.

No—her incisors closed on the mercenary's head, and when she tossed *her* head, his went flying like a child's ball.

In a bare handful of seconds, the two humans and three coursers turned the space between the stables and the wall into an abattoir where nothing lived. And then the blood-splashed coursers swept around the stables' eastern edge after the fleet-footed enemies who'd escaped their wrath.

✧ ✧ ✧

At least ten men came scrambling towards the veranda.

No one would have accused them of being in any sort of formation—not surprisingly, given the chaos behind them and the knots of royal guardsmen and assassins coalescing in furious swirls of combat around the main lodge. But no one could have accused them of hesitation, either, and if their coordination wasn't perfect, it was good enough to overwhelm Leeana.

The first mercenary beat all of his fellows up and over the edge of the veranda, and Leeana's left-hand sword flashed in a crimson-streaming arc as she gave him the victor's prize. Then she whirled in the same flowing motion to face a man coming at her from the right. She engaged his sword with her right-hand blade, parrying it high barely in time, crashing into him chest-to-chest, and her left hand came up. She switched her primary attack from right to left, as instantly as Dame Kaeritha herself might have, and the man who'd just tried to kill her collapsed as she thrust up under their locked blades and drove the sword in that hand home in his armpit.

He slithered off her steel, and she turned, swaying aside purely by trained instinct, as another sword whistled through the space her head had occupied an instant before. She backpedaled, knowing she had to give ground while she regained her balance, yet painfully aware of the wall behind her. She couldn't back far, and so she set herself, taking a chance, bulling in on her new opponent before she was fully centered herself. A blade scored her ribs as she twisted her torso aside, and then he, too, went down, clutching at his face and screaming as her right-hand sword drove into his open-faced helmet. It wasn't a fatal wound, but blood fountained between his fingers as he clutched at his butchered eyes, and she kicked him aside as three more mercenaries came at her.

Her finely focused, steely purpose never faltered, but despair welled up behind it. All three of them were armored, whereas she could already feel the blood flowing down her left side in proof that she was completely *un*armored, and they advanced on her with coordinated menace.

She backed slowly, unable now to pay attention to the larger fight, watching them, poised to take any opening, however tiny, however fleeting. But they gave her no opening, and she felt the edge of the veranda looming up behind her. She drew a deep breath, and then—

The mercenary at the left end of the short advancing line screamed. He rose on his toes, then stumbled forward, going to his knees, and Sir Jerhas Macebearer's riding boot slammed between his shoulder blades, kicking him out of the way. The white-haired Prime Councilor slid through the gap he'd created, his back protected by the lodge's front wall, slotting in at Leeana's left, and she noticed that he'd left his cane behind.

Despite his age, he was past the mercenaries, covering her left side, before they even realized he was there, and the worn, wetly gleaming saber in his right hand was rock-steady.

Leeana noted all of that from the corner of her left eye, her attention locked on the men in front of her. They hesitated—only for an instant, barely noticeable to any observer—as their brains adjusted to the old warrior's unexpected appearance, and in that instant, she attacked. She uncoiled in a full-extension lunge that drove her right-hand sword through the closer mercenary's mouth and into his brain, and he dropped like a string-cut puppet. But her sword stuck briefly in the wound. It pulled her arm down, dragged her off balance, opened her to his remaining companion's attack, and it was his turn to lunge forward.

He never completed that lunge. In the instant that he launched it, Macebearer's bloody saber flicked into his helmet opening. There was no nasal, and the saber chopped through the bridge of the mercenary's nose. It struck his forehead with stunning force, not quite cleanly enough to cut through the bone, and the would-be assassin went down on one knee. He retained his sword, but his left hand clutched at his mangled face. Leeana couldn't tell if it was a simple reaction to the pain or if he was trying to clear his eyes of the sudden flow of blood, and it didn't matter. In the instant he was blind, the Prime Councilor's wrist turned, and the blade the mercenary never even saw drove through his unguarded throat from the side.

✧ ✧ ✧

Tellian and Dathgar rounded the corner of the stable block first.

The courtyard was a chaos of bodies and blood. There were no more mercenaries coming over the wall, but at least sixty of them were already inside it, driving in on the main lodge . . . and the King. More than a dozen of Swordshank's armsmen were down, lying amid the bodies of their enemies, and the survivors had been pushed back against the lodge, fighting furiously to hold the doors. At least two of the unarmored courtiers of the King's party lay with those still, twisted armsmen, and others fought to hold the building's windows.

And on the veranda, fighting before the front door itself, was his daughter, the left side of her white shirt soaked in blood, with the Kingdom's white-haired Prime Councilor at her side.

Bodies sprawled in front of them, but even as he caught sight of them, another clutch of mercenaries separated itself from the confusion and charged towards them, seeking to rush the door.

Something screamed beside him like a wounded direcat, and then Gayrfressa went bounding forward like a chestnut demon.

There was no time to discuss it with Dathgar . . . nor was there any need. They were one, and as the mare charged, they thundered out into the courtyard behind her with Hathan and Gayrhalan at their side.

✧ ✧ ✧

Leeana felt Gayrfressa coming, but she dared not look away from the fresh attackers swarming across the veranda towards her and Sir Jerhas.

"Take it to them, Milady!" a sharp, clear voice said from beside her. "I've got your back!"

She didn't waste time nodding. She simply went to meet her foes, and Sir Jerhas Macebearer came behind her.

Their sudden advance took the mercenaries by surprise, and Leeana pressed that fleeting advantage ruthlessly. She feinted to her left, then drove forward with her right, and another assassin collapsed as she thrust eight inches of steel into his thigh and his leg folded beneath him. Her booted heel came down on his sword wrist with bone-shattering force as he hit the veranda's blood-soaked planks, and she pivoted left, taking the man she'd first feinted towards from his suddenly unprotected flank. He gave ground, interposing his own sword frantically, but her left foot came up. The toe of her boot slammed up between his legs, and he cried out, staggering in sudden anguish. She tore through his wavering guard, ripping out his throat with both blades at once, and he sprawled across the man she'd crippled.

She recovered with desperate speed, aware of yet another opponent coming at her from the right, but Sir Jerhas was there. His saber engaged the mercenary's heavier longsword in a flurry of steel that would have done credit to a man half his age, turning the other's attack. Steel belled on steel in a lightning exchange of cuts and parries, but the younger, stronger mercenary pushed the older man back.

Not quickly enough. Leeana Hanathafressa was a war maid, and just as ruthlessly pragmatic as her husband. Honor was undoubtedly all very well, but she saw no reason to let the unarmored Prime Councilor fight it out with a man half his age and armored to boot. As Sir Jerhas gave ground, backing past her, she swiveled and struck with a viper's speed, driving a short sword home just below the mercenary's ear.

✧ ✧ ✧

Gayrfressa was crimson to the knees, and more blood streaked her throat and blew in a scarlet froth from her nostrils, as she took the mercenaries in the courtyard from the rear. Two tons of chestnut fury rolled over them like a boulder, pounding them into the dirt, crushing anyone who stood between her and her chosen sister, and Dathgar and Gayrhalan fanned out behind her.

One moment, the attackers had known they hovered on the brink of success, despite far heavier losses than they'd ever anticipated. At least half the King's armsmen were down and they were driving remorselessly forward, fighting in the very doorway of the lodge with the defenders melting like snow before them. And then, with no warning, three blood-soaked juggernauts slammed into them.

The coursers rampaged through them, killing as they came, and the mercenaries in that courtyard were in no better state to meet them than the ones they'd trapped between the stables and the outer wall. The only difference was that *these* mercenaries had room to run, and they did. The shock of that sudden, unexpected attack broke them, and the survivors fled madly towards the gate, flinging up the bar, spilling through it with Dathgar and Gayrhalan thundering in pursuit.

Less than thirty of them made it.

Chapter Thirty-Six

Cassan Axehammer sat on a fallen tree at the top of a steep bank, trying not to fidget impatiently as his armsmen watered their horses from the chuckling stream at the foot of the slope. He begrudged the halt, and the tension within him was coiling ever tighter as they drew closer to the hunting lodge. Despite that, he could scarcely fault Stoneblade or Horsemaster. They'd made remarkably good time since he'd informed them of his "suspicions," and they had a Sothōii's eye for their horses. It would no more occur to them to arrive for a fight on blown, exhausted mounts than it would to leave their swords at home, and they were right, if not simply for the reasons they knew about. If all went well, they'd be riding after the fleeing assassins soon enough, and they'd need horses capable of overhauling them.

Not that recognizing that made it any easier for Cassan to sit, waiting. His normal chessmaster's patience had deserted him, and he needed to be *doing* something, moving forward now that the moment of decision had arrived. He'd managed not to snap off anyone's head, but his armsmen knew him well enough to give him space and privacy. They worked steadily and quickly with the horses, and he flipped bits of dead bark moodily into the water while he waited.

"Milord Baron."

Cassan stiffened and his head whipped up. There was no one to be seen, however, and his eyes widened as they darted around, searching for the speaker. He *knew* that voice, but how—?

"Down here, Milord."

The voice was tiny, yet sharp, peremptory, and Cassan looked down, then paled as he saw the perfectly ordinary-looking gray squirrel sitting upright on the leaves, an acorn clasped in its forepaws while it gazed up at him with a fixed, unblinking stare. A chill of sheer terror went through him, and he put his palms on his tree-trunk seat and started to shove himself upright.

"*Don't!*" the voice snapped with a commanding edge, and this time it came unmistakably from the squirrel. The baron froze, and the squirrel dropped the acorn and flirted its tail.

"Better," it said, and Cassan swallowed hard as he recognized Master Talthar's voice coming from the small creature. It was suddenly hard to breathe, and perspiration beaded his brow as he stared at the confirmation of the truth he'd so carefully avoided acknowledging to himself for so many years.

"Yes," the squirrel said with Talthar's voice, "I'm a wizard. Of course I am! And you're a traitor. Would you like me to confirm that for your enemies?"

Cassan looked around, eyes darting frantically towards his armsmen, and the squirrel snorted.

"You're the only one who can hear me...so far," it told him. "I can always broaden the focus of the spell, if you want, though."

The baron shook his head almost spastically, and the squirrel cocked its head as it gazed up at him.

"Frankly, I would have preferred to let you remain in blissful ignorance, since we both want the same thing in the end, anyway," it said. "Unfortunately, we have a problem. The King's armsmen realized Arthnar's men were coming. They managed to hold off the initial attack and inflicted heavy losses on them. Half of Swordshank's men are down, as well, but I'd say the odds are at least even that your 'allies' aren't going to be attacking again anytime soon. I could be wrong about that, but what should matter to you is that a dozen or so of them have been captured, including at least one of their officers. And contrary to what you may have believed," the wizard's biting irony came through the squirrel's voice perfectly, "they think *you're* the one who hired them. Which is true enough, in a way, isn't it?"

Cassan turned even paler as he remembered his conversation with Horsemaster and realized the pretext for massacre he'd invented had become a reality after all.

"Understand me, Milord," the squirrel told him. "I want you to succeed, and if you do, I'll be delighted to continue to support you as effectively—and discreetly—as I always have. But for you to do that, you'd better get a move on."

✧ ✧ ✧

"Well, that was almost worth it," Varnaythus said, sitting back in his hidden chamber with a sour expression. He'd released his link to the squirrel, which had promptly scurried off into the forest once more, but the wizard's gramerhain showed him Cassan's expression quite clearly, and it was still nearly as stunned as it had been when the squirrel first spoke to him. "I thought he was going to have a heart attack."

"Are you sure that was a good idea?" Sahrdohr asked in a careful tone, looking up from his own stone, where he'd been monitoring the advance of Trianal's army across the Ghoul Moor. Too much was coming together too quickly for either of them to keep an eye on everything, and the fact that they'd planned it that way made things no less hectic. Now he met his superior's gaze, and Varnaythus shrugged.

"No," he acknowledged. "I don't see how it could hurt, though, and it should at least keep him from changing his mind at the last moment."

Sahrdohr frowned thoughtfully, but then, slowly, he nodded. "It does rather burn his bridges for him, doesn't it?"

"More to the point, it makes sure he *knows* his bridges are burned. Now he can't even pretend he doesn't know he's been cooperating with wizards. Any real interogation by one of Markhos' magi will prove that, and that's just as much high treason as regicide, as far as the Sothōii are concerned. There's no way back for him unless he succeeds, and a man like Cassan will figure that if he *does* succeed he'll be able to find a way to be rid of us eventually. That should stiffen his spine."

"I noticed that you didn't mention anything to him about what Tellian and Hathan did to Trâram's men."

"No, I didn't, did I?" Varnaythus smiled nastily, then shrugged. "On the other hand, they ought to be less of a problem for him. The two of them may have ridden Trâram's mercenaries into the ground, but his armsmen know how to fight wind riders. Especially when they have lances and the wind riders don't... not to mention outnumbering them a couple of hundred to one! Under *those* circumstances, I'm not that worried about even his ability to deal with them."

He shrugged again, and Sahrdohr nodded again.

"You didn't mention Trisu or the war maids, either," he pointed out.

"Of course not." Varnaythus snorted. "Why cloud the issue for him? It's unlikely the threat of them would turn him back at this point, but it might. Besides, it's not as if we really want him to get away with this. We need at least some of Trisu's armsmen to escape with word of Cassan's treachery if we're going to touch off a proper civil war."

"And if they get there before he's had time to kill Markhos?" Sahrdohr asked. The war maids and armsmen from Kalatha and Thalar Keep had faced a far shorter journey than Cassan, and they'd ridden hard enough to cut their arrival time shorter than he'd originally estimated.

"That could be unfortunate," Varnaythus conceded, "but there aren't enough of them to stop him. And if it looks as if they might, there's always the kairsalhain, isn't there?"

✧ ✧ ✧

Erkân Trâram looked at what was left of his company and managed somehow not to curse out loud.

It wasn't easy.

At least I'm not going to have to worry about having enough horses for the final run to the river, he thought savagely. *Fiendark take those damned wind riders!*

"I make it seventy-three, Sir." Sergeant Selmar's voice was flat, and Trâram winced.

That was even worse than he'd been afraid it would be. He'd expected to take significant losses to Markhos' guardsmen getting over the wall, but his employer hadn't mentioned any wind riders in full plate! In fact, he thought sulfurically, he'd been specifically told that any wind riders who might be present would be courtiers who would never be so gauche as to bring armor on a hunting trip with their King.

And this is what I get for trusting someone else's information about something like that. Even assuming the bastard told me the truth—*as far as he knew it, anyway—I should've planned from the perspective that he might just be wrong.*

His teeth grated as he considered Selmar's numbers. No wonder even the tough-minded noncom sounded half-stunned. If they were down to only seventy-three effectives, then he'd lost over a *hundred* and seventy in that murderous exchange.

And I'll bet those frigging wind riders took down half of them all by themselves.

He glowered down at the bloodstained bandage around his left forearm. He was lucky the pile-headed arrow had punched a neat, round hole through the meat and muscle without hitting bone. A broad-headed arrow would have shredded the limb, but his surgeon had cut the shaft of the one which had actually hit him and drawn it the rest of the way through the wound. It hurt like Phrobus, but it was unlikely to cripple him, and at least he was right-handed. He could still fight . . . unlike entirely too many of the men he'd brought north with him.

"All right, Gûrân," he growled finally. "Get them organized into two platoons."

The sergeant looked at him wordlessly for a moment, then drew a deep breath, squared his shoulders, and nodded.

"Aye, Sir," he said, and Trâram turned to Somar Lararik, who was no longer simply his senior lieutenant but the only one he still had.

"Well?"

"The best I can give you is a guess, Sir," the lieutenant said. He shrugged. "Mûrsam's estimate is probably the best."

Trâram nodded. Corporal Fûrkhan Mûrsam was as hard-bitten and experienced as they came. He'd never been promoted above corporal because he found it difficult to remain sober in garrison, but he never drank in the field. Indeed, he seemed to get steadily more levelheaded and focused as the crap got deeper and deeper.

"He says he personally saw at least twenty and probably twenty-five of Markhos' armsmen down, and maybe as many as a half dozen of his damned 'guests' and their servants. That matches *fairly* well with what I'm getting from the others, although I'm inclined to think it may be a little overly optimistic, myself. And that doesn't include the Phrobus-damned wind riders."

Trâram nodded again. Assuming the corporal's estimate was correct, there couldn't be more than a score of armsmen left, and he had fifteen of his surviving crossbowmen bellied down in the woods within fifty yards of the gate. The Sothōii had already lost two more armsmen they were in no position to spare discovering he had no intention of allowing them to *close* that gate once again. They'd declined to lose any more in the effort, which at least meant he wasn't going to have to go across the wall if he tried a second attack.

If not for the wind riders, he wouldn't have hesitated, and he'd have mounted the followup as quickly as possible, while the defenders had to be at least as disorganized as *he* was. Of course, if it hadn't been for the damned wind riders, he wouldn't have *needed* to launch a second attack, either. On the other hand, he knew about them now. They wouldn't have the advantage of surprise the second time around, and he still outnumbered Markhos' guardsmen by at least three-to-one. And for that matter, the wind riders' presence made it even more urgent that he get in there and finish them off along with the rest of the hunting lodge's occupants.

If he gave this operation up as a bad idea now, he rather doubted they'd simply decide to let him go. No, they'd do everything they could to lay him and his men by their heels, and it was distinctly possible they might figure out where he was headed. If they did, and chose not to ride directly after him, it was all too likely that something with a courser's speed and endurance could reach the Spear at one of the riverside towns downstream from his rendezvous with the barges well before he could sail down the river past them. And if they managed that, it wouldn't be difficult for the authorities to send boats to Nachfalas, his only way down the Escarpment from here, to wait for his arrival. Assuming, of course, that they didn't have enough boats on hand to simply come after him in midstream themselves.

As long as those accursed coursers were in a position to do that, he couldn't count on breaking contact and getting away clean. Even if he could, his employer was unlikely to be pleased. The assassination of a king was a serious matter, and if the mission failed, he might decide it was time to snip off any loose ends that could lead back to him. Trâram had no desire to spend what remained of his life looking over his shoulder, waiting for the dog brothers to catch up with him.

There are only two *of them, Erkân,* he reminded himself. Of course there was that third *courser* to worry about. But now that he knew it was there, and now that his crossbowmen could bring their own missile weapons to bear through the open gate, the enormous chestnut was simply one more unarmored horse.

It was the other two coursers and that heavy barding of theirs. If he could just come up with a way to take *them* out of action, or at least find a way to get close enough to hamstring them without getting trampled into red mud first . . .

He paused, eyes narrowing suddenly, then stooped and picked up a handful of the forest's deep leaf mold. He looked at it for a moment, then closed his fist and listened to the dry leaves crackle as he crushed them, and he smiled.

✧ ✧ ✧

Leeana looked up as Dathgar and Gayrfressa arrived almost simultaneously at the veranda rail while Sir Jerhas Macebearer tied off the bandage on her gashed ribs.

The cut wasn't especially deep, although it had bled freely, but she was grateful for the dressing. She was also more than a little surprised the Prime Councilor had insisted on personally assisting her with it.

Not that there weren't more than enough wounded to keep everyone else with any healing skill busy, she reflected grimly, listening to the moans of the wounded and dying men littered across the courtyard. She gazed at that carpet of writhing bodies—and the ones which would never writhe again—and knew her childhood memories of Chergor would never be the same.

"Leeana?" Her father had raised the visor of his helmet, and his voice was sharp with the same concern she felt welling out of Gayrfressa.

Macebearer glanced up over his shoulder.

"Your daughter's going to be fine, Tellian," he said, and Leeana's eyebrows rose as he called her that.

"It's more than a scratch, but it's also shallow and clean," the Prime Councilor continued as she lowered the bloodied shirt she'd raised to let him get at the wound. "We've both seen people take far worse in their first fight, at any rate." His lips twitched in something midway between a smile and a grimace. "And we're lucky she was here to take it; without her, they would've carried the veranda and gotten to the King after all. It hurts my pride to admit it, but she's not just better with a blade than I am *now*. I'm afraid she's better than I *ever* was. And"—the fleeting almost-smile disappeared and his voice went harder—"the number of these bastards the two of you killed between you should convince just about anyone that *you* weren't the one behind the attack."

"I hope you don't expect some of them to *admit* that," Tellian said, never looking away from Leeana.

"Probably not," the Prime Councilor replied, standing back and leaning against one of the veranda's supports while he watched Leeana tuck her shirt back in. "It's a point *I* intend to make, however, since your daughter's warning—not to mention her sword skill—means I'll be around to make it."

"That's the second time you've called her my daughter," Tellian observed, and Macebearer shrugged.

"Did you think I thought you'd stopped loving her just because she became a war maid? I'm sure it would shock any number of our lords warden to hear me say it, but at the moment I don't really care very much." He snorted a sudden chuckle. "No doubt I'll get over it in the fullness of time, but at least for the moment, I think it's more important for her to be who the two of you think she is than who the *law* says she is."

Tellian looked at him for a long, still moment, then nodded and looked back at his daughter. She saw the worry in his eyes, the darkness deep within them as he tried to keep them from clinging to the blood on her shirt and the stain where it had run down over her breeches.

"Are you really all right, love?" he asked in a much gentler tone, and she knew he was asking about far more than a cut.

"As close to it as anyone could be," she told him honestly.

She looked down at her right hand, wondering why it wasn't quivering the way it felt it ought to be, thinking about how many of those dead and dying men in the courtyard had been put there by that very hand, and tried to understand her own feelings. She didn't—not really—and if she didn't understand them herself, how was she supposed to explain them to him? She thought about that for a moment, then looked back up at him.

"I'll *be* all right, anyway," she said. "That's probably the best anyone can say after his—or *her*—first fight, isn't it?"

"It is."

She'd never heard her father sound quite like that, and a deep, heart-melting surge of love went through her as their eyes met. She was his daughter, and the daughters of Sothōii nobles were supposed to be protected, cherished—kept safe. He'd never in his worst nightmare expected to see his daughter, the treasure of his heart, whirling through a cauldron of blood, screams, and shearing steel. And yet, despite the terror he must have felt, despite the bone-deep training which insisted in his heart of hearts, whatever his mind might tell him, that women—and especially *his daughter*—had no business shedding their blood, or anyone else's, he was fighting *so* hard to keep that dread, that fear, from showing. He was failing, but that only made her love him even more for trying.

"Sir Jerhas is right," Tellian continued, looking at the bodies sprawled on and about the veranda. "Without your warning, they would've overrun us before we even knew they were here, and that doesn't even count *this*." He gestured briefly at the bodies. "If it's all the same to you, I don't think we'll be discussing this in any great detail with your mother, and at the moment I find myself really wishing you'd never become a war maid, but"—he looked straight into her eyes—"I'm proud of you."

"I had good teachers," Leeana said.

"I'm sure you did. But I've just decided what to give you and Bahzell for a wedding present." Leeana cocked her head, and he snorted harshly. "If you're going to be a wind rider, you need the armor to go with it, and I happen to have friends in Dwarvenhame. I'm sure they can help us out with that."

<*And the sooner the better,*> Gayrfressa agreed tartly. The blood-soaked mare glared at her chosen rider. <*Two-foots! And you were worried about* me?!>

<*Of course I was,*> Leeana replied silently, reaching up to stroke the courser's neck as Gayrfressa leaned closer, touching her nose to her chest and blowing heavily. <*You're a bigger target than I am.*>

<*Oh, really? And* which *one of us came through without a scratch?*>

Leeana laughed just a bit shakily and turned back to Macebearer.

"I appreciate the bandage, Sir Jerhas. I only hope you didn't shock the rest of the King's gentlemen *too* severely."

"I'm sure some of them will be suitably horrified later," the Prime Councilor said dryly. "For now, I doubt somehow anyone's likely to make any . . . inappropriate remarks. And as for the propriety of it," his blue eyes twinkled suddenly as they cut briefly to Tellian's face, "my younger daughter is at least ten years your senior, young lady. I believe I can put a bandage on your ribs without being overwhelmed by lust."

Leeana blinked at him. For a moment, she was certain she'd

imagined his last sentence, but those blue eyes gleamed, and she heard something shockingly like a crack of laughter from her father's direction as the Prime Councilor stroked his luxurious mustache and returned her goggle-eyed look with a bland smile.

"I see you have hidden depths, Milord," she told him finally, and he chuckled. But then he sobered and shook his head.

"I won't pretend I suddenly approve of the entire notion of war maids," he said, "because I don't. But without you, my King would be dead. Whatever I think of the choices you've made, nothing can erase that debt."

"No, it can't," another voice said, and Leeana turned quickly as King Markhos stepped out onto the veranda.

The King looked around the body-littered courtyard, his expression hard, and anger smoked in his eyes. Anger made even worse, Leeana realized, because he'd been denied the right to strike a single blow in his own defense.

She doubted Swordshank could have enforced that edict if Markhos had brought along his own armor. It had been difficult enough as it was, yet the King had been forced to acknowledge the overriding logic of his personal armsman's argument. If he fell, their attackers won, whatever their losses; if he lived, then his guardsmen won, even if not one of them survived. He owed it to those guardsmen—and especially to the ones who were certain to fall in his defense—to live. To make their sacrifice count. And so while every instinct cried out to join the battle, he'd made himself accept the far harder task of waiting at the center of his defenders' ring of swords while they died to protect him.

"I can think of very few men, noble or common, who have ever served the Crown as well as you have this day," he said now, turning back to Leeana. He glanced up at her father, but his eyes came back to meet hers, and his voice was level. "And I can think of none at all who have ever served it *better*. I stand in your debt, and my house remembers its debts."

Leeana flushed and shook her head quickly.

"Your Majesty, I'm scarcely the only—"

"Of course you aren't," he interrupted her, looking out over the courtyard once more, watching a half dozen of Swordshank's surviving armsmen dragging wounded assassins out of the pile of dead and dying. His bodyguards' expressions suggested those prisoners would soon be telling their captors everything they knew, and his eyes hardened with grim satisfaction as he continued speaking to Leeana.

"The Crown owes a debt to a great many people today, and I'm afraid it isn't the sort anyone can truly pay. But I overheard at least a portion of your conversation, and Sir Jerhas is right. Without you and your wind sister, *all* of my armsmen would have fallen in my defense . . . and they would have fallen in vain. Your father"—the King's expression didn't even flicker as he called Baron Tellian that—"has always served me and the Kingdom well, yet there have been times, especially of late, when that service has threatened to turn the entire Kingdom topsy-turvy, as well. I suppose there's no reason I should expect his daughter to be any different in that regard."

Leeana opened her mouth. Then she closed it again, and Macebearer chuckled.

"I think—" he began, then broke off as Gayrfressa's head snapped up. The mare wheeled, looking to the east, and her remaining ear went flat.

<*Smoke!*> she told Leeana, and green eyes widened as Leeana smelled the same scent through the courser's nostrils.

Chapter Thirty-Seven

Trâram watched the first flight of flaming arrows trace lines of smoke across the sky and smiled thinly. He hadn't had many archers to begin with, and it had become painfully evident in the assault across the wall that the ones he did have weren't as good as King Markhos' armsmen.

Fortunately, they didn't have to be for what he had in mind.

The steeply pitched, cedar-shingled roofs of the main lodge, the stables, and the enclosed barracks showed clearly above the cursed ornamental wall. They were big targets, and the plunging arrows struck firmly into them. Within seconds, more smoke began to curl upward, and Trâram's smile broadened. The defenders had economized on manpower by defending the buildings, firing from cover as his men crossed the wall and falling back on the doors and windows as the attack rolled in. But large and ornate as the lodge was, the entire area enclosed by its wall wasn't all *that* spacious, and after the casualties they'd taken in the initial assault, the King and his guardians couldn't possibly have enough manpower for firefighting on top of everything else. Once the buildings were nicely alight, they'd be driven from cover, forced to huddle in the limited space where nothing would burn, and hemmed in by torrents of heat and smoke. They'd find their defensive options badly cramped when that happened.

Flames began to leap and dance along the roofs, the columns of smoke growing thicker and denser, beginning to billow on the fires' growing updraft. He watched those columns climb and waited.

✧ ✧ ✧

Some of the armsmen and servants dashed for the watering troughs and the lever-arm pumps that served them. It was an instinctive reaction, but one Leeana knew instantly was futile. There were simply too many arrows, too many separate pools of flame spreading across those roofs, and her heart sank as she pictured what the heat and smoke were going to do to their ability to defend the King.

But then she heard a sound even more horrifying than that thought—the screams of panicked horses.

"*The stables!*" she shouted, and ran madly across the courtyard, ignoring the scattered rain of burning arrows hissing out of the heavens. More feet pounded behind her, following her towards the stables with the bone-deep instinct of all Sothōii.

Hooves thundered on box stalls, more whistling screams of terror rose from within the smoke, and Leeana heaved desperately at the bar across the stable doors. Someone skidded to a halt beside her, helping her, throwing the locking bar aside, grabbing the huge double door panels and hauling them wide. Smoke, heat, and those bone-chilling screams billowed out of them, and Leeana coughed as she ran into the heart of chaos.

She flung open the stalls nearest to the entrance, dodging frantically as the horses in them threw their weight against the opening doors. Those horses saw light, knew where the door was, and terror gave them wings. They thundered out of the stable, fleeing madly from the crackling flames, and Leeana coughed again, harder. The smoke was incredible, and the stablemaster had stored a loft full of hay against the coming winter. Burning bits of shingle and roofing timber spilled into the loft, and the dried hay caught instantly. White smoke joined the seething coils of wood smoke, and it was suddenly impossible to see more than a foot or two through the choking, suffocating waves of heat.

<*Come back!*> Gayrfressa cried in the back of her brain. <*Leeana! Sister*—come back!>

Leeana heard her hoofed sister, but even Gayrfressa's voice was lost and far away, somewhere beyond the immediacy of her mission. She staggered in the blinding smoke, finding the stall latches by feel more than by sight, throwing them open, but these horses couldn't see the entrance, and even if they could have, crackles of flame danced and leapt between them and the stable door. The path to escape and life lay between those flames, but they eyed the wall of smoke with its ominous red glare, and the panicky horses shied away from the visible menace. They reared and trumpeted madly, deadly in their terror, and Leeana jumped aside, barely in time, as one of them blundered blindly deeper into the death trap of the burning stables.

She caught another by the halter, and was nearly dragged from her feet by the terrified creature. She managed to hang on, wishing desperately that she could somehow bandage its eyes, but that would have taken an extra set of hands. All she could do was speak to it as soothingly as the tumult of sound and her own coughing breath would allow while she dragged it towards safety.

She'd managed to get it almost all the way to the entrance when a flaming bit of debris landed on its croup. The fiery piece of wreckage wasn't especially large, but the burned horse squealed and bolted forward, nearly trampling her as it broke free of the stable. She staggered, almost falling, then started back into the roaring inferno once more.

Something hit her. Already off-balance, she fell, and barely managed to tuck a shoulder before she hit the ground. The cut on her ribs sent a stab of pain through her, but she ignored it, shoving herself back up onto her knees, starting for the stable again.

"No!" a voice shouted in her ear.

She coughed, trying to understand, and felt hands on her shoulders, dragging her back. She turned her head and found herself looking into a face she knew.

"No, Milady!" Tarith Shieldarm said. He shook his head, tears washing pale lines through the soot on his face. "No . . . it's too late."

<Listen to him! Listen *to him, Sister!>*

Leeana twisted, trying to pull free, the hideous screams of the horses still trapped in that vortex of flame washing over her, but he wouldn't let her go.

"No," he said once more. "You can't! It's too late!"

The words broke through to her at last, and she sagged, suddenly aware that she wasn't simply coughing. She was weeping wildly as those shrieks of agony rolled over her, and the man who'd been her personal armsman for so many years gathered her into his arms and held her tightly.

"There, lassie," he murmured in her ear, stroking her singed, ash-smutted hair with one callused hand. "There. You did what you could. Come away now."

✧ ✧ ✧

"No, here—*here!*" Hathan Shieldarm shouted.

"Leave the horses!" he heard Tellian bellowing. "Fiendark take it, *leave the horses!*"

Hathan winced at the pain and rage in his wind brother's voice, but the baron was right. They couldn't save all the horses, whatever they did, and in trying to save *any* they played directly into the hands of the men trying to kill the King. He snarled, beating at one of the King's armsmen with the flat of his saber, hard enough the man staggered and nearly fell. He came back up, his face a mask of fury, then stopped when Hathan struck him again. The armsman shook his head, and reason flowed back into his expression.

Reason... and hate. Hate directed at that moment against the wind rider who'd stopped him from running into that roaring, crackling furnace.

Reason won. The armsman shook his head, then nodded and staggered back towards the King.

"Into the corner!" Tellian shouted. "Get the King into the angle—now, damn you! *Now!*"

Sir Frahdar Swordshank's voice joined the baron's, whipping the remaining armsmen and courtiers into something resembling organized motion. They dragged the wounded with them, trying to keep low, under the smoke, as they backed into the southwestern corner of the walled enclosure. The wind—such as there was of it—was out of the west, pushing the worst of the smoke away from them. The rolling, roaring flame which had engulfed the main lodge was to their right front, and the wall itself was to their left. It was a pathetic excuse for a defensive position, but it was the best they had.

<They're moving, Brother,> Gayrhalan told Hathan. *<They're moving.>*

They were, and the wind rider heaved a mental sigh of relief. Then his head came up as a huge chestnut mare loomed out of the smoke beside him. Leeana leaned against Gayrfressa, coughing, her face streaked with tears, and Hathan's heart twisted as he saw her. He started to reach out to her, but there was no time. The best he could do was give her a nod of encouragement before he and Gayrhalan crossed to Tellian.

The baron looked up grimly as Gayrhalan drew up beside Dathgar.

"She's all right," Hathan said quickly.

"So far," Tellian grated. His face was as filthy as his armor, smeared with ash, and his eyes were hard, as close to despair as Hathan had ever seen them.

"They'll be coming again . . . soon," the baron continued, wrenching his thought and heart away from his daughter, focusing on the desperation of the moment. "This time, it'll be the gate."

"Unless they decide that's what we're going to expect and they use the cover of the smoke to come over the walls again," Hathan replied.

<*It will be the gate,*> Gayrhalan said flatly. Hathan looked down, and the courser turned his head far enough to look up at him with one eye. <*We hurt them too badly on the walls last time, Brother. They won't come in scattered that way a second time.*> He flicked his ears in the equine equivalent of a shrug. <*The gate will let them come in together, and they'll expect the smoke to keep us from seeing them until they're right on top of us.*>

"Gayrhalan's right," Tellian said harshly as Dathgar relayed the gray stallion's argument. "Even if they don't use the gate, they'll come in concentrated this time, and that means they'll have to cross the courtyard to get to the King. That's when it will be up to us."

Hathan looked at him for a moment, then turned and peered into the rolling walls of smoke and flame and nodded in slow understanding.

✧ ✧ ✧

Leeana finished tying the water-saturated cloth across her nose and mouth. It helped—some—and she pressed her face into Gayrfressa's shoulder, trying to shut out the horrible sounds still coming from the stable.

<*You did all you could,*> Gayrfressa told her quietly. <*You did all you could.*>

<*It wasn't enough,*> Leeana replied silently, hearing the sob in her own mind voice.

<*Of course it wasn't. But I'm selfish, Sister. I want you alive, not dead in that stable.*>

Leeana flinched, hearing the terror in the courser's voice and knowing it wasn't for herself. She stroked the huge mare's flank, her hand trembling, and started to say something more, but there was no need for it.

And there was no time, either.

✧ ✧ ✧

Trâram waved his men forward.

They obeyed his hand signal without eagerness, but there was no hesitation, either. It wasn't just about the money anymore. They'd lost two-thirds of their companions, and they wanted vengeance for those deaths.

They moved forward, faces swathed in water-soaked cloth, eyes squinted against the stinging smoke. The gate loomed before them, like an apparition seen through driving snow, and expressions tightened and stomachs knotted as they headed for it. It was time—

A bugle sounded suddenly behind them, and Trâram whipped around just in time to see a mounted Sothōii armsman crashing out of the forest behind him with his lance couched.

✧ ✧ ✧

"The King! *The King!*" Cassan Axehammer shouted, and his armsmen charged.

The waves of smoke rising above the trees had spurred them forward, and Cassan's heart had risen with every furlong. The hunting lodge must be engulfed in flame, and that very possibly meant Markhos and Tellian were already dead. Even if it didn't, the confusion it engendered could only aid his own plans, and the warning Talthar had issued through that accursed squirrel drove him like a lash. If Talthar had told him the truth—if the assassins truly believed Cassan was the one who'd hired them—those assassins had to die, and die quickly. And so he'd launched his armsmen into the mercenaries' backs at the gallop without wasting a precious moment trying to order or control their formation.

Surprise was total. Trâram and his men had been entirely focused on the burning hunting lodge. The sudden, soaring notes of the bugle, the drum roll of hooves, and the thunder of war cries swept over them, and a merciless steel stormfront of lanceheads and sabers was close behind.

Some of the mercenaries turned, striking at their enemies with the fury of despair before they were ridden over by steel-shod hooves, lanced, or cut down by furiously driven sabers. One or two, closest to the flanks of their formation, bolted for the woods, only to be cut off and slashed down by outriders of the main charge.

Most of them never had the opportunity to do even that much. Taken completely unawares from behind, they died almost before they ever realized they were under attack.

✧ ✧ ✧

Tellian and Hathan stared at each other in confusion and speculation as the bugles continued to sound.

"Trisu?" Hathan said, but Tellian shook his head.

"It might be, but I don't think so. It sounds to me like there's too many of them for that."

<*You're right, I think, Brother,*> Dathgar said. <*There are at least several hundred of the lesser cousins out there—more than Lord Trisu could possibly have assembled.*>

"Then who the Phrobus *is* it?" Hathan demanded as Gayrhalan relayed Dathgar's remarks. The dark-haired wind rider grimaced. "Not that I'm not grateful, you understand, but something about having that many armsmen turn up all unannounced at the very moment people are trying to kill the King turns me all suspicious."

"And me," Tellian agreed grimly.

"So what do we do?"

"That, Brother, is a very good question." Tellian drew a deep breath, his eyes worried, then exhaled noisily and looked down as Frahdar Swordshank appeared at his stirrup.

"The King needs your advice, Milord," the guardsman said, and Tellian nodded curtly.

Dathgar turned without any instruction from his rider, picking his way through the armsmen between him and Markhos. The courser halted beside the King, and Tellian bowed from the saddle.

"Your Majesty?"

"I suppose we should be grateful," Markhos said, his tone flat, "but we've had unpleasant surprises enough for one day. I can't quite rid my mind of the thought that this might be another one."

"I think there are too many of them for it to be Lord Trisu," Tellian replied. "Which presents the question of who *else* it might be. It's always remotely possible someone else realized what was happening and rode to your rescue, but it seems . . . unlikely, I'm afraid."

"You think it may be whoever *sent* the assassins," the King said, looking Tellian straight in the eye. "After all, whoever it might have been"—the unspoken name of the baron they both knew it had to be hovered between them—"wouldn't want any inconvenient loose ends dangling about."

"That's what I'm afraid of, at any rate," Tellian admitted.

"And I," Sir Jerhas Macebearer put in from the King's side. "But we might all be wrong. And even if we aren't, how many men could . . . whoever is behind this have trusted with the truth?"

"That's a good point," Tellian said after a moment. "Dathgar"—he patted the courser's neck—"thinks there are at least 'several hundred' horses out there. His ears are a lot better than mine, and I trust his judgment. But no one could have brought that many armsmen fully into his confidence about something like this without some hint of it leaking out. Or, at least, no one would take the risk that it *might* leak out. And whoever might command them, those are *Sothōii* out there, Your Majesty. They won't take kindly to the notion of attacking the King."

"Meaning what?" Markhos asked, his eyes narrowing.

"Meaning that someone has to go out there, find out who they are, and get a grip on the situation before there's an . . . unfortunate accident."

"And who did you have in mind?" Markhos demanded, then snorted harshly at Tellian's expression. "That's what I thought. And the answer, Milord, is that it *isn't* going to be you."

"But—"

"No," the King said flatly. His nostrils flared. "First, I cannot and will not risk one of the Kingdom's four barons at a time like this. And, second, Milord, if that should happen to be who both of us are afraid it might be, the *last* person we need to send out to talk to him is you."

"But—"

"I'll go, Your Majesty," Hathan said quietly.

Tellian's head snapped around. He hadn't heard his wind brother approaching, nor had he realized Hathan had heard the conversation. He opened his mouth quickly, but Hathan shook his head.

"His Majesty's right, Tellian. We can't risk you, but it has to be someone whose word will carry weight not just with whoever their commander might be, but with those armsmen themselves. But neither Sir Jerhas nor any of the other of the King's guests have armor, and even if that's Trisu himself out there, accidents can happen. A hasty archer could put an arrow right through any of them if they were sent out as His Majesty's envoy, and we need Sir Frahdar right where he is. I, on the other hand—"

He tapped his steel breastplate with a gauntleted fingertip, smiling thinly at his wind brother, and Tellian gritted his teeth.

"Dathgar and I are just as well armored as you are," he pointed out bitterly.

"Yes, you are. But if that *is* Cassan," Hathan smiled grimly as he finally said the name out loud, "seeing you is far more likely to push him over the edge. He wouldn't be *happy* to see me, either, of course. But if you're still in here with His Majesty, he's going to be less tempted to try to arrange an 'accident' than he would if you came into reach. Especially if he hasn't informed his men of what he's really up to. And if he does do something hasty, Gayrhalan and I are well enough protected—and fast enough to have a better chance of getting back here in one piece than anyone else you could send."

✧ ✧ ✧

Cassan watched Stoneblade reforming his armsmen and tried not to fidget.

The baron had hoped to carry straight on into the lodge, riding to the King's rescue in the sort of confusion most likely to create a tragic accident which could be safely blamed on Tellian of Balthar after all the inconvenient witnesses were dead. But the collision with the mercenaries had disordered and slowed his armsmen, and Stoneblade was too good a field commander. He was only too well aware of what could happen in that sort of situation, and he had no intention of allowing it. He'd had his buglers sounding the recall almost before they'd hit the mercenaries, and Cassan's teeth ground together as he watched his senior captain in action.

I should have told him what we're really after, he thought grimly. *Either that, or I should've left him the hell home!*

Unfortunately, he hadn't, and Horsemaster's company had obeyed Stoneblade's bugle calls without even thinking about it. The men were confused and anxious, and their horses were spooked by the smell of smoke and burning horseflesh. They were grateful for the promise of control and command those bugle calls offered.

Now how do I get them back into motion? Cassan wondered. *There has to be a way, but I've got to be careful. I can't afford—*

"Milord!" Tarmahk Dirkson pointed suddenly, and Cassan looked up as a smoke-stained, soot-streaked wind rider rode slowly through the open gate. Cassan's jaw tightened with a sudden burn of fury, but then he relaxed slightly. It wasn't Tellian's dark bay; it was that other bastard Hathan's gray, and his mind worked feverishly as he watched the wind rider come to a halt twenty or thirty yards outside the gate.

"Sir Garman," the baron said, turning to his captains. "Until we know more about the situation—especially the *King's* situation—I want us prepared for any eventuality. You and Sir Kalanndros remain here and make certain you keep the men under control. I trust you to use your own judgment—and especially to see there aren't any accidents until I get back here."

Stoneblade looked at him for a moment, then nodded, obviously relieved by his baron's determination to keep anything untoward from happening.

"Of course, Milord."

"Very well, then. Tarmahk?" Cassan glanced at his personal armsman, and Dirkson nodded back, then gave his squad a stern look.

"On your toes, lads," he said.

✧ ✧ ✧

<*Wonderful,*> Gayrhalan growled as he and Hathan saw the crossed battleaxe and war hammer on the banner above the small, close-spaced cluster of horsemen walking their mounts towards them.

<*It could be worse,*> Hathan replied.

<*Really? How?*>

<*Give me a day or two and I'll think of something.*>

Gayrhalan snorted, but there wasn't time for another exchange before Cassan and half a dozen armsmen in his personal colors reached them.

"The King, Sir Hathan? Is the King all right?"

Hathan blinked at the raw fear in Cassan's harsh, quick question. It certainly sounded sincere.

"The King is well . . . so far," he replied after a moment, and watched Cassan sag in the saddle.

"Thank the gods!" The baron shook his head. "I was certain we were going to be too late. Thank the gods we got here in time after all!"

<*Careful, Brother.*> Gayrhalan said. <*I think he's lying—his lips are moving!*>

"You *did* get here just in time, Milord." Hathan kept any awareness of his companion's comment out of his reply. "We're grateful you did."

"And you're wondering how it happened." Cassan's expression turned grim, and he shook his head. "I don't blame you. Tomanāk knows there's enough bad blood between me and Tellian to make anyone suspicious. I won't pretend I'm sorry about that, or that

I'm anything except his enemy, either. Or even that I wouldn't do just about anything to get the better of him. And that spills over onto you, of course." He met Hathan's eyes levelly, his expression unflinching, then drew a deep breath and squared his shoulders. "But we serve the same King, however we feel about one another, and the last thing either of us needs is a return to the Time of Troubles."

Hathan's eyes narrowed at the other man's open admission of hostility and sensed his courser's matching surprise at the baron's frankness.

"I'm sure Baron Tellian would agree with you in at least that much, Milord," he said.

"And very little else, I'm certain." Cassan managed a thin smile, but then he exhaled noisily and shook his head again.

"I don't suppose any fair minded man could blame him for that. But this time he and I are going to have to work *together* if we want to prevent just that from happening."

"I beg your pardon?"

"I discovered—too late, I was afraid—that my kinsman Yeraghor's strayed into dangerous waters." Cassan's tone was that of a man admitting something he manifestly wished he didn't have to. "It may be at least partly my fault. He knows how bitterly I hate Tellian, how far I've been willing to go to get the better of him, and he's allied his fortune to mine. That probably opened the door to what's happened . . . but I believe he's been manipulated by someone else. Someone who would be delighted to see the entire Kingdom disintegrate into the Time of Troubles all over again."

He paused, and Hathan cocked his head. He never would have expected Cassan to implicate Yeraghor in something like this!

"Manipulated, Milord? By whom?"

"I can't be sure," Cassan replied in that same unwilling tone, "but something his lady said in a letter to my wife struck me as . . . odd. I had my agents in the East Riding look into it very cautiously. Two of them seem to've disappeared without a trace. The third came to me with a tale I dearly wanted to disbelieve, but I fear he was right."

The baron's nostrils flared.

"There's wizardry afoot in Ersok, Sir Hathan," he said flatly. "I don't believe Yeraghor realizes it, but I have conclusive evidence. I believe someone from outside the Kingdom—someone who knows all about my enmity for Tellian—has used sorcerous means to influence him. It was the last thing I wanted to believe, but when my agent reported that Yeraghor had actually dispatched assassins to murder the King, I couldn't take the chance that he might be wrong." Cassan's shoulders sagged. "I turned out my armsmen and we rode as fast as we could. The whole way I was praying my agent was wrong, but these"—he waved wearily at the bodies of the dead mercenaries littering the ground—"look like exactly the assassins my agent described."

<*Toragan!*> Gayrhalan said. <*Do you think* Cassan of Frahmahn *might actually be telling the* truth?>

<*Anything's possible, I suppose. And he* did *say wizardry was involved,*> Hathan replied, yet he couldn't quite produce his normal acerbity.

"And what, precisely, do you suggest we do about it, Milord?" he asked harshly.

"The first step has to be to see to the King's safety," Cassan replied. "And after that, it must be the dispatch of Crown magi to Ersok to investigate and smell out any wizardry."

He was clearly uncomfortable saying that—not surprisingly, Hathan thought, given his well-known hostility towards the magi.

"It's the only way to be certain we know what's truly happening," the baron continued. "I'm almost certain Yeraghor doesn't realize he's being manipulated and controlled by someone else."

He shook his head again, sadly, and moved a little closer to Gayrhalan. His warhorse was smaller than the towering courser, a fact Cassan would normally have bitterly resented and done everything he could to avoid acknowledging. Now he reached out and upward, laying one hand almost beseechingly on Hathan's armored forearm.

"I'm *almost* certain of that," he said softly, so softly Hathan had to lean towards him to hear him. "But I'm not positive. Gods, I wish I was! The truth is, I'm afraid he may realize *exactly* what he's done, and if the Kingdom learns one of the four barons willingly resorted to the use of sorcery, the gods only know how it will react!"

Hathan nodded slowly, forced against his will to acknowledge Cassan's point.

"It will be essential for Tellian and me to present a united front if that's the case," Cassan said, his expression bitter. "And I won't pretend that thought pleases me one bit. But if the two of us stand together, the fact that we can't agree on anything else in the world should at least cause the lords warden to accept that none of the other barons are dabbling in sorcery. And if it turns out Yeraghor is being manipulated unknowingly, or even against his will, it's still going to take Tellian and me together to either keep it from becoming general knowledge or to deal with its repercussions when the truth leaks out."

<*Now* that *sounds more like Cassan,*> Gayrhalan said. <*The "repercussions"* he's *worried about probably mostly have to do with the fact that Yeraghor's* his *cousin!*>

<*Maybe,*> Hathan replied. <*Even probably. But that doesn't make him wrong. If Yeraghor* is *the one who used wizardry against Borandas and now he's tried to assassinate the King, the Kingdom could all too easily tear itself apart hunting for other traitors and hidden wizards. And he's right about something else, too; if he and Tellian present a united front, everyone else will have to take them seriously!*>

"I trust you won't take this wrongly, Milord," he said out loud, "but I think Baron Tellian—and the King—are going to want to see this evidence of yours about Yeraghor."

"Of course they are." Cassan gave a harsh chuckle. "If the position were reversed, *I'd* certainly want to see it. It'll take some time to assemble all of it, but I brought along a copy of my agent's report." He took his hand from Hathan's forearm and reached for his belt pouch. "I think the best thing to do at this point is for me to keep my armsmen safely outside the wall while you take the report back to the King and show it to him and Tellian. Once they've had a chance to look at it, then—"

The hand reaching for his belt pouch darted suddenly to one side. It closed on the hilt of a dagger, and before Hathan could react, the dagger came out of its sheath, drove in through the open visor of his helmet and thrust through his left eye socket into his brain.

Gayrhalan was as surprised as his rider. His head swung to the side, trying to bat the dagger aside before it could thrust home, but he was too late. Cassan and his armsmen had planned quickly but carefully on the ride to meet the King's envoy, and in the instant the courser was totally focused on Cassan, Tarmahk Dirkson flexed his right hand. The short-bladed dagger in the spring-loaded sheath strapped to his forearm snapped into his hand and he lunged in a single supple movement. The blade went home, stabbing through the eye opening in Gayrhalan's steel plate chamfron.

A heartbeat after Hathan stiffened and started to slide from the saddle, Gayrhalan collapsed under him.

"*Treason!*" Cassan screamed, wheeling his horse back towards his shocked armsmen. "Treachery! *They've killed the King!*"

Chapter Thirty-Eight

"Hathan!"

The agonized cry burst from Tellian Bowmaster as Dathgar and Gayrfressa felt Gayrhalan's death. The coursers echoed the helpless protest, screaming their rage, and Leeana tasted blood as her teeth sank into her lip.

She and her father stared at one another, each feeling the other's pain. It was all they could do for what seemed like an eternity, but then Tellian gave himself a savage shake and turned to the King.

"Hathan is dead," he said in a voice of hammered iron. "So is Gayrhalan. Cassan murdered them both."

Markhos' face turned to stone.

"How?" he demanded.

"*Cassan*," Tellian spat. "Cassan spun a tale about *Yeraghor* being behind all this—spun it well enough even *I* might have believed there was some truth in it. He offered to show Hathan 'proof' . . . and then put a dagger through his eye. He's mine, Markhos—*mine!* This time I'll have his blood!"

"This time you'll have his blood, Milord," Markhos promised. King and baron gazed into one another's eyes for a long, icy moment, and then Markhos smiled humorlessly. "Of course, first we both have to live long enough for you to collect it."

✧ ✧ ✧

Cassan thundered back to Stoneblade and Horsemaster, then drew rein so hard his horse half-crouched, skidding on its rear hooves. Both captains stared at him, eyes stunned, and he pointed back at the fallen courser and wind rider.

"The bastards have killed the King!" he snarled.

"Are you *sure* of that, Milord?" Stoneblade demanded, his expression shocked.

"*Sure* of it?!" Cassan looked at him incredulously. "The son of a whore admitted it to me!"

"He *admitted* it?"

Cassan gripped his reins fiercely, battling his own impatience. But he had to handle this carefully. He had to carry Stoneblade—and all of his armsmen—with him if he meant to succeed.

"Not at first," he said harshly. "At first, he insisted the King was well. You saw us talking! He said the King was suspicious of our 'timely' arrival—that was why he'd been sent out to find out who we were, why we were here. He wasn't happy to see *me*, I assure you! But he *pretended* he was . . . at least until I suggested the King would be safer out here. That was when he told me he'd been instructed by the King to invite *me* into the lodge to 'confer' with him and Tellian. Look at that smoke, those fires! D'you really think the King would invite me into the middle of all that instead of getting out of it himself as quickly as possible?! Besides, he insisted the King had invited me by name . . . after admitting he'd been sent to find out who we were! It was ridiculous!"

He spat on the ground.

"I told him that with the hunting lodge burning down around the King's ears, it would be far better to get him safely out of it, and that's when he started getting evasive. He came up with one excuse after another, every one of them thinner than the one before. So I told him I needed some assurance—some proof—the King was still well and in control of his own fate. That's when he cursed me and reached for his sword. It was only the gods' own grace I'd been suspicious enough to see it coming! I couldn't reach my saber in time, but I got my dagger into his helmet before he could clear the scabbard. And somehow Tarmahk managed to drop the courser before he could take my arm off with his jaws."

Stoneblade's eyes were narrow, and he looked at Horsemaster.

The junior captain had been staring at Cassan. Now he looked at his fellow armsman, his brain racing. Silence hovered for a moment, and then Horsemaster drew a deep breath.

"I saw Hathan reach for his sword," he said softly.

Cassan's expression never altered, but triumph flooded through him. He hadn't dared hope Horsemaster would commit himself, and he wondered how much of it was an armsman's loyalty and how much was cold calculation. Horsemaster must realize that by the simple fact of being here, suspicion must attach to him and Stoneblade if their liege was proven a traitor. Loyalty to his baron would be a thin defense against the charge of regicide, even among the Sothōii, but if Cassan was in a position to control the story emerging from this day's work...

Stoneblade's expression was still shaken, but his eyes hardened and he looked back at Cassan.

"Your orders, Milord?" he asked crisply.

✧ ✧ ✧

Leeana's hands were rock-steady as she nocked an arrow to her string once more, but tears trickled down her cheeks. Hathan had been a part of her life since she'd learned to walk—her father's closest friend, her personal armsman's cousin, her own adoptive uncle. A man of unyielding honor, the very shieldarm he'd been named. A man Cassan of Frahmahn could never have defeated in battle... murdered by a coward and traitor, and his wind brother with him.

She felt Gayrfressa's rage and grief melding with her own, but the mare wasn't with her. She and Dathgar—and Tellian—had circled around behind the still-blazing main lodge despite the smoke and the heat. It was bad enough for the humans; it was far worse for someone with a courser's senses, and Gayrfressa lacked the barding which had protected Dathgar from flying cinders. Now the coursers waited, shrouded in blinding, choking smoke and surrounded by roaring flame. Any normal horse would have been overcome by the smoke, even assuming it hadn't been driven mad with panic, but Dathgar and Gayrfressa weren't horses. They closed their eyes, enduring, drawing on their link to the energy which sustained the entire world, and somehow they bore it.

Leeana didn't know how. Even with her link to Gayrfressa, she couldn't understand how the coursers could do it, but they did, and she blinked her own eyes furiously clear of tears as bugles sounded outside the lodge once more.

✧ ✧ ✧

The warhorses were skittish.

No, Cassan thought, they were far worse than that—they were half-panicked, and he knew Stoneblade had been right. It would have been far better to dismount his armsmen and take them in on foot. However little they might care for the prospect of fighting on their own feet, his men would have found it enormously easier than trying to control warhorses who were terrified by the smell of smoke and the roar of flames. And it would have been far easier to control them, as well.

Which was why Cassan had insisted on a mounted charge. He wanted—*needed*—as much confusion as he could possibly get. All of the King's guards had to die in the melee, and the chaos would cover Dirkson and his squad as they made sure Markhos himself was dead.

He could hardly explain all of that to Stoneblade, of course. Instead, he'd pointed out that they didn't know for *certain* the King was dead. He *might* simply be a prisoner... so far, at least. And if that was the case, they had to break in and settle this as quickly as humanly possible, before a desperate Tellian did kill his captive.

It was a risky argument, in some ways, but it was a pretext with which Stoneblade was unable to quibble. The armsman remained manifestly unhappy about his baron's choice of tactics, but he could scarcely argue with Cassan's motives. Nor could he dispute Cassan's insistence that even if they were to lose half their men, it would be a bargain price if they got King Markhos back alive.

And if there are any inconvenient little problems, I'm sure I can count on Tarmahk to see to it that Stoneblade isn't around to become one of them, the baron thought grimly. That, too, would be a bargain price if it came to it.

Even with Stoneblade's acquiescence, it had taken longer than he liked. Not that it had actually taken as long as it had seemed to, he told himself, and—

The bugles sounded.

"*For the King!*"

✧ ✧ ✧

"Here it comes!" Swordshank shouted. "Ready, lads!"

Leeana recognized the bugle call, and she shook her head. Much as she respected her father, she'd questioned his sanity when he predicted Cassan would attack mounted. How could any Sothōii be stupid enough to drive horses into something like *this?!*

But they were doing it, and her jaw tightened as she raised her bow. It was going to be ugly.

Swordshank had put his surviving armsmen to work even before Hathan rode out to his death. They'd dragged every obstacle they could find in the smothering smoke out into the courtyard, littering the area in front of them with blocks of stone levered loose from the veranda's steps, wheelbarrows from the groundskeeper's storage shed, picks and shovels, firewood, even blazing roof beams dragged out of the inferno. Leeana's hair was even more badly singed and scorched from helping them, but Swordshank had harshly ordered her away when they started moving the burning timbers. Unlike the armsmen's armored gauntlets, she had only riding gloves, and she'd burned her left hand badly before Swordshank realized what she was doing. Fortunately, it was the *back* of it she'd damaged. Using it hurt, but she could still grip, and she settled herself firmly as the oncoming hooves thundered through the wide-open gate.

The smoke was thinner than it had been, and she and the defenders had the advantage of familiarity with the lodge's ruins. They didn't have to look for their enemies—they knew where they had to be, and the first volley of arrows was fired almost before they saw their targets.

✧ ✧ ✧

Horses screamed as the arrows drove into them.

However wide the gate in that wall might be, putting a cavalry charge through it was like trying to thread a needle with an anchor hawser. The galloping column of horses, all of them already half-maddened by the smell of smoke, was squeezed together. Over a score of warhorses peeled away from the column, completely refusing to pass through that narrow opening. Half a dozen more ran into the gate posts, or were crowded into them by their fellows and reeled aside with broken legs . . . or necks. But others got through, bursting into the courtyard, spreading out again, wheeling as their riders sought their enemies.

And as they wheeled, the arrows found them.

Cassan's armsmen were armored; their horses were not, and Swordshank's orders had been cold and brutally pragmatic. His armsmen wasted no arrows on targets protected by breastplates and boiled leather.

They shot at the horses.

Leeana tried to close her ears to the tortured screams of horses riven and torn by arrowfire. They couldn't understand what was happening, and she wished she couldn't, either. Wished those screams wouldn't come back to her in nightmares. Wished she hadn't been forced to murder innocents rather than the traitors on those horses' backs.

Yet even through her tears, she picked her targets unflinchingly, and the entire front rank of Baron Cassan's armsmen crashed down in ruin.

✧ ✧ ✧

The weight of fire astonished Cassan.

He'd been positive Markhos' armsmen had to have taken heavy casualties against the mercenaries, and he'd known they no longer had any buildings to use for cover. What kind of lunatics would stand in the open and try to use *bow*fire to break a cavalry charge?!

Yet that was precisely what they'd done... and it worked.

Less than half the horses who went down were actually hit by arrows. The others crashed into their dead or wounded fellows, falling, spilling their riders, in all too many cases rolling over those riders and crushing them in their own collapse. Here and there, a handful made it through without being hit or falling over another horse—only to encounter the obstacles strewn in their path. Some of them reared, throwing their riders, squealing in panic as they found flames directly in their path. Others broke legs on wheelbarrows or heaps of firewood, invisible to them in the smoke until far too late.

Cassan swore viciously, watching as the attack slithered to a halt. It stalled in a drift of dead or screaming horses, and the column behind them packed itself solid, unable to advance, losing its momentum and wavering in confusion.

✧ ✧ ✧

"*Your Majesty!*"

Leeana spun as Sir Jerhas Macebearer shouted. The Prime Councilor had claimed a fallen armsman's bow to thicken the defensive fire, as had most of the surviving courtiers and servants, and positioned himself on one flank of their perilously short line. He stood to Leeana's left and rear... in the last line before the King.

And too far away to intervene when Sir Benshair Broadaxe, Lord Warden of Golden Hill, dropped his own bow, drew his dagger, and turned on the King.

Macebearer's shout warned Markhos, but Golden Hill was already inside the reach of the King's saber. Markhos dropped the sword, reaching for the dagger, then gasped as Golden Hill got past his grappling hand. It wasn't a clean strike—the King had managed to partially block it, divert it so that it drove into the meaty part of his shoulder instead of his heart—but Golden

Hill recovered the blade with a snarl, and no one else could reach him in time. He bored in again, desperate to finish the King and make his escape in the confusion of combat, and—

A short sword drove into his spine. He twisted, mouth open in a silent scream, dropping the dagger, and Leeana Hanathafressa kicked his body off her blade and turned to face Cassan's armsmen.

✧ ✧ ✧

"*Now!*"

Not even choking smoke and crackling flame could overwhelm instincts trained on half a hundred battlefields. Tellian Bowmaster and Dathgar could read the tempo of a battle the way a bard read an epic poem. Neither of them could have explained how, but they knew the exact instant when Cassan's charge spent itself. When it recoiled, its strength compressing upon itself like a bow stave bent to the very edge of breaking.

And in that moment, *they* charged.

It was ludicrous, of course. There were only two coursers and a single wind rider, and there were almost a hundred mounted armsmen packed into that courtyard. Huge, coursers might be, and powerful, but not even they could face those odds. It was obvious.

But no one had told *them* that, and even if someone had, they wouldn't have cared. Not with the deaths of two brothers burning in their hearts and souls. Not with their daughter and wind sister fighting for her own life. Not with their King's life hanging in the balance.

They slammed into the stalled warhorses like thunderbolts. Tellian's saber stayed sheathed. Instead, he'd chosen a battleaxe, standing in his stirrups, swinging with both hands and all the power of his back and shoulders, trusting his armor to turn any blows someone landed in return while he cropped heads and hands and arms. Blood sprayed as he sheared through flesh and bone, and Dathgar was a battering ram. He ripped into the warhorses with a high, whistling scream of rage, like a dray horse running over children's ponies.

"*Markhos!* Markhos! *For the King!*"

The horses squealed, trying frantically to get out of Dathgar's way, but there was no room to dodge, and Tellian bellowed his war cry as he and his courser literally rode down Cassan's mounted armsmen. They clove a chasm of crushed and broken bodies—horses and men alike—through the heart of their enemies' charge, and Gayrfressa charged beside them. Bigger and stronger even than Dathgar, the blue star of her missing eye glaring with blinding fury, hooves like hammers, jaws like axes, and filled with a rage that was terrifying to behold. She rampaged across the courtyard like a chestnut hurricane, and then she and Dathgar burst through the far side of the column, turned hard to their left, and braked to a halt on one flank of that short line of armsmen.

It was too much.

Cassan's *armsmen* might have been willing to continue that charge, to continue to attack, but their horses were not. They recoiled, turned, and fought their way back out of the hunting lodge's confining walls and the smoke and the fire and the blood which had consumed so many of their fellows, and they took Cassan and his armsmen with them.

✧ ✧ ✧

Cassan wrestled his stampeding mount to a halt.

The warhorse trembled under him, snorting, shaking its head, still fighting the bit, but the baron dragged it under control with an iron hand. He turned it, forcing it back, and saw Stoneblade pulling his own mount to a stop beside the lead troop of the company he'd held in reserve. The captain's breastplate was splashed with blood—someone else's, obviously—and Cassan's jaw tightened as he drew rein beside the armsman and saw Stoneblade's expression . . . and no sign of Horsemaster.

"You were right," he said quickly, before Stoneblade could speak. "We should have gone in on foot."

The admission seemed to defuse at least some of the captain's anger, and Stoneblade drew a deep breath.

"Done is done, Milord." His grim voice was harsh. "But I think we'd best organize a bit better for the next attack."

"Agreed," Cassan said curtly.

The captain seemed to hover on the brink of saying something more, and tension crackled between them for a moment. Then that moment passed and Stoneblade looked away.

"I'll see to it, then."

He gave his baron a brusque nod and began barking orders, and Cassan watched him. Then he glanced at Tarmahk Dirkson, and his personal armsman looked back . . . and nodded slowly.

✧ ✧ ✧

"Oh, stop fussing, Jerhas!" King Markhos said testily.

"But, Your Majesty—"

"Stop fussing, I said." The King shook his head. "It hurts, all right? I admit it. But I'm not exactly in danger of bleeding to death, and we have other things to worry about."

The Prime Councilor looked as if he wanted to argue, but he clamped his jaw, and Markhos grunted in satisfaction. The bandage over the deep wound in his shoulder made an ungainly lump under his bloodstained tunic and he looked just a little pale, but his blue eyes were clear and snapping with anger.

"We won't be that lucky a second time," he told Tellian flatly, and the baron was forced to nod.

"Probably not, Your Majesty. Even Cassan's going to be bright enough not to pack cavalry like that again. They'll either push an infantry column through the gate or come at us over the wall, the way that first lot did."

"Why in Phrobus' name didn't they do that the first time?" someone demanded, and Tellian shrugged.

"Because he thought his way would work," he said. "And because all this smoke"—he gestured at the thick columns rising from the fires—"is going to attract *someone's* attention. And when it does, the people who see it are going to remember the King's visiting here. He needs to finish this before any unfortunate witnesses happen along."

"I think there may be another reason, Milord," Leeana said, carefully not calling him father. He looked at her, and she grimaced. "The confusion," she said.

"To create an opportunity for Golden Hill, you mean?" Macebearer said, glaring at the elegantly dressed corpse one of Swordshank's armsmen had dragged away and heaved onto the pile of bodies heaped into a grisly breastwork for their position.

"No, Milord." Leeana shook her head. "Or not *primarily* for him, at least. I'm not at all sure he was part of the plan from the beginning. I think he simply realized his patrons' position is hopeless if His Majesty survives. He thought he saw an opportunity to make sure you didn't, Your Majesty, but I doubt Cassan even realized he was here. And even if Golden Hill was part of the plot from the beginning, how could Cassan have been confident he was still alive?"

"Then why create confusion?" the Prime Councilor asked.

"Not for Golden Hill," Tellian said slowly, his eyes on his daughter's face. "For his own people."

"That's what I think," Leeana agreed. She looked back and forth between Markhos and Macebearer. "We know the lies he spun for Hathan and Gayrhalan before he killed them, but we don't know what he told his own armsmen *after* he murdered them. And when they charged, Your Majesty, they were shouting 'For the King.' I think he told his armsmen that *we've* either killed you or taken you prisoner. Most of those men think they're trying to rescue or avenge you . . . and he wanted enough confusion for someone he trusts to get close enough to kill you before the others realized you weren't already dead."

There was silence for a moment, and then Macebearer nodded slowly and looked at Tellian.

"A remarkable daughter you've raised here, Milord," he said.

"I've always thought so," Tellian acknowledged with a faint smile.

"But if she's right—and I think you are, Milady," Markhos said, "—then the way to beat him is simple enough. All I have to do is show myself to his men and call on them to lay down their weapons."

"No," Tellian said immediately. The King looked at him, eyebrows raised, and the baron shook his head. "At least some of those men out there *do* know why they're here, Your Majesty, and every one of those armsmen has a bow."

"They wouldn't dare—not in front of so many witnesses who aren't part of any plot against me," Markhos shot back.

"Your Majesty, they don't have anything to lose," Macebearer pointed out. "Any of them who were part of this from the beginning know your magi will get to the bottom of it in the end . . . if you live to order the investigation. And they know the penalty for treason. Any of them with a bit of backbone—or enough desperation—is going to figure he has a better chance of surviving if he engineers an 'accident' for you, no matter how suspicious the accident in question might appear."

"That's as may be," Markhos said, "but it doesn't change the fact that losses or no losses, he's still got two or three hundred armsmen out there and we have less than thirty in here, even counting those of us who don't have armor." He swept one hand in a circular motion, indicating the surviving grim-faced, scorched and bedraggled men standing around him with bows and swords in hand. "Eventually, they're going to simply overwhelm all of you, and when that happens

I think it's unlikely I'll get out of this alive any more than the rest of you." He smiled crookedly. "I don't doubt all of you are prepared to die defending me, but I'd really prefer you don't. Especially not if I'm not going to survive anyway."

"Your Majesty, you're the King." Tellian's voice was flat. "You don't have the right to risk your life the way other men do—not when the stability of the entire Kingdom depends upon you."

"I have a son, I have a brother, and I have two daughters," Markhos replied in an equally flat tone. "I *am* the King, Milord Baron, but there are others to bear the Crown, should I fall."

"Your Majesty, we can't—"

"Baron Tellian, we *can*."

Blue eyes locked with gray, and tension crackled between them.

✧ ✧ ✧

Cassan exhaled in noisy relief mingled with anger.

Stoneblade had moved with maddening deliberation as he organized the fresh attack. He'd used a dagger to scrape a diagram of the hunting lodge's layout onto a cleared patch of ground, and he'd methodically questioned the survivors of the first attack to fill in the details. Then he'd assigned objectives to each troop of dismounted armsmen and made sure their troop commanders understood what they were to do.

Cassan was confident Dirkson and his squad had already known what *they* were to do, but Stoneblade's careful organization was going to make their task more difficult. That was bad enough, but the baron suspected his captain was deliberately delaying the assault. Something about Stoneblade's eyes, the set of his shoulders, shouted a warning to Cassan's instincts.

He wanted to snap out the attack order, override Stoneblade's dragged-out preparations, but he dared not. If the captain truly did suspect the truth, a peremptory order might be enough to turn reluctance into open resistance, despite his personal oath to Cassan. No. Better to wait. If Stoneblade refused to order the charge, that would be time enough to take drastic action. Once the captain *did* order the attack, he'd be just as committed as Cassan—or just as guilty of treason, at any rate—and a man like Stoneblade didn't do things by halves. Besides—

A bugle blared suddenly out of the forest behind him, and Cassan wheeled his horse in shock as a long line of cavalry walked slowly out of the shadows towards him with lances ready.

He'd never met the burly, fair-haired man riding beside the gray-and-white banner, but he recognized the arms of the Pick-axes of Lorham. The full-moon banner of the Quaysar Temple streamed on the breeze beside it, and the woman riding beneath that banner wore the surcoat of an Arm of Lillinara.

His heart sank, but he faced the newcomers with the courage of a man who had nothing left to lose.

"Stand where you are!" he snapped.

The oncoming banners halted a hundred yards away and he heard his own armsmen climbing quickly back into their own saddles behind him, yet that upright thicket of lances never wavered.

"What's your business here?" Cassan shouted across the distance.

"A question I might fairly ask you, Milord Baron," the man who must be Trisu of Lorham replied coldly. "This is the *West* Riding, not the South."

"I know perfectly well where we are. And I ask you again—*what brings you here?*"

"A threat to the Kingdom," Trisu said flatly. "One I believe I'm beginning to fully understand."

"A threat to the Kingdom, is it?" Cassan shot back and barked a contemptuous laugh. "The only threat to the Kingdom *I* see here is you, Milord! You and that traitorous bastard you serve!"

"Have a care, Milord! Baron or no, any man who names me traitor will answer with his life!"

Cassan sneered as he realized how badly outnumbered Trisu actually was. Even supported by the Quaysar Temple Guard—and how dangerous could armsmen who took orders from *women* truly be?—he had fewer than half the men Cassan still retained.

"I'll call you whatever I choose," he said harshly. "Your baron's already murdered the King! No doubt you were part of the same plot. I order you in the name of the Crown to lay down your weapons and surrender now or pay the penalty for your crimes!"

"If you think you can take our arms, come and try," Trisu's voice was a glacier grinding mountains into rubble, and the upright lances shivered and came down all along the front of his line.

"Very well—on your own head be it!" Cassan drew his saber and looked over his shoulder at his armsmen. "Take them! For the King!"

"*For the King!*" his men thundered, and they charged.

A baron had no business in the front line of a cavalry melee, and Cassan let his armsmen charge past him. Trisu's men and the

Quaysar guards spurred to meet them, and Cassan smiled thinly as the two forces slammed into one another and he realized the newcomers were even more badly outnumbered than he'd thought. He actually owed that idiot Trisu a vote of thanks! Stoneblade would be committed now, whatever else happened, and it wasn't as if—

"Kalatha! Kalatha! *Kalatha for the King!"*

Cassan twitched and twisted in the saddle as the forest stretching along his right flank came to sudden life. The fresh voices shouting that war cry were higher and lighter but no less savage, and he stared in disbelief as the war maids of Kalatha swarmed out of the trees. They were on foot, not mounted, and a Sothōii's instinctive contempt for infantry—especially unarmored infantry*women*—welled up within him as he realized who and what they were. But only for an instant, for *these* women were past mistresses of the art of light infantry tactics and concealment. They'd filtered soundlessly forward in the shadows of the trees while Trisu occupied his attention, putting themselves in a perfect position to hit his own men from behind, and he hadn't seen a thing. Not a thing! How in Fiendark's name had they managed to get this close without his even *seeing* them?!

And then they were upon his armsmen, and they didn't seem to care that they were on foot.

Warhorses screamed afresh as the war maids piled into the fray, short swords and daggers flashing ruthlessly, hamstringing the horses of men who were already locked in combat with Trisu's mounted troops and helpless to defend themselves against an attack from the rear. The shrieking horses went down, spilling their riders, and the war maids were waiting when those armsmen fell. They swarmed over them before they could even start to rise, and if those armsmen were armored, that did them little good when they were taken two or three to one. War maids fell, as well, but they flooded through the ranks of Cassan's men like the sea, and the surprise was devastating.

He gawked in disbelief as his entire right flank crumpled in chaos and confusion, and even as he watched, Trisu's left pivoted, swinging in on the rubble of his own right, charging past their war-maid allies to slam into the back of his *left* wing.

It was too much for men who were already confused, who knew they were far from home... who'd had one surprise too many. Sabers began to go up, raised hilt-first in token of surrender, and once it began, it spread like wildfire. Perhaps a third of his armsmen refused to yield, grimly determined to take as many of their enemies with them as possible, but there could be only one possible outcome.

For one endless moment, Cassan of the South Riding stared at the disastrous collapse of all his plans. Then he wrenched his horse's head around and drove in his spurs.

✧ ✧ ✧

"*Stand where you are!*" Baron Tellian bellowed as Swordshank's armsmen started to race towards the gate and the bedlam of combat. They halted, staring over their shoulders at him, and he glared at them. "Get back into your positions! If those are friends of ours out there and they win, well and good! But that's their job; *your* job is to protect the King!"

The armsmen stared at him for another handful of seconds, and then they slunk meekly back into their original lines. Yet even as they did, a chestnut courser with an eye of blue flame went bounding past them and out the gate with a red-haired wind rider in its saddle.

"*Leeana!*" Tellian shouted, but Gayrfressa was already through the gate in a rolling thunder of hooves.

✧ ✧ ✧

Cassan turned his head, peering over his shoulder once more. There was no sign of pursuit yet, but it would be coming all too soon. He needed enough of a head start for his tracks to be lost in those of all the other fugitives who would shortly be fleeing the scene of his debacle. Where he'd go, what he'd do, in the wake of such utter disaster was more than he could begin to calculate at the moment, yet the first order of business was clear enough: to escape. To—

A huge chestnut mare burst through a screen of trees behind him, and he swallowed a strangled curse. His warhorse was already at full stretch, galloping all-out despite the dangerous terrain, but the courser closed quickly, eating up the distance between them effortlessly, and blue fire glittered from its right eye socket. He didn't know what that fire was, but somehow he knew he couldn't escape it—that glittering flame would find him wherever he went, wherever he hid.

Despair flooded through him, and with it came a towering rage. It was over. Tellian had won. Everything Cassan had fought for throughout his entire life was gone, snatched away by the man he hated most in all the world. And on that courser, charging after him, was Tellian's hradani-loving whore of a daughter—a woman who'd never trained to fight on horseback and who wasn't even armored.

He bared his teeth, turning, bringing his horse back around and drawing his saber once more. Perhaps he'd lost, but he could take this one last exquisite vengeance. He could lay Tellian's daughter dead on the ground and turn his triumph to dust and ashes in his mouth!

"Come to me, bitch!" he screamed, and charged to meet her.

They flashed towards one another, and he snarled triumphantly as he realized she didn't even have a sword in her hands! He'd have to be careful of the courser, but he didn't really care whether he lived or died now—not any longer. All that mattered was that he kill *her* before he died, and the fool was making it *easy!*

He rode right at her, saber extended in a long, straight lunge, anticipating the shock in his wrist as the steel drove into her and—

She wasn't there.

Cassan's eyes started to widen in astonishment as Gayrfressa broke to her right, impossibly quick for something so huge, and Leeana twisted sinuously in the saddle. His saber drove past her harmlessly, and he was still turning his head, trying to understand what had happened, when Gayrfressa thundered past him in the opposite direction and Leanna's left foot came up under *his* left foot and heaved with savage power. The sudden pressure unbalanced him, and his saber flew from his grip as he clutched desperately after the pommel of his saddle.

It was too late. Surprised, already off-center from the lunge which had missed its target, Leeana's lifting foot unbalanced him completely. He hit the ground with bone-crushing force, crying out as something shattered in his right shoulder. Slivers of anguish rocketed through him, and he shook his head groggily, dragging himself up as high as his knees. He had to get back on his feet, he had to—

Something flashed over his head. A kneecap rammed into his shoulder blades like a maul, and his left hand clawed uselessly at his suddenly blood-slick throat as the war-maid garrotte bit deep. He gurgled, twisting frantically, and Leeana Hanathafressa crossed her wrists behind his head, set her shoulders, and twisted with all her strength.

The last sound Cassan Axehammer ever heard was the crunching snap of his own neck.

Chapter Thirty-Nine

Varnaythus stared into his gramerhain, jaw tight while echoes of disbelief reverberated deep in his eyes.

Impossible. Everything had gone perfectly—*perfectly!*—and that bastard Tellian had turned it around on him anyway. After all his years of effort, his plans, the risks he'd run—after he'd gotten every piece into position despite all the obstacles and every one of his Lady's demands—all of it had been torn apart by the last-minute interference of one miserable mage, a mangy pack of war maids, one minor lord warden... and a single meddling wind rider who seemed to be almost as hard to kill as her never-to-be-sufficiently-accursed *husband!* It couldn't have happened, yet it had.

Disbelief turned into crackling fury as a tall, slim, red-haired young woman and a huge chestnut courser cantered up to the smoking ruins of a hunting lodge. The young woman slid from the saddle, crossed to where her father stood beside the King of the Sothōii, and dropped something round at Markhos' feet. The King rolled the round object to one side with the toe of his boot, and Cassan Axehammer's dead, astounded eyes stared up at the monarch he'd tried to murder.

"*Bitch!*" the wizard hissed, all the years of wasted effort that severed head represented crashing through him in a torrent of rage, and his hand twitched towards the carved-bone wand lying on the desk before him.

"Would that be wise?" a quiet voice asked, and Varnaythus' head swiveled. Sahrdohr met his gaze and shrugged ever so slightly. "It's your decision, but as soon as we activate the kairsalhain, everyone in Norfressa will know exactly who was behind all this. Or every mage—and Wencit—will, at any rate, and even with Her orders, the Council won't like that."

Varnaythus glared, but even as he did, he knew his anger wasn't truly—or shouldn't be, at any rate—directed at the magister. Sahrdohr simply happened to be close enough to serve as a focus, and Varnaythus forced himself to leash his temper. It wasn't easy, under the circumstances, but no one could attain the rank of master wizard without learning how to govern his own passions.

"Point," he said after a moment, his voice sharp, and his nostrils flared as he inhaled deeply. Then he turned back to his own gramerhain.

Arm Shahana's image glowed with the silver-shot blue of Lillinara, and a fresh lava flow of anger rippled through him as he watched her lay hands upon Markhos Silveraxe. The glowing blue corona ran down her arms to her hands, lapping about the King, and Varnaythus could actually *see* his wound closing. Somehow the healing of that wound—the wound which was the visible proof of how *close* they'd come to hurling the Kingdom of the Sothōii into civil war and destruction—actually helped him throttle the fuming embers of his rage.

He inhaled again, more naturally, and gave himself a shake. It was because watching her heal Markhos put everything back into focus, he decided. It punctuated the failure of Athnar's assassins—and Cassan—and forced him to consider everything afresh, with all the hard-earned dispassion he'd learned in his long, ambitious life.

They'd moved everyone out of the ruins of the hunting lodge as the last of the flames gnawed away at the remaining fuel, but they hadn't gone very far. Nor would they, with so many wounded men. Shahana would heal the worst hurt, but a single arm of Lillinara wasn't going to be able to heal very many of them, and moving injured men over Sothōii roads would be an agonizing ordeal for the wounded. Messengers had been sent galloping off to Balthar and Sothōfalas, and he was certain additional armsmen and healers would swarm towards Chergor as soon as those messengers reached their destinations. Eventually, of course, Markhos would retire either to Balthar or to his capital, but no Sothōii king would leave a field where so many had fallen in his defense until he'd personally seen all the survivors properly cared for. That meant Markhos would be anchored to the vicinity of the burned hunting lodge for at least the next day or two, and all he really needed to be was within a half mile or so.

The kairsalhain Varnaythus had carefully planted under the hearth in the main lodge was undoubtedly buried under collapsed, charred timbers and masonry, but the most intense mortal fire would scarcely affect the stone. It was formed of the same crystal as his gramerhain, fused in the heart of a working beside which the most powerful lightning bolt was but a weak and pallid thing. And, like his gramerhain, it had come from the working with an affinity for the art. It was sensitized, attuned to the art—no larger than a child's thumb, yet capable of focusing and storing workings that could have destroyed a city the size of Trōfrōlantha itself. Yet that was only one of its possible functions. Kairsalhains could be—and often were—used as repositories for such spells, as well as... more subtle ones, but they could also be used as beacons, anchors, or keys.

Varnaythus was still uncertain exactly how the mage wind-walking talent functioned, but it was clearly different from the spells of teleportation available to a wizard, for a wind walker could travel to places he'd never been, never even seen, if he made the journey in short enough stages. A wizard couldn't. The art needed a focus, an aiming point, and (also unlike wind walkers) it cost a wizard dearly in gathered power and concentration to teleport himself over long distances even *with* a focus; trying to transport anyone else at the same time drove the cost upward exponentially. Almost anything could be used as a focus at need, as long as the wizard had prepared it properly before he or someone else deposited it at his intended destination, but a kairsalhain was best, because it could be charged before it was placed. The wizard could draw upon the energy stored in the stone rather than expending freshly gathered (and sometimes... unruly) power, which let him arrive undrained, with his command of the art unimpaired—not a minor consideration when colleagues who wished one ill might be awaiting one's arrival.

There were other advantages to using kairsalhains, of course. A wizard's wards created a shielded area into which no teleportation spell could reach, for example. But if he'd placed a kairsalhain within it and properly attuned it to the individual idiosyncrasies of his wards, he or an ally with the correct words of command could still pass directly through them without difficulty and without the need to *lower* those wards and expose himself to someone else's attack. And teleportation spells weren't the only workings a kairsalhain could store.

Like the one under the heat-cracked hearth of a burned hunting lodge.

He touched his wand again, stroking it lightly, feeling the power quivering against his palm. He had only to speak the word of command here in his working chamber, and hundreds of leagues away that stone would awaken in a blast of heat and fury like the very kiss of Carnadosa. The crater would be almost a mile across. The forest around the lodge would be flattened, splintered, turned into a roaring inferno that burned for days. And Markhos and Tellian and Arm Shahana and Leeana Hanathafressa would be wiped from the surface of the earth as if they had never existed.

He felt the aching need to do just that, to crush the opponents who'd defeated his tools without ever even realizing who their true enemy was. To show these Norfressans the true power rising once again in Kontovar. But Sahrdohr was right. Satisfying as it might be in the short term, it carried enormous risks, risks the Council of Carnadosa was loath to run . . . and the greatest of which was Wencit of Rūm.

Varnaythus could have lived with the thought of forewarning Norfressa that Kontovar was once again prepared to move. Without wizards of their own, there would be little the Norfressans could do with that warning. But that had been true for centuries, and still the Council had waited, watched, planned, and spied but never dared to step out of the shadows and into the open, and the reason it had not was named Wencit of Rūm.

For twelve hundred years, Wencit had held the wizard lords of Kontovar at bay, and his very name touched altogether too many of them—including one named Varnaythus, he admitted—with terror. No wand wizard in his right mind would willingly face a *wild* wizard, not in arcane combat. Wencit's sheer power would have been enough to frighten any sane opponent, but he held more than power in those scarred, ancient hands of his. He held the keys—the keys to the spells which had strafed Kontovar, seared cities and fortresses into bubbled plains of glass, burned forests, melted mountains, turned glaciers to steam and rivers to desert. He'd *created* those spells for the Last White Council. He alone knew their secrets, knew their innermost workings . . . and they remained active to this day.

The Council of Carnadosa had probed them with the utmost caution. Tested to determine that they still stood ready to his hand, awaiting his command. They dared probe no deeper than that, but the connection was there, the conduit was open, singing with the unmistakable vibrations and imprint of his power, and Wencit was a wild wizard. It had taken the entire Council of Ottovar to raise those spells under his direction; a wild wizard would need no one else's aid to use them a second time.

But the old bastard doesn't want *to use them*, Varnaythus reminded himself. *He remembers last time too well, remembers how the sky burned above Kontovar for weeks, how the smoke choked a world in The Year That Had No Summer. He remembers the screams, the destruction, the walls of flame marching across a continent. He watched it all in his grammerhain, saw every instant of it; it haunts him still, and that's his ultimate weakness, the chink in his armor. He doesn't ever want to call down that devastation a second time . . . but that doesn't mean he* won't. *He did it the first time; drive him hard enough, and he might yet do it again, despite his memories. Carnadosa only knows what provocation it would take to drive him to it, but none of us ever wants to find out.*

And that was the risk of using the kairsalhain, for in its own way, the entire continent of Kontovar was one huge kairsalhain for Wencit of Rūm. He could reach his fist into its bedrock and twist any time he chose, any time he was willing to kill enough millions of the wizard lords' servants and slaves. And if those wizard lords used the art too openly here in Norfressa, he might decide that time had come.

"We'll wait," he said softly, taking his hand from his wand, sitting back in his chair. "It was never anything but our ultimate fallback plan, anyway—like the kairsalhain under Markhos' throne room in Sothōfalas—and the Council won't be pleased if we're driven to using it in the end."

Sahrdohr nodded, his relief obvious despite his carefully controlled expression, and Varnaythus' lips twitched in a sour smile. The magister was right; the Council *wouldn't* be pleased if they used the art so openly . . . yet he could live with that if he must. His orders came from Carnadosa Herself, and whatever the Council might think, that was all the protection from its wrath he would need. Wencit wouldn't be swayed by it, of course, but at least his fellow wizard lords would have no choice but to accept the deed once it was done.

Yet *She* wouldn't like it either, really, if not for the same reasons as the Council. No, even though it would be precisly what She'd commanded him to do, She'd still be furious because the prize would be so much less valuable than the one She'd set out to claim. But if he waited, if he held his hand long enough to see what happened on the Ghoul Moor, he would be able to divert Her anger to a much safer target, for the failure against Bahzell would be Anshakar's failure, not his. Bahzell had always been the main focus of this entire elaborate operation, and he could always point out that he'd warned Anshakar of the danger Bahzell presented, cautioned him not to take his task too lightly, too overconfidently.

He would have done all *he* could to make the attack a success, and then—and only then, after Krashnark's servants had failed in every aspect of *their* mission—he would bring Her the death of Bahzell Bloody Hand's wife. That prize, purchased at whatever price in the open use of the art, would be far, far better than to bring Her nothing at all.

And who knew? If Tellian and Markhos both died—and especially if he used the kairsalhain under Sothōkarnas to destroy the fortress, half of Sothōfalas, *and* Markhos' wife and children, as well—the Kingdom might yet dissolve in civil war after all. There was still Yeraghor to think about. He'd be desperate when word of this reached him, and if that was followed by a power vacuum, an adroit advisor might well be able to convince him that...

"Markhos' assassination was secondary to our main objective, anyway," he told the magister, "and we damned nearly succeeded in it despite that bastard Brayahs and Tellian and his bitch of a daughter." He shrugged. "Bahzell was always the main target, and no meddling mage is going to change a single damned thing that happens on the Ghoul Moor. It would take a *god* to change that!"

He bared his teeth, tapping his gramerhain, summoning up the view of Tellian's marching army once more.

"We'll wait," he repeated, gazing intently down on the tiny, crystal-clear images in the heart of the stone. "If Anshakar is half as mighty as *he* seems to think he is, we won't need to worry about Markhos or the Sothōii. And if it should happen Anshakar *isn't* strong enough to deal with Bahzell, there'll still be time to kill the King and his precious family. And just between the two of us, Malahk," his eyes were hard and hating as he glared at those distant images, "I find the notion of killing Bahzell's wife and father-in-law curiously soothing at this particular moment."

✧ ✧ ✧

At least it wasn't raining.

Bahzell Bahnakson would have been much happier if he'd been able to convince himself the absence of clouds was simply a natural change in the weather. Or, failing that, that it was because whoever or whatever had caused all those dreary days of rain had been dismayed by the steady advance of no less than three champions of Tomanāk and decided to take the rain—and himself—elsewhere.

Unfortunately, he could convince himself of neither of those things.

<Neither can I, Brother,> Walsharno thought at him. *<But at least it means we can see whatever's coming before it gets here. And our two-foots' bow strings won't be wet!>*

"No, that they won't," Bahzell replied, his voice pitched too low for anyone else besides—possibly—Brandark, riding beside him, to hear. "And truth be told, I'll take whatever it is we can get, and grateful I'll be for it. Not that I'd be finding it in my heart to complain if it should happen we were offered more."

<Nor I,> Walsharno agreed, tossing his head in assent. *<Nor I.>*

Bahzell stood in his stirrups, stretching and simultaneously trying (vainly) to see a little further. Not that he expected to see very much. The Ghoul Moor was both more uneven and more heavily overgrown with scattered clumps of trees than the Wind Plain. In fact, it reminded him very much of the land further north and west, around Hurgrum, except for the absence of farmsteads. Ghouls did raise some crops, as winter fodder for their food animals, and Trianal's mounted foraging parties would be keeping a lookout for any such sources of supply they could sweep up along the way. But those crops tended to be closer to the ghouls' occupied villages, and the villages in the area here along the Hangnysti had been largely deserted since midsummer.

They'd scouted this region cautiously over the last week or two, confirming that the villages in it remained empty. Since the rain had finally eased, though, their scouts had found tracks churned across the mud, indicating that quite a few ghouls had at least passed through it. Nor was that all they'd indicated, unfortunately. Ghouls were scarcely known for tactical or strategic sophistication, yet at least some of those tracks clearly suggested they'd been sending out scouts of their own, keeping an eye on the allied expedition. The possibility that the other side might know more about *them* than they knew about *it* for a change wasn't exactly comforting, but the Sothōii scouting parties had at least turned up sufficient tracks to suggest conclusively where the ghouls had gone. They were gathering along the Graywillow River, a tributary of the Hangnysti about three hundred miles west of its junction with the Spear, which made entirely too much sense from their perspective.

The Graywillow was scarcely two hundred miles long, but it had a lot of small, winding tributaries which drained an extensive, often marshy floodplain, and the main stream was close to seventy yards across where it joined the Hangnysti. That made it a significant water barrier, and the terrain along its course—especially as it neared the Hangnysti—was rough, its banks lined with thick, tangled thickets of the willows from which it took its name. Farther upstream the willows gave way to dense stretches of mixed evergreens and hardwoods which could provide dangerously effective cover for troops as irregular as ghouls... and which would break up the formation of any infantry which tried to go in after them. Taken all together, it was an unfortunately good defensive position. On the other hand, with all the rain which had beset the Ghoul Moor in the last month or two, the Graywillow had to be running high and deep—probably deep enough to be a barrier even for ghouls, if they could catch them between their own advance and the stream.

Beyond the riverline, between the Graywillow and the Spear, a rolling expanse of grasslands stretched east and south almost to the border of the Kingdom of the River Brigands, offering grazing space for enough meat animals to supply an enormous horde of ghouls, assuming any imaginable power could force the ghouls in question into some sort of cooperative effort. Which was a sobering thought, given what appeared to have been happening.

With the information available to him, Trianal had seen no choice but to move down the southern bank of the Hangnysti to the Graywillow. If that was where the enemy was, then that was where they had to go to find him. At the same time, however, he'd stayed within sight of the Hangnysti the entire way, using barges to carry food and fodder. And, with Tharanal's enthusiastic assistance, he'd turned a score of barges into heavily armored missile platforms, with stout wooden bulwarks pierced by firing slits for arbalesteers and raised firing platforms mounting the much more powerful sort of crew-served ballistae Axeman cruisers mounted. *Those* arbalests threw quarrels up to five feet long for as much as four hundred yards, with steel heads capable of driving through a foot and more of solid, seasoned oak. Not even a ghoul would enjoy meeting one of them. And there were even a dozen barges fitted with catapults capable of hurling banefire, the dreadful incendiary compound of the Royal and Imperial Navy. With them to cover his riverward flank—and, for that matter, to provide supporting fire if they had to close with the mouth of the Graywillow—Trianal could afford to concentrate his army's attention on threats away from the Hangnysti as they moved through the empty, deserted spaces between them and the ghouls' suspected position.

And it's no complaint they'd hear out of me if the bastards were never after coming back here, Bahzell thought grimly as he settled back down in the saddle. *If they'd sense enough to stay clear of the river and leave us be, then it's happy enough I'd be to leave* them *be, in return. But as soon as ever we've sent these lads home . . .*

Very few of the men in the expedition would have shared his willingness to let the ghouls alone, and he knew it. For that matter, *he* had no illusions about the creatures' willingness to live in peace with any set of neighbors, and he knew it would be no more than a matter of time—and not much of it—before the hradani or the Sothõii would be forced to invade these same lands again to prune back the threat to their borders and their people. Yet however this year's incursion ultimately worked out, all too many of the men marching and riding about him would be dead or crippled by its close. No number of dead ghouls could truly be an equitable trade for that, and his nerve-eating certainty that something as dark as it was powerful lurked behind the rain and the ghouls' bizarre activities and tactics made him fear how high the final cost might be.

"Did you ever think that perhaps the *smart* thing for us to do would be to just go home for the rest of the summer?" Brandark asked lightly from beside him. Bahzell looked at him, and the

Horse Stealer shrugged. "I know we have it to do eventually, Bahzell, but do we really have a deadline? We're not going to be barging anything through here before next year, anyway. Maybe whatever's been behind all this Phrobus-taken rain would get bored and go away over the winter? I know *I'd* go away rather than face a Ghoul Moor winter!"

"I'm thinking it's a mite late to be suggesting such as that, my lad," Bahzell observed mildly. "And if that's the way your thought is setting, why, there's naught to be keeping you here. I'm sure as how Tharanal's bargemasters would be happy enough to be giving you space aboard, if it should happen you're so inclined."

"I was simply pointing out that it would be the smart thing to do," Brandark replied. "The problem, though, is that doing the smart thing requires the person doing it to *be* smart." He shook his head mournfully. "And *I*, unfortunately, seem to've been associating with Horse Stealers too long." He heaved a vast sigh. "Who would've thought that I, of all people, could find myself swept away into foolishness like this by the childlike enthusiasm of a batch of hradani—oh, and let's not forget the Sothōii!—too stupid to come in out of the rain and the mud?"

"Is that the way of it, then?" Bahzell cocked his ears at his friend, and Brandark shrugged.

"One way to explain it, anyway. And another way"—his tone darkened and his hand dropped to the hilt of his sword—"is to point out that whatever's out there isn't likely to go away whatever we do. I'd just as soon deal with it here before we find it moving up the Hangnysti towards Navahk and Hurgrum." The Bloody Sword smiled grimly. "Call me silly, but I'd rather fight it somewhere none of our women and children are likely to get caught in the slaughter."

"Aye, there's something to be said for that," Bahzell agreed.

He started to add something more, then broke off as a five-man section of Sothōii cavalry swept over the crest of a low ridge perhaps two miles ahead of them and headed towards their main body in a mud-spattering gallop. Hradani had excellent vision, and his ears came up and his eyes narrowed as he peered at them. Then his jaw tightened, Walsharno wheeled under him, and Brandark blinked in astonishment as the courser disappeared in a shower of mud all his own.

✧ ✧ ✧

"What is it, Bahzell?" Trianal Bowmaster asked sharply as the huge roan half-slid to a halt beside his command group.

"There's a scouting party coming in yonder," Bahzell replied tersely, jabbing a thumb to the south-southeast. "They're coming fast, like all Sharnā's demons were at their heels, and there's the stink of something else coming on behind them." He bared his teeth. "It's in my mind it won't be so very long before we've proof enough of whatever it is as has been playing with the weather."

"Bahzell's right, Milord," Vaijon said. He was gazing off to the southeast, his eyes focused on something no one else could see.

"And whatever it is wouldn't be heading this way if it didn't figure it could take us head-on," Sir Yarran Battlecrow said flatly.

"My very own thought," Bahzell agreed, and his expression was grim. "More than that, it's the very stink of evil that's coming behind them." His ears flattened in frustration. "It's an arm I'd give to know just what it is I'm feeling, but I've still no better idea than I had this morning. Except that whatever it is, it's closer than it was then."

"It's not just closer, Bahzell," Vaijon said. The others looked at him, and the younger champion shrugged. "It's not just *of* the Dark—it *is* the Dark," he said harshly. "And there's more than one of it, whatever it is."

<He's right.> Walsharno tossed his head. *<In some ways, he's more sensitive to it than we are, Brother. I hadn't realized until he said it, but he's right. I sense at least two of it now, both headed our way, and they're both strong.* Very *strong.>*

<As strong as that bastard of Krahana's?>

<Stronger,> Walsharno replied flatly. <Much *stronger.>*

Bahzell's jaw clenched as he recalled their encounter with Krahana's servant. Jerghar Sholdan had been quite strong enough for his taste. Indeed, it had taken all the power he and Walsharno together could channel to defeat him, and they might not have even then if he'd realized in time that he faced not one champion of Tomanāk, but two.

<True, Brother.> Walsharno had followed his thoughts yet again and tossed his head in agreement once more. *<But he had the souls of an entire courser herd at his disposal... and they still had their link to Wencit's "magic field" to draw upon when he forced them to serve him. Whatever these may be, they don't have that. They're... individuals. Very strong, but reliant upon their own strength and no one else's, I think.>*

"Walsharno's after agreeing with you, Vaijon," Bahzell told the others. "He's the scent of at least two. It's powerful they are, he says, and it won't be so very much longer before they're up with us."

"That's good enough for me." Trianal's voice was like iron, and he turned to his personal bugler. "Sound 'Stand and form,'" he said.

"Yes, Milord!" the bugler replied, and the urgent notes flared across the muddy grassland as he sounded the prearranged signal.

Trianal's augmented force had been moving in the reverse of a typical mixed formation of horse and foot. The standard clouds of mounted scouts had been thrown out, but instead of stationing formed cavalry on the flanks away from the river to protect the infantry from surprise attacks, the *footmen* had been formed on the army's right in column of battalions, with the cavalry between them and the river. Hradani infantry was simply better suited to taking the shock of a charge of blood-crazed ghouls, and it was important to protect the horses which provided the Sothōii's mobility. The mounted archers would be able to fire over the heads of even Horse Stealer foot soldiers, supporting the hradani while they held their shield wall; there'd be time enough for cavalry charges once the ghouls recoiled.

The supply wagons, pack train, and—especially—the mules loaded with additional arrows for the Sothōii moved along the very bank of the Hangnysti, covered by infantry and cavalry alike. There'd been some—not many, but a few—among Trianal's men who'd felt his youth had made him overly cautious, even timid, to adopt such a cumbersome formation, especially now that he had almost twenty thousand men, horse and foot, under his command. None of his senior officers or battalion commanders had been among those critics, however, and orders rang out as the bugler sounded the signal for which they'd been waiting half impatiently and half anxiously for the last two days.

The infantry stopped in place, and two-thirds of its battalions faced right and advanced two hundred yards further inland from the Hangnysti. The front ranks went to one knee, bracing their shields before them, and a triple line of arbalesteers formed in open ranks at their backs. Half the arbalesteers would double as pikemen once the melee was joined, and the wagons assigned to each battalion drew up behind them, unloading thickets of pikes and stacking them where they'd be ready to hand when needed.

Each arbalesteer had three feet of clear space on either side of him; another man in the next line stood directly behind each of those clear spaces; and a metallic clicking rose above them as thousands of Dwarvenhame-built arbalests were spanned and quarrels were fitted to the strings.

The two infantry battalions forming the rear of the column wheeled in place, facing northwest, back the way they'd come, and deployed into a line covering the newly formed battle line's right flank with their left while their own right was anchored firmly on the Hangnysti. The pair of battalions leading the column did the same, except that they anchored themselves to the battle line's *left* flank and faced southeast, covering the main formation's left. The remaining infantry battalions formed into solid, compact squares, half of them spaced evenly behind the battle line to simultaneously cover the supply wagons and form an infantry reserve at the middle of the three-sided rectangle.

Not all the infantry faced west, away from the river, however. The Hangnysti provided less protection against ghouls than it might have against most other foes, given how well the creatures swam. The river could still be counted upon to break them up, especially as they struggled ashore through the soft mud and sand along the banks, but it *couldn't* be counted on to *stop* them. That was why the other half of Yurghaz's infantry faced the river, not inland... and also the real reason for those heavily armed barges pacing Trianal's army on the Hangnysti itself.

The cavalry moved just as quickly, coordinating with their foot-bound fellows with the precision and polish of long practice and mutual confidence. They knew exactly where they were supposed to be, and they went there. Four thousand spread themselves along the rear of the battle line, where they could support the infantry with arrow fire, and three thousand more formed in the spaces between the blocks of reserve infantry, ready to pounce on any ghouls which might swim the river and get past the infantry or to intercept any enemy penetrations of the battle line. A thousand more were held back in a reserve position under Trianal's personal command, ready to be dispatched to wherever they might be most needed. They were also earmarked for quick exploitation if the enemy should break, of course... not that anyone expected the ghouls to be breaking anytime soon. And even as the infantry and cavalry formed, the missile-armed barges which had been pacing them on the Hangnysti began shifting position. Many moved downstream, towards the Spear, placing themselves to sweep the front of the short, heavy line protecting the army's left, but most anchored a few yards offshore, where the missile troops could cover the bank against swimming ghouls as well as forming as a final reserve for their land-bound fellows.

The catapult-armed barges positioned themselves with special care, farther out into midstream, and the catapult crews had loaded their practice rounds even before their barges anchored. As soon as those anchors splashed down into the Hangnysti's mud, the catapults thumped, hurling their inert rounds far over the heads of the infantry and cavalry. Those practice rounds had exactly the same weight and ballistic characteristics as the banefire rounds waiting to follow them, and Bahzell smiled with grim satisfaction as they thudded into the mud a hundred yards and more beyond the infantry's front ranks. The gunners aboard the barges launched a second wave of rounds, making certain of their range and firing bearings. Then they loaded with banefire and stood ready.

The speed with which the entire formation shifted would have astonished anyone who hadn't seen Trianal's "expedition" turning into an "army." This was a tightly integrated, smoothly articulated force, one with confidence in itself and in its commanders but no illusions that it faced an easy task because its opponents were "only" ghouls, and Bahzell felt a surge of pride not just in Trianal, but also in Vaijon and Yurgazh, for making it so.

Their march formation had been planned to make it as fast and straightforward as possible to shift into battle formation, and the fact that the river covered their backs simplified things immensely. But all the planning in the world wouldn't have produced this result without the merciless, unremitting drill to which they'd subjected their men for just this moment. Even the Sothōii levy Trianal had brought down from the Escarpment had been slotted efficiently into their overall organization, taking its lead from the armsmen who'd been part of the expedition from the beginning. The newcomers weren't as well drilled and disciplined as they might have been, but if all went well their primary function would be as missile troops, and any Sothōii armsman had literally grown up with a bow in his hands.

The same bugle calls which had shifted the army's formation

had recalled the troops of cavalry who'd been scouting beyond its right flank on the march, and individually designated companies of infantry opened access points in the battle line to admit them. They trotted quickly across to their own assigned positions, joining their fellows, and the scouting party Bahzell had seen galloping back passed through an opening of its own to reach the command group.

"Thousands of them, Milord," the senior man said harshly, his face white as he reined his weary horse to a halt and slapped his breastplate in salute to Trianal. "Never seen so many of them in one place! Phrobus, I never thought there *were* so many of 'em!"

"How *many* thousands?" Trianal asked calmly, and gave the scout a crooked smile when the man stared at him. "I realize you didn't have time to actually count the number of legs and divide by two, Sergeant. A rough estimate will do."

Two or three of his officers chuckled, and even the scout smiled. But he also shook his head.

"Milord, we couldn't get close enough to tell how many. I'd say there had to be—what? Six or seven thousand?—this side of the Graywillow." He looked at the other members of his section of scouts with an eyebrow raised, and heads nodded. "Problem is, they were already throwing those nasty javelins of theirs at us. They were pushing us back—pushing hard—and more of 'em were boiling out of the woods along the river like maggots. I'd be lying if I said I could tell you any more than that, but it seemed to me I'd best be getting the lads back here to tell you what we'd already seen."

Without trying to see more and getting them all killed, he didn't say, but Trianal nodded.

"Information's a hell of a lot more valuable than dead troopers, Sergeant," he agreed, and the scout's shoulders relaxed almost imperceptibly.

"Should I assume they're following along behind you?" Trianal went on, and the sergeant nodded back to him.

"Aye, Milord. I'd say they're not in all that tearing a hurry—given how fast the buggers can run, you'd've seen 'em already if they were. But they'll be along. And, Milord, they're using drum signals."

"I see." Trianal glanced around his command group's faces for a moment, then turned back to the scouts.

"You've done well, Sergeant. Now get your men back behind the supply element and rest your horses." He smiled again, more thinly. "I think it's time for the *rest* of us to do our jobs."

"Aye, Milord. Thank you!"

The sergeant beckoned to his section, and the five of them splattered off across the muddy grass while Trianal, Bahzell, and the rest of the command group looked at one another.

"Drum signals," Trianal repeated, as if the two words were an obscenity, and Bahzell snorted.

"Well, we'd signs enough already as how these aren't your *ordinary* ghouls, lad," he pointed out, and shrugged. "I've no doubt at all, at all, as how these bastards are going to prove a right handful, and that's a fact. Still and all, it's in my mind the tactical situation's simple enough to be going on with. It's not so very likely all the drum signals in the world are to matter all that much."

"I'm afraid Prince Bahzell's got *that* right, Milord," Yurgazh said sourly. He looked out in the direction from which the scouts had come for a moment, then grimaced and looked back at Trianal. "I think it's time I was joining my infantry, Milord."

"Agreed." Trianal nodded at him and gave Sir Yarran a glance.

"I'm off, I'm off!" the older Sothōii said, raising one hand in a mock defensive gesture. "Just you be remembering what bugles, staff officers, and couriers are for, young man!"

"I'm not planning on leading any desperate charges," Trianal said dryly.

"What I really want to hear is that you're planning on *not* leading any desperate charges," Yarran said even more dryly. "Under the circumstances, though, I suppose I'd better settle for the best I can get, hadn't I?"

"Not much point hoping for anything else, any road, Sir Yarran," Yurgazh said even more sourly, and glanced at Vaijon. "I don't suppose you could convince my idiot prince to get his unmarried arse back aboard one of those barges, could you?"

"Not unless you want me to have him physically dragged," Vaijon replied with a tight grin. "Hurthang and a couple of the other lads are probably big enough to do it, but I can't guarantee he wouldn't get banged up around the edges in the process if he took offense. Which he probably would."

"And then there's Prince Yurokhas." Trianal's tone was even more sour than Yurgazh's had been as he glanced over his shoulder at the wind tube gryphon standard in the colors of the royal house floating above the compact, neatly formed block of the Order of Tomanāk.

"I might be able to order *him* onto a barge," Vaijon admitted, following the direction of Trianal's gaze. "He is a member of the Order, if not our chapter, and I am a champion. Although, now that I think about it, Bahzell's senior to me. If anyone's going to do any ordering, I think it ought to be him, since he's at least older than Yurokhas on top of everything else."

"And because you've got a pretty damned good idea how he'd react to the 'order,' too, I imagine," Trianal said darkly.

"And because of that," Vaijon acknowledged with a fleeting smile. Then the smile faded. "The truth is that in cold-blooded political and dynastic terms, he's actually more expendable just at the moment than Arsham, Trianal. And he's a member of the Order, too. Whatever's coming this way, it's exactly what the Order is pledged to fight." He shook his head. "I can't justify ordering him to safety without some overriding reason—like his place in the succession—and as a member of the Order, he has a *right* to be here."

"I know," Trianal sighed. "I know. Just . . . try to keep him in one piece if you can, all right? The King would be upset if anything happened to him. And more to the point, he's my prince and Uncle Tellian loves him. Tomanāk, *I* love him, come to that!"

"We'll do what we can," Vaijon promised, and chuckled harshly. "Besides, if our masterful battle plan works, what could possibly go wrong?"

"The enemy, lad," Bahzell said with a grim smile. "That's why we've the habit of calling him 'the enemy.'"

Chapter Forty

The ground trembled as the devil named Anshakar followed the howling ghouls towards their prey. The massive drums—sawn sections of hollow log, the drum heads made of the tanned hide of ghoul tribal chiefs and so massive that carrying them required four ghouls to bear each of them, slung between them on poles—throbbed and bellowed, beaten by the ghouls' new shamans to the glory of their new gods. He tasted the mingled terror, hunger, and rage swelling about him, and if most of that terror and much of that rage were directed against him and his two fellows, Anshakar could not have cared less. Terror was terror, and rage was rage; both were chained by desperate obedience, and when the moment came to unleash it, it wouldn't matter in the least who had spawned it. Besides, it was always useful for sword fodder to be more frightened of its commanders than of the swords it faced.

He bared his fangs, nostrils flared as he raised his head, sucking in air, seeking that first delicious scent of the prey he'd been brought here to take. Eagerness tingled, burning in his blood like fire, and the hideous light of his eyes rippled and glared. The ghouls who'd learned to worship him meant nothing. Nothing! They were only a means to an end, and this—*this*—was what his Lord and Master had created him to be and do! It had been far too long since last he'd tasted the blood of a foe worthy of his hatred. Perhaps this new champion, this *Bahzell Bloody Hand*, would slake the need for destruction and slaughter that fumed at his core like a furnace.

His gaping, bare-fanged grin spread wider, lips wrinkling with contempt as he remembered the puny wizard's warnings. Warnings! *Warnings* for Anshakar the Great! What did *he* care for a *wizard's* repeated failures to rid this puling world of its so-called champions?! For the incompetence of creatures who followed that bitch Krahana, or the gutless pygmies who served Sharnā the Timid? This world—this universe—was ripe for the taking. He could smell it, *feel* it, already taste the blood and destruction. His kind were even more sensitive to such things than those contemptible wizards. If the cusp point wasn't here yet, it was coming, in no more than a few of the mortals' little decades. That was the true reason his Lord had sent him and Zûrâk and Kimazh here, whatever the wizard or his mistress thought—to seize that point, to twist it out of the other Dark Gods' grasp and give it over solely to Krashnark, where it belonged. And if this *Bahzell* was powerful, what did it matter? Anshakar was powerful, too, and far more ancient and experienced than any mortal champion of Tomanāk could ever hope to be. His very name—Anshakar—meant "World Breaker" in the tongue of his own folk, and he'd earned it well. He—*he!*—had led the final assaults which had given no less than two universes to the Dark. Now he would give it a third, and feast on the flesh of any feeble champion who'd dared to stand in his path!

✧ ✧ ✧

Nausea clenched and roiled in Bahzell Bahnakson's belly. It wasn't terror, though he was no more a stranger to fear than the next man. No, this was more than that. It was a sickness, a revulsion. He'd felt its like before, but never this strongly. The demons he'd faced and defeated, Krahana's shardohns and servants—they'd carried the same reek, the same taint of corruption and vileness he felt spinning its way towards him like a tornado. Yet for all their power and foulness, they'd been but a shadow of the darkness and despair that loomed above the Ghoul Moor like a mountain range of desolation, ribbed with agony and soaked in hopelessness and unending misery. He could feel three of them, now; three separate pustules burning their way across the land like acid, searing a deep wound filled with snail-slime poison in their wakes.

<*Whatever it is, Brother,*> Walsharno's soundless voice was harsh, <*it knows your name.*>

"Aye, that it does," Bahzell agreed grimly. He, too, could feel the focus in the heart of the darkness, feel it reaching for him, seeking him. And it wouldn't be the first time a servant of the Dark had done that, either. "It's half-tempted I am to go out and meet it where none of these lads would be caught betwixt us."

<*Understandable, but pointless.*> Walsharno shook his head. <*With all those ghouls coming with it, I doubt whatever it is is planning on meeting us in single combat.*>

"No, you've the right of it there."

Bahzell's jaw muscles tightened, and he fitted an arrow to the mighty composite horse bow he'd finally learned to use. He wasn't the most accurate archer in the world yet—indeed, he was far from it—but no lesser arm could have drawn that recurve bow, and he could fire it far more rapidly than even he could span an arbalest. Walsharno moved under him, striding slowly and steadily southeast, towards the short section of line facing directly towards the Graywillow. They moved up into the ranks of horse archers behind the hradani infantry, followed by Brandark as they took their place beside Sir Kelthys Lancebearer and his courser brother Walasfro. The two coursers loomed above the normal warhorses around them, and Sir Kelthys smiled grimly.

"Kind of them to bring music to the dance," he remarked, and Bahzell snorted a mirthless laugh. The army had continued its advance towards the Graywillow until Trianal had ordered it to form for battle. Now the land before them rose to the southeast, climbing gently but steadily to the ridgeline Bahzell had watched the scouts cross, still perhaps five hundred yards in front of them, where it broke sharply downward once more towards the Graywillow's marshy floodplain. The ghouls were not yet in sight beyond that ridge, but the monstrous thudding of their drums was clearly audible, and Bahzell's hradani ears heard the howling shriek of ghoulish war cries on the wind.

"From the sound of things, there's Fiendark's own horde of them," Sir Kelthys remarked in that same conversational tone.

"Not so much Fiendark's as his brother's, I'm thinking," Bahzell replied, and somehow, as that avalanche of evil drew closer, he knew it was true. He couldn't have said how he knew, but there was no doubt in his mind. "This is after being Krashnark's work."

"Krashnark?" Sir Kelthys looked at him, one eyebrow arched. "You're certain?"

"That I am," Bahzell said harshly.

"Then I suppose we should feel honored." The human wind rider's smile turned crooked. "I don't believe there's been a single devil sighting since the Fall. In fact, there's never been one in Norfressa at all, if memory serves."

"And it's in my mind to wonder just what it is makes us so all-fired important to be changing that," Bahzell rumbled.

"Oh, I think I can probably hazard a guess," Brandark said from his other side. "I mean, ever since you and I left Navahk, someone on the other side's been trying to kill you, after all. Well, and *me*, I suppose. Much as it irks me to admit it, however, I think they've seen me more as a case of collateral damage."

"Brandark has a point," Sir Kelthys observed reasonably. "It's not as if they haven't been trying progressively harder to stop you and your father—and Baron Tellian, come to that—for years now. And before you start feeling all responsible for what's going to happen here, Milord Champion, you might consider that anything that pisses the Dark off badly enough for them to send devils after you—for the first time in twelve hundred years, mind you!—has to be worth doing in its own right."

"Not that we'd *object* to facing some weak, contemptible, easily vanquished, merely mortal foe just once, you understand," Brandark assured him. "A platoon of halflings, perhaps, or even a regiment of crazed gerbils, hell-bent on world conquest." Then his smile faded. "Which doesn't change the fact that Sir Kelthys is right. No one ever told us there wouldn't be risks, Bahzell. And the last time I looked, most of us thought it was a good idea when we agreed to come along."

Bahzell shot him a sharp glance, but the Bloody Sword only looked back steadily until, finally, the Horse Stealer was forced to nod. Then he returned his attention to that empty, sloping rise before them. From the sound of things, it wouldn't be empty very much longer.

✧ ✧ ✧

"Get ready!" Tharanalalknarthas zoi'Harkanath bellowed.

He knew it wasn't technically the right order—the pained look from his second in command, an experienced artillerist, was proof enough of that—but he had a good voice for bellowing, rolling up out of the thick, powerful chest of his people, and his eyes glittered. Although he'd served his required time in Silver

Cavern's standing army, Tharanal himself had been an axeman in the ranks and then a combat engineer, not an artillerist, and as a general rule, he left the arcana of catapults and ballistae to those who knew how to use them without killing themselves instead of their intended targets. For that matter, the man who was Dwarvenhame's senior liaison to Prince Bhanak and the Northern Conferderation had no business in the impending battle at all. It wasn't his task, and all false modesty aside, he knew Kilthan and the other Silver Cavern elders were going to peel a long, painful strip off of his hide for risking such a valuable asset coming even this close to the fighting.

None of which meant very much to him at the moment or changed the fact that he'd put himself in command of all the barges, which made him responsible for the men who crewed them. Even if that hadn't been true, many of the men in that formation along the riverbank had become friends of his, and this project had long since become vastly more than simply the most challenging assignment of his entire life. It was important—it *mattered*—in even more ways and to more people than he'd imagined when he first set out. And even if it hadn't, he, too, could sense the darkness sweeping towards the army of hradani and Sothōii who awaited it. He was a follower of Torframos, not Tomanāk, and no champion of any god, but Stone Beard's hatred for the Dark burned just as deep and just as hot as his older brother's, and so did Tharanalalknarthas zoi'Harkanath's. He could no more have avoided this clash than he could have flown.

The deck under him vibrated as the crew of the anchored barge dumped more heaps of the ballistae's huge, javelinlike darts beside their weapons, ready to hand. He watched one ballista crew as the humans assigned to crank the windlass spat on their palms while the dwarven gunner bent slightly and squinted to peer through his ring-and-post sight at the shore, eighty yards away. There were six of the dart-throwers mounted along the barge's centerline, and a thick, head-high wooden bulwark had been raised along the clumsy vessel's side. There were firing slits in that bulwark for arbalesteers, and a fighting step to allow infantry to defend the barge against boarders. Eighty yards of riverwater might have seemed sufficient protection to someone who'd never fought ghouls, but the creatures swam entirely too well for anyone who *had* fought them to make that comfortable assumption. That, after all, was the reason they'd brought so many barges in the first place, to cover the army's back, and no one had suggested that was going to be a simple task. Even the barges with catapults, substantially farther out in the river, were far from safe havens, and Tharanal checked the baldric of his own battleaxe, making certain the weapon would be ready to hand if—when—he needed it.

The dart-thrower's gunner grimaced and straightened, then lifted the dart already in the firing tray and bent a thunderous scowl upon it.

"This thing's got a broken vane," he growled, waving it under his loader's nose. "The damned thing's hanging by a thread! How in Torframos' name d'you expect it to fly true? We're going to be firing too damned close to their line for that kind of crap!"

"Sorry," the loader—another dwarf—said, tossing the offending dart over the side. "Didn't see it. I'll keep a closer eye on the others."

"Damn right you will," the gunner told him with a ferocious glower, and Tharanal smiled faintly, then looked back towards the shore once more.

✧ ✧ ✧

Darnas Warshoe felt no temptation at all to smile. Indeed, it was all he could do not to curse out loud.

He'd never counted on the transport barges being incorporated into Trianal's battle plans. He'd chosen his role as a crewman who wasn't exactly a stranger to warfare as a way to insert himself into the Ghoul Moor in a fashion which would draw no attention to him yet make him valuable as a shore-based longshoreman who could be expected to look after himself in a fight. He should have been able to slip away from the field force's shore-based freight handlers and attach himself to the mule trains hauling the cavalry's extra arrows without drawing too much attention. That would have put him right in the heart of the upcoming battle's confusion and chaos, ideally placed to take his designated targets with an arrow of two of his own. Instead, he'd been drafted as one of the infantry defending the catapult barges. There'd been no way to refuse without drawing entirely too much attention to himself, which was how he came to be stuck in the middle of a Phrobus-damned river instead of close enough to carry out his assignment for Baron Cassan.

He wasn't concerned about the baron's reaction to his failure once he'd explained what had happened. Well, that wasn't quite true. He wasn't concerned that the baron would hold that failure against *him*, under the circumstances, but he was a man who prided himself on accomplishing his tasks. And, perhaps even more importantly, he'd been told it was just as important—even *more* important—that Yurokhas die as it was for him to kill Trianal. If it came to a choice between them, if only one target could be taken, then he was to choose the prince over Tellian's heir, despite all the enmity and hatred between Cassan and his despised rival, and that told Warshoe all he needed to know. There could be only one reason for an attack on the royal succession, whether his patron had seen fit to explain that to him or not, and if King Markhos died and *Yurokhas* didn't...

He growled again, silently, but then he stopped and gave himself a mental shake. Perhaps all wasn't lost after all, he thought, and glanced at the loaded catapult behind and above his position at the barge's bulwark. He was no trained artillerist himself, but how much training would it require to arrange an "accident" that tragically hit the Order of Tomanāk's command group once the fighting got sufficiently confused? Of course, he'd have to exercise a certain caution about how he contrived it, but he was a capable fellow... and almost as good a swimmer as a ghoul. That was a point eminently worth keeping in mind, since the northern bank of the Hangnysti happened to be a part of the *South* Riding.

✧ ✧ ✧

"Oh, shit."

Bahzell wasn't certain who'd said the two words. He knew it was one of the Sothōii sitting their horses about him, but only from the accent. The words came out almost conversationally, quietly yet with a certain heartfelt fervor, as the ridge crest before them turned suddenly black and swarming with ghouls. The tall, gangly, ungainly-looking creatures paused for just a moment as they found Trianal's army drawn up in battle formation before them. It was almost comical, in a way... or might have been if there'd been a few thousand less of them. They'd clearly hoped to catch the entire force on the march, spread out, and the leading ranks of the creatures skidded in the muddy grass when they saw those unshaken, armored lines of infantry, arbalesteers, and mounted archers waiting for them, instead.

Unfortunately, the reason their feet skidded was that the thousands upon thousands of additional ghouls coming on behind them hadn't seen the waiting humans and hradani. They kept charging straight ahead, slamming into the ones who'd tried to stop to reconsider their options. Assuming that was what those front ranks had done, that was. It seemed unlikely, ghouls being ghouls... but no more unlikely than the tall, narrow diamond-shaped shields altogether too many of them carried.

"Shields?" he heard Brandark mutter from beside him. "*Ghouls* with *shields?* That's against the rules, isn't it?"

"As to that," Bahzell's ears twitched in amusement at the other hradani's aggrieved tone, "I'm thinking whoever's put these lads together isn't so very much concerned about the rules."

"No, I suppose not," Kelthys said from his other side, raising his bow but not yet drawing it. "I agree with Brandark though. It offends my sense of the way things are supposed to be."

"I'll not argue with you there," Bahzell conceded. He hadn't raised his own bow yet. The targets he was waiting for had not yet put in an appearance, but for others in the army—

"Arbalests *ready*!"

Only a hradani's bull-like voice could have produced that thunderous bellow, and the strange, singing tension of the Rage's steely purpose rang through it like a bell. Bahzell felt his own Rage stirring, raising its head as he summoned it to him, and the front rank of arbalesteers seemed to shiver as the weapons were raised, butt stocks pressed shoulders, heads bent so that cold, focused eyes peered over their sights.

"*Brace!*" platoon leaders and sergeants in the foremost rank of infantry shouted, and the kneeling hradani leaned forward, driving their shoulders against their close-spaced shields.

Drums thundered beyond the the ridge. A vast, bestial, yelping chant rose from thousands of ghoulish throats in a massed war cry no human or hradani had ever before heard. And there was something else behind it, a howling something, a sound that was both more and less bestial than the ghouls themselves. Bahzell had heard its like before, and so had Walsharno, and Vaijon, and Brandark, and Hurthang. Not exactly the same thing, of course, for this one was deeper, a vehicle for commands and not simply an undifferentiated howl of elemental fury and hunger. Yet there was no mistaking it.

<Strange how much like demons devils sound, isn't it?> Walsharno said calmly in the back of his brain. *<Given how much they're supposed to hate each other, you'd think they'd at least* try *to sound different.>*

"I'm none so sure *we* sound any different—humans from hradani, I'm thinking—in *their* ears," Bahzell replied.

<Probably not. But I don't think it's quite that complicated, Brother. When you come down to it, evil only has one voice.>

Bahzell flicked his ears in agreement, and then the ghouls came spilling down the western side of the ridge, waving their crude weapons in a flint-edged tidal bore of hate. Those who'd hesitated hesitated no longer. They raced forward with the loping, deadly speed of their kind, screaming their hatred... and their hunger.

"Arbalesteers!" The deep voice bellowed once more as the ghouls foamed down the long, gentle slope. Five hundred yards separated them from the waiting army. Then four hundred. Three hundred. Two—

"*Looooooose!*"

KEERRWHUNNNG!

Two hundred steel-bowed arbalests fired as one, driving their flat, lethal quarrels into the ghouls' faces. Those diamond shields were little more than woven wicker covered with leather. They didn't even slow the steel-headed shafts, and deeper, bubbling shrieks—of agony this time, not simply hate—erupted in sprays of torn flesh and blood. Scores of ghouls went down, many of them tearing at the wounds those quarrels had ripped through them before going on to strike yet other targets, somewhere behind them. More of the creatures, coming on behind them, stumbled and fell, and any ghoul who fell in the face of that swarming avalanche never rose again. Its own companions' taloned feet trod its shredded corpse into the mud.

The first rank of arbalesteers stepped back through the open gaps in the second and third ranks behind them. They slung their arbalests across their backs and picked up the pikes stacked ready between the infantry and the horse archers.

"Second rank—*loose!*"

A second deadly volley sleeted into the ghouls, tumbling still more of them, caving in the front of the charging horde like an ocean wave devoured the wall of a child's castle of sand. But the ghouls were no static wall. For every creature who fell, two more stormed forward across its bleeding body, driven by their own fury and the merciless will of the devils behind them.

Bows began to sing as the range fell and the the mounted Sothōii arced their first arrows up to come driving down deeper into the mass of ghouls like steel-pointed rain. The third rank of arbalesteers stepped forward and fired a third murderous volley while the second rank reloaded. Then it was the second rank's turn once more. The third. The second. And even as they fired, that arching canopy of arrows slashed down in lethal waves.

Gaps appeared, filled in almost instantly, and still the endless flood swept over the crest, pounding closer, absorbing quarrels and arrows alike. It was like watching a landslide or a tidal wave, not flesh and blood, however brutish that flesh and blood might be. The ghouls simply absorbed the fire and drove onward, closing the range with all their fearsome speed, getting close enough to bring their enemies into their own reach and force the hradani to abandon their missile weapons.

Showers of flint-tipped javelins hissed upward as they drew closer. Most of them glanced off of the front rank's shields or the arbalesteers' breastplates and helmets. But not all of it, and men and hradani grunted or cried out in anguish as sharp-edged stone sheared flesh and muscle. The screams of wounded warhorses added themselves to the hellish din, and Walsharno twitched as one of those javelins hammered off the close-linked chain barding a courser could carry with relative ease.

Sir Kelthys' bow sang again and again in Bahzell's ear. Flint spear points and flint- and obsidian-edged war clubs thudded against the front rank's shields. The kneeling hradani thrust upward through the narrow chinks between them, driving longswords deep into the ghouls' vitals.

The arbalesteers who'd snatched up the waiting pikes stepped forward as their companions filtered to the rear, slinging their own arbalests to take up shields or pikes of their own. Those with pikes joined their fellows, thickening their line to present an impenetrable, glittering wall of pikeheads, while those with shields formed into reserve squads, ready to reinforce the fighting line's front ranks at need. The pikemen's weapons reached out above their companions' shields, punching into the enemy, filling the air with the reek of riven bowels and blood. Some of the ghouls reached across the tops of the front rank's shields, fastening their talons on the shields' edges, trying to wrench them away from their bearers... or to drag the infantrymen out of their formation and into the maw of the ghoulish vortex of destruction. Here and there, they succeeded, but the pikemen held the gaps until more shield-bearing swordsmen could fill them. And even as the mound of bodies began to grow before the shield wall, the Sothōii, well behind the vicious melee, continued to send their looping fire far back into the ghouls' ranks.

Stymied by that wall of shields and stabbing pikes, the ghouls swept around the angle of the army's formation, flowing down its long western face. Some of them swung in, trying to break the angle itself, but Trianal and his officers had anticipated that. That angle was held by the Horse Stealer warriors of Clan Iron Axe, men of Prince Bahnak's own household, armed with sword and shield and all the controlled fury of their Rage. They might be killed, but they *would* not be broken, and their swords reaped a grisly harvest from the ghouls who tried.

Yet if they held, thousands of additional ghouls streamed past and around them, turning in, flinging themselves bodily against the rock-steady line of infantry further south. Arbalest bolts hissed to meet them, pike heads thrust and bit deep, swords sheared and stabbed, yet there were far more ghouls than any of them had truly believed was possible. No one had ever seen—no one had ever *imagined*—anything which could force fifty thousand of the creatures together into a single, unified horde. Trianal's troops were outnumbered by better than two to one by enemies bigger and stronger—and faster—even than Horse Stealer hradani, and *these* ghouls seemed willing to absorb any casualties rather than break and run. They threw themselves bodily against their foes, no longer trying to wrestle the infantry's shields away from them but content to simply bear those shields down by weight of numbers. To bury them under the massive weight of their own dead flesh if that was the only way to open gaps in that unflinching line.

And here and there, especially along the long southern face, they succeeded.

✧ ✧ ✧

WHUNNNNGGGG!

The ballistae aboard Tharanal's barge thumped and thudded, throwing their vicious darts into the ghouls. Each of those atrocious missiles plowed a furrow through the creatures, rupturing chests and torsos, ripping heads completely off, taking down a dozen or two dozen of them in a single shot. But they *were* single shots, individual thunderbolts rather than a massed volley, and it took time to re-span the weapons between shots.

Tharanal watched the two humans on the ballista he'd observed earlier. They flung themselves on the windlass cranks almost before the spring steel bow stave stopped vibrating. The handles blurred with the speed and fury of their efforts, yet it still took time, and the dwarven gunner danced impatiently, his loader waiting to slam a fresh dart into the firing tray, as the enormous bow bent once more. The cocking mechanism locked, the windlass men stood back, and the loader leapt in, dropping the dart with a skilled shove to make sure it was properly seated, then jumped out of the way himself.

"Clear!" the gunner shouted, raising the gimbal-mounted weapon, peering through his sights as he trained it on the enemy pressing the eastern end of the line. He drew a deep, steadying breath and took took one more moment to aim, and then—

WHUNNNNGGGG!

Tharanal watched the dart whizz across the river in its flat, fleeting trajectory. He watched it disappear into the mass of ghouls in a fresh shower of blood. A score of them went down in a ruler-straight line, parallel to the fighting line and barely fifteen yards from it . . . and the horde simply absorbed the blow and kept right on coming.

THUMPPP!

His head came up as one of the catapult barges launched a beer-keg-sized clay vessel in a high, graceful arc. Smoke and flame trailed behind it as it sailed across the entire width of Trianal's army and into the forest of enemies pressing in upon it. The projectile struck like an angry meteor, bursting the instant it hit the ground, sending its inextinguishable contents across the ghouls in a gouting, liquid river of fire.

The banefire clung, burning, consuming, impossible to remove or put out. Not even rage and hate, not even the driving will of Anshakar and his fellows could stop the shrieking victims' desperate efforts to escape the agony. They whirled in place, clawing at their own flesh. They ripped it off in gobbets, yet that only gave the flowing banefire fresh fuel to consume, and they howled in torment, turning to flee as if they could somehow run away from the torrents of flame running down their own bodies. But there was no escape from that clinging holocaust, and in their flight they brushed up against dozens of others, spreading the banefire to fresh targets, new torches. The stench of blazing flesh, the black smoke of burning, rose all along the line, and *still* fresh waves of ghouls pressed forward in the chinks between those dreadful pools of fire.

"Ware the water!" someone shouted. "*Ghouls in the water!*"

Tharanal looked down just in time to see the first ghoul explode upward out of the river like a leaping salmon, claws reaching for the top of the barge's bulwark.

Three different arbalest bolts struck it in midair, and it shrieked, falling back to dye the water with its own blood. Yet even as it thrashed and flailed, three more followed it up from the depths. Then more—and more! Dozens of the creatures hurled themselves at the barge, enough to set even its broad hull and tonnage rocking in the water, and war cries rose as the infantry detailed to man the bulwarks hacked and hewed frantically at their attackers.

✧ ✧ ✧

Darnas Warshoe *did* swear this time, but he was scarcely alone in that. His saber slashed the throat out of the first ghoul up his barge's side, and the creature's talons opened, surrendering their grip as it splashed back into the river. Another lunged up in its place, and another. The arbalesteers and archers on the elevated platforms behind him continued to pour out quarrels and arrows, but most of their fire was reserved for the ghouls throwing themselves ashore to get at the army's back. The waiting infantry and cavalry met them with lance, pike, and sword all along the riverbank, yet they came in waves—disorganized, uncoordinated, but still deadly—and the water nearer the shore turned crimson as the barges' fire ripped into them.

But the ghouls attacking the barges themselves were more elusive targets. Swimming deep underwater, they were invisible to the archers until they burst from the river's surface to claw their way up the vessels' sides. That was why so many infantry had been assigned to their defense, yet no one had anticipated there would be so many *attackers*, and Warshoe swore again as three of the creatures hurled themselves straight at him.

An axe-armed hradani appeared at his side from somewhere, swinging his battleaxe with silent, vicious power and the relentless speed of his people's Rage. Ghoul hands and arms and heads flew in grisly profusion, and Warshoe stepped back a pace. He knew when he was outclassed, and he let the hradani take his place while he guarded the other man's flanks and rear. He heard more screams and shouts rising all along the barge's shoreward side, but he dared not look away from his own front. Either the other defenders would hold their ground or they wouldn't, and there was nothing he could do about *their* fight, anyway.

A ghoul's arm came over the bulwark, stabbing at the hradani's side with a flint dagger. The hradani never saw it coming, but Warshoe lunged forward, bringing his saber down with all the elegance of a meat axe on the ghoul's wrist. Its thick, warty hide was like a treetrunk, but the dagger flew as tendons sheared and bone shattered, and the arm disappeared back over the side in a spray of blood. Warshoe whirled, leaping to intercept another attacker—then screamed as a talon came out of nowhere. It avoided his breastplate and ripped through his leather armor as if it were paper, shredding his left shoulder, splitting the shoulder joint in a scarlet fountain of blood and agony.

He turned his head, seeing the ghoul who'd struck him, hearing its howl of triumph. It drew him towards its gaping maw, and he smelled the stench of its breath, saw the spittle running between its fangs. He'd seen more than enough maimed and broken bodies in his time to know what the hot spray of arterial blood from his own sundered flesh meant. There was time for him to realize he wouldn't be completing any more assignments for Baron Cassan, and then he snarled and twisted his body, pivoting on the agonizing talon driven through his shoulder, and slammed the tip of his saber into that wide-open mouth. The point came out the back of the ghoul's head as the saber's basket guard slammed into its fangs, and then both of them pitched over the side into the water waiting below.

✧ ✧ ✧

"Oh, that's just *wonderful!*" Brandark shouted in Bahzell's ear as a towering monstrosity loomed up among the ghouls. It thrust its way through them, trampling them underfoot, crushing those unable to get out of its way. It bellowed its fury as it came, shaking its massive horned head and waving a huge iron mace. Sickly green fire licked about that weapon's flanged head, glowing even in the bright sunlight, running down its shaft and dripping from its end like tears of poison.

The ghouls tried desperately to clear its path, but they were packed too tightly. Sothōii arrows sheeted out at the thing, skipping and glancing from its shaggy, hairy hide. One or two of them *didn't* bounce. They sank into that hide—no more than an inch or two, far too little to possibly injure something its size, but it howled its fury at the flea bites. It lowered its head, sweeping those horns through the ghouls in its path, scything them out of the way in a bow wave of shattered, screaming bodies and blood, and its eyes flashed with crimson and green fire as it cleared a way to the prey it truly sought.

"*That*, I presume, is a devil?"

The Bloody Sword's voice was calm, almost detached, but his sword had appeared in his hand as if by magic.

"Aye," Bahzell said grimly. "Mind, I've not seen one of them before this my own self, but trust a well-read lad such as yourself to get it right. Sometimes, any road."

The monster raised its head, ghouls and bits and pieces of ghoul dripping from its horns, running down its grotesque face, and those flaming eyes glared across the bodies and the blood between it and Bahzell.

"*Bahzell!*" The horrendous voice rolled like thunder over all the other sounds of battle, all the other shrieks, all the other screams. "Face me, Bahzell! Face me and *die*, coward!"

"Well, at least it has a more extensive vocabulary than a demon," Brandark observed, but Bahzell wasn't listening.

<Are you ready, Brother?> he asked silently.

<Take what you need,> Walsharno replied simply, and once more, Bahzell Bahnakson reached deep. Deep into the core of who and what he was. Deep into the determination and the unyielding will of a champion of Tomanāk. Deep into the focusing and purifying power of the summoned Rage, and his own anger, and his own rejection of all that creature was and stood for. And as he reached into that great, mysterious well, his hand met another. Walsharno reached back to him, melding his own unique strength and dauntless purpose with Bahzell's. They fitted together, becoming a single alloy, an amalgam that fused seamlessly and reached out to another, even greater fountain of power.

<I am here, my Swords,> a hurricane voice rumbled deep, deep within them both, and a gate opened. Energy flamed into them in a universe-spanning flood of azure fire. It pulsed through their

veins, frothed in their blood, and every possible color flashed at its heart like coiled lightning.

"*Tomanāk!*"

Walsharno's shrill, high whistle of defiance and rejection matched his chosen brother's bull-throated bellow, and Bahzell Bahnakson drew his bow at last. No human arm could have bent that bow, and precious few hradani ones. Four hundred pounds—that was the draw of Bahzell's bow—and his shaft was sized to his stature, the next best thing to four feet in length.

He drew the string to the angle of his jaw, gazing down that long, straight shaft at the horned devil ripping its way through its own terror-maddened army to reach him. And as he gazed, the bladed steel arrowhead began to change. Blue lightning crackled from Bahzell's right hand. It ran down the string, dripped from the fletching, danced down the shaft, coalesced in a seething corona around the arrowhead. And as it coalesced, it changed, taking on other colors. *All* the colors—the colors of Wencit of Rūm's witchfire eyes.

Brandark shrank away from his friend, eyes wide as he recognized the sizzling, hissing fury of the wild magic. He stared at Bahzell, and his ears went flat as he saw the same incandescent light glitter in the pupils of the Horse Stealer's brown eyes.

And then Bahzell Bahnakson released his string.

Over the years, he'd been ribbed mercilessly by his closest friends as he learned to master the mysteries of the bow. It wasn't as simple as an arbalest, and his accuracy with it remained considerably less than the sort of pinpoint performance he routinely turned in with the weapon he'd favored for so long. But there was no sign of that now—not in *that* shot.

The arrow leapt from the string. It shrilled through the air, no longer an arrow but a lightning bolt, and it rode a flat, explosive concussion of thunder. It flashed across the wounded ranks of infantry holding back the tide of ghouls, and the creatures beyond that hard-held line screamed, cowering down, their bodies bursting into flame as that fist of fury streaked over their heads. It slammed into the center of the mammoth devil's stupendous chest, and the creature's flame-shot eyes flew wide in astonishment.

Fresh thunder rolled. A blast of energy blew back from the point of impact, spreading in a cone-shaped fan, and the ghouls caught within it had no *time* to shriek as they flashed instantly into charred bone and drifting flecks of ash. At least fifty of the creatures vanished in that instant, but it was only the backblast, only the echo.

A holocaust enveloped Bahzell's towering enemy. It exploded up out of the monster's ruptured chest. It wrapped about him in a corona like a python of wild magic, and unlike the ghouls, he *did* have time to shriek.

He staggered back. He dropped his glowing mace, crushing another dozen ghouls to death. He clutched at the light-gouting wound in his chest, taloned hands etched against the brilliance as they tried vainly to staunch that deadly gash. He stared at Bahzell, but this time there was no rage, no hunger in his eyes—only disbelief, shock . . . and fear.

Bahzell lowered his bow, half-reeling in the saddle, feeling even Walsharno's immense vitality sag under him, but he never looked away from his foe, and his brown eyes were harder than flint and colder than the dark side of the moon.

The horned monstrosity sagged, still clutching at his chest, going to his knees. Ghouls scattered in every direction, clawing their way up and over one another in their panic. At least a score were unable to escape, and his massive body crashed down across them. He landed on his back, spine arched in agony, and that same holocaust of light gushed from his opened mouth as he screamed.

Then there was a final, earsplitting crash of thunder, a flash of brilliance that blinded every eye that looked upon it . . . and when the blindness cleared, there was only a crater blasted into the muddy, bloody trampled grass of the Ghoul Moor. Twenty yards across, that crater, its lip crowned with seared and tattered charcoal scarecrows which had once been ghouls, and smoke and steam poured up out of its depths.

Chapter Forty-One

The ghoul shaman pounding the enormous drum directly in front of Anshakar looked up as his new and terrible god halted abruptly. Looked up—then wailed in terror as the devil's head snapped erect, his nostrils flared, and a horrific bellow erupted from him.

That wail was the last sound the shaman ever made. It was still bursting from him when Anshakar brought both massive fists crashing down upon the earth. They hit wrapped in haloes of green fire, like whirlpools of poison that gyred out in all directions, and smashed the shaman and the drum-bearers into bloody ruin. Half a score of other ghouls were sucked into those whirling vortexes with squeals of despair, their bones licked clean of flesh in the single heartbeat before the bones themselves dissolved into dancing ash, and at least fifty more scrambled desperately away from the yard-deep craters those fists punched into the muddy ground.

How? *How?* The question hammered Anshakar's brain as furiously as his fists had pounded the Ghoul Moor. He'd felt Kimazh's destruction—not simply his death; his *destruction.* Nothing of the horned devil remained. Not a trace of his physical being, not a scrap of his essence—not in this universe or any other. He was gone, blotted away even more utterly than any soul Anshakar himself had ever consumed!

He straightened slowly, glaring around at the cowering ghouls who surrounded him. They quailed before his flaming eyes and turned away, surging towards their enemies once more under the lash of his will, and he scowled, feeling the empty place where Kimazh had once dwelt.

He'd never liked Kimazh. The horned devil had believed brute strength on the physical plane was all that really mattered, and while he'd possessed that in abundance, he'd never been noted for his intelligence or any *other* sort of strength. Of all the trio Anshakar's Master had sent into this world to serve his purposes, Kimazh had been the stupidest and—physical strength aside—the weakest. Anshakar would shed no tears for Kimazh, and when he returned to his own place, he would cheerfully seize all the power and all the slaves which had once been Kimazh's. Yet his companion's obliteration suggested that perhaps he himself had underestimated the opposition of this Bahzell Bahnakson.

Kimazh's destruction carried the taste of Bahzell, the scent Anshakar had been given to hunt him down if he'd been wise enough to decline to come to Anshakar. No doubt Kimazh had scented it as well. He'd seen Bahzell within reach and thought to take him now, as his own prey, devouring the champion's power and claiming Krashnark's reward for himself alone. Well, greed and overconfidence had earned their just reward, yet the nature of his fate was sobering. Nothing Anshakar had ever seen suggested the power and ability to simply wipe away a greater devil as if he'd never even existed. Slay one's physical avatar, even banish one's essence back to the universe from whence it had come in tatters that might take centuries to heal, yes; that he'd seen before, although never a foe who could have done it to *him*. But the power to simply . . . extinguish Kimazh? Blot him out like a candle flame? No. No, that was something new, something neither Anshakar nor any other devil, so far as he knew, had ever seen or experienced.

Yet a blow of that devastating power could not have come cheaply. Tomanāk's champions were but mortal. To channel that much power, release that much destruction, had to have drained any mortal conduit to the point of *self*-destruction, as well. And not even the greatest of mortal champions was proof against more mundane means of death.

The idiot Kimazh had been *supposed* to feed his ghouls into the furnace, break the mortals' line, draw Bahzell into the melee. No champion of Tomanāk could resist that situation! Their simpering sense of "honor" would compel them forward, lending their aid to those in need, and when it did they would expose themselves to the edged, blood-hungry flint and obsidian of the ghouls' weapons. Let them be struck down, wounded—weakened, or even slain—and even the mightiest champion's soul would be easy to take. And if these worthless, terrified ghouls proved incapable of even that much, the champion would still be distracted, forced to defend himself against purely physical threats, when their true foes finally struck. It was a strategy which would see thousands upon thousands of ghouls slaughtered in the doing, but what were they to Anshakar and his fellows? They existed only to be used, and he bellowed his own rage and hatred as he sent them crashing against the shield wall of Trianal Bowmaster's army like hurricane-driven surf.

✧ ✧ ✧

"What was that?" Prince Yurokhas demanded, staring southwest to where a boil of light reared itself above the confused battle.

"*That*, Your Highness," Vaijon Almerhas replied dryly, "was Bahzell and Walsharno." He shook his head like a man trying to throw off the effects of a hard, straight punch. He'd felt Kimazh's destruction and the enormous surge of Bahzell and Walsharno's combined attack just as clearly as Anshakar. Indeed, the echoes rolling out and reverberating from that eruption of power could have been felt by any champion of Tomanāk within a thousand leagues. "Whatever we've been sensing may have been, there's only two of them now."

"Are *they* all right?" Prince Arsham asked urgently from where he sat his horse beside Yurokhas' Vahrchanak.

Even the burly, powerfully built Prince of Navahk looked like a youngster perched on his first pony beside the towering courser, but he and Yurokhas had taken to one another more strongly than anyone would have cared to predict before they'd met. More to the point at the moment, the concern for Bahzell and Walsharno in his voice was completely genuine, and Sharkah Bahnaksdaughter looked up quickly from where she stood in the ranks of the Order's foot troops.

"So far," Vaijon said a bit more grimly. "Whatever they did, though, it took a lot out of them. They're going to need time to recover before they can do it again."

"Lovely."

At that moment, Arsham sounded a great deal like his countryman Brandark, Vaijon reflected. The Navahkan shook his head and grimaced.

"I don't suppose you happen to know just what 'whatever they did' was, would you?" he continued, and Vaijon shook his head.

"We each have our own technique," Vaijon said almost absently, looking away from the prince to where the tempo of screams, war cries, and the ululating howls of ghouls had just redoubled. The Sothōii horse archers between the Order and the long, southern front of the army's formation were beginning to move slowly forward, and those in the front two or three ranks were casing their bows and drawing lances from their saddle boots. "None of us come at it quite the same way. And Bahzell is more... improvisational than most of us."

"Somehow I can believe that," Arsham said.

"So can I," Yurokhas added, readying his own heavier, longer lance. "I think it might be a good idea for you to begin thinking about an approach of your own, though, Vaijon."

Vaijon nodded, his eyes hardening and his jaw muscles tightening as he saw the huge four-armed, spike-skinned, cat-headed shape looming up beyond the crossing showers of javelins and flights of Sothōii arrows. He leaned from the saddle to take his own lance from one of the Order's Horse Stealers and then looked at Hurthang.

"Get ready to clear me a path," he said quietly, and Hurthang nodded.

"Aye," he promised grimly. "We'll just be doing that."

He slapped Vaijon's armored thigh, then turned away and began bellowing orders of his own.

"You'll oblige me please, Your Highness—*both* Your Highnesses—by staying alive, if you please," Vaijon said, never looking away from that cat-headed monstrosity. "If I thought it would do any good, I'd have some of Hurthang's lads drag the pair of you out to one of the barges."

"It's a little late for that now, Vaijon," Yurokhas pointed out with a thin smile.

"Besides," Arsham added, looking over his shoulder at the combat raging along the riverbank just as another flaming charge of banefire flew overhead, "it looks like at least half the barges are under attack, as well."

✧ ✧ ✧

The devil named Zûrâk squalled like the universe's largest panther as twenty gallons of banefire hit him squarely in the belly. The impact alone was enough to stagger even something his size, and he found himself wishing he'd brought along at least one shield instead of the swords and battleaxes clutched in all four of his hands. The banefire ignited instantly, running down his iron-plated hide, clinging and burning with enough purely physical pain to make him howl in anguish. His seared scales replaced themselves almost as quickly as they were consumed, but that did little to slake his flaming torment or the devastation dripping from him to lick over and consume the tight-packed ghouls about him.

He glared furiously at the barges anchored in mid-river, at the catapult crews and arbalesteers continuing to pour fire into the bleeding ranks of ghouls even as others of the creatures hurled themselves upon the vessels. Three of those barges had been swamped, their defenders butchered, but the others still held out and continued to sweep the western face of the defending army with their murderous darts. And the catapult barges, farther out, rained fire and destruction far into the ranks of his own terrified force.

He, too, had felt Kimazh's destruction, but he'd been even closer than Anshakar. He knew it hadn't been Bahzell alone; the deed had required Bahzell and Walsharno both. And he could sense the *other* champion, the one called Vaijon, before him on the far side of the infantry line which had finally begun to crumble. Vaijon... who had no courser champion to aid *him*.

"On!" he shrieked from his cocoon of flame, screaming the command at the desperately drumming shamans. "*On!* Break them—*break them now!*"

The shamans heard him, and the drums thundered and rolled, pounding out their commands and the fury of the shamans' god. They swept over the ghouls, gathered them up, and hurled them straight into the teeth of the defenders' shields, swords, and pikes. It was death to charge that unyielding line... yet there were some things worse than simple death, and one of them was named Zûrâk.

✧ ✧ ✧

"Stand! *Stand your ground!*"

Yurgazh Charkson's thunderous shout carried clearly even through the tumult of battle and the deafening boom of the drums. It was probably the most superfluous order he'd ever given, he thought, remembering other fields and other battles. He'd won his officer's rank by holding even Rage-maddened hradani firm in the face of defeat, but there was no comparison between the foes he'd fought then and the ones his men faced today. Bahnak Karathson's infantry had been hard, dangerous opponents, but they'd been *men*, not red-fanged creatures driven and goaded by something out of nightmare.

He drew his own sword and settled his shield as the avalanche of shrieking ghouls hurled themselves forward with redoubled fury. Around him, his staff and runners did the same. They'd learned, as Prince Bahnak had demanded, that generals—even hradani generals—had no business surrendering control of their forces by wading into the middle of a melee. Unfortunately, this time it looked like the melee was going to be wading into *them*.

✧ ✧ ✧

The ghoulish charge slammed into the hradani infantry like a battering ram. War clubs, spears, talons, and fangs came at them in a wave of fury beyond belief. They obeyed their general, those infantry. They *stood* their ground, as only hradani riding the Rage could, but standing their ground wasn't enough. Not this time.

Hundreds of them died where they stood that ground, and the line directly in front of Zûrâk broke.

✧ ✧ ✧

Bugles sounded, their notes rising clear and clean above the yammering thunder of battle, summoning the reserves. But in that instant, in that moment when the line broke, there was no time for any of those reserves to respond.

A torrent of ghouls exploded through the break, foaming out, swinging to take the pikemen to either side in flank and rear. Squads of infantry posted immediately behind the line turned to face them, battling to hold the influx until more powerful reinforcements could arrive, but they were driven back, forced to give ground step by bleeding step. And through the middle of that break, straight into the teeth of the Sothōii behind it, came a creature out of nightmare, still wrapped in its glaring corona of banefire and shrieking its fury.

Arrows and arbalest bolts streaked to meet it from either side, but the men directly in front of it were too busy fighting for their lives, and the Sothōii armsmen who'd exchanged bows for lances surged forward. A mounted trooper's most valuable weapon was momentum. They would have been fools to take that charge standing, but neither did they have the time and space to build speed. Against something with the physical size and power of ghouls, that was a fatal shortcoming. Their light lances gave them the advantage of reach even over something with arms that long, but they lacked the velocity to drive home a true countercharge. Scores of the creatures went down, shrieking and twisting, clutching at the lances which had transfixed them. But they also took those lances with them, dragging them out of the hands of the armsmen who'd felled them.

The veteran armsmen released their weapons rather than try vainly to retain them. Sabers swept out of scabbards all along the Sothōii front, thrusting and hewing desperately, but now it was the ghouls with their unnaturally long limbs who had the reach advantage. Stone-edged weapons hacked wildly—with a minimum of skill, but enormous speed and power. Some of them shattered on steel breastplates; more of them found the more vulnerable leather armor protecting arms and legs. The screams of wounded men rose to meet the howls of wounded and rampaging ghouls. Horses shrieked as throats were torn out or legs were hewn out from under them. Armsmen were snatched from saddles, disappearing into the flood of destruction. Dismounted hradani infantry fought desperately to reach them, a millennium of mutual hatred forgotten . . . and most of those infantry died in the process.

The rupture of the army's line spread, widened. The last of the mounted Sothōii went down, and Zûrâk bellowed in triumph from the heart of his shroud of banefire as his creatures engulfed their foes like the Spear River in springtime flood.

And then the Order of Tomanāk charged.

"*Tomanāk!*"

The massed battle cry cut through the incredible din of battle like summer thunder, and Zûrâk shrieked his fury at the sound of that hated name.

Although the Hurgrum Chapter of the Order had grown steadily over the years since its founding, it remained the smallest single contingent attached to Trianal's army. It counted less than five hundred warriors, against thousands upon thousands of ghouls, and over four hundred of its total strength was infantry, not cavalry. But those infantry were *hradani* infantry, with a training and discipline even Bahnak Karathson's army had yet to attain, and that relative handful of cavalry were overwhelmingly Sothōii cavalry... and all of it had been trained and mercilessly drilled by Vaijon Almerhas.

Unlike the Sothōii who'd been stationed immediately behind the original line to support it with bowfire, the Order had almost a hundred yards to build velocity. That wasn't a great deal of distance for horses to build maximum speed, but it was more than enough for Horse Stealer and Bloody Sword hradani riding the cold, mercilessly focused fury of the Rage.

The Order went into the triumphant ghouls like a thunderbolt—like the very mace of the deity it served. It struck not in a meticulously dressed line but in an even more meticulously ordered *wedge*, driving its point into the disorganized, swirling tide race of the victorious ghouls like the prow of a ship. The Order's small cavalry force covered the wedge's flanks, for even now the whirlpool of ghouls overspread the Order's entire formation, but the tip of that wedge was made of Horse Stealers in full, articulated plate, gift of the Dwarves of Silver Cavern, and armed with the great daggered axes of Clan Iron Axe. Flint and obsidian were no match for tempered steel, and the men behind those axes were almost as big, almost as strong, and far, far better trained than the ghouls themselves.

The creatures recoiled as that juggernaut crashed into them, hurling them back in windrows of broken bodies. Many of those to either side of the Order's wedge were seized by the same panicked reaction as their unfortunate fellows directly in front of it. The more immediate terror of slashing steel, especially when they'd finally tasted victory only moments before, was enough—barely—to overcome even their terrified obedience to Zûrâk's driving will. They turned, tried to scatter and flee, but they were too tightly packed, too congested, and the Order's infantry thundered their battle cry as they hewed mercilessly at their enemies' backs.

Yet not all of the ghouls *could* flee. They simply couldn't get out of the way, and as the infantry wedge drove forward, trampling dead and wounded ghouls underfoot, the rearmost ranks taking time to slash off heads to be certain "dead" ghouls stayed that way, it moved deeper and deeper into the swirling torrent of its enemies. Infantry battalions from Trianal's central reserve moved at a dead run to reinforce the hideously outnumbered Order, but they were still minutes away, and minutes were eternities on that field.

Ghouls who found themselves squeezed between the still-resisting infantry on the flanks of the original breakthrough and the angled faces of the Order's wedge turned upon their foes with the redoubled fury and power of desperation. They sought any opening, any gap, and some of them—a handful, at first, then dozens, and finally scores—spurted out through the mercilessly closing spaces between the Order and Yurgazh Charkson's infantry and burst into the open area at the heart of the army's rectangular formation.

They were far too intermingled with the defenders for archery, and the reserves charging to the Order's support were still too far away to engage them, yet it was obvious even to ghouls that those inside the army's lines were doomed if the Order succeeded in plugging the breakthrough. They turned, leaping forward with all the speed and agility of their kind, to swarm around the wedge's flanks and sweep into its center from behind.

It was a close-range, brutal battle, even more ferocious in its way than the combat swirling around the point of the wedge. Hurthang and Vaijon had detailed a single thirty-man platoon—all they could spare from the wedge itself—to cover the charging infantry's backs, and its members turned in place, fighting furiously to hold off the threat. Even more of the struggle, however, fell upon the Order's small cavalry force, and Yurokhas of the Sothõii and Arsham of Navahk were at the heart of it.

Vahrchanak and his rider fought as one being, with steel-shod hooves, shield, lance, and sword. They *were* one, seeing through one another's eyes, hearing through one another's ears, with an awareness of the fury and confusion about them impossible for any single individual to attain. Only a handful of warriors, even among the elite ranks of Sothõii wind riders, could have matched the skilled deadliness of Yurokhas Silveraxe, and the most superbly trained warhorse in the world was no match for the intelligence and training of a courser. Vahrchanak screamed his own equine rage and fury as he trampled ghouls into bloody mud, lashed out with his heels in perfectly timed kicks, reaped limbs and heads with his own ferocious jaws. His barding absorbed blows that would have felled any unarmored horse, and he and his rider were so closely linked that Yurokhas anticipated his every move. The prince adjusted balance and seat automatically, and his shearing sword and the hammer of his shield guarded Vahrchanak's flanks while the stallion rampaged through their enemies.

Prince Arsham was twice Yurokhas' age and, despite the Sothōii prince's training and skill, far more experienced and much, much stronger. Individually, he was almost certainly even more deadly than Yurokhas, but his mount, for all its willingness and courage, was no courser, and Arsham knew it. He glued himself to Vahrchanak's side and rear, helping to cover the courser and his rider while they reaped their bloody harvest, and his own sword ran red as the mad tide of combat raged around them.

The assault on the wedge's flanks reached a crescendo and began to ebb as more and more of the attackers were cut down and others turned hopelessly to face the reserves charging down upon them. But those still attacking the Order redoubled their own efforts, frantic to somehow break the wedge and escape back through the gap they'd torn in the original fighting line.

One of those ghouls went down, left arm severed by the sword of Arsham of Navahk. It screamed in pain and lashed out with its remaining set of talons... and disemboweled Arsham's mount.

The mortally wounded horse shrieked as it collapsed, spilling its rider. Arsham managed to kick free of the stirrups and land in a semi-controlled roll. He retained his sword and came back upright almost instantly, despite the weight of his armor, but *almost* instantly wasn't good enough. A trio of ghouls launched themselves directly at him even as he regained one knee and started to stand, and he snarled through the corona of his Rage as he managed to block the first murderous war club whistling towards his head.

His counterstroke chopped through his attacker's knee and the ghoul collapsed with a keening wail. That left Arsham open and unguarded against the other two, however, and his eyes glittered as he saw death coming for him. An obsidian-headed spear thrust straight for his throat with the darting, deadly speed of a striking adder and there was no time to dodge, no way to block.

Four feet of bloody, tempered steel sheared through the spear shaft and continued onward into the ghoul spearman's chest. The double-edged blade carved its way through the ghoul, then looped back up in a perfectly timed backstroke that took the head completely off the third ghoul.

Arsham's eyes widened at the brutal efficiency of his rescue, but more attackers were driving into the momentary open space that deadly sword had created. He hurled himself fully to his feet, turning instinctively to put his back to his rescuer's. The two of them stood, an armored rock throwing back the last, desperate surge of the river of ghouls which had been cut off by the Order's charge, and even as he fought for his life, a tiny corner of Arsham's brain reflected on the irony of it.

Who would have dreamed, in the days when he was his father Churnazh's least trusted but most lethal general, that he would someday owe his life to Sharkah Bahnaksdaughter of Hurgrum?

✧ ✧ ✧

Zûrâk recognized the failure of the ghouls' breakthrough as the hated Order of Tomanāk sealed off the gap. A third of the Order's infantry might have been killed or wounded in the doing, but they'd done it. The ghouls between him and the enemy continued to fling themselves forward, still more terrified of him than of the relatively clean death of battle, yet they were a spent force, and he knew it.

But he didn't care. They'd served their purpose, for they'd drawn the Order into the melee where Zûrâk could get at it directly. The banefire eating at his armored hide might send waves of torment sizzling along his unnatural nerves, and fury might fill his brain, but his focus and purpose remained and he waded forward.

The ghouls before him quailed away from his faceless, flaming shape, and his swords and axes swept aside any who were too slow to evade him. They were mere encumbrances, an inconvenient obstruction between him and his true target, and he roared his challenge as he came.

✧ ✧ ✧

Vaijon—once of Almerhas, and now of Hurgrum—sat his warhorse behind the center of the wedge formation of the Order he'd spent the last seven years of his life training. He'd made himself sit there, waiting, letting his sword brothers—and his single sword *sister*—face the enemy while he held aloof.

It was the hardest thing he had ever done in his life.

The Hurgrum Chapter was his family, even more than if they had been his own bone and blood. He knew them all. He'd trained with them, led them, watched them come together—Hurgrumese and Navahkan, hradani and Sothōii, forgetting centuries of hatred and bloodshed to become one in the service of the god of battle—and now he'd watched them bleed and die while he waited. Somewhere in the very back of his mind behind the singing silence of discipline and the focused purpose of a champion of Tomanāk, he remembered an arrogant young man who would have felt only contempt for "barbarian" hradani and little more respect for the Sothōii. That young man was far away from this day and place, and even as he felt his sword companions bleed and die about him, he was grateful for every step of the journey which had brought him here in that young man's place. Here to confront the enemy he'd been born to face.

A pretty toy, a voice rumbled into the silence within him, *but the steel is sound enough under all the fancy work.*

Despite the carnage about him, despite the fire-wrapped shape striding towards him, despite even the deaths the Order had suffered, Vaijon smiled within his open-faced helmet as the words from a long-ago day flowed through him.

"I've tried, at any rate," he told Tomanāk, and heard a silent, approving flicker of laughter.

Yes, my Sword, you have. Bahzell was right about you, and so was I. Are you ready, Vaijon?

"I am," he said calmly.

Together, then.

Vaijon felt a mighty hand rest upon his right shoulder. His mind and heart reached out to that hand in return, and a sheath of glittering blue light swept down his own right arm. It licked out along the shaft of his lance, gathering in a coruscating halo about its leaf-shaped blade, and he drew a deep breath.

"*Now*, Hurthang!" he shouted, his voice cutting through the deafening tumult as cleanly as a sword, shadowed and carried by the echo of the War God's own voice, and Hurthang Marahgson heard him.

"*Open!*" Hurthang bellowed, and the point of the wedge—the *reason* the Order had charged in a wedge aimed directly at Zûrâk—opened. The armored axemen who had formed it, those who survived, stepped back and to the rear instantly, and the handful of ghouls between them and Zûrâk, found themselves face to face with something even more terrifying than Horse Stealer axes.

"*Tomanāk!*"

Vaijon of Hurgrum's war cry sounded like a trumpet and his horse bounded forward.

That horse had been Tellian of Balthar's gift, and any prince would have paid a fortune to possess it. Yet it was no courser, and there was no way even a courser could have reached full speed in so little space. There simply wasn't enough distance.

It didn't matter. Somehow, in a way those who saw it happen knew even then they would never be able to describe even to themselves, Vaijon's warhorse went from a standing start to full gallop in a single bound, and the glittering head of his lance went before him.

The tattered screen of ghouls between him and Zûrâk flung themselves aside, frantic to avoid the azure apparition thundering towards them. A handful were too slow; the halo of blue lightning crackling around Vaijon's lance head touched them, and they twitched, transfixed, soundless mouths opened in screams they had no time to utter before they exploded into clouds of ash.

Then they were gone, and Zûrâk's eyes blazed green and crimson through the seething curtain of banefire as he bellowed his hunger and charged to meet his foe.

They met in an eruption of bright, clean blue light and the sickly green of corruption, and dozens of men were bowled off their feet by the silent concussion of that collision. The glaring lance head drove past Zûrâk's reaching arms. It hammered into him, and he shrieked in a greater agony than he had ever experienced. The cleansing light of Tomanāk ripped outward from it, tearing at him, consuming him. He was tougher and far, far more powerful than the ghouls who'd been destroyed by that halo's lightest touch, but his glaring eyes bulged incredulously as he felt himself disintegrating—flaring into nothingness—as that devouring incandescence ravened its way through him.

He shrieked again, but even in his torment, his mind was clearer than Kimazh's would have been. He struck with both swords and both axes—not at Vaijon, but at the shaft of Vaijon's lance. Livid green fire enveloped all of his weapons as they thundered down, and a fresh boil of light exploded outward as the lance shaft shattered.

The blue volcano demolishing Zûrâk's very being vanished. He was hurt, more dreadfully wounded than he'd ever imagined he might be, but he howled his triumph as he struck his enemy's weapon from his hands. He heaved himself back upright, straightening and raising his own weapons once more... ready this time to strike directly at his foe. Without the fire of that horrific lance, no mortal could stand against him, and once this hated champion was gone, he would sweep through the ranks of infantry and cavalry to take Bahzell and Walsharno from behind while Anshakar came at them from the front. And once *that* happened—

Vaijon never hesitated. He dropped his shattered lance and, for the first time ever, he did something he'd seen Bahzell do dozens of times.

"*Come!*" he thundered, and his longsword materialized in his empty hand as he deliberately hurled himself directly into Zûrâk's embrace.

He ducked under the sweeping swords in the devil's upper set of hands as his warhorse went down without even a scream under the savage, scissoring blow of Zûrâk's battleaxes. But the blow came too late. Vaijon was already inside Zûrâk's reach, driving himself up and out of his crumpling horse's saddle. The devil dropped his weapons, closing his arms, driving his talons through the back of Vaijon's armor, desperate now to rend and destroy his enemy, but Vaijon of Hurgrum, champion of Tomanāk, had known that was going to happen. He had only one purpose... and he accomplished it.

Zûrâk shrieked as that magnificently bejeweled and glittering blade, caparisoned in a far greater sapphire splendor, drove upward through his unnatural lungs and heart and backbone in a blinding flash of cleansing fury. His spine arched as that same fury erupted back out of his chest, sprayed out between his shoulder blades, and exploded upward through his torso and squat, thick neck. He stood a moment longer, a headless, shredded shape belching the brilliant blue of Tomanāk's rage and rejection... and then he folded forward over the body of his foe.

Chapter Forty-Two

<*Vaijon!*>

Walsharno's silent, agonized cry echoed Bahzell Bahnakson's pain. A golden strand, as much a part of him as his own pulse, snapped, its broken end whipping away even as he grasped vainly after it. It was gone, vanishing between one breath and the next, and he felt the anguish of its passing even through the focus of his Rage.

Yet there was no time to let themselves feel it fully, for even as Vaijon fell, taking one of the remaining focuses of the Dark with him, a screaming battering ram of ghouls smashed into the hard-pressed battle line in front of them. The line bowed, stretched, began to break . . . and beyond it, striding towards them, wrapped in its own sick green fire, came the last and greatest of their foes.

✧ ✧ ✧

Anshakar snarled as Zûrâk was blotted away as thoroughly as Kimazh had been. The wizard had lied to them, he realized. Even as he'd whined and warned them that these were no ordinary champions of Tomanāk, he'd never once suggested they were soul-killers. Perhaps he hadn't realized it himself—not then, at least—but Anshakar knew it now. He'd never seen it before, but he recognized what had happened. It wasn't the same as the Dark's soul-killers, for Zûrâk and Kimazh had simply been obliterated, not consumed, but the difference mattered little in the end. In theory, this Bahzell and his courser companion could destroy even Anshakar the Great.

But *only* in theory, for he was more than close enough now

for his senses to confirm the way in which destroying Kimazh had drained both Bahzell and the courser. They were recovering quickly—more quickly than he would have believed possible—but it would still be many minutes, probably as much as an hour, before their mortal frames could once again channel and generate enough power to destroy one such as him. Hurt him, yes; they could do that. But actually slaying him would be beyond them, and so he whipped his slaves on before him, eager to grind his way through the defending infantry and reach his prey.

✧ ✧ ✧

Bahzell's brown eyes were bleak as yet another monstrous shape loomed up amid the gradually thinning ranks of the ghouls. He knew as well as Anshakar how killing the first devil had drained both him and Walsharno, and this one was far stronger than the first had been. Its power reached out towards them like a strangler's hands, battering at them, trying to crush them with the fear of its coming. That same fear reached out to the defenders in front of him, causing even the hardiest hradani to quail, despite the buttress of the Rage. They stood their ground, their Sothōii allies with them, but the ferocity of their defense faltered, and in that moment, Anshakar launched his own final reserve at their throats.

"They're coming through," Brandark said at Bahzell's side.

"Yes, they are," Sir Kelthys agreed.

The human wind rider tossed his bow aside, something no Sothōii would have done except under the direst of circumstances, to swing his shield into position. Walasfro stamped one forehoof under him, and Kelthys drew his sword.

Bahzell glanced at his two companions, then back at the oncoming Anshakar as one of the huge javelins from the ballistae-armed barges struck him squarely. It drove two feet into the naked devil's side, but he only plucked it out, licked his own blood from it, and then hurled it back at the barge from whence it had come. It struck the arbalest which had launched it, shattered its windlass, drove through the vessel's deck and completely back out the other side of its hull below the waterline.

"Stay behind us, the pair of you," he said harshly. "Just you be keeping them off our backs."

"Are you sure about that?" Brandark asked quietly, without a trace of his usual banter, and Bahzell smiled grimly.

"You'd best be taking my word for it this once, little man," he said. "You'd not like what would happen if you were to be finding yourself betwixt us and that bastard yonder."

The Bloody Sword took one look at his friend's expression and nodded soberly. Then he looked at Kelthys, and the Sothōii nodded back.

"We'll keep them off your back," Brandark promised.

✧ ✧ ✧

The frenzied assault smashed into the frontline infantry just as the terror radiating from Anshakar struck the defenders. The weight of that double blow was too great, and the decimated battalion holding the front crumbled. It didn't break, didn't run, even then; it simply disintegrated into dead bodies and isolated knots of still-desperately fighting men as the ghouls drove them back by sheer force of numbers and suicidal ferocity. Fresh bugle calls sounded, sending two-thirds of Trianal's remaining reserve thundering towards the breakthrough under Sir Yarran Battlecrow. But once again, it would take precious minutes for the reinforcements to arrive, and those were minutes Bahzell Bahnakson and Walsharno didn't have.

"*Stand clear!*"

The sheer, ear-stunning volume of Bahzell's thundered command roared out through the bedlam of battle. Walsharno's fierce whistle came with it, and the mounted Sothōii armsmen between them and Anshakar obeyed that double command without even thinking about it. It wouldn't have mattered if *they'd* wanted to hesitate, not with Walsharno's will fastened upon their warhorses with all the ruthless authority of a courser herd stallion and a champion of Tomanāk. Those horses scattered to either side, and Walsharno, son of Mathygan and Yorthandro, chosen companion of Bahzell Bahnakson of the Horse Stealer hradani, came through that gap like thunder.

✧ ✧ ✧

Anshakar's eyes widened in surprise as the mounted troops in front of him scattered rather than advancing to meet the ghouls. He hadn't expected them to break *that* quickly, that easily, and the ghouls who'd broken past the still-resisting knots of infantry howled their own astonished victory—and vast relief—as the armsmen in their path dispersed.

But then a single horseman erupted from that opening, and the ghouls' relief vanished in wailing panic as they saw him.

He came at them in an earthshaking, rolling, mud-spattering

thunder and a dreadful corona of blue fire. It crackled about him, streaming on the wind of his passage, running down the mighty stallion's legs, pooling around his hooves and splashing outward with every booming stride. It reached out to either side, that fire, and stretched out before him, and wails of panic turned into shrieks of agony at its touch.

The ghouls enveloped in that glittering wave of power twisted and contorted, writhing and burning like grass in a furnace. It consumed their flesh, seared their bones, dropped their scorched skeletons into the mud and the blood and the grass. Bone crunched under the surviving infantry's boots as that same glaring tide pushed *them* none too gently out of the horseman's path, as well, and a mighty sword appeared in his hands.

"*Tomanāk!*"

Bahzell Bahnakson and Walsharno thundered toward Anshakar, and that blazing blue bow wave came with them.

✧ ✧ ✧

Anshakar was taken aback by the fury of his puny foes' charge. He would have expected even one of Tomanāk's champions to have played for time, tried to stay away from him long enough to recover the strength to face him. Yet it seemed this Bahzell, this Walsharno, were even more foolish than their fellows, and he spread his arms and loped to meet them with a hideous smile. That blue stormfront might terrify ghouls—might even be deadly to such contemptible creatures—but it held no terror for Anshakar. It was far too weak to so much as injure one such as him, far less *destroy* him.

✧ ✧ ✧

Bahzell felt Anshakar's searing power rise higher and fiercer as he and Walsharno hurtled towards it. He'd known this enemy was stronger than the devil he'd already vanquished, yet its sheer, stunning potency was even greater than he'd feared. He and Walsharno were no fit match for it, not in their present state, and both of them knew it.

Few of my champions die in bed.

The warning Tomanāk had given him so long ago, the night he explained why he wanted a barbarian hradani as a champion, echoed in some deeply buried corner of Bahzell's mind. He couldn't pretend he'd ever known or thought differently. Yet all men died—even men as good as Vaijon—and it was given only to a few of them to choose their deaths. To know beyond shadow or doubt that that which they died to save was worth the saving, the evil worth the fighting... the death worth the dying. That was what drew a champion to Tomanāk—that knowledge, that *understanding*—and neither Bahzell Bahnakson nor Walsharno could see *this* evil and refuse to fight it, even knowing they must die in the doing.

There were no words from Tomanāk. Not this time. There was only his hand at their back, his war cry in the thunder of their hooves, and his bright, fierce determination welded to their own wills like steel.

"*Tomanāk!*" Bahzell bellowed yet again, and the sword in his hands turned into a glorious cascade of azure flame.

✧ ✧ ✧

Anshakar flinched from that hated name, but he sneered at the hradani who'd dared to utter it.

"*Krashnark!*" he bellowed back in a voice fit to break the heavens themselves, and the ghouls cowered down, covering their ears' with their talons. "Come to me, Bahzell! *Come and die!*"

✧ ✧ ✧

Bahzell heard Anshakar's challenge, heard the hunger and the confidence in it, and knew that confidence was justified. He could sense the vast tide of Tomanāk's presence and power, feel his deity's willingness to offer all of himself that he and Walsharno might channel, but they were still too spent. They couldn't reach deep enough, channel enough of it, to defeat this enemy. Yet perhaps they might at least wound it badly enough to drive it back from whence it had come, badly enough for the remainder of Trianal's army to survive. It was a threadbare hope, but all they could give their companions.

Anshakar was a towering inferno of sick emerald fire, consuming the world, straddling the horizon, and they arrowed straight for the heart of it with one heart, one mind... one soul.

And then, suddenly, there was *another* soul, another presence. It flared deep within them, like a sudden streamer of golden flame, part of them and yet apart, and they recognized it.

Sir Vaijon Almerhas, commander of the Hurgrum Chapter of the Order of Tomanāk, touched them. It was fleeting, that touch across the wall of death, impossible for anyone to sustain, but in that instant, it opened another conduit to Tomanāk, and fresh strength—more strength than any mortal could ever have channeled—scorched through them.

"Tomanāk! *Tomanāk and Vaijon!*"

✧ ✧ ✧

Sudden fear stabbed through Anshakar's confidence as he heard the terrible joy in that thundering voice. The presence and power coming at him doubled, then *re*doubled, roaring up with all the roiling fury of the sun itself. His taloned feet skidded in the Ghoul Moor's mud and bodies, but it was far too late for that.

Bahzell and Walsharno struck him like a typhoon.

That bubble of blinding blue brilliance was a battering ram. It bowled him off his feet, hurled him backward for a dozen yards. Nothing had ever done that before, and the sodden ground erupted in a spray of steaming mud as he landed on his back and the impact blasted an enormous crater. He reached out to either side, like a man fallen into deep snow, claws scrabbling as he tried to thrust himself back upright, but there was no time for that, either.

Wind rider and courser, champions both, souls linked, Bahzell and Walsharno loomed up, impossibly vast, impossibly huge, enormous enough to dwarf even Anshakar the Great. A flaming hoof, vaster than a boulder, crashed down on Anshakar's chest, and he screamed as flesh burned, ribs crumpled in crushed ruin, and an agony he'd never imagined tore through him. He reached up, clawing desperately, talons raking through Walsharno's chain barding, but the stallion only brought his other forehoof down like Tomanāk's mace, and Bahzell leaned from the saddle. That flaming sword sheared one tree-trunk arm at the elbow, and Anshakar screamed again as the stump of his arm gouted blood. His other arm rose, almost feebly now, batting at Bahzell's blade in futile self-defense, and Bahzell lopped it off as well even as Walsharno rose high on his back legs.

The stallion towered there, an immense, fiery sapphire sculpture, looming against the heavens, and then both forehooves came down as one. They landed in a holocaust of blue fury, and Anshakar the Great's head exploded in a fountain of flame.

✧ ✧ ✧

"*No!*"

Varnaythus of Kontovar brought both fists crashing down on either side of his gramerhain.

"Fiendark fly away with their souls! Krahana lick their bones!" he snarled.

So close—they'd come so *close!* First the failure against Markhos, and now *this!*

Trianal's army had hovered on the brink of defeat. A quarter of the supporting barges had fallen to the ghouls. The riverbank had been littered with the bodies of Sothōii and hradani, and the ghouls' unrelenting pressure had been driving the remaining defenders back from the water's edge step by step, despite the barges. That Krahana-damned bastard Vaijon of Almerhas had been crushed—*crushed!*—and Bahzell and Walsharno had been too weak, *far* too weak, to stop Anshakar by themselves! He'd seen it, been able to taste it himself through the gramerhain, and yet, somehow, at the last moment, that bastard hradani had slipped aside and avoided destruction yet again. *Again!*

He made himself straighten, made himself inhale deeply, and looked up from the crystal as the ghouls scattered like windblown chaff. Many of the creatures, maddened by battle and blood lust, continued to attack, but they were less than a tithe of the original horde. No power on earth could have stopped the rest of them from fleeing now—not when their new gods had been slain, for the compulsion those gods had wielded had vanished with Anshakar's death, and the terror of his destroyers was upon them.

Malahk Sahrdohr looked back at the older man, gray eyes stunned. He'd watched the same battle, seen the same signs Varnaythus had seen . . . and now *this*.

"Well," the senior wizard said finally, his voice harsh, "it seems Anshakar and the others aren't going to kill Bahzell after all." He showed his teeth. "And Vaijon by himself isn't going to be enough to keep Them happy."

Sahrdohr shook his head in mute agreement, and Varnaythus' nostrils flared as he contemplated the act he'd hoped so desperately to avoid.

Well, at least you're in an even better position to lay the blame on Anshakar and his idiots than you thought you'd be, he told himself. *And you've got even better reason to rip out that bastard Bahzell's heart with his wife. Yes, and Yurokhas, as well!* His eyes glittered like shards of ice. *Let's see how the pair of them deal with* this.

"It's time," he said out loud. "We'll take Chergor first, then Sothōfalas."

Sahrdohr's expression was acutely unhappy. Obviously, he'd hoped as strongly as Varnaythus that it would never come to this, and he had a few reservations about the strength of their wards. They'd be dangerously close to the blast that would gut the city, and the wards in question were Varnaythus', not his. No wizard truly liked to trust his own precious skin to the craft of another, but he only nodded and murmured a command into his own gramerhain.

The images in it changed, focusing tightly on the smouldering ruin where the kairsalhain lay buried. The crystal itself burned crimson in Sahrdohr's stone, despite the wreckage and tumbled stonework hiding it from any mortal senses, and as Varnaythus gazed into the gramerhain over his companion's shoulder, he felt the kairsalhain's potency beat against him like waves of heat even through the intermediary of the scrying spell.

"All right, let's—"

Varnaythus never completed the sentence.

It was like being locked in a cage with a bolt of lightning. In one shattering instant, a cataract ripped through the warded chamber's defenses as if those formidable workings were so many cobwebs in an autumn storm. Varnaythus cried out in torment as the collapsing wards backlashed through the wizard who'd erected them in the first place. It was only a trickle, only a minute fragment, of the total power he'd poured into them, far less the brutal fist of wild magic which had just torn them asunder, yet it was enough to blast him off his feet and hurl him bruisingly into the chamber's wall. His head hit stone, hard enough to stun, and he slid down as a white-haired man with eyes of flame appeared in the middle of his sanctum in worn Sothōii leathers.

Sahrdohr threw himself out of his chair, eyes wild with shock and fear, but he was a wizard lord, and despite his total surprise, his hands came up. A wand appeared in them, swinging to point at the apparition, but the flame-eyed man simply reached out towards him, closed his hand into a fist wrapped in a nimbus of wild magic, and made a ripping motion.

Sahrdohr shrieked. He rose on his toes, his body arched, and something flashed from him into that clenched fist. Then his eyes rolled up, his knees collapsed, and he crumpled to the stone floor like a discarded puppet.

Varnaythus pushed himself shakily to his feet, staring at the intruder while he tried to force his stunned mind to function.

It wasn't possible. Even for Wencit of Rum, this simply wasn't *possible*. He'd set those wards himself. Yes, wild magic could break them, but not without probing them first, sampling and analyzing them, learning who'd erected them, how he'd woven them. Not without employing enough power to destroy every living thing within a thousand yards, at any rate! Not even Wencit of Rūm could have tested them thoroughly enough to avoid that without Varnaythus sensing him at it. And even if that had been possible, this chamber hadn't so much as existed before Varnaythus created it, and no one—*no one!*—could simply teleport himself into a place he'd never been before.

Yet there Wencit stood, and Varnaythus felt terror shiver through him as he found himself face-to-face with the last white wizard in all the world. He reached out in the desperate hope that he might somehow have time to activate one of his own teleportation spells before Wencit annihilated him, but his shoulders slumped as he encountered a fine-meshed barrier, stronger even than his own wards had been, enclosing what had been his sanctum in a prison of wild magic.

"So," Wencit said finally, his voice soft. "I've been looking forward to this, Varnaythus of Kontovar."

Varnaythus twitched, although why he should be surprised—especially in the wake of everything *else* that had just happened!—that Wencit knew his name eluded him at the moment.

"I suppose I should be flattered, then," he heard himself say, and Wencit smiled. It was a cold smile, and his witchfire eyes blazed.

"A professional courtesy first, if you please," that voice which sounded like his own continued.

"What?" Wencit asked, with a complete calm and assurance Varnaythus found more terrifying than any threat.

"How?" Varnaythus waved at the chamber about them, and that cold smile grew even colder.

"You aren't the only one who knows how to create a kairsalhain. But you *were* kind enough to build your working chamber on top of one of mine."

Varnaythus' eyes flickered in shock. Then he shook himself.

"That's not possible," he said flatly. "I created this chamber myself. No one else—not even Sahrdohr—knew its physical location, and even if you'd found it, no one could get a kairsalhain inside its wards without my sensing it!"

He heard the outraged professional pride in his own voice and knew vanity was a foolish prop at a moment like this. But professional pride was all he truly had, here at the end of things, and he glared at Wencit, daring even a wild wizard to dispute him.

"You weren't listening," Wencit replied. "I didn't get anything 'inside its wards.' I didn't have to. You built it *on top* of my kairsalhain. It's been waiting here for over seven hundred years, Varnaythus."

The Carnadosan's eyes didn't flicker this time; they bulged. Seven hundred years? Wencit had been here—buried a kairsalhain here—*seven hundred* years before? That was... that was—

"I said I've been looking forward to this," Wencit said. "As it happens, I've been looking forward for quite a long time. And speaking of time, it's time for me to deliver a message to your colleagues back in Trōfrōlantha."

"A message?" Varnaythus felt like a parrot, yet despite himself, he also felt a faint tremble of hope. A message implied a messenger, after all.

"Your friend Malahk will deliver it for me," Wencit said, watching the hope die in Varnaythus' eyes. "In fact, he'll be part of the message."

"What... what do you mean?" Varnaythus thought of all the inventive ways a wizard's artistically dismembered body could be delivered—and how long the unfortunate wizard could be kept alive during the dismembering process—and shuddered. Perhaps he was going to be more fortunate than Sahrdohr after all.

"Oh, he'll be just fine... physically," Wencit replied, still with that icy smile. "But you and the Council crossed a line this time, Varnaythus. There are some things I will not tolerate, and Malahk will deliver that message. And as an indication that they should take it seriously, I've stripped his Gift from him."

Varnaythus swallowed hard, although he supposed there was no reason one more impossibility should bother him after so many others. Stripping a wizard of his ability to wield the art was the cruelest punishment of all, far crueler than simple physical death, and it could seldom be done *without* killing the victim. Even when it could, it took weeks of preparation and the shared and focused abilities of at least a dozen other wizards.

"And the message?" he asked.

"It's very simple." Wencit's voice was flat. "You will never—*ever*—again attempt to attack Leeana Hanathafressa with the art." Varnaythus stared at him, and there was no smile on Wencit's face now. "I'll know of any attack even before it's launched, just as I knew of this one, and there will be no more warnings. I still control the spells that strafed Kontovar a thousand years ago. At the next attack on her I will not simply destroy the wizard who carried it out, but blast Trōfrōlantha for a second time. I will leave no stone atop any other stone, and there are no wards so strong, nor working chambers so deeply buried, that I won't be able to reach them. And should that prove insufficient warning, if any Carnadosan should be so foolish as to attack her a *third* time, I will lay waste that entire continent in a wall of fire that will dwarf its first destruction. I will burn out my own magic—a *wild wizard's* magic—to power that destruction, and it will be ten *times* a thousand years before Kontovar rises from *those* ashes."

Varnaythus was white. It had required the fall of the greatest empire in Orfressan history, the conquest in fire and blood of an entire *continent*, to drive Wencit and the Last White Council to strafe Kontovar. Yet as he looked into Wencit of Rūm's flame-cored eyes, he knew the wild wizard meant it. Even if it cost his own life, he would scour Kontovar down to clean, bare stone—kill every green and growing thing, every animal—if the Carnadosans dared even to attack, far less *kill*, a single young woman. What could possibly...?

Those eyes told him that question would never be answered. There had to *be* an answer, a reason Wencit would make that dreadful promise for Leeana's sake but not for Bahzell's or for any other person he'd known and loved in all the dusty centuries of his life. Yet Varnaythus of Kontovar would never know it.

Wencit raised his hand, and a spray of wildfire erupted from it. It reached up, then flowed outward, coating the chamber's stone walls, enveloping them within a glorious canopy of light that flickered and danced.

"My name," the wild wizard said in ancient Kontovaran, "is Wencit of Rūm, and by my paramount authority as Lord of the Council of Ottovar, I judge thee guilty of offense against The Strictures. Wouldst thou defend thyself, or must I slay thee where thou standest?"

A strange, shivering sort of calm seemed to fill Varnaythus. He wondered, for an instant, how many other wizards had heard that same challenge in that same voice over the centuries. He didn't know...but none who'd heard it once had ever heard another voice again.

He bowed ever so slightly, then drew his own wand. He raised it, summoning his power, and hurled the most deadly spell at his command. A wrist-thick cable of green lightning that would have given even a creature like Anshakar pause, might even have blasted him back into his own universe, streaked across the scant twelve feet between him and his foe.

It had no effect on Wencit of Rūm at all.

The ancient wild wizard simply raised one hand, almost negligently, and that vortex of ravening destruction shattered on his callused palm. It splintered into all the colors of the rainbow, and then it was gone, banished as if it had never even existed.

Varnaythus staggered, sick and emptied of power, and stared at the white-haired old man with the terrible wildfire eyes.

"So be it." Wencit's executioner voice was colder than Hope's Bane Glacier. "As thou hast chosen, so shalt thou answer."

The terrible flash of those flaming eyes was the last thing Varnaythus ever saw.

Epilogue

No one had ever seen a gathering quite like it.

Bahzell Bahnakson and his wife stood on the battlement of East Tower and looked down into Hill Guard Castle's main courtyard as the next contingent of unlikely visitors clattered through the main gate. The newcomers seemed oddly undersized in comparison to their escort of armsmen in the colors of the House of Bowmaster. Pony-mounted dwarves had a tendency to look that way when they were flanked by Sothōii warhorses, but the visitors' sartorial splendor and the banners cracking above them in the brisk north wind made up for any deficiencies of stature.

"I see old Kilthan's after arriving," Bahzell said. "The bald fellow yonder, in the orange tunic."

"Under the waterwheel banner?" Leeana asked, and Bahzell nodded.

"Aye, and that's Thersahkdahknarthas dinha'Felahkandarnas next to him." Bahzell had paused for a moment before bringing out the full name of the head of Clan Felahkandarnas. Brandark himself couldn't have done it better, and Leeana looked up at him and batted her eyes in admiration.

"I hadn't realized I'd married such a sophisticated man," she said, and Bahzell chuckled and laid an arm around her shoulders to draw her in against his side.

"Now, that you haven't," he told her, bending to press a kiss to the top of her head. "It's naught I am but a backwoods boy from Hurgrum, lass, and you'd best not be forgetting it."

"I'm sure I won't, given the pains you take to keep reminding the rest of us what a bumpkin you are. You're not really fooling anyone, you know."

"No?" Brown eyes twinkled down at her for a moment, then he shrugged. "I'll not say as there isn't maybe a mite of truth in that, but only think how lost poor Brandark would be finding himself if I was to suddenly come all erudite on him. It's a dreadful mischief he might do himself."

"Oh, we couldn't have *that!*" Leeana agreed, and looked back down at the courtyard as the latest covey of visitors drew up before the great keep and a fanfare sounded.

"I wonder where Mother's going to put them all?" she mused as the Baron and Baroness of Balthar emerged from the keep to greet their guests. "King Markhos already has the North Tower, and *your* parents already have the South Tower, and the *West* Tower's running over with war maids." She shook her head. "I know Mother's always enjoyed entertaining, but this is getting ridiculous, Bahzell!"

"Well, we've a month or so yet before first snowfall," Bahzell pointed out philosophically. "I'm thinking pavilions on the parade ground might be working." He smiled. "And now I've thought of it, I'll wager it would be fair speeding things along, wouldn't it just, with a Wind Plain winter coming on and them under canvas?"

"That's an awful thing to suggest," Leeana told him sternly. "Not that you don't have a point."

"Dreadful practical, we Horse Stealers are," Bahzell assured her, and she snorted. Then her expression turned rather more serious.

"You're not the only ones," she told him. "Or perhaps I should say *we're* not the only ones, since I've married into the family this way." Her lips quirked another smile, but her eyes were grave as she looked down into the courtyard once more. "I have to say, though, it's a good thing. Not that I ever thought practicality or—even worse!—reason would dare to rear its ugly head where *Sothōii* were concerned."

"Best be striking while the iron's hot," Bahzell responded with a shrug.

"Oh, indeed," a third voice said, and the two of them turned as a fiery-eyed, white-haired man stepped out onto the battlements behind them. He was far more simply, even drably, dressed than any of Hill Guard's other visitors.

"And it's wondering I've been where you'd gotten yourself to," Bahzell said.

"Listening with bated breath while Sir Jerhas beats the speaker of the Kraithâlyr about the head and ears—figuratively speaking, of course—about the Crown's new attitude towards war maids," Wencit of Rūm said. He shook his head. "I'm getting just a bit tired of sitting around ominously while he does that."

"Sure, and I'm thinking that's what you're after getting for being such a figure of legend, and all," Bahzell told him, and the old wizard snorted.

"'Figure of legend,' is it, Bahzell Bloody Hand? At least no one's trying to call *me* 'Devil-Slayer'!"

"And if it's all the same, I'd sooner no one would be calling me that, either," Bahzell said in a much grimmer tone, and Leeana laid one hand on his forearm.

"No one's forgetting all the others who died on the Ghoul Moor, Bahzell," Wencit said much more gently. "And no one's forgetting what happened at Chergor, either, Leeana." He inclined his head slightly to her, although his eyes remained on Bahzell's face. "But the truth is—and you know it as well as I do, Bahzell—that it's what happened there that makes all of this possible."

He waved one hand at the courtyard, where the Dwarvenhame delegation was in the process of being ushered up the steps into the main keep, and after a moment, Bahzell nodded.

As Sir Kelthys had observed that dreadful day, no one had truly seen one of Krashnark's greater devils since the Fall of Kontovar itself. Indeed, their appearances even in Kontovar had been more matters of legend than confirmed fact. But with twenty thousand witnesses, not even the most skeptical Sothōii was inclined to doubt that was exactly what Trianal's army had faced.

The price that army—and the Order of Tomanāk—had paid to stop them had been horrific. Vaijon was only one of the eight thousand dead they'd suffered. Yurgazh Charkson would not be returning to Navahk. Over half the Hurgrum Chapter had died. Sir Yarran Battlecrow would spend the remainder of his life with one leg. Half of Tharanalalknarthas zoi'Harkanath's barge crews had died, and Tharanal himself had lost his left hand to a ghoul's jaws. He'd been thrusting a dagger down the creature's throat at the moment those jaws closed.

Losses among the hradani infantry who'd held that line against the avalanche of ghouls had been especially heavy. Hurgrum would be years recovering from all the sons she'd lost that day, but their deaths had accomplished far more than simply clearing the line of the Hangnysti for the Derm Canal project. The Sothōii who'd been there with them, who'd shared that day of blood and carnage, had carried the tale of that grisly field back to the Wind Plain, and those battle companions had been . . . disinclined to listen to any more anti-hradani bigotry. It wasn't just the fighting men of the West Riding anymore, either. Prince Yurokhas and his royal brother had seen to it that the truth of that fight had been spread far and wide.

It had come hard on the heels of the news of the assassination attempt at Chergor. Of the treason of Baron Cassan . . . and of the King's rescue by the despised war maids of Kalatha. Some had tried to give the credit to Trisu of Lorham, instead, but Trisu would have none of it. Stubborn and stiff-necked he might be, but no man who lived could doubt Trisu of Lorham's honesty or call him liar, and he'd already thrashed one particularly bigoted minor lord warden within an inch of his life for daring to impugn the war maids' contribution.

They were the ones who'd discovered the plot in the first place, he'd told the spectators, standing over the semiconscious body of his opponent in the middle of the lists. It was a *war maid*, not one of his armsmen, who'd carried the warning to Chergor in time. Who'd fought—unarmored and on foot—to save their King. Who'd claimed the traitor's head and delivered it to King Markhos. And it was her sisters who'd taken Cassan's armsmen in the flank and produced the victory his outnumbered armsmen—and, he'd added rather pointedly, the Quaysar Temple Guard and the Arm of Lillinara who'd commanded it—could not have won without them. In fact, he'd finished, one foot resting on the breastplate of the opponent who'd finally begun to stir once more, without the war maids of Kalatha, King Markhos would be dead, and Baron Tellian with him, and the traitor who'd killed them might very well have been named regent for Crown Prince Norandhor.

It had been quite a performance, and he'd capped it by escorting Shahana Lillinarafressa to the great banquet Baron Tellian had decreed (with King Markhos' strong support) in honor of those selfsame war maids. He'd danced no less than six of that evening's dances with Shahana, as well, and Bahzell had spotted the two of them with their heads together over tankards of beer well after everyone else had left for home or rolled unconscious under one of the tables. (With so many war maids in attendance, it had inevitably turned into *that* sort of party before the night was over.)

The sheer shock of the attempt on Markhos' life, not to mention the disreputable nature of his rescuers, had rippled through the Kingdom of the Sothōii like the outrider of an earthquake. And then had come the terrifying news that greater devils had been seen for the first time in twelve centuries—and seen *here*, in Norfressa.

The majority of Norfressans had half-forgotten that they and their ancestors had ever lived anywhere else. They knew the tales and they sang the ballads, but aside from the historians among them, Kontovar was no longer truly real to them. It was a legend, a cautionary tale, something that had happened long ago to someone else entirely, and they'd grown accustomed over the centuries to coping with the handful of the Dark's servants and creatures who emerged into the Light from time to time without sparing much thought for the Council of Carnadosa or the wizard lords of Kontovar who lay on the far side of an ocean, half a world away from Norfressa.

It was probable, Bahzell thought, that the *majority* of Norfressans still felt that way about it, but not the Sothōii. Not anymore.

It hadn't happened overnight, although it probably seemed that way to many. It had actually begun with Krahana's attack on the Warm Springs coursers, he knew, although he wasn't surprised no one really seemed to have noticed at the time. Shīgū's strike at the Quaysar Temple of Lillinara and the war maids had been far less disturbing to the Sothōii in general than the murder of so many coursers, yet not even the coursers' deaths had been enough to pull most of the Sothōii away from their concentration on their hatred for their more traditional enemies at the foot of the Wind Plain. Not even the Hurgrum Chapter's role in freeing the coursers' souls had been enough to change *that*. Not quite.

But like the first stones in an avalanche, those events had started something far greater than anyone would have guessed at the time. Not all of the Sothōii had gone peacefully back to sleep afterward. Some had started paying attention, and when Tellian, Kilthan, and Bahnak had begun their great canal scheme, others had paid heed, as well. Not all of them *happily*, perhaps, but it had gotten them looking in the right direction.

And then had come the Battle of the Hangnysti and the

proof—the *proof* no one could ignore—that the threat of the Dark remained only too real . . . and that the Dark was determined that those trying to bring peace between hradani and Sothōii would fail.

They were a stubborn people, the Sothōii. It wasn't in them to change their minds quickly or easily. Indeed, they were uncomfortably like Bahzell's own people in that regard. But whatever else they might be, they weren't stupid. No one doubted that the Dark had been involved in the attempt on Markhos, as well, especially since the mage investigators probing that plot had already confirmed that Cassan had been involved with at least one dark wizard. And if the Dark who'd tried to murder their King also wanted to prevent them from somehow achieving a just peace and friendship with the hated hradani, why, the Sothōii were more than stubborn enough to do just that and laugh in the Dark's teeth.

A bitter price Trianal's army had paid, but what it had bought—what it was buying—was worth the cost, and he knew it. Not in his heart, where the aching emptiness of so many missing friends was still unhealed, but in the considered judgment of a champion of Tomanāk who knew victory when he saw it.

"Aye," he told Wencit now. "Aye, it's the folk who died as made this come together. But not a one of them had the doing of it for fame or bards' tales any more than me . . . or Vaijon."

"Of course not," Wencit said gently, reaching up to put a hand on Bahzell's shoulder, and smiled crookedly. "Don't you think I, of all people, understand *that?*"

The wizard shook his head, and Bahzell snorted softly as the question put his own discomfort with the songs already circulating about his "mighty deeds" at the Hangnysti—not a one of them, curiously, by Brandark Brandarkson—into perspective. He'd been at this championing trade for less than ten years, after all; *Wencit* had been in the legend-making business for over twelve *centuries.*

"On the other hand," Wencit continued, almost as if he'd just read Bahzell's mind, "you do seem to do things in more . . . concentrated doses than I do. I really wouldn't object if you slowed down just a bit for, oh, a decade or two."

"I wouldn't really object to that, either, Bahzell," Leeana chimed in, and Bahzell chuckled.

"No more would I," he assured them.

"That's what you *say,*" Wencit said darkly, "but I've noticed these things tend to seek you out."

"Well, at least this time *you'd* no need to be getting involved," Bahzell pointed out affably, and Wencit smiled.

"No," he agreed, glancing at Leeana. "No, this time *I* didn't have to get involved at all. Very peaceful, it was."

"For some," Leeana said tartly, and the wizard gave her a small, ironic bow.

"Have the war maids decided how they're going to select their delegate to the Great Council?" he inquired by way of a change of subject.

"Not really." Leeana shook her head, accepting the change. "Some of us are still too deeply in shock that the Kingdom's lords warden haven't all dropped dead from apoplexy at the mere notion for us to think very constructively about it ourselves yet. I know we're going to have to come up with a solution, but it would have helped if the King had decided to give us some guidelines."

"Actually, I think it was much wiser of him to leave it up to you," Wencit disagreed. "Whoever you end up nominating is going to have to have Crown approval, but you war maids aren't really accustomed to the top-down way the Kingdom as a whole does things. Better for you to come up with your own way of choosing your nominees. Besides," the old wizard grinned suddenly, "I've been around long enough I'm accustomed to taking the long view, and I'm thoroughly in favor of opening the door—just a crack, you understand—to the notion of the kind of Parliament the Axemen have."

"Mother, Wencit!" Leeana laughed out loud. "You *would* have the lords warden dropping in droves if you suggested something like *that!*"

"Which is why I have absolutely no intention of doing anything of the sort, even—or perhaps especially—to Markhos or Sir Jerhas." The wizard snorted. "Not that I'd have to mention it to your father or your father-in-law, my dear. Trust me, they're already thinking about it."

"Aye, like as two peas in a pod, they are," Bahzell agreed, glancing back down at the courtyard where several days ago the first hradani prince ever to be received peacefully on Sothōii soil had exchanged bows with the first Sothōii king who'd ever greeted a hradani without a sword in his hand. "And not done scheming yet, either of them, I've no doubt at all, at all."

"I'd be disappointed if they were," Wencit told him cheerfully. Then he gave himself an obvious mental shake.

"I'd be disappointed," he said more briskly, "but I really didn't come up here to discuss politics with the two of you."

"No?" Bahzell said a bit warily.

"Oh, don't worry, Bahzell! I have no fell designs on you, your wife, or your time together." Wencit smiled at them. "I only wanted to ask if you've given any thought to a proper wedding gift for Sharlassa and Trianal?"

"Why?" Leeana asked.

"Because if you haven't, I have a suggestion."

"That sounds ominous."

"Don't be silly." The wizard looked at her severely. "It's just that you're now sept to Clan Hûrâka by marriage, courtesy of your husband's adoption by Duke Jâshân. That being the case, I thought you might ask your sister-in-law Zarantha to give them exactly the gift they need."

"Zarantha?" Bahzell's ears twitched in surprise, and his eyes narrowed. "And what gift would that be?"

"Training for Sharlassa," Wencit said in a suddenly much gentler tone. "She's a mage, you know."

"*Sharlassa?*" Leeana stared at him, and he shrugged.

"I suspect she has only one talent, or possibly two, and they've been late manifesting, Leeana. But trust me—I know more about recognizing the mage talent than most. I don't think her talents are strong enough for her to have a very severe mage crisis, but I do think it would be a very good idea for Trianal and her to honeymoon at Zarantha's academy."

"Thank you," Leeana said after a moment. She gave her head a shake. "Thank you very much!"

"You're very welcome." Wencit smiled. "I've had quite a strong interest in the magi for quite some time, you know. Part of that long view of mine, I suppose. And now, I have to run. I promised His Majesty I'd put in an appearance at this afternoon's conference. More sitting around ominously in the background, I imagine. It's really quite amusing, you know. I don't actually have to *say* anything. I've discovered over the centuries that most of your normal, bickering aristocrats really know what they *ought* to be doing; they just have no interest in actually doing it. All I have to do is sit there and look at them sternly and they suddenly start falling all over themselves to do what they ought to have done all along."

"Amusing," Bahzell repeated, cocking his ears at him. "It's a strange, strange man you are, Wencit of Rūm."

"Of course I am. I'm a wizard."

Wencit gave them another smile, then disappeared down the winding stair into the tower, and Bahzell and Leeana turned back to the courtyard.

It was emptying rapidly now, and she leaned her head against him, one arm around his waist.

"Sharlassa as a mage." She laughed softly. "*And* as a future Baroness of Balthar and Lady Warden of the West Riding. I'm amazed she hasn't already stolen a horse and fled to hide among the Wakūo!"

"Or the war maids," Bahzell agreed with a chuckle. "But she's made of sterner stuff than ever she thought, I'm thinking."

"Not to mention the fact that Trianal would hunt her down wherever she hid," Leeana acknowledged. Then she cocked a devilish eyebrow up at her towering husband. "And what about *your* sister, Milord Champion?"

"As to that, it's early days," Bahzell replied comfortably. "I'll not say I've aught against the notion, mind, and it's sure I am my Da can see the advantages clear as ever Arsham can. But Sharkah's a mind of her own, too, and neither Father nor Mother would be pushing her into a thing, even if they'd any notion they could."

"But Arsham seems interested in her for more than just 'reasons of state,'" Leeana pointed out.

"Aye, so he does. And she's more than a mite interested in *him*, I'm thinking." Bahzell shrugged. "But she's after being a mite stubborn, you've no doubt noticed. I've no notion where she comes by it, reasonable as all the rest of my family's after being, yet there it is, and years it's been she's had her heart set on the sword maid's path. I'm thinking it'll need a mortal lot of patience on Arsham's part to talk her round to the notion of settling down as anyone's princess."

"Well, I don't suppose he could have survived under Churnazh as long as he did if he weren't a patient fellow," Leeana said thoughtfully, and Bahzell chuckled.

"Aye, so he is. And it's in my mind as Sharkah knows it, too. I'm thinking she's minded to see just *how* patient he's after being. And she's naught but in her early fifties. She's time to let him be wearing her down properly."

Leeana looked up at him in amusement, then frowned.

"But if she does marry him, would she have to leave the Order?"

"As to that, the decision would be up to her," Bahzell said much more soberly. "She'd not have to give up her sword oath, but it's like enough the Hurgrum Chapter would be releasing her. And she'd not agree to wed if she'd any notion but to be meeting the duties as came with wedding a ruling prince. It's not at all surprised I'd be if she's already discussed it with Hurthang."

Leeana nodded. Hurthang had become the commander of the Hurgrum Chapter following Vaijon's death. It wasn't a responsibility he'd wanted, for a lot of reasons, but as Bahzell had pointed out upon occasion, a follower of Tomanāk was one who did what needed doing, and there'd never been any doubt who the Chapter itself would choose as Vaijon's successor. And it was probably just as well there'd been no confusion about its leadership, since the Chapter—despite its losses at the Hangnysti—would soon be far larger than it had been. The Battle of the Hangnysti had done nothing but increase its renown, and its human membership was growing by leaps and bounds.

And the fact that Prince Yurokhas has joined the Hurgrum Chapter hasn't hurt its recruiting here in the Kingdom one bit, she reflected.

"Vaijon would be proud of them, I think," she said softly, and Bahzell smiled.

"Aye, that he would. A rare popinjay he was, when first we met, but a finer man I've never known."

<*Well, if that's so, you had quite a bit to do with the way it turned out,*> a voice said suddenly from behind them, and they turned quickly, eyes widening.

<*No need to look as if you've just seen a ghost,*> Vaijon told them with an impish smile. He stood on the battlements, the East Tower's steeply pitched roof just barely visible through him, and a soft blue glow clung to him, bright enough to be visible even in the sunlight.

"Lad—" Bahzell began, then stopped.

<*What? You've finally encountered something that can shut you up and Brandark isn't even here to see it?*>

Vaijon laughed, and the bright, joyous sound went through them both like a cleansing wind.

"I've no doubt you'll be dropping in on him to tell him all about it," Bahzell said after a moment.

<*There are some things a champion of Tomanāk doesn't do to another champion of Tomanāk, and giving Brandark that kind of ammunition comes under that heading, I think,*> Vaijon told him. <*Besides, that's not why I'm here.*>

"No?" Leeana touched the silver sprig of amethyst-leaved periwinkle she wore in her hair. She seemed preposterously calm to Bahzell, but Vaijon only smiled at her. "Why *are* you here, then?"

<*To tell this big lummox you're married to not to fret,*> Vaijon said. He turned back to Bahzell, and his smile turned softer. <*It's not your fault, you know. I always wanted to serve Tomanāk, and you were simply kind enough to straighten me out.*>

His smile faded away completely, but his blue eyes were warm as they met Bahzell's.

<*Bahzell, there's not a moment of my life—or my death—since that day in Belhadan that I've regretted. You gave me my life, the one I always wanted, and no man ever had a friend or a brother he loved more than I love you. I died doing what I was born to do, and I'm not entirely sure I'm done doing it yet. I'm still working on understanding the rules, and you may recall that I can be a little bit of a slow study. But tell Hurthang and the others how much they meant to me, and that the other lads and I will be waiting for them—and you, of course.*> He smiled again. <*Not that I have any grim portents of impending doom for any of you.*>

"And—" Bahzell paused and cleared his throat. "And I'm sure it's glad they'll all be to hear it," he told his friend just a bit huskily.

<*Probably.*> Vaijon agreed. <*But in the meantime, I'm sure you'll find plenty of things to keep you busy. In fact, I see one—Well, never mind. That would be telling.*>

"I can see as there are some things even dying doesn't change," Bahzell said much more dryly, and Vaijon laughed.

<*Of course not, Bahzell! Where would be the fun in* that?> His body began to thin, becoming increasingly translucent, and his smile turned impish once more. <*But don't worry! I'll be keeping an eye on you. What else are friends for?*>

He was almost invisible now, and Bahzell seemed to feel a hand resting on his shoulder. It squeezed for just a moment, then released him, and he heard Vaijon's laughing voice one last time.

<*After all, I'll need to take lots of notes for the nights I spend helping Brandark work on new verses, won't I?*>

Gods of Light and Dark

The Dark Gods

Phrobus Orfro

Called "Father of Evil" and "Lord of Deceit," Phrobus is the seventh child of Orr and Kontifrio, which explains why seven is considered *the* unlucky number in Norfressa. No one recalls his original name; "Phrobus" ("Truth Bender") was given to him by Tomanāk when he cast Phrobus down for his treacherous attempt to wrest rulership from Orr. Following that defeat, Phrobus turned openly to the Dark and became, in fact, the opening wedge by which evil first entered Orfressa. He is the most powerful of the gods of Light or Dark after Tomanāk, and the hatred between him and Tomanāk is unthinkably bitter, but Phrobus fears his brother worse than death itself. His symbol is a flame-eyed skull.

Shīgū

Called "The Twisted One," "Queen of Hell," and "Mother of Madness," Shīgū is the wife of Phrobus. No one knows exactly where she came from, but most believe she was, in fact, a powerful demoness raised to godhood by Phrobus when he sought a mate to breed up his own pantheon to oppose that of his father. Her power is deep but subtle, her cruelty and malice are bottomless, and her favored weapon is madness. She is even more hated, loathed, and feared by mortals than Phrobus, and her worship is punishable by death in all Norfressan realms. Her symbol is a flaming spider.

Carnadosa Phrofressa

"The Lady of Wizardry" is the fifth child of Phrobus and Shīgū. She has become the goddess of black wizardry, but she herself might be considered totally amoral rather than evil for evil's sake. She enshrines the concept of power sought by any means and at any cost to others. Her symbol is a wizard's wand.

Fiendark Phrofro

The first-born child of Phrobus and Shīgū, Fiendark is known as "Lord of the Furies." He is cast very much in his father's image (though, fortunately, he is considerably less powerful) and all evil creatures owe him allegiance as Phrobus' deputy. Unlike Phrobus, who seeks always to pervert or conquer, however, Fiendark also delights in destruction for destruction's sake. His symbols are a flaming sword or flame-shot cloud of smoke.

Krahana Phrofressa

"The Lady of the Damned" is the fourth child of Phrobus and Shīgū and, in most ways, the most loathsome of them all. She is noted for her hideous beauty and holds dominion over the undead (which makes her Isvaria's most hated foe) and rules the hells in which the souls of those who have sold themselves to evil spend eternity. Her symbol is a splintered coffin.

Krashnark Phrofro

The second son of Phrobus and Shīgū, Krashnark is something of a disappointment to his parents. The most powerful of Phrobus' children, Krashnark (known as "Devil Master") is the god of devils and ambitious war. He is ruthless, merciless, and cruel, but personally courageous and possessed of a strong, personal code of honor, which makes him the only Dark God Tomanāk actually respects. He is, unfortunately, loyal to his father, and his power and sense of honor have made him the "enforcer" of the Dark Gods. His symbol is a flaming steward's rod.

Sharnā Phrofro

Called "Demonspawn" and "Lord of the Scorpion," Sharnā is Krashnark's younger, identical twin (a fact which pleases neither of them). Sharnā is the god of demons and the patron of assassins, the personification of cunning and deception. He is substantially less powerful than Krashnark and a total coward, and the demons who owe him allegiance hate and fear Krashnark's more powerful devils almost as much as Sharnā hates and fears his brother. His symbols are the giant scorpion (which serves as his mount) and a bleeding heart in a mailed fist.

The Gods of Light

Orr All-Father

Often called "The Creator" or "The Establisher," Orr is considered the creator of the universe and the king and judge of gods. He is the father or creator of all but one of the Gods of Light and the most powerful of all the gods, whether of Light or Dark. His symbol is a blue starburst.

Kontifrio

"The Mother of Women" is Orr's wife and the goddess of home, family, and the harvest. According to Norfressan theology, Kontifrio was Orr's second creation (after Orfressa, the rest of the universe), and she is the most nurturing of the gods and the mother of all Orr's children except Orfressa herself. Her hatred for Shīgū is implacable. Her symbol is a sheaf of wheat tied with a grape vine.

Chemalka Orfressa

"The Lady of the Storm" is the sixth child of Orr and Kontifrio. She is the goddess of weather, good and bad, and has little to do with mortals. Her symbol is the sun seen through clouds.

Chesmirsa Orfressa

"The Singer of Light" is the fourth child of Orr and Kontifrio and the younger twin sister of Tomanāk, the war god. Chesmirsa is the goddess of bards, poetry, music and art. She is very fond of mortals and has a mischievous sense of humor. Her symbol is the harp.

Hirahim Lightfoot

Known as "The Laughing God" and "The Great Seducer," Hirahim is something of a rogue element among the Gods of Light. He is the only one of them who is not related to Orr (no one seems certain where he came from, though he acknowledges Orr's authority... as much as he does anyone's) and he is the true prankster of the gods. He is the god of merchants, thieves, and dancers, but he is also known as the god of seductions, as he has a terrible weakness for attractive female mortals (or goddesses). His symbol is a silver flute.

Isvaria Orfressa

"The Lady of Remembrance" (also called "The Slayer") is the first child of Orr and Kontifrio. She is the goddess of needful death and the completion of life and rules the House of the Dead, where she keeps the Scroll of the Dead. Somewhat to her mother's dismay, she is also Hirahim's lover. The third most powerful of the Gods of Light, she is the special enemy of Krahana, and her symbol is a scroll with skull winding knobs.

Khalifrio Orfressa

"The Lady of the Lightning" is Orr and Kontifrio's second child and the goddess of elemental destruction. She is considered a Goddess of Light despite her penchant for destructiveness, but she has very little to do with mortals (and mortals are just as happy about it, thank you). Her symbol is a forked lightning bolt.

Korthrala Orfro

Called "Sea Spume" and "Foam Beard," Korthrala is the fifth child of Orr and Kontifrio. He is the god of the sea but also of love, hate, and passion. He is a very powerful god, if not overblessed with wisdom, and is very fond of mortals. His symbol is the net and trident.

Lillinara Orfressa

Known as "Friend of Women" and "The Silver Lady," Lillinara is Orr and Kontifrio's eleventh child, the goddess of the moon and women. She is one of the more complex deities, and extremely focused. She is appealed to by young women and maidens in her persona as the Maid and by mature women and mothers in her persona as the Mother. As avenger, she manifests as the Crone, who also comforts the dying. She dislikes Hirahim Lightfoot intensely, but she hates Shīgū (as the essential perversion of all womankind) with every fiber of her being. Her symbol is the moon.

Norfram Orfro

The "Lord of Chance" is Orr and Kontifrio's ninth child and the god of fortune, good and bad. His symbol is the infinity sign.

Orfressa

According to Norfressan theology, Orfressa is not a god but the universe herself, created by Orr even before Kontifrio, and she is not truly "awake." Or, rather, she is seldom aware of anything as ephemeral as mortals. On the very rare occasions when she does take notice of mortal affairs, terrible things tend to happen, and even Orr can restrain her wrath only with difficulty.

Semkirk Orfro

Known as "The Watcher," Semkirk is the tenth child of Orr and Kontifrio. He is the god of wisdom and mental and physical discipline and, before The Fall of Kontovar, was the god of white wizardry. Since The Fall, he has become the special patron of the psionic magi, who conduct a merciless war against evil wizards. He is a particularly deadly enemy of Carnadosa, the goddess of black wizardry. His symbol is a golden scepter.

Silendros Orfressa

The fourteenth and final child of Orr and Kontifrio, Silendros (called "Jewel of the Heavens") is the goddess of stars and the night. She is greatly reverenced by jewel smiths, who see their art as an attempt to capture the beauty of her heavens in the work of their hands, but generally has little to do with mortals. Her symbol is a silver star.

Sorbus Kontifra

Known as "Iron Bender," Sorbus is the smith of the gods. He is also the product of history's greatest seduction (that of Kontifrio by Hirahim—a "prank" Kontifrio has never quite forgiven), yet he is the most stolid and dependable of all the gods, and Orr accepts him as his own son. His symbol is an anvil.

Tolomos Orfro

"The Torch Bearer" is the twelfth child of Orr and Kontifrio. He is the god of light and the sun and the patron of all those who work with heat. His symbol is a golden flame.

Tomanāk Orfro

Tomanāk, the third child of Orr and Kontifrio, is Chesmirsa's older twin brother and second only to Orr himself in power. He is known by many names—"Sword of Light," "Scale Balancer," "Lord of Battle," and "Judge of Princes" to list but four—and has been entrusted by his father with the task of overseeing the balance of the Scales of Orr. He is also captain general of the Gods of Light and the foremost enemy of all the Dark Gods (indeed, it was he who cast Phrobus down when Phrobus first rebelled against his father). His symbols are a sword and/or a spiked mace.

Toragon Orfro

"The Huntsman," also called "Woodhelm," is the thirteenth child of Orr and Kontifrio and the god of nature. Forests are especially sacred to him, and he has a reputation for punishing those who hunt needlessly or cruelly. His symbol is an oak tree.

Torframos Orfro

Known as "Stone Beard" and "Lord of Earthquakes," Torframos is the eighth child of Orr and Kontifrio. He is the lord of the Earth, the keeper of the deep places and special patron of engineers and those who delve, and is especially revered by dwarves. His symbol is the miner's pick.

Characters

Ahnlarfressa, Sharral—a war maid; Mayor Yalith's assistant.

Almerhas, Sir Vaijon of—champion of Tomanāk and head of the Hurgrum chapter of the Order of Tomanāk.

Amber Grass, Lord Warden of—see Sir Jerhas Macebearer.

Anshakar—a senior, powerful devil servant of Krashnark.

Arrowsmith, Halahk—one of Baron Cassan Axehammer's vassals.

Axehammer, Cassan—Baron of Framahn and Lord Warden of the South Riding. Most powerful noble of the Sothōii South Riding and an implacable rival and foe of Tellian Bowmaster.

Axehammer, Felytha—Baroness of Frahmahn; wife of Baron Cassan Axehammer; younger sister of Rulth Blackhill.

Axehammer, Lynaya—Baron Cassan Axehammer's younger daughter.

Axehammer, Sir Seralk—Baron Cassan Axehammer's son and heir.

Axehammer, Shairnayith—Baron Cassan Axehammer's elder daughter.

Bahnaksdaughter, Lady Adalah—Prince Bahnak Karathson's fifth daughter and ninth, and youngest, child.

Bahnaksdaughter, Lady Halah—Prince Bahnak Karathson's fourth daughter and eighth child.

Bahnaksdaughter, Lady Marglyth—eldest daughter of Prince Bahnak Karathson; Prince Bahnak's Justicar and a senior member of his council.

Bahnaksdaughter, Lady Maritha—second daughter and third child of Prince Bahnak Karathson and Princess Arthanal; Prince Bahnak's treasurer.

Bahnaksdaughter, Lady Sharkah—Prince Bahnak Karathson's third daughter and sixth child; a member of the Order of Tomanāk.

Bahnakson, Prince Bahzell—fourth son and seventh child of Prince Bahnak of Hurgrum of the Horse Stealer hradani; a champion of Tomanāk and wind rider of courser Walsharno.

Bahnakson, Crown Prince Barodahn—eldest son and heir of Prince Bahnak Karathson.

Bahnakson, Prince Thankhar—Prince Bahnak Karathson's second eldest son and fourth child.

Bahnakson, Prince Tormach—Prince Bahnak Karathson's third eldest son and fifth child; Prince Bahnak's primary liaison with Kilthandahknarthas of Silver Cavern.

Bahranafressa, Selistra—a war maid; Tomarah Felisfressa's freemate.

Balthar, Baron of—see Tellian Bowmaster.

Battlecrow, Sir Yarran—Lord Festian's scout commander and marshal; one of Baron Tellian Bowmaster's most trusted field commanders.

Blackhill, Rulth—Lord Warden of Transhar. Baron Cassan Axehammer's brother-in-law and political ally.

Borandas, Baron—see Borandas Daggeraxe.

Bowmaster, Hanatha—Baroness of Balthar; wife of Tellian; mother of Leeana.

Bowmaster, Leeana Glorana Syliveste—daughter of Tellian and Hanatha. Later Leeana Hanathafressa as war maid (see also Leeana Hanathafressa).

Bowmaster, Tellian—Baron of Balthar and Lord Warden of the West Riding. Most powerful noble of the Sothōii West Riding. Father of Leeana Hanathafressa and wind rider of courser Dathgar.

Bowmaster, Sir Trianal—Baron Tellian Bowmaster's nephew; adopted as his heir after Leeana became a war maid.

Brandarkson, Brandark—poet, scholar, and swordsman of the Bloody Sword hradani; Bahzell Bahnakson's closest companion and friend.

Broadaxe, Sir Benshair—Lord Warden of Golden Hill.

Bronzebow, Tahlmah—Sharlassa Dragonclaw's personal maid.

Cassan, Baron—see Cassan Axehammer.

Cathman the Peddler—an alias of Master Varnaythus whose persona is that of an itinerant peddler who dabbles in charms and potions.

Chanharsadahknarthi zoihan'Harkanath—senior stone herd (sarthnaisk); attached to the "Gullet Tunnel" and one of Kilthandahknarthas' close kinswomen.

Charaksdaughter, Farmah—Hurthang Marahgson's wife, the maid Bahzell rescued from Navahk.

Charkson, Yurgazh—a one-time mercenary member of Prince Churnazh's personal guard who has become a ranking member of the new Royal Army of Prince Bahnak.

Chersa, Lord Warden of—see Garthmahn Ironhelm.

Churnazhson, Arsham—Prince of Navahk following the death of Prince Churnazh.

Daggeraxe, Borandas—Baron of Halthan and Lord Warden of the North Riding. Most powerful noble of the Sothōii North Riding.

Daggeraxe, Master Brayahs—Borandas Daggeraxe's first cousin (son of Borandas' deceased father's younger brother). A mage in the service of the Crown.

Daggeraxe, Myacha—Baroness of Halthan; second wife of Baron Borandas Daggeraxe.

Daggeraxe, Sir Thorandas—Baron Borandas Daggeraxe's eldest son and heir.

Darakson, Arhanâk—Lady Maritha Bahnaksdaughter's husband; Prince Bahnak Karathson's son-in-law.

Darhanfressa, Barthyma—a war maid; one of the barmaids at the Green Maiden in Kalatha.

Dathgar—Baron Tellian's bonded courser. The name means "Thunder Grass."

Deep Water, Lord Warden of—see Sir Kelthys Lancebearer.

Dirkson, Tarmahk—Baron Cassan of Frahmahn's personal armsman.

Dragonclaw, Jahsak—Lord Warden of Golden Vale. A wind rider and Tellian's choice to take the wardenship of Golden Vale following Saratic Redhelm's removal by the Crown. Rider of courser Kengayr.

Dragonclaw, Jahsakan—Lord Jashsak and Lady Sharmatha Dragonclaw's youngest child.

Dragonclaw, Sir Mahrlays—Lord Jashsak and Lady Sharmatha Dragonclaw's second eldest son.

Dragonclaw, Sir Salmahn—Lord Jashsak Dragonclaw's eldest son and heir.

Dragonclaw, Sharlassa—Jashsak and Sharmatha Dragonclaw's daughter.

Dragonclaw, Sharmatha—Lady Warden of Golden Vale; Jahsak Dragonclaw's wife.

Dronhar, Lord Warden of—see Welthan Handaxe.

Farlachsdaughter, Princess Arthanal—Bahnak Karathson's wife; Bahzell's mother.

Felisfressa, Tomarah—a war maid; Kalatha's most successful seamstress and dressmaker.

Felytha, Baroness—see Felytha Axehammer.

Firearrow, Mahrahk—alias of Magister Malahk Sahrdohr.

Framahn, Baron of—see Cassan Axehammer.

Gayrfressa—"Daughter of the Wind" or "Wind Daughter." Walsharno's younger sister. Becomes the companion of Leanna Hanathafressa.

Gayrhalan—Hathan Shieldarm's bonded courser. His name means "Storm Souled."

Glanharrow, Lord Warden of—see Sir Festian Wrathson.

Golden Hill, Lord Warden of—see Sir Benshair Broadaxe.

Golden Vale, Lord Warden of—see Jahsak Dragonclaw.

Gorsandahknarthas zoi'Felahkandarnas—the senior engineer on the Derm Canal to the Hangnysti River.

Green Cove, Lord Warden of—see Sir Shandahr Shaftmaster.

Greenslope, Doram—Baron Tellian Bowmaster's stable master for Hill Guard Castle.

Gurlahnson, Sarkhan—Gurlahn Karathson's older son. Often serves as a sort of deputy and troubleshooter for his Uncle Bahnak.

Hallafressa, Balcartha—a war maid; commander of five hundred; the senior officer of the Kalatha town guard.

Hallafressa, Dalthys—a war maid; town administrator of Kalatha.

Halthan, Baron of—see Borandas Daggeraxe.

Hanatha, Baroness—see Hanatha Bowmaster.

Hanathafressa, Leeana—a war maid and the first female wind rider. Rider of courser Gayrfressa. (See also Leeana Bowmaster).

Handaxe, Welthan—Lord Warden of Dronhar, one of Baron Cassan Axehammer's vassals.

High Tranith, Lord Warden of—see Tarlan Swordsmith.

Hollow Cave, Lord Warden of—see Garthan Warbridle.

Horsemaster, Sir Kalanndros—a senior armsman and captain of Baron Cassan of Frahmahn.

Horsemaster, Trebdor—one of Baron Cassan Axehammer's vassals.

Hûrâka, Duke Jâshân of—a powerful Spearman noble and supporter of Bahzell Bahnakson. Father of Zarantha of Hûrâka.

Hûrâka, Mistress Zarantha—adopted sister of Bahzell Bahnakson and a powerful mage. Founder of first Spearman mage academy.

Hurthangson, Gharnal—Hurthang Marahgson's firstborn child.

Ironhelm, Garthmahn—Lord Warden of Chersa in the East Riding. An ally of Baron Cassan Axehammer and former Prime Councilor to King Markhos.

Ironsmith, Barlahn—Garlahna Lorhanalfressa's lover and freemate.

Jâshân, Duke—see Jâshân of Hûrâka.

Johlanafressa, Taraiys—a war maid; Commander of Five Hundred Balcartha Evahnalfressa's current aide.

Karathson, Gurlahn—Prince Bahnak's only living (younger) brother. Serves as Bahnak's chief of staff.

Karathson, Prince Bahnak—Ruler of Hurgrum and the Northern Hradani; Bahzell's father.

Karmathson, Jarthûhl—Lady Marglyth Bahnaksdaughter's husband; Prince Bahnak Karathson's son-in-law.

Kengayr—courser companion of Lord Warden Jahsak Dragonclaw. His name means "Born of the Wind."

Kilthandahknarthas dihna'Harkanath—lord of Clan Harkanath of the Silver Cavern towards.

Kimazh—a senior, powerful devil servant of Krashnark.

Lancebearer, Sir Kelthys—Lord Warden of Deep Water; a cousin of Baron Tellian Bowmaster and wind rider of courser Walasfro.

Larark, Lieutenant Somar—a Spearman mercenary in the pay of Arthnar Sabrehand. Erkân Trâram's second-in-command.

Lillinarafressa, Shahana—the arm of Lillinara sent to keep an eye on Quaysar following Dame Kaeritha Seldansdaughter's rescue of the temple from Shīgū.

Lorham, Lord Warden of—see Sir Trisu Pickaxe.

Lorhanalfressa, Garlahna—a war maid from Kalatha; one of Leeana Hanathafressa's closest friends.

Macebearer, Sir Harahmohr—oldest son of Sir Jerhas Macebearer and his steward in Amber Grass while Sir Jerhas is occupied in Sothōfalas.

Macebearer, Sir Jerhas—Lord Warden of Amber Grass and Prime Councilor to King Markhos.

Maglahnfressa, Theretha—a war maid glassblower from Kalatha.

Mahrlafressa, Saltha—a war maid serving in the Kalatha City Guard. A member of Leeana Hanathfressa's platoon.

Marahgson, Hurthang—Bahzell Bahnakson's cousin and the senior member of the Hurgrum Chapter of the Order of Tomanāk in Balthar.

Myacha, Baroness—see Myacha Daggeraxe.

Pickaxe, Darhal—previous Lord Warden of Lorham. Trisu Pickaxe's deceased father.

Pickaxe, Salthan—Trisu Pickaxe's cousin, senior magistrate, and librarian.

Pickaxe, Sir Trisu—Lord Warden of Lorham; a vassal of Baron Tellian Bowmaster.

The Quaysar Voice of Lillinara—like all voices, the "new" Voice at Quaysar has given up her original name.

Rahnafressa, Erlis—a war maid; commander of three hundred; Commander of Five Hundred Balcartha Halafressa's second-in-command.

Redhelm, Saratic—former Lord Warden of Golden Vale. One of Baron Cassan's vassals, stripped of his title by King Markhos.

Rianthus of Sindor—Commander of Kilthandahknarthas' personal security force; a human ex-major in the Royal and Imperial Mounted Infantry. Detailed as chief of security for the Gullet Tunnel and as Kilthan's military liaison with Prince Bahnak of Hurgrum.

Sabrehand, Arthnar—a senior chieftain and current First Captain of the River Brigands (i.e., king). Also known as Arthnar Fire Oar.

Sahrdohr, Magister Malahk—also known as Mahrahk Firearrow. An associate of Master Varnaythus, also from Kontovar and a servant of Carnadosa.

Salgahn—a dog brother (assassin) working with Varnaythus.

Sarthayafressa, Lanitha—a war maid; the Kalatha librarian and senior schoolteacher.

Seldansdaughter, Dame Kaeritha—a champion of Tomanāk.

Selmar, Sergeant Gûrân—a Spearman mercenary in the pay of Arthnar Sabrehand. Senior noncom of Captain Erkân Trâram's company.

Sermandahknarthas zoi'Harkanath—the senior engineer on the Gullet Tunnel. Kilthandahknarthas'nephew.

Shaftmaster, Sir Shandahr—Lord Warden of Green Cove; one of Baron Tellian Bowmaster's vessels. His son, Sir Wahlandys Shaftmaster is the Lord of the Exchequer and Keeper of the Privy Purse for King Markhos.

Shaftmaster, Sir Whalandys—the oldest son and heir of Sir Shandahr Shaftmaster, Lord Warden of Green Cove; Chancellor of the Exchequer and Keeper of the Privy Purse in Sothōfalas.

Shieldarm, Hathan—Baron Tellian Bowmaster's wind brother. Tarith Shieldarm's cousin. Rider of courser Gayrhalan.

Shieldarm, Tarith—formerly Leeana Bowmaster's personal armsman; now commander of Baron Tellian Bowmaster's personal armsmen. Hathan Shieldarm's cousin.

Silveraxe, Queen Jalythya—second (current) wife of King Markhos.

Silveraxe, King Markhos—King of the Sothōii.

Silveraxe, Crown Prince Norandhor—four-year-old son of King Markhos and Queen Jalythya.

Silveraxe, Princess Rahana—King Markhos' second daughter by Queen Shathmyra.

Silveraxe, Princess Shathmyra—King Markhos' older daughter by Queen Shathmyra.

Silveraxe, Queen Shathmyra—first (deceased) wife of King Markhos.

Silveraxe, Princess Verylys—the younger child of King Markhos and Queen Jalythya.

Silveraxe, Prince Yurokhas—wind rider and younger brother of King Markhos and, after his infant nephew, next in line for the throne. Rider of courser Vahrchanak.

Stoneblade, Sir Garman—a senior armsman and captain of Baron Cassan of Frahmahn.

Stonecastle, Yeraghor—Baron of Ersok and Lord Warden of the East Riding and a kinsman and ally of Baron Cassan Axehammer.

Swordshank, Sir Frahdar—the commander of King Markhos' personal guard.

Swordsmith, Tarlan—Lord Warden of High Tranith. One of Baron Cassan Axehammer's vassals.

Swordspinner, Sir Jahlahan—Baron Tellian Bowmaster's seneschal at Hill Guard Castle.

Talafressa, Raythas—a war maid in the Kalatha city guard. A member of Leeanna Hanathafressa's platoon.

Talthar, Master—Master Varnaythus' alias for his dealings with Cassan and Yeraghor.

Tamalithfressa, Yalith—a war maid; Mayor of Kalatha.

Tellian, Baron—see Tellian Bowmaster.

Tharafressa, Shallys—a war maid; innkeeper; proprietor of the Green Maiden, Kalatha's largest and most popular inn.

Tharanalalknarthas zoi'Harkanath—a much younger kinsman of Kilthandahknarthas; one of Kilthan's most trusted aides and his main liaison with Banak of Hurgrum.

Thersahkdahknarthas dinha'Felahkandarnas—lord of Clan Felahkandarnas of the Silver Cavern dwarves.

Thregafressa, Ravlahn—a war maid; commander of one hundred; Commander of Three Hundred Erlis Rahnafressa's lieutenant.

Transhar, Lord Warden of—see Rulth Blackhill.

Trâram, Captain Erkân—a Spearman mercenary in the pay of Arthnar Sabrehand.

Vahrchanak—Prince Yurokhas' courser companion; his name means "Snow Thunder."

Varlonsdaughter, Tala—Bahzell Bahnakson's housekeeper.

Varnaythus, Master—a black sorceror and priest of Carnadosa with ties to the Dog Brothers.

Walasfro—Kelthys Lancebearer's courser. His name means "Son of Battle."

Walsharno—the first courser champion of Tomanāk and Bahzell's bonded courser. His name means "Battle Dawn," "Dawn of Battle," "Battle Sun."

Warblade, Sir Altharn—Captain in the service of Lord Warden Trisu.

Warbridle, Garthan—Lord Warden of Hollow Cave. One of Baron Cassan Axehammer's vassals.

Warshoe, Darnas—a trusted spy, agent, and assassin in the employ of Baron Cassan.

Wrathson, Sir Festian—Lord Warden of Glanharrow. One of Tellian's staunchest supporters.

Wrathson, Lady Harlahssa—Lady Warden of Glanharrow. Lord Festian Wrathson's wife.

Wrathson, Sharlys Hanatha—Festian and Harlahssa Wrathson's daughter; twin sister of Yarran.

Wrathson, Yarran Trianal—Festian and Harlahssa Wrathson's son, heir to Glanharrow.

Yeraghor, Baron—see Yeraghor Stonecastle.

Zûrâk—a senior, powerful devil servant of Krashnark.